Universal Ac

C.J. CHERRYH'S

DEVIL TO THE BELT

HELLBURNER AND HEAVY TIME

*

"Cherryh does to the future military establishment what she did to future corporations: gives a close and skeptical look at what it's like to be at the bottom of the pyramid."

—Locus

*

"Excellent. . . . Cherryh, who evokes more tension and danger in one verbal confrontation than most writers can manage in a dozen space battles, maintains a fast pace throughout."

—Publishers Weekly

*

"Marvelously skillful . . . exactly the thing her fans will hope to find."

—Philadelphia Inquirer

*

"Taut, gripping, realistic work."

—Kirkus Reviews

*

"Smoothly written. . . . The characters are intriguing . . . the plot complex. . . . Cherryh's short, reverberant sentences have the feel of the best tough-guy detective fiction, and she is marvelously skillful in establishing her characters' motivations."

—Cleveland Plain Dealer

*

more . . .

"Highly recommended. . . . [Cherryh's] singular ability to create a believable vision of a spacefaring future is exceeded only by her talent for populating that vision with 'real' people."

—Library Journal

*

"Gritty adventure, strong characterization, and Machiavellian dealings aplenty. . . . [*Heavy Time* is] vintage Cherryh."

—Locus

*

ONE OF THE MOST ACCLAIMED AUTHORS

IN THE HISTORY OF SCIENCE FICTION–

C.J. CHERRYH

*

"The top of the field in both world-building and characterization. . . . [Merchanter is] one of the best built and most lived-in futures in science fiction."

—Chicago Sun-Times

*

"[An] unequaled ability to imagine what it would be like to live and work in space . . . old-fashioned SF at its very best."

***—Publishers Weekly* (starred review)**

*

"Cherryh's gifts are many. She creates believable, sympathetic, and altogether imperfect characters and scrambles them well, creating gut-wrenching interpersonal conflicts and tensions."

—San Diego Union-Tribune

*

"Cherryh writes intelligent, realistic science fiction."

—Columbus Dispatch

*

"Her ability to create deeply developed characters in a fully realized universe makes for absorbing, insightful reading."

—Flint Journal

*

"Cherryh understands human nature under stress and has a gift for conveying the immediacy of interaction, concerns, betrayal, and forgiveness."

—Science Fiction Age

*

Also by C.J. Cherryh

Cyteen

Tripoint

Rider at the Gate

Cloud's Rider

Finity's End

Available from Warner Aspect

C.J. CHERRYH

DEVIL TO THE BELT

A Time Warner Company

Warner Books, Inc., 1271 Avenue of the Americas, New York, NY 10020

Visit our Web site at www.twbookmark.com

Printed in the United States of America

First Printing: December 2000

10 9 8 7 6 5 4 3 2 1

Library of Congress Cataloging-in-Publication Data
Cherryh, C.J.
[Hellburner]
Devil to the belt / C.J. Cherryh.
p. cm.
Compilation of 2 previously published books: Hellburner and Heavy time.
ISBN 0-446-67653-5
1. Space warfare—Fiction. 2. Science fiction, American. I. Cherryh, C.J. Heavy time. II. Title.

PS3553.H358 A6 2000
813'.54—dc21 00-043646

Introduction

The Company Wars

Earth sent out colonies via pusher-ships to what became the Hinder Stars, a series of minor stars that provided the essentials of space-faring life: metals and life chemicals. That anchored bases for the far-traveling sunlight ships that took very, very long to complete what became the Great Circle trade, back to Sol and out again . . . hence the symbol of the EC, the Earth Company, a circle of stars.

Earth wanted to regulate the pusher-ships, wanted to dictate who flew and who didn't, wanted to install the crews, wanted to own the ships—but the crews who spent their lives on the long, slow traverse of the Great Circle weren't Earthers any longer, not by the time they reached a port many of them had never seen. Earth-based crews had to start out on their own ships, because the longtime pusher crews weren't willing to come ashore: Their homes were their ships, their lives stretched long between the stars, their cultures unique to the ship of their birth.

The inhabitants of the far-flung stations grew just as isolate, just as locally minded.

But Earth was the only source of luxury goods, and the only source of a mother-culture that held civilization together.

The discovery of Pell's World at what became known as Pell's Star ended the dependency of the colonists on Earth. A new earthlike planet redefined everything—and made a second Circle Trade with a loop ending at Pell. Earth no longer dictated.

And then a scientist at a farther base came up with faster-than-light, and ships left the Circle to convert to the new technology.

Earth found it out when a faster-than-light starship arrived in its port.

Everything changed. Earth saw wealth out there it thought it ought to be able to tax.

The colonists disagreed.

Earth began losing its brightest and best to emigration . . . and started requiring visas and restricting travel.

The brightest and best at the nearest stars, those Earth could most easily reach, ran farther and fast to get out of Earth's reach—and established a wildcat colony at Cyteen.

Earth tried to seize control of the merchant ships that served the colonies. Certain ships and stations agreed with Earth and feared the strangeness of Cyteen, and certain of the Hinder Stars attempted to enforce the visas on the merchant ships.

The merchant ships, notably *Finity's End*, resisted. There were fatalities, trade shutdown, and finally shots were fired. Cyteen began building merchant ships.

So did Pell.

Certain forces inside Earth's many governments knew they were losing control not only of their colonies, but also of a situation that could spiral way out of control. They could survive being cut off from trade—but they would have to surrender to any armed starship that showed up on their doorstep. They saw a future in which Earth might be ruled from outside, by interests as foreign to their own as any alien they had ever dreamed of meeting.

They had to do something.

They had the resources. They had to do something, do it fast, do it secretly and throw support to those spacefarers who were still loyal to the idea of Earth. If they didn't, they would lose their last allies, either to defeat, or to pragmatic acceptance of the new powers in the deep Beyond.

Their survival hinged on supplying those loyal forces. Not everyone on Earth understood that. Not every government and every leader believed it . . . but enough did. Not every government in the solar system was following the same agenda: Sol Station's Earth Company and Mars saw a chance, while pursuing their collective survival, to get power into their own hands and away from the nations of Earth itself.

And there were, inevitably, the venal and self-interested, and those who hoped that if they ignored the threat it would just go away.

The Earth Company had its own motives: By jostling the nations of Earth into this and that decision for its own benefit, it had made itself a war it had to win. Its center was Sol Station, orbiting around Earth, where it acted on decisions the many governments of Earth were still debating and made deals with corporations that grew about it. Its local source of supply was local space. And Earth itself had so limited an idea of what was happening above its blue skies.

C.J. Cherryh
April 2000

HEAVY TIME

CHAPTER 1

It was a lonely place, this remote deep of the Belt, a place where, if things went wrong, they went seriously wrong. And the loneliest sound of all was that thin, slow beep that meant a ship in distress.

It showed up sometimes, sometimes missed its beat. "She's rolling," Ben said when he first heard it, but Morrie Bird thought: Tumbling; and when Ben had plugged in the likely config of the object and asked the computer, that was what it said. It said it in numbers. Bird saw it in his mind. You spent thirty years tagging rocks and listening to the thin numerical voices of tags and beacons and faint, far ships, and you knew things like that. You could just about figure the pattern before the computer built it.

"Got to be dead," Ben Pollard said. Ben's face had that sharp, eager look it got when Ben was calculating something he especially wanted.

Nervous man, Ben Pollard. Twenty-four and hungry, a Belter kid only two years out of ASTEX Institute when he'd come to Bird with a 20 k check in hand—no easy trick, give or take his mother's insurance must have paid his keep and his schooling. Ben had bought in on *Trinidad*'s outfitting and signed on as his numbers man; and in a day when a lot of the new help had a bad case of the Attitudes and expected something for nothing, damned if Ben didn't wear an old man out with his One More Try and his Bird, I Got an Angle—

Regarding this distress signal it wasn't hard at all to figure Ben's personal numbers. Ben was asking himself the same questions an old man was asking at the bottom of his mortgaged soul: How far is it? Who's in trouble out there? Are they alive? And . . . What's the law on salvage?

So they called Base and told Mama they had a Mayday, had she heard?

Base hadn't heard it. That was moderately odd. Geosyncs over the Well hadn't heard it and ECSAA insystem hadn't picked it out of all the beeps and echoes of tags and ships in the Belt. Base took a while to think, approved a course and dumped them new sector charts, with which Mama was exceedingly stingy: Mama said Cleared for radio use, and: Proceed With Caution. Good luck, Two Twenty-nine Tango.

Spooky, that Base hadn't heard that signal—that she claimed that was a vacant sector. So somebody was way off course. You lay awake and thought of all the names you knew, people who could be out here right now—good friends among them; and you asked yourself what could have happened and when. Rocks could echo a signal. Lost ships could get very lost. That transmitter should be the standard 5 watts, but a dying one could trick you—and, committed, boosted up to a truly scary *v*, about which you could also have second thoughts, you had a lot of things on your mind.

The rule was that Base kept track of everything that moved out here. If your radio died you Maydayed on your emergency beeper and you waited til Mama gave you clear instructions how she was going to get you out of it—you didn't expect anybody to come in after you. Nowadays nobody went any damn where out of his assigned sector without Mama confirming course and nobody used a radio for long-distance chatter with friends. You get lost in the dark, spacer-kids, you go strictly by the regulations and you yell for Mama's attention.

That ghosty signal was doing that, all right, but Mama hadn't heard . . . and by all rights she should have. Mama said it could be a real weak signal—they were running calculations on the dopplering to try to figure it . . . Mama claimed she didn't hear it except with their relay, and that argued for close.

Or, Mama said, her reception could have a technical problem, which at a wild guess meant some glitch in the software on the big dishes, but Mama didn't talk about things like that with miners.

Mama didn't talk about a lot else with poor sod miners.

"You remember those 'jackers?" Ben asked, waking up in the middle of Bird's watch.

"Yep," Bird said, working maintenance on a servo motor; he tightened a screw and added, then: "I *knew* Karl Nouri."

"You're kidding."

"Only twenty years back. Hell, I drank with him. Nice guy. Him and his partner."

That got Ben, for sure. Ben slid back into his *g-1* spinner and started it up again. But after a while Ben stopped, got out, hauled on his stimsuit and his coveralls and had breakfast, unshaven and shadow-eyed.

A man felt ashamed of himself, disturbing the young fellow's rest.

But the remembrance of Nouri went on to upset Bird's sleep too.

No one was currently hijacking in the Belt—the company had wiped out Nouri and his partners, blown two of them to the hell they'd deserved, luring help in with a fake distress signal, killing crews, stripping logs for valuable finds and ships for usable parts—

Nouri's operation had worked, for a while—until people got suspicious and started asking how Nouri and his friends were so lucky, always coming in with a find, their equipment never breaking down, their ships real light on the fuel use. Careful maintenance, Nouri had insisted. They did their own. They were good at their work.

But a suspicious company cop had checked part numbers on Nouri's ship and found a condenser, Bird recollected, a damn 50-dollar condenser, with a serial number that traced it to poor Wally Leavitt's ship.

They'd shipped Nouri and five of his alleged partners back to trial on Earth, was what they said, company rules, though there'd been a good many would have seen Nouri himself take a walk above the Well.

But worse than the fear in the deep Belt in those days, was the way everybody had looked at everybody else back at Base, thinking: Are you one of Them? or . . . Do you think *I* could be?

One thing Belters still argued about was whether Jidda Pratt and Dave Marks had been guilty with the rest.

But the company had said they were. The company claimed they had solid evidence, and wrote down personable young Pratt and Marks in the same book as Nouri.

After that, hell, freerunning miners and tenders hadn't any rights. The company had never liked dealing with the independents in the first place: the company had made things increasingly difficult for independent operators once it had gotten its use from them, and the Nouri affair had been the turning point. No more wildcatting. Nowadays you documented every sneeze, you told Big Mama exactly what you'd found with your assay, they metal-scanned you when you went through customs, and you kept meticulous log records in case you got accused of

Misconduct, let alone, God help you, Illicit Operations or Illicit Trading. If you helped out a buddy, if you traded a battery or a tag or a transponder back at Base, you logged the date and the time and you filled out the forms, damn right you did: you asked your buddy to sign for a 50-cent clip, if it had a serial number on it, and the running unfunny joke was that the company was trying to think up a special form for exchange of toilet paper.

Nowadays it was illegal to keep your sector charts once you'd docked: Mama's agents came aboard and wiped your mag storage, customs could strip-search you for contraband datacards if it took the notion, and you didn't get any choice about the sector you drew when you went out again, either—'drivers moved, by the nature of what they were, you had mandated heavy time, no exceptions, and Mama didn't send you to anything near the same area. It was illegal to hail a neighbor on a run. You spent three months breathing each other's sweat, two guys in a crew space five meters long and three meters at the widest, so tight and so lonely you could hear each other's thoughts echo off the walls, but if one freerunner tried to call another a sector away from him, he and his partner went up on Illegal Trading charges faster than he could think about it, it being illegal now to trade tips even with no money or equipment changing hands: the company reserved the right to that information, claiming miners had sold it that data and it had a proprietary right to assign it to interests of its own—meaning the company-owned miners: to no one's great surprise the courts had sided with the company. So it was also, by the company's interpretation of that ruling, illegal to hail another ship and share a bottle or trade foodstuffs or any of the other friendly deals the Nouri crackdown had put a stop to.

So when they'd advised Base they wanted to move out of their assigned sector on a possible ship in distress, Mama had taken a nervous long time about giving them that permission. BM—Belt Management—was a sullen bitch at best, and you *never* tried to tell Mama you were doing something purely Al-truistic. Mama didn't, in principle, believe that, no'm. Mama was suspicious and Mama took time to check the records of one Morris Bird and Benjamin Pollard and the miner ship *Trinidad* to find out if *Trinidad* or either of her present crew had demonstrated any odd behaviors or made any odd investments in the recent past.

They could use their radio meanwhile to talk to the beep. Mama would permit that.

And evidently Mama finally believed what they heard—a 'driver ship fire-path crossed the charts she sent, which might well explain an accident out there, and *that* could make a body a little less anxious to go chasing that signal, but it seemed a little late now to beg off: they had the charts, they'd seen the situation, they couldn't back down with lives at stake, and Mama had set all the machinery in motion to have them check It out.

Right.

Mama couldn't do a thing for them if it did turn out to be some kind of trouble. Mama had indicated she had no information to give them on anybody overdue or off course, and that was damned odd. The natural next thought was the military—they asked Mama about that, but Mama just said Negative from Fleet Command.

Meanwhile that beep went on.

So Mama redirected a beam off the R2-8 relay, boosted them up along what Mama's charts assured them was a good safe course, and they chased the signal with the new charts Mama fed them, using the 'scope on all sides for rocks or non-rocks along the way—there was a good reward if you could prove a flaw in Mama's charts; if you had the charts legally, then you could work on them: that was the Rule.

At this speed you just prayed God the flaw didn't turn up directly in your path.

But as sectors went it was the Big Empty out here, nothing but a couple of company tags and one freerunner's for a long, long trip. Mama's charts were stultifyingly accurate . . . except the source of the beep, which seemed to be a weak signal. That was Mama's considered current opinion.

Meaning it was close.

Fourteen nervous days of this, all the while knowing you could make a big, bright fireball with depressingly little warning.

Naturally in the middle of supper/breakfast and shift change, the radar finally went blip! on something not on its chart, and Bird scalded himself with coffee.

The blip, when they saw it on the scope, did match the signal source.

"Advise Mama?" Ben said.

Bird bit his lip, thinking about lives, Mama's notoriously slow decisions, and mulling over the regulations that might apply. "Let's just get the optics fined down. No, we got no real news yet. We're doing what Mama told us to do. Looks like we can brake without her help. No great differential. And I seriously *don't* want Mama's advice while we're working that mother. That's going to be a bitch as is."

"You got it," Ben said with a nervous little exhalation. Ben set his fingers on the keys and started figuring.

* * *

"Looks like it caught a rock," Bird said, pointing out that deep shadow in the middle of what ought to be the number one external tank.

"Looks." Ben had been cheerful ever since optics had confirmed the shape as a miner craft. "Sure doesn't look healthy."

"It sure doesn't look good. Let's try for another still, see if we can process up a serial number on that poor sod."

"You got it," Ben said.

They crept up on it. They put a steady hail on ship-to-ship—having that permission—and kept getting nothing but that tumble-modulated beep.

It was no pretty picture when they finally had it lit up in their spots.

"One hell of an impact," Ben muttered. "Maybe a high-*v* rock."

"Could be. God, both tanks are blown, right there, see? That one's got it right along the side."

"Those guys had *no* luck."

"Sudden. Bad angle. Lot of *g*'s."

"Bash on one side. Explosion on the other. Maybe it threw them into a rock."

"Dunno. Either one alone—God help 'em—maybe 10 real sudden *g*'s."

"Real sudden acquaintance with the bulkhead. Rearrange your face real good."

"Wouldn't know what hit 'em."

"Suppose that 'driver did bump a pebble out?"

"Could be. Cosmic bad luck, in all this empty. Talk about having your name on it. What do they say the odds are?"

"Hundred percent for these guys."

Another image capture. White glared across the cameras, a blur of reflected light, painted serial designation.

"Shit, that's a One'er number! One'er Eighty-four Zebra . . ."

Not from their Base. Outside their zone. Strangers from across the line.

The tumble carried the lock access toward their lights. Bird said, "Hatch looks all right."

"You got no notion to be going *in* there."

"Yep."

"Bird, love of God, there's no answer."

"Maybe their receiver's out. Maybe they lost their radio altogether. Maybe they're too banged up to answer."

"Maybe they're dead. You don't need to go in there!"

"Yep. But I'm going to."

"I'm not."

"Salvage rights, Ben-me-lad. I thought we were partners."

"Shit."

It was a routine operation for a miner to stop a spin: and most rocks did tumble—but the tumble of a spindle-shaped object their own size and, except the ruptured tanks, their own mass, was one real touchy bitch.

It was out with the arm and the brusher, and just keep contacting the thing til you got one and the other motion off it, while the gyros handled the yaw and the pitch—bleeding money with every burst of the jets. But you did this uncounted times for thirty-odd years, and you learned a certain touch. A trailing cable whacked them and scared Ben to hell, and it was a long sweaty time later before they had the motion off the thing, a longer time yet til they had the white bullseye beside the stranger's hatch centered in their docking sight.

But after all the difficulty before, it was a gentle touch.

Grapples clicked and banged.

"That's it," Bird said. "That's got it."

A long breath. Ben said reverently: "She's ours."

"We don't know that."

"Hell, she's salvage!"

"Right behind the bank."

"Uh-uh. Even if it's pure company we got a 50/50 split."

"Unless somebody's still in control over there."

"Well, hell, somebody sure doesn't look it."

"Won't know til we check it out, will we?"

Come on, Bird, —shit, we *don't* have to go in there, do we? This is damn stupid."

"Yep. And yep." Bird unbelted, shoved himself gently out of his station, touched a toe on the turn-pad and sailed back to the locker. "Coming?"

Ben sullenly unclipped and drifted over, while Bird hauled the suits out and started dressing.

Ben kept bitching under his breath. Bird concentrated on his equipment. Bird always concentrated on his equipment, not where he was going, not the unpleasant thing he was likely to find the other side of that airlock.

And most of all he didn't let himself think what the salvage would bring on the market.

"Five on ten she's a dead ship," Ben said. "Bets?"

"Could've knocked their transmission out. Could be a whole lot of things, Ben, just put a small hold on that enthusiasm. Don't go spending any money before it's ours."

"It's going to be a damn mess in there. God knows how old it is. It could even be one of the Nouri wrecks."

"The transmitter's still going."

"Transmitters can go that long."

"Not if the lifesupport's drawing. Six months tops. Besides, power cells and fuel were what Nouri stripped for sure."

Ben's helmet drifted between them. Ben snagged it. "I'm taking the pry-bar. We're going to need it getting in. Lay you bets?"

Bird picked his helmet out of the air beside him and put it on: smell of old plastics and disinfectant. Smell of a lot of hours and a lot of nasty cold moments.

This might be the start of one, the two of them squeezing into the wider than deep airlock, which was claustrophobic enough for the one occupant it was designed for.

It truly didn't make sense, maybe, insisting both of them get rigged up. It might even be dangerous, putting shut locks between them both and operable systems; but you chased a ghost signal through the Belt for days on end, you had nightmares about some poor lost sods you'd no idea who, and you remembered all your own close calls—well, then, you had to see it with your own eyes to exorcise your ghosts. If you were going to be telling it to your friends back at Base (and you would), then you wanted the feel of it and you wanted your partner able to swear to it.

Most of all, maybe you got a little nervous when your partner started getting that excited about money and insisting they owned that ship.

Most especially since Nouri and the crackdown, and since the company had gotten so nitpicking touchy—you wanted witnesses able to swear in court what you'd touched and what you'd done aboard somebody else's ship.

Bird shut the inside hatch and pushed the buttons that started the lock cycling. The red light came on, saying DEPRESSURIZATION, and the readout started spieling down toward zero.

"Sal-vage," Ben said, tinny-sounding over the suit-com. "Maybe she'll still pitch, do you think? If those tanks are the most of the damage, hell, they're cans, is all. Can't be that expensive. We could put a mortgage on her, fix her up—the bank'll take a fixable ship for collateral, what do you think?"

"I think we better pay attention to where we are. We got one accident here, let's not make it two."

The readout said PRESSURE EQUALIZED. Ben was doing this anxious little bounce with his foot braced, back and forth between the two walls of the lock. But you never rushed opening. Oxygen cost. Water cost. Out here, even with all the working machinery aboard, heat cost. You treated those pumps and those seals like they were made of gold, and while the safety interlocks might take almost-zero for an answer and let you open on override, it was money flowing out when you did. You remembered it when you saw your bills at next servicing, damn right, you did.

The readout ticked down past 5 mb toward hard vacuum, close as the compressor could send it. Ben pushed the OUTER HATCH OPEN button, the lock unsealed and retracted the doors and showed them the scarred, dust-darkened face of the opposing lock. The derelict's inside pressure gauge was dusted over. Bird cleared it with his glove. "760 mb. She's up full. At least it didn't hole her."

Ben banged soundlessly on the hatch with the steel bar and put his helmet up against the door.

"Nada," Ben said. "Dead in there, Bird, I'm telling you."

"We'll see." Bird borrowed the bar and pried up the safety cover on the External Access handle.

No action. No power in the ship's auxiliary systems.

"No luck for them," Ben said cheerfully. "Pure dead."

Bird jimmied the derelict's external leech panel open. "Get ours, will you?"

"Oh, shit, Bird."

"Nerves?"

Ben didn't answer. Ben shoved off to their own lock wall to haul the leech cord out of its housing. It snaked in the light as he drifted back. Bird caught the collared plug and pushed it into the derelict's leech socket. The hull bumped and vibrated under his glove. "She's working," he said.

"Sal-vage," Ben said, on hissed breaths.

"Don't spend it yet."

Rhythmic hiss of breath over suit-coms, while the metal vibrated with the pump inside. "Hey, Bird. What's a whole ship worth?"

A man tried to be sane and sensible. A man tried to think about the poor sods inside, an honest man broke off his prospecting and ran long, expensive risky days for a will-o'-the-wisp signal, and tried to concentrate on saving lives, not on how much metal was in this ship or whether she was sound, or how a second ship would set him and Ben up for life. The waiting list for leases at Refinery Two meant no ship sat idle longer than its servicing required.

"130 mb. 70. 30. 10." The pressure gauge ticked down. The vibration under his hand changed. The valves parted.

Ice crystals spun and twinkled in front of them, against the sullen glow of borrowed power. Ice formed and glistened on the inner lock surfaces—moisture where it didn't belong.

"Doesn't look prosperous," Ben said.

Bird pushed with his toe, caught a handhold next to the inner valves. His glove skidded on ice. Ben arrived beside him, said, "Clear," and Bird hit the HATCH CLOSE toggle.

"Going to be slow." He looked high in the faceplate for the 360° view, watching the derelict's outer doors labor shut at their backs.

"You sure about that battery?" Ben asked.

Bird hit CYCLE 2. The pumps vibrated. "Hell of a time to ask."

"Are you sure?"

"Thirty years at this, damn right I checked. —Whoa, there."

The HUD in the faceplate suddenly showed a yellow flasher and a dataflow glowing green. The one on the airlock wall glowed a sullen red.

"CONTAMINANTS." Ben let go a shaky hiss of pent breath. "It's not going to be pretty in there. —Bird, do we have to go through with this? There's nothing alive inside."

"We're already there. Can you sleep without knowing?"

"Damn right I'll sleep, I'll sleep just fine. —I don't want to see this, Bird. Why in hell do I got to see this?"

"Hey, we all end up the same. Carbon and nitrogen, a lot of H_20."

"Cut it out, Bird!"

"Earth to earth. Dust to dust." The indicators said *740/741 mb.* and PRESSURE EQUALIZED. "Lousy compressor," Bird said, pushed the INNER HATCH OPEN button. Air whistled, rushing past the pressure differential and an uneven seal. The doors ground slowly back. External audio heard it. 10° C, his HUD said about the ambient. Not quite balmy. "Heater's going down. Heater's always next to last. —You do know what's last, don't you, Ben-me-lad?"

"The damn beeper." Ben's teeth were chattering—nothing wrong with Ben's suit heater, Bird was sure. Ben's breath hissed raggedly over the suit-com. "So Mama can find the salvage. Only this time we got it, Bird, come on, I don't like this. What if that leech pulls out?"

"Plug won't pull out."

"Hell, Bird!"

Inner doors labored to halfway open. Bird caught the door edge and shoved himself and his backpack through into the faintly lit inside.

A helmetless hardsuit, trailing cables and hose, drifted slowly in front of them, spinning in a loose cocoon of its attachments. A cable went from its battery pack to the panel, last sad resort: the occupants had had time to know they were in trouble, time to drain the main batteries and the leech unit, and finally resort to this one.

Bits and pieces of gear drifted in the dimmed light, sparked bright in their suit-spots, cords, clips—everything a tumble could knock free. Fluids made small moons and planets.

"Mess," Ben's voice said. "Isn't it?"

Bird caught the hose, tugged gently to pull the suit out of his way, and checked the suit locker. "One suit's missing."

"I'm cutting that damn beeper," Ben said. "All right?"

"Fine by me."

Stuff everywhere. Cables. A small meteor swarm of utility clips flashed in the light. Globules of fluid shone both oily-dark and amber. A sweater and a single slipper danced and turned in unison like a ghost.

"Lifesupport's flat gone," Ben said. A locker banged in the external audio, while Bird was checking the spinner cylinders for occupants. Empty. Likewise the shower.

A power cell floated past. Dead spare, one from the lock, one guessed.

A globule of fluid impacted Bird's visor, leaving a chain of dark red beads.

"Come on, Bird. Let's seal up. Let's get out of here. They're gone. Dead ship, that's all. Don't ask what this slop is that's floating. The 'cyclers are shot."

Drifting hose. More clips. A lump of blankets under the number two workstation, spotted in Bird's chest-light. "Looks like here's one of them," Bird said.

"God! Let it be! Bird!"

"Carbon and water. Just carbon and water." Bird held the counter edge and snagged the blanket.

The body drifted past the chair, rolled free as the blanket floated on to dance with the sweater.

Young man in filthy coveralls. Straight dark hair and loose limbs drifted in the slow spin the turnout gave him.

Not much beard.

Bird caught a sleeve, stopped the spin, saw a dirty face, shut eyes, open mouth. Dehydration shrank the skin, cracked the lips.

"Don't touch him!" Ben objected. "God, don't touch him!"

"Beard's been shaved, maybe three days."

"God knows how long ago—he's dead, Bird. That's a dead body."

Bird nudged the chin-lever over to sensor array, said, "Left. Hand."

The HUD showed far warmer than the 10° ambient.

Pliable flesh.

"Isn't a body, Ben. This guy's alive."

"Shit," Ben said. Then: "But he's not in control of this ship. Is he?"

Long, long door closing, with an unconscious man crowding them three to the lock, and the underpowered motors going slow and threatening breakdown. Then they could Mode 2 Override their own airlock, mixing air supplies and keeping pressure up for their passenger's sake.

"Go ahead and seal it behind us," Bird said. "Keep it just the way it was, in case Mama asks questions."

"God, we got a CONTAMINANTS flashing in *our* lock now. Why the hell don't we have a transfer bag? God, this guy's all over crud."

"We'll think of that next time. Come on, come on. Do it."

Ben swore, made the numbingly slow seal of the wreck's doors, then pulled their leech free and hit HATCH CLOSE on their own panel, sending One'er Eighty-four Zebra toward an electronic sleep, still docked with them, her last battery on the edge of failure.

"Man was a total fool," Ben muttered. "He should've hooked the ship in to feed that suit, not the other way around. Should have let her go all the way down."

"Would've made sense," Bird said.

"So where's the partner?"

"God only. Push CYCLE. I can't reach it."

Ben got an arm past him and the rescuee and hit the requisite button. Their own compressor started, solid and fast, a healthy vibration under the decking.

Then the whole chamber went red and a blinking white light on the panel said INTERNAL CONTAMINANT ALERT.

"Shit," Ben groaned.

"You got that right."

"Bad joke, Bird. That stuff got past the filters!"

"Just override. Tell it we're sorry, we can't help it."

Ben was already punching at the button. Ben said, "We don't need any damn corpse fouling up our air, howsoever long he takes to get that way. —God, Bird, we *own* that ship!"

"Just let's not worry about it here." Bird felt the slight movement in his arms. Hugged the man tight, thinking, Poor sod. Hold on. Hold on awhile. We got you. You're all right. He said to Ben, "He's moving."

Ben drew an audible breath. "You know, we could put him back in there. Who's to know?"

"Bad joke, Ben." The PRESSURE EQUALIZED lit up. "Hatch button. Come on, give me a hand, huh? I can't turn around."

"We can't damn well afford this!" Ben said. "We're into the bank as far as—"

"Ben, for God's sake, just punch the damn button!"

Ben punched it. The hatch opened, relieved the pressure at Bird's back, gave him room to turn and haul their rescuee inside. He carefully let the man go and let him drift while he sailed back into the lock and secured the leech into its housing. Then he drifted back through and shut the inside hatch.

Ben was lifting his helmet off—Ben was making a disgusted face and swearing. Their air quality alarm had the warning siren going and the overhead lights flashing—it was that bad. Ben grabbed their guest by the collar and started peeling him out of his clothes.

Bird got his own helmet off and let it float, stripped off his gloves and helped Ben peel the unconscious man to the skin, trying not to breathe, bunching the coveralls and stimsuit continually as they peeled them off, trying not to let them touch the air. He hesitated whether to go for a containment bag or shove them in the washer and maybe foul the cleaning fluid for the rest of the trip. The washer was closer. He crammed them in, slippers and all, levered the small door shut and pushed the button. The stench clung to his bare hands. His suit was splotched with yellow and red stains.

He heard a faint voice not Ben's, protesting incoherently, turned and saw Ben pulling the shower door open, the young man trying to resist Ben's pulling him around. Ben pushed the man inside and pulled the door to—a knee was in the way and Ben shoved it, while their uninvited passenger, drifting behind clear plastic, slammed a weak fist against the clear plex door.

"Be a little damn careful, Ben."

Ben pulled the outside seal lever down, flung up the service panel beside the door, pushed the Test Cycle button, holding the shower door shut the while. The shower started. Their guest slammed the door with his fist again, drifted back against the wall as the water hit him.

"What's the water temp?"

"Whatever you left it."

"I don't remember what I left it. —Cut it, Ben, he's passed out."

"He's all right, dammit! We've spent enough on this fool, I'm not living with that stink! It's my money too, Bird, in case you forget! It's my money right along with yours we spent running after this guy, it's my money pays for those filters, and that smell makes me sick to my stomach, Bird!"

"All right, all right. Take it easy."

"It's all over us!"

"Ben, —shut up. Just shut up. Hear me?"

The air quality siren was still going. It was enough to drive a man crazy. They were having a zero run, hardly anything in the sling. They'd spent nerve-wracking hours getting the ship linked and now Ben had gotten so close to money he could taste it. Ben got a little breath, looked as if control was still coming hard for him, as if he was somewhere between breaking down and breaking something.

Bird shoved over to the lifesupport control panel and cut the siren. The silence after was deafening. Just the shower going and their own hard breathing.

Ben was a hard worker, sometimes too hard. Bird told himself that, told himself Ben was a damned fine partner, and the Belt was lonely and tempers got raw. Two men jammed into a five by three can for months on end had to give each other room—had to, that was all.

Ben said, thin-lipped, but sanely, "Bird, we got to wipe down these suits. We have to get this stink off. It's going to break down our filters, dammit."

"It won't break down our filters," Bird assured him quietly, but he went and got the case of towel wipes out of the locker. The shower entered its drying cycle. The guy was floating there, eyes shut, maybe resting, maybe unconscious. Bird reached for the door.

Ben held the latch down and pushed the Test Cycle a second time.

"Ben," Bird protested, "Ben, for God's sake, the guy's had enough. Are you trying to drown him?"

"I won't live with that stink!"

The man—kid, really, he looked younger than Ben was—had drifted against the shower wall and hung there. He was moving again, however feebly—and maybe it was cowardly not to insist Ben listen to reason, but a small ship was nowhere to have a fight start, over what was likely doing the kid no harm, and maybe some good. You could breathe the mist, you could drink the detergent straight and not suffer from it. Dehydrated as he was, he could do with a little clean water; and cold as he'd been, maybe it was a fast way to warm him through.

So he said, "All right, all right, Ben," and opened the box of disinfectant towels, wiped his hands and chest and arms and worked down.

"I can still smell it," Ben said in a shaky voice, wiping his own suit off. "Even after you scrub it I can still smell it."

"That's just the disinfectant."

"Hell if it is."

Ben was not doing well, Bird thought. He had insisted Ben go over there with him and maybe that had been a mistake: Ben wasn't far into his twenties himself; and Ben might never have been in a truly lonely, scary situation in his whole stationbound life. Ben had spooked himself about this business for days, with all this talk about hijackers.

On the other hand maybe an old dirtsider from Earth and a Belter brat four years out of school weren't ever going to understand each other on all levels.

They shed the suits. They'd used up three quarters of their supply of wipes. "Just as well our guy stays in the shower," Bird said, now that he thought calmly about it, "until we have something to put him in. His clothes'll be dry in a bit." He cycled the shower again himself, stowed his suit and floated over to the dryer as it finished its cycle. The clothes were a little damp about the seams, and smelled of disinfectant: the dryer's humidity sensor needed replacing, among a dozen other things at the bottom of his roundtoit list. He read the stenciled tag on the coveralls. "Our guy's got a name. Tag says Dekker. P."

"That's fine. So he's got a name. What happened to his partner, that's what I want to know."

Maybe that was after all what was bothering Ben—too many stories about Nouri and the hijackers.

"He wasn't doing so well himself, was he?" Dekker, P. was drifting in the shower compartment, occasionally moving, not much. Bird opened the door, without interference from Ben this time, and said, quietly, before he took the man's arm: "Dekker, my name's Bird, Morrie Bird. My partner's Ben. You're all right. We're going to get you dressed now. Don't want you to chill."

Dekker half opened his eyes, maybe at the cold air, maybe at the voice. He jerked his arm when Bird pulled him toward the outside. "Cory?" he asked. And in panic, bracing a knee and a hand against the shower door rim: "Cory?"

"Watch him!" Ben cried; but it was Ben who caught a loose backhand in the face. Dekker jabbed with his elbow on the recoil, made a move to shove past them, but he had nothing left, neither leverage nor strength. Bird blocked his escape and threw an arm around him, after which Dekker seemed to gray out, all but limp, saying, "Cory, . . ."

"Must be the partner," Bird said.

"God only. I want a shower, Bird." Ben snatched the half-dry coveralls from him and grabbed Dekker's arm. "Hell with the stimsuit, let's just wrap this guy up before he bashes a panel or something."

"Just hold on to him," Bird said. Bird caught the stimsuit that was drifting nearby, shook the elastic out, got the legs and sleeves untangled and got hold of Dekker's arm. "Left leg, come on, son. Clean clothes. Come on, give us some help here. Left leg."

Dekker tried to help, then, much as a man could who kept passing out on them. His skin had been heated from the shower. It was rapidly cooling in the cabin air and Ben was right: it was hard enough to get a stimsuit on oneself, nearly impossible to put one on a fainting man. He was chilling too fast. They gave that up. By the time they got him into the coveralls and zipped him up he was moving only feebly, half-conscious.

"Not doing real well, is he?" Ben said. "Damn waste of effort. The guy's going to sign off—"

"He's all right," Bird said, "God, Ben, mind your mouth."

"I just want my bath. Let's just get this guy to bed, all right? We get a shower, we call Mama and tell her we got ourselves a ship!"

"Shut up about the ship, Ben."

A long, careful breath. "Look, I'm tired, you're tired, let's just forget it til we get squared away, all right?"

"All right." Bird shoved off in a temper of his own, drifted toward the spinner cylinders overhead, taking Dekker with him—carefully turned and caught a hold, pulling Dekker toward the open end. "Come on, son, we're putting you to bed, easy does it."

Dekker said, "Cory, —"

"Cory's your partner?"

Dekker's eyes opened, hazed and vague. Dekker grabbed the spinner rim, shaking his head, refusing to be put inside.

"Dekker? What happened to you, son?"

"Cory, —" Dekker said, and shoved. "I don't want to. *No!*"

Ben sailed up, grabbed Dekker's collar on the way and carried him half into the cylinder, Dekker fighting and kicking. Bird rolled and pushed off, got Dekker by a leg, Dekker screaming for Cory all the while and fighting them.

"Hold on to him!" Ben said, and Bird did that, holding Dekker from behind until Ben could unhook a safety tether from the bulkhead, held on while Ben sailed back to grab Dekker's arm and tie it to a pipe.

"Damn crazy," Ben said, panting. "Just keep him there. I'll get another line."

"That's rough, Ben."

"Rougher on all of us if this fool hits the panels. Just hold him, dammit!"

Ben somersaulted off to the supply lockers, while Bird caught his breath, and kept Dekker's free arm pinned, patting his shoulder, saying, "It's all right, son, it's all right, we're trying to get you home. My name's Bird. That's Ben. What do you go by?"

Several shallow breaths. Struggles turned to shivers. "Dek."

"That's good." He patted Dekker's shoulder. Dekker's eyes were open but Bird was far from sure Dekker knew where he was or what had happened to him. "Just hold on, son." A locker door banged, forward. Ben came sailing up with a roll of tape.

"I'm not sure we need that," Bird said. "Guy's just a little spooked."

Ben ignored him, grabbed Dekker's other arm and began wrapping it to the pipe. "Guy's totally off his head." Dekker tried to kick him, Dekker kept saying, "My partner—where's my partner?"

"Afraid there was an accident," Bird said, holding Dekker's shoulder. "Suit's gone. We looked. There wasn't anybody else on that ship."

"No!"

"You remember what happened?"

Dekker shook his head, teeth chattering. "Cory."

"Was Cory your partner?"

"Cory!"

"Shit," Ben said, and shook Dekker, slapped his face gently. "Your partner's dead, man. The suit was gone. You got picked up, my partner and I picked you up. Hear?"

It did no good. Dekker kept mumbling about Cory, and Ben said, "I'm going down after a shower. Or you can."

"I'm scared we left somebody in that ship."

"You didn't leave anybody in that ship, dammit, Bird, we're not opening that lock again!"

"I'm not that sure."

"You looked, Bird, you *looked*. If there was a Cory he's gone, that's all. Suit and all. We've done all we can for this guy. We've spent days on this guy. We've spent our fuel on this guy, we've risked our necks for this guy—"

"His name's Dekker."

"His name's Dekker or Cory or Buddha for all I care. He's out of his head, we got nowhere safe to put him, we don't know what happened to his partner, we don't know why Mama doesn't know him, and that worries me, Bird, it seriously does!"

It made sense. Everything Ben was saying made sense. The other suit was gone. They had searched the lockers and the spinners. There were no hiding places left. But nothing about this affair was making sense.

"Hear me?" Ben asked.

"All right, all right," Bird said, "just go get your shower and let's get our numbers comped. We have to call in. Have to. Regulations. We got to do this all by the book."

"Don't you feel sorry for him. You hear me, Bird? Don't you even think about going back into that ship."

"I won't. I don't. It's all right."

Ben looked at him distressedly, then rolled and kicked off for the shower.

Bird floated down to the galley beside it, opened the fridge and got a packet of Citrisal, lime, lemon, what the hell, it was all ghastly awful, but it had the trace elements and salts and simple sugars.

It was the best he knew to do for the man. He drifted over to Dekker, extracted the tube and held it to Dekker's lips.

"Come on. Drink up. It's the green stuff."

Dekker took a sip, made a face, ducked his head aside.

"Come on. Another."

Dekker shook his head.

Couldn't blame him for that, Bird thought. And you damn sure didn't want anybody sick at his stomach in null-g. He tested whether the cord and the tape were too tight, decided Dekker was all right for a while. "We'll let you loose when your head clears. You're all right. Hear me? We're going to get you back to Base. Get you to the meds. Hear me?"

Dekker nodded slightly, eyes shut.

Exhausted, Bird decided. He gave the man a gentle pat on the shoulder and said, "Get some sleep. Ship's stable now."

Dekker muttered something. Agreement, Bird thought. He hoped so. He was shaky, exhausted, and he wished they were a hell of a lot closer to Base than they were.

The guy needed a hospital in the worst way. And that was a month away at least. Bad trip. And there was the investment of time and money this run was going to cost them. Half a year's income, counting mandatory layouts.

Maybe Ben was right and they did have a legal claim on this wreck—Ben was a college boy, Ben knew the ins and outs of company law and all the loopholes—and maybe legally those were the rules, but Bird didn't like thinking that way and he didn't like the situation this run had put them in. If it was a company ship they had in tow and if it was the company itself they were going to be collecting their bills from—that was one thing; but the rig with its cheap equipment wasn't spiff enough for a company ship. That meant it was a freerunner, and that meant it was some poor sod's whole life, Dekker's or somebody's. Get their expenses back, yes, much as they could, but not rob some poor guy of everything he owned. That wasn't something Bird wanted to think about.

But Ben could. And Ben scared him of a sudden. You worked with a guy two years in a little can like this and eventually you did think you knew him reasonably well, but God knew and experience had proved it more than once—it was lonely out here, it was a long way from civilization, and you could never realize what all a guy's kinks were until something pushed the significant button.

CHAPTER 2

The old man went away. Dekker heard him or his partner moving about. He heard the shower going, over the fan and the pump noises in the pipes beside his head. The ship was stable. That was a feeling he had thought he would never have again. He had dimmed the lights, cut off everything he could and nursed it as far as he could til the 'cyclers went and the water fouled.

And here he was free of the stimsuit, light as a breeze and vulnerable to the chill and the lack of *g*. He was off his head, he knew that: he scared the people who had rescued him, he knew that too, and he tried not to do it, but they scared him. They talked about owning his ship. They might kill him, might just let him die and tell the company sorry, they hadn't been able to help that.

Maybe they couldn't. Maybe he shouldn't care any longer. He was tired, he hurt, body and soul, and living took more work than he was sure he wanted to spend again on anything. He had no idea how long and how far a run was still in front of him getting home. He didn't think he could stand being treated like this all the way. Everything smelled of disinfectant, and sometimes it was his ship and sometimes it was theirs.

But Cory never answered him wherever he was, and at times he knew she wouldn't.

The old man drifted up into his sight again, put a straw in his mouth and told him to drink. He did. It tasted of copper. The old man asked him what had happened to his partner. Then he remembered—how could he have forgotten?—that she was out there and that ship was, he could see it coming—

"No!" he cried, and winced when it hit, he knew it was going to hit, the collision alert was screaming. He yelled into the mike, "My partner's out there!" because it was the last thing he could think of to tell them.

"Your partner's dead!" somebody yelled at him, and another voice, angry, yelled, "Shut up, dammit, Ben! You got no damn feelings, give the guy a chance. God!"

He was still alive and he did not understand how he had survived. He hauled himself to the radio, he held on against the spin as long as he had strength. "Cory," he called on the suit-com frequency, over and over again, while the ship tumbled. Maybe she answered. His ears rang so he couldn't hear the fans or the pumps. But he kept calling her name, so she would know he was alive and looking for her, that he'd get help to her somehow . . .

As soon as he could get the damned engines to fire.

Or as soon as he could get hold of Base and make that ship out there answer him. . . .

Ben said, "We're *due* salvage rights, whether he's company or a freerunner, *no* legal difference. It's right in the company rules, I'll show you—"

Bird said, carefully, because he wanted Ben to understand him: "We'll get compensated."

"Maritime law since—"

"There's the law and there's what's right, Ben."

"*Right* is, we own that ship, Bird. He wasn't in control of it, that's what *right* says."

Ben was short of breath. He was yelling. Bird said, calmly, sanely, "I'm trying to tell you, there's a lot of complications here. Let's just calm down. We've got weeks yet back to Base, plenty of time to figure this out, and we'll talk about it. But we're not getting any damn where if we don't get our figures in and tell Mama to get us the hell home. Fast."

"So how much are you going to spend on this guy? A month's worth of food? Medical supplies? We're going to bust our ass and risk our rigging for this guy?"

Bird had no answer. He couldn't think of one to cut this off.

"This is my money too, Bird. It's my money you're spending. Maybe you own this ship, maybe I'm just a part-share partner, but I have some say here." Ben flung a gesture toward Dekker, aft. "That guy's going to live or he's going to die. In either case he's going to do it before the month is up. Much as I want to be rid of him, there's no need busting our tails—we have double mass to move, Bird, and hell if I'm dumping the sling—"

"All right, we're not dumping the sling. Not ours, not his either, if we can avoid it."

"And we're not putting any hard push on the rigging. There's no point in risking our necks. Or putting wear on the pins and the lines. We don't call this a life-and-death. We can't cut that much time off. And hell if I want to meet a rock the way this guy did."

It made better sense than a lot else Ben had been saying. Bird took that for hopeful and nodded. "I'll go with you on that. A hard push could do more harm than good for him, too."

"Guy's going to die anyway."

"He's not going to die," Bird said. "For God's sake, just shut up, he can hear you."

"So if he doesn't? A month gets him well, and we pull into station and he looks healthy and he says sure he was managing that ship just fine—"

"Just let it alone, Ben!"

"I'm going to get pictures."

"Get your pictures." Bird shook his head, wishing he could say no, wishing he had some way to reason with Ben, but if getting a vid record would make Ben happier, God, let him have the pictures. "We have the condition of that ship out there, we have the log records over there—"

"Charts—" Ben exclaimed, as if that was a new idea.

"We're not touching that log. No way. That part of the law *I* know."

"I'm not talking about that. Look—look, I got an idea."

An idea was welcome. Bird watched doubtfully as Ben punched up the zone schema, pointed on the screen to the 'driver ship and its fire-path to the Well, the same thing that scared them even to contemplate. "*That's* got a medic. That's got a friggin' company captain in charge. We just ask Mama to boost us over there just across the line and *they* can take official possession."

"Damn right they would. The company doesn't run a charity."

"It's an R1 ship! They're obligated to take him. They have no choice. The law says a 'driver is a Base: they can log us right there for a find if we bring it in, and this is a find, isn't it? Same as a rock. We can turn it in, money in the bank, and we can apply to do some clean-up along with its tenders for the rest of our run—that's damn good money. Sure money. And we got the best excuse going."

"Ben, that's a 'driver captain you're talking about. They don't *have* to do anything. You want him to tell us we've still got to turn around and take this guy in to Base, maybe clean to R1, if he takes it in his head—he can do that. You want him to tell us he'll hold Eighty-four Zebra for us—and then contest his fees in court when he shows up three years from now with one hell of a haulage charge? We got this run to pay for, we got serious questions to answer, because there's a whole lot that's not right about this, and I'm not taking my chances with any Court of Inquiry back at Base with all the evidence stuck out on a 'driver that for all we know isn't coming in for three or four more years. If you want to talk law, now, let's be practical!"

Ben's mouth shut.

"A 'driver does any damn thing it wants to: Three years' dockage charges, supposing they're on the start of their run. Three years' haulage. You want to try to pry a claim away from the company then? Not mentioning the cost of getting it there. We're short as is. You want to hear them say ferry it back ourselves anyway? Twice the distance? Or get us drafted into its tender crew on a *permanent* basis? You know what they charge a freerunner for fuel?"

Ben looked very sober during all of this. Ben bit his lip. "So that's out. You know, we could just sort of knock that fellow on the head. Solve everybody's problem."

Ben, who was scared to death of looking at a body.

"Yeah, sure," Bird said.

And from aft: "What time is it? What's the time?"

Ben glanced up. "Now what does he want?"

Bird checked his watch. "2310," he shouted back.

"I want my watch."

"God," Ben muttered, shaking his head. "We have four weeks of this guy?"

"I want my watch!"

Ben yelled: "Shut up, dammit, you're not keeping any appointments anyway!"

"Patience," Bird said, but Ben shoved off in Dekker's direction. Bird sailed after, arrived as Dekker said quietly,

"I need my watch."

Ben said: "You don't need your watch, you're not going anywhere.

It's 23 damn 10 in my sleep, mister, you're using our air and our fuel and our time already, so shut up."

"Ben, just take it easy."

"I'll shut him up with a wrench."

"Ben."

"All right, all right, all right." Ben took off again.

Dekker said, "I can't see my watch."

Bird floated over where he could read the time on Dekker's watch. "2014. You're about three hours slow."

"No."

"That's what it says."

"What day is it?"

"May 20."

"You're lying to me!"

"Bird," Ben said ominously, and came drifting up again to reach for Dekker, but Bird grabbed him.

"I can't take four weeks of that, Bird, I swear to you, this guy's already on credit with me already."

"Give *me* a little slack, will you? Shut it down. Shut it up. Hear me?"

"I've dealt with crazies," Ben muttered. "I've seen enough of them."

"Fine. Fine. We get this guy out of a tumble, he's been whacked about the head, he's a little shook, Ben, d'you think you wouldn't be, if you'd been through what he has?"

Ben stared at him, jaw clamped, grievous offense in every line of his face.

Ben was in the middle of his night. That was so. Ben was tired and Ben had been spooked, and Ben didn't understand weakness in anybody else.

Serious personality flaw, Bird thought. Dangerous personality flaw.

He watched Ben go back to his work without a word.

Good partner in some ways. Damned efficient. Good with rocks.

But different. Belter-born, for one thing, never talked about his relatives. Brought up by the corporation, for the corporation.

Talk to Ben about Shakespeare, Ben'd say, What shift does he work?

Say, I come from Colorado—Ben'd say, is that a city?

But Ben didn't really know what a city was. You couldn't figure how Ben read that word.

Say, I went up to Denver for the weekend, and Ben'd look at you funny, because weekend was another thing that didn't translate. Ben wouldn't ask, either, because Ben didn't really want to know: he couldn't spend it and he wasn't going there and never would and that was the limit of Ben's interest.

Ask Ben about spectral analysis or the assay and provenance of a given chunk of rock and he'd do a thirty-minute monologue.

Damn weird values in Belt kids' mindsets. Sometimes Bird wondered. Right now he didn't want to know.

Right now he was thinking he might not want Ben with him next trip. Ben was a fine geologist, a reliable hold-her-steady kind of pilot, and honest in his own way.

But he had some scary dark spots too.

Maybe years could teach Ben what a city was. But God only knew if you could teach Ben how to live in one.

Bird was seriously pissed. Ben had that much figured, and that made him mad and it made him nervous. He approved of Bird, generally. Bird knew his business, Bird had spent thirty years in the Belt, doing things the hard way, and Ben had had it figured from the time he was 14 that you never got anywhere working for the company if you weren't in the executive track or if you weren't a senior pilot: he had never had the connections for the one and he hadn't the reflexes for the other, so freerunning was the choice, . . . where he was working only for himself and where what you knew made the difference.

He had come out of the Institute with a basic pilot's license and the damn-all latest theory, had the numbers and the knowledge and everything it took. The company hadn't been happy to see an Institute lad go off freerunning, instead of slaving in its offices or working numbers for some company miner, and most Institute brats wouldn't have had the nerve to do what he'd done: skimp and save and live in the debtor barracks, and then bet every last dollar on a freerunner's outfitting; most kids who went through the Institute didn't have the discipline, didn't refrain from the extra food and the entertainment and the posh quarters you could opt for. They didn't even get out of the Institute undebted, thank *God* for mama's insurance; and even granted they did all that, most wouldn't have had the practical sense to know, if they did decide to go mining and not take a job key-pushing in some office, that the game was not to sign up with some shiny-new company pilot in corp-rab, who had perks out to here. Hell, no, the smart thing was to hunt the records for the old independent who had made ends meet for thirty years, lean times and otherwise.

Namely Morris Bird.

Freerunning was the only wide gamble left in the Belt—and freerunners, being from what they were, didn't have the advantage of expert, up-to-date knowledge from the Institute—plus the Assay Office. But with Morrie Bird's thirty years of running the Belt, his *old* charted pieces were bigger than you got nowadays, distributed all along the orbital track, and he got chart fees on those every month, the company didn't argue with his requests to tag, and those old charted pieces kept coming round again, in the way of rocks that looped the sun fast and slow. Sometimes those twenty-four- and twelve-year-old pieces might have been perturbed, and if somebody tried to argue about the claim, your numbers had to be solid after all those years—besides which, to find the good chaff that might remain to be found, you had to have more than guesswork. That was the pitch he had to offer along with 20 k interest-free to finance some equipment Bird badly needed; that was why Bird should take a greenie for a numbers man in a time when experienced miners went begging: company training, the science and the math and the complete Belt charts that Assay got to see—and they had done damned well as a team—*damned* well, til they'd got one of those absolutely miserable draws Mama sometimes handed you—a sector where there just wasn't much left to find but a handful of company-directed tags on some company-owned rocks.

So right now they were in a financial slump, Bird was under a strain, and Bird had odd touchy spots Ben never had been able to figure—all of which this Dekker had evidently hit on with his crazy behavior and his pretty-boy looks. Dekker was up there in their sleeping nook mumbling about losing his partner (damned careless of him!) and now Bird was mad at *him*, acting as if it was *his* fault the guy was alive and the find that might have been their big break turned out complicated.

Maybe, he thought, Bird did want that ship as much as he did, maybe Bird was equally upset that this fellow was alive, Bird having this ethic about helping people—Bird might well be confused about what he was feeling.

Dangerous attitude to spread around, Ben thought, this charity business—and unfair, when Bird even thought about forgoing that ship for somebody who owed him and not the other way around, at his own partner's expense. It was a way for Bird to get had, and a man as free-handed as Bird was needed help from a partner with a lasting reason to keep him in one piece.

"Bird?" he called out from the workstation. "I got your prelim calc. No complications but that 'driver and our mass."

Bird came over to him, Bird said he'd finish it up and call Mama.

Bird touched him on the shoulder in a confusingly friendly way and said, "Get some sleep."

Ben said, because he thought it might make Bird happier, "You. I'm wired." At the bottom of his motives was the thought that a little time next to Dekker's constant mumbling about Cory and his watch might make Bird a little less charitable to strangers.

But Bird said, "You. You're the one needs it most."

"What's *that* supposed to mean?"

"It means what it means. You're tired. You've worked your ass off. Get some rest."

"I don't think I'll sleep right off. That guy makes me nervous. This whole situation makes me nervous."

"Bad day. Hard day."

He decided Bird was being sane again. He was relieved. "You know," he said, "we might just ought to get a statement out of this guy. You know. Besides pictures. I'm going to get a tape of this whole damn What-time-is-it? routine, show what we got to cope with. Might just prove our case."

Bird shook his head.

"Bird, for God's sake."

"Ben," he said firmly.

Ben did not understand. He flatly did not understand.

"Just go easy on him," Bird said.

"So what's he to us?"

"A human being."

"That's no damn recommendation," Ben muttered. But it was definitely a mistake to argue with Bird in his present mood: Bird owned the ship. Ben shook his head. "I'll just get the pictures."

"You don't understand, do you?"

"Understand what?"

"What if it was you out there?"

"I wouldn't be in that damn mess, Bird! You wouldn't be."

"You're that sure."

"I'm sure."

"Ben, you mind my asking—what ever happened to your folks?"

"What's that to do with it?"

"Did *they* ever make a mistake?"

"My mama wasn't the pilot. —That ship's not going to be book mass, with that tank rupture. Center of mass is going to be off, too. Need to do a test burn in a little while, all right? I don't want to leave anything to guesswork."

"Yeah. Fine. Nothing rough. Remember we have a passenger."

Ben frowned at him, and kept his mouth shut.

Bird said, pulling closer, "I got to tell you, Ben, right up front, we're not robbing this poor sod. He's got enough troubles. Hear me? Don't you even be thinking about it."

"It's not robbing. It's perfectly legal. It's your rights, Bird, same as he has his. The same as he'd take his, if things were the other way around. That's the way the system is set up to work."

"There's rights, and there's what *is* right."

"He's not your friend! He's not even anybody's friend you know. Bird, for God's sake, you got a major break here. Breaks like this don't just fall into your lap, and they're nothing if you don't make them work for you. That's why there's laws—to even it up so you can work with people the way they are, Bird, not the way you want them to be."

"You still have to look in mirrors."

"What's mirrors to do with anything?"

"If we're due anything, we're due the expenses."

"Expenses, hell! We're due haulage, medical stuff, chemkit, and a fat salvage fee at minim, we're due that whole damn *ship*, is what we're due, Bird."

"It won't work."

"Hell if it won't work, Bird! I'll show it to you in the code. You want me to show it to you in the code?"

Bird looked put out with him. Bird said, with a sigh, "I know the rules."

Bird had him completely puzzled. He took a chance, asked: "Bird, —have I done something wrong?"

"No. Just give me warning on that burn. I'm going to shoot some antibiotics into our passenger, get him a little more comfortable."

Ben said, vexed, figuring to argue it later, "Better keep a running tab on the stuff, if that's the way you're playing it."

"There isn't any damn tab, Ben! Quit thinking like a computer. The guy can have kidney and liver damage, he can have fractures, he can be concussed. You can calc a nice gentle burn while you're at it. We're not doing any sudden moves with him."

"All right. Fine. Slow and easy." Ben tapped the stylus at the keys, with temper boiling up in him as Bird left—downright hurt, when it came to it. He tapped it several times on the side of the board, shoved away from the toehold and caught up with Bird's retreat. "Bird, dammit, what in hell have I done?"

Bird looked at him as if he were adding things in his head.

Maybe, Ben thought, maybe Bird just didn't like to be argued with. Or maybe it was that pretty-boy face of Dekker's. Dekker was a type he thoroughly detested, because for some people there didn't need to be any sane reason to do them favors, didn't matter they were dumb as shit or that they'd cut your throat for their advantage, people believed them because they looked good and they talked smooth. It suddenly dawned on him that Bird was acting soft-headed about this guy with no good reason; and he decided maybe Bird taking care of Dekker himself wasn't a good idea at all. He said, quickly, quietly, "It's the bank I'm worried about. And this guy's intentions. He's not in his right zone. He's a long way from it. We don't know him. Maybe he was thrown here, maybe he wasn't. We don't know what he is. He could be some drop-off from the rebels—"

"There aren't any 'jackers, Ben. And he isn't any rebel. What's he going to spy on? A ship you can see from deep out with any decent optics? You've heard too many stories."

"All right, all right, he's one of the good guys. You want him tucked in safe and sound, you want a dose of broad-spectrum stuff and maybe some vitamins in him, I'll take care of it. *You* set up the burn."

"You're already running on it."

"I said I'll take care of him!"

Ben kited off toward the med cabinet, and Bird's first thought was, So maybe I talked some human sense into him. And then, cynically: Maybe at least he figures he's precarious with me right now, and covering his ass is all he's doing. You don't change a man that fast.

Then he saw Ben fill a hypo and thought, God, he wouldn't!

Bird kicked off from the touch strip and sailed up beside Ben. "I'll do it."

"I'll take care of it."

Bird snatched at the bottle. It floated free. It turned label-side toward him as he caught it and it *was* antibiotic Ben had been loading.

Ben scowled at him. "You're acting crazy, Bird. You're acting seriously crazy, you know that?"

"I'll handle it," Bird said. "Just wait on that burn a few minutes."

Ben scowled at him, shoved off from the cabinet and sailed backward toward the workstation. Offended, Bird thought, with a twinge of irritation and of conscience at once—not sure what Ben really had intended. Ben had no patience or sympathy for Dekker or anyone else—so he'd thought.

Or was it just plain jealousy Ben was showing?

Ben belted back in at his keyboard. Ben was not looking at him, pointedly not looking at him.

Bird kicked off to the side, drifted up to Dekker—Dekker looked to be asleep, Bird hoped that was all. At least he'd given up asking what time it was. Bird popped him on the arm with the back of one hand.

Dekker waked with a start and an outcry.

"Polybact," Bird said, showing him the needle. "You got any allergies?"

Dekker shook his head muzzily. Bird gave him the shot, snagged the Citrisal pack out of the pipes where air currents had sent it, uncapped the stem and put it in Dekker's mouth.

Dekker took a sip or two. Turned his head. "That's all."

"We're going to do a test burn. After that we'll be doing a 140, going to catch a beam home. Has to be our Base, understand, unless we get other instructions. We're out of R2."

Dekker looked at him hazily. "No. No hospital. 79, 709, 12. That's where we were. We had a find—big find. *Big* find. I'll sign it to you. Just go there. Pick my partner up."

"Your partner was outside when the accident happened?"

Dekker nodded.

"What happened? Catch a rock?" It happened. Usually to new crews.

Another nod. Dekker's eyes were having trouble tracking. "Kilometer wide. Iron content."

Freerunning miners didn't *find* nickel-iron rocks that big. Rocks that big had been mapped by optics: those rocks all had long-standing numbers, they belonged to the company, and if they were rich, they got 'drivers assigned to them, they got chewed in pieces, and they streamed to the recovery zone at the Well by bucketloads. But Bird didn't argue that point: Dekker didn't seem highly reasonable at the moment, and he only said, "A whole k wide. You're sure of that."

"It's the truth," Dekker said. "We got a tag on it. Uncharted rock. You can have it, if you'll go back there and find her."

"Cory's a her."

"Cory. Yes." He was going out again. "God, go back. Go back there, listen to me, anything you want . . ."

"You want another sip?" Bird asked, but Dekker was out again, gone. Bird shoved off and arrowed down to grab a handhold by Ben's workstation, but Ben said:

"I'm already ahead of you. Man said 79, 709, 12? No signal in that direction but the 'driver."

Nothing but the 'driver, Bird thought. God. "Hear any tag?"

Ben shook his head.

Bird bit his lip, wondering—

Wondering, dammit, how long that particular 'driver had been there. A while, damned sure. But Mama only told you what you needed. You could work out the rest from what you could gather with your own ears and your radar, but who wanted to?

Who, in a question about a company tag and a private claim, —wanted to?

Ben said in a low voice, "Do you suppose that fool tried to skim the company on a rock that size?"

Bird thought, I want out of here.

But what he argued to Ben was: "We just don't ask. We don't know anything and we sure as hell aren't getting in their way. Whatever claim's out there already has a 'driver attached."

"Makes other claims kind of moot, doesn't it?"

"Don't even ask."

Company prerogatives, secret company codes and direct accesses—company ships could talk back and forth at will; bet your life they could.

And count that that 'driver ship was armed—if you counted a kilometer-long mass driver as a lethal weapon, and Bird personally did. You didn't want to argue right of way or ownership with a 'driver captain. They were ASTEX to the core and they were a breed—next to God.

Ben said, "Told you we should have left this guy on the other side of the lock. It's still not too late."

"Cut the jokes. It wasn't funny the first time."

"Bird, there's a hell of a lot more than he's telling. Big find, hell. They were skimming a company claim."

"We don't know that."

"Well, that's all I want to know. Suddenly I'm damn glad we haven't been talking to that 'driver. I don't like this, damn, I don't."

"I don't know anything. You don't know anything. We didn't look at that log. Thank God. Let's just get us out of here."

"We could offer to give evidence."

"We don't know what we're swearing to. We don't *know* what happened."

"We *could* look in that log."

"Sure, a skimmer's going to log his moves. What's he going to write? '1025 and we just blew a chip off a 1 k rock'? If we touch that panel over there we'll leave a record of that access, and maybe that's not a good idea. Do I spell it out? Don't be a fool."

"I can fix that log. I think I can bypass that access record if you really want to know."

"Don't depend on it. 'Think' isn't good enough. No. We don't run that risk. Best claim we've got is that we haven't seen those records and we don't know a thing. We don't have a problem if we just keep clean. No shady stuff. Nothing. Clean, Ben."

"Knock that guy in the head," Ben muttered. "Be sure there's no questions. Then there's no problem."

God, he thought. Is that what they teach this generation?

The ship jolted.

Dekker yelled aloud, struggling to get free. Someone—a familiar voice now—shouted at him to shut up.

Another, gentler, said, "That was just getting in position, Dekker. Take it easy."

He had another blank spot then, woke up with the nightmare feeling of increasing *g*, not knowing where it was going to stop, or what had started it. Something pressed into his back and he thought, God, we're spinning—

"Cory!" he yelled.

"Shut up, dammit!"

"Dekker." This came gently then, with a touch at his shoulder. A smell of something cooked. Freefall. He blinked and looked at the gray-haired man, who let a foil packet of something drift near his face.

"We've done our position," the man said to him, he couldn't remember the name, and then did. Bird. Bird was the good one. Bird was the one who didn't want to kill him. "We're going to catch our beam tomorrow and we're going home. Seems Mama thinks we're in no hurry or something, damn her. I'll let you loose if you can keep awake." Another pat on the shoulder. "You know you've been off your head a little."

"What time is it?"

"Shush," Bird said, "don't go asking that."

"I want to know—"

Bird put a hand on his mouth. "Don't do that," Bird said, looking him in the eyes. "Don't do that, son. You don't need to know. You really don't need to know. Your partner's just lost, that's all. A long time ago. There's nothing anybody can do for her."

He didn't want to believe that. He didn't want to wake up again, but Bird caught the packet drifting in front of his face and held the tube to his mouth, insisting.

He took a little. It was warm, it was soup, it was salty as hell. He turned his head away, and Bird let it go, leaving a tiny planetesimal of soup cooling in the air, drifting away with the current. Bird brushed at it, caught it in his hand, wiped it on his sleeve.

Blood everywhere, shining dark drops. . . .

Everything was stable. Clean and quiet. Nothing had ever gone wrong here. Nothing had ever *been* wrong. He kept his eyes open for fear of the dark behind them and tried another sip of what Bird was offering him, while the first was hitting his stomach with an effect he was not yet sure of.

Why am I here? he asked himself. What is this place? This isn't my ship. What am I doing here?

Maybe he asked out loud. He didn't keep track of things. "To Refinery Two," Bird told him.

He shook his head. He got a breath and thought, Cory's still in the ship, they've left Cory back in the ship—

He reminded himself, he could do it now with only a cold, strange calm: No, Cory's dead— Not that he could remember. He kept telling himself that over and over, but he could not remember. She was still there. She was wondering what had happened to him. She was trusting him to do the right thing, the smart thing. She was waiting for him to pick her up . . .

The dark-headed one, the young one, Ben, rose into his vision, carrying a length of thin cable and a davies clip. Ben hung in front of his face and reached behind his neck with the cable.

"Hell!" he yelled, and used a knee, but Ben grabbed a handful of his coveralls and it missed its target.

Oh, shit, he thought then, looking Ben in the face. He thought Ben would kill him.

Bird said, from the other side, "Easy, son. It's temporary. Hold still."

He had thought Bird was all right. But Bird held him still and Ben got the cable around his neck. The clip clicked.

"There," Ben said. "You can reach the necessaries . . . reach anything in this ship but the buttons. And you don't really want those, do you?"

He stared eye to eye at Ben and wondered if Ben was waiting to kill him while Bird was asleep. He remembered hearing them talk. He wondered whether Ben was going to hit him right now.

"You understand me?" Ben asked.

He nodded, scared, and likewise clear-headed in a tight-focused, adrenaline-edged way. He stayed very still while Ben started untaping his left wrist from the pipe. He didn't think either ahead or backward. It was just himself and Ben, and the old man saying, holding tightly to his shoulder, "I apologize. I sincerely apologize about this, son. But we can't have you wandering around off your head. Ben's not a bad guy. He really isn't."

He remembered what he'd overheard. He had thought Bird wanted to keep him alive, and now he wasn't sure either one of them was sane.

Ben freed his left arm. Bird untied the right. Moving both at once hurt his chest, hurt his back, hurt everything so much his eyes teared.

Ben went away forward. Bird stayed behind, put a hand on his shoulder. "No difference between our config and yours, the standard rig, by what I saw. Anything you can reach, you can use. Wouldn't use the spinner with that cable attached, understand, but you got *g* while you were tumbling, God knows probably more than enough. Your stimsuit's clean, but you'd as glad be free of it a day or so, wouldn't you? You're probably sore as hell. —Right? Just don't try to use the shower, cable won't let it seal, we'll have water everywhere. Anything else you got free run of. Copy that?"

"Yeah."

Bird gathered up the trailing cable, put it in his hand, closed his fist on it. "When you're moving about the cabin, do kind of keep a grip on that. We don't want you hurt. Hear? Don't want that cable to pull you up short. We're not going to do a burn without we warn you, but all the same, you keep a hand to that. Hold on to it."

Just too many things had happened to him. He could not figure what his situation was or what they wanted. He shoved off, drifted away from the bulkhead to get the packet of soup that had come adrift. Braking with his arm against a pipe was almost more than he could do. He let go the cable, confused, and banged his head,

Someone caught his foot and pulled, gently. It turned him as he came down and he saw Bird with a packet of soup in his own hands.

"There's solid food," Bird said, "when you can handle it. Use anything from the galley you need. You got pretty dehydrated."

He hated all this past tense, implying a major piece of time he didn't remember. From moment to moment he told himself Cory was gone, and every time he did that he felt a sense of panic. He brushed a touchpad with his foot, stopped, drank a sip and watched Bird sip from his own packet. He kept thinking, They're lying to me, they're not taking me home. . . .

Finally he asked Bird, "What 'driver is it out there?"

"What about a 'driver?"

"You were talking about a 'driver. What 'driver were you talking about?"

Ben yelled up from below, "Don't tell him a damn thing, Bird. He hasn't earned it."

He looked from Ben down at the workstation up to Bird, resting by the bulkhead.

"Ben's excitable," Bird said. "Just have your breakfast. Or supper, as may be."

But Ben was drifting up to them. Ben braked with the shove of a hand against the conduits. "I'd like to know," Ben said, "what you've got to pay for this trip. Eat our food, breathe our air, take up our time and our fuel. We're aborting a run for you. We just got effin' *started* and we're headed back to Base, damn near *zeroed* on your account, mister. You got any assets to pay for this? Or just debts?"

"We have money," he said, and then knew he shouldn't have said that to these people. He said, desperately catching up the thread of his thought—he hoped he hadn't lost anything between: "So what 'driver is it?"

Ben said, "How much money?"

"Ben," Bird said.

"I want," he said carefully, "I want you to call that 'driver and ask about my partner."

"Ask what about your partner?" Ben asked.

"Ask if they—" He stuttered on the thought. He never stuttered, and still he could not get it out. "—if they p-picked her up."

"So why should they? What were you doing here, poaching in another Refinery's zone?"

"We w-weren't." Dammit. "*It* was."

"What do you mean, 'it was'?"

"Ben," Bird said, and then, looking at him: "Forget he asked."

He didn't understand. He was so weak he couldn't track what they were saying from moment to moment, and hostile questions, zero *g* and unaccustomed food were all one confusion of balance and orientation. There was a constant buzz in his head that rose and fell like the fan-sounds. From moment to moment he knew Cory was alive, and from moment to moment he thought about the time and wanted to check his watch to be sure.

But that was crazy. He began to know it was. The only hope Cory had now was that 'driver ship. Maybe it had picked her up. Maybe it had.

"He's not telling the story he started with," Ben said. "Man's lying somewhere. A collision with a rock, he said. An explosion took one whole damn tank out. The other one's got a bash you could park a skimmer in. You want to see the videotape, man? I can show you the tape."

"Didn't hit a rock," he said, shaking his head. He had no idea where this was going. He had no idea what they were accusing him of, whether this was going on record or what they wanted from him.

"Why would it explode?"

"The 'driver clipped us."

"Facing *away* from the Well? Whose Zone were you in?"

"R1."

"'Driver, hell. You ran it into a rock, didn't you? Just plain ran it onto a rock."

"No."

"Ben," Bird said, "take it easy. The guy's confused."

"'Take it easy.' —Some people with trouble deserve it, you know."

"We don't know anything," Bird said. "His memory isn't going to be all that good, with what he's been through."

"Looks healthy enough. Looks damned well healthy enough on our air and our food. Looks like he's making real good progress."

Ben talked about claiming the ship, he recollected that—they were after the ship and they claimed they were taking him to R2, not home; now they were talking about other debts—

They talked as if they wanted to put him to work for them. He had heard about Nouri. It had happened before in the Belt. Guys with all sorts of kinks went out in ships . . . and when they were ready to come in to Base, they might not want to take the evidence with them.

God, he thought, and looked off toward nowhere. The only thing in the vicinity was that 'driver ship. If they had never reported finding Cory—

The instruments . . . something coming at him over the horizon—

Explosion like a fist hit them. *G*-force. He reached after the fire controls.

No power. Nothing . . .

Ben left him. Bird left him. He saw Bird talking with Ben, holding on to Ben's arm, he couldn't make out what they were saying.

Then Ben shouted, "We own that ship!" and Bird: "Just shut it down, Ben, shut it down, for God's *sake*, Ben!"

They started arguing again, yelling at each other about money, about what they were spending on him, and Bird took his part, saying, over and over again, "It's not your damn decision, Ben!"

He watched, turning so he could see, phasing in and out of clear awareness, the fan-sound going in his ears, the soup he had drunk lying queasy on his stomach. He was afraid at one point Ben was going to hit the old man, and that Ben was going to end up in control of the ship.

The argument broke up. He grayed out awhile. He came to with something near him and looked into a cyclopic glass lens, a camera pointed at his face, Ben's face behind it. That scared him. He stared back, wondering whether Ben had a real kink or whether Ben was just a hobbyist. He was afraid to object. He just stared back and tried not to throw up.

Then Ben cut the camera off and said,

"Got you, you son of a bitch," and drifted off.

He thought, This guy's crazy, he's absolutely crazy . . . Ben wanted his ship. Ben wanted him dead. He had this cable around his neck, that Ben had put there. He was afraid to sleep after that, afraid Ben was going to do something stranger still, and adrenaline kept him focused for a while. But things started going away from him again, he was back in the dark with the tumbling and the pressure building in his head, and then he was back again with that lens in his face and Ben going crazier and crazier . . .

He had no idea how long those times were or whether he had dreamed the business with the camera. When he looked, Bird was sleeping in a makeshift net rigged down toward the bow, and Ben was back at the workstation keyboard as if he had never moved, never had done anything in the least odd. He watched Ben for a while, wondering if he had hallucinated, wondering if it was safe to move with Bird asleep, because he was beginning to feel an acute need of going down to the head, and he was scared to do anything that Ben might conceivably object to.

Finally he shoved off very slowly and drifted down feet first toward the shower/toilet.

Ben looked around at him. He touched the other wall and caught the shower door, and Ben seemed not to care.

Don't use the shower, he remembered that—he kept the cable in his left hand the way Bird had said, but for a space he lost track of where he was again: then he was inside the shower where the toilet was, finishing his business. He thought for a panicked moment. They're lying, this is our ship all along. It was even the same ribbed pattern on the green shower wall. He could feel it when he touched it, real as anything he knew. He thought: Cory can't be dead, she isn't dead, there isn't any other ship—

But there was the cable snaking out the door, there was the clip that wouldn't come off—he tried to brace himself with his feet and his shoulders while he worked, he pulled the clip cover back to squeeze the jaws with his bare fingers, but he could get no leverage on it and all the while Cory was out there with no way to get back—

He looked at his watch. It said 0638. It said, March 12. He thought, The damn watch is wrong, it can't be March 12. I'm back where I started. Cory's going to die. Oh, God—

The clip cover slipped and he pinched his finger, bit his lip against the pain and thought, I've got to get rid of this, got to get hold of the ship, get the radio—

He looked around him for leverage, anything that could double for a pliers and put a pinch on the jaws with the clip cover retracted. He tried the soap dispenser, pried the small panel up, worked himself around upside down with his foot braced against the wall, pulled the spring cover back from the jaws with the fingers of his left hand, and held the pressure point under the metal edge of the panel with the leverage of his right hand, pushing the panel edge down on the clip, hard as he could, trying not to let it slip—

CHAPTER 3

Came a thump from the shower, and Ben thought to himself: He's been in there a long time.

He slipped his seat belt off, shoved off in that direction and snatched a handhold at the shower corner, catching a hazy image of Dekker upside down and crosswise in the stall.

What in hell? he wondered. He flung the door back—could make no sense at first of what Dekker was doing. Then he saw the bloody fingerprints on the locker door, the whole angle of Dekker's neck and arm forcing the soap dispenser panel shut on the clip. Dekker let it go of a sudden, the panel banged, and Dekker came off the wall at him, grappling for a hold, trying, he realized in panic, to get the cable looped around his throat.

He yelled, flailed out and caught the cable, their tumble winding them both into the cable Dekker was trying to get around his neck, and in sheer panic he hit him, hauled up on the cable and kept hitting him, hard as he could.

"Ben!" Bird yelled. He half-heard it: he just kept pounding away, his fist gone numb, his breath so choked he had no idea whether he was snagged in the cable or not. Bird grabbed his arm, yelling, "You're going to kill him! —Ben, dammit, stop!"

He realized then that Dekker was no longer fighting. Bird pried him out of his grip, Dekker floating loose and limp. Bird shook at him again, said, "God, have you lost your mind?"

Sympathy for a damned lunatic—no thanks for stopping Dekker from killing them. He was shaking from the scare Dekker had given him, he hurt from Dekker's hitting him, and Bird took Dekker's part.

"That sonuvabitch tried to pry the clip loose!" he said and shook free of Bird's grip, grabbed Dekker, hauled him up again where the pipes and conduits were, and fumbled the roll of tape out of his hip pocket. Dekker was still limp as he started wrapping his wrist to a cold-water pipe, but he hurried, afraid he would come to.

"Stop it!" Bird cried, and came up and shoved him away.

His hand hurt. Bird was taking the lunatic's part. So he went down and got into stores and dispensed himself a beer: he didn't speak to Bird, he didn't trust himself to say anything at the moment. His jaw was sore. A tooth felt loose. His lip was cut. He had never had a fight in school and it had not been his idea to have one this late in his life, except a guy wanted to kill him. He yelled up at Bird, "Don't you let that sonuvabitch loose! Don't you do it, Bird!"

He took a gulp of beer, still shaking, his legs and arms jerking spasmodically, his breath so erratic he had trouble drinking. Not scared, mad, that was all. Damned mad. The guy tried to kill him and Bird shoved him off and started making sympathetic noises at the guy that had meant to do them both in. Bird owned the ship. Bird gave the orders. And Bird thought they could trust this sonuvabitch. . . .

"Toss me up a cold pack," Bird yelled down.

He did that: he opened up medical and sent it up to Bird and Bird didn't even look at him.

Bird cut the penlight. At least Dekker's pupils were the same size and they both reacted, which was about all he knew to look for. Dekker was bleeding from the nose in little droplets. He mopped the air with his handkerchief, to keep it out of the filters, wiped Dekker's chin, then caught the cold pack and applied it to Dekker's face and the back of his neck.

Dekker began to show signs of life, confused, struggling with the tape for a moment before he reached over with his free hand and started tearing at it. Bird grabbed that hand, restrained it, saying, so only Dekker could hear, "Easy, easy, just stay quiet, it's all right. Just take it easy—you're not doing any good that way. Cut it out, hear?"

Dekker was breathing hard, staring at him or through him, he had no idea. Dekker wanted loose, couldn't fault him for that—couldn't be sure he was sane, either; and God only knew what was going on with Ben. Dekker gave a jerk at the wrist he was holding.

"Uh-uh," he said. "Just stay still. You leave that tape alone for a while. Hear? Just let it be."

Dekker said, "Liar."

"Yeah, right." You went to sleep and things were halfway under control and you woke up with two guys trying to kill each other and it wasn't highly likely to make sense. "You're bleeding into our filters. Just stay still—damn!" as Dekker choked and sneezed beads of blood. He snagged them with the handkerchief, one-handed, pressed it against Dekker's face. "I don't know what you did, son. Did you do something to piss Ben off?"

Dekker only shook his head, denial, refusal, he had no idea. Dekker blew blood into the handkerchief, gasped a bubbly breath and mumbled, "Cory. Call Cory."

"Not likely she's answering." He shoved Dekker's hand at his face. "Hold that." He snagged the ice-pack that was coming back after its impact with the wall, and gave Dekker that too. "Just keep the cold on it. If you're going to bleed, bleed into the handkerchief, all right? Don't blow at it. Just let it be."

Dekker looked at him past the bloody handkerchief and the cold pack. Sane for a moment, maybe. Or just too miserable and too short of breath to be crazy for a while.

He collected himself and his headache and the remnant of his patience, shoved off and drifted down to Ben. Ben intended to keep his back to him, it seemed—so he turned, touched a cabinet and changed course. You got used to reading faces upside down or sideways. Ben's was sour, upset, and Ben was trying not to notice being stared at—only drinking his beer and trying to be somewhere else.

"I got a problem," he said. "Ben?"

"We both got a problem," Ben said shortly, as if he was not going to say much else. But Ben said then: "The guy was trying to kill us. He damn near had that clip undone, with a panel edge for a pliers. What was he going to do then, huh, Bird? You reckon that?"

"God only. Just go easy. We got a long way back."

"Go easy," Ben scowled. "Listen, I saved and did without all my life to get that 20 k, you understand? Nobody ever handed me a break, nobody ever gave me a damn thing, and here we have the best break anybody could look for—"

"It doesn't say we own that ship. It doesn't."

"God, Bird, —"

"We'll be all right." He could understand Ben's panic, on that level: the 20 k was hard come by, all right, so was everything. "We won't go under."

"Go under! You're old enough to know better, Bird. I put my whole life savings into this operation!"

"So have I," he said shortly, and hauled himself down and turned so he could see Ben's face rightwise up. "Thirty plus years' worth. And listen to me: you don't go hitting the guy again. He's had enough knocks to the head."

"So who is he? Who is he that you owe him a damn thing, Bird? Is there something about this guy I don't know? Somewhere you've met this guy before?"

He looked at Ben with this feeling they were not communicating again: he listened to Ben's single-minded craziness with the uncomfortable feeling he might yet have to take a wrench to his partner.

But just about the time he thought Ben might really blow, Ben gave this little wave of his hand and a shake of his head. "All right, all right, we're going in, abort our run—forget it, forget I said anything."

"What day is it?" Dekker asked from across the cabin. "Cory? *Cory?*"

"The 21st," he told him. "May 21st."

Ben raked his hand through his hair, rolled an anguished glance toward Bird. "I want rid of him. God only knows what happened to his partner. Or if there ever was a partner."

"Cory?"

"Shut up!" Ben screamed at Dekker. "Just shut it up!"

Bird bit his lip and just kept it to himself. There were times you talked things over and there were times you didn't, and Ben certainly didn't act in any way to discuss things at the moment.

"Just get our confirm out of Base," Bird said, and ventured a pat on Ben's shoulder. "It's all right, Ben. Hear?"

"Shut him up," Ben begged him. "Just shut him up for a while."

Dekker worked at the tape on his wrist, such as he could—his fingers were swollen, his ribs hurt, and he could not understand how he had gotten this way or whether he had done something to deserve being beaten and tied up like this—he flatly could not remember except the shower, the green ribbed shower, the watch—it was that day, something was going to happen to Cory—if it was that day . . . but Bird said May, not March.

January has thirty days. No, 31. February 28. March . . .

Thirty days hath September . . . April, March, and November . . .

"April, *May*, and November. Shut *up!*"

March 12. Thirty-one days. 21 less 12.

No, start in January. That's 30, no, 31, and 28—or 29 if it's leap year —is it leap year?

"It's not a leap year!"

28 and 12—no, start again. Thirty days in January—

"It's May effin' 21st, Dekker!"

Reckoning backward—twenty-one days in May—

Couldn't happen. Couldn't be then—

"You reset my watch, damn you! You're trying to drive me crazy!"

Bird came drifting up to him, put his hand on his shoulder, caught the cold pack that was drifting there and made him take it again. Bird said, quietly, on what previous subject he had no idea at all, "Time doesn't matter now, son. Just take it easy. We're about ready to catch our beam. You'll hear the sail deploy in a bit."

"Refinery Two," he said. He remembered. He hoped he did. He hoped it wasn't all to happen again.

"That's right." Another pat on his arm. Bird might be crazy as Ben, but he thought there was something decent in Bird. He let Bird tilt his head over and take a look at his eye, the right one, that was swelling and sore.

"Bird, do me a favor."

"You're short on favors right now, son. What?"

"Call my partner."

"We're doing all we can."

He didn't believe that. He especially didn't believe it when Bird pulled another cable loop out of his pocket and grabbed his other wrist. He resisted that. He tried to shove Bird off, but when he exerted himself he kept graying out and losing his breath. "Let me go," he asked Bird, quietly, so Ben wouldn't hear. God, his ribs hurt. "Let me loose."

"Can't do that, son. Not today. Maybe not for a while. Ben says you've been bashing things." The cable bit into his wrist and one clip snapped.

"Ben's a liar!" No. He hadn't meant to take that tack. He tried to amend it. A second clip snapped—woven steel cable looped around a pipe or something. He tried not to panic. He tried to be perfectly reasonable. "He's right. I was off my head awhile. But I'm all right now. Tell him I'm sorry. I won't do it again."

"I'll do that." Bird squeezed his shoulder in a kindly way. "Nobody's going to hurt you, son. Nobody means you any harm. We just got three people in a little ship and you're a little confused. Try to keep it a little quiet. You'll be all right."

The oxygen felt short. He tried not to panic. He didn't want them to tell him he was confused. "Bird," he said, before Bird could get away. "There's a 'driver right where I came from. Isn't there?"

"I wouldn't know that, son. I don't know for sure where you came from."

"79, 709, 12."

Bird nodded slowly. "All right. Yes. There is a 'driver near there."

He found his breath shorter and shorter. He said, calmly, sanely, because he finally found one solid thing they both agreed on. "All right. I want you to call it. Ask about my partner."

"You sure you *had* a partner, son?"

Reality kept getting away from him. Time and space and what had happened did. He fixed on Bird's gray-stubbled face as the only reference he had. "Just call the 'driver. Just ask them if they picked up my partner. That's all I ask."

"Son, . . . I honestly don't know what you might have been doing out there in a 'driver's assigned territory. You understand me?"

He didn't. He shook his head.

"How long have you been in the Belt, son?"

"Couple years." He wasn't sure of that number any longer either. He was sure of nothing in regard to time. He thought again—look at my watch—got to know—which direction to reckon.

"Freerunner?"

"Yeah."

"You ever make any money at mining?"

Ben asked those kinds of questions. "Maybe."

"Haven't ever done any skimming, have you?"

His heart jumped. He shook his head emphatically, wanting Bird to believe him. "No." He couldn't remember what conversation they were in, what they had just said, why Bird was asking him a thing like that.

Bird said, "We're just damn close to that 'driver's fire-path, understand, and if we got one accident, we sure don't need another, you read me?"

Things were dark awhile. Bird gave him more of the soup, told him it was breakfast and they were all right. He wanted to think so, but he didn't believe it any longer. He heard voices near him. He thought he remembered Bird asking him questions after that. He wasn't sure. He dreamed he answered, and that Bird let him loose awhile to get to the toilet. But maybe that was the other time.

From time to time he remembered the collision. His muscles jumped, and then he would realize that was long past and he was still alive. "What time is it?" he asked, and Bird caught him by the side of the jaw, made him focus eye to eye.

"Son, *don't* cross Ben again. Don't ask him the time. Don't ask me. Your friend's dead. She's *dead*, you understand me?"

Bird's grip hurt. Bird was angry and he didn't know why.

"We got the confirm from Base," Ben shouted up.

"Yeah," Bird called back, and patted Dekker's face. "Got a draft coming from that vent. I'll get you a blanket, tuck you in—we're about to catch the beam."

"Yeah," he said. He was confused again. He thought that Bird had said that would be some time yet. But he'd given up knowing where they were. He hung there, nowhere for a while, listening to Bird move around. He heard hydraulics working, heard that series of sounds that meant a sail deploying. He thought, So we're going in. He didn't really believe it. It wasn't going to happen. It wasn't possible any longer. He couldn't come back from this. He just kept seeing the shower wall, the watch on his arm, perpetual loop, maybe because he *was* dead . . .

Bird came back with an armful of blankets and jammed one between his head and the pipes, one at the small of his back. "Don't lose that," Bird said, and took a bit of webbing and tied it around him and the blankets and the conduits, telling him he had to, it was for his safety, but he had stopped believing Bird. He thought about Sol Station. Mama coming home from work. Cory meeting him at Refinery One dock. Hi, there, she'd say. I'm Cory. And a person who'd been a lot of letters and a lot of postage would be flesh and blood . . .

If he could get to dockside, if they brought him that far, she'd be there . . . if he could get to the 12th he could get there again . . .

He'd run out on his mother, Cory had run away from hers. His mother just let him go. Cory'd sent those letters that would always be stacked up in her mail-file and waiting for her . . . He'd say, Don't read them, but Cory would. Then she'd be down with a guilt attack for days, and go off by herself and spend hours at a rented comp writing some damn letter home—but he wouldn't. There was a lot he should have said when he'd had the chance. But it was Cory that didn't get any more chances, and that wasn't fair.

"Stand by," Bird yelled up at him. "Dekker? Hear me? We're about to catch the beam. You all right up there?"

He thought he answered. He was thinking: We're not going home. We're not ever going home again. There's going to be all these letters stacked up and waiting for Cory, and Cory won't ever read them. They'll just tell her mother . . . and she'll kill me . . .

"Dekker! Dammit, pay attention!" Ben's voice. "Answer!"

"Yeah," he said.

"Dekker!"

He said it louder. The acceleration pressed his body against the blankets Bird had tucked between him and the pipes. The tape cut off circulation and his fingers on that hand went numb. He began to be dizzy: the ship was going unstable—all of it came back, the explosion and the ship tumbling, things flying loose—

"Cory!" he yelled; or maybe that was then. He had no more idea. Someone told him to shut up and he remembered that he had been rescued, but he had no idea where they were going or whether he was going to live.

Finally the pressure let up and he hung there with his head throbbing and the feeling slowly returning to his hands. Pressure in his sinuses and behind his eyes built to a blinding headache when he tried to wonder what was happening or where he was.

"What time is it?" he asked, but no one paid attention to him. He asked again, his voice cracking: "What time is it?" and Ben sailed up into his vision, grabbed him by the knee, grabbed him by his collar and hit him across the face.

"Shut up!" Ben yelled at him. He tried to use his knee and turn his face to protect himself. Ben hit him again and again, until Bird came in from below and pulled Ben off him, yelling at Ben to stop it. Bird said, "Go back to sleep, Ben." And Ben yelled back: "How can I sleep with What time is it? What time is it, God, I'm going to strangle him before the hour's out—I'm going to fuckin' kill him!"

"Ben," Bird said quietly, taking Ben by the shoulder. "Ben. Easy. All right. —Dekker, . . . *shut the hell up!"*

After that, it could have been next day, next week, a few hours, he wasn't sure. Ben came floating up to him, carefully took him by the collar and gathered it tight, and calmly said, right in his face, "It's my watch now, hear me? We're all alone. Do you hear me, Dekker?"

He nodded. He looked Ben in his close-set eyes and said yes again, in case Ben hadn't understood him.

"You want to know what time it is, Dekker?"

He shook his head. He remembered that made Ben crazy. Ben wound his grip tighter, cutting off the blood to his head.

"If you ask the time just one damn more time I'm going to break your neck. You understand me, Dekker?"

He nodded. The edges of his vision were going. Ben went on looking at him with murder in his eyes.

He remembered—he was not sure—Ben taking pictures of him while he was unconscious. He thought, while Ben was shutting the blood away from his brain, This man is crazy. He's crazy and I'm not that sure about Bird. . . .

"Hear me?" Ben said.

He tried to say yes. Things got grayer. The ship was spinning. Ben let him go and went away. Then he gulped several lungfuls of air and started shivering. He wished Bird would wake up, he wished he knew where he was going now, and whether Cory would be waiting on the dock. They said Refinery Two, but that was like saying Mars or the Moon: places were different, and you didn't know where you were going even if you knew the name.

The Belt was like that. It was always like that. The rules changed, the company tried to screw you, but Cory always did the figuring, Cory had had college, Cory knew the numbers, and he didn't.

He wished they had never taken him off that ship. He wished they had never found him. Or maybe he was dreaming. He had no idea now what was real.

Dekker was off his head again, mumbling to himself, just under the noise of the pumps and the fans. Ben put a hand over that ear and tried to concentrate on the charts, feeding in info that was going to come in handy, because Big Mama didn't like to tell freerunners anything except what she had to—but with a spare and illicit storage, an enterprising and close-mouthed freerunner could vastly improve on Mama's charts, look at the sector she offered you, and *tell* which runs to take at any cost and which to lease out if you had any choice.

So you paid close attention while you were running, you listened to the sectors you were passing through blind and used your radar for what it was worth, on all the sectors around you while you ran on Belt Management's set, (they swore) safe course out and home; and you filed every piece of information you could get your hands on, listening for the older tags, making charts of the new, figuring where good rocks might cluster, assembling the whole moving mass of particles around you, because when Jupiter swept the Belt on his twelve-year course, slowing rocks down, speeding rocks up, and now and again changing certain orbits by a million or so k or flinging certain rocks clear out of the Belt, those all-important numbers did change. It was Sol's set of dice, but Jupiter did make the game interesting, and the freerunners with the best numbers and the best records were the freerunners that survived. Rocks hit each other now and again, 'driver-tenders got careless, and now and again you might find an uncharted big bit of some old rock long since ground to bits and used, a chunk still running the old orbit path, give or take what rocks did to each other and what Jupiter did and what the occasional 'driver did when it went firing loads through the Belt to the Well: not much to hit out here, but now and again, generally thanks to some 'driver, they did, with shattering results. Sometimes, again, strange rocks just wandered through, old bits of comets, Oort Cloud detritus, God only: every rock had its path, they all danced with Sol, but some were distant partners—and with the mass they were hauling now, you just hoped to hell Mama liked you, and gave you solid numbers.

"We're not real easy to stop," he had said to Bird, among other things.

"We could brake," Bird had said.

And he: "Yeah, yeah, and we're carrying more mass than those cables are rated for."

"Won't happen," Bird said.

Thinking like that infuriated him. The thought of the rigging failing, the thought of, at best, a walk outside for repairs, at worst, the whole sail failing beyond repair—*Trinidad* taking, at this heading, the long, long fall into the Well—made him crazy. He was already holding on to his temper with his fingernails and Bird came out with *It won't happen.*

He had fantasies of killing Dekker.

Maybe Bird.

But that was as crazy as Dekker was.

He kept feeding in the information. He kept building and refining his portable record. He ignored Dekker as much as possible. Thing about null-g, you couldn't get your finger to stay in your ear. Not easily. He thought about his earplugs, over in the cabinet, but those worked too well for his peace of mind.

He cast a glance askance at Bird sleeping so quiet in his net, where they had strung it between the galley and the number one workstation, Dekker being just too close to the spin cylinders. Dekker might have been crazy long before this—and Bird just might be soft enough to let the guy loose on his watch. That was all it took, let Dekker near a wrench or, God forbid, get his hands on something sharp.

All that blood in the ship, all those little red splatters on the suits—did a cut on the forehead bleed like that?

He had to have it agreed with Bird. They had to keep that guy confined—somehow, someway. They couldn't sleep in nets for a month, they needed the spinners: and the idea of being blind and tucked in a spinner for six hours wondering what Dekker was doing on Bird's watch already upset his stomach.

And, damn, he intended to keep every move logged, everything they did, everything this Dekker did, every spate of What time is it?

Dekker would get the time, all right. Logged on and logged off.

He'd get the expenses written down, too, exactly the way he knew how to do it in a record Management would accept—because Benjamin J. Pollard wasn't letting an old man's softheadedness rob them of a break like this. Hell. No.

Refinery Two was only slightly prettier than a rock, but it did come welcome—that k-plus wide sooty ring that you only caught sight of on camera—and most to Bird's knowledge were eager to see it, and did turn the optics on, long before it was regulation that you had to get visual contact. There she hung, magnified in the long lens, spinning with a manic vengeance, with her masts stuck up like spindles and her stationary mast surfaces bristling with knobby bits that were pushers and tenders, and shuttles from the Shepherds and such. A few, hardly more than ten or so at any one time, counting company rigs waiting crew change, were ships a lot like *Trinidad*, a whole lot like *Trinidad*, if you took plan B on your outfitting, and opted for green in the shower.

A lot of the fitting inside Refinery Two was a lot like *Trinidad*, too, except, one supposed, if you got down to corporate residence levels, and there was about the same chance of freerunners seeing that in person as getting a guided tour of the company bunker on Mimas.

Belters lived and Belters died and Refinery Two just rolled on, this big factory-hearted ring which was the only close to *g-1* place miners and tenders in R2 zone ever got back to. She swallowed down what the Shepherds gathered in, she hiccuped methane and she shat ingots and beams and sheet and foam steel. She used her own plastics and textiles or she spat them at Mars, in this year when Jupiter was as convenient to that world as Sol Station was. But nobody knew what went to Mimas. Some said what was down there repaired itself and had more heart than any company exec—but that was rumor and you didn't want to know. Some said it wasn't really the ops center it was reputed to be, in case of something major going wrong at the Well: some said it was the ultimate bunker for the execs—but you didn't say *war* in polite society either and you didn't think too much about the big frame that sat out there aswarm with tenders and construction craft, a metal-spined monster that took rough shape here at the source of steel and plastics before it moved on to final rigging at Sol. You called what was going on out in the Beyond a job action or you called it a tax strike or you called it damned stupid, but if you were smart you didn't discuss it or that ship out there and you didn't even think about it where Mama might hear.

A-men.

"Well," he sighed, "she's still here. Kept the porch light on and the door open."

Ben didn't say, What's a porch light? You never could get a rise out of him like that.

"Used to sit outside at night," Bird said, "look up at the stars—you know what a shooting star is, Ben, lad?"

"No." Ben's tone said he was not at the moment interested to know. He was working approach, as close as his second-class license would let him. "I'm about ready to hand off. You got it?"

"Yeah."

"Dockmaster advises they copy on the request for meds. They're on their way."

"Good on that." He saw Ben furiously ticking away at the comp. "—I got your handoff. Take it easy."

"Take it easy. We got meds and customs swarming in here, we have to have the records straight."

"Everything's in order. I checked it. You checked it. —You're sure they copy on that mass."

"Yeah. I made 'em say-again." Ben was going through readout. No papers. Everything was dataflow. BM wanted forms, and it was all dataflow, not at all like the old days when if you fouled up some damn company form you got a chance to read it over slow and easy and say it right. Now in this paperless society the datalink grabbed stuff and shoved new blanks at you so fast you didn't have time to be sure all your answers made sense.

"You got all that stuff," Bird said. "And welcome to it. Damn, I hate forms."

"No worry."

Ben had a sure instinct for right answers. Ben swore it was a way of thinking. Ben input something and said, "Shit! Shut him up!"

He only then realized Dekker was talking, mumbling something in that low, constant drone of his. "I can't half hear him, he's all right."

"I can hear him! I can damn well hear him— Where are we? Where are we? What time is it? I tell you—"

"Easy."

"I've *been* easy. I'm going to kill him before we make dock, I swear I am."

"No, you're not. He's being quiet. Just let him alone."

"You're losing your hearing. You can't hear that?"

"Not that loud."

"The guy's crazy. Completely out of it. Only good thing in this business."

"Ben, . . . just—drop it, Ben. End-of-run nerves, that's all. Just drop it, you mind?"

There was a cold silence after that, except the click of buttons. And Dekker's voice, that *was* loud enough to hear now and again once you thought about it.

Long silence, except for ops, and approach control talking back and forth with them, walking them through special procedures.

"I'm sorry," Ben said stiffly.

Maybe because they were closer to civilization now. And sanity.

"Where are we?" Dekker asked.

"God!" Ben cried, and leaned far back in his seat. He yelled up at Dekker: "It's June 26th and we're coming into Mars Base, don't you remember? The president of the company's going to be at the party!"

"Don't do that," Bird said. "Just leave the poor guy alone."

"He's alone, all right, he's damn well alone. Another week and we'd be as schitz as he is."

Another call from Base: *"Two Twenty-nine Tango* Trinidad, *this is ASTEX Approach Control: tugs are on intercept. Stand by the secondary decel."*

"Approach Control, this is Two Twenty-nine Tango. We copy that decel. We're go." He shut down his mike, yelled: "Dekker! Stand by the decel, hear me?"

"Break his damn neck," Ben muttered.

There was no time for debate. They had a beam taking aim. Approach Control advised them and fired; pressure hit the sail and bodies hit the restraints—they weren't in optimum attitude thanks to that ship coupled to them, and it was a hard shove. Dekker yelled aloud—hurt, maybe: they had him padded in and tied down with everything soft they could find, but it was no substitute.

It went on and on. Eventually Dekker got quiet. Hope to hell that persistent nosebleed didn't break loose again.

"Two Twenty-nine Tango Trinidad, *this is ASTEX Approach Control: do a simple uncouple with that tow."*

"Approach Control, this is Two Twenty-nine Tango. We copy that uncouple. Fix at 29240 k to final at 1015 mps closing. O-mega."

Bird uncapped the button, pushed it, the clamps released with a shock through the frame, and One'er Eighty-four Zebra went free—still right up against them, 29240 k to their rendezvous with the oncoming Refinery and they were going to ride with the tow awhile, until the outlying tugs could move in and pick it off their tail.

Ben muttered. "I got everything customs can ask on that ship. Got all the charges figured, too."

"Just leave it, Ben."

"I want that ship, Bird. I want that ship. God, we got the proof—I got all the proof they need—"

"Ben, —"

"Look, they do their official investigation. But this guy's *incompetent*, he was *incompetent* when we boarded. What's he going to do, ask 'em the time? The law's on our side." Ben was cheerful again. "We got it, Bird, we got it."

"Let the guy alone," he said. "Forget about that ship, dammit!"

"I'm not forgetting it. Hell if I'll forget it. We're filing on it. Or I am. You can take your pick, partner."

"There's such a thing as wanting things too much. You can't ever afford to want things that much. It's not healthy."

"Healthy, hell. *I'll* take care of us. All you have to do is sit back and watch me go, partner, I know the law."

"There's things other than law, Ben. —Just stow the charts, hear me?"

"I'm not stowing the charts."

"We're going to get searched, dammit, just put the damn things in the hole or friggin' dump 'em, we can't get 'em off this time—"

"Guys run 'em in all the time, customs doesn't give a damn—just say they're vidgames. They don't even boot to check."

"Ben, dammit!"

"I haven't spent all this work to give up those charts. They're going to go over us with a microscope, Bird, —"

"Thirty years nobody's found that hideyhole, not customs and not the lease crews. Just drop 'em in. You think they're going to go at us plate by plate over a rescue?"

"Two Twenty-nine Tango Trinidad, *this is ASTEX Approach Control: tugs are 20 minutes 14 seconds, mark."*

"Approach Control, this is Two Twenty-nine Tango. We copy: 20 minutes 14 seconds. No problem, tow is clear. Proceeding on that instruction."

Ben said, "You got an Attitude this trip. I don't understand it, Bird, I swear I don't understand it."

"You know Shakespeare, Ben?"

"Haven't met him."

They were still speaking as they made dock. Barely.

"We got 'er," Ben said.

Several significant breaths later Ben said, "I'm sorry, Bird."

"Shakespeare's a writer," Bird said.

"One of those," Ben said.

"Yeah."

"You got him on tape?"

"There's a tape. Hard going, though."

"Physics?" Ben asked.

"Two Twenty-nine Tango Trinidad, *this is ASTEX Dock Authority, check your pressure. Will you need a line?"*

"We copy 800 mb, B dock. No line, we're 796."

"Trinidad, *we copy 796. Medical units standing by on dockside. Stand by life systems sample."*

"Shit," Ben groaned, "they're going to stall us on a medical. They damn well better not find some bug aboard, I'll skin him."

"Won't find any bug. Get our data up, will you?"

They were nose to the docking mast. *Trinidad* shuddered and resounded as the cradle locked. She hissed a little of her air at the sampler.

ASTEX said: *"Welcome in,* Trinidad. *Good job. Stand by results on that sample."*

The dockside air went straight to the back of the throat and stung the sinuses, icy cold and smelling of volatiles. It tasted like ice water and oil and it cut through coats and gloves the way the clean and the cold finally cut through the stink Bird smelled in his sleep and imagined in the taste of his food. Time and again you got in from a run and the chronic sight of just one other human face, and when you looked at all the space around you and saw real live people and faces that weren't that face—you got the sudden disconnected notion you were watching it all on vid, drifting there with only a tether and a hand-jet between you and a dizzy perspective down the mast—worse than EVAs in the deep belt, a lot dizzier. Dock monkeys kited about at all angles, checking readouts, taking samples, talking to empty air. Bird's earpiece kept him informed about the meds inside the ship, the receipt of the manifest and customs forms at the appropriate offices—

"Morris Bird," the earpiece said, thin voice riding over the banging and hammering of sound in the core. "This is Officer Wills, Security. Understand you found a drifter."

He hated being sneaked up on, hated the office-sitters that would blindside a man and made him look around to see where they were—or whether they were there and not a phone call. He turned and saw three of them in ASTEX Security green, sailing his way down the handline.

"Yessir," he said, before they got there. "Details have already gone to BM. Any problem?"

"Just a few questions," Wills said. Before he got there.

CHAPTER 5

"You have any theories to explain what happened?" Wills asked. The cops hung face to face with him, all of them maintaining position with holds on the safety-lines, and you about needed the earpiece to hear at the moment over the thundering racket from a series of loads going down the spinning core. Bird, mindful of the Optex Wills was wearing, shrugged, shook his head and said, mostly honestly: "Could've caught a rock. Helluva bash on one side. On the other hand, the bash could've been secondary. Maybe he was working real close in and just didn't see another one coming, dunno, really, dunno if it's going to be easy to tell. We didn't go outside, just got a look on vid. We did make a tape."

"We'll want that. Also your log. Did you remove anything from the wreck?"

"We took out the rescuee and the clothes he was wearing. Nothing else. We washed 'em and he's still wearing 'em. He had his watch, and nothing in his pockets. He's still wearing the watch. Anything else we left aboard, even his clothes and his Personals. You wouldn't want to open up without a decon squad. It's a real mess in that ship."

"Any idea where the partner is?"

"Evidently she was outside when the accident happened. He kept trying to call her, kept trying when he was off his head, I guess he tried til he couldn't think of anything else. They're from R1. Her name was

Cory. That's all we ever figured out. His life systems were near gone, ship was tumbling pretty bad. He'd taken a lot of knocks." He hoped to hell that would cover Ben's ass about the bruises. He felt dirty doing it, but he would have felt dirtier not to. "Kid was pretty sick from breathing that stuff, kept hallucinating about having to call his partner—evidently did everything he could to find her, sick as he was." He tried to put Dekker in the best light he could, too, fair being fair. "When we got to him, I guess he just finally realized she was gone. Fever set in—he's been off his head a lot, just keeps asking over and over for his partner, that's all."

"What would he say?"

"Just her name. Sometimes he'd yell Look out, like he was warning someone. Kid's exhausted. Like when you give up and then the adrenaline runs out."

"Yeah," Wills said. "Didn't happen to say why they were out of their zone?"

"He didn't know they were out of their zone."

"So he did say something else."

"We had to explain we were taking him to R2. It upset him. He was lost, disoriented. The accident must've happened the other side of the line."

Cops never told you a thing. Wills grunted, monkeyed along the lines toward the hatch as if he was going inside. The other officers followed. But one of the blue-suited meds was outbound, towing a stretcher with Dekker aboard, and the other meds were close behind. The cops stopped them at the lines just outside the hatch, delayed to look Dekker over, talk to the meds, evidently asked Dekker something: there was a lot of machinery noise on the dock—they must be loading or offloading—and he couldn't hear what they said or what Dekker answered. They only let the meds take him away, and that course came past him.

They had wrapped Dekker up in blankets, had him strapped into the stretcher, and Dekker looked wasted and sick as hell. But his eyes were open, looking around. The meds brought the stretcher to a drifting stop and said, "You want to say goodbye?"

It was one of those faces that could haunt a man, Dekker's lost, distracted expression—but Dekker seemed to track on him then.

"Bird," he said faintly through the noise and the banging overhead. "Where're they taking me?"

Dekker looked scared. Bird wanted it over with, wanted to forget Dekker and Dekker's nightmares and the stink and the cold of that ship, not even caring right now if they got anything for their trouble but their refit paid. He sure didn't want an ongoing attachment; but that question latched on to him and he found himself reaching out and putting a hand against Dekker's shoulder. "Hospital. That's all, son. You're on R2 dock. You'll be all right."

Bird looked at the meds, then gave a shrug, wanting them to go, now, before Dekker got himself worked up to a scene. They started away.

"Bird?" Dekker said as they went. And called out louder, a voice that cut right to the nerves, even over the racket: *"Bird?"*

He exhaled a shaky breath and shook his head, wanting a go at the bar real bad right now.

Ben came out of the hatch with their Personals kits. The police stopped him and insisted on taking the kits one by one and turning them this way and that. They were asking Ben questions when he drifted up, and Ben was saying, in answer to those questions, "The guy was off his head. Didn't know what he'd do next. Screaming out all the time. Thinking it was his ship he was on. We had to worry he'd go after controls or something."

He scowled a warning at Ben, but not a plain one: there was the Optex Wills was making of every twitch they made. Ben was looking only at the officers. He said, to explain the scowl, "You'd be off your head too if you'd been banged around like that."

"In the accident," Wills said, fishing.

"Ship tumbling like that," he said. "The wonder is he lived through it. *Couldn't* have helped his partner. All he looked to have left was his emergency beeper, and when that tank blew, it didn't go straight—you got this center of mass here, see, and you get this tank back here—"

You got too technical and the docksiders wanted another topic in a hurry.

Wills said, interrupting him, "Go into that with the Court of Inquiry. We'll want to log those kits. Leave them with us and we'll send them on to your residence. What's your ID?"

"On the tag there." Ben indicated his kit. "1347-283-689 is mine. Bird here's 688-687-257. Ship's open. Look all you like."

"You can go now."

You never got thanks out of a company cop either. Bird scowled, looked at Ben, and the two of them handed their way up lines toward the hand-line. A beep meant a boom was moving. Red light stained the walls. But the alarm was from the other end of the big conduit- and chute-centered tunnel that was the cargo mast. You could get dizzy if you looked at the core itself, if you let yourself just for a moment think about up and down or where you were. Bird focused on the inbound gripper-handle coming toward him, ignored the moving surface in the backfield of his vision—caught it and felt the first all-over stretch he'd had in months as it hauled him along. Ben had caught the one immediately behind him—he looked back to see.

"Customs," he remarked to Ben, in a lull in the racket from the chutes. "I hope they've talked to the cops."

"No trouble. We haven't even got our Personals. Cops've got 'em. Cops have got everything. They gave me this receipt, see?" He used his free hand to tap his pocket. "Hell, we're just little guys. What are we going to have? We'll get a wave-through. You watch."

"They'll give us hell."

"So don't tell 'em it was out-zone. We reported it where the rules say. We got rights. Meanwhile we're gone into a public contact area and there's no use for them to check us, is there?"

"Rights," he muttered. "We got whatever rights Mama decides to give us, is what we got. —What did you tell that cop about Dekker? Did you tell them he was crazy?"

"Hey, they don't need my help to figure that. The meds belted him in good and tight when they took him away."

"What did you tell them?"

"I said he wasn't too clear where he was. They asked about the bruises, and I said he got loose, all right? I said he was after the controls and he's crazy, besides which he fought us when we had to get him back and forth to the head."

"That's a couple of times, Ben, for God's sake . . ."

"Hey. We got this guy tied to the plumbing, bruises all over him, all ages, what are we going to say, it was a month-long party out there?"

"Yeah," he said, and shut up, because the chute was sucking another load down, and down here you could hear the hydraulics. His stomach was upset. It had been upset for the last week, when it had been clearer and clearer Dekker was not going to be able to support a thing they said, that Dekker was liable to say anything or claim they'd met eetees and seen God. This is it, Ben had said when Dekker had tried to get at the engine fire controls. They'd put Dekker to bed taped hand and foot: Dekker had screamed for an hour afterward, and Ben had gotten that on tape too.

He had wanted to erase that video. Dekker had enough troubles without that on permanent record with the company: Dekker could lose his license, lose his ship, lose everything he had, and he didn't want to hand BM the evidence to set it up that way—but Ben had said it. Dekker wasn't any saner than he had been. Dekker would have been dead in a few days if they hadn't found him, and as much as they'd done to patch the kid together, he didn't seem likely to need much of anything but a ticket back to the motherwell and a long, long time in rehab.

"Poor sod," he said.

Ben said: "Good riddance." And when he frowned at him: "Hell, Bird, I've seen schitzy behavior before, I've seen damn well enough of it." There was profound bitterness behind that: he had no idea why, or what Ben was talking about, but Ben didn't volunteer anything else. Ben was talking about the school, he decided, or the dorms where Ben had spent what other people called childhood. It didn't matter now. The trip was over, Dekker was with the meds, the whole business was out of their hands, and Ben knew Shakespeare wasn't a physicist. Good for him. They'd patch up their partnership and take their heavy time while somebody else leased *Trinidad* out—and paid them 15-and-20 plus repairs and refit: could do that all the time if they wanted, but you didn't get rich on 15-and-20 while you were sitting on dockside spending most of it.

Got to give up sleeping and eating, he was accustomed to joke about it.

Ben would say, intense as he always was when you talked about money, We got to get us a break, is what.

They got off the line in customs, explained they didn't have their Personals, the cops had them, no, they didn't have any ore in their pockets and they didn't have any illegal magmedia on them, all the records were on the ship, yes, they had contacted another ship out there, they'd hauled a guy in, they hadn't taken anything off it, no, sir, yes, ma'am, they'd tell Medical if they got any rashes or developed any fevers or coughs, Medical had already told them that, yes, sir.

God, no, they didn't volunteer to customs that it was an out-zone ship, yes, sir, they'd reported the contact, no, it was an instructed contact: the agents' questions were strictly routine and the stress-detectors didn't beep once.

Customs validated their datacards, logged them both as active in R2, and they went back to the hand-line for the lifts.

Ben said, conversationally, while they were each trailing by a gripper handle, Ben in front this time: "You can quit worrying about the charts. Got the card in my pocket."

His heart went thump. "Dammit, Ben, —"

"Hell, it was all right."

"I told you leave it!"

"Where the cops'd find it?"

"You could've said. God!"

"Hey. You're a lousy liar. Was I going to burden your conscience? You passed the 'detectors—so did I, right?"

Ben could. Stress detectors depended on a conscience.

"You're just too damn nervous, Bird."

"You could've left 'em under that plate, dammit. You could've done what I told you to do—"

"You want to get caught, *that's* the way to do it—conceal something on the cops. I didn't conceal it. It was right in my pocket. God, Bird, *everybody* does it. If they wanted to clamp down, why do they let us have gamecards? Or vid? Why don't they check that? I could code the whole thing onto a vidtape."

"If too many people get too cocky, just watch them. Some nosy exec gets a notion, and you can walk right into it, Ben, you can't talk your way out of everything."

"Everything so far."

"Hell," he muttered. They were coming to the end of the hand-line, where you got three easy chances to grab a bar and dismount in good order instead of (embarrassment) shooting on down to the buffer-sacks that forcibly disengaged a passenger before the line took the turn.

Ben was first on the bar, swung over and pushed 8-deck on the lift panel before he caught up. "I'll ride down with you."

"So where else are you going?"

"Where do you think?"

"Shit, Ben."

"Somebody will. Probably there's a line of creditors on the ship. But we'll at least get the 50/50. Damn right we will."

"You're bucking for back trouble, and you won't get a damn thing. There'll be a rule."

"Young bones. I won't stay long. And there's no real choice, Bird, you have to file the day you get in. *That's* the rule."

"So file at the core office."

"Trust those bastards? No do. Corp-deck's it."

"Out of your mind," he muttered as the car arrived. They floated in, took a handhold. The car sealed, clanked and made its noisy, jerky interface with the rotating heart of the core, and started solidly off down the link. He didn't argue any more with Ben. If Ben had the fortitude to go down a level past helldeck an hour after dock and stand in some line to file to claim the poor sod's ship, he didn't know what to do with him. He only sighed and stared glumly at the doors and the red-lit bar that showed them approaching another take-hold.

"Bird, you got to take better care of yourself. What have you got for your old age?"

"I'm in it, and I don't plan to survive it." The car clanked into the spoke, and they shot into it with the illusion of climbing, until they hit that queasy couple of seconds where distance from R2's spin axis equaled out with the car's momentum as far as the inner ear was concerned. Then the ear figured out where Down was, the car's rolling floor found it a half-heartbeat later, and bones and muscles started realizing that the stimsuits you worked in, the spin cylinders you slept in and the pills you took like candy didn't entirely make up for weeks of weightlessness. Knees would feel it; backs would. The red-lit bar that showed their distance from the core was shooting toward 8-deck.

Meg and Sal were on 6; he had found that out on their way in. He'd left a message for them on the 'board, and he planned on company tonight. That and a drink and a long, long bath. Maybe with Meg, if she answered her messages.

If she wasn't otherwise engaged.

The car stopped. He got out, on legs that felt tired even under 8's low *g*, muscles weary of fighting the stimsuit's elastic and now with *g* to complicate matters. Ben got out too, and said, "Meet you at the 'Bow."

Ben didn't even slow down. He just punched the button to go on down as far as the core lift went, to 3.

Bird shook his head and headed off down 8-deck—damned if he was even going to call up his mail before he hit the bar at the Starbow. Mail would consist of a bank statement and a few notes from friends as to when they'd gone out and when they'd be back. His brother in Colorado wrote twice a year, postal rates out here being a week's groceries and Sam not being rich. It wasn't quite time for the biannual letter and outside of that there wasn't mail to get excited about. So screw that. He just wanted a chance to get the weight off, get a drink, see a couple of familiar female faces if fate was kind, and never mind Ben's wet dreams. Ships didn't come without debts, probably multiple owners, not mentioning the bank, and the company would find some technicality to chew up any proceeds they could possibly make from the ship, til it was hardly worth the price of a good rock, plus expenses. Ben was going to work himself into a heart attack someday, if ulcers didn't get him first.

* * *

The meds said, and the Institute taught you, some null-*g* effects got worse every time you went out; your bones resorbed, your kidneys picked up the calcium and made stones, and the body learned the response—snapped to it faster with practice, as it were, and Ben believed it. Science devised ways to trick gravity-evolved human systems, and you took your hormones, you spent your sleeptime in the spinner and you wore the damn stimsuit like a religion. Most of all you hoped you had good genes. They told gruesome tales of this old miner whose bones had all crumbled, and there was a guy down tending bar in helldeck who had so many plastic and metal parts he was always triggering the cops' weapon scans. He didn't intend to end up like that, nossir, he intended eventually to be sitting in a nice leasing office collecting 15-and-20 on *two* ships, free and clear of debt, and letting other poor sods get their parts replaced. He had no objection to Morrie Bird sitting in that office as vice president in charge of leases, for that matter: Bird had the people sense that could make it work, and Bird couldn't last at mining forever: they'd already replaced both hips.

So Bird went off to the easy adjustment of 8-deck in blind trust that Mama would do the right thing and assay their take in the sling and record all the data they'd shot to the offices during their approach—while the one of them who'd worked for Mama for two years and knew the way Mama worked took the immediate trip down to 3-deck, and the frontage of the debtors' barracks he'd once lived in. Oddity was endemic hereabouts—you could look down the strip now and spot a guy dressed head to foot in purple, but he wasn't necessarily crazy—at least you could lay money he didn't claim the company'd done this or that or ask you the time every five minutes.

God, he hated remembering this place. But he still kept an ultra-cheap locker there, with a change of clothes—

Because you had to dress if you were going to go call in debts, nothing rad or rab, just classic. Good sweater, good pants, casual coat. Real shoes. You had to look like solid credit to get what he was after. And his legs were in good enough shape, all things considered: he'd foreseen this, and taken his pills and worked out all the way back—burning off the desire to strangle Dekker, Bird had probably thought, regarding those unusually long sessions on the cycle and the bounce-pads.

But he could walk, at least. He could peel out of the coveralls and the stimsuit, shower in the public gym, dress himself in stationer style and go down past helldeck to 1, where he weighed Earth-normal, walking like an old man, it might be, but he'd taken a painkiller while they were coming in, and it was just a matter of taking it easy—going where Mama knew damned well a spacer directly back from a run wasn't comfortable going—which was why so many tricky little company rules said you had to sign the forms in person, on the day you docked, at the core office if you wanted Mama to take her time—or in the main offices if you wanted Expedition. The inner decks being notoriously short of lawyers, a lot of spacers never even realized Expedition was possible.

You could put in a company-backed claim on salvage, for instance: go to the general office, file to have the company run procedures and wait it out; but that threw it into ASTEX administrative procedures, which ground exceedingly slow, and put it in the hands of ASTEX Legal Affairs, which usually found some t uncrossed or i undotted. Up there you could file a claim for expenses, but you only got that after Mama had adjudicated the property claims, unless you knew to file hardship along with it; and you could file for salvage, but you had to know the right words and be sure the clerk you got used them: half the low-level help at the core couldn't spell, let alone help you with legalese.

Best of all, you could pay a call on an old classmate from the Institute, break the queue *and* get the precise by-the-book words on the application.

8-deck was transient and gray and lonely: you might see a handful of miners in from their runs, not to mention the beam-crews and the construction jocks and whoever else worked long stints in null; you saw the occasional Shepherds and 'driver crews, transiting to their own fancy facilities, and a noisy lot of refinery tenders and warehouse and factory workers and dock monkeys on rest-break (there were a lot of refinery operations on 8)—and sometimes, these days, some of the military in on leave—but you didn't get anything like the flashy shops or the service you had down on helldeck. Here you kind of bounced along between floating and walking, being careful how fast you got going, being careful of walls and such—your brittle bones and your diminished muscles and your head all needed to renew acquaintances with up and down—slowly, if you were smart.

The public part of 8 was all automats, even the sleeperies—no enterprising station freeshop types behind the counters, even for the minim shifts that Health & Rehab would let a stationer work on 8. It was robot territory, just stick your card in a slot and you got a sleepery room or a sandwich or the swill that passed here for bourbon whiskey: but that was all right for a start, everything was cheaper than helldeck and your whole sense of taste was off, anyway, for the first bit you got used to refinery air.

You found no luxury here that didn't come out of an automatic dispenser, unless you were working for the company—in which case you saw a whole other class of accommodations, the adverts said: they said a whole lot better came out of the vending machines behind those doors—but Bird had never seen it. 'Driver crew and Shepherds didn't need the waystops that miners did—if they were up here they were slumming, on a 1-hour down from some business in the mast; but generally they went straight to helldeck, where big ship officers and tech crew had cushy little clubs and free booze, and Access with all sorts of perks on the company computers.

Adverts said you could get at least a sniff of those perks, even as a miner—if you let the company own your ship and provide your basics; but that meant the company could also decide when you were too old or you didn't fit some profile, and then you were out, goodbye and good luck, while some green fool got your ship. God help you, too, if Mama decided you weren't prime crew on that ship, and some company-assigned prime crew got shunted out to work tender-duty for three years at a 'driver site—which effectively dumped all the relief crews back at the Refinery onto the no-perks basics, to do time-share in a plastics factory. Work for the company and you could fill in your time swabbing tanks in the chemicals division til you got too old, and then they set you down on retirement-perks and let you sweep floors in some company plant to earn your extras.

Hell, no. Not this old miner.

But a lot of years he had been coming back to 8, and he'd seen changes—or maybe he had felt livelier once upon a time. 8 these days echoed to footsteps, not to music and voices. The bright posters had all gone years ago, the month the company had gone over to paperless records-keeping. The company favored gray paint or institution green, except for pipes that came wrapped with hazard yellow and black.

You used to get the unofficial bills here too, the pasteups that would appear overnight—saying things like TOWNEY LIES and FREE PRATT & MARKS—Mama hadn't liked those in the best days, nossir, the bills that said things like EQUAL ACCESS and the take-one flyers that used to give you the news the company wouldn't. They'd all gone. No paper.

You still found the old barred circle, you still found PEACE and FREE EMIGRATION scratched in restroom plastic, right alongside the stuff you could figure Neanderthals must've carved in Stone Age bathrooms—you found MINIM and RABRAD and SCREW THE CORP, along with other helpful suggestions in the toilets . . . far more frequent here than down on helldeck, he guessed because sanding down the panels in light *g* made a bitch of a lot of dust, and spray paint was as bad. Or maybe it was because Security didn't come up here much and the ordinary maintenance crews were contributing to it too. So the crud and the slogans stayed in the bathrooms, not even covered by paint, while 8-deck got nastier and dirtier and showed its age like some miners he knew.

He was in a sour mood—maybe the cops, maybe Ben's stupid chance-taking with the datacard, maybe just that he was tired of the shit and tired of feeding a company that was trying to blow itself to hell; and right now specifically because the cops had their Personals, which meant he was stuck in the stimsuit and his day-old coveralls until the cops turned his kit loose: damned if he was going to buy new knee and ankle wraps at vending machine prices.

But he did buy a bottle of aspirin, a cheap men's personals pack, and a far too expensive bottle of cologne: the hips were gone, the ankles were going, the hair was gray and thinning, but the essentials still worked and he did have hopes. He walked into the bar in the front of the ambitiously named Starbow Hotel and, with his card in the slot at the desk, punched Double and Guests Permitted.

In the midst of which transaction somebody grabbed him from behind and swung him around, clean off his feet.

"Hey!" he yelled, as the turn brought him face to face with dusky-skinned Sal Aboujib, who grabbed him the same as the one behind—

That *had* to be Meg Kady.

He hugged Sal back in this bouncing unstable minim-*g* dance. He said, "Damn, you're both fools!"

But he'd hoped with all his heart they'd got his message.

"Old friend of Marcie Hager's," Ben said at the counter, down in Records. "Is she in?"

The clerk looked over his shoulder, looked at him, looked at the line that stretched out the door, said, uncertainly: "She might be."

"Thanks," he said warmly, smiled, and on an adrenaline rush and a dogged determination not to show the pain, walked cheerfully past the counter, through clerk territory and on back to the hallway: men in good suits didn't stand in that line. Ben Pollard didn't. He walked as far as an office that said *M. Hager, Technical Supervisor*, wiped the sweat off his face, rapped on the door, opened it and leaned in the doorway.

"Hello there, beautiful."

Marcie Hager looked up from the desk, looked nonplussed for an instant. Then: "Ben Pollard. God, I thought you'd shipped out to Mars or something."

"Mind if I sit?"

She said, after a second's consideration, "Of course not. Come on in. Coffee? —Are you all right? You're white."

"First day back. Came down from 8. —You're looking good."

"Last time I saw you, you were in Assay." Marcie got up, poured two instant coffees. "White? Sugar? —Back from where?"

"White. Plain. —Assay for a while. Then I bought into a ship."

Marcie's brows went up. Estimation of his finance clearly did. So did her interest. "Social call?"

He grinned, sat down with the coffee, said, after a deliberately slow sip, "I ran into a piece of luck. I thought you might be able to help me."

You went to the company school, you learned what bought what from whom: some were cheap and some cost more than a freerunner could possibly pay, but you always kept track of your old classmates and, on call, you did favors such as Marcie Hager was about to—because favors got you favors, and that, for one thing, meant he didn't have to stand in that line.

"Yeah?" Marcie said, and sat down and sipped her own coffee. "Sounds interesting."

Meaning Marcie thought somebody with a ship equity four years out of school just might be going somewhere even a Technical Super in Records might find useful—even if freerunning was as high-risk an investment as there was, it was disposable cash and high-interest returns in the short term; and it was capital that a Technical Super in Records, with all her Access perks, couldn't lay hands on—

But not as if Marcie was going to ask cold cash for favors. In Marcie's position, subject to company scrutiny, you never left a datatrail.

"Just a little expediting. A claim for salvage. I don't want to be at the bottom of the list of creditors. This guy owes us, big—"

Marcie's left eyebrow titled. "Like in—major salvage."

"Ship salvage." He leaned back, eased a very sore set of muscles in his back, took another slow sip of coffee. "Number's One'er Eighty-four Zebra."

"Mmmn. Not from this zone, Benjie. That's a *long* procedures delay. Where in *hell* have you been?"

"Yeah, well, —but—" He turned on his nicest smile. Rule One: you didn't deal in plain words. Rule Two: you were careful about cash. Rule Three: you didn't ask favors of prigs—but Marcie certainly wasn't that.

Marcie said, "Just so you know," and turned on her terminal. Marcie's kind might not trade in cash, but Marcie said, while she was idly tapping her way through a chain of accesses, "What ever happened to Angie Windham, you know?"

"Don't know. But you know Theo Pangoulis went bust? He bet everything he had on that shop—could have told him nothing succeeds in that location."

Marcie scowled. That wasn't the kind of offering you gave: they were seriously negotiating now, and her fingers stopped moving.

He said, "On the other hand, I do hear from Harmon Phillips."

"Do you?"

"You know he's on Aby Torrey's staff. Up in Personnel."

"That's interesting," Marcie said. "—Have you got your numbers ready?"

It was swill, but there was *g* enough to keep it in the glass and you in your seat if you sat easy, and there was sure as hell good company—the two prettiest sights in the belt, Bird swore: Soheila Aboujib, a grin gleaming on her dark face, her ears and fingers aglitter with her reserve bank account, laughed, elbowed Meg in the ribs and said, "He's been out there too long."

"Let me tell you," he said—and did, in the light traffic of the Starbow's autobar: they were in a crowd of dockers and tender- and pusher-jocks. The piped music adjusted itself up, affording a little privacy to people at the back corner table.

"Yow," Meg said, when she had the essentials. "So Ben's down in Admin, is he?"

"If he didn't break a leg," he said. "I tell you, I'm worried about him. He's been acting like a crazy man from the time we linked on with that ship."

"I dunno." Meg was what the young folk called rab, and the hairdo this time was what his generation called amazing, shaved bare up the sides, red as fire atop, a mass of curls trailing down her neck and all these bangles on her ears. With Meg you'd never know what you'd see—sometimes it was braids and sometimes that hair turned colors. Meg Kady, she was, Hungarian on one side, Sol Station Irish on the other, Meg said—but sometimes it was Scots; and once, overheard in a bar, she'd said it was Portuguese Martian. God only knew about Sal Aboujib, who had a coffee complexion and coffee-black eyes: with Sal it was braids today, a hundred of them, with metal clips, but you never knew—sometimes that hair changed styles and colors too.

Either one of them was too pretty for a gray-haired, brittle-boned old wreck—had to be his brains they were after picking, he was sure: get him drunk and ask him questions, buy a dinner and try to get specific coordinates out of glum, close-to-the-chest Ben—neither one of which had ever been too successful. But you never figured what made friends: you just took up with people, found out who you could trust, and if you found a good one you kept those contacts polished, that was all—never could remember how they'd taken up with him—well before Ben, back when he'd been working with various hire-ons, something to do with a mixed-up drink order (he'd been far gone and so had they) and a game of pitch-the-penny in quarter *g* with a crowd of equally soused tender-jocks.

Never could remember who'd finally gotten the bill.

"From over the line?" Meg asked, regarding the strayed ship, and he said, "One'er number. Clean-talking kid, real young, maybe twenty, twenty-two. Partner's dead out there. Tank blew. His partner was outside."

"Brut bad luck," Sal said with a shake of her braids. A little grimace. Then: "You seriously got rights on that ship?"

"Ben thinks so. Thinks so enough to risk his knees. He's been working out for weeks. I figured he was going to pull this, but I did think he'd at least check in first."

Meg said: "Want us to track him? We've been scuzzing along on 6, in no hurry, figuring on a friend showing up—could've done 3 two days ago. We can go down . . ."

"He'll get back. If he doesn't I'll call the hospital."

"You two feuding?"

"Ben gets a little over-anxious."

"Yeah, well. That's Ben. —But if it worked, if you did get salvage—can you just take the ship?"

"It's not going to work. Company'll find an angle. You watch."

"Que sab?" Meg said. "But if it did—"

"Meg, he's been damn crazy. Ever since we found that ship. I tell you, I was afraid—" He'd been too long away from a drink. He hadn't dared indulge, on the return trip, and this one hit him like a hammer. He almost said: Afraid of him, —but that word could get back to Ben, and he didn't want that. He said, instead, "Ben works real hard. But sometimes he gets to looking most at where he's going, not what he's doing."

Meg reached out and laid a hand on his arm. "Yeah, well, cher, you want us to talk to him?"

"No, no, it's between him and me. Let him get this bug out of his works. He's going to find nothing but a string of bills to that ship's account. It's probably in hock for its last fuel bill. If we get expenses I'll be happy."

"Can't blame him for trying," Sal said. "Hell, I'd brut kill for a chance like that."

You never knew on some things whether Sal was kidding.

"Look," Meg said, squeezing his wrist. "What say you screw the medregs, cancel here and come down to 6 with us?"

"Meg, my old knees—"

"Old, hell. We got a nice berth there at the Liberty Bell. You just stay here and collect Ben when he comes in. We'll party tonight. Get the spooks out. We knew we were waiting for somebody."

"Yeah," said Sal. "Just give us a little time to clean up the room."

"Clean up, for God's sake—what are we? Strangers?"

Meg elbowed his arm, getting up. "Hey, we just got to get a few things out of it. Female vanity."

He gave a shake of his head and sipped his bourbon. A few things out of the room. The things might well be male. But he charitably didn't suggest that.

And it was (charitably) true Meg and Sal might do some feminine fussing-up in the place; and it was no real surprise that Meg and Sal might bounce a casual acquaintance or two in favor of him and Ben—they were simpatico, for some reason God only knew; they were also on *Trinidad*'s leaselist, though they were just in themselves, and in no position to take a ship out for another month or three.

"See you below," they said, and went.

Pretty woman like that could've talked him down to helldeck tonight if she'd insisted: pretty woman like that—

Who lied like a company lawyer.

Meg was an ex-shuttle pilot, native to Sol Station (or Mars)—accused at Sol Station of political agitation (or arrested for smuggling, depending on how many Meg'd had). Either one in fact could've gotten her deported down to the motherwell if they'd gotten the evidence she'd evidently managed to dump. In either case, the company had (she said) invited her to leave places conveniently close to sources of luxuries. Meg had taken up with Sal when she got here—Sal herself had gotten bounced out of Institute pilot training, Sal never had said why, but it didn't matter: there were a number of things Sal *would* have done, and you could take your pick. Sal was smart, she'd had at least her class 3 license, and by his reckoning, she had what the good numbers men had: she went past the numbers to *see* the Belt in her head. It was formal schooling and experience Sal lacked—and the way Sal had been getting it, in the School of Last Resort, you just hoped to live long enough.

He was sure the pair skimmed, occasionally—just clipped a little off another freerunner's tag if they didn't know him personally.

But not from their friends. Or if they had—he figured they'd pay it back when they had it to pay and never tell you they stole it. That was the kind they were, even Sal, who was real loose about a lot of things, and he counted that honest. Everybody got desperate enough sometime. He'd done it himself once or twice or three. And paid it back to the guys he'd done it to, without ever telling them he'd done it. He understood that kind of morality.

So he'd lease *Trinidad* to Meg and Sal now and again—a classier ship than they could generally get, with equipment other rigs didn't have. They were learning. They took advice. He'd lease to them this time, if they'd been ready to go—he *liked* them, that was reason enough.

But all of a sudden there was this other ship: he'd seen that idea light up in their eyes—that if by some stroke of cosmic luck they did get a second ship, then *somebody* had to be leasing it, didn't they, maybe on a primary basis? Surely he wasn't going to sell it to the company. God only how far their imaginations took those two.

Damn, he asked himself, what was the jinx on that ship, that it made Ben crazy and now it had Meg and Sal thinking about something they just weren't damn-all good enough yet to ask for?

While nobody gave two thoughts to the poor sod in hospital who was screwed out of everything he had, not to mention the owners and the lease crews over at R1 who might be screwed.

Sometimes he thought he was too old and too far from his beginnings. Sometimes he dreamed about pine trees and sagebrush and sunsets.

But he dreamed very realistically about poverty too—recalled what it was to scrape and save to get up to space for schooling; then by desperation and some fast talking to make it out to Asteroid Exploration, Inc., to a program that let you lease-purchase: they'd been that desperate for miner pilots then, desperately looking, in the start-up of the current push.

Most of them that had come out then were probably dead now: he knew about the ones on R2, and he was the last of that lot. The plain station labor that had gone into refinery jobs and processing—God only: maybe a lot of them were dead too. He remembered young faces; he remembered the talk about what they were going to find, how they were all going to get rich on company wages.

Yeah. And now that the mapping was mostly done and the company had its 'drivers working real smoothly, the company didn't want the freerunners anymore. E-co-nomics, they said. Freerunners didn't fit the system the way it had grown to be, all company-run, and ASTEX stacked the deck any way it liked. You couldn't complain and you couldn't get clear—because that took money you didn't have; or if you did sell your ship back to the company you got to Sol Station with, after passage, 50, 60 k in pocket, back at your starting place aged 50 plus with your bones all brittle and that 60 k all you had for your retirement and your medical bills.

But he read his brother's letters and he knew beyond a doubt that thirty years was too long an absence for anyone: Earth had changed, attitudes had changed—people worried about things that didn't worry him and they didn't worry where he knew they should. Earth was at war with its colonies, shooting hell out of human beings, while Earth-folk argued whether the eetees at Pell had souls, and blamed the government for the market crash when company merchant ships went on strike about the damn visas. You had the rabs walking around in shave-jobs and glitter and scrawling slogans because society was going to hell and the human race with it; you had the Isolationists who wanted to shut down the far star-stations and not speak to anybody but Earth and Mars and the Belt; and you had the Federationists and the Separationists and the pacifists and the neo-nationalists and the New Evangelicals all of whom thought they knew how to reform the human race; you had the Euconomists and the anti-geneticists and the ones that claimed there was a youth drug from space that the governments had embargoed, but the rich could still get it; and you had various defense departments in the United Nations and United Internationals building those bloody huge warships to enforce the embargoes against the rebels in far space, while the Free Trade Party that had won the election in the PanAsian Union wanted to get rid of all the embargoes, cancel the visas and let people go where they wanted to go—but out there in deep space things changed, things changed constantly, faster than anybody could keep up with. He had not quite been born when somebody out at Cyteen had discovered Faster Than Light and rewritten the book, and hell if he understood FTL physics *or* its politics, but the company built its ships out of the metal he'd found. They'd armed the traders of the Great Circle before he was born, and right now they were building those new trans-light carriers to Teach the Colonies a Lesson. All this had been going on near a hundred years, but it was breeding at FTL rates now—they'd shot the rab reformers at the company doors back in the '15, they'd established the visas, they'd shunted Earth Company operations out into half a hundred subsidiaries like ASTEX that only tangled the company's books beyond the capacity of any single Earth-based government to audit, and nobody was responsible for a damned thing. They'd had draft riots at Sol Station a year ago, four kids killed, they'd had two officials up for falsifying military supply records, so the rumor had been, —while out here in the Belt there were construction workers and those great steel skeletons you weren't supposed to talk about, that eventually, after a handful of years, powered up and pushed themselves on toward Sol Station for finishing. All this went on. But if you looked at the vid on the wall and wondered what else might be going on you didn't know about, the company News & Entertainment division was running a program on hydroponic gardening.

Damn crazy life. Sometimes you sat out there in the Belt with one other guy in a little ship and wondered what would happen to you both if humanity did go crazy and blow itself to hell. Lately you kept an anxious ear to the news Mama doled out daily and tried to figure out who was actually running things in the motherwell, because damned if the company was going to tell you about it in so many words: ASTEX, Asteriod Explorations, was part of the Earth Company, which had the whole damn United Defense Command on its leash; the whole thing was a damn alphabet riot—ASTEX, EC, SS, U1, MEX, and FN, for starters, and everybody was sleeping in more than one bed, governmentally speaking—

Which he preferred not to. Maybe the kids in the colored hair and the glowpaint and the nose-rings were right. Maybe humankind would blow itself up. Maybe Belters would survive out here and breed themselves a whole new human race—

One that thought Shakespeare was a physicist.

He got up and carded himself a drink—canceled the rez for himself and Ben at the Starbow, while he was at it, since he hadn't used the key that had dropped from the slot; and seriously wondered if his back was going to take it on 6—in various considerations.

"Bird?"

Well, so Ben had survived. Ben was back with excitement bubbling in his voice. He turned around as Ben stopped and caught his balance against the vending machine.

"Bird, we got a chance. We got a real chance." A gasp for breath. "Broke my neck getting up here." Another breath. "Ship's got a double registry—over on Refinery One. Paul Dekker and Corazon Salazar. *She's* Cory, *she's* the partner—and his title's completely clear."

"You're kidding. He's no more than a kid."

"Dunno what she was, but they owned that ship. They owned her clear—no liens, no debt, nothing, Bird, we got it! We got the only claim against it! We're first in line!"

He picked up his drink out of the dispenser and just held it in a shaking hand. You didn't think about things like that, you didn't ever start wanting something that just couldn't happen. But knowing they had bills to meet and the company paying claims so slow nowadays—

God forgive, he started thinking then—if Dekker was crazy—if they really were *due* that ship . . .

"Your name's Dekker," they asked. Meds. He remembered them. But how he had gotten here he couldn't remember. He didn't know how long he had been here. He didn't know how long he had been out just now. He asked questions back, but he never got much help from their answers.

Sometimes he thought he was on a ship like his own ship; sometimes he thought he had been hallucinating all of it. "Bird?" he asked sometimes. Sometimes he was afraid Ben was going to come floating up and hit him.

Sometimes he thought Bird and Ben had been something he'd dreamed in this place, and he simply couldn't figure how he had gotten here, unless Cory had somehow gotten the ship straightened out and brought him in. He felt tranked. He thought, This is a hospital. This is Base. We're home. We're safe. . . .

"Where's your partner?" someone asked him.

He slitted his eyes open, lifted his head so far as he had strength to do. He saw a white coat, a man writing on a slate.

"Where's your partner?" the med asked him. "Do you remember?"

Black. An alarm screaming. The ship jolted and spun—he struggled against the weight of his own arm to reach the controls, wondering whether the autopilot could possibly straighten them out or if it had engaged already. He didn't know. He hit the switch. Something jolted the ship, threw him against the workstation—

"Mr. Dekker. Do you recall what happened?"

Green-walled shower. The watch showed March 12.

"What day is it?" he asked. But they didn't answer him. He tried to see his watch, but he couldn't move his arms. "Bird, what time is it? For God's sake, *what time?*"

The man in white wrote on his slate and said, "What time do you think it is?"

"Give me my watch. Where's my watch?" It wasn't on his wrist. It had lied to him. Or it was his only way back. "Where's my watch, dammit! —I want my watch!"

The man left. Others came in and shot something into his arm. After that he could hear his heart beating heavier and heavier, and he was slipping into dark.

"Bird?" he asked, thinking Ben must have something to do with this. "Bird, wake up—Bird, help me—*Bird, wake up and help me!*"

CHAPTER 6

Glass touched glass, in the Liberty Bell, on 6. "Here's to friends," Sal said, and Bird, telling himself it was far too soon to plan on anything, had made up his mind not to tell Meg and Sal a thing.

But that had gone by the side the minute they'd seen Ben's smugly cheerful face.

"You got it!" Meg said, before they even got their drink orders in.

"We're at least tracking," Ben said. "We're gaining on it. They're going to expedite the claim."

For the life of him, Bird couldn't figure how Ben managed to get around people in offices. But he did.

So here they were, on their way to feeling no pain at all, .7 *g* be damned.

It wasn't as if Meg and Sal would leave them cold tomorrow if the deal fell through. They weren't that kind. But they sure as hell enjoyed the party tonight.

They enjoyed it afterward too, piled into two adjacent rooms in the Bel—actually the party traveled and they had to throw this one pair of tender-jocks out twice, who complained they'd been invited.

"No, you weren't!" Sal Aboujib said. And shut the door and slid down it, laughing. Meg was laughing too much to help her, so they hauled her up and picked her up, Sal yelling that they were going to drop her on her head.

So they fell on the bed—which at low *g* meant a slow bouncing, all of them, while up and down went sort of alcoholically crazed for a moment.

"God," Bird said, falling back on what he thought was mattress. "I'm zee'd."

Meg fell on him with a vaporous kiss and he stopped caring which way was up.

Turned out when they waked it was Ben and Sal's bunk they were in, but that was no matter, Ben and Sal had just gone off next door. But they had last night's sins to pay for—a hangover in low *g*, with your sinuses and your ears playing tricks, was hell's own reward.

"Cory?" Dekker asked. "Cory?" But he was not in the ship, he was inside white walls with white-coated medics who asked him over and over "What happened to Cory?" and he couldn't altogether remember what their truth was, or what they wanted him to say. He asked for Bird, and they asked him who that was, but someone said in his hearing that that was the man who'd brought him in.

From where? He tried to remember where he had left Bird, or what had happened, but it always went back to that shower stall, the watch showing him the time . . . March 12. And it was his choice what would happen that day . . .

He slept again. He was more comfortable when he waked. His hands were free and they let him sit up and gave him fruit drink. A man came and sat down by his bed with a slate and started asking him questions—How old are you? Have you any relatives? all rapid-fire. It was the sort of thing they asked if you'd had an accident, something about next of kin. It scared him. The shower in this room wasn't the shower he remembered, he could see the white walls through the door. He'd jumped ahead. Cory wasn't with him, and he was in a hospital having to go through these questions like some actor in a vid. It couldn't be real. God, he didn't want his mother to hear he was lying in a hospital somewhere she couldn't help, he'd screwed up enough: he just said he was from Sol Station and shut up.

"What was your relationship with Corazon Salazar?" they asked him then, cold and impersonal. He said, going through the ritual, "She's my partner."

But if he went on answering, they'd write it down as true and he'd be here, he couldn't go back to the shower, he'd be out of the loop and he'd have no chance to fix it: Cory would be dead then. No way back.

The man asked, "Did you have relations with her?"

That made him mad. "That's not your business."

The man asked: "Did you ever quarrel?"

"No."

The man made a mark on his slate. "What did you invest in that ship?"

He didn't understand that question. He shook his head.

"Did you put any money into it?"

He shook his head again. "That wasn't the way it worked. Cory was the money." Cory was the brains too, but he didn't admit that to a stranger. Cory was the one who had no question what she wanted. But the man didn't ask that. The man said, "What happened out there?"

He couldn't go back to the shower now. No green walls. White. He thought, What should I tell them? And the man said, "Does that upset you? You said Ms. Salazar was working outside the ship. Why?"

He said, not sure what he might have changed, "We were working a tag."

"Did Ms. Salazar regularly do the outside work?"

"I'm the pilot." Two answers right. He felt surer now.

"I see. So she hired you. And gave you half interest in her ship. For nothing."

He nodded.

"Where did you meet?"

"We wrote letters back and forth. We'd been writing a long time. Since we were kids."

Another note on the slate. "Then it was more than a business relationship."

"Friends."

"You didn't have a falling-out, did you?"

He looked at his watch. But it wasn't there. They'd taken it.

The man said, "Did you quarrel?"

"We never quarreled."

"She always did what you wanted? Or didn't she, this time?"

He didn't understand. He shook his head. He thought about the shower, but it wasn't vivid this time. Even the green seemed faded.

The man asked: "Why did you cross the line? To cover what you'd done?"

He didn't understand what they were getting at. He shook his head again, looked furtively at his wrist, remembered he mustn't do that. It upset people. Like Ben. It upset Ben a lot. . . .

"Tell me the truth," the man said. "What were you doing out there?"

"We had a tag," he said. "We were working it."

He lost the room of a sudden. It was dark and there were the boards lighting and blinking. He tried to find the safe white wall again.

"Did you leave her there?" the man said. He couldn't remember what he'd just said, he could only see the boards, and someone was holding him down. He got an arm free. People were yelling. There were flashes of the white room, there were faces over him and they were all holding him. He yelled: "Let me go!" and felt a sharp explosion against his shoulder, but they kept holding him, telling him to calm down.

He said, out of breath, "I'll be calm. I'll be calm, I don't want any more sedatives—"

Because when they drugged him he had no idea where he was or how long he was out or where he went in that dark . . .

He opened his eyes again with a terrible leaden feeling, as if he weighed too much and he couldn't wake up—but he knew where he was, he was in the hospital. Two very strong men were holding him down and asking him how he felt now.

He was out of the dark. He said, when he had gotten a whole breath, "I'm fine. I'm fine. Just don't give me any more shots, all right?"

"Will you talk to us? Will you behave?"

"Yes," he said.

The man in white leaned over him then, took hold of his wrist and asked him, "Are you still worried about your watch?"

His heart gave a little thump, making him dizzy. But he knew it was a test. He wasn't supposed to ask the time. They beat him when he did that. Or gave him shots. He shook his head, wanting to stay awake now.

The doctor said, "We're going to take some readings while we talk. Is that all right?"

Another test. He made up his mind then: it didn't matter what the truth was. If he didn't say exactly the right thing they'd give him shots. He'd been in trouble in his life—but this was serious. This was a hospital and they thought he was crazy.

The doctor asked him, "Are you still worried about your watch?"

Black. The siren going. He heard something beeping wildly. A timer was going off and he didn't remember setting it. He could see the doctor frowning at him—he tried to track on the doctor: he knew how important it was. And when he did that, the beeping slowed down.

"That's better," the doctor said. "Are you all right? Do you want to tell me what just happened?"

He got a breath. He said, calmly, trying to pay no attention to the beeps, "Cory was outside. We were working this tag—"

"On which side of the line?"

"On this side." Stupid question. The beeps went crazy a moment, when his heart did. He got it calm again. "We were working this tag. A big claim. Big. Kilometer wide . . ."

"Are you sure, Mr. Dekker?"

"It was that big. And we were out there. We'd shot our tag, but it wasn't a good take. Cory said—" The beep sped up again and he slowed it down, staring at the wall, remembering Cory saying, We're not letting those sons of bitches— "—We had to fix it. And she was going to go in—"

"You couldn't handle a rock that size."

"It was stable. Not that bad." Again the beep. He said, before it could get away from him, "But this damn 'driver—he wasn't on the charts—he wasn't slowing down. I said—I said, 'Cory, get in here, Cory, he's still not answering me, Cory, get inside—' "

"Get the trank," the doctor said. The beep became a steady scream. Like the collision alert. Lights were flashing.

"I said, I kept saying, 'You sonuvabitch, my partner's out there, my partner's outside, I can't pull off—' "

They hit him with the trank. Two of them were holding him. But he kept screaming, " 'I can't pull off, you sonuvabitch!' "

"It's not working," somebody said.

The doctor pushed his eyelid up, leaning close, said, looking elsewhere, "Get the chief," while breath came short and the monitor was beeping a steady panic:

"They didn't list it," he said. "It wasn't broadcasting—"

The doctor said, "Make up another dose. 50 ccs."

"It wasn't on the damn charts—"

"Easy," the doctor said. "We understand you. —Cut that racket."

The beeper stopped. He took an easier breath.

"Good. Good." Another dark space then.

Somebody had had an accident, an R1 ship turned up in R2 zone, probable 'driver accident—which should be BM's job, but it was in William Payne's day-file, straight from Crayton's office, in General Administration.

The memo said: Handle this. We need minimal publicity.

Payne paged through the file. A freerunner pilot in hospital—making wild charges about a 'driver captain violating regulations . . .

God. The Shepherd Association was hardnosing it in contract talks, the company trying to avert a strike—Payne shook his head. Not quite his job, but it was very clearly an information-control situation, and that *was* his department, as executive director of Public Information. One could even, if one were paranoid, suspect a set-up by the Independents—but it seemed the pilot's physical condition was no fake, and a miner was dead.

Bad timing—damned bad timing for this to come in.

The question was how far the rumors had already gotten. Freerunners had done the rescue. That was one problem. News & Entertainment could run another safety news item, give the odds against a high-*v* rock, remind everyone it was a remote possibility—or maybe best not to raise the question. The Shepherd Association wanted an issue. It was begging for a forum. Meanwhile the police were going over the wreck, poking about—*that* was a department Public Information couldn't entirely handle. Best keep them away from the issues in the case.

A release from the pilot was the all-around best fix. Evidently BM had a crack team going over that ship—that was good: if there was a mechanical fault, settle the problem there, no problem. Get a statement from the pilot, fix culpability if there was any—

Not with a company captain, damned sure, and not in a lawsuit that could bring the Shepherd Association in as friends of the court. That certainly wasn't what Crayton meant by "settlement."

A hand touched Dekker's face. It gave him the willies. He couldn't do anything about it. Couldn't even open his eyes yet.

"Mr. Dekker, would you answer a question for me? There's something I don't understand."

He got a breath. Two breaths. Did get his eyes open, marginally. "What?"

"Why the watch?"

"Kept the time."

"Mr. Dekker."

Clearer and clearer. It was the doctor again. He made a try at sitting up, inched higher on the pillows.

"How are we feeling, Mr. Dekker?"

"Like shit."

"You were talking about the watch."

Beep.

"*Explain* to me about the watch, Mr. Dekker. Why does it upset you?"

He wished he knew the answers to that one. The doctor stood there a long time. Finally he thought, Maybe this one's going to listen. He said, tentatively, "We had some stuff linked to the main board. *Way Out* was old. The arm didn't work off the main board. It was supposed to be a three-man, you know, the way some of the ships used to be . . ."

"Go on, Mr. Dekker. The watch."

"You couldn't work the arm and see the log chrono. Real easy to lose track of time when you're working and we didn't trust her suit indicators. So we used my watch." His voice shook. He was scared the doctor was going to interrupt him and order him sedated if he lost it. And he wasn't sure if he was making sense to the man. "It only timed an hour, you know, the alarm was a bitch to set—so we'd set it to January 1. —What day is it?"

"July 15th, Mr. Dekker."

He despised crying. He didn't. He wouldn't. The doctor was getting impatient. He took deep breaths to help him. "Don't give me any shots. I need to figure—how far is it . . ."

"Don't distress yourself, Mr. Dekker."

January has thirty-one days. February is 28. March, 12.

71.

Out there in space. Seventy-one days. She'd have been out of air in 4 hours. Oh, God, . . .

"Mr. Dekker."

"March has thirty days. Or 31?"

"31."

12 from 31 is 19. Nineteen days in March. April is—

Thirty days hath September . . . April, *June*, and November . . .

The doctor patted his shoulder. One of the orderlies came back.

"No!" he yelled. "I've almost got it, dammit!"

They shot him with it anyway. "Be still," they said. "Be still. Don't try to talk now."

49. They found me on the 21st. 49 and 21. Do you count the 12th twice?

I'm losing it . . . start again.

Or can I trust my memory?

It was still 6-deck and still a waiting game. Every day Ben went down and checked the lists. Every day it turned up nothing but PENDING. *Trinidad* herself was still hung up in the investigation—there was no way they could lease her, no matter that there were a dozen teams applying; there was no way they could even start her charge-up, and every day she sat at dock she was costing money instead of earning it. Bird haunted the supply shops, pricing the few small parts she needed; but they couldn't even get access to her, the way Bird put it, to fix the damned clothes dryer.

"You can't hurry the police," Ben said, trying to put a reasonable face on things. "It can't be much longer."

And Sal, between sit-ups—they were working out in the gym: "I thought you could fix anything."

"Not in my range of contacts," he said, frustrated himself. Nudging Security was asking for more investigation.

"Hell," Bird said, mopping his face, leaning on the frame of a weight machine. "I sincerely hope they just get something decided. My heart can't stand much more of this prosperity."

Meg didn't say anything but, "Easy, Bird."

Payne said: "No, dammit, just don't answer. Tell Salvatore—no, *don't* tell Salvatore. I'll talk to him. . . ."

Hell of a day. A Shepherd crew and a tender crew mixed into it in a bar and a bystander was in hospital; and *this*—

Some clerk in R1 had return-sent the Salazar kid's mail as Deceased, Return to Sender, and the sender in question, Salazar's mother, had hit the phone asking for information on her daughter. The operator in ASCOM, knowing nothing about it, had sent the call to Personnel, the confused clerk that took the call in R1 Personnel there couldn't find Salazar's file and insisted to the bereaved mother there was no such person, while *her* supervisor had tried to stall for a policy clarification out of R1's Administrative levels, then realized she was out of her depth and tried to send it through to a higher level, after which it had bounced confusedly from department to department until a secretary in Legal Affairs put the call on hold and the woman hung up.

Salazar's mother was on the MarsCorp *board*, for God's sake. Nobody had told him. Nobody had told Towney. Nobody had flagged the dead miner as a problem—

Alyce Salazar's next phone call had hit the president's desk. Not Towney's, in ASTEX. *Hansford*, in the Earth Company's Sol Station headquarters. Hansford had called Towney, Towney had had to release the file, and Hansford's office had released the details to MarsCorp.

Alyce Salazar had found out Dekker had survived, and immediately claimed it was no accident, he was a scoundrel who'd seduced her daughter, kidnapped her to the Belt, and killed her for her money.

Which turned out to have been a fair amount, before expenses. There was a binding surviving-partner clause—

But Alyce Salazar was an angry woman, one *damned* angry

woman . . . and lawyers were talking to lawyers at very expensive phone rates.

"Mr. Crayton is on the line," Payne's secretary said.

God, . . .

"Mr. Crayton, sir, . . ."

Crayton said, "Have you got the letter?"

"Yes. I have it up now."

"One went to Security."

Oh, my God, . . . "I'm sorry, sir. I certainly didn't . . ."

"Not from your office. From Ms. Salazar. She wants that boy's head. You understand the implications? We *need* this mess cleared up. We don't want him in court. I want you to patch this up. Get the facts straight. We've got to have an answer for this one."

Still no police clearance. And on a certain afternoon in the Bell, when Ben was in the bar doing some technical reading, Meg slipped into the chair across the table, leaned both arms on the table and said, "Benjie, cher, let's go do talk."

He'd thought at first Meg was just bored, Bird being out of sorts for the last couple of days; and he wasn't totally surprised, back in her room, to end up in bed in mid-shift, —not the first time for him and Meg, but it was all the same unusual, even if he was entirely sure—and he was—that Bird wouldn't take exception. The side-shaving was a turn-on. The mop on top and down the back was several shades brighter than elsewhere, but it was beyond a doubt Meg's right color; and she had some kind of creature tattooed around one leg—snake, Meg had told him once, early on in their acquaintance. Bird had told him what kind it was and said if it bit you, you were dead in three minutes. He thought that might well fit Meg, if you got on her bad side.

But he wasn't on her bad side. He had it figured by then that Meg had ulterior motives, though Meg wasn't the sort to hold a man off while his brains scrambled—he swore he couldn't do anything until she'd told him what was going on, but she proved that wrong: she had him truly gone before she started asking him about the ship, about Dekker, about the way Bird was stewing and fretting—

"Bird's severely upset," Meg said. "You think there's a chance on that ship? —Because if there isn't, you got to talk to him."

"Dekker's brain's gone. No question. Yeah, there's a solid chance on that ship, there's a good chance."

"Bird says if you get anything it'll have to be in court. Bird's saying you won't win. That it's all just a waste. But he doesn't act it. —Is there anything the company can turn up? I mean, you didn't seriously transgress any regs out there . . ."

So that was what was bothering Meg. Meg and Sal had to be looking for a lease for their next run, if that ship wasn't going to come through—or if they were only going to sell it to the company. Meg and Sal hadn't been betting elsewhere: that was what he suddenly figured, and they were down to decisions. "There isn't going to be any court, I promise you. You know what Bird's problem is? He's scared he's going to make money. Every time you get to talking about it—he just looks off the other way. If I hadn't filed on that ship, you think he'd ever have done it? Hell, no. He'd have waited till he got his legs. Then he'd have said, well, it's too late, there'd be other creditors—you tell me what goes through his head, Meg. I swear I don't know."

"Dirtsider."

"So?" One of Meg's stories had her born on Earth, too. But that didn't seem to be the version Meg was using today. "Are they all like that? Is it something in the water?"

"Bird grew up poor."

"So I grew up an orphan. So what's that got to do with anything?"

"It's habit with him: when he gets enough—that's all. That's all he wants from life. He doesn't want to be rich. He just wants enough."

It didn't make any sense—not at least the why of it. He held the thought a moment, turned it over, looked at its underside, and decided he wasn't going to understand. "Well, it's not enough for me. Damn well not enough for me."

Meg sighed. "Haven't ever seen enough to know what enough is."

"Damned short rations," he said. "That's what Bird's 'enough' comes to. And it doesn't keep you fed when your legs and your back give out. Doesn't get you insurance."

"Insurance," Meg chuckled. "God, jeune fils. . . ."

"That's a necessity, dammit! Ask me where I'd have been if my mama hadn't had it."

"Yeah, well. —She was a company pilot, wasn't she?"

"Tech." He rolled over. He didn't like to talk about things that were done with or people that didn't come back. They didn't matter. But the example did, "You don't get any damn where halfass protected. Insurance—my company schooling—Bird's knowing who to lease to—"

"Like us?"

Oh, then, *here* was the approach. Meg was looking at him, chin on hands, putting it to him dead-on, with no Bird for a back-up. He didn't want to alienate Meg and Sal—especially Sal. They weren't the best miners in the Belt, but they had other benefits—not all of them in bed. And he kept asking himself if he was using good sense, but the answer kept coming up that there might be miners better at their job, but if you wanted a couple of stick-to-a-deal, canny partners, present company and Sal weren't damn bad.

Some of Bird's friends, now—had his affliction. And they were going broke or had gone.

Meg said, "You suppose you could put in a word with Bird, explain how we'd be reasonable. We'd work shares."

Not every day somebody as tough and canny as Meg needed something from him—seriously needed something. He toted it up, what the debts might be, what the collection might be. If one looked to have a long career leasing ships—one needed a couple of reliable partners who knew the numbers. And Sal in particular had possibilities—if Sal could get a grip on her temper and shake out that who-gives-a-damn attitude. Sal also had useful contacts. While Meg—

He said, he hoped after not too long a pause: "I could talk to him. What are friends for?"

"Wake up." Someone shook at Dekker's shoulder. "Come on, Dekker. Come on. Come out of it."

He didn't want to come back this time. It was more white coats. He could see that with his eyes half shut. But there was dark green, too, and the gleam of silver. That didn't match.

A light slap at his face. "Come on, Dekker. That's fine. —Do you want an orange juice?"

It never was. It was a cousin of that damned Citrisal. But his mouth was dry and he sipped it when they put a straw between his lips and elevated his bed. *G* felt heavier here. He thought: This isn't the same place. We're deeper in.

"How are you feeling?" his doctor asked him.

But he was looking suddenly at the company police, realizing what that uniform was.

"Paul Dekker?" the head cop said. "We want to ask you a few questions."

He heard that beep again. That was him. That was the cops listening to his heartbeat, and it was scared and rapid.

"Have you found her?" he asked. Cops always came with bad news. He didn't want to hear what they might have to say to him.

But one of them sat down on the side of his bed. That man said, "What did you do with the body?"

"Whose body?" For a moment he honestly didn't know what they were talking about, and the monitor stayed relatively quiet. Then his pulse picked up. "Whose body?"

"Your partner's."

The beeps became hysterical. He hauled the rate back down again, saying calmly, "I couldn't find her. They hit us. I couldn't find her afterward."

"Mr. Dekker, don't play us for fools. We'll level with you. Don't you think it's time you leveled with us?"

"This ship ran us down—"

"—and it wasn't on the charts. Come now, Mr. Dekker, you know and I know you had a motive. College girl comes out here with her whole life savings, and here you are—not a steady job in your life, no schooling, not a cent to your name. How'd you get here? How'd you get passage?"

"Cory and I were friends. From way back."

"So she puts up the equity, she just insists the ship go down as joint ownership, with a death provision in there—"

"No."

"Or was that your idea?"

"I don't even know what you're talking about."

"You signed it. We've got your signature right at the bottom."

"I didn't read it. Cory said sign, I just signed it!"

The officer had reached for a slate the other cop had. He pressed buttons. "We have here a deposition from your port of origin, from one Natalie R. Frye, to the effect that you and Ms. Salazar quarreled over finances the week you left. . . ."

"Hell if we did!"

"Quote: 'Cory was mad about a bill for a jacket or something—' "

"I bought a jacket. She thought I paid too much. Cory'd wear a thing til it fell apart. . . ."

"So you quarreled over money."

"Over a jacket. A damn 38-dollar jacket. We fought, all right, we fought, doesn't everybody?"

"Ms. Frye continues: 'Cory had been sleeping around. Dek didn't like that.' "

"Screw Natalie! She wasn't a friend of ours. Cory wouldn't spit on her."

"*Did* Ms. Salazar 'sleep around'?"

"She slept where she wanted to. So did I, what the hell?"

"Well, that wouldn't matter to anyone, Mr. Dekker, except that she never got back."

The beeps accelerated, not from shock: a fool could see where this was going. He was shaking, he was so mad, and if he went for the bastard's throat they'd trank him and write *that* down, too.

"Cory's lost out there," he said doggedly. "A ship ran us down—"

"Mr. Dekker, there was no other ship in that sector."

"That's a lie. That's a damn lie." He reached frantically for things they couldn't deny. "Bird knew it was there. Ben knew. We talked about it. It was a 'driver, was what it was—it wasn't on my charts—"

The officer said, dead calm: "Bird and Ben?"

"The guys that picked me up!" He was scared they were going to tell him *that* never happened either. But *someone* had brought him in. "I called that sonuvabitch, I told it we were there, I told it my partner was outside—"

"Are you sure the rock didn't block the signal?"

"No! —Yes, I'm sure! I had it on radar. Why in hell didn't it see me?"

"We don't know, Mr. Dekker. We're just asking. So you did see it coming. And did you advise your partner?"

They made him crazy, changing the rules on him. One moment they accused him. Then they believed him. Sometimes he seemed to lose things.

"Didn't you say you'd hit a rock? Wasn't that your story at one point?"

He was lost and sick and the drugs still had him hazed. The beeps increased in tempo. He wasn't sure whether it was his heart or something on com.

"So where did you manufacture this ship, Mr. Dekker?"

"It was out there."

"Of course it was out there," the officer said. "You had it on your charts. Your log showed that. How could we doubt that?"

He was totally confused. He put his hands over his ears, he tried to see if the alarm going was his heart or something in his head. "Call the 'driver, for God's sake. See if they picked Cory up."

"Didn't you call?" the cop asked.

"Yes, dammit, I called, I called and it didn't answer. Maybe my antenna got hit. I don't know. I called for help. Did anybody hear it?"

"A ship heard you. A ship picked you up."

"Different." He was tired. He didn't want to explain com systems and emergency locaters to company cops. "Just call the 'driver out there."

"If there is a 'driver out there," the cop said, "we'll ask. But if they had picked up your partner, wouldn't they have notified their Base? Don't you think they'd have called that in?"

He thought about that answer. He thought about the way that ship had ignored warnings. He thought about it not answering his hails. He thought—It's not hours, is it? It's months, it's been months out there.

The alarm sounded again. He wanted it calm, because when he didn't do that within a certain time they sedated him, and he was trying to be sane for the police. "I don't know they heard me. Just call them."

"We're going to be calling a lot of people, Mr. Dekker." The cop got up from his bed. "We're going to be asking around."

They walked to the door. The doctor went with them. He lay there just trying to keep the monitor steady and quiet, on the edge of hysteria but a good deal saner than he wanted to be right now. He remembered Bird, he remembered Ben. He was relatively sure he had come here on their ship. But sometimes he even feared Cory might not have existed. That he had always been in this place. That he was irrevocably crazy.

CHAPTER 7

If 8 was gray and automated, 6 was green paint and a few live-service restaurants and shops, but the time still dragged: you worked out in gyms, you hit the shops til you had the stuff on the counters memorized, you skipped down to 3-deck for a while and maybe clear to 2 for an hour til your knees ached and your heart objected. The first few weeks after a run were idle time, mostly: you didn't feel like doing much for long stints. You'd think you had the energy and then you'd decide you didn't; you sat around, you talked, you filled your time with vid and card games and when you found your legs, an occasional grudge match in the ball court or sitting through one of the company team games in the big gym on 3-deck was about it. But mostly you worked out til you were about to drop, if you had to wrap your knees in bandages and pop pills like there was no tomorrow—and that was what Bird did, because the younger set was chafing to get down to heavy time that counted, down in the neon lights and fast life of helldeck—down in the .9 *g* on 2 that was as heavy as spacers lived—specifically to The Black Hole, that was the accommodation they favored, and the hour Mike Arezzo called and said he had two rooms clear, adjacent, no less, they threw their stuff in the bags and they were gone.

Checking in at The Hole felt like coming home—old acquaintances, a steady traffic of familiar faces. Mike, who owned the place and ran the bar out front, kept the noise level reasonable and didn't hold with fights, pocket knives, or illegal substances. Quiet place, all told. Helldeck might have shrunk from its glory days: worker barracks and company facilities had gnawed it down to a strip about a k and a half long, give or take the fashionable tail-end the corporates used: that was another ten or fifteen establishments—but you wouldn't find any corporate decor in The Hole; no clericals having supper, not even factory labor looking for a beer. The Hole was freefaller territory: dock monkeys and loaders, tenders, pushers, freerunners, construction crew from the shipyard and the occasional Shepherd—not that other types didn't stray in, but they didn't stay: the ambient went just a bit cooler, heads turned and the noise level fell. It went the other way when lost sheep turned up.

"Hey, Bird!" Alvarez called out, and heads turned when they walked in. Guys made rude remarks and whistles as Meg sauntered up to the bar and said, "Hello, Mike."

Mike said, accurately, "Vodka, bourbon, vodka and lime, gin and bubbly . . ." and had them on the bar just about that fast.

Home again for sure. Close as it came.

"How's it going?" Mike asked. "Persky says you got a distress call out there. Pulled some guy in."

"Yeah. Young kid. Partner dead. Real shame."

Alvarez said, "What's this with *Trinidad* hanging off the list? The cops impounding her?"

God, the other thing helldeck was good for was gossip.

"Nothing we did," Ben said, fast. "But Mama's got her procedures. You contact a ship from across the line—"

"Across the *line*—"

Some parts of a story you saved for effect. They were worth drinks, maybe supper. "Wait, wait," Alvarez said, "Mamud and Lal are over at The Pacific, I'll phone 'em. Wait on that."

—You got one grounded bird here, Bird had used to joke, when it came to getting about in *.9 g*: hard as null-*g* was on the body, you got so frustrated with walking on helldeck—it took so *long* to get anywhere, and the Trans was always packed. Food and drink didn't have to be chased—that was the plus. But when you first got in you always felt as if you'd forgotten your clothes: you got so used to the stimsuit moving with you and fighting every stretch, you kept checking to make sure you were dressed. Air moved over your skin when you walked. And how did you spot a spacer in a fancy restaurant? Easy. He was the fool who kept shaking the liquid in his spoon just to watch it stay put—or who set something in midair and looked stupid when it didn't stay there.

He was also the poor sod always in line at the bank, checking his balance to see if Assay or Mining Operations had dropped anything into his account—or, in this case, down at the Security Office to see if, please God, the technicalities had been cleared up and some damned deskpilot might just kindly sign the orders to get his ship out of port.

No.

And no.

The 28th of *July*; for God's sake, and the cops hadn't finished their search.

And when he decided to stop by the bank and check the balance, to see if the last of the 6-deck bills had come in, dammit, the bank account showed a large deduct.

So . . . the aforesaid spacer hiked the slow long way to the Claims Office, and stood in line in this scrubby-poor office to find out the state of affairs with *Trinidad*'s claimspending and its tags. Ben had gotten into his nice office-worker suit and gone clear around the rim to say hello to friends in Assay who just might hurry up the analysis—and you'd sincerely hope it wouldn't run in reverse.

"Two Twenty-nine Tango," he told the clerk, who said, "*Trinidad*, yeah, Bird and Pollard, right?"

"Right."

The clerk keyed up and shook his head. "I hate to tell you this—"

"Don't tell me we got a LOS. You don't want to tell me that."

"Yeah. —You got a pen? I'll give you the number."

"I got my list," he said, and fished his card out of his pocket and stuck it in the reader on the counter.

"That's number T-29890."

"Shit!" he said, and bit his lip. On principle he didn't cuss with friendly clerks. But it was the second best tag they had, a big rock for these days. Iron. And he had been careful with it. He raked his hand through his hair and said, "Sorry. But that one hurts, on principle."

"Maybe better news tomorrow. They do turn up again."

"Yeah," he said, "thanks."

So they'd lost a tag. It happened. You sampled a rock, you took a sample in and ran your on-site tests, and if you liked it and thought Mama would, you called and told her you had potential 'driver work here. You got your big bounty when your second, official Assay report confirmed your work; and you got a certain monthly fee just for having it on the charts; but you didn't get paid percentage on the mineral content until some 'driver finally got around to chucking it back in bucket-loads, until the Shepherds got it in, and the refinery reported what it *really* had. Which happened on the company's priorities, not yours.

And if you had a Loss of Signal that meant Mama had to do the bookkeeping on it, and Mama had to re-tag it, pick it up on a priority, or let it go until another pass—all that was shitwork Mama didn't like to do, when a nice neat tag that stayed on was what you got that bonus for, and back it came unless you personally could firm up those numbers and keep track of it. If it got perturbed out, as did happen, you could lose it altogether, or have to fight it in Claims Court.

So, well, this one was too good to let slip or leave to chance. Maybe a little computer work could find it. There was a remote chance it could just be occulted for a while, something in the way that wasn't on the charts—a LOS could sometimes put Recoveries onto another find, in which case you got that credit; it happened in the long ago; but generally a rock just, in the well-known perversity of rocks, got to turning wrong, and managed to turn in some way that the strip transmitter was aimed to the 3% of the immediate universe Mama's ears didn't cover—or the transmitter could have died: they didn't live forever, especially the junk they got nowadays.

So it was hike over to Recoveries and pay a couple more c's out of the account for the technicians to pull up a file and figure probable position and talk to it and listen with a little more care, first off, in the hope of getting contact, before they went to the other procedures. Meanwhile the bank didn't pay interest on what Mama had taken out, that was why they did immediate withdrawals these days: every damn penny they could gouge.

"Odd-shaped rock," he typed on the form, and invoked the data up out of Mama's storage. Photos. And mass reckoning. And the assay report on the pieces they'd knocked off it.

The Recoveries clerk took the dump, looked at it, and lifted an eyebrow. "Thorough. Makes our job a lot easier. We might have a real chance of waking this baby. Or getting a 'driver on it before it gets out of reach. Real nice piece, that."

That made him feel better at least. You kept the people in Recoveries happy and they maybe paid a little more attention to getting you found or a little more urgency to getting you picked up—unlike the guys who took only one sample and that from the only good spot on the rock.

A lot of novice miners had gone bust that way—talk Mama into a whole lot of expensive tags on junk, just collect the bounties and puff up the bank account and buy fancier analysis gear—and a few took the real risk and outright falsified the samples. It paid off in a few instances—but the sloppy work that usually went along with that kind of operation sooner or later started showing up in reprimands and fines, and a crew got back to Base some trip to find out their bank account had been holed while they were gone—Mama didn't ask you to write a check these days: under the New Rules, she just took it, and you could sue if you thought you'd been screwed—if you could afford to hire the company's own lawyers.

And you'd never say that 'drivers ever, ever cheated in reckoning the mass they'd thrown; and you'd never *ever* say that a refinery would short their receipts. 'Driver captains and refinery bosses never, ever did things like that.

But you did do real well to get a reputation for being meticulous, taking multiple samples, being clean with your records, making it so 'drivers and tenders *knew* your tags were worth going after. Knowing your mass. Photographing all the sides, including after the tag was on. Most of all knowing the content—rocks being their individual selves and damned near able to testify in court who their parents were.

No skimmer liked to mess with his claims, no, sir—because Morris Bird was real friendly, he was on hailing terms with most of helldeck; and when he got a few under his belt he told everybody far and wide how he kept accidents from befalling his claims and how suspicious it was if it came in short.

There had only been one or two uncharitable enough over the years to remark that sleeping with the two most likely to do the skimming couldn't hurt. But he had stood up for Meg and Sal, and so had no few others.

It made him happier just thinking about it—

Made him outright laugh, thinking how that had probably done more to reform Meg Kady than all the Evangelicals and the Islamic Reformeds who handed out their little cards on helldeck.

Sal, now, he thought—reforming Sal was a whole different proposition.

You got all kinds on helldeck—except you didn't walk it in any business suit, not if you didn't want to get laughed out of The Hole. So Ben shed it at the locker he kept on 3-deck, put on his casuals and his boots, after which it was safe to go home.

Change of clothes, change of style—Ben Pollard went most anywhere he cared to go on R2 and nobody would find him out of place.

But fact was, helldeck was where he most liked being—down in the hammering noise and the neon lights. He'd been scared as any company clerk when he'd first laid eyes on it, at 14, even if his mama had belonged here—but even at that age he'd known sure as sure that Ben Pollard was never going to have the pull to get out of the company's lower tiers. He'd learned how it really was: the ideal the company preached might be classblind; but funny thing—kids without money ended up like Marcie Hager, in the middle tiers, where you had certain cheap perks, but you'd never get a dime of cash and you'd never get further—and aptitudes and institute grades had damned little to do with it. President Towney's son, for an example, was about as stupid an ass as had ever graduated from the Institute and they put him in a vice-presidency up in the methane recovery plant . . . while Ben Pollard, a Shepherd's kid, got a stint at pilot training (at which he was indifferent) and geology, at which he was good; and a major in math, thank God. But he couldn't get into business administration, not, at least, tracked for the plum jobs. They went to relatives of company managers. They went to company career types, who had paid their dues or whose parents had, or who tested high in, so he had heard, Company Conformity.

Shit with that. He took a little jig step on his way back from the Assay office, and on helldeck nobody took exception to a little exuberance—if a guy was happy, that guy must have reason: in a society that lived on luck you wanted to brush close to whoever looked to have it, because that guy might lead you to it.

What he had was a card in his pocket that said they had a couple of nice pieces, and that money was going into the bank, dead certain. You tagged things and you didn't know how long it was going to be til the 'driver got there, but what you had in your sling was money—and in this case, a good chunk of it.

Yeah!

"Meg or Sal in?" he asked Mike at the bar when he got to The Hole—he knew where Bird probably was, where Bird had been this time of day for the last week.

Mike said, "They aren't, but the cops were."

He looked at Mike a moment. It was hard to change feet that fast. "Cops."

"They weren't in uniform. But they had badges. Anything I should know?"

He sighed, said, because, hell, you needed the local witness on your side if it came to trouble: "All right, Mike. The guy we rescued—out in the Belt. We got a claim in on the ship. He owned it. Sole survivor. The guy's crazy. God only knows what he's said. Police are probably checking us out to be sure we're on the straight."

Mike looked a shade friendlier at that. And interested. "Claim on the ship, is it?"

He tapped his key on the bar. "More of a long, long story. But that part's blackholed. You, we trust. Let me go check this out."

He went back through and down the hall where the sleeping rooms were, opened the room he had (at least on the books) with Bird.

"Shit!" was his first reaction.

Not as if they had much to disarrange, but thieves could have hit and been neater. Four days to get their Personals out of police hands and here was everything they owned strewn over the sink, the lockers open, their laundry scattered on the bed—and a big bright red sticker on the mirror that said: *This area was accessed in search of contraband by ASTEX Security acting with a warrant. Please check to be sure all your personal items are present and report any broken or missing articles or unsecured doors immediately by calling your ASTEX Security Public Relations Department at . . .*

He pulled the sticker off the mirror. Paper thicker than tissue was worth its weight in gold. Literally. You could fold the thing and write important secret notes on the edges if you could find a pencil, which was equally frigging scarce.

Shit. shit. *shit!*

He opened the side door that led into Meg and Sal's room—it was technically a quad. Same mess, only more so. Meg and Sal had more clothes.

Meg and Sal were going to kill them. That was one thought going through his head. The other was outrage—a sense of violation that left him short of breath and wanting to break something.

What in hell were they looking for?

Something off that ship?

Datacard?

He had a sudden cold thought about the charts. But he had that datacard in his pocket, where he always carried it. He felt of his pocket to be sure.

Damn!

He headed out, locked the door, walked down the hall and tried to collect himself for Mike, who asked, "Anything wrong?"

"Not that I know. Be back in a bit." He kept going, to the nearest Trans to get him up to 3-deck.

He had this terrible cold feeling, all the ride up, all the walk down to the gym and the lockers. His hands were shaking when he used his personal card to open the locker. He suddenly thought: Everywhere I use this card they can trace it. Same as in the Institute. There's nothing they can't get at. . . .

He got the door open, he felt of his suit pocket—

The card with the charts was there. He'd been so excited about the Assay report he'd forgotten to switch it back.

But, God, where's it safe now?

In the room they've already searched?

Maybe they'd expect him to do that. And they might be looking for one kind of trouble—but if they found something illegal—

Damn!

Dekker opened his eyes tentatively, hearing someone in the room—realized it was his doctor leaning over him. The drugs had retreated to a distant haze.

"About damn time," he said.

The doctor moved his eyelid, used a light, frowning over him. "Mmm," the doctor said. Pranh was his name. Dekker read it on the ID card he wore.

"Dr. Pranh. I don't want any more sedation. I want out of here. — What did the police find out?"

Pranh stood back, put his penlight in his pocket. "I don't know. I suppose they're still investigating."

"How long?"

"How long what?"

"How long have they been investigating?"

"Time. Does that still bother you?"

It still touched nerves. But he was able to shake his head and say—disloyal as it felt to say—"I know Cory's probably dead. Right now I want to know why."

Pranh's face went strangely blank. Pranh looked at the floor, never quite at him, and started entering something on his slate.

"You haven't heard from the police," Dekker said. It was hard to talk. There was still enough of the drug in him he could very easily shut his eyes and go under again, but he kept pushing to stay awake. Pranh didn't answer him, and he persisted: "How long has it been?"

"Your partner *is* dead. There's no probably. Denial is a normal phase of grieving. But the sooner you get beyond that—"

"I don't know she's dead. You don't know. For all I know that ship picked her up. I want to talk to the police. I want a phone—"

"Calm down."

"I want a phone, dammit!"

"It's on the record. A rock hit you, a tank blew."

"There wasn't any rock—"

"You said there was. Are you changing your story?"

"I'm not changing anything! There was a 'driver out there. It didn't answer our hails, it ran right over us—"

"Denial," Pranh said quietly. "Anger. Transference. I've talked to the investigators. There's no 'driver. There never was a 'driver near you. One was working. It's possible there was a high-*v* rock. A pebble."

"Pebble, hell! I want to talk to the police. I want to know what that 'driver captain says! I want a phone!"

The doctor went to the door, leaned out and spoke to someone outside. And left.

"I want to talk to somebody from Management!" he yelled at the empty doorway. "Dammit, I want to talk to somebody who knows what's going on out there!"

But all that came through the doorway was a pair of orderlies with a hypo to give him.

He swore when they laid hands on him and when they gave him the shot; and he swore all the while he was sliding back down again. He felt tears running on his face, and his throat was raw from screaming. He thought of Cory, Cory shaking her head and looking the way she did when something couldn't be fixed.

Can't do it, Dek.

And he said to himself and to Cory, Hell if not.

Two pieces of news Ben had for Bird when he walked into the *Hole*, and good as one was, the bad won. Hands down.

"We got an LOS on a big one," Bird muttered as he sat down on his bed. He threw that out flat, because it was completely swallowed up in this. "Sure it was cops?"

"They left a note. A sticker." Ben showed it to him, folded, from his pocket. "It was worse than this. I straightened up some—folded Sal and Meg's stuff."

"Got them too."

"Got them too."

"Damn." He shook his head. It was all he could think to say.

"Maybe," Ben said, "maybe they're just checking us out. I mean, legally, they can search anything they want—and we have this claim in—"

"Legally I'm not sure they can," he said, tight-jawed. "But the complaints desk is hell and away from R2." Then he thought about bugs, signed Ben to hush, got up and took him out and down the hall to a table in the bar. By that time he figured Ben knew why. Ben looked worried as he sat down.

"Two beers," he said to Mike Arezzo. And brought them back and sat down. He said to Ben: "They could have bugged the place. But if we ask to move, they'll be asking why and they'll get interested."

"I don't know why they're on us in the first place," Ben said. "It's that damn Dekker, I know it is. No telling what story he's telling them."

"We don't know that."

"Well, it would be damn useful to know. I can talk to somebody in—"

He laid a hand on Ben's arm. "Don't try to fix this one. I don't care who you know. It's too dangerous."

"Dangerous, hell! We haven't *done* anything but save that guy's neck!"

Ben really believed in some things. Like The System and The Rules he regularly flouted. "You remember you asked me about Nouri and his lot. And I said that wasn't that long ago. Police can do any damn thing they want to. They did then. They still can. Your company education tell you that?"

"There are regulations they have to follow—"

"That's fine. There's regulations they sometimes don't follow. Remember Nouri? Wasn't anything they didn't search on these docks; and you didn't say, I got my rights. The company has its easy times and it has its crackdowns, and both of us can remember when toilet paper didn't have stuff in it to break it down so you can't make presspaper anymore, you got to use those damn cards you stick into these damn readers that we don't know where the hell they connect to; *I* can remember when ships could kind of work in and out of the sectors and you could link up and share a bottle: now they'll slap a fine on you you'll never see the top of. I can remember when they didn't care about this stupid war with people clear the hell and gone away from here, that they say now can just come in here and blow us to hell, and once upon a time we didn't have the company bank taking LOSes out of your account if you paid for a search, not until Recovery turned up an absolute no-can-do. I've seen a hell of a lot change, friend. I've heard about how the company has to do this and the company has to do that, and if we organize and everybody stands together the company's going to give in. Hell! We're not the Shepherds, the company doesn't have to give in. The company can replace us, the company's *aching* to replace us, and if it wasn't for the charter that says they have to deal with independents on a 'fair and equitable basis' they'd have screwed us all right out of existence. They teach you that in company school?"

"There are still rules. They're still accountable to higher management."

"Yeah, they're accountable. The only accounting that matters is the balance sheet. We shouldn't have filed on that ship, Ben. We shouldn't have done it."

"You're not making sense. It's the company's rules. They set up the salvage rules. You're saying they're not going to follow them?"

"Ben, the rules aren't supposed to cost the company money. *That's* the Rule behind the rules. I've had a bad feeling about this whole business from the beginning. You don't win big. You never win big."

"If you don't take the breaks you have you damn sure don't win anything!"

"You're all shiny new and bright polished. I was that a long time ago." He took a mouthful of the beer and swallowed. "I remember when they started making this stuff, too. You don't want to see the vats this came from."

"Yeah, well, maybe everything you remember was better. Maybe everything now is shit. Or maybe it was always like this."

"We didn't always have the company on our necks. We didn't always have them gouging every penny they can get their hands on, we didn't always have a friggin' military shipyard next door making us a target—we haven't always had all this damn happy stuff on the vid all the time, when we know nothing *happy* is going on back home, Ben!" It was too much to say, even out in the bar, where bugs weren't likely. It was too much even to think about. Ben looked confused.

"Here's home, Bird. This is home."

"Yeah," he said. "It's mine, too. But sometimes I'd like to kick its ass."

Meg and Sal came in the door. They had to explain to them how it was.

Sal said, "Sons of bitches," meaning, he hoped, the cops. But Meg and Sal were smarter than Ben in some ways. They shut right up, and said a dinner would patch things—

Funny, he thought then, that they had never even once thought that the cops could have been searching after something Meg and Sal had done, and them almost certainly skimmers, and just back from a run. But the company never minded skimming much, the way it never minded how Sal took money from guys—Sal just didn't do favors for free, unless she was your partner. And truth be known she got a bit out of Ben, the way they'd just gotten their dinner paid for. Company brats understood each other.

The gals didn't even look much upset, just kind of shrugged it off and shook their heads as if two guys who got into somebody else's trouble could expect police. Or maybe they were just trying to keep everybody level-headed, you never knew with women. They might be madder than hell and thinking how they'd like to break certain guys' necks, but they'd think about it awhile and figure they were *owed* for this, more than a couple of beers.

So they said they'd go straighten up, and they left. Ben lingered a minute finishing his beer and then said he'd go check the bank and make sure the money got logged right, which was an excuse: God only knew where Ben was really going.

Bird said, "Don't you try anything."

Ben said yeah and left.

Maybe he should have warned the gals about bugs. Probably they were chewing up him and Ben right now. But maybe it was better they did talk in the room, make whoever might be bugging the place think that they didn't suspect a thing. They knew about the ship, all right. But they didn't know what else there was to worry about.

Like that 'driver sitting out there where that ship had come from.

'Driver chewing away at what miners found—extracting and sorting and sending bucketloads to old Jupiter, who slowed it down again so the Shepherds could bring it in to be sheet and foam and such. Mama always assigned sectors according to the 'drivers' work patterns, so you knew there was one somewhere by, but *between* you and the Well, with its business end pointed the other way. Anytime you thought about going near a 'driver's actual fire-path, you had to think about how big it was and how small you were and how what it threw came so fast you'd never know what hit you. 'Driver paths were the one item of information Mama gave out for five or so sectors away, not even regarding the line that divided R1 work zone from R2. Every firing of the 'drivers had to be logged and reported to Mama as to exact time. You couldn't move a 'driver without Mama's permission. You sure couldn't hide one.

So Mama just forgot to put a 'driver on Dekker's charts? It had been on the ones Mama dumped to *Trinidad*—right where Dekker had given them the coordinates for the accident.

Damn, you didn't want to have thoughts like that.

Lot of pressure on Mama lately—a lot of crazy behaviors out of ASTEX's upper echelons—like mandatory overtime in the factories, like trying to revise the contract with the Shepherds, to let them install a few company-trained crew members on Shepherd ships—a fool could see where that was heading. None of the Big Shakeups had ever made sense, but damn-all anybody could do if the Earth Company got behind it. *They* could change the rules, they could change the *laws* if there was one in their way. The EC had so many senators in its pocket and the EC was so many people's meal ticket in one way or another, especially with this ship construction boom; and there were so many blueskyers bone ignorant about space and politics—

Living down at the bottom of the motherwell like his own brother did, writing him once a year about the wife and the kids and two pages at Earth to Belt mail rates about how he was putting in green beans this spring. God. Did people still think about things like that?

"Just sign this," they said, and shoved a slate under Dekker's hand—they had raised the bed up, propped him with pillows, but the trank was still thick and he could hardly focus. It was heavy *g* this time. It felt hard to breathe.

"What is this?" he asked, because he hadn't gotten cooperation out of anybody in this place and he didn't trust any of them. It might be a consent for them to go cutting on him, or giving him God knew what drug, and damned if he was going to sign it unread, in this place heavy as 1-deck.

They said—the *they* who came and went sometimes, cops, doctors, orderlies, he wasn't clear enough to figure that at the moment—"It's just so you can get out of here. You want to get out of here, don't you?"

"Go away," he mumbled, sick at his stomach.

"Don't you want to leave?" He had dropped the stylus. They put it back in his fingers.

He tried to get a look at it, then. It took a lot of work to make out the letters out of the general haze. But it said: AFFIDAVIT. Legal stuff. He worked some more at it. Finally he saw it was an accident report.

Accident. Hell.

He threw the thing. Maybe he broke it. It hit the wall and fell with a clatter like broken plastic. He thought, It wouldn't do that upstairs.

He said, "I'm not signing anything without a lawyer."

* * *

Hell of a mess they'd left. Meg was maddest about the jewelry. She sat there untangling earrings and swearing. "Ought to say we're missing something. Serve the cops right."

And Sal, sorting through the stubs of makeup pencils: "Blunted every damn point. Corp-rat pigs."

"We haven't done anything." It took some thinking, but that was the case. Meg unwound tiny chains and felt an upset at the pit of her stomach. "Sons of *bitches*, why the hell'd they toss everything together. . . ."

Sal came over and leaned on her fist on the bed. Signed, fast and sharp, Careful. Which didn't help the feeling in Meg's stomach at all. If they were bugged, and the way things were going she'd believe it, they could make those bugs vid as well as audio.

They didn't need this trouble. They *wanted* a chance at that ship, but they sure didn't need this trouble, and trouble for the guys was what it smelled like.

They could move out. There were sleeperies besides the *Hole.* They could kiss Ben and Bird off and go find another lease after all; but if that second ship did come Bird's way—

Then they'd want to cut their throats, was what. Bird and Ben were the best operation they had a chance with: no chance for her in the company. Not much for Sal either: with a police record you could work as a freerunner, but you didn't get any favors and you didn't fly for the company, and if anything went wrong on the deck you were on, you were first on the cops' list.

Just about time something went right for a change. There'd been enough bad breaks.

Like the sector they'd just drawn, which got them a nice lot of ice and rock, in which Mama wasn't keenly interested, no, thank you. That was the kind of allotments lease crews got lately: There were thin spots in the Belt, they were passing through one, and the ship owners took the good ones if they had to break health and safety regs to get out again.

Well, hell, you hung on. You stuck it. You skimmed when you had to and you did your damnedest. Meg Kady swore one thing: she wasn't going to die broke and she wasn't going to be spooked by any company cop throwing her stuff around.

Her hands got real steady with the little chains. She felt her mouth take on this little smile. Fa-mil-iar territory. Amen. "Cops on Sol are higher class," she said to Sal, right cheerfully. "These shiz don't take any courses in neat, do they?"

"Sloppy," Sal said. "Severely sloppy."

* * *

Salvatore sank into his chair, shoved a stack of somebody's problems aside, and took his inhaler from the desk drawer and breathed deeply of the vapors—enough to set himself at some distance. He took a deeper breath. The drug hit his lungs and his bloodstream with an expanding rush, reached his nerves and told him to take it easy. He hated scenes. Hated them. Hated young fools handing Security more problems and doctors who invoked privilege.

Most of all he hated finding out that there was more to a case than Administration had been telling him.

The phone beeped. He took another deep breath, let it go: his secretary would get it; and he hoped to hell—

"Mr. Salvatore," his secretary said via the intercom. "Mr. Payne."

Third call from PI that day. This was not one Salvatore wanted, and he knew what Payne had heard. God, he wasn't ready for this.

He punched in, said, "Mr. Payne, sir."

"I'm told we have a problem," the young voice on his phone said: Salvatore's office didn't have vidphones—he was glad not to have. Payne was junior, a bright young man in the executive, V.P. in charge of Public Information and PR, directly under Crayton, who was directly under Towney himself, and there was absolutely no doubt somebody else had been chewing on his tail—recently, Salvatore decided. So Payne passed the grief down *his* chain of command, to Security. "That damned fool is going to keep on til we have a corporate liability. This isn't going to help anyone, Salvatore."

"I understand that."

"Look, this is coming from upper levels, you understand *that?*"

"I do understand that, yes. . . ."

"This is getting to be a damn mess, is what it's getting to be. The girl's mother is after that kid and the whole company's on its ear. We've got contracts to meet. We've got schedules. We need that release. We need this case settled."

"I'm advising him to sign it, Mr. Payne." Salvatore took a deep breath—of unadulterated office air, this time. God, who was Payne talking to? "We're working on it. There's a possibility, the way I see it—" He took another headclearing breath and took a chance with Payne. "There's an indication the kids might not have been where their log said they were. It could have been a mistake, it could have been deliberate. I think they may have been skimming."

There was a long silence on the other end. God, he hoped he'd not made a major mistake in saying that.

"What we have," Payne's voice said finally, quietly, "is a minor incident taking far too much company time."

"Yes, sir."

"I can't be more plain than that. We *don't* need an independent involved in the courts, especially a kid with camera appeal. I've got the data on my desk, I'll send it over to you. There *was* no 'driver. We have the log. There was no such entry. I'll tell you what happened out there, captain, these two kids were up to no good, very likely skimming, probably scared as hell and taking chances with a rock way too large for their kind of equipment. Dekker either screwed up and had an accident that killed his partner, or there was a mechanical failure—take your pick of the safety violations on that ship. Maybe we should be prosecuting on negligence and probably on skimming, but I can give you the official word from Legal Affairs, we're not prosecuting. The kid's been through enough hell, there's no likelihood that he's going to be competent to testify, or that he won't complicate things by raising extraneous issues in a trial, and we're not going to have this drag on and on in a lawsuit. Salazar's or his. There's people on this station would love that, you understand me, captain?"

"I do, sir."

"So get this damn mess cleared up. You hear me? I want that release. I'm sending you the accident report. You understand me? We have elements here perfectly willing to use somebody like Dekker. I don't want this blown out of proportion. I want it stopped."

He thought about the recorder on his desk. His finger hesitated over the button. He thought better of that move. But he wanted to make Payne say it. "Stop the investigation?"

"Put out the fire, Mr. Salvatore. We have a damage control situation here. I want this resolved. I want this problem neutralized. Hear me?"

"Yes, sir," Salvatore said—which was pointless, because Payne had hung up. He punched in a number, the outer office. He said to his aide: "Get me Wills on the phone. *Now!*"

Dammit, if the kids were skimming—charge them. You skim from the company, you get busted. Period. But the girl's mother insisted not. The girl's mother insisted *her* daughter wouldn't involve herself in a shady operation. Beyond a doubt Dekker had murdered her daughter for the bank account.

Good point, except it was one doggedly determined killer, who'd wrecked his ship and sent himself off the mental edge for an alibi. He'd seen miners do crazy things, he'd investigated one case that still gave him nightmares, but nobody had held Corazon Salazar here at gunpoint and nobody had any indication Dekker was after money. By what his investigation had turned up, the girl had quit college, taken money from a trust fund, paid *Dekker's* way out here and laid down everything she had for an outdated ship and an outfitting—

A mortal wonder they'd gotten back alive the first time—and if anybody'd been kidnapped out here, it sounded more like Dekker . . . who was just damned lucky to have been found: physics had been in charge of that ship, the second those tanks ruptured: damned sure the kid hadn't—and God and the computers knew why it had stayed in the ecliptic, but it didn't sound like good planning to him.

Hell, Dek didn't handle money, one of the interviewees had said, in the investigation on R1. *He just flew the ship. Always tinkering around with it. . . .*

Social? Yeah, he'd be with Cory, but he'd be doing vid games or something—he used to win bar tabs that way. Real easy-going. Sometimes you'd get a little rise out of him, you know, showing off, that sort of thing, but he always struck me as downright shy. The games were his outlet. He'd be off in the corner in the middle of a crowd, Cory'd be at the table talking physics and rocks, yeah, they were a real odd pair, different, but it was like Cory did the headwork and Dek was all realtime—

Yeah, Dek had a temper. But so did Cory. You never pushed her.

Yeah, they slept together—but they weren't exclusive. Minded their own business—didn't get real close to anybody. People tried to take advantage of them, them being kids, they'd stand their ground . . . Cory more than Dek, actually. She'd draw the line and he'd back her up . . . not a big guy, older guys used to try to hit on him—he'd stand for about so much, that was all, they'd find it out.

Honest? I don't know, they weren't in anything crooked I ever heard . . .

There *was* a 'driver out there. He had the up to date charts. Company records had it arriving March 24 and the accident as March 12. But the ships' logs were tied up in BM regulations and the mag storage had been dumped. A panel by panel search of the two ships hadn't turned up any illicit storage, and Wills hadn't found any datacards in the miners' rooms.

Which didn't mean no datacards had gotten off the ship. *Hell* of a case for customs to wave past. Administration could come blazing in demanding answers on that.

But no one had told him early on there was any question about the charts; and he consequently hadn't told Wills. And now the evidence was God knew where. Or if it still existed. You tried to do some justice in this job. There was a kid in hospital in more trouble than he was able to understand, up against a woman with enough money to see him hauled back to Sol—and into courts where Money, the military, dissatisfied contractors, and various labor and antiwar organizations were going to blow it up into an issue with a capital I.

Salvatore understood what they were asking him to do. Found himself thinking how they didn't demote you down, just sideways, into some limbo like an advisory board no one listened to, out of the corporate track altogether.

He had a wife. A daughter in school, in Administrative Science—a daughter who looked to her father for the contacts that would make all the difference. Jilly was bright. She was so damned bright. And how did he tell her—or Mariko—this nowhere kid in hospital was worth Jilly's chances?

He took another deep breath from the inhaler, thought: Hell, Dekker's been no angel. He's got a police record on Sol, juvenile stuff. Mother bailed him out. Nothing he's done that we can prove . . .

But kids don't know what they're doing. If the kid can't use good sense, use it for him.

He felt the slight giddiness the inhaler caused: don't overdo it, his doctor said, and rationed the inhalers: his doctor didn't have William Payne on his back. Or a wife and daughter whose lives a recalcitrant kid could ruin.

If Dekker had used his head he wouldn't be where he was. Salvatore knew kids: kids never made mistakes, kids were too smart to make mistakes—but this kid *had* made a mistake, he was in far over his head. His partner was dead, a lot of survivor-guilt was wound around that—give the kid an out, that was the answer. No kid was going to understand politics and labor unions and defense budgets. Dekker had nothing to win that way and nothing but grief if he tried. Give him an excuse, offer him a way not to be accountable for his mistakes.

Before his mouth put him in real trouble.

The Department of Statistics says that the rise in birth rates this year reflects the rising number of females in the population, which will only continue to rise. Commenting on this, a spokesman for James R. Reynolds Hospital said today that the company should place contraceptives on the general benefits list. The average number of hours worked has fallen 10% during the last five years while the standard of living has continued to rise . . .

"Screw that," Meg said.

"That's what they don't want you to do," Sal said.

. . . population increase of 15% during the last decade. . . .

"Then why in hell are they doing overtime?"

. . . President Towney declares that R2 is facing a population crisis, and urges all women to consider carefully their personal economic situation. Statistics prove that women who postpone childbearing until after age 30 will on average enjoy a 25% higher standard of living. President Towney reminds all workers whether male or female that those who desire to advance in the company should Be Careful. . . .

"Think they'll advance us if we're careful?" Meg snorted.

"Maybe we should go tell them we're waiting," Sal said.

You got the vid blasting away in the gym. You couldn't escape it. They were sitting there sweating, waiting the breath to do the next round with the machines, and Towney was blithering again.

On the other hand . . .

Meg looked at her nails. It was a hobby, growing nails in heavy time. They all got clipped when you went to serious work. Or they broke off, eventually, in the dry cold.

Mostly she didn't want to look up, because there was this chelovek just come in that she sincerely didn't want the notice of. *This* gym, Sal wanted. And she'd said to Sal she'd as soon do something a little less exclusive.

"Sal."

"Yeah, I see 'im."

Meg looked from under her brows, tried to look like furniture; heart thumping.

Tall guy, hair shaved up, Nordic or something: his name was Mitch, he was a Shepherd tech chief, and he was a friend of Sal's. Not of hers—most definitely not of hers. Mitch had seen them and done this little take, just a half a heartbeat, and gone on over to the weights.

"I think I'd better evaporate," she said to Sal.

"No. Sit."

It was fairly well Shepherd territory they were in, this little gym near the end of helldeck. It was a gym Sal had always had rights in. She didn't. And this Mitch—Mitch never had approved of their partnership . . . mildly put.

Sal got up and went and talked with him. Meg tried not to be so forward as to read lips, but she could read Sal, and it wasn't thoroughly happy.

Then Sal put her arm around Mitch and steered back toward her.

"Meg," Mitch said.

It was her cussed nature that she wouldn't stand up. She strangled a towel, tilted her head to get a look at him against the lights and gave him a cool smile. "B'jour, Mitch, que pasa?"

He did rab the way Shepherds did, fash. He meant the same in his way. He didn't speak the speech, damned sure. Didn't do the deeds. He said, "Kady. How are you doing?"

"Oh, fair."

"That's good. That's good, Kady. No noise, no fusses. You're friend of a friend of a friend, you understand. That's gotten you this far. I must say I've been impressed."

"You're a sonuvabitch, Mitchell. Nice not seeing you lately."

Mitch smiled. Good-looking sonuvabitch. And having the authority to toss her out of here, and out of Sal's life.

"Don't screw up, Kady. You're on tolerance. You've run the line damned well so far. I've told Sal, there's a real chance on you."

"Take it and screw with it. I'm *not* on your tolerance."

Mitch's brows went up. Then he got this down-his-nose look, shrugged and walked away.

Meg rubbed the bridge of her nose, not wanting to look at Sal. She didn't know why she'd done that. Honestly didn't know why. It wasn't outstanding good sense.

"Sorry, Aboujib."

"Yeah, well." Sal dropped down to her heels, arms on knees. "He asked, he got, he knew he was pushing. He's all right."

"Yeah. I know how all right he is. Sumbitch. Little-*g* god. Shit-all he's done for you."

Silence from Sal a moment. She'd gone too far with that one. Finally Sal said, "They've heard about the upset in our room. Mitch wants us out. Says lease and go, get out. They're worried."

"Hell if!" Meg said. "We're *close*, dammit. What's he bloody care?"

Sal's dark face was all frown. "We do got a warning."

"Yeah, well, Aboujib."

"Severe warning."

"Wants me out of here, too, let's be honest. *You* get a lease, *I'll* stay here and hold us a spot on the ship."

"Didn't say that."

"I'm not saying split, dammit, I'm saying I stay here and hold us a spot and you keep your friends happy."

"He's advising both of us."

She took a tag end of the towel, mopped her forehead, an excuse to gather her composure. "We're that close. Dammit, Sal, you don't get that many breaks. There won't be another."

Sal didn't say anything for a moment. Meg sat there thinking, Sal's break's with them: her real break is with them, if she toes the line. Damn sons of bitches. Couldn't help her. Couldn't take her in. Toss a kid out like that . . . make her turn spirals til she's proved herself—hell if, Mitchell.

Sal said, finally, "Come on. Out of here."

On the walk, out in the noise and the traffic of the 'deck: "I don't think there's a bug there—Mitch wouldn't talk, else. But there's a word out, Meg: I got to confess, I maybe said too much."

"About what?"

"Ben got data off that they got when they were after that ship. He's been working with it and he doesn't give a damn what it is to anybody else, it's his charts and he's not going to see it dumped. He said that."

Meg took a long, long breath. "Merde. That's what you told Mitch?"

"Mitch came to me. They wanted a copy."

"Ben'd kill you."

Sal kept her voice low, beneath the noise and the echoes. "Yeah. I know it. But they won't make the same use of it—just the information, just those chart numbers. You got to fund me, Kady. Mitch's got my card right now. Access to our locker for the next while."

"Shit, Aboujib!"

"On the other hand—"

"This thing's got too many hands as is!"

"On the other hand, Shepherds have got their eyes on us after this. Dunno what they can do with those charts—but they're thinking there's something just damn ni-kulturny about Bird's ship being tied up, about this kid getting killed out there, about the cops looking through the stuff—"

"You told him this. You went to him."

Sal ducked her head. "I was worried. Worried about whether we shouldn't cast off and get clear of this, if you want the truth. You ask yourself why the cops would turn our rooms upside down, ask yourself if there's any damn thing we've been involved in out of the ordinary except we got two friends trying to file on a ship."

"Aboujib, —"

"Yeah, I know. I was just asking a question. I said I thought it could be data they're looking for—"

"Aboujib, do you seriously mind telling me in the hereafter when you're going to pull a lift like this?"

"Yeah, well, I figured you'd worry."

"I'd have killed you. —Ben know?"

"No."

"So how long before he finds out? God, Aboujib, that jeune fils is no fool. He could've bugged the damn card."

Sal pursed her lips. "Did."

"Then he does know?"

"Neg. Of course not. He and I *both* came through the Institute."

It was tests: put the washer on the stick, fit the pegs in the stupid holes. Add chains of figures. Dekker knew what they were up to when they gave him the kid toys.

"Screw that," he said, and shoved the whole box onto the floor—wishing it was lighter g. But it made a satisfying racket. He looked up at the disconcerted psychologist and said, "Screw all of you. I'm not taking your tests until I see a lawyer."

He stood up and the orderlies looked ready to jump, the petite psychologist frozen, slate held like a shield.

He coin-flipped the washer he had in his hand. Caught it before it fell, then tossed it toward the corner, looking at the orderlies.

"You want to come along?" Tommy said. He was the one who talked.

"Yeah," he said, shrugged, and walked over to the door where Tommy and Alvie could take hold of him. They had worked it out: he walked and they didn't break his arms.

If he was quiet they kept the restraints light and he could keep his hands free. It was hell when you couldn't scratch.

"Vid," he said when they were putting him to bed. There was vid in this room. Tommy turned it on for him. He didn't even want to ponder where he'd been, what they were doing, it was just one more try, no different than the rest.

But it scared him.

Another doctor walked in, turned off the vid. He'd never seen this man before. But it was a doctor. He had the inevitable slate, the pocketful of pens and lights and probes. And a name-badge that said Driscoll.

Driscoll walked over, sat down on the edge of the bed.

"Don't get friendly," Dekker said. "I'm not in the mood."

He enjoyed seeing the bastard sit back and take on an offended surliness. He was down to small pleasures lately. Driscoll consulted his slate mysteriously. Or Driscoll was the one who had the memory problems.

"I understand your impatience," Driscoll said.

"I'll talk to a lawyer."

"We have your test results."

"You didn't run any test."

Driscoll looked at his slate again: "Impaired motor function, memory lapses. . . ."

"That's bullshit."

"Mild concussion, prolonged isolation, oxygen deprivation, exposure to toxic materials—a possibility of some permanent dysfunction—"

"Bullshit!"

"Inappropriate behavior. Hostility."

"Get the hell out of my room. Where's Pranh?"

"Dr. Pranh is on leave. I'm taking his cases." Driscoll made a note on the slate. "I take it you'd like to get out of here."

"Damn right."

"I'll order the forms."

"I'm not signing any forms."

Driscoll got up, reached the door and hesitated. "Try to control those outbursts, Mr. Dekker. Staff understands your problem. But it would be all around easier if you'd make an effort. For your own sake. —Are the hallucinations continuing?"

Dekker stared at him. "Of course not," he said. He thought, That's a damn lie.

But it scared him. It pushed his pulse rate up. They'd turned off the beep, but that didn't mean they weren't listening, or that it wasn't going into storage somewhere.

Eventually a younger man came in, with another slate—walked up to the bed and said, "How are you feeling?"

The badge on this one said Hewett. He hardly looked twenty. He had a pasty, nervous look. Maybe they'd told him he was crazy.

Dekker didn't answer him; he stared, and the young man said,

"I've got your release forms." He offered the slate. "You sign at the bottom—"

"I'm not signing this thing."

"You have to sign it."

"I've asked for a lawyer. I'm not signing that thing."

Hewett looked upset. "You have to sign it, Mr. Dekker."

"No, I don't."

"You want out of here, don't you?"

"They want me out of here." He was cold. The air conditioning seemed excessive. He thought if there was a pulse monitor going it must be going off the scale. "I'm not going to sign that thing. Tell them they can do it. They've lied about everything else."

Hewett hesitated this way and the other, said, in hushed tones, "Just sign it. That's all you have to do."

"No." He shut his eyes. Opened them again as Hewett left.

He wanted out of here. He no longer thought he was safe from anything here. But he didn't see a way.

Rush for the door? If he got to the outside, especially if he hit anybody, the cops would have him on charges, God knew what. Sign the form and then go for a lawyer? A signed form was all that mattered to these people. It was all they listened to. And what kind of legal help was he going to get here? A company lawyer? Company witnesses?

He'd had a brush with the law on Sol Station—kid stuff. He'd learned about lawyers. He'd learned about hearings. Judges went in with their minds made up.

Another white coat came in. With a slate. This one walked up, held it out, and said, "This is for your medical insurance. Sign it."

He eyed the slate, eyed the woman suspiciously.

"It just authorizes payment of your bills. You're damned lucky you have it. You're a hundred percent covered."

He took it, looked at it. It looked legitimate. It listed him and it listed Cory. He signed the thing, and he remembered fighting with Cory, an outright screaming argument about that policy, saying, We don't need insurance, Cory, God, if you have an accident out here, that's it, that's all—it's a damn waste of money . . .

And Cory had said, the college girl, from just a different way of life than his: I've never been without insurance. We're at least having medical. I don't care what it costs. If we need it, it'll always be there . . .

In the crazy way Cory did things—argue about a damn jacket and spend a thousand dollars a year on a company policy that wasn't going to do them a damn bit of good. He started crying. He didn't even know why. The medic stood there staring at him a moment, and he put his arm over his face and turned as far over as he could. She left. But he couldn't stop.

Tommy came in and said, "Do you want a shot, Mr. Dekker?"

He grabbed his pillow and buried his face in it. So Tommy went away.

"Got something for you," Marcie Hager said, in her office in Records, with that peculiar smugness that Ben remembered. He came away from the door frame—he had come to the Records office on a cryptic Drop by—from Marcie. This after a *nice* bottle of wine that showed up with a buzz at Marcie's door some days past. You never paid Marcie's kind in funds. But you did want to be remembered.

Marcie said, a very faint whisper, "Got a little flag on your claims case. Seems Dekker's license has just been pulled."

He pursed his lips. "Grounds?"

"Doesn't say. Just turned up on the flag."

"Mmmn," he said. He winked at Marcie, said: "Thanks," with a little lift of his brows. "Big thanks."

Marcie looked self-satisfied. "I did enjoy that." Meaning the wine, he was sure. But it didn't mean the wine paid everything. Marcie had her sights set on promotion—something to do with personnel. He didn't forget that.

So Dekker's license was being pulled.

He walked out of the Records, hands in pockets, reckoning what he knew and who he knew, and finally decided to stroll over to a certain small office in Admin—nothing much. Records.

But Fergie Tucker worked there.

Fergie was just plain bribable.

"Hello, Fergie," he said, leaning on the counter. "How about lunch?"

"The guy's got no license now," Ben said, over a sandwich in Io's flashing neon decor. You never could tell what you were eating in here—everything flashed red and orange and green and the music made the wine shake in the glasses, but Tucker liked it. "He's out on a medical. Psych, if you ask me. He was crazy, out of his head all the way back—no way in hell he was in control of that ship."

Tucker took a drink. Strobe light turned the wine black, then flashed red on Tucker's face as he set the glass down, a jerky movement synched with the bass flutter down the scale. The wine shook. The air quivered. Tucker said, more loudly than he liked, "What exactly do you want?"

"Ex-pe-dition," he said, leaning close.

"Huh?" Tucker said. Tucker's hearing had to be going.

"Expedite!" he said, over the bass line. "There's no damn way he was in control. That's the law. He has to be in control, or we own that ship."

"I know the law."

"Well?"

Tucker shrugged, and took a big bite of his sandwich. Which left him sitting there while he disposed of it. Tucker had been a pig in school and he was still a pig. But he was a high-ranking pig. And he could move data along if he wanted to.

"Everything in order?" Tucker asked finally, when the mouthful was down.

"That application's so clean it squeaks. Vid. Before, after, and during. Clean bill from the cops."

"Court of Inquiry?" This around a mouthful.

"We haven't gotten any complaints. Nothing filed on us. On him, maybe. But I know that title's clear. It's *his*. The partner's dead, died out there. Sole title's with the guy, there aren't any other liens on it. We're *it*."

Tucker's face was orange now, with moving shadows. Sitar run. Clash of cymbals. Bass in syncopation.

"So what are we talking about?"

"Just slip it ahead in the queue."

Tucker swallowed. Said, slowly, "Has to have a grounds. Give me one."

He said, carefully, "What's grounds?" and inclined his head as far across the table as he could get it. The music was on a loud stretch.

"Where is this ship? What's its status?"

"At dock. Lifesupport's a mess. Tanks are blown. Filthy as hell and the cops have it."

"Chance of ongoing damage?"

"Could be. Depends. Have we got a better one?"

"Hardship."

"On who?"

"The claimant? Have you suffered damage?"

God, it was so close he could taste it. "Financial?"

"Any kind of damage? Can you document it?"

"Yes!" He winced. The music vibrated through the table top. He held the explanation a moment, then shouted, "We spent our reserve getting that mother in. We're short at the bank, we couldn't lease our ship out when we came in because the cops had it impounded, now we don't know what to do—she's past time she should have gone, you know, here we are a good way through our heavy time, but she's sitting idle; we got crews stacking up want to lease, and we need the money, but you only get a percentage on a lease if we do let her go out."

"So? Where's the hardship?"

"We could have to be here because of legal questions on the other ship—we're trying to be in compliance with the rules, but we don't know which way to jump. We've already lost a big chunk of our capital and we're scared to leave for fear of sending the whole deal out the chute, you understand what I'm saying? We've been waiting months already. We're coming to the time we should be out of here and we can't be."

"Yeah," Tucker said. "You know, somebody else could even slip in with a bid and take that ship, if word got out she was up for claim, if you weren't around to, sort of, oil the gears."

Tucker was a real bastard. He stared at Tucker, thinking, Don't you think about it, you scum, —while the music went from green to red and his blood pressure went up and up.

"Yeah," he said, "but we *are* due a Hardship."

"Yeah, well, you know those things are hell to fill out. You have to use the right words, say exactly what the clerks around in Claims like to hear. And you have to have somebody take it over there, that can put it on the right desk."

"Guaranteed?"

"Guaranteed." Tucker's pig eyes looked him up and down. "Ship owner has collateral like hell. Never has anything in pocket. How're your finances running?"

"Five hundred."

"Five thousand."

"The hell!"

Tucker shrugged, slid his eyes away, filled his mouth with sandwich. The bass fluttered up and down the scale.

"All right!" Ben yelled.

Trinidad was free. That had come through this morning. Thank God. Bird nursed the beer to the bottom and the last lean froth—wanted a second one, but the tab at The Hole was already too high. August friggin' 15th, and *Trinidad* was still at dock.

Meg patted his shoulder, went over to the bar. He figured what she was doing, then, and turned half around to protest, but Mike was already drawing the first one, and Sal Aboujib laid her hand on his from his other side. "Beer's cheap," Sal said. "Let her buy this one. We owe you a few."

He had a slateful of figures that wouldn't balance, Ben was still arguing about staying on, Dez Green and Alvarez and a good many of the other independents who'd been in when they arrived had all checked out on runs, and he was trying right now to decide whether old bones could run the risk of shortening their own time here, or whether they should just lease *Trinidad* out to Brower and his mate and sit at Base running up sleepery and food bills—maybe even lease her to Meg and Sal. *Promise* them the new ship if they got it. In that consideration they were short of supplies, the bank was not cooperating, and the damned LOS never had turned up again. They could try one more thing to get Recoveries to wake it up, but that computer time was expensive—and he just wasn't sure it was worth it. They'd had another minor LOS yesterday, not on one of their own, but on one they had a 15-and-20 on, on Peterson's lease; and he wished to hell he knew whether it was just bad luck, Peterson's fault, or whether there'd been any assignment in that sector when the thing went dead: the company just didn't like to hand out that kind of information. There were hotheads on helldeck that'd go for somebody if they got the wrongful or rightful notion they'd been robbed. Couldn't blame Mama on that one. Fights with chains and bottles were hell on the cops.

So they took the second LOS and they were going to have to tighten belts, that was all. And he knew why Meg and Sal were moping around with him and Ben instead of out running down a lease or even hitting on them for *Trinidad*, when that would have been the logical thing.

Hard at this point to tell them they weren't good enough to make enough to rate any prime lease, and they'd better go court somebody else, when Meg and Sal were courting them with all the finance they had and they were, dammit, day by day letting them do it, standing by them when anybody else would have called them fools.

You know, he'd told them more than once, at the first; I got to be honest with you: I don't think that ship of Ben's going to come through.

Did that drive them off? Hell no.

He should have said, plain and cold: Meg, I hear you're one hell of a pilot, and Sal, you're not bad at the numbers, but you just haven't got the years—haven't got the math, haven't got the sense of how things work—

Should have said, a long time ago: You two shouldn't ever have made a team: two greenies in the same ship is never going to get better fast enough for what you want.

But he knew what kind of slimespots they'd already shipped with before they'd proved on *Trinidad* that they could go it alone, and started getting leases: and Meg had courted him real hard just before Ben showed up with the cash and the schooling—he still flinched when he recalled having to tell Meg that; and Meg taking it real well, though she looked as if she'd got it in the gut. Maybe Sal even knew. And she and Sal had stayed teamed, even so.

They'd take good mechanical care of a ship, and bring her back sound and clean. Last lease he'd had with Hall and Brower, you couldn't say that. And they might do better with decent charts—and a little help from Ben.

Sal and Ben were a close pair lately. Those who knew Ben might snicker; and those who knew Sal would never in a million years win a bet on what really went on for some of those hours in the room, which was Ben talking numbers and Soheila Aboujib ticking away with her rented comp, with her lip caught in her teeth and this frown that would break glass—Sal could look madder than any individual he knew except Crazy Bob Crawford. Ben was hard to shake when he got an idea, but when it came to plain determination to make it, Aboujib and Meg Kady both were right up there with the cussedest.

We could do worse, Ben kept saying—when who to lease to had never been Ben's department, just which draws to lease and which to work—but he couldn't say Ben was wrong, except today it came to him that they'd blown near two months here, and they only now got *Trinidad* free. He and Ben could go ahead and make a run—

Yet here they both were, with karma piling up with the pair who'd stayed by them. He couldn't figure how he'd gotten into this, or when it had gotten too late—but when the cops had raided them and thrown Meg and Sal's stuff all over, that had been a real bad time to tell them shove off and forget it—

It seemed a worse time this morning, with their account bleeding money and him into Meg for a beer. He knew he ought to say, coldly as he could: Meg, Sal, don't you buy me a damn other drink this morning, because you're not getting what you're after, and you're wasting your money on what isn't going to come through—

But Meg set the mug down in front of him, patted him on the shoulder and sank into the chair beside him. "We got an idea, Bird. You and Sal go out in *Trinidad*. Ben and I stay here to keep that application alive and take care of problems—we get us a little finance, put what Sal and I got in the pot with yours—make sense?"

"I got to say—" was as far as he got toward a desperate *I don't think this is a good idea, and I can't take your money*

—when a familiar step came up behind him and a hand slapped a paper down in front of him.

His eyes must be going. For a moment it failed to make sense as what it was. A piece of real paper. With official print.

And Ben landing in the chair on his other side, grabbing his arm, shaking him and saying, "We got it! We got it, Bird!"

"The ship?" Of a sudden he knew it was a ship title. He'd handled *Trinidad*'s—years ago, before he put it in the bank vault. "It says Two-Two-Ten-Charlie. That's not the number. . . ."

"Same ship. Same ship with the blown tanks. They renumbered it. Like she was new. New start. Everything. We can sell her or we can fix her. We got her, Bird!"

He felt a little dizzy. He took a drink of the beer. Meg grabbed his arm from the other side. Sal was on her feet hugging Ben, and Ben was ordering drinks.

"Wait a minute!" he said, "wait a minute! Free and clear?"

"Free and clear," Ben said. "We got a few charges to pay, but hell, we got the collateral, now!"

"What charges?"

"We got—8, 9 k to pay . . . plus the dockage."

"Nine *thousand!*"

"Administrative. It's nothing, Bird, *—nothing*, against the value of that ship. Figure it! It's ours!"

"I don't believe it."

Ben pointed on the paper, where it said: *joint ownership*, and both their names. That wasn't the terms of the split they'd always had, but, hell, he thought, Ben had hunted down the forms, Ben had done the legwork, Ben had pushed the thing when he never thought it would happen.

Mike came over, Mike heard how it was, and gave them a round of drinks on the house—The Hole never did that. But Mike did now.

They had more than was good for them.

Which was when Ben said how he'd heard Dekker was going to be in hospital a long, long time. How he'd gotten his license pulled.

Brain damage, Ben said.

"Shit," he said, suddenly sick at the stomach.

"Hey, I told you," Ben said. "Dekker's a certified mental case."

"They pull him all the way?" Sal asked.

Ben shrugged. "Close as makes no difference. *If* he gets re-certified there's no way they give him a class 1. D3, maybe, but no way he can ever be primary pilot. Ship's *ours*, on account of it was a tumbling wreck when we got it, and just because he was inside it is im-ma-terial. He was just baggage. He couldn't stop it and he was in no shape to help himself."

Poor guy, he thought.

"Fact is," Ben said, "we *still* got a stack of bills against his account. And if he's gone for a long walk, he doesn't need the money: they'll just ship him out to the motherwell. I got an attachment on his bank account."

That was too much. "Now, wait a minute, Ben, we *got* the ship."

"And the repair bills. And our fuel and our dock time and *its* dock time, don't forget that. They'll stick us with all those bills."

Unpleasant thought. "And the cleanup inside," he said. "God, have you got any figure what that's going to cost?"

"I dunno," Ben said. "But we can get our expenses back."

He was disgusted with himself, being happy to hear that. Maybe there was a lot of disgust at the table. Meg and Sal had gotten real quiet.

But Ben pulled out his pocket slate and started running figures. "What we can do, we do the repairs ourselves, we use the reserve cash—"

"Whoa, wait a minute. That's our private insurance fund."

"You don't have to think like that now. That *ship* out there's our insurance fund. We got flexible capital now, Bird, sure we want a reserve, but we got to get that thing in running order. We risk it now, while it's in this shape; we don't lease *Trinidad* this run, we can do that work in a month if we push it, and we build back our fund. It'll work."

"Hell," he said, "I don't know. This poor guy—"

"It's not our problem," Ben said.

"Ben, . . ."

Ben gave him a bewildered look.

"We don't take anything more from that guy. That's flat. No more charges against him."

Ben didn't say anything for a moment. Ben looked as if he were worried about the objection, or confused. Finally: "Yeah, well, all right. But we're talking about a guy that may not make it out of the psych ward."

"If he does."

"Yeah, if he does, fine. So we're all right, so we collect it and if he gets out we can stand him a stake. If not, who cares?" Excitement got the better of him, he broke out in a grin and slapped Bird on the shoulder. "We got it, Bird, we got it, we got it made."

The guys went off to somewhere, talking about checking out prices on tanks, happy, mostly—they all should be. Everything had worked.

But Meg sat there with Sal turning her glass in a pointless circle and scared for a moment that didn't clearly make sense. She wasn't superstitious, as a rule. Maybe she'd gotten to distrust a winning hand: it always seemed to be the big breaks that stung you, the ones that made you lose your sense of reality and pushed you to commit to big mistakes—like the break that had had her believing that sumbitch back at Sol.

"No damn luck at all," she said. "Poor bastard's had all up and down, isn't he? Good old MamBitch. Screwed him good."

"Yeah," Sal said. "Didn't Mitch say?"

"Suppose he *is* crazy?"

"Ben swears he is."

"Brut bad luck for him."

"Company'd only get that ship. That's who we're screwing."

"That's the truth."

"Bet MamBitch passes a reg real fast says this can't happen again. Bet MamBitch never severely figured somebody'd get through the shit-work and file all those forms. They don't count on us knowing how."

"Ah, but they paid off. That proves MamBitch is honest, doesn't it? Then she'll pass her rule."

Sal gnawed her lip, tilted her head to one side, a clash of metal-clipped braids. "That gives Mama credit for brains. That's never been proved."

"That's the truth. True here, true everywhere."

Clink of glasses.

"Here's to one more poor bastard," Sal said. "Up the corp's.

"Yo," Meg said. "Here's to regulations."

"Stupidity," Sal said.

"Inefficiency."

"Venality."

"Is that a division?"

"Right under the corp-rat president."

Clink. "Here's to somebody Responsible."

"Must be on Mars."

"Sure ain't here."

A quiet snort. And a look in Sal's eyes that was dead serious.

"Screwed," Sal said.

"Yeah," Meg said, "but what's new? Maybe he'll get lucky. Maybe they'll ship him back to his zone, let him re-train."

"Lay any bets? He could have *friends* there."

"No takers," Meg said, and stirred a water-ring with her finger.

Sal said: "Worth a nudge."

Meg looked at her then, and Sal made a little shrug, gave her a lift of the brows with this smug look in her eye.

"You let it alone, you and your friends."

"No worry, Kady."

"Yeah." Cold as ice, Sal was; but sometimes you got this feeling she was thinking of something that risked her neck and she was breathing it in like an oxygen high. Sal was a Shepherd's daughter. Sal was also an orphan—in one deep dive into the Well.

That was worth remembering, too.

CHAPTER 9

They'd asked his shoe size at breakfast. Now they turned him out of bed, gave him underwear and socks that came folded, likewise a cheap little Personals kit, a pair of brand new boots (black) and coveralls (blue) with foldmarks all over, so he looked like a mental case. They let him shave himself this time, but his hair hung around his ears and down into his collar: he didn't even remember the last time Cory had cut it. He just stood there in front of the mirror staring at a hollow-cheeked, wild-eyed stranger and didn't understand what Paul Dekker had to do with this gaunt crazy person. He didn't remember that small white scar on his temple, didn't understand how it could have healed so far without him ever knowing he'd gotten it. . . .

Tommy took him gently by the arm—he liked Tommy more than Alvie. Alvie just did his job; Tommy cared. Tommy always gave him that little moment to get his balance, that moment to figure out that he had to do what they wanted, because Tommy had his orders, but Tommy was never rough with him, and Tommy guided him now with a real concern for his comfort.

"Where are we going?" he asked.

"Just down the hall," Tommy said. "It's all right, Mr. Dekker."

"Not going to be any more tests."

"No, sir. Just down to the office."

Things kept echoing in his head. He said, "Tommy, did they give me something?"

"When they did the tests this watch, yes, sir. Still a little groggy?"

"Dizzy," he said.

"Yes, sir. We'll just take it slow, all right? Good chance you're going to be leaving this afternoon."

That scared him. He thought, Where to? Where is this place? They'd let him out and he'd be somewhere he didn't know and Tommy wouldn't be there. Just strangers.

Tommy opened a door for him and brought him into an office. He didn't want to stay here. He didn't want to be alone with any more doctors. Tommy set him down in a chair and he grabbed on to Tommy's arm. "Stay here," he said.

Tommy patted his shoulder. "It's all right." The doctor was coming in from the other door, same stamp as all the others. Tommy had said the doctor's name and he didn't care, he just wanted out of here. But Tommy stayed, right there with his hand on his shoulder a moment and when the doctor ordered him, Tommy left him there.

"How are we doing?" the doctor said.

"Screw you," he said—couldn't muster any enthusiasm about it. He felt as if he was floating.

"Don't like this place, do you?"

That question wasn't even worth answering. He wanted to go back to bed. Wanted to watch vid or something. Or sleep.

"Still having the memory lapses, Mr. Dekker?"

He honestly didn't know. He shook his head.

"I'm Dr. Visconti. Outpatient Services. Dr. Driscoll says you're doing much better."

Maybe he was supposed to say something about that. He didn't. He just nodded.

Visconti said, "There's an answer here from Management, on your request for a Court of Inquiry. Do you want me to read it to you? Do you want to read it?"

"I'll read it," he said, and Visconti pulled a card from his pocket, slipped it into the slate that was lying on his desk and offered it to him. It said,

Mary Finn, Special Judge
Legal Affairs Technical Division
Re inquiry: Belt Management, Div. 2,
Mining & Recovery

ASTEX
MEMO TO:
Mr. Paul F. Dekker
c/o James R. Reynolds Hospital
R2/ASTEX MINING

8/01/23

Dear Mr. Dekker:
We have investigated your claims regarding the fatal accident that occurred on or about March 12th of this year. We enclose the testimony of 1) Recoveries, which has attempted to trace the course of 1-84-Z and to determine the location of the accident; 2) the testimony of Mohammed Fahdi, range officer and Lyle Xavier Manning, senior captain of the ship Industry, *which was the only ship of its class operating near that path; 3) the testimony of Frances E. Rodrigues; Chief of Operations of BCOM/R1; 4) the report of Gianpaulo Belloporto, chief examiner, ASTEX R2 DIV ECSAA. It is the determination of this office that a catastrophic failure of the main intake value caused an explosion of the number two primary tank of 1-84-Z, which hurled the vessel in an unanticipated acceleration toward charted asteroid 2961. . . .*

"This is a damn lie. This whole thing is a lie—"

"Mr. Dekker."

"There wasn't any catastrophic failure."

"Mr. Dekker. There *was* no 'driver in your vicinity at the time. The report doesn't find you culpable. It was a very unfortunate double system failure. The pressure in that tank was building up during your maneuvering while your partner was outside. The valve had failed. The warning should have sounded. There's no evidence it did. The blowoff apparently didn't function—that part of the tank is missing and there's no way to check—"

"What are you, a psych or a mechanic?"

"It's part of our job, Mr. Dekker, to determine what did happen before we offer advice. The investigators don't find any evidence of negligence, and they don't blame you in any wise for the accident."

He shut up, just stared at the wall. Useless to argue. Absolutely useless.

"It simply wasn't your fault, you understand? It wasn't any one person's fault. There's going to be a thorough investigation at R1 maintenance—but most serious accidents, they tell me, involve a triple failure, either of human beings or of equipment. As I understand it, the pressure warning didn't sound. They're sure of that from the log recorder. The blowoff can't have functioned properly. It says here they're investigating the possibility of a primary cause in a cross-wiring of a control module in an attitude control unit—the chance that the safety interlock system actually caused a pressure increase instead of a system shutdown. If it's any comfort to you, there's going to be a design review and a mandated inspection on that particular module. Whatever the technicalities—as the experts explain it, it was bound to happen at some point during a period of frequent brief firings—the investigating board thinks when you were moving in to pick up your partner. So it's absolutely not your fault, Mr. Dekker. There's no way you could have detected the malfunction: no way you could have anticipated it, nothing you could have done when it did happen. It's not a question of blame. And you've *carried* a great deal of personal blame, haven't you, Mr. Dekker?"

"Anything you say, doctor."

"It's called transference. A terrible experience, a long period of disorientation, periods of unconsciousness. Guilt for what you didn't do. A 'driver accident is something every miner's afraid of—something you can't defend against, a shot arriving out of nowhere, faster than anything can warn you. A loss of personal control. Just like that explosion. That fast. Cory's gone—"

"Not Cory."

"Not Cory?"

"What's the matter? Her being dead puts you on a first name basis with her? Go to hell, doctor!"

"Of course you'd have protected her. You're still protecting her. But you have to accept you're not to blame. Something blew up. There may be culpability on someone's part, but it's not with you. There was a 'driver, but it was a sector away. It wasn't firing. The events you've fantasized just didn't happen. They don't *have* to happen in order for you to be innocent. You have to turn loose of that fantasy. Your partner's gone. There's no chance she's alive now. There's no hope. There hasn't been from the first few hours after the accident. You have to give that up. You have to take care of yourself, now, Mr. Dekker."

"It's a damned lie," he said. "You haven't been here all the while, have you? They used to say there wasn't a 'driver at all. Now it's a different story."

"It's a different story, Mr. Dekker, because records are kept by zones and by sectors. You were almost correct, but you were remembering a recent position. The mind will do that to you. There wasn't a 'driver in the vicinity. The BMO at R1 and here at R2 have compared records. They know your course now. They didn't, at the start. Now they're sure the 'driver wasn't anywhere near the accident."

He couldn't answer that. His hold on what had happened had become too precarious. He decided to keep his mouth shut, before they argued him out of another piece of his memory.

The doctor took the slate, put in another card. "Are you ready to get out of here, Mr. Dekker?"

"Damn right I am."

"You'll be in outpatient for a while." The doctor passed him the slate. "You'll have a prescription to help you sleep—I understand you still have trouble with nightmares. That's only normal. You have to work these memories out. You have to remember and deal with this tragedy. I think you understand that. But you will have the prescription, if you need it." He reached forward and offered a stylus. "Sign the bottom of the document and date it."

Dekker pushed the button, scrolled back. It said, . . . *agree to the findings hereabove stated* . . .

"No," he said, and shoved the slate at the doctor. "I don't agree."

"You don't feel you're ready to be released."

The doctor didn't take the slate. It stayed in Dekker's hand and his hand shook. He thought, If I sign this lie nobody will ever pay for what they did. They'll have killed Cory, and I'll have run out on her, finally even I'll have run out on her . . .

But if I stay in here they'll make me crazy. They can tell any damn lie they want.

What's justice? What's justice, when there's nobody can call them liars?

He set it in his lap, shaking so badly he could hardly write his name, but he signed it. His eyes blurred. He handed it over.

"Can you say, right now," the doctor said, "at least *maybe* it was an explosion? *Maybe* it was an accident? Can you get that far, Mr. Dekker? Can you admit that now?"

He nodded.

"Mr. Dekker?"

"Yes," he said.

"Good," Visconti said, and took the datacard from the slate and put it in his pocket. He got up from the edge of the desk. "Come with me, Mr. Dekker. I'll take you to Dismissals."

He got up. He hurt in every joint. They went out the side door and into a corridor he hadn't known was there. He only wished Tommy had been there. He would have liked to have Tommy with him.

"Don't mind a little stiffness," Visconti said while they were walking. "I want you to walk. I want you to do low-impact exercises—you don't need any broken bones to complicate matters. No jumping. No jogging. If there is any pain in the back, stop. The card we're going to give you has all your prescriptions, with dosages and cautions. I don't have to warn you about calcium depletion, kidney stones, that sort of thing. The calcitonin regulators you're surely familiar with. What I've given you shouldn't have any interactions, but take any symptoms seriously, follow the exercise routines I've laid out exactly, precise number of repetitions. If you get any undue amount of sleep disturbance, see me, if you get blood in the urine, if you get sharp headaches, blurred vision, hallucinations or pain in the chest, put that card in the nearest reader, punch 888, and don't leave that reader. An emergency crew will find you."

"888."

"That's right. I'm your doctor of record. Don't hesitate to call me." They reached a counter in a hallway that stretched on toward the light. "This is patient Dekker, Paul F. Would you find his file and his belongings?" Visconti put out his hand. "Good luck, Mr. Dekker."

Maybe it would have been braver to have told Visconti go to hell. But it might have landed him back in the other hall again, with more stuff being shot into him and the doctors saying, Are you still having those memory lapses?

He shook Visconti's hand and waited at the counter alone when Visconti went away. His legs were shaking. His ears were buzzing. He was afraid he was going to fall and they were going to put him back to bed, so he sat down on a molded bench that made his back hurt and waited until someone at the window called his name.

They gave him his datacard and wanted him to sign another release, that he'd received his Personals and his card and his prescriptions. They handed him a bag of prescription bottles and another sack that had his watch and his old coveralls and stimsuit, he signed, and they wanted his card in the slot on the counter.

He punched Validate. He punched Read, to know what it would show him, and the reader screen showed two things valid: the ASBANK account number and his insurance. It said it was August 15. It said: ALL ACTIVE ACCOUNTS ARE IN PROCESS OF TRANSFER TO ASBANK R2 DIV.

And below that: PILOT CREDENTIALS: INVALIDATED.

He couldn't move for a moment. The clerk said, "Mr. Dekker?" and asked if he was all right.

He couldn't think. There was just a door to a lobby, a way out, and he took his card back, shoved away from the counter and walked for the light.

He had no idea where he was when he left the hospital, he only walked for a while down wide beige hallways with no clear thought in his head except that he was out of the hospital and nobody had stopped him.

But a cop did. The cop blocked his path and asked for his ID card, and he stood there scared they were going to take him back, while people in business suits walked past ignoring the situation.

The cop inserted the card in his pocket slate, with that expression that said he had to be a thief at best and that if there was anything wrong on this whole deck he had to be a prime suspect. Then the cop, still with that dead expression, stared off down the way and said to no one he could see, "Yeah. Yeah. Copy that. Thanks." Then the cop gave the card back with marginally less chill and pocketed his slate. "Just out of hospital, is it?"

"Yessir."

"You need any help, Mr. Dekker?"

"No, sir. I'm all right."

"Where will you be staying?"

"Don't know. Helldeck."

"Trans is down the way, about a hundred meters. You'll want the last car. About your fourth, fifth stop."

"Thank you," he said, and walked on in the direction the cop had pointed. ASTEX didn't want a spacer walking on their clean deck, fingerprinting their beige paneled walls. He understood the rules. He didn't even spit on the floor. He made it to the Transstation, leaned on the wall and waited til the Trans showed up and the doors opened. People in suits got off, he stepped aboard, into an empty car, and sat down. One woman got on, sat down opposite, didn't look at him, even if there was nothing else to look at. The Trans started up, whipped along to its next stop on the rim. Somebody else got in. Eventually all the business types got off and spacer and worker types got on: the screen said NEXT STOP 2 as the Trans started off in the other direction and climbed.

If would help if he could ask his way. But people didn't do that. People kept their mouths shut in the Trans, the same here as at R1. Ads lit the info screen, advertising upcoming facilities; music blared. The first stop listed mostly BM service offices. The second was commercial. The third listed sleeperies, gyms, and bars, and that was where he got off, into the echoing noise of helldeck.

He wobbled a bit when he walked, but that wasn't unusual here, for one reason or another. He looked like a lunatic and carried plastic sacks full of everything he owned, and that wasn't unusual here either—ordinary helldeck traffic. Some religious type jostled him, a religious type who yelled something about God and judgment and aliens and wanted him to come and hear a tape. But he didn't, he just wanted to be let alone, and the guy told him he was going to hell.

For a while he was just lost—he could believe there had never been a hospital, there had never been a wreck: everything around him sounded and felt like home Base for the last two years—but the names were all different—

Cory had never existed here. His eyes and his ears kept telling him he had finally come home; but people around him were busy with their own lives, in shops with different names.

He walked, going through the motions people who belonged here went through. He didn't know what he wanted. His knees and his feet and his shoulders began to ache with the unaccustomed exercise, and he recalled, out of the long nightmare of the ship, that he had wanted a beer very badly then. So, in the process of picking up his life, he walked into a comfortable-looking bar—The Pacific, it said, with plastic colored fish and plastic coral reefs and blue lights over the bar. The customers—there were ten or so—were tenders and dock monkeys, mostly. The shapes and shadows of creatures he'd never seen reminded him vividly of Sol Station, where he had a mother who honestly might care if she saw the mess he was in.

She'd say, Paul, didn't I tell you so? Didn't I say you were being a damned fool?

She'd say, teary-eyed and exasperated beyond endurance: Paul, now, how in hell am I going to get you out of this one? You cost me everything I ever got in my life. You've done every damn thing you could to screw up. What am I supposed to do for you now?

But he'd have been drafted if he'd stayed on the station. No essential job, 18, no medical reason not, they'd have taken him; and she hadn't wanted that either, they'd agreed on that. She'd kissed him goodbye and he'd been embarrassed and ducked away, the last time he'd ever seen her—humiliated because his mother had kissed him in public. He understood now how he'd been a pain in the ass, and after all the grief she hadn't deserved, the last thing Ingrid Dekker needed was her grown son calling up, saying he was coming home—to get sucked up by the military after all, if they wanted a certified schitz—

So what the hell good could they do each other? He wouldn't take any more of her money. Or her peace of mind, whatever it was now. And she couldn't help him.

He ordered a beer and handed the bar his card, hoping the hospital hadn't cut off alcohol—not good for a man on trank, but he didn't care. The bartender looked at him and stuck the card into the reader, where he could find out as much as a bartender needed to know, namely could he pay for what he'd just ordered, and had he any active police record?

A Medical showed up. He could see the screen from where he was supporting himself on the bar. But the guy didn't argue about the beer, just drew one and gave it to him; and he found himself a vacant booth and fell into it, sipped his beer, shut his eyes and sat there awhile in relative null before his brain started to conjure pictures he didn't want to recall. So he looked at the stuff the hospital had given him—took his watch out of the bag and put it on.

It said, 06/06/23: 15:48:10. 15:48:11: he watched the seconds tick along, thought, No, that date's not right. It's August. August 15.

Cory's somewhere out there. All that black. All that nothing around her.

She'd have seen the explosion, seen the ship—it could have run right over her—

Dammit, no! she wouldn't have, because that wasn't what had happened, that was the doctor's story. There wasn't any bad valve, there'd been a 'driver . . . he'd argued with it: This is our claim, hear us?

Instruments went crazy, collision alert sounding—he yelled over and over again, *A-20, Mayday, Mayday, my partner's out there—*

You damned ass! What do you think you're doing?

He ground the heels of his hands into his eyes, thinking how the log would show those instrument readings. The doctors kept saying something different, but maybe the cops hadn't even gotten into the ship—the doctors wouldn't know shit about the technicalities and they didn't care, they just made up stuff they thought was going to shut him up—it was their job, and they didn't want him complicating it. The way the company worked, the cops probably hadn't even looked, either, just some judge took all these reports from a 'driver that didn't want any record of what it had done and operators in BM who didn't want to admit—

—admit a 'driver had jumped a claim.

His head ached with a vengeance. He shied away from the company's reasons. He thought about the pills and sorted through the lot, reading labels.

But beyond that . . .

He looked at the time again, August 15th. The accident—

(No accident, dammit.) That was the 12th of March.

March 12 to March 31 is twenty days. 20 plus 30 in April is 50. 50 plus 21 in May is 71.

January 1 to March 12. Thirty-one days in January, 28 in February, they said it wasn't a leap year, 12 in March. 31 and 28 and 12 makes seventy-one days. Seventy-one days til they found me. Seventy-one days from January 1st to the accident. No. From the accident—that was why the watch read out the 12th. The numbers are a match—that's all. And between then and now—is it coincidence? Or do months always do that? What do 30's and 31's have to do with anything sane?

He couldn't think. His mind slid off any long track it tried to take. It made his head ache. He took his datacard and used its edge to reset his watch. August. The 15th. That was it. It said August 15 and Cory was out there somewhere, while he was sitting in an R2 bar. Half a year was gone, part of it lost in the dark, part of it on the ship, part of it in hospital. The 15th of August. And his card was active here, on R2, and they hadn't said a word about sending him home: he supposed they didn't want the expense.

Or they didn't want him talking.

Screw that—if he knew anyone to tell anything to on helldeck—

If they'd gotten his ship in, if—he had anything to live on—

He remembered the license suspension—the doctors said it was oxygen deprivation and nerve damage because he dumped a stupid box on the floor and pissed off some doctor with an Attitude, that was what had gotten written down on his records. Or they'd pulled it because of the accident—but they'd cleared him of that. He could fix the license part of his problems, get the shakes out, get some sleep and do a few days in the gym—

All he had to do was sign up and pass the operationals again. No problem with that.

Except the hours requirement. . . .

The company was going to be reasonable? The thought upset his stomach.

Retake the medical exam, maybe, *put* the damned washers on the stick, this time. He could prove it never should have been pulled. Getting the ship in order might take everything he had—tanks blown, all that crud when the lifesupport went down—but he could do a lot of the cleanup himself—but the dock charges . . . they'd come in, when? July 26th? *June* 26th?

God, he didn't want to think about time any longer, didn't want to add numbers or sweat finance right now or figure out how much he'd lost. But now that he'd started thinking about it he couldn't let it go. He couldn't keep any figures straight in the state he was in, and he had no idea what the tanks were going to cost. Twenty, thirty thousand apiece, maybe, counting the valves and controllers and hookups: some value for the salvage on the old ones, but it was going to take bank finance, and they had his account tied up—it might be smarter to sell it, buy in on some other ship—

The bar had a public reader. He got up with his beer and his bag of pills and his belongings, and went and put his card in, keyed past the surface information for detail this time.

APPLICATION MADE FOR FUNDS TRANSFER: 47,289.08 in ASBANK R1 branch to ASBANK R2. ACCESSIBLE AFTER 60 DAYS. PUBLIC NOTICE POSTED 08/15/23. CURRENT AVAILABLE BALANCE: 494.50.

Sixty days. God. What could take 60 days? He wanted to know where his ship was, what berth, what those charges were so far. He typed: 1-84-Z: STATUS.

R2's computer answered: UNAVAILABLE.

Screwups. There wasn't a thing in his life that some damned agency hadn't messed up.

He took his card, went back to the bar, said, "Can I use the phone?"

The bartender held out his hand, he surrendered his card for the charges and the guy waved him to the phone on the wall at the end of the bar.

He punched up INFORMATION, asked it: DOCK OFFICE, pushed CALL, waited through the Dock Authority recording, punched Option 2, and patiently sipped his beer while his call advanced in queue. A live human voice finally acknowledged and he said, "I'm Paul Dekker, owner of One'er Eighty-four Zebra. Should be at dock. I'm getting an UNAVAILABLE on the comp, can you tell me what—"

"Confirm, One'er?"

"Yes. Towed in. Might be in refit."

"Just a minute. You say the name is Dekker?"

"Paul Dekker."

"Just a minute, Mr. Dekker."

He took another sip of the beer, and leaned heavily on the counter, his breath gone short. He'd had enough of incompetence, dammit, he'd had enough of doctors arguing with him what he had and hadn't seen and he wasn't ready to start a round with the Dock Authority. A ship *Way Out*'s size was a damned difficult object to misplace.

"Mr. Dekker, that ship was here. I'm not finding any record of it. Just a minute."

A long wait while he sipped his beer and his heart pounded.

"Mr. Dekker?"

"Yes."

"Are you sure that ship hasn't gone out?"

He was on the edge of crazy now. He said, "I'm an owner-operator. No, it hasn't gone out. It *shouldn't* have gone out. Try Refit."

"I'll check." The operator sounded concerned. Finally.

The barman was looking at him. A bunch of military drifted in and took his attention. He hadn't seen them on R1. But they were customers. He was glad of the distraction. He was in no mood for a bartender's questions.

The bartender served the other drinks. The hold continued. The soldiers settled in at a table. The barman signaled him: Refill?

He slid the empty mug down the bar, still waiting, still listening to inane music.

"Mr. Dekker?" the phone said.

"Yes."

"I'm going to put my supervisor on. Please hold."

He had a bad feeling, a very bad feeling. The beer came sailing back to him, and he stopped it and sipped at it without half paying attention.

"Mr. Dekker?" A different voice. Older.

"Yes."

"Mr. Dekker, that ship's number was changed. I'm looking at the record right now. You're Mr. Paul F. Dekker. Would you confirm with your personal ID, please."

"12-9078-79."

"Yes, sir. That title was transferred by court order. It was claimed as salvage."

He couldn't breathe for a moment. He took a drink of the beer to get his throat working downward again.

"Mr. Dekker?"

"Did the guy who claimed it—happen to be named Bird? Or Benjamin-something?"

"I'm not supposed to give out that information, Mr. Dekker. I can give you the case number and the judge's name. If you have a question, I'd suggest you go to the legal office. We don't make the decisions. We just log what they tell us. I'm very sorry."

"Yeah." He was having trouble with his breathing. He didn't have his card to take the note the Dock Office was putting in. He didn't want to involve the barman to get it. It went wherever it went when you didn't key a Capture. "Thanks."

"Good luck, Mr. Dekker."

The Dock Authority hung up. He pushed the flasher, keyed up Information and keyed into Registry. Took the 1 choice this time and asked the robot for M. Bird.

Bird, Morris L.: *2-29-T* berth 29 and, *2-210-C* in Refit.

He signed Registry off and keyed up information on Morrie Bird. It gave a can-be-reached-at phone number.

He called it. The voice that answered said: *"Black Hole?"*

"Is this a sleepery?"

"Sleepery and bar. Help you?"

He hung up. He drank a big gulp of beer and picked up his sacks off the bar. He asked the barman: "Where's The Black Hole?"

"About three doors down. Something the matter, mister?"

"Yeah," he said.

And left.

CHAPTER 10

Heavy time was, for a very major thing, a desperate chance at all the vids you'd missed, at food that Supply Services hadn't blessed, at faces you wouldn't see day after day for three months, and at the news you didn't get out there where Mama's newscast was the only gossip you got, telling you crap like, Gas production in R2 is up .3%; or: There was a minor emergency in core section 12 today when a hose coupling came loose, releasing 10,000 liters of water—

The mind conjured intriguing images—but they were thin fare to live on. Heavy time was real life: the reviews Mama radioed you out in the deep Belt of vids in the top ten only let you know what was a must-see when you got back. A stale rehash of handball scores was no substitute for seeing the interdivisional games, and electronic checkers with your shipmate was damn sure no substitute for sex.

Heavy time was anything you could afford besides your hours in the public gyms and your socializing in the sleeperies and bars and your browsing in junk shops—precious little you could buy except consumables and basics, because a miner ship had no place to store unusefuls, and mass cost fuel: but experience didn't mass much except around the waistline—so those were the kind of establishments you tended to get on helldeck, those that catered to the culturally, sexually, and culinarily deprived.

And if a couple of your partners turned up absent since quitting time into supper, with a sudden lot of credit in the bank, you knew it was probably one of the above.

Even if it left you doing the supply shopping and handling the guys wanting a lease, you couldn't blame him too much, and Bird didn't: Ben had never been inclined to do it, Ben had worked hard on the legal stuff and the filings, and Ben had finagled a deal with a company repair crew to get the tanks installed.

But leaving him with the phone calls . . .

The regular lease crews wanting a piece of *Trinidad* or *Way Out*—those you could explain to. They weren't overjoyed, but they understood. It was the horde of part-time unpartnered would-be's, most of whom you wouldn't trust to find their way up the mast and back, who called up every time a ship went on the list; and who, finding out that *Trinidad*, newly on the list, wasn't to lease, argued with you; and, worse, that a brand-new ship, *Way Out*, was already first-let to one Kady and Aboujib, of less seniority and a certain reputation—

Well, it told you that you sure didn't want to lease to those hotheads anyhow. He said to the latest such to call, "Screw you, too, mister. Hell if you ever get any ship I'm handling," and hung up.

After which he walked past the looks from the other tables, back to the table by the door and the figures he was working with Meg—bills and bills, this week, pieces and parts of *Way Out*, mostly. He sat down and shook his head.

"Another fool," he said, and punched up the Restore on the slate beside his plate, trying to recall his previous train of thought, and wishing to hell they still gave you paper bills, instead of damn windows on a slate that caught the glare from the ceiling lights. "Wayland Fleming. I never let to that son of a bitch and right now I'm damn glad. —Where in hell's Ben and Sal off to, anyway?"

"Vid, I think."

"Spending money." He shook his head. "I don't know what's got into Ben."

Meg looked up with raised eyebrows and said, "Now, Bird, you *know* what's got into Ben."

No, he honestly hadn't had it figured until Meg said that—and it somewhat upset his stomach. Ben and Sal? Cold, cool Ben?

With Sal Aboujib?

"You *didn't* have it figured?" Meg said. "Come on, Bird."

That they were sleeping together, hell, yes—going at it non-stop, absolutely, but that was youthful hormones. What Meg implied was something else. A guy like Ben, who'd saved every penny all his life, out spending it on a woman?

Ben, his best-ever numbers man—being courted by Kady's? And advising him who to lease to, against his better judgment?

Meg had toted up the expense figures while he was at the phone: she had a better head for bank balances than he did, she was damned pretty, and sometimes, looking at her, even if an old blue-skyer's eyes had to get used to fire-red hair shaved up the sides and bangles up the ears, it was the likes of Meg that could keep a man interested in living.

But what was he doing suddenly sleeping steady with Meg Kady, when there were whole stints ashore he'd spent without a woman so much as looking at him? And what was Ben doing spending his money on Sal?

He was afraid he did have the answer to that, and maybe he ought by rights to be mad. Maybe he ought to throw Meg Kady out on her scheming ear and rescue Ben from Sal's finagling.

The problem with that scenario was—

A hand landed on his shoulder, jerked him around and out of his chair.

A fist sent him back over the table. He had his foot up to stop another attack, but he *knew* the wild-eyed lunatic that was standing there wobbling on his feet. Everybody in the room was out of their chairs, Meg had hers in her hands, Mike was probably calling the cops, and Dekker was standing there looking as if standing at all was an effort.

"Where's my ship?" Dekker yelled at him.

Bird got a cautioning hand up before Meg could bash him. "Ease off," he said, and yelled at Mike Arezzo, behind the bar: " 'S a' right, Mike, I know this crazy man."

"You're damn right you know me!" Dekker said. "I get out of hospital, I call the dock to get my bills, and what have I got?"

The jaw wasn't broken, but teeth could be loose. He rolled off the table and staggered to his feet with Meg's hand under his arm.

"Is this Dekker?'" Meg asked.

"This is Dekker," he said. "—Sit down, son, you look like hell."

"I've *been* there." Dekker caught a chair back to lean on, getting his breath. "You damned thief."

"Easy. Just take it easy."

"Easy! You went and stole my ship, you lying hypocrite!"

It wasn't a kind of thing a man wanted to discuss in front of neighbors. Mike Arezzo asked, from over at the bar: "Want me to call the cops, Bird?" At tables all over the room a lot of people were listening. "I'm not having my place busted up."

"Why don't you?" Dekker gasped. "Prove I'm crazy, this time, so you don't have me to deal with. They can do the rest of the job on me—that's what you wanted, isn't it? That's what you set up for me. You took everything else. Why don't you just finish the job?"

"Mike, I'm buying this guy a drink. I want to talk to him. He's all right."

"I don't want to talk to a damn thief!"

"Beer, Mike, that's what he's been drinking. —Sit down, Dekker. Sit!"

Dekker breathed, still leaning on the chair, "I need those log records. Just give me the log records, that's what I want—"

"I don't have 'em," he said. And when Dekker just stood there looking at him: "She was cleaned out when they turned her over. God's truth, son. They're not going to give somebody else's log over to anybody else—I don't know if they got it stored somewhere, but her whole tape record was clean when she came to us. Zero. Nada. Everything's out of there."

Dekker was absolutely white. "The damn company killed my partner, they're saying there never was a 'driver near us—they *erased* my log—"

"Kid, shut up and sit down."

"You know that 'driver was out there! You know what the truth was before they changed it—"

Meg pulled at his arm. "Bird, —"

"Ease off, Meg. —Just sit *down*, son." People were headed for the door. People were clearing the place.

Dekker slumped against the chair back, bowed his head, shaking it no, and Abe Persky said, brushing up close on his way out, "Not bright, kid. Understand?"

Abe left. Mike was pissed about his customers, *and* the noise—he brought the drink over and said, "Shut this guy up. We don't need this kind of trouble in here."

"We got him," Meg said, got Dekker by the shoulder and steered him for the chair. "You just calm down, hear? Bird's not a thief."

"The company's the thief—you just—"

Meg said, "Shut it down, just shut it down, jeune fils. We hear you. Listen to me. Sit fuckin' *down*."

Dekker fell into the chair, caught his head against his hands, in an ambient quiet even The Hole's music couldn't drown.

"Dunno if he ought to have this," Mike said. "I give you guys a break and you give me a crazy?"

Dekker said, looking up: "I'm not crazy!"

"Them's the ones to watch," Mike said, and set the beer down.

Dekker was honestly sorry he'd hit Bird. It was Ben he wished he'd found, before the cops came and got him. He might have killed Ben. And that might have satisfied him.

But Bird had told the bartender not to call the cops, for what good that would do, the red-haired woman had made him sit down at their table and they gave him a beer he didn't need—

God, his head was pounding. His eyes ached.

The two of them—Bird and this woman with the red hair, who might be a Shepherd—sat at the table with him and told him how the company would have taken everything he owned anyway, how he had to be smart and keep his mouth shut, because he was only making trouble for people who didn't have any choice . . .

"So what have *I* got?" he asked.

"Hush." Bird grabbed his wrist, squeezed hard, the way Bird had done on the ship, telling him shut up, to keep Ben from killing him, and his nerves reacted to that: he *believed* in Bird's danger, he *believed* in Bird's advice the same helpless, stupid way he'd found himself from one moment to the next believing what the doctors told him, and he knew then he was lost. He said, pleading with Bird for help: "They're lying to me."

Bird whispered, "Hush. Hush, boy. So they're lying. Don't make trouble, if you have any hope of getting that license back."

He didn't remember he'd told Bird about his license. He couldn't even remember how long he'd been sitting here, except his hand stung, which told him how long ago he'd hit Bird. Holes in his memory, the doctors said. Brain damage . . .

"Whatever's happened," Bird said quietly, still holding his arm, leaning close, "—whatever's happened, son, we're not against you. We want to help you. All right?"

He was alone in this place, he didn't know anybody on R2 but Bird and Ben, a handful of doctors and Tommy. He sat there with Bird holding his wrist and keeping him anchored in reality, or he might go floating off right now. Bird said he wanted to help. Nobody else would, here; Belters didn't; and he couldn't get back to R1—couldn't go back home without Cory even if they'd send him. Their friends would say, Why did you let her die? Why didn't you do something? And all those letters waiting from her mother . . .

"Guy's gone," the woman's voice said.

"He's on something." Bird shook his arm. "Dekker, you on drugs?"

"Hospital," he said. He was staring at something. He could see a haze. He had no idea why he was staring, or how he was going to come unlocked and move again, except if Bird would realize he was in trouble and bring him back. . . .

Bird said, "Dekker?"

"Yeah?"

"Look, where are you staying?"

That question required some thinking. It brought the room a little clearer. "I don't know," he said, asking himself if it mattered at all. But Bird shook at his arm, saying,

"Listen. You're pretty fuzzed. How are you set? You got any funds?"

He tried to think about that, too. Recalled the 60-day delay—when he'd been on R2 longer than that, dammit, and he didn't know why the bank had waited til he got out of hospital to start transferring his account. He had no idea how he'd even bought the beers a while back. He had no idea how 500-odd dollars had arrived in his account—whether it was his, or whether he just didn't remember. . . .

Bird said, "We could put you up a few days—not that we owe you, understand? Let's be clear on that. But I don't really blame you for coming in here mad, either. Maybe we can work something out, put the arm on a few guys that might help, you understand what I'm saying?"

It sounded better than Pranh or the rest of them had offered, better than the cops had given him. Bird had always seemed decent—Bird was the one who'd told him about the 'driver.

"Out there," he whispered, trying to turn his head and look Bird in the eyes to gauge his reaction, but he couldn't manage the movement: "Out there—you saw. You remember what happened. . . ."

Bird closed down harder on his wrist, numbing his fingers, hurting his arm, reminding him Bird had another face. "Better you concentrate on where you're going, son, and not think about anything else. You can't help your partner now. She's gone. Best you can do is get yourself clear. You think about it. Your Cory would want you to use your head, wouldn't she? She'd want you to be all right. Isn't that what she'd say?"

That made him mad. Nobody had a right to put words in Cory's mouth. She'd hate it like hell. But he couldn't get back from where he was. He said, staring off into nowhere, "Screw you, Bird."

"Yeah, well," Bird said. "Try to help a guy—"

Another hand landed on his arm, pulled him around until he was looking at brown eyes, shaved head, dark red crest—rab, radrab, Shepherd or whatever she was, he didn't know. He was fascinated—wary, too. He'd been rab once. But Cory hadn't approved—Cory was too frugal, too Martian to waste money, she'd say, or to waste effort on the system, even screwing it.

That senator—Broden—saying, when they'd opened fire on the emigration riots—"No deals with the lawless rabble—"

Newsflashes, when he'd been—what? Ten? Twelve? First real political consciousness he'd ever had, seeing people shot down, blood smeared on glass doors . . .

Rab style and rabfad was one thing. Shepherds wore it modified, he guessed because it annoyed the exec, and they would. But this one, extreme as she was, with marks of age around her eyes—"You're from Sol Station," the woman said. "Right?"

"Yeah."

She stared at him a long time. It felt like a long time. She might be thinking of trouble. Finally she said, her hand having replaced Bird's on his wrist without his realizing. "Severely young, severely stupid, cher juene fils. Company'll chew you up. Bird's all right. If Bird's telling you, you *do*. Or are you looking for MamBitch to save you? That's *fool*. That's sincerely *prime* fool, petty cher."

Rabspeak, from years ago. From before Cory. From a whole different life. Rabfad had turned into respectable fast-fad, except if you didn't get it out of the trend shops, except if you were truly one of the troublemakers—

Dress like that on helldeck was a statement—a code he couldn't cipher anymore, not what the colors were, what the earrings said, what the shave-job tied you to . . . like this woman, who looked him in the eyes and talked to him—as if she saw what he had been before Cory—a damned fool wearing colors and politics he hadn't then known the meaning of—

A stupid kid, skuzzing around the station, no aims, nothing but mad and trouble on his mind—screw the system, make trouble, get high on the outside chance of getting caught—

He'd been so smart then, he'd known everything, known so much he'd gotten himself arrested, tracked into the System as a juvie Out of Parental Control—himself and his mother tagged for deportation to the well, til his mother paid everything she'd saved to get them both bailed out.

(God, Paul, you've been nothing but a disaster to me, you've done nothing but cost me from the time I knew I was carrying you—)

They'd put him in a youth program, special studies, writing letters to kids on Mars—

My name is Cory. I live at Mars Base. . . .

"Hear me, jeune rab? Do you read?"

He said, "Yeah. I hear you."

"Good," Meg said, patted his face and looked away, at someone else. "Kid's gone out. Beer's not a good idea."

Someone else came up close beside him. He could hear the footsteps. "Not doing real well, is he?"

He didn't know that voice.

"Kid's a little buzzed." That was Bird. Something hit his face. Jolted him. "Dek-me-lad, pay attention. This here's Mike Arezzo, owns The Hole. —Kid's had a bad break. Just out of hospital."

"This is the guy, huh?"

He could see this Mike when Mike moved back past Meg's shoulder. But he couldn't recognize him. He was only sure of Bird.

Then there was another voice he knew. "What in hell's going on here?"

His heart turned over. He couldn't move. He couldn't think. Ben was on him, saying, "Call the cops, get this guy out of here. . . ." and Bird said, "Calm down, Ben, just calm down."

Ben was going to kill him. He still couldn't move.

Another voice said, clear and female, "Dekker, huh?"

Dark-skinned face. Hand holding his jaw, turning his head, making him look her in the eyes.

"Skuzzed out," the dark woman said. She had a thousand braids, clipped with metal. She was right. He was entirely skuzzed out. He said, dim last try at sanity, "Trank. Hospital. Beer."

She said: "Fool."

Jack Malinski had grabbed Ben's arm, him and Sal out shopping the 'deck, just walking home; Malinski had said, "Ben, some guy just pasted your partner down at The Hole, talking wild about that ship you got—"

He'd run. He'd outright run, getting here, Sal racing along with him—gotten here out of breath. He'd thought it was some guy mad about the lease-list. But they got to the door of The Hole and it was Dekker, no question—Dekker, sitting in a chair at their regular table, and Bird getting up to grab his arm and pull him aside before he hit the bastard. "I got to talk to you," Bird said, and when he said it that way, Ben had this sinking feeling he knew exactly what Bird was going to say in private, Bird with his damned stupid guilt about that ship.

Bird said, "Dekker's a little upset. They turned him out of the hospital."

"Fine, let's call the cops."

"He's all right. The guy's just at the end of his tether."

"Tether's *snapped*, Bird, for God's sake, a long time ago, nothing we can do—nothing we're *qualified* to do."

"Give him a chance, Ben. Guy's just mad. Mad and upset."

"Homicidal is what he is!"

"No. No. He's not. Come on, Ben."

"Come on, hell! Your mouth's a mess."

Bird blotted his lip with the back of his hand, looked for traces. "Can't say I blame him. Guy's lost his partner, lost his ship, lost his license—"

"It's not our fault!"

"Ben, I got to look at myself in mirrors. You understand? It's not our fault, but it's not like we didn't get something from him, either."

"That's life!"

"Ben. . . ." Bird looked utterly exasperated with him, with *him*, as if it was his fault, Bird just closed off from him again, he had no idea why, and it upset him. He knew he wasn't likable: there weren't a lot of people who had ever liked him—while other people got what they wanted just by the way they looked. Dekker was one of those people, the sort that scared him when they got anywhere near somebody he liked—dammit, he had everything he owned and everything he wanted tied up in Bird. And in Sal. And he was willing to fight for it, if he could figure out how to do that.

Go along with it? Or pull strings in Admin, use whatever points he had to get the guy back in hospital—

Bird had his shoulder to him, looking mad, watching the table where Meg and Sal were both making over Prettyboy. You could figure. Women would—though he'd remotely hoped Sal had better sense. He gritted his teeth and said, "Bird, what do you want to do?"

"Just—" Bird was still upset. But Bird did look at him. "We got a chance to help the guy. Doesn't cost us much—give him a chance to get his bearings and get his records in shape. You can pull those strings. You know how."

It hit too close to what he was already thinking—in a completely opposite direction. "Look at him!" he cried. "The guy's gone! He's off the scope! You're thinking about financing *him?* My God, Bird!"

"Not finance. Just get him introduced around, get him a start, maybe get him partnered up with somebody decent . . ."

"We don't know what happened to the last one! Nobody damn well knows, Bird!"

Bird caught his arm and leaned close, saying, half under his breath: "Cut it. We know it wasn't his fault—"

He said, under his: "We know what he said. But he hasn't made a whole lot of sense. That's the trouble, isn't it?"

"For God's sake, Ben, give the kid a chance—you said yourself, if we got the finance, give the guy a stake—"

I don't know why you want to hand this guy the keys to everything we own and say help yourself! What about me? What about the guy that's tossed all his funds into this well, huh? This guy could be a slash-killer for all we know, and you're wanting to use our credit on him?"

"Shut up, Ben."

He shut up. Bird turned him loose and went over to talk to Mike at the bar. Mike stood there scowling. Dekker was still sitting there with his mind bent, staring off into deep space.

Meg was in the next chair talking to him. *Sal* was leaning over him, showing cleavage. He walked over to Dekker, laid a hand on his shoulder, ready to jump if Dekker wanted to throw a punch. He squeezed Dekker's shoulder, said, casually, "Hello there, Dek. Remember me? Ben Pollard. How are you doing?"

He flinched, and he *could* move: he turned his head very slowly to look up at Ben, remembering they were not in the ship, they were in a bar in a sleepery on R2, and he'd just punched Bird. He figured Ben wanted to punch him, but Ben wasn't doing it because this was a public place.

He said, "Hello, Ben." He could almost come out of the haze. Ben was far clearer to him than the women had been. He was actually glad when Ben moved a chair and sat down, leaning into his face, holding his arm.

Ben said, "Well, how've you been, Dekker?"

"Not good," he said; and, fighting to get back from where he was, he tried desperately to be civil so long as Ben was being: maybe he *had* been crazy. Maybe Ben was honestly trying to start things over. "You?"

"We're fine. We're real fine. Sorry about the ship."

He figured Ben was trying to make a point. He wasn't going to accept it. But numbness gave him a self-control he wouldn't have had otherwise. "Yeah, well," he said.

Ben squeezed his arm. "A little zee'd, are we?"

"They gave me something." Dekker held up white plastic sacks. Ben took them from him. Prescription bottle showed through the plastic. "I'm supposed to take those."

"Not all at once," Meg muttered. "He's had enough damn pills and excessively too much beer. Man needs to get up and walk, is what he needs."

He thought, All right, let's keep people happy, give this guy a chance to show out crazy as he is—the poor little pet.

So he stood up and pulled at Dekker. "Come on, Dekker, on your feet. Walk the happy stuff off."

Dekker didn't argue. He stood up. Ben got an arm around him before the knees went.

"The Pacific called," Bird came over to say. "Seems he left his card there. They're holding it."

"Guy's got a card." Ben felt a little better then, hoping there was finance on it. "Has he got a room there?"

"No, I worked something out with Mike."

Ben stopped, with his arms around Dekker.

He thought: *Shit!*

CHAPTER 11

Dekker waked, eyes open on dark, *g* holding him steady. But it wasn't the hospital, it didn't smell like the hospital. It didn't sound like the hospital. It sounded like helldeck, before they'd left. His heart beat faster and faster, everything out of control. Nothing might be real. Nothing he remembered might be real.

"Cory?" he yelled. "Cory?" And waited for her to answer somewhere out of the dark, "Yeah? What's the matter?"

But there was no sound, except some stirring beyond the wall next to his bed.

He lay still then, one hand on the covers across his chest. He could feel the fabric. He wasn't in a stimsuit. He wasn't wearing anything except the sheets and a blanket. He lay there trying to pick up the pieces, and there were so many of them. R1. Sol. Mars. The wreck. The hospital. The Hole. His whole life was in pieces and he didn't know which one to pick up first. They had no order, no structure. He could be anywhere. Everything was still to happen, or had. He didn't know.

A door opened somewhere. Someone came down the hall. Then his opened, the ominous click of a key, and light showed two silhouettes before the overhead light flared and blinded him.

Bird's voice said, "You all right, son?"

"Yeah." His heart was still doing double-time. He put his arm up to shade his eyes. Time rolled forward and back and forward again. He began to figure out for certain it was a sleepery, and he remembered being in the bar with Bird and Ben. It was Bird and the red-haired woman in the doorway, Bird in a towel, the woman—Meg—in a sheet. Ben showed up behind them in the doorway, likewise in a sheet, looking mad. Justifiably, he told himself, and said, "I'm sorry."

"Clearer-headed?" Bird asked.

"Yeah." Things are still going around. He recalled walking up and down the hall behind the bar, up and down with Ben and Meg and a black woman, remembered eating part of a sandwich because Ben threatened to hit him if he didn't stay awake—but he didn't remember going to bed at all, or how he'd gotten out of his clothes. He had hit Bird in the mouth. Bruised knuckles reminded him of that. "Sorry. I'm all right. Just didn't know where I was for a second."

"Doing a little better," Bird said.

"Yeah." He hitched himself up on his elbows, still squinting against the overhead light. "I'm all right." He was embarrassed. And scared. The doctors said he had lapses. He didn't know how large this one might have been or how many days he had been here since he last remembered. "Thanks."

Bird walked all the way in. "You're sounding better."

"Feeling better. Honestly. I'm sorry about the fuss."

Ben edged in behind Bird, scowling at him. "Beer and pills'll do that, you know."

"Yeah," he said. He earnestly didn't want to fight with Ben. His head was starting to ache. "Thanks for the rescue."

"Good God," Ben said. "Sorry and Thank you all in one hour. *Must* be off his head."

"I've got it coming," he said. "I know." He slipped back against the pillow, wanting time to remember where he was. "Leave the light on, would you?"

Ben said, "Hell, if it keeps him quiet—"

They left then, except Bird. Bird walked closer, loomed between him and the single ceiling light, a faceless shape.

"You had a rough time," Bird said. "You got a few friends here if you play it straight with us. Watch those pills, try to keep it quiet. Owner's a real nice guy, didn't call the cops, just took our word you're on the straight. All right?"

He recalled what he'd done. He knew he had maybe a chance with Bird, maybe even with Ben, if he could keep from fighting with him. "Tell Ben—I wasn't thinking real clear. Didn't know what ship I was on."

"You got it straight now?"

"I hope I do." His head was throbbing. He wanted desperately for them to believe him. He didn't know whether he believed *them*—but no other way out offered itself. He put his arms over his eyes. "Thanks, Bird."

Bird left. The light stayed on. He didn't move. In a while more he took his arm down to fix the room in his mind. It was mostly when he shut his eyes that he got confused; it was when he slept and woke up again. He kept assuring himself he was out of the hospital, back with people who understood, the way the doctors didn't, what it was like out there.

And the two rabs, who might be Shepherds, but who didn't talk like it—he wasn't sure what they were, or what they wanted, or why they zeroed in on him. They worried him the way Ben worried him—not the dress: the mindset—the mindset that said screw authority. No future. Get high. Get off. Get everything you can while you can, because the war's coming, the war to end all wars.

Hell, yes, Cory had said, it could end Earth. But it *won't* get the human race; that's why we're going, that's why we're heading out of here . . .

People in boardrooms had started the war over things nobody understood. And the rab had just said—screw that. And rattled hell's bars when and as they could until the company shot them down. He hadn't known that when he was a kid. He hadn't understood anything, except he was mad at what they said was happening to the human race. He'd hated school, hated the have's and the corporate brats—he'd understood corruption, and pull, all right; he'd thought he was rab and scrawled slogans on walls and busted a few lights with slingshots, gotten skuzzy-drunk a few times and lightfingered a few trinkets in shops before he'd figured out what the rab was and wasn't, and why those people had died trying to get through those doors—he'd been thirteen then, nothing could touch him and he'd be thirteen, forever . . .

Til Cory.

And Cory—Cory wouldn't at all have understood him sitting at the table with two women like that. Cory would talk to him later and say, the way she'd said more than once, Stay away from that kind, Dek, God, I don't know where your mind is . . . we don't want any trouble; we don't want anything on our record—

Meg, the older one's name was. Meg. With the red hair and the Sol accent he'd never realized existed until he'd gotten out here and heard Cory's Martian burr and heard the Belter's peculiar lilt. There might be a heavy dose of Sol in Bird's speech. But none in Ben and none in the black woman—all of them the last types you'd ever think to be hanging around with a plain guy like Bird—or with each other. *Not* likely Shepherd women—who might drink with miners, maybe—but far less likely sleep with them . . . when women were scarce as diamonds out here and available, good-looking women could take their pick clear up to the company elite if they wanted, if they didn't have a police record. They didn't have to live on helldeck—unless they wanted to.

Maybe Bird didn't understand the rab . . . wreck everything, take what you wanted, rip the company—

So much for ideals and causes. Same here as at Sol. Same in the Movement as in the company boardrooms. No difference.

He squeezed his eyes shut, felt tears leak out. Raw pain. He had no idea why. He thought—

—screw all of them. Company and not.

But he didn't mean it the stupid way the kid on Sol had meant it, 13 and stupid and tired of bumping up against company types, scared as hell about the rumors that said his generation wasn't going to have a chance to grow up—he'd gotten a knot in his stomach and lain awake half the night, the first time he'd heard how the colonies didn't have to fire a shot—how the rebels could just drop a rock out of jumpspace, a near-*c* missile aimed right at Earth or Sol Station. Nobody could see it coming in time. *That* for Earth—that for all the history they were supposed to memorize, all the rules, all the laws. Over in five minutes. So why learn anything that was going to be blown up? Why try for anything except grabbing as much as you could before it went bang?

But nobody'd do a thing like that. Nobody'd really hit Earth, nobody'd really hit a station and kill all those people. Of course they wouldn't.

Cory would say—just get me far enough, fast enough. Cory had told him about places he'd never cared about until she made it sound like there was an honest chance of getting there—if you had the funds. If you could get the visa. If the cops didn't stop you at the last minute and say, Wait a minute, Dekker, you have a record—

The Earth Company said no more free rides, and you had to pay off your tax debt before you could get a visa. Then your own government, the only time you'd ever see anything from your government, wrote you down as belonging to the ship you'd bought a share on, and you could go.

—Where there'll be something left, Cory would say— Cory had an absolute conviction that Out There was much better than where they were—

—on a ship that had no use for an insystem pilot. He didn't know whether that was living or not. Truth be known, he had never had any idea what he was going to do then—keep balancing on one foot, he supposed, saying yes and meaning no, going with Cory because Cory was going somewhere—and he didn't trust the draft wouldn't take the miners, too, once those ships were built—haul him off to live in a warship's gut and get killed for the company, blown to hell for the company—

Step at a time, Tommy had used to tell him when he was too zee'd to walk. Step at a time, Mr. Dekker . . .

Dammit, he wanted to fly, that was all, just get that back—get his hands back on the controls again—

The last few moments he'd thought—he'd thought, clear and cold, not at all afraid, that he could still pull it out—

That he could still make that son of a bitch pay attention to his com—

Wake somebody up on that damned ship, rattle their collision alerts if that was what it took—

He looked at the ceiling tiles. He supposed they were real. He supposed he'd gotten this far away from the wreck. But no matter how far he stretched it, time just looped back and sank into that moment like light in a black hole. One single moment when things could have worked and didn't. . . .

Those sons of bitches on that 'driver had known he was there. Had known they'd hit a ship. They must have. Even if it had never heard him—if somehow his com wasn't getting through to them—if nothing else, when the tanks blew they'd have known it wasn't a rock they'd hit.

And if *his* com wasn't reaching them—wouldn't they have listened to the E-band after they'd hit a ship? Wouldn't they have heard Cory's suit-com?

Damned right they had.

Meg leaned close to the mirror, painting a thin black line beneath her bottom lashes. Hell to keep the eyes from running right after makeup: she blotted with her finger, tried again. The next door over opened and shut. Ben and Bird were off to breakfast, everybody dressing where their wardrobe was. Sal, mirrored past her shoulder, was putting her boots on. "We got a day to do," Meg said, with a flourish at the corner of her eye. "But we can take second shift. I vote we feel out the novy chelovek."

"Severe spook."

"Decorative spook." Eyebrow pencil. Auburn. Hard to come by out here. If you were broke you used grease pencil, and *that* was expensive. "He came straight last night, after the bogies. *Seemed* to be coming in focus. . . . Bird talked to him."

"After the things he shouldn't have said in the bar, Kady, a serious lack of governance there—*everybody* was talking about it."

"He was drunk. Gone out. Everybody knows that."

"So he's got no failsafes? Shit, Kady! Ben's got severe misgivings on this."

"Tsss." She did the other eye with three even strokes, heard Sal get up and caught her reflection with a rap of the knuckle at the mirror. "Remains to see. Later's time enough. Bird says."

"Bird says. Bird says. What's Bird have in his head, here? 'Find him a partner.' Ben can't scope it. And brut put, I don't like this 'partner' talk and I sincerely don't like Bird close with this jeune fils, whose tab I don't know why we're paying, with *our* funds, while he's got a card and access, thank you."

"So do *I* understand?" But she figured she did, more than Sal would. She looked at Sal, eye to mirrored eye, then turned and leaned against the counter, taking the mandatory three thoughts before a body should commit truth—as the saying went. But Sal was seriously upset this morning—Sal had had her eye on that ship, and Sal had been talking to Ben last night, in these rooms, that was point one, and scary enough—if that was all of it, and there were enough angles with Sal on a thing like this she wasn't at all sure. "We got to talk, Sal."

Sal stared at her a couple of beats, still hot, shrugged and picked up her jacket. "Na. Rather breakfast, actually."

Meg didn't move. Sal didn't like brut talks, especially when she'd just snapped to a judgment about a thing, but Sal constitutionally didn't like mysteries. She said, to Sal's back, "Sal—do you want to know quelqu' shoze?"

She waited, *knew* Sal was going to turn around with an exasperated look and say—

"*What* should I want to know?" As if there couldn't possibly be anything worth the nuisance. Sal came at some things with her mind as tight as her fists.

She gave the room a significant glance around, then pushed buttons she knew were buttons with Sal. "Tell you later on second thought."

Sal had this look like she'd knife something; but that only meant Sal's mind was working again; and they'd been severely careful about bugs since the cops had torn the room apart. She snagged her jacket up. They walked out into the hall and through the door into The Hole proper, where the guys had a table in the shiftchange rush—Ben and Bird already into their breakfast. You went over to the hot table at the end of the bar, you told the second shift cook, Price, that you were breakfast, and he dumped whatever-it-was into a plate while you drew your own coffee.

They took their plates and their cups to Bird and Ben's table and sat down. " 'Morning," Bird said. " 'Morning," Meg said back, and thought how that, too, was one of those things native Belters didn't just naturally say.

Spooky kind of partnership, when you got to thinking about it.

Spookier still, just as they sat down, that Dekker showed up in the doorway. He came part of the way to their table and made a cautious little gesture like Can-I-join-you?

Bird waved his hand, swallowed his mouthful. "Grab your plate."

Dekker was clean shaven, hair wet and combed back—quiet and polite. That was a plus. Good bones, under a jumpsuit that didn't fit. A woman did notice things like that, if she was alive.

"Could do with feeding," Bird said.

Ben made a surly shrug. Meg tried to think of something cheerful, took a forkful of The Hole's best stand-in for sausage and eggs and a sip of not bad coffee, while they were all waiting for a lunatic to come and sit down with them.

"Want to bet he'll ask the time?" Ben asked.

"Don't you open your mouth," Bird said sternly.

"Did I say a thing?"

"Nice rear," Meg said.

"Doesn't impress me," Ben said.

"Quiet."

"Yeah, he'd do that for hours."

"Ben, . . ."

"All right, all right. He's doing just fine. Hasn't jumped Price or anything."

"Ben."

Dekker came back, with his breakfast and his coffee—into a sudden quiet at their table.

"How are you feeling?" Bird asked him as he sat down.

"Hung over," Dekker said, sipped the coffee with a grimace, and, from vials in various pockets, started laying out a row of pills: not unusual, for spacer-types—bone pills, mineral pills, vitamin pills; but Dekker's collection was truly impressive.

"Dekker?" Ben said. "You having eggs with your pills, or what?"

Dekker gave this defensive little glance up, the cold sort that made Meg's nerves twitch toward a knife she didn't carry now—didn't quite meet anybody's eyes. "Yeah. Thanks, whoever put the crackers by the bed. Lived on them last night. My stomach was upset."

"They give you a doctor's number?" Bird asked

Dekker nodded, swept up a fistful of pills, chased them one after another with coffee, and didn't ever answer that. Bird shrugged. Dekker ate his eggs. They ate theirs. Finally Dekker got up and went back to his room, saying something about needing his rest.

"Yeah, well," Ben said, staring after him.

"Man's hung over," Bird said.

Ben didn't say a thing to that except, "Are we going in to the docks?"

"Yeah," Bird said. "Afraid they're not going to move if we don't push. And we can pull those panels, right now. We can do that. But four's too crowded up there."

They were close to viable now on *Way Out*. They'd gotten the tanks mated three days ago, they'd gotten the interior blown out and certified for access, they'd gotten everything well toward completed, if they could just get the refit crews to keep after it and get the value assemblies connected . . . but when it was a case of getting skilled help on free time, it wasn't easy. It took inducements and constant look-ins to make tired crews on overtime look sharp and do it right.

"We'll be back about suppertime," Bird said. "And if you two wouldn't mind to be staying here . . ."

"Hey!" Sal held up a hand. "Don't make us responsible for this guy!"

"Don't let him cross Price. Or Mike. All right?"

"No!"

" 'Appreciate that." As Bird and Ben got up quickly and beat a retreat.

"Well, *hell!*" Sal said.

"There's worse."

"I'd *rather* vac the cabin."

"Hey. Don't judge too soon. That's *good* bone structure."

Sal gave her a flat, disgusted stare.

Meg said, "You can go up if you want. I can hold it here. Or we can take a walk and I can tell you what I won't say in the room."

"Yeah," Wills said, on the phone, *"yeah, we did find him."*

Salvatore got a breath. "Damn right you'd better have found him."

"Yessir."

"So where the hell is he?"

"Sleepery, sir, just hadn't paid a bill yet. No problem."

"There'd better not be. You listen to me. If you can't tag him any other way you keep somebody on it. You don't let that guy slip. Understand?"

"Yessir. Report's coming to you right now." Wills sounded upset. But he'd been on it, when a routine print had shown no card use for a sleepery. Couldn't particularly fault Wills: Dekker wasn't the only case Wills had on his lap, a couple of them felonies, while Dekker was Minimal Surveillance. But Human Services had dropped 5 whole C's onto that card for the sole purpose of making sure Dekker stayed traceable, and it was embarrassing to the department to have him slip in the first couple of hours, in a place where he had no friends, no contacts, no credit and no way to get it.

Wills asked: *"You want Browning to ask a few questions?"*

Salvatore scanned the report, how Dekker had spent 5-odd dollars in a helldeck bar, 5.50 on beer and phone calls, and nothing else—

Browning had talked to The Pacific, who'd referred Dekker down the row to The Black Hole, and sent his card there when the management at The Hole had called for it. Browning had had the sense to query Wills before any next step, and Wills had told Browning not to follow that lead too closely: Dekker was apparently still there, The Hole was a quiet place with no apparent reason to lie to The Pacific, but Dekker hadn't used the card at The Hole after he'd gotten it—which indicated Dekker must have some acquaintance there—or that he'd found some means of support—meaning hiring out for something, ditching the card for a while, not an uncommon dodge for a man evading the cops: prostitution was the ordinary way for somebody with reason to duck the System—or if not that, he had to have friends.

Wills said: *"Bird and Pollard are staying there. We checked them earlier."*

Bird and Pollard. Salvatore searched his recent memory.

"The ones that claimed his ship," Wills said. *"The ones that brought him in. Ship claim went through. The company paid. But Bird and Pollard saved his life. My guess is he looked them up, with what idea I don't know, but evidently it wasn't war. He's staying there, evidently on one of their cards."*

Not necessarily looking for trouble, then—searching out the only two people he knew made perfect sense. Healthy sense, even. Salvatore sipped at a cooling cup of coffee, thought about it, and said: "All right, all right, the boy's got himself settled. Long as he's quiet, understand? Just get a list of the current residents. Run backgrounds. That sort of thing."

"Copy that," Will said. *"We can do it on a tax check."*

"Do it."

They'd gotten the lawsuit dropped—the report had convinced the EC board, a closer call than the kid knew about. But he'd signed the accident report—he was out of hospital and if he just for God's sake got a job and settled, he was fine. Visconti said rehab might not be productive right now. There was a lot of hostility.

So let him run through the Human Services money. Let him settle and think about surviving. There wasn't any negligence, there wasn't any charge to file, and Dekker didn't go to trial, however much Alyce Salazar wanted his head. Salazar was threatening civil suit now, to tie up the bank account and the insurance, but Crayton's office said don't worry about it: the daughter was over 18, the partnership was signed and legal, with a survivor's clause, and the account was jointly acquired, anyway. Dekker was safe: there was no legal way Salazar was going to get at him.

That card could go in the pending settlement stack.

Strolling along the frontage spinward of The Hole, Sal had things of her own to say. And for openers, since Meg wasn't getting started: "I'll tell you this, Kady, we got to get him out of there, God, of all places for him to come!"

"Natural enough."

"Natural! He said it, they friggin' took every lovin' thing he owned—what's he going to do, forget it?"

Meg walked a few steps further. Kicked at a spot on the decking. "Dunno. Difficult to say. But what are we going to do, throw him out? That's brut sure he won't forgive."

"Forgive, hell!"

Another silence. "You know, brut frank, Sal—there's a difference in Ben and Bird."

"We're talking about Dekker. Or why are we out here?"

"We're talking about that. Calmati, calma, hey?"

"So say! Doesn't make sense so far!"

"I tell you, I never had any use for the motherwell. You less."

"Damn right."

"Watch it go, right? Screw it all, all that shiz. —But—I get out here,

Sal, I dunno, thinking it over—I *know* why Bird paid for this guy a room."

"So? Why did he?"

"You know you don't say 'morning."

"Of course I say 'morning. And what's that to Flaherty, anyhow?"

"You say it because I say it. You didn't come saying it. Or 'evening. Brut different, Sal."

"So?"

"Different the way Bird's different from us. Never saw how the motherwell matters til I figured that."

"That's shit." Sal hated soppiness. This was getting soppy, it wasn't like Meg, and it was making her increasingly uncomfortable.

"May be shit," Meg said. "But I know why Bird paid."

"Because the motherwell makes you crazy."

"Dekker's from the motherwell. At least from Sol Station—which is close enough for 'mornings."

"Accent tells you that."

"Yeah. But we *think* in accents. That's what I'm talking about. Yours and mine. I can turn my back on the motherwell, I can take what I want and leave the rest. Bird's not rab, Bird's just norm, but I know how his mind works—I dealt with there, remember."

"Are they all fools?"

"Fools, peut et'. But not the only. You mind me saying, Sal—you're going to be a skosh bizzed at me over this—"

Puzzles and puzzles. A body could be irritated at motherwell Attitudes, too. "All right. So we got this deep secret difference. It's worth five. Go."

"Head-on, then—MamBitch is scamming her kids."

"Is that new?"

"It is when you don't see it. You know, even the vids that get out here, they're pure shit, Aboujib, they're company vids. They're slash-vids, cop-chasers, fool-funnies, salute-the-logo shit, intensely company, intensely censored—you understand me? MamBitch has been robbing you all along, little bits and pieces. Robbing me too. Those sods brut *like* what's rab. Rab's no trouble to them, hell, rab's where they're going—forget Earth. Forget what's old garbage. —Only out here the *company's* going to pick what's rab. Capish'?"

"Neg." She looked at Meg with the slight suspicion Meg was talking down a long motherwell nose at her, a long thirtyish nose at that. But Meg hadn't made sense enough yet to make her mad. "This going somewhere significant eventually?"

"It's the Institute, all over again. Understand? You didn't take the shit there. But you don't say 'morning—"

"F' God's sake, Kady, good morning, then!"

"But Belters don't say it. Bird remarked it to me once: Belters don't and Sol Station will. Belters don't give you a second cup of coffee without you pay for it. On Sol Station you expect it. Belters don't give you re-chances. You screw up once, you're gone, done, writ off—"

"E-vo-lution. Don't let fools breed."

"*Corp*-fad, Aboujib. It wasn't always that way."

Down a damned long motherwell nose.

"You take a look at corp-rat executives the last couple of years, Aboujib? Seen the clothes? Rab gone to suits."

"So? Poor sods still got it wrong."

"No. No. They got it *right*. I don't say on purpose—I'm not sincerely sure they have that many neurons compatible—but they *like* the rab. In their little corp-rat brains, shit, yeah, dump the past, let the company say what's fad, what's rab, and what's gone—they don't ever like some blue-sky lawyer citing charter-law at 'em, so that's gone. Don't teach anybody about the issues: all us tekkie-types and pi-luts need is slash-vids and funnies, right? Tekkies don't need to know shit-else but their job. Hell, the rab never said dump all the smarts, we said Stop thinking Earth's it, wake up and see what's really going on out there; but the stupid plastics said, *Dump the past.* We said Access for the People, and the plastics say *Grab it while you can.* Corp-fad. Plastic *is*, Aboujib, plastic *sells*, plastic doesn't ask questions, plastic's always dumber than the management, and hell, no, management didn't plot with its brain how to take us over, they just wobble along looking for the easy way, and damned if we didn't give it to them."

Corp-fad made an ugly kind of sense. The Institute was without question MomCorp's way of making little corp-rat pilots—she'd seen that happening: she wouldn't salute the logo and they'd found a way to can her, right fast.

"I'm 35," Meg said after a moment or two of walking. "I'm an old rab. Eight, nine years ago they shot us down at the doors and the politicrats in the company's bed said that good old EC was within their rights, it was self-defense, the rab was breaking the law and endangering a strategic facility, d' you believe that? Corp-rat HQ is a strategic facility? —Time the miners *and* the Shepherds had the guts to tell the whole damn company go to hell, turn the whole operation independent. But where are they, Sal? Where are they? Freerunners are mostly gone. Brut few coming out here now: the company's training the new generation, paying their bills and giving them the good sectors til they get it all in their pocket. The Shepherds let the company handle their outfitting and now they're fighting to hang on to the perks they have. The rab got themselves shot to hell in the '15 and here we got these damn synthetics swaggering around with the company label all over. The plastics don't know what we were. They turn us into clothes. Into *corp*-fad. Damn young synths make the music without the words. The Movement's probably dead back at Sol. Old. Antique. And where do I go?"

"Brut cold," she said, and put her hands in her pockets, walking step for step with Meg, Meg seeming to have finished her say. Crazy as it sounded, she wondered if the Institute *had* censored the things it didn't want them to know, on purpose, and when she thought about it, rights damned sure had changed—

Things like abolishing crew share-systems, the way they'd used to be on Shepherd ships. Like the bank refusing to honor cash-chits, the way Shepherds had paid out bonuses, and kept money outside the bank card system.

She thought about the courses she could have sailed through if she'd kissed ass. She thought about her mama and her papa's friends, Mitch among them, who'd said . . . You're a fool, kid. Should have kept your head down til you graduated. We can't make an issue, you understand? A kid with a reckless endangerment on her record isn't it. . . .

So she was a fool and the instructors washed her out, told her the same as they'd told Ben: Insufficient Aptitude. She was learning from Meg—she'd learned more from Meg than she ever let on with the licensing board; and when the time came Meg couldn't teach her, then she'd go to Mitch a hell of a lot better than Mitch ever thought she was . . . flight school washout, Attitude problem and all.

But meanwhile her mama's and her papa's friends were going grayer and thinner and more brittle, some dying of the lousy shields they'd had in the old days, the old officers and crew hanging on to their jobs because they were the skilled crews the company urgently needed—

But the company was training new techs fast as they could, and the new head of MamBitch was talking about substituting Institute hours for the experienced Shepherds' years, requiring re-certifications every five years after you were forty.

The Shepherds had naturally told MamBitch where they'd send the cargoes the hour they did that and the company threatened to pass those re-cert rules if the Shepherds ever did it—but the company didn't have enough pilots to plug in those slots right now that wouldn't dump more than cargo into the Well, or fry themselves and their ships by pure accident. Yet.

So Big Mama had had to assign her shiny new tech crews to tend the 'drivers for now, because Shepherd crews wouldn't fly with the corp-rat cut-rate talent straight out of 'accelerated training'—and because the military was hot on Mama's neck about schedules. But time and the Belt were taking their natural toll and the day was coming, even a dumb-ass Attitudinal washout could see it ahead, when there'd be just too few of the old guard left to make a ripple in the company's intentions: some-day company was going to pass its New Rules, and she was the right age to be caught in it. She didn't like Meg's line of thought at all, and she couldn't figure how it had much to do with anything present—which was what Meg had promised her.

"So?" she said. "So what's this leading to? What's this to do with our problem?"

"If you want to figure Bird," Meg said, "you seriously need to understand, blue-skyers don't know what short supply *is*. They don't think by the numbers: air's free and they got nothing but heavy time, so they give it away—they give it away even if they haven't got it, because that's their pride, you see? They have to say they can, even if they *can't*, because natural folk can, and anything less they won't admit to."

"Way to starve," Sal said. "Way to end up on a company job. That's pure fool, Kady. And Bird isn't."

"Air's free on Earth. Feet can go."

"If you don't mind dirt. And they got laws that say where you can go. I heard Bird say."

"Yeah, well." Meg walked a few more steps. Sal remembered then that, old business at Sol Station notwithstanding, Meg was a whole lot closer to blue sky than she ever could be, and she worried that maybe she'd cut Meg off with that zap about dirt.

But Meg went on as if she hadn't taken offense: "That's how it is for corp-rat execs, isn't it? Air's free wherever they are. Short for them is when they run out of their Chardonnay '87—I know. Hell, I used to run that freight. I know what those sons of bitches are eating, them with their Venetian antiques and their mink bedspreads."

"Venetian?"

"Italiano. Ochin expensiv. Fragil. Minks are fuzzy live crits. You wear their skins."

Sal looked at her. Sometimes Meg scammed you when she was in a mood. Hard to be sure.

"No shit. I used to freight it. Pearls, fancy woods, stuff like that. If you skimmed that stuff, you could black market it to starships or you could sell it right back to guess where?"

Sal lifted a brow.

"I guess the corp-rat got his apartment furnished," Meg said. "Or he got a cheaper source. SolCorp didn't want me going to trial, hell no. They told me I could come here and fly for myself or I could pilot some pusher back and forth off Mars for good old EC if I sincerely didn't want to go do mining."

That was half what Meg had said and half what she'd never said—that she had been dealing black market with some exec, and it was that guy who'd blindsided her.

Things you found out, after this many years.

She liked Meg hell and away better than she had those years ago, that was sure—understood a good deal more of her thinking; but not all of it, never all of it, and she wasn't entirely sure she wanted to know where Meg had been or what Meg had been trained to do. Dive into a planetary well or bring a ship out of one—the thought gave a Shepherd's daughter the chills.

"So, well, Bird's got a little ahead at this guy's expense, he's short—Bird's not going to say no, isn't going to make this guy ask, either. Machismo. Something like. Fact is, *I've* been where this guy is and it makes me a skosh mad, Sal. It sincerely does."

"Well, I'd agree with you I don't like to see the guy screwed, hell, I put it on Mitch, and *they're* bizzed about it—but they're going to do a real fast hands-off after what he did. I'll tell you the word I don't like, Kady, it's what I heard from Persky—the guy yelled out about Bird and Ben knowing a 'driver was out there—"

"Yeah, well, he was drunk."

"Doesn't matter if he was drunk, Kady, dammit, I got very scarce favor points with Mitch—"

"Screw Mitch."

"Yeah, the hell with Mitch—Mitch'll give me a choice, get out and away from Bird, that's what he'll tell me."

"Would you do it?"

"It's all over the damn 'deck what he said—"

"Tss. They drugged him stupid, Aboujib."

"We got a live charge here, Kady. We can't afford this. *They* can't!"

"All right, I'll tell you what Bird said to me. This is a confidence. Black-hole it."

"Go."

" 'Driver's sitting out there right where the accident happened.

Dekker gave 'em the coordinates. Said he and his partner had found a big rock. Class B. That's where that thing is sitting, chewing it up and spitting it at the Well, fast as it can. Few more months and it won't be there."

"Why in *hell* didn't you tell me?"

"I *am* telling you. I found it out from Bird last night. That's what you can see on those charts you lifted."

"Shit!" —But that doesn't make sense. Something rolls in from Out There—yeah, rocks like that happen, but *we* don't get 'em. Those things show up on optics."

"So somebody slipped—assigned the kids to it. MamBitch can't make a payout like that to a freerunner. You want to know how many'd be kiting out here? *Buying* passage out here? If it *was* iron, the way Dekker claimed, that's a friggin' national debt!"

She let a breath go between her teeth. "God."

"You know MamBitch's help. Some lowlevel fool in BM screws up, puts this freerunner out there and then his super finds out. And does any freerunner call in til he's got his sample? Not the way you and I do it: we're not having the Bitch say no, don't pursue, and then have her hand the good stuff to her lapdogs . . . and give the kids credit for *some* savvy about the system. They wouldn't trust the Bitch. They'd go on and sample it—get a solid assay on that thing."

"Dangerous as *hell* for a ship their size. Maybe it *was* the rock that got 'em, maybe they were just rushed . . ."

"Possible. I dunno. The jeune fils isn't thinking so."

"And a rock like that—untagged—where'd it come from? Thing had to have an orbit way the hell and gone. And iron?"

"We don't know shit what it was. We do know one kid is dead and MamBitch wiped the log. But those loads are going to hit the Well any day now. Drop *that* on Mitch."

"I can drop it, for what it's worth. But with a mouth like that—"

"Severely young, severely green, Aboujib. We can pull him in line."

"Kady."

"I'm telling you. Tell you something else. We *have* to pull him in line: *they* know where he was last night."

"What are you talking about?"

"*MamBitch*, Aboujib. MamBitch. He *came* there. He checked in. He knows Bird and Ben—"

"Oh, God."

"Yeah, 'Oh, God.' I've *been* through this. They've got a line on him. Not a short one, maybe, but that depends on what he gets into. And what are we going to tell Bird? Excuse us, Bird, but you sincerely got to pitch this guy out, on account of MamBitch is looking for trouble and on account of Sal's slipped Ben's charts to the Shepherds?"

"Dammit, why didn't you say something?"

"How can I say what I didn't know? I didn't hear the word ''driver.' I didn't see those charts. I didn't hear the word 'rock' til last shift—"

"Dammit!"

"You want another thought to sleep with? We're going out of here in a couple weeks, and what's *he* going to be doing—or saying—while we're out there? Can we stop him?"

"God."

"What's Mitch going to say about that?"

"I don't know!"

"We could shut him up for about three months, say."

"What are you saying? Take him *with?*"

They walked past a noisy bar doorway. Meg said, the other side: "Well, here's what I'm thinking: the jeune fils needs his license back. Say he passes the ops. He's got to have board time. Couple hundred hours. Gets him off the 'deck. Gets him shut up."

"Yeah, and where's Ben in this figuring? Ben'll *kill* that guy."

"Who said Bird and Ben?"

"Oh, God. You're out of your head, Kady."

"Look. Bird's got this debt—and *we* can pay it for him. We make it like a favor. Then Bird's got karma for us. So does this guy—who's also from the motherwell."

"Who's also bent. And we get tagged with him!"

"Tell Mitch what we're doing. Tell him we're going to bend this guy around the right way. Do *they* want him now? I don't think so. We can solve Dekker's problem, solve Bird's problem, solve Mitch's problem. *Our* rep can't get too badly bent. That's where we're useful. We get this jeune fils' sober attention and he's no problem."

Meg rolled her eyes. *Hell* of a situation wrapped around that ship that they were so close to—

Decorative is one thing, she thought. But where's the payout? —Meg hands out this air-is-free and everybody-works-partners stuff, like the preacher folk. But what's this guy really bring us?

They walked along, looking at displays in spex windows, in the deep bass rhythm of music blasting from the speakers, bouncing off the girders overhead.

She said to Meg: "I'll tell you one thing, that chelovek better not have been skimming. *We* got rep enough. And he *damn* sure better not come into The Hole on drugs again. He really better not be that kind."

"Couldn't say that this morning," Meg said.

"Couldn't say he was on the beam, either. I hate those quiet types. No joke, Meg, if we get out there and he does go schitz—what in hell are we going to do? We don't know we *can* get him straight. That guy could get severely strange out there. Then what do we do?"

"Keep him tied to the pipes, the way the guys did? I could go for that."

She caught a breath. "Warped, Kady!"

"Well, hey, —he isn't useless, is he?"

"Hell!"

"Gives Mitch three whole months. Do you want this jeune fils loose on the 'deck the way he is, talking about Bird and Ben and 'driver ships?"

"Point."

"So we just got to figure how to sign him in, with MamBitch."

"What the hell do we call him? Ballast?"

Lascivious grin. "Systems redundancy?"

"Rude, Kady."

"Yeah." Meg grinned, with a sideways glance.

"Don't con me! We got more than a small problem here. Say we get this guy straight, we *still* got him in the middle of things—we got Ben, who's seriously put out, here . . . Ben's *not* going to go easy on this, he's *not* going to go shares with this guy."

"Ben better not push Bird on this. Don't expect him to figure it, just he shouldn't push. Everybody needs some room sometime."

"Serious room, here. Major with Ben, too."

"He doesn't have to work with Ben."

"Who's going to work with him? We got guys starving on the list, and any numbers man needing a pilot wants one who doesn't see ee-tees, f' God's sake. That jeune fils made himself a rep yesterday that he's got to live down a *long* time before they forget that—"

"There's always Yoji Carpajias."

"God." Yoji was a great numbers man. But he didn't bathe. "We'd have to steam and vac all over."

"Yeah. But there is Yoji. There's others. Leave Ben on prime with *Trinidad*. Us on prime with *Way Out*. If MamBitch lets Dekker re-certify, then quiet is exactly what she wants. And Dekker with his license back—is a whole lot more credible, isn't he?"

"Yeah, and how do we keep a line on him? He's poison right now. But we don't know him. We don't know *what* way he's going to turn."

"Dekker's from Sol. He's a lot more like Bird. You got to take into account he'll do things for Bird-type reasons. He's stuck by his partner, hasn't he? He'll owe us. Major karma."

The idea got through to her then, what Meg was saying. "Karma, hell. If Bird gives that sumbitch board-time, he can charge for it. Take it out of his hide, he can. Either Dekker's got finance to pay that time or Bird's for sure got a pilot on a string. That old sonuvabitch!"

"I don't think that's why Bird's doing this."

Sal gave Meg a look, thinking that through the loop a couple of times, wondering if she was following Meg through everything she'd been saying. "Yeah, but are *we* that crazy? Bird owns *Way Out*—but *we* own our time. We log that guy's board-time, and we own him til he can pay his charges with us—that's the law, that's the only damn useful thing the Institute ever taught me. We debt that guy to us for time, *we* get him re-certified, and the company won't friggin' get him, how's that for charitable?" She came to a dead stop on the decking, hands in pockets, with a whole new idea taking shape. Mitch, and *Way Out*, and a deal higher-value cards to deal with. "Maybe that's why MamBitch left the preacher-stuff out of pilot training, you think?"

Bad business, working null, floating around for hours on end compromising everything your heavy time was supposed to mend, but, hell, the meds who made the health and safety regulations hadn't priced help these days. Zero unemployment, the company claimed, or near enough as didn't count: and you could hire some real zeroes to come up and scrub, all right, but they'd play off on you and steal what wasn't bolted on, and to Bird's way of thinking and Ben's as well, it was better to take the extra dock time, do the steam and vac themselves and see what damaged systems they could fudge past the inspectors that really could be repaired instead of replaced—turn it over to a refitter like Towney Brothers, and you'd have a one hell of a bill, not least because Towney was in the pocket of half a dozen suppliers.

A-men.

So they didn't replace the shower, they just unbolted the panels and took them to the rent-a-shop on 3-deck where they could sand down the edges—no way you could tell it from new, once you screwed it back together. They took things apart and ported it down to 3, cleaned it and reassembled it, right down to the electronics. And you steamed and you vacced, and steamed and vacced and took apart and put together. Likely Ben was learning more about a ship's works than he'd ever opted for.

That was where Ben was right now, porting a big load of work down to 3 for the gals to handle or for them to do when they got down there after lunch.

Maybe they could put Dekker on time and board, if he could keep straight and if he was physically able: a miner pilot worth anything at all had to be a fair mechanic. Meanwhile—

"Bird?" Meg said out of the ambient noise of the core. He missed his purchase on a bolt and caught his finger with the power driver. He said something he didn't ordinarily say and sucked the wounded finger, looking around at the open hatch, which they had half shut and plastic sheeted to keep the warm air in and the dock noise out.

"Sorry." Meg drifted in, held the plastic aside, pretty sight in that lacy blue sweater. She turned herself so they were looking at each other right side up. "I'm sorry, Bird. —You want some help with that?"

"Doing fine," he said. He turned around again, seated the driver and put the screw home on the board he was re-installing. He took the next off the tacky-strip. "Aren't you cold, woman? And who's watching Dekker?"

"Sal and I got this idea," Meg said.

Which said it was something halfway serious. He wasn't sure he was going to like this. He reached over and snapped the tacky-strip out of the air before air currents that blew and drew from the plastic Meg was holding sent it somewhere inconvenient.

"We got this idea," Meg began again, "a kind of a partnership deal."

He heard it out. He didn't say a word while Meg was telling it: he slept with this woman and he figured he was going to hear it all night if he didn't hear it now. It moderately upset his stomach.

Meg said, "Can't help but make money, Bird."

"Yeah, saying this guy is fit to go out this soon. Saying he can get his license back. Put you and Sal off in a ship with him for three months? Bad enough with Ben and me. You gals—all alone out there—"

Meg blinked and said in a considerate way: "Yeah, but we won't take advantage of him."

"Be serious, Meg."

"We're major serious."

"You're letting out the heat, Meg."

"Listen to me. We can make this contract with him, Sal says it's perfectly legal: we charge him his board-time for training, he'll pay us in cash or he'll pay us in time—"

"Indenture."

"Huh?"

"It's called indenture. I read about it. When we friggin' *had* paper, before they made the toilet tissue fall apart. You're talking about indenture. We got the guy's ship. Ben wanted to put a lien on his bank account. Now you want *him?* That *stinks*, Meg."

Meg got quiet then. Offended, he was sure. He picked off another screw and drove it into the hole.

"So what other chance has he got?" Meg asked. "Bird? —Who but us gives a damn what happens to that guy?"

He drove it in and looked around at Meg, suspicious now—it was worth suspicion when Meg Kady started talking about her fellow man.

"What's this 'us'?"

"Earthers."

It was at least the third time he'd heard Meg change her planet of origin. He was polite and didn't say that.

Meg said: "Dekker's out of the motherwell too, isn't he? Same as us."

"Sol, the way he talks."

"So you figure it, Bird—a greenie like him, paired up with another kid—she must have been. They never, ever got it scoped out, what the rules were. Worst kind of pairing he could make, nobody to show him the way—the guy didn't set out to screw up. He just didn't have any advice."

There'd be soft music next. What there was, was the heater going and money bleeding out onto the cold dock. "You want to close that plastic, woman?"

Meg ducked back and closed it. It gave him time to think there had to be something major in it for Meg and Sal. It didn't give him time to figure what it was.

"All right," he said. "We've heard the hard sell. Now what's the deal?"

Meg hesitated, rolled her eyes in a pass around that meant, We'd better not talk here, —and said, "Bird, what're you doing for lunch?"

CHAPTER 12

Dekker drowsed in the muted music-noise of the bar outside, lay in a .9-*g* bed half awake, having convinced himself that there wasn't anybody going to come through the door with hypos or tests or accusations. That was all the ambition he had: he was safe in this place and maybe if he just stayed very quiet there wasn't going to be anybody interested in him for a while, including Bird and including Ben.

Please God.

He got hungry, and hungrier—breakfast hadn't been much. Finally he looked at his watch, just looked at it awhile—didn't know the right hour, Bird had told him it had been off. But it was August 16th. It stayed August 16th. He knew where he'd gone off, and how absolutely unhinged he'd come—would never have thought he was capable of going off that far, would have hoped better of himself, at least. He'd kept a sort of routine on the ship once he'd slowed the tumble with the docking jets—enough to move about a little, do necessary things—irrational things, he thought now. Some of them completely inane, because Cory would have. God, he'd near killed himself doing housekeeping routines—because Cory would have.

He wasn't sure how much he'd forgotten. There were some holes he never seemed likely to patch. Other memories—weren't in any kind of order. He was scared to try to sort them—afraid he'd find some other memory to leap up and grab him by the throat, like that damned flash on the shower wall, the watch—he couldn't even remember if he'd had a shower the day of the accident. No, he thought, there'd been too much going on—

Hole there. Deep hole. Scary one. His heart was thumping. It was just the green wall, the place aboard Bird's ship that looked exactly like his own. That was where he'd gotten lost—but there were so many other places. The bar outside, the 'deck, the people he didn't know—he was hungry and he didn't want to go out and face people and questions and strangers. So he lay still a long while and listened to the beat of the music, and finally took his pills when he figured it must be time.

Then his stomach began to be upset in earnest: he figured he should go get something to eat to cushion the pills, so he ventured out as far as the bar—no one out there that he remembered but the owner, who didn't meet him with any friendliness—

No, they didn't serve lunch. There were chips. Dollar fifty a package. Want any?

He took a package and a soft drink—wanted them on his card, but the owner said he was on Bird's, and wouldn't take no.

He didn't want a fight. He took his card back and moused back to his room, upset, he didn't know why, except he didn't know what the terms were or why he was too scared to demand the damn chips go on his card—but he was, and he was ashamed of himself. He ate the chips with a lump in his throat, sat there on the bed and thought about taking a sleeping pill and just numbing out for a few hours, because he'd been dislocated out there, nothing and no one out there was familiar. He couldn't sit here and go around and around in mental circles all day, he *hadn't* the routines that had kept him sane, he was sitting here waiting for something he didn't know what, and he couldn't keep out of mental loops.

He took out the sack of pills—looked at the size of the bottle that was sleeping pills—God, he thought. What are they doing? How many of these are there?

In which curiosity, he poured the pills out on the counter and counted them.

212 pills.

Didn't intend for me to want refills on that one for a while.

He might be a little microfocused. He tended to do that lately. Maybe it was brain damage. But his amusements had gotten very narrow in hospital—bitter, constant harassment. Move, and counter. They moved. You moved. You didn't trust them. They never made consistent sense.

He spilled pills out onto the nightstand and started counting. Vitamin pills, potassium, 30 or so each. The calcitropin stuff, enough for a month . . . Big bottle labeled: Stomach Distress: As needed. Another labeled: For Pain: 1 every 4 hours. 40 of those. Decongestant: 45 pills: 1 every 4 hours. Diuretic: 60 pills: 1 daily. Drink plenty of liquid. Anti-inflammatory: 40 pills, Take 2 before meals. Depression: 60 pills: Alcohol contraindicated.

He sat there with those piles of pills, the one of them making this towering great heap on the counter, and he stared at it, and he stared, and he thought: 212 sleeping pills?

What did they do, misread the prescription?

No.

That's not it, is it?

Cory's dead, they tell me I'm crazy, they take my ship and take my license and tell me I won't fly again, and they give me 60 uppers and 212 sleeping pills?

They really don't want me to screw up my exit.

He hadn't known where he was going or what he was doing until he'd stared at that heap of pills awhile.

He thought: First they kill Cory. Then they want me dead—

The hell with that.

He raked the pills into the appropriate bottles, wondering if there was a way to get into the corporation level—

No, that *was* crazy: really crazy people went into places and killed people who didn't have anything to do with their problems. Some innocent little keypusher or some smooth corp-rat bastard—neither one was going to get to the people responsible—

Somebody was outside; somebody knocked on his door and cold panic shot through him.

"Dekker?"

"Yeah?" he said.

"Dekker?" A woman's voice—one of Bird's friends: he didn't know why his hands were shaking, he didn't know what he'd just been doing or thinking that deserved it, but his heart went double-time and reason had nothing to do with it. "It's Meg Kady. You want to open the door?"

He raked the pill bottles into the plastic bag, the bag into the drawer. Not all of it fit. He made it.

"Dekker?"

Severe spook, Sal had called him, and face to face with him, Meg was very much afraid Sal might be right. He opened the door a crack, listened with a dead cold expression while she explained she and Sal wanted to buy him a drink. "Thought you might be tired of the walls. Come on. Get some air. Have a drink or two."

He looked as if at any second he was going to slam that door and lock it in her face—maybe with reason, Meg thought: the man must know Ben didn't like him, and he might have real suspicion about the rest of Bird's friends.

"Hey," she said, and gave him her friendliest grin. "You're not afraid of *us?*"

If that and the sweater she was wearing didn't get a man out of his room she hadn't got a backup.

Dekker muttered under his breath, looked rattled, and felt over his pockets. "This place safe to leave stuff?"

"Yeah. Anybody boosts stuff from The Hole, he's Mike's breakfast sausage. —How're you feeling?"

"All right."

Dead tone: All right. Dekker came out, let his door lock, walked with her down the hall to the bar like he was primed and ready to jump.

Severe spook. Yeah. Or suspicious of them and their motives.

Sal was waiting. Easy to capture a table with space around it—traffic at this hour was real light, most people being about their business. They went through the social dance, Hello there, good looking, how're you feeling? Sal pulled a chair out, got up, he sat down, she sat down, Meg sat. Mike, thank God, got right over for the orders.

"Spiced rum?" Dekker asked.

"Premium price," Mike said.

Dekker hesitated, reached for his card. Meg put a hand in the way. "Let us buy."

Upset him. He slowly put his card on the table. "Put it on mine. All of it. Rum and whatever they're having."

Meg shot a look at Sal, and gave Mike a shrug. "What the man wants," she said, thinking: Pricey tastes he's got.

Mike took the card. Dekker started to lean back, arm over the chair back—like it was a fortified corner he wasn't going to be pried out of; but the hand was shaking. He put it on the tabletop.

Sal said, "What do you go by?"

"Dek—to friends."

"Dek." Sal reached out across the table. "Sal. Aboujib, if you got to find me."

He hesitated, then made a snatch forward and solemnly shook Sal's hand.

Meg reached hers out. "Magritte Kady." Cold fingers. Scared spitless. "Meg'll page me anywhere. There's only one on R2. —You been out of that room today?"

"Lunch," he said.

"Any good?"

He shrugged.

Mike got the drinks over, fast, thank God, a merciful few beats without conversation. Dekker picked up his drink. Meg lifted her glass with a flourish.

"Welcome to R2, Dek."

"Thanks," he said faintly.

"Thanks for the drinks. —You remember us at all?"

He nodded.

Sal said, "We'd better say, before anything else, we're the ones that have *Way Out* leased."

He didn't react at all to that, just kept looking at Sal.

"I'm the pilot," Meg said. "Sal's my numbers man. You were the primary license on your team, right?"

Dekker nodded glumly, watching them, every move. He held the rum in one hand, the other arm over the chair back. "Yeah. I was."

"Excuse." She leaned her elbows on the table and cut down the distance. "Let's be frank here. They busted your license. Bird and Ben claimed your ship—but they haven't cut you off cold, either. They risked their financial asses saving your life. Understand? Lot of expenses."

"Yeah."

"So we got a lease on what used to be your ship, and probably you aren't real happy with us."

Dekker said tonelessly: "Yeah, well. Not your fault. No hard feelings."

"But," Sal butted in, "we got to thinking how we could do you and us both some good."

Meg said, quickly: "We figure you want your license reinstated. Which you got to have board time for. Which could be expensive, if you had to get it from the company—and you still might need some help to get past the bureaucrats."

Dekker gave her a quick, plain, a what-in-hell-are-you-up-to stare.

"Chelovek," she said quietly, because even in the bar, even with the music going, you had to worry about bugs lately, since the cops had searched the place, "you ran into real trouble—got ground up in the gears entirely, you *and* your partner. —Where are you from? Sol Station?"

Dekker nodded.

"Neo out here?"

"Two years." His jaw was set, not going to say a syllable more than he had to. Improvement on yesterday, she thought.

"Brut put, Dek, you got yourself in one helluva mess, and there's beaucou' guys on R2 who'd pick your pocket the rest of the way. But as happens we're not them, and Bird's a blue-skyer, so he knows where you come from. —Not that we owe you, mind. But Bird doesn't like to take advantage. There's some things we can't fix. But suppose we could—what's prime business on your mind right now? What can we do most for you?"

He shook his head, staring elsewhere.

"Mad, I don't blame you, jeune fils. But are you going to spite yourself? What can we do to even things up? Anything you need?"

Another shake of the head.

"Yeah, well. You know what the corp-rats want, don't you?"

That got a look, a nasty one.

"They want you all theirs, jeune fils. They really don't like the independents. Their charter makes 'em have to accept us, but they got you right down to signing with the company."

"They won't sign me with the company. I haven't got a license."

"Oh, they'll give it *back* to you, jeune fils. When you're theirs. ASTEX regulations screwing you over and ASBANK ready to lend you money. What are you running on now? Mind my asking?"

"Yeah, I mind."

"Good. Do mind. But do you want to get that license without them?"

A little reaction there. Not a word.

"We got a deal for you. You get time at our boards, you take our help, you, me, Sal, Bird and Ben, we all make our own little arrangement that gets you working again, gets you fed, boarded, and eventually reinstated. How's that?"

Interest, at last. Hostility. "Why? Goodness of your heart, rab?"

"You pay us cash for our time if you can pay us, or you pay us a share plus lease after that—that's Bird's word on it, if you pass muster by Sal and me."

He looked somewhere else. She let the silence hang there a moment, then said: "We're not hard to get along with, Dek. We're fair good company."

"My partner's dead, do you bloody mind?"

Sal said, "She fond of you starving? Cold *bitch* jeune rab."

Dekker looked bloody death at her but Sal sailed right on:

"But I'll guess she wasn't a cold bitch at that, and she wouldn't like what you're doing to yourself, if she was here, which she isn't, nor will be hereafter. She's signed *off,* man, we all do. Death's life, you know, and it keeps on."

"Shove off." Dekker pushed his chair back and got up. Meg did, laid a hand on his arm: he slung it off. Mike, over at the bar, was probably reaching for the length of pipe he kept.

She said, quietly, lifting both hands, "Easy. Easy. No cops here. No offense. Help, here. That's all."

"You're an antique, you know it? You're a friggin' antique. Rab's gone. You're not *in* it anymore."

She actually felt a painful spark of interest—the jeune fils more lately from Sol and more in the current. "True?" She tilted her head, took a damn-you stance and said, "You got better, little plastic?"

He was twenty, maybe—you wouldn't tell it by the eyes; but the body, the way he let himself be jerked off course, scared as he was, that was all young fool. Maybe he didn't really even want to care about what she thought now: he'd only attack blind, young-fool-like, and for just a single unquiet moment—knew she'd just attacked him back.

"Come out of it. It's the twenties."

"So? What's the twenties got to offer us the '15 didn't? Corp-rats in fancy suits? Here at R2's still the teens. Maybe I don't like your tomorrow, little corp-rat."

"It's 2323 on Sol and they're building warships to blow the human race to hell. Lot you changed, whole fuckin' lot you changed!"

"So what's the word, little plastic?"

"The word's business suits, the word's grab it before it goes. That's Sol. That's all the good you did."

Bitter news, no better than she already knew. But she balanced on the balls of her feet, hands in belt, shrugged and said, "It goes *on*, young rab. Didn't we tell you, back in the '15, wake up! You're going to fly for them?"

"I'm not flying for anybody."

"You'll be living off the corp-rat sandwich lines the rest of your life if you do the fool now. They'll own you—and you'll be flying some damn refinery pusher til you're older than Bird." She added quietly, gently: "Or you can sit down, jeune fils, listen to me, and use your brains for more than ballast."

He stood there without saying anything. Meg thought, with Sal in the tail of her eye, God's sake, don't move, Aboujib, keep your friggin' mouth shut, kid's going to blow if you draw breath.

Dekker looked away from her, then, hooked a leg around his chair front and melted down into it.

Meg heaved a sigh, sank into the chair next to him, where he had to look her in the eyes. "Let us make up, jeune rab. Let's not do deal right now. Let's just take you out on the 'deck and show you the cheap-shops."

"I don't feel like it."

"Not far. Relax. We're severely reprehensible, but we don't take advantage. Won't push you. Just a little walk."

Kid was scared white. And he managed not to look her in the eyes.

"Come on," she said. "You've seen too much of hospitals. Sal and I'd like to spend a little, see you get fixed up with a bit more'n a friggin' plastic bag for a kit—like to stand you a few Personals, you copy? Even if you decide not to take the rest of our offer."

She figured Sal was having a stomach attack right now, knowing Sal. Meg, Sal'd say, you want to pass out tracts too?

Dekker's breathing grew calmer after a moment. He said, "Shove off."

"You telling us you want to go with the company. We should leave you alone, just stay out of your life?"

A few more breaths. He picked up the glass with a shaking hand, drained it and set it down empty, except the ice. Then he nodded, and seemed to fall in on himself a little. "Yeah, all right, whatever."

Like they could chop him up in pieces if they wanted to, he didn't care.

She put her hand on the back of his chair, stood up, and he stood up. She showed him toward the door with: "Mike? Tell Bird we're shopping."

And Sal, damn her, with the nerve of a dock-monkey, locked on to Dekker's arm as they headed him out the door, saying, "I know this place. Absolute first-rate. You got to see. All right?"

"Medium," he told the dealer, embarrassed by his company, exhausted by the walk, not sure he wasn't going to be had in various ways, some possibly dangerous—but he couldn't prove it. He'd broken what Cory called Rule One, going off with Belters he didn't at all know, into shops they did know, taking their word about who to deal with and who to trust—he didn't know whether they were on Bird's side of things or not. Ben's, for all he knew, but they were having a good time and he was out of the funk he'd tried to sink into—

Drifting, a little, maybe. But they'd gotten him moving, they'd made him mad, but they'd done more for his nerves than all of Visconti's pills. He was alive. He was thinking about something besides Cory, overwhelmed with music, with colors and textures and excited, cheerful voices—

He was halfway happy for a moment.

"Now, no shiz, Pat, you give him our deal, now," Sal told the guy, whatever that meant, and Meg called after him, "No corp-rad, now! Something serious!"

The dealer brought back pants and a bulky sweater. The pants said medium. They were gray stretch and they didn't half look medium. The price said 49.99, middling high for a cheapshop.

"That's too much," he objected. The dealer whisked out another pair of pants with diagonal stripes, black and red, that looked like a rab's nightmare. Laid that out with a blue sweater.

"God," Meg said, "not blue. Red. Can you match?"

"Let's try for coveralls," he said. "Blue or gray. Something that fits."

"Oh, work stuff," Meg said. "Dull, dull. No fun. —Try the gray pants, come on, Dek. You got the figure."

"Starvation," he muttered. He told himself he should stop this, just get the coveralls traded for something that fit. But they were both set on him trying the gray, they shoved sweaters at him, and in their enthusiasm it was just easier to do it, make a fool of himself and prove once and for all it wasn't going to work.

But the mirror showed him a walking rack of bones that actually didn't look bad in the pants, and that could use a sweater twice its useful size to hide his thin shoulders.

He wasn't sure, though, about the big slash stripes on the sweater. He stepped out of the changing booth to get the dark blue one, self-conscious as hell, and the women made appreciative sounds. "*Rab* sweater," Meg said. "Oh, I do like that."

He suffered a crisis of judgment, then, looking in the mirror outside the dressing-booth, and before he could reorganize, Sal said, "Suppose he'd fit those metal-gray boots? He's got small feet."

He didn't really want a wide striped sweater. He hadn't set out to get metal-gray boots that belonged on a prostitute. He damned sure didn't need the bracelet Sal shoved on him, but: "This is my treat," Sal said. "Man, you got to. Push the sleeves up."

"I need work clothes worse. Blue. On *my* card—"

"He's trading in the coveralls," Meg said to the dealer. "Can you just size him down?"

"Yeah," the dealer said, and hauled out a pair that said small. "If these don't fit you can exchange. You're a real small medium."

That wasn't what a man wanted to hear, who'd worked hard enough getting the size in the first place. But he decided he might be, after the hospital. He got the bracelet. He bought some cheap underwear and a pair of thermals, a plain gray stimsuit, his old one having been washed to a rag—that was expensive; and he ended up with the blue sweater too, along with a pair of black pants (stretch, like the gray) and black docker's boots, used. He was tired now, dizzy, and shaking in the knees; he was ready to go back to his room and collapse, the man was toting up the charge and he felt a moment of cold panic as those numbers rolled up. He wasn't sure now what he'd just done, wasn't even sure he dared wear what they'd talked him into: he'd had his turn with rab when he was thirteen—but not here, where rab was a statement he didn't know how to deal with—where it was corporate or where it was a badge of things he didn't understand . . .

I'm a fool, he thought. He thought how Bird and Ben were going to look at him when he got back—and the rest of the boarders at The Hole, some of whom might take serious exception to a show-off with no license: he'd forgotten his troubles, they'd made him forget for a few dazed moments and damned well set him up.

"I think we'd better go back," he said, wanting time to think. His head was going around. But Meg said, "Neg, neg, you can't go shaggy. Let's get that hair trimmed."

"Cut off that pretty hair?" Sal said, the way he'd protested once himself—when he was thirteen. "No!"

"Not all of it," Meg said. "Come on, Dek. Let's go get you fixed up. It's on the way. Won't take fifteen minutes."

"No," he said.

Which ended him up in a barber's chair dizzy and remembering he'd missed at least one batch of pills, with two women telling a helldeck barber how he wasn't to take too much off, "—except the sides," Meg said.

He'd given up. It was like the hospital. He was just too tired to fight on his own behalf, and they were right, the shoulder-length hair and the shadows under his eyes made him look like a mental case. If the cut was too extreme he could trim the top himself, with a packing-knife or something, God, he didn't care right now, it was a place to sit down.

Cory and he had cut each other's hair, to save money, conservative,

Martian trim—just practical. He watched what was happening in the mirror in front of him and kept thinking, in the strobe of the barbershop neon, Cory wouldn't like this. Cory would get that disgusted, high-class look on her face and say, *Really* not your style, Dek.

Cory's first letters had told him she didn't like the rab. When she'd sent her picture and he realized he had to send his back—with the long hair and wild colors and, God, the gold earring, he'd forgotten that—

But he'd been thirteen. He'd seen a serious, soft-eyed girl as sober and as kind as the letters. So in another crisis of judgment he'd gone to a barber and borrowed a plain blue pullover—gotten a serious job, he'd forgotten that too—tried to hide it from his friends, but they found out and thought it was damned funny.

He hadn't had those friends after that. Hadn't had many friends at all after that—except Cory; and he'd never met her face to face.

Stupid way to be. He hadn't planned it. He hadn't been happy with his school, his work, with anything but flying. Worked the small pushers for the shipyard—he was *supposed* to be loading them: the health and safety regs didn't let kids outside the dock there. But he'd got his class 3. And the super let him sub in until he was subbing in for a guy that ran a pusher into a load of plate steel . . .

". . . up the sides," Meg said. "Yeah. Yeah!"

Sal, with her metal-clipped braids, leaned to get a direct look at him, flashed a white grin and said, "That's optimal!"

It didn't hurt a guy's feelings to have a couple of women saying he looked good, but what was developing in the mirror in front of him was someone he'd never met before: it was 2315 again—but he wasn't 11, he was 20—It was the way the deep-spacer had said, the one they'd gotten in to talk to the class back then: You live on wave-fronts. You live on a station, you ride the local wave—the time you know. You go somewhere else, it's a different wave. Maybe a whole set of waves, coming from different places, different times. There's an information wave. There's fads. There's goods. There's ideas. They propagate at different rates.

Some dumb kid had made a joke about propagation.

The merchanter had said, dead-sober, So do stationers. Some shouldn't. And there'd been this scary two beats of hostile quiet and an upset teacher, because that was what deep-spacers were notorious for, on station-call, and what stationers were fools to do—especially with deep-spacers, who moved on and didn't care. Cory's mother had—and look what came of it. . . . a girl who'd made up her mind that Mars was irrelevant. Who said that rab was irrelevant. Cory had used to say: The rab can't really change anything. They can't build. They're saying reform Earth's politics—but it won't work. Worlds are sinks, they're pits where people learn little narrow ideas—Luna Base was a mistake. Mars Base was. Once we'd got off Earth we shouldn't ever have sunk another penny in a gravity well—

Cory had said more than once, I'd rather a miner ship for the rest of my life than be stuck on a planet—

He focused on the mirror where it wasn't *Way Out*'s cabin, it wasn't Cory's face he was seeing, and the thin, shadow-eyed stranger who got out of the chair looked like someone who might have a knife in his boot. He wasn't sure Cory would recognize him. He wasn't sure Cory would ever have liked him if she'd met him like this.

"Serious rab," Meg said, with a hand on his shoulder. She looked past his shoulder into the mirror, red hair, glitter and all. Sal was at his other side.

He stared at the reflection, thinking, I'm lost. I don't know where I am.

This is who survived the wreck. It's somebody Cory wouldn't even want to know.

But it's who is, now. And he doesn't think the way he used to—he's not going your direction anymore, Cory. He can't.

I've seen crazy people. Faces like statues. They just stare like that. People leave them alone.

He doesn't look scared, does he? But he is, Cory.

God, he is.

CHAPTER 13

He'd spent money he didn't want to spend, that sliced deep into all he had to live on for the next sixty days; he had Meg on one arm and Sal on the other both telling him he looked fine, and maybe he did, but he wasn't sure his legs would hold him—wasn't sure he wasn't going to fall in a faint—the white noise of the 'deck, the echoes, the crashes, rang around his skull and left him navigating blind.

Sal kept a tight grip on his left arm, Meg on the right, Sal saying in the general echoing racket that he looked severely done; and Meg, that they shouldn't have pushed him so hard.

"We can stop in and get a bite," Meg said.

"I just want to get home," he said. They had his packages, they kept him on his feet—he had no idea where he was, and he looked at a company cop, just standing by a storefront, remembering the cop that had stopped him outside the hospital, the fact he was weaving—a fall now and they'd have him back in hospital, with Pranh shooting him full of trank and telling him he was crazy.

God, he wanted his room and his bed. He wanted not to have been the fool he'd been going with these people—he wanted not to have spent any money, and when he finally saw familiar territory and saw The Hole's flashing sign, he could only think of getting through the door and through the bar and through the back door, that was all he asked.

It was dimmer inside, light was fuzzing and unfuzzing as he walked, only trying to remember what pocket he'd put his key in, and praying God he hadn't left it in the coveralls back at that shop—

But Bird and Ben were sitting at the table they'd had at breakfast, right by the back door. Meg and Sal steered him around to their inspection and Ben looked him up and down as if he'd seen something oozing across the floor.

"Well."

Bird said: "Sit down, Dek."

"I'm just going back to my room."

"*His* room, it is, now," Ben said; and Meg, with a deathgrip on his arm:

"Ease off. Man's severely worn down. He's been shopping."

"Yeah." Ben pulled a chair back. "It looks as if. —Sit down, Dekker."

His knees were going. But Ben suddenly took as civil a tone as Ben had ever used with him, walking out on him didn't seem a good idea, and he was afraid to turn down their overtures, for whatever they were worth—there damned sure weren't any others. He sank into the offered chair, Meg and Sal pulled up a couple of others, and he gave up defending himself—if they wanted something, all right, anything. Ben would only beat hell out of him, that was all, and Ben didn't look as if he was going to do that immediately, for whatever reasons. The owner—Mike—came over to get his drink order—Bird and Ben were eating supper, and Bird suggested through the general ringing in his ears that he should do the same, but it was already too late: he couldn't get up and stand in the line over there and he wasn't sure his stomach could handle the grease and heavy spices right now. He remembered the chips. He said, "Beer and chips."

"Out of chips. Pretzels."

"Yeah," he said, "thanks. Pretzels is fine." Maybe pretzels were a little more like food, he had no idea; and beer was more like food than rum was. Anything at this point. God.

"That all you're going to eat?" Bird asked.

Ben nudged him in the ribs and said, "Must be flush today. Who's buying the pretzels, Dekker?"

Meg said, "Ease off, Ben. He's seriously zee'd."

"That's nothing new," Ben said, and Bird:

"Ben."

"I just asked who's buying the pretzels."

"I am," Dekker said. "If you want any, speak up and say please."

Ben whistled, raised a mock defense. "Oh, well, now, yeah, don't mind if I do. God, you're touchy."

He'd have come off the chair and gone for Ben, under better circumstances. He didn't have it. It wasn't smart. But something took over then and made him say, with a set of his jaw: "I didn't hear please."

"Oh. Please." An airy wave of Ben's hand. "Passing charity around, are we, now? Paying off our debts? Did finance come in?"

"Not yet. But it will. You want my card?" He pulled it out of his pocket, tossed it onto the table. "Go check it out, Pollard. Take whatever you think I owe you."

Ben looked at him, and Bird turned his head and called out, "Mike, get those beers right over here, Ben's had his foot in his mouth. —Excuse him, son. You want to get the pretzels, we'll get the drinks."

"I'll pay my own tab," he said. Too harshly. He was dizzy. He wished the drinks would hurry. He wished he was safe in his room and he wished he knew how to get there before he got into it with Ben. Mistake, he told himself, serious mistake.

"We mentioned to him about the board-time," Meg said. "He says he wants to think about it."

"What 'think'?" Ben said. "He's got no bloody choice."

"Ben," Sal said, sounding exasperated, "shut up."

"Well, there isn't." Ben was quieter, scowling. "Try to help a guy—"

"Ben," Bird said.

"We're buying his effin' drink!"

"Ben," Meg said, and slammed her palm on the table, bang, a hand with massive rings on each finger. "We talked about the lease, and the jeune fils is thinking it over, that's his privilege. Meanwhile he's *offered* to pay his own tab, all right? So don't carp. —Don't pay him any mind, Dek. Sometimes you seriously got to translate Ben. He means to say Trez bon you're on your legs again and mercy ever-so for the pretzels."

The beer and the pretzels came. Dek picked his card off the table and shoved it at Mike, said, "Put it all on mine," and tried not to think what his account must look like now.

Bird said: "You don't have to do that, son."

"It's fine," he said. He picked up his beer and felt Ben's hand land heavily on his shoulder, the way Ben had done on the ship when Ben was threatening to kill him. Ben squeezed his shoulder, leaned close to touch glasses with him.

"No hard feelings," Ben said.

He didn't trust Ben any further than he could see both his hands. His stomach was upset, he was all but shaking as was, and the glass Ben had touched the rim of suddenly seemed like poison to him, but he sat still and took the requisite polite sip of his beer.

Ben said, "So do you want the board time?"

He looked at Bird, asking without saying anything whether this was Bird's idea too. Bird didn't deny it.

"Yeah," he said.

"So there's strings to be pulled," Ben said. "Short as the time is, we have to expedite, as is, or you won't get the ops test before we're out of here—and if you don't do those forms right, they're not going through. Now, as happens, I know the people you need. You do the work in the shop—"

"What work?"

"Thought you'd talked to him," Bird said.

"I said we'd mentioned it," Meg said. "We didn't exactly get down to that point."

"Well, now we have," Ben said. "There's no other way to do it, Dekboy. Only deal going. So you've agreed. We're waiting to hear how you're going to pay for it. Time? Or money? Or the pleasure of your company?"

They were coming at him from all sides. He wasn't sure there wasn't a moment missing there—his ears were ringing, they were all looking at him, Ben with his hand on his chair back—he lost things, the meds said he did; and he sat here surrounded by these people who as good as had a gun to his head. If they helped him he might have a chance—but if they figured out he did forget things, the word would get around and it was all over, he'd never get reinstated, he'd end up doing refinery work . . .

"You any good as a mechanic?" Bird asked.

"I kept *Way Out* working."

"As a pilot?"

"I was good." He didn't expect Bird would believe him. He added, self-consciously, "We weren't broke." Bird had seemed the best of them, Bird had kept him alive and argued for him with these people. He was desperate for Bird to take his side now. And if they robbed him, there were worse alternatives. "Cory and I had 47 k in the bank. Not counting the ship free and clear. R1 bank's sending it, but I can't draw on it for another fifty, sixty days."

"47 k," Ben jeered. "Come on, Dekker."

He didn't look at Ben. He looked at Bird and Sal, clasped his hands around the wet chill of the beer glass. "Cory's mom was pretty well set. Cory had her own account—trust funds. The hour she turned 18, she took it and she called me and bought my ticket and hers. She came out from Mars, I came from Sol—we met out here and we bought the ship. Paid a hundred fifty-eight k for her. Another 40 in parts. We made a few mistakes. We hadn't made many runs—only been out here two years. But Cory knew what she was doing. She nearly had her degree in Belt Dynamics. 28 of that 47 k we didn't have when we came out here. We were doing pretty well."

"Damned well." Bird said.

"College girl," Ben said, "come on, the company'd have snapped her up."

"She didn't admit to it. She didn't want a company slot."

"With that kind of money? She was a fool."

"Ben," Bird said.

"Well, she was."

He set his jaw, *made* himself patient. "She just didn't want it. The fact is, she wanted a share in a starship."

"Oh, for God's sake!" Ben said.

"She wanted into the merchanters. You have to buy in. Her trust fund wasn't enough—wasn't enough for both of us. And she had this idea, it was all she'd listen to."

"Why?" Sal leaned forward, chin on clasped, many-ringed hands, neon sparking fire on her metal-beaded braids. "Why, if she was rich?"

"Because," was all the answer he could manage. There was a knot in his throat and he thought if Ben opened his mouth he'd lose it. Cory had been so damned private. Cory didn't tell people her reasons. But they went on listening, waiting for him, so he shrugged and said, "Because she hated planets. Because her father was a deep-spacer—her mother wanted a kid, she didn't want a husband and she didn't want anybody in Mars Base to have that kind of claim on Cory. Cory was a solo project. Cory was her mother's doing, start to—"

—finish. That word wouldn't come out. He said, watching condensation trickle on the beer glass: "Didn't even know his name. Cory sort of built on her own ideas. Stars were all she talked about. Wanted to do tech training. Her mother wouldn't have it. So she studied astrophysics. She had the whole thing planned—getting the money, coming out here—getting us both out."

Ben said, quietly, "Hell, if she could buy a ship, she could have gotten it faster working for the company. What's the rate? Eighty, ninety thou to get your tax debt bought?"

And her mother there, he thought, her mother on MarsCorp board to pull strings, get her broke and get her back. But he didn't say that. He said: "They'd have drafted me if I'd stayed at Sol. That was part of her reason. We were going together. That was the plan."

"That crazy about you, was she?"

"Ben," Meg said, "shut up. . . ."

"I don't know why everybody's telling me to shut up. It *wasn't* the damn brightest thing she could have done. She could have gotten to Sol Station, probably bought straight into a ship with what she had—she expected to make it rich here freerunning?"

"Her mother," he said, "wanted Cory back in college. Wanted—God only." His stomach hurt. He had a sip of the beer to make his throat work. "She was under age. Couldn't get an exit visa over her mother's objection. This was as far as she could get. Til she was twenty-one."

"The ship and 47 k in the bank," Ben began. "What *do* those sons of bitches want for a buy-in, anyway?"

"Maybe a couple hundred k apiece. With the ship, we had it for one of us, tax debt to get the visa, you've got to pay that off to the government before you ever get down to paying the ship share—and Cory's was high: she had a degree. Another 70 k each to get back to Sol. I told her get out—I saw on our first run it was no good. We didn't know how hard it was out here. We *wouldn't* have done it this way—but by then we'd sunk so much into the ship . . . and just buying passage to Sol would eat up everything she had . . ."

He'd yelled at her the night before their last run, he'd said, The war's getting crazier. They've got these damn exit charges, God knows when they're going to jack them higher—if you don't go now, there's no telling what they'll do next, there's no guarantee you can *get* out . . .

He'd begged: Just leave me what's left over. I'll buy in on some other ship, work a few years—whatever ship you're on will come back here. I'll join you then—

He'd been lying about the last. She'd known he was, she'd known he didn't want to go. And she'd known he was right, that both of them weren't going to make it. She'd known she was going alone, sooner or later, or they were going to do what every freerunner ultimately did do—go into debt. That was why the shouting. That was why she'd burst into tears. . . .

"—And she said?" Meg asked.

He'd lost the thread. He blinked at Meg, confused. He honestly couldn't remember what he'd been telling them. He picked a pretzel out of the bowl, ate it without looking at them. Or answering.

Bird said, "The lad's tired."

"Yeah," he said, remembered that he was behind on his medicine, remembered that the company management were all sons of bitches and *they* were the ones that handed out the licenses. Even that was in their hands.

Bird reached out, thumped a grease-edged fingernail against his mug. "Want another round? A beer? On us? To sleep on?"

"You're right," he said. "I'm pretty tired." He thought about his room. He thought about the bed and the medicine he was supposed to take.

All those sleeping pills . . .

Meg hung a hand on his right shoulder, leaned close and said, "We better get you to bed."

He couldn't answer. He shoved her hand off and got up and left.

"Man's in severe pain," Meg said under her breath, looking over her shoulder.

"Looked all right to me," Ben said. "Looked perfectly fine, out spending money like there was no tomorrow."

She muttered, "Yeah, add it up, Ben." Across the table Bird looked mad. She figured Bird had somewhat to say and she shut up for several sips of beer.

Bird didn't say anything. Ben set his elbows on the table in an attitude that said he knew he was on Bird's bad side, but he looked mad too.

Things were going to hell fast, they were.

"Excuse us," she said, and got up and took a pinch of Sal's sleeve. Sal read a full scale alert and came with her over to the end of the bar where the guys couldn't lip-read. "Aboujib, we got a severe problem."

"Yeah. Men!"

"Easy, easy. We got a partner/partner problem developing here."

"You know Ben's a good lay. But he's being a lizard."

"I sincerely wasn't going to say that."

"I don't mind saying it. I'll bust his ass if Bird doesn't. I *told* Ben what I'd carve off him if he got too forward with me. And Bird *damn* sure won't take it."

"Bird can handle him."

"Yeah," Sal said and got a breath. "With a wrench. I tell you, I'm not putting up with this act. And I'm not standing in the fire zone either. I vote we go out to a show, leave the boys to one room."

Sometimes Sal made real good sense. "Yeah," Meg said. "Sounds good."

"I got a serious concern," Bird said.

"Yeah, well," Ben said, looking at the table. "Sorry about that, Bird."

"Why'd you push on him?"

"Hell if I know," Ben said, and didn't know, actually. Meg and Sal came back to say they were leaving: "You guys work it out," Sal said. And that made him madder. He watched them walk out. He had no notion where they were going, but he felt the ice on all sides of him.

"I don't know what the hell it is," he said without really looking at Bird. "I don't know what it is that the guy's got, but it seems to get in the way of people's good sense." He hadn't liked this partners idea from the time Sal had showed up at the 3 deck shop telling him how dealing with Dekker was going to set them all up rich, how it was such a good idea, Dekker getting his license back and all—and he'd liked it less than that when pretty-boy came sauntering in here all manicured and looking like trouble.

Bird didn't say anything for a while after that. Finally: "Maybe some people can't figure out why you got it in for him."

"Because he's crazy!" Ben said. "Because we're going to take this loony out there where he can get his ship back—cut the girls' throats and run that ship back over the line . . ."

"You've been seeing those lurid vids again. What in hell's he going to say about two more missing persons over at R1? 'Excuse me, they took a walk together'?"

"He doesn't have to have a good excuse! He's crazy! Crazy people don't have reasons for what they do, that's why they're crazy!"

"They still have to explain it to Belt Management."

"It doesn't do Meg and Sal any fuckin' good!"

"My money'd be on Meg and Sal."

"Don't be funny, Bird, it's not funny."

"I think it's damned funny. We got a 95 k mortgage on *Way Out* with the bank, we got nothing but dock charges on *Trinidad* for the last several months, we still aren't past inspection on the refit and we still got a filing to go before we can think about getting out of here. In case you haven't noticed, Ben-me-lad, we could seriously use another pair of hands here. We're bleeding money, with two ships sitting at dock."

"Meg and Sal do just fine. We *don't* know about this guy. And we'd have had *two* pair of hands today if Meg and Sal weren't out spending money on this guy. He's *trouble*, Bird, he's been trouble from the first we laid eyes on him."

"We can always say no, if he turns out to be trouble. We got time yet at least to find it out. Let's just put him to work, see how he gets along."

"You *can't* say no, Bird, you got this severe problem with saying no. You crawl ass-backwards into what's going to cost you money. If I didn't—"

"I can say no real good, Ben, if you recall. I said no to Meg and I said no to quite a few would-be's before I took you on. Now, you and me being partners, I give you a lot I wouldn't give just anybody—but being partners goes both ways. And right now I'm asking you to just give me a little more line."

"To do what? Wait until his money comes through? Then he'll pay for his own bills? That's real convenient, Bird, that's real damned convenient. He doesn't get to pay anything, he doesn't do anything, and we're buying his meals!"

"Ben, —"

"I don't know why you believe him over me, that's all!"

"Ben, —I dunno whether the gals are right about this deal: they could be. Here I am trying to figure whether I trust Dekker, and you're acting so damn crazy I end up defending him. I can't hardly take *your* side, without having him off down the 'deck in a fit now, can I?"

"It'd be good riddance!"

"Yeah, and what if the gals are right and this guy's a good steady prospect?"

"Steady, hell! Bird, *who* are we going to get to go out with Dekker? 'What time is it? What time is it?' Who's going to put up with that?"

"The guy really got to you out there, didn't he?"

He *hated* being patronized. "He didn't *get* to me."

"Good," Bird said. "Good."

"Dammit, don't—"

"—don't what?"

Cut me off like that, Ben thought blackly. But what he said was, "All right, all right. We'll see how he does the next week or so." He took a pretzel out of the bowl. "Guy didn't take 'em." Wasteful habit. It was like somebody who had money, who was used to having it. And on the thought of the 47 k Dekker claimed to have: "If he's got the funds he claims, he's a damned walking bank. Where'd he get it, except this rich college girl? He had a lot to gain by her dying, you know."

"Yeah, looked like he was having a real good time out there, didn't it?"

He hated it when Bird got surly with him. It made him figure maybe he wasn't being reasonable.

Bird said: "The Nouri thing, you know, changed a lot. Cops with warrants to do anything they wanted, the news full of friends informing on friends . . . I don't think there was half the under the table stuff going on that the company claimed—like we were some major leak in the company accounts. We weren't. We were making it. You understand? People used to help each other, that's what was going on, then. If you got in trouble and you needed a part, you didn't go to the bank, you went to a friend. You could borrow under bank rates, if you kept your promises, if you ran a good operation and paid your debts—and damn sure people knew if you did. We were making it, and the company wasn't. Now you tell me who's the better businessmen." Bird lifted a shoulder and took a sip of a dying beer. "Now we've got a generation coming off Earth with the Attitudes. We got a generation coming out of the Institute that never heard of Shakespeare—"

"God, so give me a tape, Bird! I swear I'll listen to the sumbitch."

Bird looked at him oddly, then reached across the table, took hold of his hand, man/woman-like, which was odder still, scarily odd, coming from Bird, from the guy he shared a ship with. Bird said, "Ben, you're a good guy. You really are. *Stay* that way."

Ben rescued his hand, shaken. "What's that mean?"

Bird only said, in that same peculiar way, "Ben-me-lad, I'll look you up that tape."

Dekker stared at the ceiling and thought about a sleeping pill, thought about the whole damned bottle—but hell if he'd give the company the satisfaction.

Ben wasn't going to let him alone. That was the way it was, that was the way it was going to be. Ben didn't like him, and with Belters, that well could be the final word on it. Ben had taken his ship and now Ben had him down as trouble—that was the way it was going to be, too.

He didn't know why Ben set him off like that. He didn't know why he'd said what he had, he didn't know why he'd talked about Cory's business, or whether he had a chance left with them, under any terms now he'd walked out—and he didn't know what Bird might be thinking.

If nothing else—that he and Ben together were a problem: he had no question which way Bird would go if Ben wanted him out.

And Ben talked about getting his license back, with no dollar figure on it. Everything he had, he was sure—*if* they still took him after the blow-up out there. Ben thought he was crazy, Ben thought he'd crack if he got out there again, and, honestly speaking, he wasn't sure of himself. The deep Belt was no place to discover you'd grown scared of the dark; and handling a ship making a tag was no time to have a memory lapse, to find the next move wasn't there—-or not to remember where you were in a sequence or what you'd already done. You didn't get other chances. The Belt didn't give them.

He didn't know himself what would happen when the hatch shut behind him, whether he'd panic, whether he'd be all right—whether he'd think he was all right and, the longer he was out in that ship, slowly unravel between past and present, the way he had in the shower—*that* shower, the same surroundings, nothing but his current partners' presence to anchor him in time.

Everybody seemed to be asking him to collect himself, get on with his life as if nothing had happened. It seemed to be the way everybody got by—they numbed themselves to feeling, made themselves deaf and blind to what the company got away with, just kept their mouths shut, chased what money they could get, and got used to seeing a lying sonuvabitch in the mirror every morning, because that was the only kind that had a chance in this place.

He didn't know whether he could do that. He didn't even know whether he could keep out of that pill drawer and stay alive tonight, or whether the gain was even worth it anymore.

Cory, he'd said that time they'd had the argument, maybe I don't want to go. What in hell am I going to do on a starship? I failed math. I failed physics. I don't have your brains, Cory, it was your idea all along. They won't have work for me, I'll be dead mass, the rest of my life, Cory. What kind of life is that?

She'd set him down, told him plain as plain he hadn't any chance in staying, she'd told him the company was crooked, the company was screwing the freerunners, screwing the pilots, screwing everybody that worked for them. Cory had handled big money, she knew how banks worked with the big operations. She'd told him what ASTEX was doing with their electronic datacards and their policies on finds. She'd tried to explain to him exactly what that direct-deduct stuff on LOSes did to accounts and interest, and how they were skimming on the freerunners in ways that had nothing to do with rocks.

She'd said, Dek, don't be a fool, you've no future here. They're killing the freerunners, they'll get the Shepherds in not too many years—there's no hope here.

She'd said, Don't ever think I'll leave you behind . . .

Sal sipped her drink in the blue neon of Scorpio's—the vid had been not-too-bad, chop and slash, the way Meg said, but not a long one, and as she had put it, it was way too early to chance walking in on the boys, besides which she had a word to drop on some friends next door. It was her favorite lounge—Shepherd territory, right next to the Association club—pricey, spif: you got the usual traffic of office types who went anywhere au courant on the edge of helldeck, but the Shepherd relationship with Scorpio's was longstanding: Shepherds got the tables in the nook past the glass pillars, and Shepherd glasses came filled to the brim, no shorting and no extra water, either.

Not a place they could afford as a steady habit, damn sure, not unless they picked up some guys with Shepherd-level finance, and they weren't shopping to do that this time.

No danger of walk-up offers this side of those pillars either, thank God: the women to men ratio on helldeck meant Shepherds were used to being courted, not the other way around, and two women who weren't signaling didn't get the pests that made sane conversation impossible in a lot of the cheaper bars, God, you got 'em in restaurants, in vid show doorways—this shift some R&R bunch was in from the shipyard, and the soldier-boys on leave down at the vid were the damn-all worst. They'd had a glut of male fools for the last few hours and Scorpio's was a refuge worth the tab, in her own considered opinion.

"I tell you," she said over an absolutely genuine margarita, "my instinct would be to take this Dek a tour before we go out, you know, personal, just friendly. Rattle him and see what shakes. I think that's a serious safety question. But we got Ben in the gears, damn 'im."

"You want my opinion, Aboujib?"

"Po-sess-ive?"

"Vir-gin, Aboujib. You're probably the first that ever asked him."

"Hell, he's that way with Bird!"

"Yeah."

She saw what Meg was saying, then. "That way about a lot of things, isn't he?"

Meg stirred her drink with the little plastic straw. "Man's got a serious problem. Hasn't cost us yet. But it's to worry about. Ni-kulturny, what he pulled on Bird tonight."

"Ochin," Sal agreed with an uncomfortable twitch of her shoulders, sipping her margarita, thinking how they weren't doing as ordinaire with Ben, how if it was anybody else but the best numbers man on R2, she'd have handed him off to Meg—switch and dump, the old disconnection technique. But, dammit, Ben was special, the absolute best, and Meg with Ben didn't do them any good. Meg didn't know the right questions and she didn't do the calc as well.

Besides which it wasn't Meg who made Ben crazy enough to show her things the Institute hadn't, that *he'd* figured, that he wouldn't hand out to anybody. She'd never met a case like Ben—you felt simpatico with him one minute and the next you wanted to break his neck. She'd never met anybody she *trusted* the way she did Ben—except Meg and Bird; Ben was the only one but Meg and Bird she'd feel safe going EV with—and, counting his crazy behavior, she couldn't figure that out.

At least he wasn't like the greasy sumbitch who'd threatened not to let her back in the ship unless she did him special favors. Numbers men were always at a disadvantage, always got the problems until you were as good as Ben, that *no*body wanted to lose. Meg had never been through that particular trouble—a numbers man didn't dare antagonize his pilot, if he had any sense; and he didn't send his pilot walkabout either—but a numbers man definitely could get out with some severely strange people in this business; and if you had some few partners you were sure of, you didn't let them go—didn't try to run their lives for them, not if you wanted all your fingers back, but hell if you wouldn't go to any length to hold on to them, to keep things the way they were.

Kill somebody? If it came to it, if you ever would—then you would. And trying to keep two tallish young guys from killing each other out there . . .

"What are we going to do, Kady?"

Meg pursed her lips. "Just what we're doing. Let Bird handle it."

Someone brushed by their table. Touched her shoulder. "Aboujib?"

God. A walk-up? Meg's frown was instant. Sal looked around and up an expensive jacket at a Shepherd—one of Sunderland's crew, friend of Mitch's—she didn't know the name. He said, very quickly, slipping something into her pocket, "That question you left?"

"Yeah," she said—different problem. *Same* problem. She held her breath. Felt something flat and round and plastic in her pocket, her heart going doubletime.

"This is Kady?"

"Yeah," she said. "You can say."

"Word is, problem's gone major. You're tagged with it. Go with it the way you said. Time's welcome. But when you get your launch date . . . you let us know. Very seriously."

The guy walked off then.

God.

"What the hell?" Meg asked.

"I dunno," she said, thinking about a shadowy 'driver sitting out there spitting chunks at the Well. And MamBitch, who prepared the charts *and* their courses, and shoved them up to *v* and braked them.

"I dunno." Her stomach felt, of a sudden, as if she'd swallowed something very cold.

"Is that what I think I heard?" Meg asked. "They think we could be in some kind of danger?"

"I don't know."

"Oh, God, great!"

"Let's not panic."

"Of course let's not panic. I don't effin' like the stakes all of a sudden."

She leaned forward on the table, pitched her voice as low as would still carry. "Meg. They're not going to let us run into trouble."

"Yeah," Meg whispered back. "Let's not hear 'run into.' I don't like the words I'm hearing. I don't like this 'Go with it.' Maybe I want a little more information than we're getting into."

"They're saying we're doing the right thing—"

"Yeah, doing the right thing. We can be fuckin' martyrs out there, is that what they want?"

She reached across the table and grabbed Meg's hand, scared Meg would bolt on her. "We got a real chance here—"

"What real chance? Chance your high and mighty friends are going to hold us a nice funeral? Chance we can collect the karma and they stay clean?"

"Meg, I can get you *in*."

"Screw that." Meg jerked her hand back. "I don't take their charity."

"Meg. For God's sake don't blow it."

Meg set her jaw. Took several slow breaths, the way she would when she was mad. "What's their guarantee? Shit, we could be bugged here—"

Sal took the flat plastic out of her coat pocket, which had a little green light showing. Palmed it, fast.

"God," Meg groaned.

"They're ahead of the game. They're not going to let us walk into it."

"Oh, you've got a lot of faith in them. That's contraband, dammit!"

"Meg, they're not fools."

"They must think we are."

"We made them an offer, Meg, they're *saying* they're agreeing. They're warning us."

"Yeah, 'tagged with him.' I like that. I really like that."

"Meg." She couldn't lay it out better than Meg already knew it. Meg looked like murder.

But Meg said finally: "So we're tagged with him. —Are we talking about giving up that lease?"

The answer was yes. Meg knew it. Meg knew it upside and down.

"Shit," Meg said.

"We've got what they want. They *want* him. They paid their debts. That's what they're saying. They're asking us take a risk, and we're in, Meg, they're making us an offer. If we screw 'em on this—or if we back out now—"

She was down to begging. There were pulls in too many directions if Meg skitted out on this one. God, everything she wanted, *everything*. "A Shepherd berth, Meg. One last run. We get Dek out in the big quiet for a few months and that's it. Ben and Bird set up with those ships. Karma paid. We're getting *out* of here, Meg. A chance at a *real* ship. Both of us."

That scored with Meg. Only thing that could. Meg's face got madder. Finally Meg said: "Hell if. Wake up, Aboujib."

"Hell if not. This is *big*, Meg, dammit, this is *it*."

Meg shook her head. But it meant yes. All right. We're going to be fools.

"You better be right, Aboujib. —And that jeune fils damn well better get his bearings. Fast. If they're going to make a case on him—he sincerely better not be crazy."

CHAPTER 14

Spending his sleeptime with Bird wasn't exactly what Ben had planned. Breakfast with Dekker wasn't his idea of a good time either, but Bird insisted.

So here they were, himself and Bird at the table and Dekker in line—Meg and Sal were sleep-ins: they'd gotten in *late* last shift, up to what Ben didn't try to imagine. Dekker hadn't seemed enthusiastic about their company from his side either: Dekker had answered his door, said Yeah, he'd be there, and arrived late—clipped up the sides and all.

"All he needs is a couple of earrings," Ben muttered.

"Be nice," Bird chided him, over the sausage and unidentifiable eggs.

Ben looked at him, lifted a chilled shoulder. "Hey, did I do anything?" But he reminded himself he had better bite his tongue and keep criticisms of Bird's previous pretty-boy to himself, the way he'd made up his mind yesterday that since the insanity had gotten to Meg and Sal he had as well go along with it.

Bird shot him a look that said be didn't trust him not to knife Dekker in his bed. That was the level things had gotten to. That was the primary reason he figured he had better go along with it.

Until Dekker slipped up. Then he was even going to be charitable about "I told you so," he sincerely was—so long as Bird saw it clear when it happened and came to his senses.

So Dekker walked up with his cup of coffee and his eggs, not quite looking at either of them, kicked back a chair and sat down.

"I have to apologize," Dekker said first off, still without looking at them.

Ben manfully kept his mouth shut.

"I sort of wandered off yesterday," Dekker said.

Bird shrugged, but Dekker wasn't going to see that gesture, looking at his plate like the zee-out he was. Bird said, "Pills will do that."

"I'm going off them," Dekker said. His hand with the fork was shaking. Badly. —A real mess, Ben thought. Wonderful. We're supposed to go out with this guy. This is going to be at the controls out there.

Dekker did look up then, shadow-eyed as if he hadn't slept much. "I cut you off yesterday. If the offer's still open—I'd like to talk about it."

"Offer's open," Bird said. Ben thought: Hell.

Dekker didn't say anything for a moment, just stirred his eggs around on his plate. Then a second look at Bird. "So I want my license back. What's the time worth?"

"Depends on your work," Bird said.

Ben did a fast calc, what Dekker had, what gave them a solid return on putting up with him. "10 k flat. With a guarantee you *get* the license."

Dekker looked bewildered—maybe a little overcome at the price and *not* understanding the quality of what he'd just thrown in. *He* wasn't exactly sure why he'd thrown it in—except he'd had this nanosecond of thinking he'd asked high and Bird was already on his tail. So it just fell out of his mouth: There you are, fancy-boy, *I* can fix it, *I* can, so you damned sure better mind your manners with me.

Bird didn't say anything, Dekker didn't, so Ben added, with a certain satisfaction, "Fair, isn't it? Guaranteed, class 1."

Bird looked a little worried. But he still didn't say anything.

"Whose guarantee?" Dekker asked.

Ben gave him a cold stare. "Mine. On the other hand, if you ask anybody the time, Dekker, if you pull *any* shit on us out there, you'll take a walk bare-assed."

"Ben," Bird said.

"I'm serious," he said, and Dekker looked worried.

"Ben's all right," Bird said. "He really is."

Dekker said, finally, "I haven't got any other offers."

"Small wonder," Ben said, and realized that he'd broken his resolution a tick before Bird glared at him.

Dekker glared at him too. Dekker said, "I'll pull my weight."

Ben said, "Damn right you will. You'll do whatever you're told to do. And you'll put up with whatever shit you're handed, whatever you think of it—with no gripes."

Bird said, "Ben, —"

Dekker glumly reached across the table. It took a moment before Ben realized he wanted his hand, that Dekker was truly calling his bluff and taking the deal.

Damn, Ben thought. He had as soon stick his hand in a grinder, but things with Bird were precarious. So he made a grimace of a smile, gave Dekker his hand and they made a limp, cheerless handshake across the plates.

No one looked convinced, not Dekker, not Bird. *He* certainly wasn't. But he said, "All right, if we're going to do this, let's get that re-cert application in right now. I take it you haven't done that."

"No craters," Meg said as they walked out into the bar. They'd come in late last shift, they'd slept late, gotten up and come out on the absolute tail end of breakfast. No Dekker, no Bird, no Ben. Meg shoved her hands into her pockets and looked at Mike over at the bar. Sal looked too, with a lift of the eyebrows.

"They kill each other?" she wondered.

Mike said, dishing up the last of the rubbery eggs, "Left like old friends, all three. Said tell you they were going up to the dock. They're leaving you a pile of scrub-up and sanding in the shop."

"Fun," Sal sourly.

"Ben with Dekker?" Meg said, with a gathering worry. "Not damn likely. We got a problem here."

Sal poured her own coffee and took the plate Mike handed her. "Kady, I think we got to use strategy."

"What strategy? I vote we shoot Ben."

"Na, na, he's playing along with Bird." Sal took the plate and the coffee back to the table and hooked a chair out, as Meg did the same. "We got, what, three weeks if we push it. If Dek's able to pitch in. The guys are going to be trouble. Trez macho."

"Trez pain in the ass. If *Bird* takes a position you need a pry-bar."

"We can't have Ben and Dekker in the same ship. That's prime."

"So Bird takes Dekker—and *we* take Ben." That, come to think of it, wasn't at all a bad idea. They'd been after Ben's numbers for two years. *That* was solid and Shepherd promises were come-ons and maybes.

Besides which, if there was anybody who could keep Dekker in line—

Sal ducked her head, checked in her pocket a beat—God, *smooth* move, there, Meg thought, with a knot in her stomach; and Sal looked up with the devil's own ideas in her eyes. "*I'll* tell you what we do, Kady, we apply to go out tandem. *All* of us. I'll tell you why." A jab of Sal's finger on the tabletop. "Because Bird doesn't want Dekker sliced and stacked. Because Bird's had one trip with Ben and Dekker already and if we give him the out to break that up—we ask for even split on the board time, just to make him believe it, we set it up with the Bitch, and we get Ben and his numbers *and* access to Dekker."

"Hell, we have got a ship coming out of refit. Shakedown run."

"That's the grounds. Only reason they'll do it."

"A skosh noisy. Do we need MamBitch's special attention on us? I *don't* think a special app is a good idea."

"Kady, we *got* the Bitch's attention. I'll ask my friends, but I don't know what worse we can do. And *if* they say do it, and if She'll let us—hell, if we can get out there tandem, we can just do our job, just ride it out while the shit flies, as may, and figure things are getting taken care of—they're *not* going to arrange anything on the way out, not unless they're pushed, and if the Association brings it up as an issue, damn *sure* the Bitch isn't going to run us into a rock on the way back. There's coincidences and there's coincidences. They're just a little from having the EC down their throats."

You had to wonder whether more understandings might have passed in that little encounter at Scorpio's than Sal had even yet admitted: and MamBitch beaming them up to *v* on a heading MamBitch picked—on charts that might have a little technical drop-out right in their path—hadn't helped her sleep at all. MamBitch was finally admitting in the news how she might go grievance procedures with the Shepherds to settle the outstanding complaints and patch up the sore spots—MamBitch having this severely important production schedule to meet, because the Fleet High Command was breathing down her neck.

That was the public posture. Behind the doors in management there were careers on the line.

There was the Shepherds' whole existence on the line.

"I tell you," she said to Sal over the eggs, "I'd sincerely like to know if you know anything additional—now or in future."

"If I know you'll know." A solemn look. "I swear."

"Thanks," she said. She did try to believe it.

A berth with the Shepherds, Sal said. It was already an endangered species. And they themselves were fools to think otherwise: you got out of the habit of longterm thinking—when the only out you had was a break in a business that was already taking the deep dive to hell. Freerunners weren't going to last forever. Go with the lease deal or go for broke Sal's way—*see* if the Shepherds kept their bargains, or if there was a bargain—or if the Shepherds were still independents when the shakeout came.

Sal had wanted this break, God, she'd chased it for years—blew it once, by what she knew, and those sons of bitches relatives of hers had kept Sal on a string for near six years, sure, let the kid be eyes and ears on helldeck, let Aboujib run their errands and risk arrest, let Aboujib sweat long enough to be sure she took orders—

Aboujib had gotten a severe warn-off from the Shepherd Association when she'd taken up with her—and being Aboujib, she'd locked on to her mistake and damned the consequences. Her high and mighty friends had said, Drop Kady, and Sal had gone to talk to some officer or other—God only what she'd said in that meeting, or what they'd said or threatened, but Sal had stormed out of their exclusive club and not talked about a berth with the Shepherds for the better part of a month.

They'd survived the ups and down since, gotten hell and away better than they'd started—things had looked so clear and so possible, til yesterday, til the Association dangled Sal's dream in front of her, the bastards—

She'd said yes to Sal last night. She had the sinking feeling this morning she'd been a chronic fool, and committed herself to something she wouldn't have, except for those two margaritas. But she hadn't exactly come up with an effective No this morning, either, both of them sitting here betting their necks on that little green light—Sal was dead set.

She still couldn't open her mouth and say, Sal, no deal. We're going with the lease.

Didn't know if you'd call it friendship. Didn't know what was wrong with her head—but the way things were getting to be on R2, the freerunners didn't have that many more years. She could worry about Bird—you couldn't call it romance, what she had with Bird. Mutual good time. And a guy she'd no desire to see run up against a rock, dammit: if Dekker was the problem, . . . they were all tagged, as the Shepherd had put it: Bird, Ben, *all* of them. The Association might be using them—but the Association might be the only protection a handful of miners had—the *Shepherds* were the only independents with any kind of leverage.

That—was enough to advise keeping one's mouth shut. And not to say No.

Couldn't tell Bird. Bird wasn't good at secrets. Damn sure not Ben.

What had the Shepherd said? The problem's major? The problem's *gone* major?

Something had shifted. Ben's charts? Something the company had done?

The dumbasses in the fire zone didn't get that kind of information.

Turn in the re-cert application, Ben had said. Move on it. *Way Out* was headed for soon-as-possible launch, dock time cost, Ben swore he had friends who could get the test scheduled within the week, and Dekker decided, in Bird's lack of comment, that Ben might be telling the truth.

So it was a good idea to do that, Dekker supposed: and found himself sitting in a Trans car between Bird and Ben, nervous as a kid headed for the dentist—only beginning to calm down and accept the idea of taking an ops test before he'd gotten the shakes out of his knees. Ten days was soon enough, Bird said. Give him a little time. Ten days to get his nerves together, ten days til he had to prove to BM that he still had it—that was still time enough to get the class 3 license pushed through, Ben said, which he had to have before he could count any time at *Way Out*'s boards.

God, he couldn't blow this.

Bird said: "After we get this done, we thought we'd take you up to the docks, show you the ship, all right?"

"All right," he said, in the same numb panic, asking himself what they were up to—*show you the ship* . . .

Maybe they wanted to see if he could take it. Maybe they were pushing him to find out if he would go off the edge—

Sudden memory of that fouled, cold interior, the suit drifting against the counter—the arm moving. He'd waked in the near-dark and imagined it was Cory beckoning to him.

Bird talked into his ear, talked about some of the damage on the ship, talked about what they'd done—

But the ship in his mind was the one he remembered. The stink, and the cold, and the fear—

"Admin," Ben said as the Trans pulled into a stop. "Here we are."

He got up, he got off with them into an office zone, all beige and gray, with the musty cold electronics smell offices had. They went into the one that said ECSAA Certifications, and Ben and Bird walked up to the counter with him.

"I want to apply for a license," he said.

"Recertification," Ben said, leaning his elbows on the desk beside him.

"Just let me do it." He couldn't think with Ben putting words in his mouth; he felt shivers coming on—he'd caught a chill in the Trans—and he didn't want to be filling in applications with his hands shaking. *Fine* impression that was in this office.

The clerk went away, came back with a datacard, directed him to a side table and a reader.

He went over to it and his entourage came with him, one on either side as he put the card in the slot and made three mistakes entering his name.

"Look, you're making me nervous."

"That's all right," Ben said. And when he tried to answer the next question, about reason for revocation: "Uh-uh," Ben said. "Neg. Say, 'Hospitalization.' "

"Look, the reason is a damned stupid doctor—"

"They don't *want* the detail." Ben reached over and moved the cursor back. "Don't explain. The only answer any department wants in its blanks is the wording in its rule books. Don't volunteer anything, don't get helpful, and if you don't know, N/A the bastard or shade it in your favor. Remember it's clerks you're talking to, not pilots. Say: 'Hospitalization.' "

That made clear sense to him. He only wished it hadn't come from Ben.

" 'Reason for application'?" Ben read off the form, and pointed: "Say: 'Change in medical status.' "

He hadn't thought of having to pass the physical again. The idea of doctors upset his stomach. But he typed what Ben said.

"Sign it," Ben said. "Put your card in. That's all there is to it."

It left a lot of blank lines. "What about 'Are there any other circumstances. . . ?' "

"This is a 839-RC," Ben said, and tapped the top of the display, where it had that number. "An 839-RC *applies*, that's all it does. It doesn't explain. It's not a part of the exam. Just send it."

"Have you ever filled out one of these?"

"Doesn't matter. I worked in Assay. Answer by catch-phrases. *Don't* pose the clerks a problem or it'll go right to the bottom to the Do Pile. Don't be a problem. Send the bastard."

"Do it," Bird said.

He keyed Send. In a moment the screen blinked, notified him his account had been debited 250.00 for the application and told him he had to pass the basic operationals within sixty days, after which he had to log 200 hours in the sims or at the main boards of a working ship, by sworn affidavit of a class 1 pilot—

And take a written exam.

Someone had as well have hit him in the gut. He stood there staring at the message til Bird laid a hand on his shoulder and said they'd go on to the core now.

He was down to 95 dollars in his account, he hadn't yet paid his bill at The Hole, and he'd never *taken* the writtens, he'd come up from the cargo pushers to the short-hop beam haulers to a miner-craft; but he'd never had to take the written exams.

Ben elbowed him in the back. "Come on, moonbeam. Don't forget your card."

He took it out of the slate, he walked out of the offices with them, in a complete haze. They got to the Transstation as the Trans pulled in and the doors opened.

"Come *on*," Ben said, and Ben taking his arm was the last straw. He snarled, "Let go of me," and shook free, wanting just to go on around the helldeck, wanting to go back to his room, lock the door, take a pill and not give a damn for the rest of the day; or maybe three or four days.

"Come on." Bird got his arm and pulled at him. The Trans doors were about to close in their faces, the robot voice was advising them to get clear. "Oh, hell," he said; and let them pull him aboard, because otherwise they were going to miss their ride and stand there til the next Trans came, asking him why he was a damned fool.

They fell into seats as the doors shut and the Trans started moving. "What in hell's the matter with you?" Ben asked. "Are you being a spook again, Dekker?"

"No," he said, and slouched down into the seat, staring at a point between them.

"You have some trouble about going onto the ship?" Bird asked him.

"No." He set his jaw and got mad, lifelong habit when people who ran his life crowded him.

Ben said: "You're being a spook, Dekker."

Probably he was, he thought. And a kid might keep his mouth shut, but a grown man in debt up to his ears and about to end up on a heavyside job had finally to realize who he owed, and how much. He swallowed against the knot in his throat and muttered, "I can't pass tests."

Bird tilted an ear and said, louder: "What?"

So he had to repeat it: "I can't take tests."

"What do you mean you can't take tests?" Ben objected, loudly enough for people around them to hear. "You had a license, didn't you?"

Screw you, he wanted to yell at Ben. Let me alone! But he said quietly: "I had a license."

"Without an exam?"

"You can do that," Bird said to Ben. "Construction work lets you do that. You can jump from class to class that way, just the operationals and a few questions. Same as I did. Not everybody comes through the Institute."

"Well, then," Ben said, "—you've been a class 1. You claim you were good. You know the answers. What's a test?"

Ben made him mad. Ben could make him mad by breathing. He tried to be calm. "Because I can't pass written questions!"

"God," Ben said, sliding down in his seat. "One of those. Can you read?"

He didn't want to know what "those" Ben was talking about. He didn't want to talk about it right now. He wanted to break Ben's neck. He stared off at the corner, past Ben's shoulder. He'd go to the ship, all right, he'd restrain himself from acting like a crazy man; he'd pass the operationals and put in his hours in Bird's ship and he'd come back and fail the damned test.

But meanwhile he'd have gotten fed. He'd have gotten in with Bird. Maybe he could get a limited license to push freight, work up through ops again, on the ship construction out there: he didn't know, he didn't even know if it was possible out in the Belt. He didn't want to worry about it right now, just take it as far as he could, and not think about the mess he was in.

Bird and Ben talked in low voices and he was the topic: he could catch snatches of it over the noise. It was two more stops til the core lift. He wanted this ride over with—*wanted* to get up to the dock, the ship, anywhere, to get them on to some other subject.

"Look," Ben said, leaning forward, "on this test business, it's easy done. It's a *system*, there's a technique—"

"Easy for you!"

"You a halfway good pilot?"

"I'm damned good!"

"Then listen to me: it's the same as filling in the forms back there. Don't give real answers to deskpilots. The whole key to forms *or* tests is never give an answer smarter than the person who checks the questions."

He took in a breath, expecting Ben to have insulted him. He couldn't figure how Ben had.

"We can get you through that shit," Ben said, with a flip of his hand. "But first let's see if you're worth anything in ops."

He didn't *want* to owe Ben anything. He told himself that Ben had probably figured out a new way to screw him—and if there was any hope at all, it was that Ben's way of screwing him happened to involve his getting his license restored.

Slave labor for him and Bird, maybe: that was all right, from where he was. Do anything they wanted—as long as it got him that permit and got him licensed again.

He thought about that til the Trans came to their stop, at the lift. They got out together, punched up for the core, and waited for the car. He tucked his hands into his pockets and tried not to think ahead, not to tests, not to the docks, not to what the ship was going to look like—

Everything was going to be all right, he wasn't going to panic, wasn't going to heave up his guts when he went null-*g*, it was just going to be damned cold up there, bitter cold: that was why he was shivering when he walked into the lift.

He propped himself against the wall and took a deathgrip on the safety bar while the lift made the core transit: increased *g* at the first and none at the end—enough to do for a stomach in itself. The car stopped, let them out in the mast Security Zone, and they shoved their cards in the slot.

The null-*g* here at least didn't bother him—it only felt—

—felt as if he was back in a familiar place, and wasn't, as if he were timetripping again: in his head he knew R2's mast wasn't anywhere he'd been before when he was cognizant—he kept Bird in sight to keep himself anchored, hooked on and rode the hand-line between Ben and Bird—

The booming racket, the activity, the smell of oil and cold and machinery—all of it could have been R1. Here and now, he kept telling himself, and by the time he reached *Way Out*'s berth in Refit, his stomach might have been upset, but he could reason his way toward a kind of numbness.

Even entering the ship wasn't the jolt he'd thought it would be, following Bird and Ben through the lock. Bird turned the lights up and the ship seemed—ordinary again. It smelled of disinfectant, fresh glue, and oil. He touched *Way Out*'s panels with cold-numbed fingers and looked around him. Everything around him was the way it had been, as if the wreck had never happened. Same name as she'd had—Cory's joke, actually—but they'd given her a new number, and she wasn't his and Cory's anymore.

Most of all there was no sense of Cory's existence here. That had been wiped out too. And maybe it was that presence he'd been most afraid to deal with.

"We've got the tanks replaced," Bird was saying, reorienting toward him. "We're stalled on one lousy part we're trying to organize on the exchange market—but we're closing in on finished."

"How does she look?" Ben asked, point blank, and he could say, calmly, without his teeth chattering, "You've done a lot of work with her."

"Want to get the feel of the boards?" Bird asked. "Main system's hooked in. Want to run a check?"

He knew then what they were up to, bringing him up here: they were running their own ops test. They wanted to see on their own whether he was missing pieces of his mind—just a simple thing, bring the boards up. Run a check. . . .

He took a breath of the bitter cold, he hauled down and fastened in at the main boards, uncapped switches and pushed buttons—didn't have to think about them, *didn't* think about them, until he realized he'd just keyed beyond the simple board circuit tests: memory flooded up, fingers had keyed the standard config-queries and he could breathe again, didn't damn well know where he was going, didn't know exactly at what point he was going to make himself terminate or whether they wanted him to run real checkouts that fed data onto the log—

—Number 4 trim jet wasn't firing—he caught the board anomaly in the numbers streaming past, the rapid scroll of portside drift; he compensated with a quick fade on 2 and kicked the bow brakes to fend off before the yaw could carry him further—*not* by the book—he knew it a heartbeat after he'd done it.

The screen went black. The examiner said: "Been a cargo pusher, haven't you?"

He said, trying not to let the shakes get started, "Yeah. Once." The examiner understood, then, what he'd done. And why.

The examiner—he was a man, and old—punched a button. Numbers came up, two columns. Graphs followed.

"You're a re-cert," the examiner said.

"Trying to be," he said. He kept his breath even, watched as the examiner punched another set of buttons.

"You can take your card out."

"Did I pass?"

"D-class vessel, class 3 permit with licensed observer." The examiner keyed out. "Valid for a year. —You in the Institute?"

"Private," he said, and the examiner gave him a second look.

"Who with?"

"Morrie Bird. *Trinidad*."

"Mmmn."

He wished he dared ask what that meant. But examiners in his experience didn't say what your score was, they didn't discuss the test, they rarely asked questions. This one made him nervous, but he thanked God the man *was* more than a button-pusher, he must be.

He left the simulator room with his card in hand, took the B-spoke core-lift down to the ECSAA office, feeling the shakes finally hit him while he was at the Certifications desk getting the license, shakes so bad he had to put his hands in his pockets for fear the office staff might see it.

Damn warning light had failed in the sim—or he'd flat failed to see it til it showed in the numbers. You never knew which. An alarm might have been blinking, he might have missed it, he might have just timed out—it felt like that, that time wasn't moving right when those numbers started going off, when he'd had to do a fast and dirty calc and just thought . . . *thought* it was a tight-in situation, he had no idea why, his brain just told him it was and he'd imagined impact where there wasn't any such thing in the simulation—

No, dammit, the sim had increased *g* sharply and for one sick moment he'd hallucinated that the engines were firing.

Maybe it was just his nerves. He wasn't sure anymore.

Maybe that was the problem.

"Uh-oh," Meg said, seeing Dekker come out and down the Admin strip. They'd taken time out of the shop to shepherd Dek back . . . in case it's bad news, she'd said, and Sal had agreed.

So knowing he was already nervous they hadn't told him they were close by, hadn't come down with him—just called and asked a Certification office secretary how long a D3 permit exam might take, and they'd come down from the 3-deck shop to be here—in case.

"Doesn't look good," Sal said; and Meg had a moment of misgivings, whether they shouldn't just duck back and try to blend with the Transstop traffic—not easy in her case and not easy in Sal's. So there was no chance for cowardice. She waved.

Or maybe on second thought they might make it away unseen. Dekker was walking along looking at his feet, off in some different universe.

She said, as he came close, "Dek? How'd it go?"

He looked up, looked dazed, as if he couldn't figure them being there, or he hadn't really heard the question.

"How'd it go?" Sal asked.

"All right," he said.

"So did you get the permit?"

"Yeah."

"So, bravo, jeune rab!" Sal clapped an arm around him and gave him a squeeze. "We said, didn't we?"

He was dead white. He looked scared—and a little zee-d. "I said I'd call up to the ship—tell Bird how it came out. I need a phone."

Deep-spaced, Meg thought uneasily. Got himself through the test in one piece and just gone out. God hope they hadn't spotted it in the office. She linked her arm through his, protective custody. "Come on. Phone and lunch. In that order."

He went with them. They found a public phone near the Transstation, and she punched through to Bird. Bird said, "Good," when he heard, and Ben said, in the background, "So what's the fuss?"

Break that man's neck someday, Meg thought. With my own bare hands.

Another damned breakdown in D-28, and a pump-connection had blown out in the mast at dockside—spraying 800 liters of hydraulic fluid into free-fall toward the rotating core surface. The super swore it was worker sabotage and Salvatore, with three more cases on his desk, had a headache.

He put a tech specialist on the investigation, poured himself a cup of coffee and told himself he had to clear his desk: the stacks of datacards in the bin had reached critical mass, Admin was having a fit over the quarterly reports being a week late, it had a Fleet Lieutenant on its lap bitching about a schedule shortfall, and he couldn't find the cards the current flags referenced.

Flag on Walker. The guy had card use near an office break-in, had no business there—no apparent relation to the crime, merely a presence that didn't make sense. Flag on Kermidge: every sign of resuming bad associations. Flags on Dekker: blew hell out of the sims.

He keyed up the subfile.

Wills' voice said, out of the comp, *"Dekker passed his D3 ops. Score shot straight to the Chief Examiner. Word is the sims jumped out of D class and ran clear up in C before the examiner terminated the test—standard if there's an overrun: the Certifications office suspects a suspension at a higher grade—started searching court records, potential inquiries to Sol—"*

Oh, shit!

"I intercepted it, told them let the license stand at a D3, pending inquiry with this office: I hope that was all right."

Thank God.

"I did check the examiner's record in the files: retired pilot, ECI training, Sol based, good record, three years in his present position, et cetera. He's clean.

"But here's another interesting development: Bird and Pollard, the ones who brought him in, that got his ship on salvage, that're staying in the same sleepery? They've filed to run pairs, refit shakedown run with Dekker's former ship leased to one Kady and Aboujib. Dekker's on that application as a D3 wanting board time.

"Here's the catch. Aboujib and Kady have records—Kady's, as long as your arm. Smuggling, rab agitator—SolCorp background, opted here on an EC transfer. Aboujib's an AIP dishonorable discharge, reckless endangerment with a spacecraft, Shepherd background, small-time morals charges, one assault, bashed some guy with a bottle. Allocations hasn't ruled yet. Deny or let-pass?"

Salvatore hit Pause, sat there with his elbows on the desk, reached for his inhaler, thinking: Son of a bitch. . . .

Not about Wills. Wills had done a good job—so far as it went. The business with the examiner jangled little alarms, no less than the immaculate Bird's shadowy associations.

Report that finding to Payne's office? Payne had said: We don't need to drag this out. The report to the ECSAA said mechanical failure, no fault of the pilot. . . .

Payne wanted the case closed; but, dammit, it kept resurfacing in the flags, and now with Wills' information came the niggling worry that where there were anomalies in official records there might also be management secrets. Salazar's threatened lawsuit, contractor disputes, the rash of incidents on the dock and in the plants—the military making demands to install Security personnel on R2—some kind of "readiness survey" involving their contracts, which was, one could suspect, strongly tied to schedule slowdowns, and, dammit, an implication of blame for *his* department—it was the whisper in the company washrooms that the Fleet was putting heavy pressure on ASTEX management, the Earth Company was worried about sabotage and slowdowns, possibly sympathizer activity—the labor agitators were looking for the right moment to embarrass the company; and damned right the radical fringes of all sorts were looking for a way to get control of the labor movement—radical fringe elements ASTEX had more than its share of, thanks to the EC's policy of letting malcontents and malefactors transfer out here—sans trial, sans publicity that might catch media attention in the motherwell, where strikes and welfare riots and lunatic religions fed on the airwaves. This Kady was probably a prime example, but monetary rather than political. *That* was no problem. Shepherd connections? Shepherds had more kids than they could find slots for. Reckless endangerment? An ECSAA violation. Not this office's province and any shift on helldeck could provide three and four assaults and a few cases for the medics.

ASTEX Security had a damn sight more on its mind than a couple of small-time malcontents and a disputed miner craft. Dekker was a watch-it, but Dekker had so far done nothing worse than show up an anomaly on a simulation—better than average. Meanwhile management had a ship over at that classified facility way behind schedule and sabotage in a plastics plant that had no damned reason except a fool of a manager.

Hell, no, it wasn't the ASTEX board that was going to take the damage: boards were never to blame—ASTEX management wasn't to blame: dump it on Security, dump it on Salvatore's desk—

So what had he got, but a missing kid with a mother on MarsCorp board, whose lawyers were threatening a negligence suit against the mechanic at R1 and trying to get those records opened. Dekker had had one incident, making wild charges against the company—but he had been quiet since then, had spent money on clothes, on food—his only current sin was applying for a re-cert in D class when he might—he read through Wills' report—have rated higher.

You did have to wonder about some ringer thrown in at higher levels, somebody working for some investigatory office, even—in these nervous days—something that should come to the attention of MI.

Blow the Dekker case wide and he could kiss his career goodbye; but if he failed to report a problem, and let something slip, his competence was at issue. Hell of a crack to be in. In his most paranoid moments he was moved to ask had there ever been a Cory Salazar—

But there was no doubt about Dekker on any level he could assess; the various departments over at R1 had his background from two years back; and no clandestine operator would be so stupid as to ring bells on a test: it didn't in any wise smell like an EC probe *or* a security problem.

Hell, Dekker had had his D1 from back in '20, he'd had working experience since, and very possibly he'd been dogging it back in '20, lying low from the military recruiters: that behavior was an epidemic among draft-age males. With that medical against him, he'd put out everything he had—and very nearly brought himself back to Ms. Salazar's attention: thank God Wills had put the stop on that.

So Dekker wanted to go back to space. It didn't seem a bad place to have him right now. You couldn't be quieter than out in the deep Belt, with no communication with anybody but BM. Alyce Salazar's lawyers couldn't serve him a summons there without a damned long arm.

Memo the doctor on Dekker's case to sign the medical release and satisfy the meddling clerk with the ECSAA rule book, get Dekker out and off the daily flags, and if Dekker went psycho out there and slash-murdered Bird and Pollard, they should have known what they were getting into. Only hope he got Kady and Aboujib with them. They didn't need the tag end of the rab acting up.

So with the push of a few keys, that was *one* problem off his desk for three months—a fix good the minute that ship cleared dock. Flag its return, flag—God!—Bird and Pollard, Aboujib and Kady, have Wills' office run down all the datatrails they might have left, at leisure. In a situation that could blow up again, on any whim of Salazar's lawyers, upper echelons could come down demanding complete files.

Pity, Salvatore thought, he couldn't sign up a few other problems for a three-month cruise in the belt . . .

Like the manager of D-28, with his dress codes and his inspections and his damned constant memos about sexual conduct off the job and his rules about mustaches, God, he'd *like* to memo Payne that Department Manager Collin R. Sabich had a private problem with kink vids, but owning the vids wasn't illegal and the fact wasn't relevant to anything but the fact Sabich was a slime. Admin knew that.

Admin had already promoted him sideways three times and evidently couldn't find anywhere less critical to put him. What else could you do with a sonuvabitch with a kink and an Institute degree in Plant Management?

God knew, maybe they'd give him an administrative office to run.

CHAPTER 15

One thing had started going right, Dekker thought, God, and another thing followed: a message turned up in the bar's mail-file at breakfast, addressed to Mr. M. Bird, from Belt Management: special permit granted for 2 ship operations in the same sector—launch permit and all, usual permits for loading and charging, et cetera, et cetera. They had a sector assignment, they'd get that and the charts when they boarded, they had a launch date, September 18th, four days from now—Bird had shaken his head over that, one of those damned do-it-now decisions from BM, no different at R2 than at R1. You expected a delay, you applied early, and you got a go-yesterday.

First the offer from Bird, then a piece of his license back, and Ben turning downright civil: now BM approved a joint run—and still nothing fell apart: Dekker sat holding his coffee cup, listening to the regulars in the bar congratulate Bird on BM's good behavior with the recollection that the last time in his life things were going this right—

But he didn't let himself think about that. He just stared at where he was and told himself that the letter had to be a sign his luck had turned, or maybe a signal from BM that management had decided to dog somebody else for a while. Who knew? Maybe somebody had slipped up and nobody had noticed he was on the crew. Maybe BM was signaling it would drop its feud with him and let him pick up his life if he just kept his mouth shut.

Don't worry about might-be's, was the way Meg put it. Just keep your head, don't make noise. MamBitch has a real shortterm crisis sense. There'll be some new sod on her grief list next week, and she'll forget all about you.

He truly wanted to believe the wreck might be a closed case, but experience told him no desk-sitter ever bothered to track and erase what some other desk-sitter had sent into files: that medical report and everything else in the files was going to surface time after time for the rest of his life, he was sure of it, a file uncatchable in its course through the company computers . . . probably every time he applied for a sector assignment. Damned sure if he tried to certify into C3.

And BM was putting him back to work, officially—still with no real resolution of what had happened, no answer, no justice. It was a cover-up Cory's mother evidently couldn't breach. He was sure she had to know by now—at least the official version. So what was *he* supposed to do that a mother on the MarsCorp board couldn't?

He thought about writing Alyce Salazar directly, send her his own account of what had happened, never mind Ms. Salazar hated him with a passion. But mail went through a lot of hands before it went out of R2. If anyone's mail found its way to special attention—his was a hundred percent certainty: he'd gotten that canny by now.

So it looked as if they were really going, and all he had to do was hold on to his nerves and stay out of trouble til launch, hope if the permit was a mistake nobody caught it in time—and try, meanwhile, to believe that Ben had really meant it just now when Ben had slapped him on the shoulder and said, in his subtle way, that in spite of him being an ass, he might actually work out.

Bird pocketed his datacard and remarked that since BM had a hurry-up on, they had a last few things to do in the shop, and they'd better get at it . . .

Sal said, "All right, all right, Bird. God, we put in fifty hours this week!" and Bird said: "Yeah, plenty all right if the shower doesn't work. Won't get any sympathy from me."

So it was a last-minute rush of things that had waited—no really vital jobs: they hadn't applied for their run without the big items latched down and *Way Out* past the mandatory ECSAA inspection: but Bird wanted some cleanup and the shop offered a refuge where a body could sit, put screws in holes and test circuits without a thought in his head except the job he was on, and he personally had no objections—anything that kept his hands busy.

Ben came and went, handling the legwork. Meg and Sal worked in the shop, raked over old lovers, the quality of hair dye, a vid they couldn't agree on—chatter, just chatter . . . human noise. They looked strained. Tired, yes. But he kept having the feeling it was more than that.

He didn't think. He didn't want to think.

Day before launch. He was holding on. Sal was frazzled. Bird grew short. "Launch nerves," Meg said under her breath. "Bird, dammit, just take it easy, we got it covered."

"It's a far walk after supplies," Bird snapped, and went off for another all-day stint on dockside, despite them arguing with him that old bones had as well get all the heavy time they could.

"Can't argue with him," Meg sighed. And Bird sent Ben down with a basket full of odd bits of *Trinidad*'s works he wanted serviced—36 hours before launch.

"Why in hell," Sal moaned, "didn't he see about this eight weeks ago?"

Ben just shook his head. "Does it every damned time. Everything's a will-pass until he gets to packing the supplies in. *Then* this latch has got too much give and he's remembered we had a condensation problem last run."

It kept their hands busy. It took their minds off the passing hours. Dekker understood Bird's state of nerves. Eventually, please God, they'd board and start launch routines and, Dekker thought, he might make it off R2 still sane.

"What kind of vids do you like?" Meg asked him, while he was testing a pressure switch.

He shrugged, figuring Meg meant they were going to rent a few for the trip, for all the spare time they weren't going to have, and he'd used to like the action stuff, but now that he thought about it, that wasn't what he wanted right now. Cory had made fun of his taste for his bloody-awfuls, that was what she had called them—but now he feared he'd never see an explosion in a vid without feeling that awful slam in the gut. He filed that away, in the odd total of silly, simple things he'd been robbed of in the wreck. Maybe he could handle it someday. But not now. Right now he just wanted to keep all that at arm's length. One step at a time, Mr. Dekker. . . .

"Dek?"

"Huh?"

"You want to go out tonight?"

He shook his head. "No," he said sharply—he didn't mean to be rude, but it was the truth—he didn't want to go watch things blow up: he didn't want any dark theater, God knew he didn't want any suspense—didn't know what he did want to do 24 hours before launch—but that wasn't it.

"Oh, come on," Sal said. "What about dinner? We can talk Bird into spending money. Something trez genteel. Candles and tablecloths. Give ourselves plenty of time to get through, get in and clean up. What d' you say? Dinner at 1900, cruise the bars, say our au'voirs along the 'deck."

"Yeah," he said, finally. Being with people tonight was probably a good idea. Meg and Sal were trying to include him in their festivities, trying to draw him into their conversation, but now that he'd committed himself he felt a kind of panic—as if by joining in he'd somehow stepped over an edge he'd really rather reconsider. He had no friends but these people, no future but what they'd arranged for him. They made their jokes, they talked to him, he answered what they asked, one side and the other of a trip for soft drinks and a package of chips.

But this Attitude kept coming over him—a blow-it-away kind of Attitude, resentment—outright rage at their trying to get at him: they had everything he owned and now they wanted his consent to it; now they wanted the resentment that had kept him alive—stupid way to feel, he thought, but their friendliness and Ben's made him mad, and he tried to figure out why, and not to be, as Ben called him, an ass.

But, dammit, everything hit nerves. Even their before-launch dinner. He'd done the same with Cory—Cory didn't make off-color jokes about the men she'd slept with—

Sore spot there. His mind was full of pits he didn't want to look into, this afternoon, pre-launch jitters triggering memories, God only knew what was going on with him—and that the tumbling, out of control feeling he'd had after the wreck was still there, making it impossible to take his life for granted—all the pieces were out of order. Everything felt new, dislocated.

Rab said do. Act. Move. Be.

But move where? Be what? Meg and Sal had their heads together, talking in low voices, protecting some secrecy they wouldn't admit him to—but they wanted him to take their lead. They'd dressed him like some damn doll—not a joke at his expense: far too serious for that. They had designs for him he didn't think had as much to do with sex as with way-of-life . . . making bitter jokes, flaunting their difference, trying to drag him away from Cory's way of doing things and back into all the blind outrage he'd used to feel—wake up, kid, join us, kid, be like us, be with, *think* like us and survive.

Maybe it *was* friendship. Be grateful, he told himself. Go out with them, mind your manners—today's enough. There's worse. There's hell and away worse to have fallen in with.

There's the people that run this place.

He was back on the ship for a moment. And back again sitting in the shop with a small valve switching assembly in his hand and no memory of whether he'd just started or just finished with it.

Panic shot a chill through him. He sat there staring at the piece and trying to figure out what he was doing with it.

"That's the last." Sal snatched it from his hand and tossed it into the basket. "God, Dek, come on, give it up. We're done!"

It wasn't anything he couldn't fix with a screwdriver if it stuck later. Nothing vital. Potential malfunction wasn't what scared him. It was the gap he'd slid into.

Damn nervous wreck, Sal thought, wiping sweat, kicking the null-*g* cart's wheels out. This one's wheels stuck. The rental office swore they didn't have another. —Get us *all* out of here—

Bang. You lifted one end and rammed it at the floor. Two times freed it up.

"Aboujib," someone said.

She turned about with an intake of breath.

Mitch's friend.

"You're still launching on the 18th?"

"Yeah."

"Don't depend on it."

"Shit! —What's going on?"

"That's the word. Keep a line on your problem. A tight line."

"*Why?*"

The Shepherd said, "You got that thing I gave you?"

"Not on me, I don't go to the core with it . . ."

"I want you to bring it to the club tomorrow. No advance word to Kady, no word to anybody. Just bring that, your friend, and your problem."

"We got a—" —launch tomorrow, she started to object. The universe turned around that point. Everything in their minds did, with manic concentration.

"Tomorrow," the Shepherd repeated.

She felt her heart sink. She thought, My God, Bird and Ben have everything they own tied up in this run . . .

They *can't* not launch tomorrow . . . Meg and me be damned, they can't not go tomorrow. "You don't back out this close, MamBitch won't change a launch date!"

"That's not in our control," the Shepherd said, and walked away.

"Why don't you come with me?" Meg asked him. "Sal's going to run that last batch up to Bird, and if he tries to give us another lot, we'll say sorry, the shop's closed. You and I can get cleared out of here and turn the keys in. I'm going to pick up a few things at Ward's, maybe stop for coffee . . ."

He shook his head. "I've got gym time to do." It was the only escape he could think of. He couldn't take Meg's company right now, couldn't risk timing out with her if that was what he had just done. He left: he didn't even realize how stupid the excuse had been until in the lift down he remembered he'd left Meg with a heavy tool case to carry to the rental office.

By then it was too late to go back and catch her, and he had no idea what to do with himself but go to the gym. Nothing seemed solid of a sudden, nothing of his life was in order—*time* worried him—he was freefalling, too scared to admit just now he'd been on autopilot and didn't know it—scared that a hatch shutting behind him was going to start him unraveling—

The blip was still moving. No question.

Cory argued with him: "It's the biggest chance we'll ever have—"

A piece of memory clicked in, quietly, just there of a sudden with that sense of frightened foolishness—he'd realized the danger in the 'driver—and he'd folded the argument, folded the way he'd folded with Sal up there. He'd had the ship completely in his hands—but he'd been afraid to be afraid, he'd let Cory's college education convince him she was right when his gut was telling him a silent, advancing 'driver the company charts didn't show wasn't playing by the rules she understood—

Cory, who knew MarsCorp inside and out, had said, We're going to call their bluff; they're in contact with BM every damn minute . . . and he'd frozen. He couldn't say, Cory, this scares hell out of me. He'd been too scared of Cory's education to say, Cory, this is just damned stupid—

She'd say, now, if she were here to say it, Well, I really blew that one, didn't I?

And he wouldn't. He couldn't—couldn't talk, couldn't get his words straight when he thought he could sound like a fool—

So he'd protected his damned soft spot. And Cory had died.

He bumped into someone. He mumbled an apology and kept walking, playing that moment over and over in his mind.

They'd been invulnerable—then. Nothing was going to turn out wrong. She'd made a bad choice, but rocks were her department, the ship was his. The company was crooked as hell, but he could call their bluff. He could make that ship listen—

He'd backed a wrong call. He'd known it and he'd done it. That was what he had to look at and look at til it burned its way into his brain.

CHAPTER 16

They waited and they waited in the bar—they'd talked Bird, practically manhandled Bird, out of *Trinidad* and into the idea of a fancy dinner, best clothes, rezzes at the Europa, a bit of bar-hopping afterward—and now Dekker went missing. Ben was mad, Sal was a nervous wreck—Dekker had been acting strange all day, Meg reminded herself glumly, and spent her own money calling the gym he reasonably should have gone to hours ago.

Of course he hadn't.

Damn.

"So, look," Bird said when she reported that fact back to the table, "we just leave word with Mike. Mike can give him directions when he shows up. He'll find us."

"Leave that guy loose on the 'deck?" Ben groaned—not the way she'd have put it, but it was another worrisome side of it. "Let's just give it a little while."

"He's a big boy," Bird said. "He's found his way around the Belt, for God's sake, he's not lost. He may not have understood it was a date."

"He understood," Meg said, and was about to say she agreed with Ben, they should give it another little while, when Mike at the bar signaled they had a call.

She stood up to take it, but Mike indicated Sal specifically, to her acute disappointment. She slid back into her chair while Sal went to take the call—probably some friend come onto R2, she decided: Dekker might call *her* if he was in a funk and he might call Bird, but Dekker asking for Sal was hardly likely.

"Probably in some bar," Ben said. "Probably drinking his way to tomorrow. Or zee'd on pills. —Dammit, Meg, think of another place."

"Pacific," Bird said

"So let's call there," Ben said, and something else, but Meg lost it. Sal hung up on her call and flashed her a come-here signal, looking seriously worried.

"Excuse me," she murmured and got up and met Sal by the phone. Sal said, head ducked and voice low, "That was Mitch. He said meet him out front. Now."

She felt a little chill. And puzzlement. "Seriously nonreg. He say anything?"

"No. Just that." Sal looked truly scared. Terrified. "Cover me with Bird. I don't know how long this may take."

"God," Meg said. "Yeah. All right."

Sal went for the door and she went back to the table.

"What was that?" Ben asked.

"Friend with a problem."

"Dekker?"

"No."

"God, this isn't getting any more organized. We're all over the damn 'deck!"

"I think we ought to make that call to The Pacific."

"Do that," Bird said, so she pulled out her card and went for the phone again.

"No," The Pacific said, ". . . Yeah, I know him. No, he hasn't been here."

Another try gone nowhere. Sal was off. Dekker was missing. Bird was as apt to go off next. Ben was right. She said to Mike, "Another round."

"Sal coming back?"

"I wish I knew," she said. "Skosh nervous day, Mike."

Mike gave a little shake of his head. "A lot wouldn't have the patience."

"Yeah," she said and went back to the table.

"Well?" Ben asked.

She shook her head.

"God, I don't know why we're putting up with this!"

"The lad's probably sorting out a few things," Bird said. "I'm not real surprised."

"Yeah, sorting out a few things . . . For all we know, the cops have got him."

"Look," Bird said. "Let's just put in a few phone calls. There's eight more gyms."

Sal came back, not looking like good news. She came up to the table and leaned against it with her hands. "Trouble," she said, very low. "They just found Dek's partner."

"Alive?" Meg asked.

"Neg. Shepherd found her drifting. At the Well."

Some things you heard and they just didn't make any kind of sense. A fool kid got killed in the far interface of the refinery zones, back sometime in March, and turned up a couple of hundred million k away in September, in a Shepherd recovery path?

"No way," Ben said.

"We have any word yet," Sal asked, "where Dek is?"

"No," Meg said, and leaned back as Mike brought the drinks.

"On my tab," Bird said to Mike, all business, and Mike cleverly made himself absent.

Ben hissed, "What do you mean, drifting at the Well? What in *hell's* going on?"

Sal shook her head, glitter and rattle of metal-tipped braids. "They don't know. Word's out on their net—codecom, to every Shepherd out there . . . you didn't hear that. They don't know if MamBitch can crack it, she gets mad as hell when they do it—but we got a seriously deviated 'driver out there."

"Fired a body at the Well?" Ben said. "God, somebody's stark crazy!"

"Worry what else they might do," Meg said. "If a general message is going out on the Shepherd net, that 'driver's going to hear the transmission, going to know the time and the PO, going to have an idea *what* that message was, even if they can't crack the code."

"*They're* not going to tell MamBitch anything," Sal said. Her voice was shaking. "But the question is how long the Shepherds can hold this quiet. This is a seriously bad time for Dek to go missing."

"If the cops haven't got him," Bird said. "Question is—does Mama know what's in that transmission? They'll pick him up."

Sal pulled two datacards from her pocket and laid them on the table. "That's from a couple of friends. We're them. They're real high Access. The word is Find Dek. Get him to the club next to Scorpio's, and don't use our cards or his."

Ben whispered, "Dammit, we got a launch tomorrow!"

"He may not make it."

We may not make it, Meg thought. The cards lay there—seriously illegal, what the Shepherds were doing and what they were risking. One kid was dead. Good chance there could be another.

She picked up one card.

Bird picked up the other.

The message stack was jammed by the time William Payne reached the office—halfway through an important dinner and three glasses of wine under his belt when the phone had rung, and he wished to hell he'd had at least one fewer. He turned on the light, slid into his chair and keyed on line, watching the flash of prioritied incomings—

His immediate superior, Crayton, with a cryptic memo: *An unexplained ship to ship message is proceeding from the Shepherds. Be alert for sabotage.*

A statement from the president of the board: *The company stands by its policy on abuse of communications.*

From Cooley, in News & Entertainment: *Continuing regular programming pending further instructions.*

From Salvatore, in Security: *Stage 1 alert in progress. Code team is assembling.*

Payne keyed on, waiting for Crayton's instructions to flow down, waiting for information to flow up from Salvatore. He was shivering. The temperature in the office was still coming up. Or it was nerves.

The Shepherd negotiations were in trouble, and *this* happened—they were clearly making a move and the company now had to break off the contract talks or lose credibility—

With agitators stirring up the dockworkers and the refinery workers spoiling for a chance to press their agendas—*real* problems in those groups. The EC insisted on dumping its touchy cases out here, and those problems didn't go away, they just recruited other problems and made demands. They opened valves in the mast. They slashed hoses. They vandalized plastics vats. Now the Shepherds committed a deliberate, massive defiance of company rules—outright challenging the company to take action, possibly even signaling the long-threatened work stoppage.

The right action, it had to be, and incoming information and outgoing instructions intersected at his desk in Public Information.

Continue the media blackout? That might keep the lid on for an hour, but it also made rumor the main source for the workers. Better to start dribbling out information as soon as he could get a policy direction out of Crayton: keep the workers glued to the vid reports and off the open decks. Some offices in the mast had equipment to hear that illicit transmission, and rumors were as quick as two workers hitting the 8-deck vending machines on coffee break. There were war jitters—and coded-com like that could set off alarms over in the shipyard, in the military base, God, clear to Earth's security zone.

He keyed up, composed a query from PI to Crayton in General Admin. *Request clearance for news release to forestall rumor and speculation.*

There were going to be hard questions for every administrator in the information chain. Every decision over the next few hours was going under a magnifying glass. The EC, the UN, UI—God only knew how far and how many careers were going down with this as it was; the Shepherds, damn them, were calling the company's bluff.

He wasn't in The Pacific, wasn't in the Tycho or the Europa or the Apollo, and so far as they could find out, he wasn't in any gym they'd ever used. They fanned out, gave up communication with each other—couldn't phone when you didn't know where to phone, and you never knew when the company was listening. I'll check 3, Meg told Ben, last time their paths crossed on the 'deck, and she caught the Trans to 3, to check the gyms there.

"Seen a dark-haired guy, rab cut, about 20, thin?"

No, no, and no. She had a stitch in her side, she had a bash on her elbow from a fast stop in .8 *g*, and she was running out of places that didn't involve the cops or the hospital. She imagined odd looks at her back, imagined the rumor starting to run the corridors: What's to do with the dark-haired rab? On helldeck she'd gotten Will I do's? from guys she asked, and the last try in the gym she hadn't—out of breath and looking like no joke at all. That wasn't good. That invited questions from the cops—especially with the Shepherds sending illegal transmissions. She took the stretch back toward the Transstation at a slow walk, catching her breath and racking her brain for where next to look, when the thought hit her that she was already on 3—and Dekker obviously hadn't done anything logical, or they'd have found him.

The cops might be tracking card use by now, and using a Shepherd card was about as nervous a proposition as using her own. But there were more Shepherds than there were Meg Kadys on R2, and a cop looking for a guy might just look past her. She about-faced and went for the core lift, used the card and rode it up with a couple of obnoxious tender-jocks who wanted to get friendly. She stared obdurately at the door, arms folded, sweating, panicked, thinking, God, no trouble, I *don't* want cops . . . *not* carrying an illegal card . . .

Up through lighter and lighter decks, where you had to take hold: the tender-jocks tried to talk her into getting off at 8 and going to a sleepery with them. She said no, very patiently, and swore she was going to hunt these guys down and kill them if she got out of this.

8. The jocks got off. Thank *God* . . . The car made the jolting transit to the core and stopped—the Access light went on and she shoved the card in, hoping to God customs wasn't on duty right now.

The door opened. She caught the grip on the line, and rode it through the numbing cold—no jacket, obviously not dressed for the core; but she'd done it before, and customs off in their warm little office had seen her come and go like this a dozen times.

Hope to God nobody's put a watch on the ships.

She was half-frozen by the time she'd braked off the line and caught *Trinidad*'s rigging-cord—hadn't even a hand-jet: she monkeyed over to the hatch, her breath coming in ragged, teeth-chattering hisses as she opened up and hauled herself through.

The damn fool was there, just doing a little wipe-down on a cabinet. He made a slow turn to look at her, all calm—like, What's the rush, Meg? What could possibly be the matter?

She brought up against a console, hauled herself steady against the recoil, out of breath, not knowing what that look meant—that he'd lost his mind and gone totally eetee, or that he was holding it together, up here testing the limits of his sanity.

"You kind of missed a dinner date," she said.

He blinked as if he were dropping into another track of thought. "God," he said, "I'm sorry."

Blank and innocent. She wasn't entirely sure he was sane right now, or that she was even safe with him in this lonely, noise-insulated place. She said, with her teeth chattering, "Dek, we got to get down and find Bird—right now. Something's come up."

"Something wrong?"

She wasn't about to explain to him here, alone. She grabbed his arm. "We just got a problem." Her teeth rattling made it hard to talk. "Come on, Dek, for God's sake, I'm freezing."

"What's going on?"

"Tell you on the way." She made a little finger-sign that meant *bug*. "Bird wants you. Now."

He disposed of the cloth he was holding. He wiped his fingers on his sweater, looking scared now.

But he dimmed the lights and followed her out of the hatch.

Message from Salvatore: *We've got some kind of stir among the military personnel on the 'deck—MP's and officers going from bar to bar, spreading out. Looks as if they're pulling their people off leave. . . .*

Payne passed the message on to Crayton's office and grabbed the phone. "FleetCom," he told it, and got one ring after another, then a robot.

"Input your priority please."

"This is Payne, ASTEX Public Information Office."

"Your call is entered in queue. Your call will be answered . . ."

Priority beeped him off. Red lights spread like plague across the phone console.

"Sir!" Salvatore said into his ear, but another priority beeped Salvatore down to autorecord.

The phone said, simultaneously with the computer, on voice: *". . . This is President Towney's office. We are in receipt of an uncoded message echoed from Shepherd craft at the Well, quote: . . . 'At 1540 hours on September 2nd, the Shepherd* Athens *picked up an anomalous object in the recovery zone. It proved to be human remains, carrying the identification of Corazon Salazar, a miner registered to R1, and reported lost earlier this year during a reported bumping incident between the 'driver* Industry *and the miner ship 1-89-Z. Our calculations indicate an origin consistent with other loads fired by the aforenamed 'driver. We are in possession of charts which indicate falsification of records. We are advising the company of these facts and we are demanding that charges immediately be filed of willful murder and attempted murder, with arrest warrants issued for the chief officers of the 'driver ship—'"*

Sweating, heart thumping, Payne keyed to Salvatore:

Whereabouts of Paul Dekker. Priority One.

CHAPTER 17

Dekker kept his jaw clamped on questions Meg clearly wasn't going to—"I don't *know* what the situation is right now," was the last information thing she'd yet said, when she'd insisted on stopping on 4-deck and walking breakneck to a lift that only took cards like the one she was using—which wasn't hers. Gold. The only card like that he'd ever seen was Shepherd Access.

He'd never seen this end of helldeck, either—where the lift let out. She led the way across the 'deck immediately to a door next to a fancy restaurant. A card-sized gold plaque was the only sign of business: the Shepherd emblem, Jupiter and the recovery track, right above the card-lock.

"What is this?" he asked.

Meg put the card in, shoved the door as the electronic lock clicked.

He ducked inside after her, into a carpeted reception room where he knew they didn't belong—by no right ought they to be here, except that card.

A blond man looked up from the reception desk.

Meg said, "This is Dek; Dek, Mitch. —Have we heard anything from the rest of us?"

"Neg," Mitch said, before Dekker could say anything, and pointed to the first door down the hall. "Wait in there. Both of you."

"I've got friends out there," Meg objected, "looking for him."

"We're *doing* something about it, Kady. We'll do it faster if you take care of him."

"Maybe you'd better tell me what's going on," Dekker said, but Meg grabbed him by the arm, said, "Dek, come on," and steered him down the hall.

"Dammit, Meg, —"

"Shit, I don't know, I don't know, come on, just awhile—sonuvabitch! I'm up to here with sons of bitches . . ." Meg took him back into an elegant deserted bar, left him standing while she turned on the lights and set up on her own, poured two fast, shaky drinks, one whiskey, one rum.

He came and leaned his elbows on the bar, said carefully: "We're not getting out of here tomorrow, are we?"

She took a sip of the whiskey and shoved the rum at him. "Drink up."

"Meg. What's happened? What are we doing here?"

She leaned on the bar, nudged his hand with her glass. "You seriously better have a little of that, jeune rab. —They found your partner."

That was it. —But the Shepherd Access, Meg's breathless rush—coming here . . . He stood bewildered. Meg came around the end of the bar and snagged him by the sleeve, pulled him to a table and set him down opposite her.

She said, "Dek, they found her at the Well. That sonuvabitch put her in a bucket and sent her a long tour of Jupiter. A Shepherd picked her up on the recovery path."

Meg sneaked up all gentle. Then she shot for the gut. His mind went blank and black—

That huge dark machine . . .

"Why in hell—" Breath dammed up in his throat. He couldn't get it out. He reached for the glass, slopped it left and right getting a drink.

Meg reached across the table, reached for his free hand as he set the glass down, squeezed his fingers til they hurt.

"Cher. Death is. Pain's life. And there's, above all, sons of bitches. Get your breath. You're not the only one who knows now. You're not alone out there. It's the independents . . . the freerunners . . . the Shepherds they were aiming at. The old, old business."

"But what in hell do they think they're doing?" His voice came out higher than he intended, hardly recognizable. "What kind of a game is this? How could they ever think they could get away with it?"

"There's crazy people. They shot us down at the company doors. News cameras everywhere. Everybody in the world saw it. How'd they get away with that, can you tell me, jeune rab? —Have your rum. The word's out on the Shepherds' com. They'll be hearing it at Sol about now. The company won't want you to talk, you understand—seriously won't want you to talk to anybody. That's what's going on. But if Mam-Bitch pushes now, the Shepherds are going to shut MamBitch down. Let the corp-rats fly the ships with their cut-rate crews. Let the company execs fly the Well."

"I want that guy, Meg."

"Close as we can come. You got the guys that launched him. *Some-body's* job's gone. Best you can do with these sumbitches."

He's reported in the core, the last report from Salvatore's office had said. They were still searching; and Payne, with Towney's office requesting the Dekker file, searched screen after screen of records generated by Salvatore's investigation.

Record score on re-certification. Cleared to retrain, shipping with the two miners who'd picked him up, plus a Kady and Aboujib, both female—

Ships both due to launch on the 18th, the sleepery owner swearing he had no idea in hell where Dekker was—Dekker has missed a supper appointment: his partners had been phoning around trying to find him. Dekker could have come and gone, the owner had no idea, he'd been watching the vid. Everybody in the bar had been watching the vid . . .

Aboujib and Pollard both had Shepherd parentage. Kady was a cashiered shuttle pilot. Bird had been a suspect in the Nouri affair, close friend of Pratt and Marks—

The file had gone to Towney's desk.

And the monkey was climbing up PI's back.

Nobody had told *his* office that Dekker was anything but, at absolute worst, a skimmer who'd gotten caught and bumped. Nobody had told him that a 'driver captain was going to make a gesture like this at the Shepherds.

He keyed up *Industry*'s record. Windowed in the second chart.

No record of asteroid 98879 prior to the incident. *Industry*'s transmission logged the discovery to the company. March 7th.

God.

Dekker had flat spooked out about the launch—that was Ben's opinion on the matter. They'd tried restaurants, game parlors, tried the bars again in the idea he could be skipping from one to the other, but the cops and the military were getting more and more visible on the 'deck.

To *hell* with that guy! Ben thought, trying to look inconspicuous while a group of military police came past the frontage. Inside, the vid was saying something about shifts held over due to "military exercises" and "a test of security procedures. . . ."

A hand landed on his shoulder. His heart nearly stopped. He spun around nose to nose with Bird.

"Don't *do* that!"

"Now *we* got a problem. We got wall to wall cops at The Hole."

He felt of his pocket, cold of a sudden. "Card's with me. We're all right."

" 'All right,' " Bird echoed him. "You got a hell of an idea of 'all right.' Have you seen Sal or Meg?"

"Not since an hour ago."

The PA blared out: *"Shifts will be held another hour. There is a Civil Defense Command exercise in progress. If you have an assigned CDC post on 3-shift, go to it immediately. If you have no assigned duty, clear the 'decks, repeat, all off-shift personnel get off the 'decks and return to quarters."*

"The hell," Bird muttered. "I've seen *this* before."

"What are they doing?"

"Cops," Bird said. "Martial law. Shit with finding the kid. They're going to shut him up, shut it down—it's Nouri all over again." Bird's hand closed on his arm. "And *we're* in it up to our ears, understand me?"

He did understand. He saw company cops moving through the crowds—saw blue-uniformed MP's too, with heavy sidearms.

Bird said, "This time we put the word out, just find some friends, spill the beans, tell them pass it on."

"Why risk *our* necks? We got enough troubles."

"That's what we said the last time."

"Bird, —those are guns out there!"

"Do you know the word 'railroad,' Ben-me-lad? Pratt and Marks were innocent. No way those boys were with Nouri's lot. Good, dumb kids. But now nobody's sure. —You do what you like."

"Where are you going?"

"Doing a little discreet talking around in various ears. The company's not hushing this one up. This time we know numbers. And dates."

His mind went scattering in panic—the launch tomorrow . . . but that wasn't going to happen. The urge to kill Dekker for involving them in this . . . but Dekker was probably the first one under arrest.

He took a fistful of Bird's coat, hauled him back. "Bird, —"

"I knew Pratt and Marks were being screwed," Bird said. "*I* had the evidence, you understand me. It could have tied *me* to Nouri—in certain eyes. Everybody was scared. Everybody was saving his own ass. And everybody lost. —Not this time."

"Bird, for God's sake—"

"This time it's *us* in the fire-path, you understand me? And we're not dumb kids. You've got that datacard. Give it to me."

Ben felt after the flat shape in his inside pocket, desperately trying to think what old classmates he knew that could fix *this* one—but there wasn't anyone. Not a damn soul who wouldn't be, the way Bird said, saving his own ass.

"*Give* it to me."

"What are you going to do?"

"Put it on the bulletin board. And pass the word."

"Shit!"

Bird leaned close and put a hand on his shoulder. "Find yourself a hole, hear me? Get down to the club. Don't know if Sal's friends'll let you in, but, hell, you've got ties there. Use 'em. It's the only hole might cover you."

Bird trying anything under the table—Bird didn't know shit about the safeguards on the computer systems, Bird didn't know shit what he was doing, dammit, those charts were their living—

They also were the only evidence that existed about where they'd been and what they'd done, and if the company arrested them and erased it—

"Hell," he said, "you've got that Shepherd card. Thing's got 1-deck Access."

"Do what with it? Hell, Ben, that thing's probably more dangerous—"

"Just leave the computer stuff to me and stay out of it, Bird, you don't know shit how to get past the lockouts. I can get into all the boards, hell, I can get it into general systems, Bird, I know the modem codes . . ."

"Where in *hell* did you get those?"

He said, "Just give me the fuckin' card, Bird, and tell 'em the filename's *Dekker*."

* * *

"Mr. Crayton is in conference," the secretary said, and Payne shot the memo through in desperation. "Give *that* to him. We've got to have a policy decision. Thirty minutes ago!"

"I believe that's the subject of the con—"

Payne hung up in frustration, and stared at the stalled press release on his screen. Then he shot it unapproved to News & Entertainment, for release.

The nature of a coded Shepherd transmission has been revealed as a query to Shepherd senior administration regarding the discovery of human remains in a Shepherd recovery zone. Company records have tentatively identified the body as likely that of Corazon Salazar, lost earlier this year in an accident near the R2/R1 boundary. Ms. Salazar, daughter of Alyce Salazar, a MarsCorp board member and prominent member of the Defense Advisory Council, was two years resident on R1. She was apparently struck and killed while EVA when a tank explosion sent her ship out of control. The ship then traveled helplessly at high velocity into R2 zone. Dr. Ronald Michaels, of the Institute, has offered the theory that the body, traveling in the firepath of the 'driver ship Industry, *was struck by one of the loads and carried along with it at a velocity sufficient to delivery it to the recovery site.*

The Shepherd discovery adds another chapter to the already tragic story of the ill-fated miner craft Way Out. *The surviving partner, Mr. Paul Dekker, was rescued earlier this year by an R2 ship dispatched to his rescue. Mr. Dekker, surviving isolation, cold and failing life-support after an amazing 71 days adrift, was released from James R. Reynolds Hospital after extensive treatment for physiological and psychological trauma. A spokesman for the hospital this shift expressed concern that Mr. Dekker has not responded to urgent attempts to notify him in advance of public release of this news. Mr. Dekker currently remains unlocatable on R2. Dr. Emil Visconti, Mr. Dekker's physician, authorized release of the news in the fear that Mr. Dekker has heard the report via other sources and appealed for Mr. Dekker or anyone knowing his whereabouts to call Security or the information desk at Reynolds Hospital immediately. Mr. Dekker is on medication and may have suffered disorientation or mental confusion due to the stress of this tragic report, and may be despondent. A spokesman for ASTEX Administration assures Mr. Dekker that he has been cleared of all fault in the accident, which occurred as the result of a catastrophic equipment failure, and urges Mr. Dekker to contact the hospital immediately. . . .*

Damn him. Damn Crayton—dumping a case like this on him with no indication at all that it had hidden problems.

Now Crayton couldn't even clear a press release. He had to put his neck on the line, *try* to keep the lid on—knowing that win or lose, this was something the company would want black-holed. Lost. Forgotten. Along with anybody in any way tainted with it.

The comp took the message. Another one windowed up, for Salvatore:

A Shepherd came and went at the core between 2041 and 2108h. Customs didn't see him. They were in the office listening to the outlaw transmission. The card belonged to a tech named Nate Chaney, who isn't answering to calls at his listed numbers . . .

No way to get to the rental comp at The Hole—but any phone would do, that had a keypad, and Io's fancy establishment had that amenity. Neon flashed, dyed the beer green and red while it shook in the glass. Couldn't hear a core blowout in this place, Ben thought, and it was crawling with low-level corporates—but he was wearing his best 'deck casuals and the corner of the bar afforded a dark area. Shepherd card first: then his:

Boot file: PROCESS. Invoke: CALL13; README5; ADD2; ADD1; ADD3

Boot memory resident file: PROCESS2. Enter.

Student pranks. The datawindow showed dots, the Egg assembling its parts and pieces.

The datawindow said: CALLME: INS TXT

INPUT: $/CHART.CUR; CHART.14; CHART.15

OUTPUT: DEKKER

The datawindow said: ENTER SYSACC

His hands trembled over the keys. He didn't think about cops. Or the corporate behind him, waiting to use the phone. He thought about data. He typed, rapidfire: *2;20;W489\209:INSTAL:C\$/$y;*BOOT3;*3.|/$;{rs/#}/p*280:#[TAG/*1]

He switched datacards—inserted the Shepherd's before the pause ran out.

Phone charge went to the Shepherd card. The Run trigger waited the first phone user after him. Nasty trick on the guy fidgeting behind him. *He'd* be out of the bar.

He sipped the beer, punched charge, extracted the card and palmed it for his, held that one up, right color for a miner, if it mattered in the blue strobe, indication to the bar he'd paid: "Thanks," he called out, drowned in the general thunder of the bass line, left his beer on the bar and went out the door.

He had the general shakes by then—but, damn, he'd really *done* it, he'd actually *run* the thing—his own tinkered-up finesse on an old Institute prank—with Assay Office bank and com direct line access numbers and a Shepherd's 1-deck phone system authorizations. The question was now whether he was ahead of the current game with the trap programs—

—and whether he could get Bird off the 'deck—whether he could *find* Bird, before the cops did.

The cops were out in force, clearing the 'deck. It was the old game, the cops said Move along, you said, Yes, sir, and you went somewhere else you didn't live—helldeck played that game, the cops knew it was a game—didn't push it too hard, helldeck crowd being what they were. They were going to have to make the sleeperies close their bars to everybody but residents, if they were serious and not just Making the Presence Felt: and *that* move would lock legitimate residents out on the 'deck and have angry confrontations left and right—not what they were after, Ben told himself; but if it was your face they might be looking for, it seemed a good idea to hang to the back of crowds, keep behind taller people and drift on when they did.

God, he thought, no knowing what Bird's puttering around into. I got to get him to cover somewhere—and if they pick us up, we just go along with it, take it easy, wait for the upper echelons to sort it out.

No way they're going to screw us for this one—too many people know the truth, too many people on corp-deck are going to be covering their asses, and to do that, they have to cover *ours*, axe that sumbitch captain out there—and any clerk they can pin it on: those are the ones who need to worry.

Maybe we can even parlay this into a company buyoff, get us that helldeck office—

Justice, hell, Bird, —it's the names you know that matter. It's where they are and what you can do to them in court.

Wipe down this card is all—

Slip it right into the trashbin.

"Screwed the kid good," Bird said, leaning close to Abe Persky, whispering over the music in the Europa. "But what they did to the girl, that wasn't any company order. That was a 'driver/Shepherd piece of business—damn sight more than letting a rock drift from a sling, this time. Shepherds are broadcasting it, outside code now—they'll hear it clear to Earth, plain as plain. *That's* what the alert is about."

"Damn," Persky said with a shake of his head.

"Listen. I dumped my charts to the helldeck board—might check it before they catch it. Filename's *Dekker. D-e-k-k-e-r.*" He nudged Persky's arm. "Pass it on, everyone you know."

"Got you," Persky said, and reached for his datacard. Nudged him back as he was leaving. "*Careful*, Bird."

Collins' table next. Collins was a company pilot now, but he didn't like being that. He came to helldeck to keep up old acquaintances. He was sitting with Robley—Robley was doing factory work now: the kidneys had gone.

He sat down with Collins and Robley, and saw Persky pay out and leave.

Just one and two at a time. But the 'deck telegraph moved like lightning.

Another call from Payne's office. Salvatore said, "Yes, sir," and, "We're trying, sir, we've thought of that, sir, we're trying that too . . ."

Payne said: "Don't tell me 'trying.' I want all the records, I want the whole file on this guy. On *all* of them. Don't give me another dead kid with relatives in MarsCorp, dammit, Administration's had enough surprises in this case! I want to know who this Dekker is, I want to know if he's got a record, I don't care if it's a misdemeanor, I want a total profile on him! You hear me? All the files, no ten-year cutoff, I want them as far back as they go, and I want them yesterday!"

Payne hung up. The comp flashed up a new message: *Workers in Textiles 2B are demanding to be let go. There's been some breakage, some pushing and shoving, manager's scared and wants some help.*

And another from Crayton's office: *Fleet Operations is recalling its personnel from liberty, stationing armed guards at two shuttle docks and at essential lifesupport and manufacturing accesses. We need immediate operations coordination. . . .*

God, Salvatore thought, and a report from Wills came in:

Morris Bird had dinner reservations at the Europa, for five. It was a no-show.

He *wanted* the inhaler. He didn't dare. "Call my wife at home," he told his secretary. "Tell her to check on my daughter. Make sure she's in the dorm." He sipped cold coffee, trying to think who he could spare to liaison with the MP's.

More messages crawled across the screen. *A man is having chest pains in Textiles 2B. Paramedics have been called. . . .*

Wills again: *Brown's turned up a witness in customs who thinks Meg Kady was in the core at about 2040h. He's not sure on that, says he saw all of them come and go the last few days taking parts back and forth—they had a permit for that, a ship in refit. We do have a confirmation on a card access for Dekker up there at 1723h. No exit. No card use at all from Kady since a phone call at 1846, from The Black Hole to The Pacific. The owner at The Black Hole claims they all left about 1900. He thinks.*

Two people slipping a security gate on a borrowed card. Happened once or twice a week, usually for assignations. The mast was a hell of a job to search, even under optimum conditions.

Textiles 2B reports a riot in progress. Manager requests additional security and paramedics . . .

Priority came through, bumped that: *Virus Alert: Technical level shutdown.*

Priority override: *A virus is copying an unauthorized file through the Belt Management System. Contents are illicit sector charts. Virus variation on COPYIT. Request computer crimes division to trace and erase proliferation through BM system.*

". . . cleared of all fault in the accident, which occurred as the result of a catastrophic equipment failure, and urges Mr. Dekker to contact the hospital immediately. . . ."

Bird gave the vid a look over his shoulder, shook his head and looked at Tim Egel. "You're a good numbers man. You believe that line?"

"No," Egel said. "Not the tooth fairy either. Shoved to the Well by a load. I'd like to see the math on that one."

"They don't teach physics in Business Ad."

"Don't teach math either, do they?" That was a tenderjock, in on it, beer in hand. "What kind of stuff is that they're giving out?"

"They want Dekker back in hospital. They worked him over with drugs. But he remembered the numbers anyway. That's what they can't cover up. 79, 709, 12. There was a bloody great rock there. That's what it was about. That 'driver came down on them while they were tagging it. Now the 'driver's sitting out there stripping that rock to loads. I'd like to match those loads with the sample Dekker had in his sling."

"Can anybody do that?"

"I got the sample. It's on record in Assay."

"This here's Morrie Bird," Egel said. "The guy that brought Dekker in."

"No shit! I heard of you! You're the *old* guy!"

Being famous got you drinks. Being famous could also get you arrested. He took a couple of swigs from the beer the guy insisted to buy him, and set it down, said, "If you're curious, check the boards for a file named Dekker. With two k's."

"Dekker," the jock said.

Egel said, in Bird's diminishing hearing, "*I'll* tell you what they're up to, friend. They weren't going to pay that rock out to any freerunner. Pretty soon they won't pay it to a company miner either. Or the tenders. When the freerunners go, there go the perks *anybody* gets on the company ticket. When they don't have to compete with independents like us . . ."

"They can't do that," somebody else said.

Time to leave, Bird thought. Getting a little warm in here. He set his drink down and slid backward in the crowd, faced about for an escape and saw cops coming into the place.

The cops waded in through the middle of the crowd yelling something about a closing order and residents only; and he stuck to the shadows until there was a clear doorway.

Outside, then. In the clear. But that was it—cops were getting just a little active.

"Where *are* they?" Meg asked the only live human being she could find in the place—no Mitch, now, just this pasty-faced guy at the desk with the phone, with no calls coming in that she'd heard. Nothing was coming in, that she could tell, not even the vid, for what good it might be.

"No word yet," the Shepherd said—guy in his thirties, serious longnose, busy with the com-plug in his ear—*not* liking real rab on his clean club carpet. He focused for a moment, lifted a manicured hand to delay her. "Ms. Kady—go a little easy on the whiskey."

She'd started away. She came back, leaned her hands on the desk. "I'm all right on the whiskey, mister. Where's Mitch? Where's my partner?"

"We have other problems."

"What?"

A wave-off. A frown on the Shepherd's face. He was listening to something. Then not.

"Look. I hate like hell to inconvenience you guys, but I have a seriously upset guy in there who's damned tired of runarounds. So am I. Suppose you tell me what's going on."

"A great many police is what's going on. They're still holding 2-shift."

"Shit."

"Don't be an ass, Kady. —That door's locked."

"Then open it!"

"Kady, get the hell back to the bar—get that kid back in there."

"Meg?"

She turned around, saw Dekker in the foyer. "Dek, just be patient, I'm trying to get some answers."

"There aren't any answers, Kady, just keep the kid entertained."

She saw a flash of total red. Bang, with her hand on the counter. "Listen, you son of a bitch—where the fuck is my partner?"

"I don't know where your partner is. If she followed orders she'd be here."

"She doesn't know we've got him! She's not on your network!"

"I don't know where a lot of people are, right now, Kady—we've got a lot more problems than your—" The Shepherd pressed his earpiece closer, held up a hand for silence.

"What?"

"They're bringing that warship's engines up, over at the 'yard. They want us out of here."

"They. Who, 'they'?"

"The *Hamilton*. There's a shuttle on the mast. But we aren't getting com with it. *Hamilton*'s saying it can't raise it. That's our contingency sitting up there."

"Shit! This is going to hell, mister!"

"Shut *up*, Kady!"

Message from CCrimes: *Ordering immediate shutdown of the banking system. The virus has entered 2-deck bulletin boards, spreading on infected cards with each use . . .*

The man in Textiles 2B had died. There was a broken leg in a fall off a catwalk, there was damage to the machinery, a woman had gone into labor—Salvatore had a view from an Optex and it was a mess. They had the phones stopped on 2, but the damn chart had proliferated from the bulletin boards to the card charge system, sent itself into every trade establishment on R2, and they didn't know if it was into the bank databank itself.

He washed an antacid down with stale coffee, and tried to placate

Payne. Payne said he had to go to a meeting. Payne said his aide LeBrun was handling the office.

Damned right there was a meeting. There had better be a meeting real soon now. With some faster policy decisions. Salvatore's hands were shaking, and he didn't know who he could trust to handle emergencies long enough for him to get to the restroom and back.

"Sir," the intercom said, "sir, a Lt. Porey to see you."

He didn't have any Lt. Porey on his list. He started to protest he wasn't seeing anybody, but the door opened without further warning, and a Fleet officer walked in on him, *with* his aide. "Mr. Salvatore," the man said. African features. An accent he couldn't place. And a deep-spacer prig Attitude, he'd lay money on it, expecting stations to run on *his* schedule.

He got up. A second aide showed up, blocked his secretary out of the doorway. And shut the door.

"Mr. Porey." He offered a grudging hand to a crisp, perfunctory grip, all the while thinking: We're going to discuss this one with Crayton. Damned if not.

"*Mr.* Salvatore, we have a developing situation on 2-deck. Rumor is loose, and some *ass* in your office is referring FleetCom to PI—"

God, a *pissed-off* Fleet prig. "That's the chain of command."

"Not in *our* operations. I want the files on this Dekker and I want the files on the entire Shepherd leadership."

"I'm afraid all that's under our jurisdiction, Mr. Porey: you'll have to get an administrative clearance for that access. I can refer you to Mr. Crayton, in General Admin—"

Porey reached inside his coat, pulled a card from his pocket and tossed it down on his desk. "Put *that* authorization in your reader."

Salvatore picked up the card with the least dawning apprehension they were in deep, EC-level trouble, and put it in the reader slot.

It said, *Earth Company Executive Order, Office of the President, Sol Station, Earth Administration Zone.*

To all officers and agents of Security and Communications, ASTEX Administrative Territories:

By the authority of the Executive Board and a unanimous vote of the Directors, a state of emergency is deemed to exist in ASTEX operations which place military priority contracts in jeopardy. ASTEX Security and Communications agencies and employees are hereby notified of the transfer of all affected assets and operations to the authority of EcoCorp, under ASTEX Charter provision 28 hereafter appended, and subject to the orders of EcoCorp Directors . . . I hereby and herewith order ASTEX company police and life services officers to place themselves directly under the order of UDC Security Office in safeguarding records and personnel during this transfer of operational authority.

Salvatore sat down and read it again.

"Effectively," Porey said, "your paycheck comes directly from the EC now. You're a civilian law enforcement officer in a strategically sensitive operation, subject to the rules and decisions of the UDC, the UN and the EC officers and board. I'm directing you to turn over those files."

"You can't have gotten an order from the EC—you haven't had the time to get a reply."

"Good, Mr. Salvatore. You are a critical thinker. There were triggering mechanisms. The transfer document has lain on my commanding officer's desk for some few days. But I'd think again about destroying files, or advising your former administrators of your change of loyalties. You have a long career with the EC in front of you if you use your head. I can't say that about all your managers." A second card hit the desk. "That goes in a Security terminal. It will make its own accesses. Can you trust your secretary?"

"I—" He saw the guns—automatics. Explosive shells. Not riot control gear. And not ASTEX any longer. "I think I'd better explain it to him," he said, and thought about his wife, about his daughter. He took the card, slid it into the computer and pressed ENTER.

The screen went to Access, and came up again with a series of dots. Porey folded his arms and watched it a moment, looked his way then with the tilt of a brow.

"The *Industry* file. Purge it, among first things."

"*Purge* it? *Erase* it?"

"It's become irrelevant. Personnel have already been transferred. Certain questions won't be asked beyond this office. That's official, Mr. Salvatore. Your career could rise or fall on that simple point. Take great care how you dispose of it. —Mr. Paget."

"Sir!"

"*Find* Paul Dekker and escort him to the dock."

"So what's the new plan?" Meg asked, she thought with great restraint, standing between Dekker's temper and some fill-in Shepherd data-jock with a rulebook up his ass who persisted in trying to get contact with a shuttle that was probably—

The Shepherd said, "They're still not getting through to Mitch—they're jamming us."

"So what do you expect? It's not just the company anymore, it's the soldiers, for God's sake, and you can't *hide* on a station—"

"You can't hide a ship, either, Kady. I'm not sure how long my ship can hold position out there—"

"Then let's get up to the dock. Play it by ear for God's sake!"

"This isn't a game, woman, we don't know if the lifts are working—"

"Sit on your ass a little longer and we won't know what *else* won't be working when we need it."

"I'm the only contact our people *have* on this station—I have my orders—Mitch is—"

"*Mitch* isn't answering, you're not contacting anybody out there, the phones are down, the soldiers are all up and down the 'deck, for God's sake—let's get the *hell* up to the dock, if that's our option!"

"It does us no good to get to the shuttle, our pilot's out there on the 'deck!"

"Is *that* your problem? Well, you're in luck, mister! You're up to your ass in pilots."

"C-class, Kady, not a miner craft—"

"Earth to orbit, ship to station, *B1*, anything you can dock at this hellhole. Let's just get the hell up there."

"Kady, there's police out there. There's armed police in front of our door. D' you have a way we're going to get past them?"

Good question.

A whole squad of soldiers passed, going somewhere in a hurry. Ben found sudden interest in a bar window, in a crowd of exiting patrons. They *were* shutting the bars, dammit. At least closing the doors.

Serious time to get somewhere. Bird might have headed back to The Hole, Bird might have been arrested by now, God only where he was.

A touch brushed his arm. His heart turned over. He looked in that direction and saw a coffee-dark face under a docker's knit cap.

Dock monkey's coveralls, too. When women were damn scarce on the docks. "What are *you* doing?"

"Getting to the club unobviously as I can, which I think the both of us urgently better. Any word on Dekker?"

"No, damn him, I'm looking for Bird right now."

"We better get him. They got soldier-boys with rifles now. They pulled those lads off liberty and they're putting some of them down by the offices."

"Damn, I don't like that."

"No argument, cher. Some of those guys are still flying a little."

"Bright. Corporate bright, there."

"Ain't corp-rat, cher, that's the so'jers—which we got gathering right down there. Don't look. Just let's stroll along and find Bird."

He hadn't been entirely scared until now. He started to walk, hearing distant shouting. People were coming out of the bar behind their backs.

A beer mug hit the 'deck and broke.

"Just keep walking," Sal said.

"Don't hold my arm. You're a guy, dammit!"

"Yeah," Sal said, and dropped it.

Try to find a match on a refinery station—

"There's candles in Scorpio's," the Shepherd said, rummaging the repair-kit.

"Not excessively helpful, mister. Never mind the screwdriver. Screw. Have you got a brass screw? Wire?"

Dekker objected, "Meg, what are you doing?"

She pulled the cover off the door-switch. "Wait-see, cher rab. God, the man has wire. What are we coming to?"

"A short's only going to start the—"

Dekker got this look then.

"Yeah," she said, winding wire about bare contacts. "Remember the '15, cher? Want you to take a few napkins, and the vodka bottles. . . . Won't take me a minute here."

"That door's going to seal," the Shepherd said, "the second the fire-sensor goes off. We'll suffocate."

"Uh-uh. Door's going to stay open. Make me happy. Say we got fire-masks in here."

CHAPTER 18

The emergency speakers said, from every other store front: *This is a full security alert. Go to your residences immediately. Go to your residences immediately. Clear the walkways for emergency vehicles.*

Sal said: "So what are we supposed to do, go home or clear the walkways? Stupid shits!"

"I don't like this," Ben said.

"Seriously time to get down to the club."

The wires sparked and melted, the door opened, Meg whipped a chair into the doorway and ducked back. Shots spattered. Dekker kept his hands steady: the toilet paper caught, the cloth fibers caught, the cloth caught, blue fire in the folds; Dekker lit the next and Meg snatched the bottle and threw it into the hall.

It shattered. Dekker lit a third vodka bottle, passed it, and Meg lobbed the second out the door and ducked back as somebody screamed in pain.

The Shepherd was on a chair with another bit of burning cloth. The smoke alarm went off inside. The fire-system started spraying, the door tried to shut as shots spattered off the edge and blew hell out of the chair back. They were down to gin bottles.

Fire-spray started outside, white chemical clouds billowing up.

"That's got it," Meg said, pulled her mask up, trod on the chair and cleared it into the smoke outside as shots went past the door.

No notion whether she'd made it, no knowledge how to dodge or duck—he just deafened himself to the shots, cleared the chair and hugged the wall in the neon-lit smoke—running shadows rushed out of Scorpio's, screaming in panic.

Shots slammed into the crowd. Bodies flew; voices shrieked above the wailing siren. He sprinted past the restaurant's blue glare, dodged runners in the mist, not caring right now if the Shepherd was behind them or not—Meg was ahead of him trying for the Emergency Shaft, Meg had the Shepherds' key, and people who'd been taking cover in the restaurant were running every which way through the mist and into the gunfire.

He saw Meg stop, saw her trying to get the key in a slot.

A shot blasted a gouge in the wall beyond her—he flinched, pressed himself as flat to the wall as he could.

"Take the lift on the next level," the Shepherd gasped, clutching at his shoulder, beside them. "They're bound to have our cards blocked— Use your own. Berth 18 if we get separated—"

People were bunching up around them in panic—somebody in a waiter's uniform had a key, shoved Meg aside. The door opened. Meg slid in with the crowd and he pushed after her, he didn't care who he knocked out of the way—there were more and more pushing at their backs, the rush shoving them past the second door and up the steps. He pulled his mask down for air, grabbed the rail to keep from being shoved down and pushed all the way into the clear, with the Shepherd close behind, around the turn and up.

"3-deck damn door isn't going to work!" the Shepherd yelled out of the clangor behind them in the stairwell. "Door's still open down there! Go for 4-deck, get a door shut behind us!"

Dekker turned his shoulders, grabbed a handhold, forced his way past panicked, flagging clerks and restaurant help—the Shepherd yelling "Go!" and shoving him from behind.

A hundred feet each deck level. No way clerks and waiters could outclimb spacer legs—on the end of four months' gym time. Meg was out of sight above them.

A siren had started in the distance—around the curvature of the 'deck. Ben couldn't see where—but, God, it was the direction of the club—where they were going.

"Come *on*," Sal cried, trying to hurry him—grabbed his hand and pulled him through the crowd coming out of the Amalthea, but steps raced behind them. "Hold it!" a shout came from close at their backs: a hand grabbed Ben's shoulder and spun him around and back, bang up against the plex front of the bar. He found himself nose to nose with a cop, with a stick jammed up under his chin.

"Pollard, is it?"

Shit, he thought, struggling for air.

Out of nowhere, Bird's voice said, "Hey! Hey, what do you think you're dealing with?" Bird came up and caught the cop's shoulder, another cop grabbed Bird and somebody in the crowd spun the cop around face-on with a beer mug.

"Hold it," Ben tried to say, "wait, dammit, *—Bird!*"

Something banged, the plex window shook to an impact, and there was blood all over—he slipped, and the cop's riot stick came away as he hit on his knees, Bird was lying there with a bloody great hole in his sleeve and a look of shock on his face. All else he could see was legs and all else he could hear was people cursing and screaming. He scrambled over, grabbed Bird's coat and dragged him up close against the frontage, Bird fainting on him, people trampling them until he had a moment of clear space and Sal grabbed his arm to pull him to his feet.

"Ben! Come *on!*"

He scrambled for his feet, pulling at Bird. Sal hauled, Bird tried to get his legs under him, and they threw arms around him and ran with the crowd, battered and staggered by people passing them, Bird doing the best he could, Sal shoving him up from the other side—gunfire and shouts echoed at their backs.

Screaming broke out ahead of them; and the crowd ebbed back at them without warning, shoved them the other way. The PA said, echoing over the shouting and the distant siren, *This is not a test. This is a real emergency—*

"Stairs," Bird gasped, and Ben thought, God, where are they? You passed them time and again, the utility accesses—between the frontages, back in the bars—

—used to use them in the Institute, up and down the dorms, you used to duck under the security cameras—

One was right next to The Hole, that was where.

His lungs were burning, Bird was losing his footing, stumbling with every step as they reached the alcove and Sal shoved at the door.

"Mike's got a key," Bird gasped.

"Hell with that," Ben said, and hit #, /, and 9 simultaneously, 8, 0, and /. Management Emergency Access.

They weren't the only ones that wanted the stairs—"Get out of my way!" Ben snapped at Sal, feeling the panic in the crowd as they pushed for the opening door—God, they couldn't climb and carry Bird between them: he got a shoulder under him and carried him solo, with Sal running the stairs ahead of him. Hysterical people shoved him from behind, shoved past, nearly knocked him down, and then somebody with sense, thank God, pulled him square again and shoved him forward when his balance faltered.

"Lock *through*, dammit!" Sal yelled—downside door shut was the only way the door up on 3-deck would open; and the guys ahead of her got out. Ben saw it through a black-rimmed blur, heard it through the ringing of the steps and the pounding in his chest, one thin feminine voice, "E-drill, *ten at a time*, you dumbass bastards!"

They had a human wave behind them. Sal was holding the door open. Sal screamed at them to get in, and the guys behind—thank God, must have had the sense to turn around in the lock and shove the tide back. The doors shut, the hallway door opened, and they had the clear cold air of 3-deck.

"Core-lift!" Sal yelled, grabbing him. He didn't know how he could do it, but Bird wasn't in any shape to carry himself. His knees and his ankles were giving and wobbling with every step, his vision was nearly gone—people were scattering past them in every direction, piling into the Trans, any way in hell they could get away. He couldn't get enough wind, he knew his knees were going, but it was close . . . he knew it was close.

He couldn't see anything but blurs—didn't even know where they were, except Sal kept him straight, and Sal hit the button when they got there and propped him on his feet—he kept blinking sweat out of his eyes, couldn't hear anything but his heartbeat and distant screams, was scared mindless the core-lift was shut off at 3 with the alarms down on helldeck, but the door opened, welcomed them with white light and cold air.

She got the door shut. He stooped, eased Bird down from his shoulder, held on to him til he could lean him against the wall—Bird's face was white even after the headdown carry, Bird's blood was soaking him, but Bird breathed something coherent about the door.

Sal was trying to card it to move. He staggered to the panel to try the E-code, but abruptly the power cut in without his touching it and the car rose—

"What did you do?" he gasped—but then the car slowed down again, on 4, and the door opened, on an out-of-breath Meg, Dekker, and a Shepherd with a key—

"God," Meg said. And: "Bird?"

The Shepherd shoved them in ahead of him and keyed them from the core as fast as Ben could get his next breath—bent double with the pain in his gut, while Meg and Sal were kneeling and trying to take care of Bird.

"We waited," Dekker panted. "Long as we could—"

Ben nodded. He didn't have the breath to tell Dekker he was an ass and it was his damned fault, he wasn't sure he could get his next gasp. He waved a helpless gesture at Bird, meaning take care of him, fool, do something for him: he couldn't straighten—while the car shot for the core and the Shepherd said, "We don't know what's going to be waiting for us up there. The minute the door's open, out and hit the handlines. If he can't hold the line—" A breathless wave of the hand in Bird's direction. "There's no way to take him."

"Screw you!" Dekker said. "We're taking him."

"There's guards on the dock up there!"

"Then screw them too!" Dekker yelled.

"Listen, kid, —"

"Shut *up!*" Meg yelled, and Ben saw the way Meg was holding Bird—how of a sudden Bird had become weight in her arms and his eyes and his mouth were still open. No, Ben thought; he couldn't move, just stood there, waiting for Bird to move, bent over with the ache in his gut, until Sal got up and took hold of him and a handhold, because they were approaching the null-zone.

Meg said, between breaths, Bird still locked in her arms, "We got a shuttle at 18, clear down the far end of the mast, dumb shits couldn't park it closer—going to take us out to a Shepherd ship. They got that carrier coming this way from the shipyard, don't know if it's got guns mounted."

"It's fast," the Shepherd said. "Too damn fast."

Their talk went past Ben's ears. It ran through his brain, as a set of facts explaining where they were going and that their chances weren't good. He thought he ought to come up with a better idea, but his brain wasn't working right—he just felt the lift reach that queasy spot and felt his gut knot up.

Bird wasn't dead, Bird couldn't be gone—it didn't make sense to him. He'd done everything he could and somehow Bird just—went out on them and he didn't know what to do with him. It wasn't damned fair, what had happened—he'd *carried* him, dammit, til his gut was full of knives, and Bird wasn't friggin' dead, he couldn't go like that—

Dekker reached in slow-motion after his arm as the car clanked into the interface. Dekker held on to him until the car stopped and the doors opened. The Shepherd made the first swing from the lift's safety grip to the mounting bar and hand-over-handed himself toward the line. Meg had let Bird go, and Meg went next—

Nothing else to do, Ben thought, with an anguished glance at Bird drifting there so white and different, among beads of blood, and grabbed the mounting bar and went, fast as he could. Without Bird.

Eerie quiet in the core. The chute was silent. You could hear the line moving in the slot, you could hear the low static hum of the rotation interface. Couldn't see anything for a moment but the line's motor housing slipping past them.

He looked back, to be sure it was all real. But Sal and Dekker were reaching for the line, blocking his view of the inside of the car.

Meg was on the line behind the Shepherd, he was three spaces back. They passed the housing out into the open, out where the core spun to a dizzy vanishing point and tricked the eye and an already aching stomach. He held on—just held on, while muscles cramped in the cold.

Past the customs zone. He kept thinking—what if someone had a gun—what if they know where we are? Nothing they could do up here. Nothing but go at the pace of the line. Cold chilled his blood-soaked clothing and turned it stiff. Fingers lost all feeling, eyes teared from the cold, more bitter than he'd ever felt it, and the line moved at the same steady pace, clank, clank, clank—with his teeth chattering and the only thought in his head now just keeping his fingers closed on the handgrip. Meg had said berth 18. 18 was hell and gone at the end of the mast. Shuttle out to a ship that was going to take Dekker and the rest of them out of here, he guessed, but the only thought that kept replaying, over and over again, was that gun going off, Bird getting hit—

He hadn't had time to stop the bleeding, dammit. Hadn't had time—Sal had known where she was going, Sal had known about the shuttle—hadn't told them, God, he should have told her to go to hell, taken Bird to the Trans, taken him to the hospital—Bird shouldn't be dead. . . .

It was *Trinidad* they were passing, now, *Way Out* mated to her for the trip they weren't going to take. They'd been so damn close—

Movement caught his eye, against the steady spin of the core, big supply can drifting free—hell! he thought, shocked by the sight, damned dangerous, a thing the size of a skimmer floating along like that with no pusher attached—

He thought—as clearly as he was thinking at all—that's wrong.

That's *wrong*, that is—

The line jolted and stopped.

"Shit!" Sal gasped, loud in that sudden silence, and Dekker thought—we're not going to get there, it's not going to work—we're hanging up here and we can't reach the shuttle—can't reach the dismount lines. . . .

"Hand off the line!" Meg yelled of a sudden, juvie lessons, old safety drill. He reached for Sal, caught her hand—saw, all of a sudden, the whole line bucking, a wave coming toward them.

Dekker yelled, "Let *go!*" and threw everything he had into the chain they made, hand to hand—he threw his whole body into that snap-the-whip twist, aimed as best he could and let *go*—

A moment of floating free, then, nothing they could do if that line hit them, if they missed the dismount-line—

The wave sang overhead and passed. The Shepherd snagged a dismount line with his foot and hauled them all toward it.

Meg called out, "Center-mast! We can't make the shuttle, we got our *own* ship there. Her tanks are charged!"

"Won't dock!" the Shepherd yelled back. "Won't *mate*, dammit!"

"Take what we can fuckin' *get*," Sal yelled. "They've turned the line loose, there's no way we can get there, Sammy, move your butt!"

Fire popped, somewhere, Dekker had learned that sound. "They're shooting at something," he called out, following Sal and Ben down the line that connected along the dockage.

Something sang past him. He thought, God, they're *fools*, there's seals where we are and they're shooting bullets—

Another ricochet—he saw Meg kicked sideways, blood spraying—thought she was going off the line, but her left hand held the line, and Sal caught up and grabbed her jacket. He made a fast catch-up to help both of them, but Meg had caught Sal's coat with her left hand, blood floating in great dark beads near her other arm. Sal screamed at Ben to get out of her way, get the hatch open.

Ben scrambled along the line and overtook the Shepherd at *Trinidad*'s entry. Sal took a swing and floated free toward them and Dekker hurled himself after, caught Meg's arm and got his hand over the bleeding as Ben and the Shepherd grabbed their clothes and hauled them into the open hatch.

"Get it closed!" he gasped, stopping with a shove of his foot on a touch-pad. "Meg, —"

Meg's own hand shoved his aside, clamped down on the arm. "I got it, I got it," Meg said between her teeth. "God, just get me a patch—get us the hell out of here! Get us to the shuttle, 18, this guy'll tell you—"

"We can't mate with a shuttle-dock!" the Shepherd cried. "We've lost it, dammit, all we are is under cover. Aboujib, get com, get contact with the *Hamilton*, tell them our situation, see if they can talk us out of this—"

"Severely small chance, Sammy."

Severely small, Meg told herself, couldn't move her arm for Ben to get a wrap on it, sleeve and all—spurting blood everywhere, real close to going out.

Like Bird.

No fuss, not overmuch pain, just—going out.

"Hang on," Ben said, and hurt her with the bandage. "Damn it, Meg, pay attention! Hold on to it!"

Grapples banged loose. She thought, Good boy, Dek, . . .

. . . Bills every damn where on the table, Bird excused himself up to the bar, talked to Mike a minute, Bird about as upset as she'd ever seen him during the days when they were trying to fix that ship. Bird was working himself up to a heart attack. Meanwhile she sat there looking at her fingernails, telling herself she was a fool for staying with this whole crazy idea.

Old anger, she told herself. So the company won another round. So another kid died. A lot of them had died—

She kept hearing the gunfire behind the raffle of glassware. Watching the rab go down. Kids, with shocked looks on their faces. The company cops with no faces, just silver visors that reflected back the smoke and the frightened faces of their victims.

Lawless rab.

Property rights. Company rules.

"We got to fix this," Bird said the day Dekker came to them. "What they've done isn't fair." And she thought, sick at her stomach, Dammit, Bird, they'll kill you. . . .

Trim jets kept firing. She felt the bursts.

The shuttle's mains kicked in, in the high lonely cold above Earth's atmosphere, the transition she loved. You knew you were going home, then, the motherwell couldn't hold you—

Up, not down—

Black for a while. She felt the push of braking, had Sal's arm around her, the aux boards in front of her, Sal trying to get her belted in. She reached with the arm that didn't hurt, took the belt and snapped the clip in, solid click. Tested it for a rough ride. She told Sal: "Get yourself belted, Aboujib, I got it, all right. . . ."

Another burst of trim jets. Dek was maneuvering, Ben was fastening his belt for him while the Shepherd—Sammy, Sal called him—was filling in at the com, saying, urgently, "They're warning us to pull back in. That carrier's moving in fast. The *Hamilton*'s powering up now—we can't make it, there's no time for them to pick us up—"

Trim jets fired constantly at the rate of one and two a second, this side and that—she had the camera view, a row of docked skimmers blurring in the number two monitor as they skimmed along the mast surface—*damn* close, there, kid—

Static burst from the general com: the Shepherd had cut B channel in. "*AMC Twenty-nine Hamilton*, this is FleetCom. You're in violation of UDC directives. Stand down—"

"Cut that damn thing off!" Ben snarled. "We got enough on our minds."

"We can't *dock*," the Shepherd yelled. Sal was belting in. Ben was. Acceleration was increasing in hammer blows from the main engines. The mast whipped past faster and faster—

Then nothing. Sudden long shove from the bow stabilizers and the mast swung back in view, retreating now—going for decel—another burst of *Trinidad*'s mains. . . .

No, she thought—*Way Out*'s mains . . . we're coupled. Double mass. —Are we giving up? Going back? Shuttle's on the mast, Dek, did we miss it. Don't get rattled, kid, . . .

Ben said something. Dek said something, and the trim jets fired another long burst, taking the ship—God, felt like a right angle to the station.

God, he's going after the *Hamilton*—

Mains again, *hard* push—pain, from the arm, real pain—

This is interesting, she thought, feeling the accel, figuring vectors. Hell of a ride, Dek, —you tell 'em we're coming?

Big shove. Dark again. She could hear the beeps from the distance indicators, the higher ready-beeps from systems on standby—she thought: that's nice, *nice* sound, that, everything's optimum config, that sumbitch interface back there worked, didn't it?

Loud argument, and the whine of the forward bay hydraulics.

"What the fuck are you doing?" a man's voice shouted. "They're ready to move, dammit, we're in their blast pattern—they got a carrier on intercept—"

Sal's voice, clear and sane: "Shut up, Sammy!"

Thank God, Meg thought, listening for the beeps and tones, easier that than keeping her eyes open. Plenty of information there: bay was open, manipulator arm was working—Sammy was saying, "God, you fool, you damned fool . . ."

Worth a look. She blinked the blurry monitors clear, saw an irregular surface, slotted with dust-deflectors and bolted-onto with tether stanchions—the arm extending out in front of them, white in the spots, shadowed onto the irregular plating—

"Go for it, go for it!" Sal said, "you got it, Ben!"

Neat touch. Hardly felt it.

Attached. To a tether stanchion. The manipulator grip closed and locked.

"*Nice* job," she said. She wasn't sure anybody heard.

The Shepherd yelled, *"Go!"*

Acceleration started, built and built.

Better dump those tanks, Dek, better just uncouple *Way Out*, let her go, and just hope to hell the arm mount holds—no way we can decel off what a Shepherd can put on us, anyway . . .

Ought to tell the kid. But just hard to get organized—hard to get the mouth to work.

Unstable load. Lot of push on. Pressure built in her arm and deserted her brain.

Going *up*, guys, going *up*, long and hard as we can. . . .

Quiet. Couldn't even hear the fans. But no more *g*.

Taste of blood.

Explosion—

But they weren't tumbling. Wasn't the way it had been. He opened his eyes, got the board in focus in this peaceful drifting—neck was stiff, muscles sprained. He turned his head and saw Ben out cold—the Shepherd beside him, headset drifting loose. If there was sound he couldn't hear it, except the fans.

Then he remembered shutting down. Remembered Meg—tried to move. There wasn't a muscle that didn't hurt. But he unclipped, pushed off and turned, getting to Meg's position.

Blood made a fine mist. She was white as a ghost and cold when he touched her face. She looked dead.

But tension came back, dead one moment, then unconscious, but *there*, by some subtle change that wasn't even movement until the eyelids showed stress. Ben was moving—number 2 boards and the best place, his and Ben's, to ride out the push.

"She make it?" Ben asked fuzzily.

"Yeah," Meg mumbled, speaking for herself. At least that was what it sounded like.

"Are we still grappled?"

"I don't know," Dekker said. "We seem stable."

Ben freed himself and drifted over to see to Sal—Sal was coming to. The Shepherd was still out. Dekker reached for the headset, heard faint static and a thin voice before he held it to his ear. ". . . alive in there?" he heard, and: "I'm hearing voices. Their com is open. . . ."

"Yeah," he said, pulling the mike into line. "This is miner ship *Trinidad*. Is this the *Hamilton?*"

CHAPTER 19

"He wasn't doing a damn thing," Ben said—there was blood all over him and Sal, blood dried on his own hands, Dekker saw, Bird's, Meg's, he had no idea. There was too much of it.

"Nothing?" the officer asked.

"Cops had *me*, dammit, he didn't need to be there, he wasn't doing a damn thing, just objected to them grabbing me, and some fool—just—pulled a trigger."

Dekker stared at the backs of his hands, seeing what he hadn't been there to see. Seeing Meg in the lift, holding on to Bird.

Sal said, "*I* saw it. They were arming guys straight off leave, some of them still higher than company corruption: green kids, didn't know shit what they were doing."

"It was a soldier."

"Damn right it was a soldier. Marine. Couldn't have been twenty."

The *Hamilton*'s purser clicked off the recorder. "We've got that. We'll send it before we make our burn."

Dekker said: "How *is* the fuel situation?"

"Not optimum," the purser said.

"Shit." Sal shook her head. The purser left. Ben didn't say anything, just got a long breath and clasped his hands between his knees.

It was as much information as they'd gotten. The same information as they'd gotten since they'd come aboard. Hadn't seen Sammy—Sammy had gone offshift, probably in his own bunk asleep or tranked out if he hadn't gotten the news yet. Sammy—Ford was his last name—had been fairly well shaken up, hadn't asked for the position he'd been handed—the situation at the dock had gone to hell, the shuttle crew hadn't answered, the 8-deck group hadn't answered, they'd suspected their com was being monitored: Mitch had gone next door to use the restaurant's phone to get contact with his crew and hadn't come back, arrested or worse, they still hadn't found out. Sammy wasn't flight ops, he was the legal affairs liaison, a Shepherd negotiator, for God's sake, who'd come aboard R2 to deal with management, if the plan had gone right, if the soldiers hadn't come in . . .

Sammy'd done all right, Dekker decided. All right, for a guy who'd probably never gotten his hands dirty. Had to tell Meg when she came to. She'd get a laugh out of it.

Another officer, this one straight past them, where they waited in the tight confines of the medstation. Right into the surgery.

Angry voice beyond the door, an answer of some kind.

"Think they've got a hurry-up," Sal muttered.

More voices. Something about paralysis and another thirty minutes. Voice saying, quite clearly, ". . . doesn't do her any good if she's dead, Hank, we haven't got your thirty minutes. Get your patient prepped, we're moving."

Man came back through the door then, looked at them, said, more quietly, "We've got your ship free, we've got a positional problem and we're doing a correction burn, about as fast as the EV-team can get in and I can get up to the bridge. Best we can do. You've got belts there. Use them. Staff's got take-holds."

Bad, then. Dekker clamped his jaw and reached for the belt housed in the side of the seat as Sal and Ben did the same. The officer was out the door and gone.

"Shit-all," Ben muttered. His hands were shaking. Sal's were clenched in her lap.

They were in trouble. No question. Headed into the Well, nobody had to say it. "Positional problem" on a Jupiter-bound vector meant only one thing, and a hurry-up like that meant they were on their own, no beam, just the fuel they had left—which wasn't a big argument against the Well's gravity slope.

Way Out's whole mass had had to go—that had been his decision: save *Hamilton* the fuel hauling it, keep *Trinidad*'s manipulator arm from shearing off at the bolts, or maybe taking the bulkhead with it: but that fuel in *Trinidad*'s tanks had been a big load—*big* load, on those bolts. He'd made a split-second judgment call, last move he'd made before he'd gone out. Maybe opening that valve had saved their lives. If that bulkhead had gone they'd have decompressed; but an uncalc'ed mass attached to *Hamilton*, three-quarters of it dumped without warning a few seconds into the burn . . . hadn't helped their situation. Computers had recomped. But their center of mass had changed twice in that accel; and when the arm gearing had fractured—they'd had to lase through the tether ring—they must have swung flat against *Hamilton*'s frame and that would have changed it again. He'd gone out by the time that had happened. Didn't know how long they'd pushed, but with a warship moving on them, they'd had to give it a clear choice between chasing them or dealing with R2.

Hamilton crew couldn't be real damn happy with their passengers right now.

The lock hydraulics cycled and stopped. A siren shrieked. A recorded voice said: Take Hold Immediately.

"All hands prepare for course correction burn. Mark. Repeat—"

"The Bitch won't give 'em a beam," Sal muttered, teeth chattering as she checked her belt. "The Bitch is damn well hoping we'll all take the deep one. Won't lift a finger."

"We're going to be all right," he said.

" 'Going to be all right,' " Ben said. " 'Going to be all right.' You know if you weren't a damn spook Bird'd be alive. Meg wouldn't be in there. We wouldn't be where we are. This whole damn mess is your fault."

"Yeah," he said, on a deep breath. "I know that."

"His damn fault, too," Ben muttered. "They weren't after him, they didn't know who the hell he was. He was clear, damn him, he was clear. I don't know what he did it for."

Engines fired. *Hamilton* threw everything she had into her try at skimming the Well.

He thought, I could just have pulled us off and out. Didn't *have* to go to the *Hamilton*. Wasn't thinking of anything else.

They'd have picked us up. But the shooting would have stopped by then. And we wouldn't be in this mess. Ben's right.

"Didn't make sense," Ben said. "Damn him, he never *did* make sense . . ."

Somebody had started shooting. The police swore they were military rounds, and Crayton's office wanted that information released immediately.

The statement from Crayton's office said: . . . *greatly regrets the loss of life* . . .

Morris Bird was a name Payne fervently wished he'd never heard. Thirty-year veteran, oldest miner in the Belt, involved with Pratt and Marks, and popular on the 'deck—a damn martyr was what they had. Somebody had sprayed BIRD in red paint all along a stretch of 3-deck. BIRD was turning up scratched in paint on 8, and they didn't need any other word. The hospital was bedding down wounded in the halls, a file named DEKKER was proliferating into places they still hadn't found and the Shepherd net was broadcasting its own news releases, calling for EC intervention and demanding the resignation of the board and the suspension of martial law.

Now it was vid transmission—a Shepherd captain explaining how the miner ship *Trinidad* had made a run for the *Hamilton*—more names he'd heard all too much about. A pilot who'd had his license pulled as impaired. A crew who'd been with Bird when the shooting happened. The story was growing by the minute—acquiring stranger and stranger angles, and N & E couldn't get ahead of them by any small measures.

. . . *A spokesman for the company has expressed relief at the safe recovery of the* Trinidad *and all aboard. The same source has strongly condemned the use of deadly force against unarmed demonstrators and promises a thorough* . . .

The door opened. He blinked, looking at rifles, at two blue-uniformed marines. At a third, who followed them in, and said,

"William Payne? This office is under UDC authority, under emergency provisions of the Defense Act, Section 18, Article 2."

He looked at the rifles, looked at the officer. Tried to think of right procedures. "I need to contact the head office."

"Go right ahead, Mr. Payne."

He doubted his safety to do that. He hesitated at picking up the phone, hesitated at pushing the button. "This *is* Administration I'm calling. Do you want to be sure of that?"

"Check it out wherever you like, Mr. Payne. Your computer will give you an explanation. Go ahead. Access Administration."

He took a breath, touched keys, windowed up Executive Access.

It said, *Earth Company Executive Order* . . .

It said Charter Provision 28, and Defense Act, Section 18, Article 2.

"We have a press release for you, Mr. Payne."

"Yes, *sir*," he said. No questions. No hesitations. He reached for the datacard the officer put on his desk and put it into the comp.

It said: *The UDC has assumed control of ASTEX operations. All workers, independent operators and contractors, and all ASTEX employees below management levels will be retained. President Towney is under arrest by civil warrant, charged with misappropriation of funds and tax evasion. Various members of the board are likewise under investigation by the EC. Residents who have information on such cases are directed to deliver that information to the military police, Access 14, on the system.*

All residents who report to the UDC office on their 'decks will have their cards revalidated and will be passed without question or exception under a general amnesty for all non-executive personnel of R2.

The UDC will meet with delegations from the independents, the contractors, and civilian employees to discuss grievances . . .

"Hell of a mess," Meg said, propped on pillows in the peculiar kind of *g* you got in small installations—still light-headed, but the fingers could move in the cast, she'd tested that.

"Couldn't tell you from the sheets when they brought you in." Sal sat down carefully on the edge of the bed, reached out a dark hand and squeezed her good one. Skins brut sure didn't match right now, Meg thought, seeing that combination, and then thought about Bird, left adrift in that lift-car. Hell of a thing to do. Bird had deserved better than that. But he'd always been a practical sumbitch, where it counted.

Water trickled from the corner of her left eye. Sal wiped it with her thumb.

"Hell," she said, and tried to put her arm over her eyes, but every joint she owned was sprained. She blinked and drew a couple of breaths. "They get us out of the dive yet?"

Sal didn't answer right off. Hadn't, she thought. Welcome back, Kady. We're still going to die.

Sal said, "We still got a little vector problem. Where'd you hear it?"

"Meds said. Thought I was out. Are we going in?"

Another hesitation. "Say we're going in a lot slower. They're having a discussion with the EC right now. Idea is, deploy the sail to half, see if we can get a line-up with the R2-23, just get a little different tack going."

"That'd be nice."

"Listen, ice-for-nerves, we got word the military's taken over—got Towney under arrest—yeah. And the board. They'll bring the beams up, they damn well have to. They're talking deal with helldeck right now—

they're asking for Mitch and Persky and some of the guys to come and talk grievances—"

"It's a trick."

"They going to put so'jer-boys to picking rocks? Beaucou' d' luck, Kady. First tag they try they'll be finding bits of some ship clear to Saturn."

"They'll deal. Maybe even get us our beam. Wouldn't be surprised. But it won't change, Aboujib. Won't change."

Sal didn't say anything for a moment. And she was on a dive of her own. Wasn't fair to Sal. Sal had real vivid nightmares about gravity wells.

She said to Sal, only bit of optimism she could come up with, "Won't be Towney in charge, anyhow."

"They're sending out this EC manager. Meanwhile it's the so'jers."

Not good news for the guys on R2. Long time til the new manager got here. Meanwhile *they* were trying their best not to fall into the Well. She wondered how good their options were. Beams going up again, yeah, if the soldiers hadn't some damn administrative mess-up that was going to wait on authorizations, or if it wasn't just convenient to the EC to have them gone. Beside which, if they were talking about a bad line, and they were having to use R2-23, they evidently were in one of those vectors where getting a beam was a sincere bitch. R2-23 was a geosync. Geosyncs at the Well were a never-ending problem, always screwed, Shepherds futzed them into line and refueled them with robot tugs, and hauled them out of the radiation intense area and fixed them when they'd gotten screwed beyond the usual—useful position, that particular beam, what odd times its computer wasn't fried—

"Got two nice-looking guys want to see you," Sal said, looking seriously fragile right now. Doing her best to be cheerful.

"Shit. I got any makeup on?"

"Forgot to pack," Sal said, squeezed her shoulder and staggered off to the door—hadn't got her ship-legs yet.

Neither had the boys. They looked like hell. Scrubbed up, at least. But limping and not walking real well, especially Ben. Good time to be horizontal, she decided, sore as she was—*Hamilton* was fair-sized, but her *g* differential still wanted to drop you on your ass, besides which your feet swelled til your body adapted. Went through it all again when you went stationside.

If they ever saw stationside again.

She patted the bedside. "Sit," she said. They sat down very carefully, one on a side of the footboard.

"Hurt much?" Ben asked. Stupid question.

"I've had nicer times in bed. You all right?"

"Fine," Dekker said. "We're fine."

"Yeah," she said, surveying the bruises. "We're a set, all right."

Course correction put them in reach of R2-23, the message from Ops said. *That's their last serious option. Calculations extremely marginal even at this point. Situation with beam goes zero chance at 0828h. We checked out that cap and their fill, and the miner-crafts' registered mass. Unless they got something from the remaining miner's tanks, they have nothing left. Cap on* Athens *indicates zero chance intercept. Dumping the tugs didn't do it.* Athens *would put itself in danger. We estimate their continuing on course is only for the negotiators. Our data appended.*

Porey tapped the stylus on the desk, called up the figures, considered it, considered a communication from the meeting in the corporate HQ, typed a brief message. *Tell their negotiators we've calc'ed* Athens *and the chances on the beam go neg at 0828. Tell them we'd be glad to provide them the figures and we're standing by our offer.*

No time for another cause with the miners. Or the Shepherds.

Good PR. Magnanimity. General amnesty, revalidate the cards, put Towney's arrest on vid, get the beams up again and get the *Hamilton* out of its situation.

The minute the Shepherds came to terms.

Breakfast.

Marmalade. Dekker hadn't tasted it since he was a kid—Ben and Sal never had. Meg said it brought back memories of her smuggling days.

"I used to run this stuff," Meg said. "Course we'd lose a jar or two now and again."

Sal made the sign for eavesdroppers, and Dekker felt it in his gut. But Meg said, "Hell, if they got time to worry about us—"

"Kind of sour," Ben said. "Bitter. Not bad, though."

"Ben, cher," Sal said. "Learn to appreciate. Life's everso prettier that way."

"I appreciate it. It's bitter. And sour. Isn't it? What's the matter with that?"

Meg rolled her eyes.

The door opened. Dekker turned his head.

Officer.

Breakfast stopped.

"Sorry to interrupt you," the Shepherd said, leaning against the doorframe, arms folded. Afro, one-sided shave job, Shepherd tech insignia and a gold collar-clip on that expensive jacket that meant he was senior-tech-something. "Thought you'd appreciate a briefing. We've got a rescue coming."

Dekker replayed that a second. Maybe they all did.

Good news?

"Who?" Meg asked.

"That carrier. Moving like a bat."

"Shee—" Meg held it.

Dekker thought, God, why? But he didn't ask. He left that to Meg and Sal, who had the credit here—who *weren't* the ones who'd put them in the mess they were in.

"Looks as if we're getting out of this," Meg said.

"God," Ben said after a moment. No yelling and celebrating. You held it that long, doing business as usual as much as possible, and when you got good news you just didn't know how to take it.

"Where's the catch?" Sal asked. "They can just overtake and haul us out?"

"Thing was .75 our current *v* two minutes away from R2. They're not wasting any time."

Dekker did rough math in his head, thought—God. And us well onto the slope, as we have to be now—

"They're talking deal," the Shepherd said. "Seems the Fleet's figured out they need us. Seems the Association's said there's no deal without the freerunners, they're hanging on to that point—they've axed Towney, that's certain now. Thought you'd want to know. —Mr. Dekker?"

"Sir."

"The captain wants to see you."

Another why? But maybe if they were out of their emergency standby . . . the captain wanted to make a serious point with the resident fool. He shrugged, looked back at Meg and Sal and Ben, with: "I'll *see* you—" Meaning that they could think about later, and being alive day after tomorrow.

God, the shakes had gotten him, too—he didn't figure what he was scared of now—a dressing-down by a Shepherd captain, good enough, he had it coming: or maybe it was suddenly *having* a future, in which he didn't know what he was going to be doing hereafter. The Shepherd might take Meg and might take Sal—even Ben turned out to have a claim.

But him?

Credit with the *Hamilton* might be real scant about now. *Trinidad* was gone, likewise *Way Out*—nothing like *Trinidad*'s velocity when they'd dumped her, but not in R2's near neighborhood by now, either, and on the same track. If she was catchable at all, the law made her somebody else's salvage. He had the bank account—but God knew what shape that was in, or what kind of lawsuits might shape up against him—corp-rats were corp-rats, Meg would say, and he had no faith the EC was going to forget him and let him be. Not with people dead and the property damage.

It wasn't a far walk to Sunderland's office. The tech-chief showed him in—announced him to a gray-haired, frail-looking man, who offered his hand—not crew-type courtesies, Dekker thought. That in a strange way seemed ominous; Sunderland didn't look angry, rather worn and worried and, by some strange impression, regretful.

That disturbed him too.

"Mr. Dekker. Coffee?"

"No, sir, thank you. I just had breakfast."

"Good you have an appetite—have a seat, there. —I confess mine hasn't been much the last while."

He made the chair, sank into it. "I know 'sorry' doesn't cover it. I shouldn't have dumped the tanks."

"We wouldn't have you if you hadn't; bulkhead wouldn't have stood it. Tried to tell you to do it. Don't know if you heard."

He shook his head. "No, sir." And thought, Just not enough hands. Not enough time.

"Things were going pretty fast, weren't they?"

"Yes, sir."

"Things have been going pretty hot and hard here, too. You know about the ship coming."

"Yessir." He felt light-headed—*g* difference. Sitting down and standing up could do that.

"Took some talking. But I didn't seriously figure they were going to let us go down. The EC wouldn't. R2-23 was an option—best we had without the EC's help, I'm sure you were following that, and a couple of exotic, chancy possibilities that we really didn't want to get down to, but when they called us this morning and told us the R2-23 computer was down, . . . I had a good idea that ship was going to move. I had a good idea they had it calc'ed down to the fine figures and they were going to carry it live on vid. Clear to Sol. The EC doesn't want us in the Well. *Bad* media, Mr. Dekker. Bad media with the miners. They've resorbed ASTEX, you've heard that, Towney's dismissed, . . . a lot of changes, a lot of them for the better. We can work with the contractors. We can work with the EC. We can work with the UDC. They know that. They just wanted the best deal they could get."

The captain called him in to talk politics?

Hell. What's he getting to.

"We've got the numbers on the accident," Sunderland said. "I don't know how much you've been told . . ."

"I'm told you'd found her weeks before you reported it." He'd found that out this morning, from Ben, and it was on its way to making him mad. "You didn't tell us, you let us go clear into prep, didn't warn us—"

"Didn't have any idea how you'd react—*whether* you could keep it together and do business as usual. Didn't know, frankly, whether Aboujib was going to jump our way or not. We thought so. But she's a hair trigger in a situation like this. And we were pushing for all the time we could, to get at records we needed. We knew about the bumping. We knew there was a miner missing. We were already comparing charts and finding discrepancies when *Athens* found your partner. We knew you were going out—quite frankly, we waited because we were still doing the legal prep. Sam Ford—you met Ford—was down there making sure the t's were crossed and the i's were dotted: when you go up against the company in a lawsuit, you'd better not have a loophole. We advised Aboujib, we set everything up for a quiet transfer hours before the thing went out over the com, we were going to get you quietly up to the dock, shuttle you aboard where they couldn't get at you and get some essential changes out of the company—I'm being altogether honest with you now—while we were helping you pursue your case against the company. Unfortunately—"

"I took a walk."

"Not that it mattered, I'm afraid, at least in the majority of what happened. We factored in the company's stupidity—we expected the military to involve themselves, but not—not that an EC order to resorb the company was already lying on FleetCommander's desk, waiting for any legal excuse it could, frankly, arrange. *They* were preparing a general audit of the company, to do it under one provision, but there was an emergency clause in the charter, that had to do with the threat to operations; and there is the Defense Act, that would let the military outright seize control if things were falling apart. And they were ready—ready because of the labor situation, ready because they thought the managers might try to destroy records—"

"They did."

"They tried. We had one piece. There were others. FleetCommander had that carrier fueled. We'd gotten that rumor. We didn't like what we were hearing. We knew when we did move we'd be dealing with the Fleet on a legal level—we even expected a confrontation at the dock. But not that they'd be as fast as they were and not that they had the legal documents to take control of the company without a time-lagged information exchange with Earth. That was eight to ten hours we turned out not to have. They had their people on R2, they had weapons on their transport, they turned out and they took the dock and our shuttle crew, and when that happened we were in deep trouble. But it *has* shaken out: we didn't anticipate dealing with the UDC this fast—but we've gotten what we were trying to force: we're dealing directly with the parent corporation, now, and very anxious defense contractors *and* the Fleet, all of whom have a budget and absolutely no personnel who can do what we do—efficiently. We can meet their quotas. We. The miners *and* the Shepherds. And the 'drivers, who *have* to come into line. Ultimately they have to. That's where it stands."

"Morrie Bird's dead. A lot of people are dead."

"We regret that. We regret that very sincerely. But we're not defense experts. We fought with what we had, the best way we knew. People *were* being killed. The way your partner was killed. You understand? ASTEX was killing miners, killing us—ultimately something would have happened. Something possibly with worse loss of life. With one of the refineries going."

He believed that, at least. He thought about it. Thought about the system the way it was and didn't believe the military was going to be better. "Bastards could have pulled us back ten hours ago," he said. "Are they better than Towney?"

"No. But they're saner."

"They let us fall for ten hours—"

"Part of the game, Mr. Dekker. We fall toward the Well at a given acceleration . . . their negotiation team meanwhile meets with ours, they won't get the beam tracking system working, the EC is hours time-lagged and not talking to us, and everybody pretends they're not going to reach a compromise. I've been through too many years of this to believe it would go any differently than, ultimately, it did. Hair's gone gray a long time ago—between the Well and the shit from ASTEX. Last few went this morning til we knew that ship was moving. But we were fairly sure. All along, all of us were fairly sure."

"Yessir," he said, in Sunderland's wait for a reaction. Adrenaline was running high, there was no place to send it. He'd gotten the rules by now. They included not expressing opinions to Shepherd captains. He looked somewhere past Sunderland's shoulder, seeing Meg and that dockside, and the blood floating there. Seeing Bird, in the lift-car. Ben covered with blood.

"I'd like, for the record, Mr. Dekker, to have your version of what happened out there, with *Industry*."

"God, I've told it. Doesn't *anybody* have the record?"

"Just in brief. For a record ASTEX hasn't touched."

That was understandable, at least. He drew a wider breath, leaned back in the chair, recited it all again. "We found a rock, we went for it, the 'driver went too, and we figured he was going to try to beat us to it. And maybe muscle us off if he didn't. So we wanted a sample on our ship before BM told us to get out. But they didn't do that. They ran us down."

"Bumped you."

"No damn bump. Sir."

"I know that. I know other details, if you want them."

"All right. Then what the hell were they doing?"

"Trying to stop an independent from the biggest find in years. Trying to keep the company from a major pay-out—that could have made the difference between profit and loss that quarter—"

"God."

"What you may not know, or may not have thought about—'drivers keep track of miners—they have *all* the charts. They are a Base. And you moved, I'm guessing—on your own engines. Maybe you made quite a bit of *v*, on quite a long run."

Another piece of memory clicked.

"True?"

He nodded, seeing in his mind all the instruments of a tracking station, a long, long move for a miner, with no request for a beam. Anomaly. Cory'd suspected BM. They hadn't thought about a 'driver monitoring what they were doing. BM did. But you could move in a sector without saying . . . if you could do it on your own engines.

Stupid, he thought, the other side of experience. Fatally stupid. But . . .

"They could have ordered us off. They could have claimed it on optics."

"Why didn't you?"

"Because—because Cory said they might not log it. They might just claim the 'driver had it first."

"Politics. Politics. They *did* log it. They gave it a number."

"Then why didn't they call us and tell us? We saw them moving. But BM didn't tell us a damned thing—not 'They've got it,' not 'Pull back,' not—"

"They *wanted* that 'driver to beat you there. Crayton's office had stepped in and said they shouldn't have logged it that way, they should undo it because they hadn't made a policy decision yet. They'd called Legal Affairs and asked for advice. We can't reconstruct all of it: the military's sitting on those records—but what I guess is there was a 'driver damned determined to get there; BM was waffling—trying to figure out how to solve it, finally figuring they were in a situation—*nobody* believes BM. Nobody'd believe you weren't screwed. It'd be all over the 'deck at R1, one opinion in management was afraid it would touch off trouble, another said otherwise—they went ass-backwards into 'letting the local base handle it'. . . that's BM code for the shit's on the captain. 'Use your discretion,' is the way they word it. That means do something illegal."

He heard the tone of voice, he looked into neutral pale eyes in a lean, aged face and thought: This is a man who's been put in that position . . .

"They just hushed it all," Sunderland said. "They left it to the 'driver. They didn't *make* a policy decision. And *he* was under communication blackout, because that's the way things go when you're 'handling it' for the company. The consensus was you'd spook and run."

"They didn't know my partner."

"Extraordinary young woman, by what I know. Extraordinarily determined. Did you call it on optics? Did you try that?"

(—we just use the fuel, Cory had said. Trusting BM to get them home.)

"We were close enough we could get an assay sample before they got there. They weren't talking to us. We figured they'd pull something with the records, so it just didn't damn well matter. We thought they'd brake, that'd give us the time. And if we had the sample aboard—and our log against theirs of when we moved—we could make a case. We knew—we were sure BM knew what was going on. We didn't except they'd run right over us."

"You understand bumpings? You know the game?"

The man thought he was a fool. There was "poor, stupid kids" in his voice. He set his jaw and said, "I've heard. I'd heard then."

"Usual is a low-*v* nudge, usually near the Refineries. Like a bad dock. Usually it's their tenders, just give you a scrape, make you spend time checking damage. But this time you'd beat him. You'd outdone his best speed even with a beam-assist. And his ass was on the line with the company. No time for nudges from his tenders. They didn't want a sample in your hands. If you had it, they wanted it dumped. Radio silence—from his side. Nothing to get on record. So he kept on course—had it all figured, closest pass he dared, bearing in mind you don't brake those sumbitches by the seat of your pants. Scare hell out of you. Get you so scared you'd do anything he said. But you moved *toward* his path, didn't you? And his Helm hadn't calc'ed that eventuality."

"What was I *supposed* to do?"

"Most would get out of the way."

"My partner was out there!"

"Some might. Some might run all the way to elsewhere. Maybe just tell BM there'd been an accident. Maybe have a 'driver tender claim a rescue."

"Hell!" But he'd known—known it wasn't quite a collision course. He'd known they were trying to shake him, he'd called their bluff—

They'd called his.

"Damn single correction," he muttered. "All they had to do. Fire the directionals and brake. Hell, he'd already braked off the beam, he was coming in well inside his maneuvering limits. He was as able to stop as I was."

"Their Helm was Belter. And that's a class A ship. Automated to the hilt. You understand me? Didn't even remotely occur to an Institute cut-rate a move like that was a choice—*he* wouldn't, so he didn't have it laid into his computer in advance. Not the directionals. Without it, running on auto—the jets won't fire if you don't take the autopilot off. He hit the jets, all right. With the autopilot on. Nothing. Some projection on the ship hit you."

"God."

"*I'd* have fired him. Damn sure. But there the 'driver was, he'd hit you. Your ship had blown a tank, you'd shot off into R2, his tenders couldn't catch you without getting a beam, you'd hit the rock as well as taken the scrape that blew the tank—they were in shit up to their necks—and Ms. Salazar was dead in the explosion. We're sure of that. —Do you want this part? You don't have to hear it. Your choice."

"I want to hear anything you know. I'm very used to the idea she's dead." But it wasn't that easy. His hands were shaking. He folded them under his arms and went on listening, thinking: The ship hit her. *I* did.

Sunderland said: "Captain Manning—that's the senior captain on the 'driver, was the one who made the decisions at this point. He had one dead. He figured your chances were zero. He had no doubt whatsoever the company was going to black-hole the whole business. And they wouldn't clear him to chase a ship that wasn't supposed to be there in the first place. BM wouldn't want that in the log. He knew he had to get rid of the body himself. So they reported they'd acquired the rock, BM didn't ask what had happened—*Registry* wasn't in the information flow. Your emergency beeper was working. BCOM upper management *knew* what was going on with the 'driver, so it wasn't asking questions. Nobody in management was going to ask, and maybe—here, I'm attributing thoughts to Manning that may not have been—but maybe he was worried you *could* be alive. At any rate he never filed a report that he'd actually hit the ship. There'd been a flash the military could well have picked up—but flashes near 'drivers are ordinary. Your radio was out, just gone—you were traveling near a 'driver fire-path, so you weren't going to be found for a long time. If any tech reported that signal of yours, I'm betting it just got a real fast silence from upper echelons for the next couple of months. You never called in for a beam, and somebody erased *Way Out* off the missed-report list. Just—erased it. You were in R2 zone, you weren't on R2's list, and nobody was going to put you there, and nobody in R2 was calc'ing your course, except that eventually the 'driver and maybe management knew you'd go into the Well, and that would be that."

"But why did he send Cory there? What the hell was he doing? What was he trying to prove?"

"My guess? His tenders had gone after Ms. Salazar's body . . . he couldn't call them back from a rescue mission. They *knew* it had been a bumping; they knew it had all gone very wrong, and Manning wanted them too scared to talk. So he made accomplices of the 'driver crew, the techs, everybody aboard—to scare them into silence; to prove, maybe, if they had any doubt—that the company was going to hush it up."

He was numb. "So they could've fired *at* the Well. They didn't have to leave a trace."

"I'm not saying Manning isn't crazy. But there's no love lost between us and the company crews. He was pissed, if you want my opinion, about the job he was sent on, he was pissed at BM, pissed at management, he was upset as hell about the accident and he had no doubt whatsoever the company'd back him against us when we did find the body—just like the bumpings, just like that, bad blood, a way of shedding some of the fallout on us—because we couldn't prove a damned thing. Even with a body—because there'd be no record. There'd be some story about a 'driver accident. Nothing would get done. It's been that way since they put company crews on those ships. And the company keeps them out there years at a run. They're bitter. They're mad. They're jealous as hell of our deal with the company. They blame us for the company losses that mean they'd been told they were staying out additional weeks. But they're not totally crazy. They had absolutely no idea you could possibly survive. It was clerks that handled the distress signal, they'd already said too much to Bird and Pollard before they'd had any higher-ups involved, and my guess is they just decided they might as well bring the ship in, get it off the books—they just didn't want Bird and Pollard telling how there was some ghost signal out there that BM didn't know about. War jitters. Nervous Fleet establishment. They decided to go on it, they panicked when they found out you were alive—but do them credit, they didn't even think of having you killed. In their own eyes they weren't killers; it really *was* an accident, and they weren't going to have you die in hospital or on the 'deck. Too bad for them. Good for us. A lot of people are very grateful to you, Mr. Dekker. —Let me tell you, no matter Cory's mother's influence, no matter anything we could do—without you staying alive, without you holding out against the company, there'd have been nothing but a body at the Well. Nothing we could prove. Ever. So you did do something. You did win. You're a hero. You and Morris Bird. People *liked* him. People truly liked him . . ."

Hard even to organize his thoughts. Or to talk about Bird. He couldn't.

"You're the ultimate survivor, Mr. Dekker. That's something near magical to Belters—and the rest of us who know what you were up against. But there's a time—maybe now—to quit while you're still winning."

"What do you mean?"

"You have an enemy, one very bad enemy."

"Manning?"

Sunderland shook his head, hands joined in front of his lips. "Alyce Salazar. She's not being reasonable. Her daughter's death—the manner in which she was found—hasn't helped her state of mind. You're not behind a corporate barrier any longer. The EC's already tried to reason with her. She pulled strings to get the UDC to investigate ASTEX, she wanted ASTEX resorbed—simply so she could get at its records, and so she could get at you. In effect, that order was under consideration, stalled in the EC's top levels, but it was lying on FleetCommand's desk principally because Alyce Salazar called in every senatorial favor she owned—favors enough to tip the balance, corporately and governmentally. And she wants you on trial, Mr. Dekker. The military's sitting on the records. It doesn't want this ASTEX situation blown up again, it doesn't want a trial, the EC doesn't want it, but the civil system can't be stopped that easily. Financial misconduct is the likeliest charge she'll try for; but she's trying for criminal negligence."

It hurt. For some reason it truly hurt, that Cory's mother was that bitter toward him.

"She doesn't have to be right, of course. She doesn't even have to win. The damage will be done. She has the money for the lawyers and she has the influence to get past the EC. They honestly don't want you in court—for various reasons. They don't want you arrested, or tried, or talking to senatorial committees—and they don't want the fallout with the miners and the factory workers and us, at a *very* strategic facility. But most certainly they don't want you on a ship headed into the Well—when R2 knows about it. They might come after us. But they *damn* sure won't let you take the ride."

It was going somewhere that didn't sound good. Same song, his mother had used to say—different verse. He asked, in Sunderland's momentary silence, "So what are they going to do?"

"Our rescue? That ship that's coming after us? —They'll pull us out. Save our collective hides. But you aren't going back to R2. They want you: the Fleet wants you. That was the sticking point the last ten hours. We tried. We've stalled, but they're moving now. We've no other options but them. God knows we can't run. And if we don't turn you over, they'll board—I have that very clear impression. In which case anything we do is a gesture, we've risked the ship, and various people can get hurt."

He had trouble getting his breath. He couldn't feel his own fingers. "Am I under arrest?"

"They tell me no. The fact is, you've been drafted."

The bottom dropped out of his stomach. "Shit!" he said before he thought who he said it to—and told himself he was a fool, they were pulling him out of the Well, they were rescuing a hundred plus people, he had damn-all reason to object to the service—

—to getting thrown into the belly of a warship and getting blown to hell that way.

"May not be altogether bad. They tell me they're interested in you for reasons that have nothing to do with the EC. They want you in pilot training."

"They want me where I won't talk. They think that'll get me aboard.

I'll be lucky if they don't arrange a training accident. A lot of people get killed that way."

"You're a suspicious young man, Mr. Dekker."

"Well, God, I've learned to be."

"And I'm one more smiling bastard. Yes. I am. —And I'm sorry. I *don't* like the role I've been cast in. I hate like hell what they're doing. But we don't have any choice. I risked my crew and my ship getting you away in the first place, because you were that important, I hung on in negotiations as long as I could, and, bluntly put, we've gotten as much as we can get, we can't help you, and it's time to make a final deal. In some measure I suspect certain offices would rather see all of us dead than you in court: in some negotiations the compromises get *too* half and half, and sanity can go out the chute. People can get shot trying to protect you. Two ships can go to hell. Literally. You understand what I'm saying?"

He did understand. He thought about the kid who'd helped Meg with the vodka bottles. The fool who'd habitually lost his temper over things he couldn't even remember the importance of, this side of things. Damned fool, he thought. Damned, dumb fool. I can't even get mad now. The mess is too complicated, too wide, it just rolls on and over people. Like Bird. Like Meg.

Sunderland said, more gently, "If they're not on the level, I think you can *put* them that way, you understand? What they tell me, your reflexes are in the top two percentile—you don't train that. That's hard-wired. They tell me . . . the speeds these FTLs operate at . . . even with computers doing the hands-on ops, the human reaction time has to be there. Mentally *and* physically. Whole new game, Mr. Dekker. And I'll tell you another reason they don't want to antagonize us. The Fleet's looking at the Shepherd pilots, the Shepherd techs—as a very valuable resource. I'm not eager for it. I'll do what I'm doing the rest of my life, and it's what I want to do. But the young ones, a good many of the young ones—may do something different before they're done."

He was in flow-through. Sunderland spoke and he believed it because he wanted to believe it. Sunderland stopped speaking, the spell broke, and he told himself Sunderland was a fool or a liar: there were a lot of reasons for the military to want Sunderland to believe that—a very clear reason for Sunderland to want *him* to believe it.

He said, in the remote chance this man was naive: "I'll be wherever it is before you. I hope it's all right." Hear me, man. Watch me. Watch what happens. It'll be important to you—

I don't trust anyone's assurances. Maybe Meg's. But you have to know her angles.

Meg knew a whole lot more than she told Bird. And Sal knew more than she ever told any of us. And Ben's figured that. That's why it's gone cold between them . . . that's why, in the shakeout, it's only partners that count.

Mine's paid out, now. Done everything I could, Cory, . . .

The interview was over. He got up, Sunderland got up. Sunderland offered his hand. He found the good grace to take it.

Hard adjustment—they hadn't *had* problems except the fact they were out of fuel and falling closer and closer to Jupiter, and in consequence of that, the morbid question whether they'd fry in his envelope before they got there or live long enough to hear the ship start compressing around them. Intellectual question, and one Meg had mulled over in the dark corners of her mind—speculation right now hell and away more entertaining that wondering what the soldier-boys were going to do with the company, and what it was going to be like in this future they now had, living on Shepherd charity.

Sal and Ben might be all right—Ben was still subdued, just real quiet—missing Bird and probably asking himself the same question—how to live now that they had a good chance they weren't going to die.

Point one: something could still go wrong. When you knew you were diving for the big one, hell, you focused on *trying* things, and you lined up your chances and you took them in order of likeliest to work and fastest to set up. But when you knew you were going to be rescued by somebody else's decisions and that it was somebody else's competency or lack of it that was going to pull you out or screw everything up, *then* you sweated, then you imagined all the ways some fool could lose that chance you had.

Point two: Sal was just real spooky right now—scared, jumpy: Sal had held out against her fancy friends once before when the Shepherds were trying to drive a wedge between them, and Sal had all the feel of it right now, wanting them so hard it was embarrassing to watch it—and Sal was hearing those sons of bitches, she was damn sure of it, saying, Yeah, that's all real fine, Aboujib, but Kady's an albatross—Kady's got problems with the EC, that we're trying to deal with in future—

—Only thing Kady can do is fly, they'd be saying; and meaning shit-all chance there was of that, with their own pilots having a god complex *and* seniority out the ass. Might be better to split from Sal, get out of her life, quit screwing up her chances with her distant relatives, and go do mining again—maybe with Ben, who knew?

But, God, it's going to be interesting times. So'jer rules, more and more. They'll make sweettalk with the miners til they got a brut solid hold on the situation, then they'll just chip away at everything they agreed to.

Dek—Dek could come out of this all right; but, God, Dek maybe hadn't figured what she was hearing from the meds, how he'd gotten notorious, how *he* was so damn hot an item it was keeping the pressure on the EC to get them out of this—couldn't drop *Dekker* into the Well, not like some dumb shit Shepherd crew that got themselves in trouble. Dekker was system-wide famous, in Bird's way of saying. And that was both a good thing and a bad one, as she could figure—majorly bad, for a kid who'd just got his pieces picked up and didn't get on well with asses.

Lot of asses wanted to use you if you were famous. Piss one off and he'd knife you in the back. She'd got *that* lesson down pat.

Good, in that consideration, if the Shepherds kept him on the *Hamilton*. But she didn't think they would—kid with no seniority, a lot of rep, and a knife-edge mental balance . . . coming in on senior pilots with a god-habit. Critical load in a week. And if they put him back on R2, God help him, same thing with the new management.

That left Sol and the EC. And that meant public. And all the shit that went with it.

She was severely worried about Dek. She kept asking herself—while from time to time they were telling each other how wonderful it was they weren't going to die and all, and Ben and Sal looked more scared right now than they'd been in all this mess—

—asking herself, too, what they were telling Dekker, somewhere on the ship.

Giving him an official briefing on his partner, maybe. Everybody'd been somewhat busy til now; and the heat being off (literally) the senior staff was probably going down its list of next-to-do's.

Or maybe they were telling him something else altogether.

The door opened. Dek came back quiet and looking upset.

"What was it?" Ben asked, on his feet. (God, she'd strangle him the day she got the cast off.)

But Dekker looked up at Ben the way he'd looked at her when she'd found him on the ship: no anger. Just a lost, confused look.

Maybe for once in his life Ben understood he should urgently shut up now.

But Dekker paid more attention to walking from the door to the end of the bed—getting his legs fairly well, she thought, better than she was, the little they let her up.

He said, "Got an explanation, at least. Pretty much what we guessed, about Cory. And it's solid, about the ship on its way. We're all right."

"*You* all right?" she asked.

He didn't answer right away. He looked down at the blanket. There was too much quiet in the room, too long. Sal finally edged over and put her hand on his shoulder.

He said, "I'm real tired."

Meg moved her legs over. "There's room. Why don't you just go horizontal awhile? Don't think. It's all right, Dek."

He let out a long slow sigh, leaned over and put his hand on her knee. Just kept it there awhile and she didn't know what to say to him. Sal came and massaged his shoulders. Ben lowered himself into the chair by the bed and said, "So is this ship going to grapple and tow us or just pick us off?"

"Tow," Dekker said. "As I gather. Thing's probably not doing all it can, even the way it's moving."

"Starship," Meg said, thinking of a certain flight. "I've seen 'em glow when they come in."

"Freighters," Sal said. "This thing's something else."

An old rab had a chill, thinking about that "something else" next that one pretty memory. Thought—Earth's blind. Earth's severely blind.

Feathers on the wind. Colonies won't come back.

Kids don't come home again. Not the same, they don't.

Lot of noise. Dekker had no idea how big the carrier was, but it had a solid grip on them, and they could move around now, get what they needed before they sounded the take-hold and shut the rotation down for the push back to R2.

But before that, they had a personnel line rigged, lock to lock, and he had an escort coming over to pick him up. The Fleet wasn't taking any chances of a standoff—while they were falling closer and closer to the mag-sphere.

Hadn't told Meg and Sal. Hadn't told Ben either. He intended to, on his way to the lock. Meanwhile he wanted just to get his belongings together. The *Hamilton* had had their personals out of *Trinidad* before they freed her, Bird's too: they'd been packed and ready to go, all the food and last-to-go-aboards stowed in *Trinidad*, that being where they'd enter and where they'd ride out the initial burn. It was all jumbled together now—*Hamilton* had had no idea who'd owned what—and he found an old paper photo—a group of people, two boys in front, arms around each other, mountains in the background.

Blue-sky. He didn't know what these people had been to Bird. He thought one of the boys looked a little *like* Bird. He didn't know what mountains they were—he knew the Moon better than he knew Earth and its geography—another class he'd cut more than he'd attended.

But he looked at it a long time. He didn't think it was right to take what was Bird's—he hadn't had any claim on him. Ben did. But you could put away a picture in your mind and remember it, years after.

If there were years after.

He took what was his. Put on the bracelet Sal had bought him—he thought that would make her happy. He didn't know, point of fact, whether they'd let him keep anything. Worth asking, he thought.

"Dek?" Sal asked.

About finished, anyway. He stuffed a shirt into the bag, wiped his hair out of his eyes and caught his balance against the lockers as he stood up.

All of them—including Meg. Sal was holding her on her feet. Ben, behind them.

"Meg, God, I wasn't going to skip out—the meds'll have a seizure."

Meg said, "Thought we'd walk down to the lift with you." In that tone of voice Meg had that didn't admit there were other choices. "Hell of a thing, Dek."

"Yeah, well, I wasn't going to worry you. —Walk you back to your cabin."

"Doing just fine, thanks. Going to check these so'jerboys out. See if we approve the company they're putting you into."

He picked up his duffel, put a hand on the wall and came closer. Familiar faces. Faces he'd gotten used to seeing—even Ben. And Meg. Especially Meg.

He leaned over, very carefully kissed her on the cheek. Meg said, "Oh, hell, Dek," and it wasn't his cheek she kissed, for as long as gave him time to know Meg wasn't joking, and that close as he'd been with Cory, it wasn't what he felt right now.

Sal kissed him too, same way. But not the same. He couldn't talk.

Ben said, holding up a hand, "If you think I'm going to, you're wrong."

You never knew about Ben. Ben saved him losing it. He got a breath, halfway laughed, and picked up the bag again, hearing the lock operating.

"Sounds like my appointment," he said. "Better move, so they can get us all under way. Risky neighborhood."

"Yeah, well," Meg said, following him, on Sal's arm. Hard breath. "They better take care of you. *Letters* are a good thing."

"May be a while," he said, glancing back as he walked. Not good for the balance. "But I will. Soon as I can. Soon as I have a paycheck. Don't know whether I'll be at the shipyard or where. Sol, maybe. I just can't say."

Trying to pack every thought he had into a handful of minutes. Thinking about the Fleet's tight security, and the tighter security around him.

"Maybe if you ask the Shepherds they can find out where I'm stationed. Maybe the captain can get a letter to me, even if I can't get one out. My mother's Ingrid Dekker, she's on maintenance at Sol—write to her, if that doesn't work. She may know where I am."

Or maybe not, he thought, as they came into the ops area, where the lift was, to take him up to the lock. Fleet uniform on the blond and two marine MP's, with pistols. Standing with Sunderland. He hoped they didn't take him off in handcuffs. Not in front of Meg, please God. . . .

"Mr. Dekker?" the crew-type said—young, insignia he couldn't read. Outheld hand. He took the offer. Didn't read any threat. "Name's Graff. Going to take you across and see you signed in."

Didn't sound like a threat. It wasn't handcuffs at least.

Graff said, "This your crew?"

"Meg Kady, Sal Aboujib, Ben Pollard." He spotted Sam Ford over to the right, Ford with his arm in a sling. "Sam Ford. Ran the com for us." He wasn't sure Ford liked the notoriety. Maybe he shouldn't have opened his mouth. But damn-all the Fleet was going to do about the rest. They were getting the one they'd bargained for, and Graff didn't look like a note-taker. He shook hands with the captain, waved a small goodbye at his shipmates, took Graff's signal they were going.

Lift took him and Graff and one guard. That was all that would fit. Graff said, on the way up, "Ops training's real glad to get its hands on you. Move of yours gave the lieutenant an attack. You didn't hear that."

He looked Graff in the face. Saw amusement. Saw the MP biting his lip.

Lift let out at the dock. Cold up here. He stood and shivered, thought then to ask, "They going to let me keep my personals? Or should I leave them?"

"Put them in stowage. Few months, you can get them back."

The lift was coming up again. It opened.

Ben came out with the other MP.

"Thought we *said* goodbye," Dekker said.

"Yeah, well," Ben said, and said to Graff, "Got room for another one?"

Different kind of ship. ECS5 was her designation—didn't have a name yet, and wouldn't, til she was commissioned. Gray and claustrophobic, huge flexing sections on the bridge. Instruments he didn't understand. Most of it was dark. The crew was minimal, evidently, or the boards weren't live yet. The personnel ring wasn't operational—it was acceleration that let them walk the deck, *g*-plus at that, with the *Hamilton*'s mass. Graff had said he'd do a walk-around with them.

Real quiet walk-around. It was a working ship. They didn't belong here. They weren't under arrest. Graff, Dekker got the idea, was doing a sell-job. "Good program," Graff said, about flight training. "They don't *want* you to come in with a lot of experience—new tech. Whole new kind of ship. Can't talk about it. Can't talk about it covers a lot we deal with."

He didn't know what he thought. The machine around him wasn't anything he'd even seen photos of.

Wasn't the only thing that puzzled him. He said to Ben, while Graff was talking to one of the techs, "Are you sure what you're doing?"

Ben gave one of his shrugs. Ben looked pale in the dark, in the light off the monitors. Sweating a little and it wasn't warm in here. "No way to get ahead. You lost the ship, Dek-boy. Debt up to our necks . . . but a man with my background—there's a real *chance* in this stuff. Military's where the edge is, the way R2's going now. Fleet's the way up, you remember I said it. There's an After to this war."

"You're out of your mind."

"Officer before I'm done. Brass pin and all. Damn right, Dek-boy. You remember you know me. You fly 'em and I'll be sitting in some safe office in Sol HQ telling 'em how to do it. Odds on it?"

"Out of your mind," Dekker repeated under his breath; and looked around him at things he wanted to understand, thinking, he couldn't help it: God, Cory should have seen this. . . .

HELLBURNER

CHAPTER 1

STOCKHOLM is a city of islands and gardens, a stunningly eclectic architectural mix, from the Rigsdagshus to the 23rd century Carlberg Museum, from the restored Riddarsholm Kyrka to the Academy gardens . . .

Founded in the mid 13th century, the city of Stockholm holds abundant evidence of a thousand years of Baltic seafaring tradition, plus a lively nightlife centered in modern Gustavsholm—

Ben indexed through the motile pictures and the text, the statistics about rainfall and mean average temperature which the Guide cautioned a visitor did not in any sense mean a constant temperature. Useless statistic—unless one contemplated Antarctica, where a mean temperature of –57° C and an average hours of sunlight only slightly better than Sol Station core meant Ben Pollard had no interest in McMurdo Base. Ben Pollard had seen a good deal of cold and dark and rock in his life. *Old* rock. This 13th century business amazed him. The whole damn human race dated itself in eighteenths of Jupiter's passes about the sun, to the astonishingly recent number of about 10k such fractions, if you took the oldest cities. ASTEX R2 out in the Belt had been a skuz old place and a friend of his had sworn it had seen better days just in *his* lifetime, but when Ben Pollard thought *old,* he thought in millions. The rock he'd handled out there was *old.* Humankind was a real junior on those terms.

He sipped real orange juice, imported up from the blue, cloud-swirled globe you could see at any hour on channel 55, along with the weather reports anywhere in the motherwell.

Weather—was a novelty. Real weather. You got weather in a station core when they were blowing cold rock down the chute. You got condensation in your spacecraft and you swore like hell and wiped and dried and tried to find the source of it. But in the motherwell condensation fell out of the sky in frozen balls or slow flakes or liquid drops depending on the low level atmospheric temperatures, and k-wide clouds threw out electrical discharges that made it a very bad notion to stand (the Guide said) as the highest point of the landscape.

Daunting thought.

The Guide said 70% of the Earth was water.

The Guide said water in the oceans was 10k meters deep in places, and because it wasn't frozen, Luna's gravity pulled it up in a hump of a wave that rolled around the globe and washed at every shore it met, enough to grind up rock into beaches.

All that unfrozen water. Gaseous nitrogen and liquid water that made all that sparkle when the sun hit the wrinkles on it that the Guide said were waves.

He planned to stand on a beach and get a good close look at that unfrozen water. On a clear day, when there were no lightnings. You could do it from the station. You could be there while you were here, but VR was a cheat, you could be a whole lot of places that weren't real. He wanted to stand at the edge of the ocean and watch the real sun disappear behind the real world, at which point he figured he would really believe he was standing on a negative curvature.

The Guide said some spacers got dizzy, with the horizon going the wrong direction. There were prescriptions for vertigo. There were preparatory programs. But hell, he'd monkeyed around the core at R2, and stared straight at the rotation interface. That had to be worse.

The clock on the screen said: 0843 June 14, 2324. And there was plenty of time this morning for coffee. Dress maybe by 0930h. Exams were done, the last score was going up today, but, hell, that was Interactive Reality Sampling and he had that one in his pocket, no question, no sweat. Probably set the curve: him or Meeker, one or the other: just let the UDC get *that* score, and Stockholm was in his pocket for sure, motherwell assignment in the safest, softest spot in the service except

Orlando. Stockholm was where Ben Pollard was headed, yeah! soon as the interviewers could get up to station.

Hell and away from the Belt, he was. Here you didn't jam two guys into a fifteen by six, hell, no, Sol Station and Admin? You got a whole effin' fifteen by six .9 *g* apartment by *yourself*, with a terminal that could be vid or VR whenever you opted. If you qualified into the Programming track in the UDC Technical Institute, you got an Allotment that afforded you 2c/d Personals per effin' seven-day week, which meant oj that was real, coffee that was *real*, red meat that was *real*, if you had the stomach for it, which Ben personally didn't—you lived like an effin' Company exec and had a clearer conscience. And if you could get that onworld posting, your tech/2 graduation rating equaled a full UDC lieutenancy in the motherwell, with an Army first lieutenant's pay to start, full grade technical/1 promotion guaranteed in a year, and access with a capital A to all the services that pay could buy. You knew there was a war out in the Beyond, but it wasn't going to get to Earth, that was what they were building that Fleet out there to stop—and even if it did nobody was going to hit the motherwell, humans just didn't *do* that. You were safe down there. You'd be safe no matter what.

He'd got his graduation With Honors, he was certain of it; he'd sweated his Security verifications, but they'd come through months ago, and nobody had come up with an objection; he'd sailed through the Administrative Service exams four weeks ago, and the only complication in his way now was the formal interview, as soon as the personnel reps from the various agencies could get seats on a shuttle up here—funding time and some legislative hearing in Admin had had the shuttle up-slots jammed with senators and brass and aides for the last three days; but that was thinning out, thank God. The agency interviewers might turn up by the end of the week, after which time—

After which he could book himself a seat for Earth on whatever assignment shook out—maybe even take his pick: Weiter had dropped him a conspiratorial word that he had three different computer divisions fighting over him, including strategic supply modeling and intelligence, and the prestigious AI lab in Geneva (which was for his personal ambitions a little too scientific and academic—give him something with a direct line to politics, God, yes. There was money in that, and a protected paycheck).

Money. A nice apartment down where you navigated a perceptually planar surface at a 300kph crawl, when he was used to thinking in kps and nanosecond intersects. Life on Earth went so much slower and death came so much later for a man who had money, brains, and position.

He'd had a partner back in the Belt, Morrie Bird, who had used to talk to him about Colorado, and cities and sunsets and Shakespeare. Bird had set a lot of personal store by Shakespeare. Bird had thought Shakespeare was important to understand. So when it had turned out of all things that he was going to the inner system, he had made it a certain point to see this Shakespeare guy—translated tapes, of course. V-vids, where you could wander around and watch the body language. And Bird had been a hundred percent right: Shakespeare really helped you figure Earthers. Blue-skyers. People who had never felt null-g, never seen the stars all the way to forever—different people, with numbers hard to figure; people who thought they had a natural right to orange juice and gravity, people who (the Guide maintained) felt the moon tides in their blood.

Getting the right numbers in a new situation absolutely mattered. On Earth air was free and ship routes and energy were what the old Earthers had fought bloody wars over. Sincerely skewed values—but you had to think about that two-dee surface constantly, and it was limited that way. Finite. Finite resources. Shakespeare helped you see that—helped you see how certain old Earthers in control of those resources had thought they could run your life, the same as Company execs. And how these king-types always talked about God and their rights, like the preachers on R2's helldeck, who snagged you with tracts and talked to you about free-shares in their particular afterlife and argued whether the aliens at Pell had souls. Only these old kings had been the preachers *and* the law *and* the bank.

Long way to come, from the Belt, from Company brat in a Company school learning nothing but Company numbers—to figuring Shakespeare and human history. But there it was, the motherlode of all living stuff and the home of humankind back when humans had been as backward as the Downers at Pell—Earth was full of museums, full of artifacts, pots and tombs and old walls graffitied with stuff that was supposed to make you live forever. The Guide said so.

Most of all, it was the motherlode of information, data, old and new. And the right numbers and enough data on the systems that ran the Earth Company and the United Defense Command could make him rich; rich made a man safe, and got him most everything Ben Pollard could put a name to.

Visitors to Stockholm may be impressed with the Maritime Museum or the Zoological Garden in Haga Park. . . .

A planet that wasn't a radiation hell was a novelty. Earth with its completely outsized moon was a novelty. And life thriving at the *bottom* of a gravity well was a radically upside down way of thinking. Life that made good wine and food that wasn't synth, a surface where plants grew and cycled the O_2 and the CO_2 on sunlight and dark; the habitats where animals lived. Fascinating concept, non-human things walking around where *they* decided to walk and looking at you with unguessable thoughts going on behind their eyes. People searched the stars for life, and there was all this life on Earth, that blue-skyers took for granted, and ate, if it didn't look too much like people.

He wanted to see a zoo. He wanted to look at a cow or a dog and be looked back at, when he'd never expect to see any real thing more exotic than miners on R&R and bugs under a lab scope.

Humans had existed such a scarily short time. With this war going on in the Beyond they seemed scarily fragile.

He wished he could talk to Bird about that. Bird had had a peculiar perspective about things. He wished he could really figure out what Bird had been, or recall half that Bird had said over the years. There was so much blue-sky attitude he still couldn't get the straight of. Baroque, was the word. Curves all over their thinking, like gold angels on the old buildings, that didn't have a damn thing to do with useful—

The message dot flashed on the corner of the screen.

God, it *could* be the interview notice. His fingers were on the Mod and the 1 to Accept Mail and the Dv and the 3 to Print faster than he could think about the motion.

It said:

TECH/2 Benjamin J. Pollard
CTS/SS/UDC 28 BAT 2
0852JUN14/24 SN P-235-9876/MLR
Report to FSO-HQ, 0930h/ref/Simons

Fleet Strategic Operations? *Fleet* Ops?

What in bloody hell?

MRL. Automatic log. No way to pretend he hadn't gotten the message. No way to query the CO. Weiter would tell him it was a report-to, he didn't have the answer, and he'd effin' better answer it and find out what the Fleet wanted with a UDC lad, hadn't he?

It *wasn't* an interview. God, no. Fleet Strategic Operations didn't need a UDC programmer tech/2 with a Priority 10 for economic/ and strategic/supply modeling. Did they?

Shit, no—the damn tight-fisted legislature insisted on trying to interface the UDC EIDAT with the Fleet's Staatentek system through the EC security screen, that was what. The Fleet Staatentek system tried to phone the UDC's EIDAT 4005 to ask for available assignees, and the 4005, behind the EC's security cloak, spat up a UDC Priority One assignee for a Fleet data entry post—

But you couldn't ignore it. You didn't want to face the interviews with an interservice screw-up or a Disciplinary in your record. Damn the thing!

No second cup of coffee. He drank the half he had left while his fingers tapped up the station map and asked it where in hell FSO-HQ was on the trans system from his apartment in TI 12 for a 0930h appointment.

9:15 2 green to 14, blue to 5-99: pass required for entry.

Hell and gone from TI, and it was already 9 o'clock. Ten effin' minutes to shave, dress and find his copy of his rating, which clearly said UDC Priority Technical/2, before the Fleet grabbed him and stuck him at Mars Base doing data entry in Supply.

He burned the beard off, pulled on his dress blues: never wear fatigues to an interservice glitch-up. He had to talk to officers, no question, before this one was straightened out, maybe all the way up the effin' C/O/C in the UDC *and* the Fleet. It could be a long day.

Envelope from UDC Technical at Geneva in the briefcase, where it belonged. He put it in his breast pocket.

Never a friggin' situation without a last friggin' minute complication. God, he didn't know why things like this happened to him. His interview appointment could come through at any hour, he *didn't* want Meeker to grab the first slot—first effin' thing he was going to do if they gave him Geneva was put the shove on that damned EC Software.

He checked his watch. 0908. Five minutes to walk to the trans. Orders *in* his pocket. Yes. And out the door.

Trans was packed. A whole wide-eyed batch of shiny new C-1's with their entry tags and their hand-baggage occupied all the seats, and Ben clung with an elbow about a pole and punched buttons on the hand reader, running down the applicable rules on interservice transfer apps.

Wasn't any reason to sweat it. Couldn't be. Weiter'd shoved him through three levels in a year. . . . He was Weiter's fair-haired baby, best Weiter had ever had in the department. Him and Meeker, neck and neck all the way. No *way* Weiter wouldn't go up the chain for him.

Green 14. He made the transfer and lost the C-1's—thank God. He got a seat, sat down and read.

Right of appeal. Ref: Administrative Appeal, Sec 14. . . . Through chain of command in service or origin.

In service of origin. Which meant the United Defense Command, which *wasn't,* never mind Fleet Captain Conrad Mazian's performance at the UN, going to let the Fleet get its hands on whatever it wanted.

Blue line now. Institution blue. The walls outside the spex in the doors grew skuzzier and skuzzier and the air that sucked in when the doors opened was cold and smelled of oil.

Descent into hell, Ben thought. Like R2 all over again. He sat in his dress uniform and watched the scenery, dark tunnel and grim flashes of gray-blue panels and white station numbers as the trans shot past stops without a call punched. Thump of the section seals. He could almost smell helldeck, all but hear the clash of metal and the hard raucous beat of the music echoing down the deck. He smelled the peculiar taint of cold machinery and kept having this most damnable feeling of—

—belonging in the dark side, living on the cheap, getting by, scamming the Company cops and *knowing* he could always slip through the system, knowing far more about the company computers and access numbers than the Company thought he'd learned. Him and Bird. —And Sal Aboujib.

Damn.

Helldeck wasn't a place you'd miss. He was someone else now. Spiff uniform and a tech/2's collar pin. Clean fingers—in all senses. He didn't do a thing illegitimate with the computers he worked with. He didn't know anybody who did, no, *sir,* didn't even dream about that h- word near the Defense Command computers.

He'd got away with it. Was still getting away with it. He'd dumped the card on R2, and it had never surfaced; he'd *gotten* his security clearance. He'd gotten his rank. Nobody was going to screw that up. Nobody could have found anything to screw him now . . .

5-99. The sign outside the doors said: SECURITY AREA. RESTRICTED. SHOW PASS.

He got up and got out in a beige, plain hallway, *warmer* here, thank

God, it wasn't going to freeze his ass off or have him shaking when he was talking to the desk. He straightened his coat, clipped his fancy-tech reader onto his belt and walked up to the only door available, under a security array that was probably reading his respiration rate and taking notes.

He put his card in the slot: the door clicked and opened. Fleet Security occupied the solitary desk in the foyer; beyond it was a potted silk palm, an abstract picture, and another beige windowless door.

"Pollard," the officer said, with no attention to the protocols in the rulebook. Or his face. Just the readout on his screen. "Benjamin J. You're carrying electronics."

"Reader."

The officer held out his hand. Ben surrendered it and watched the officer turn it on and punch buttons.

"Fancy."

Break his effin' neck getting here and this cop-type stalled him playing games with a piece of expensive and delicate equipment. He said, "I've got an appointment at 0930."

The guard said, "HQ," and motioned with the back of his hand. "Lieutenant Jackson."

Jackson, was it? Fleet Lieutenant. Which, in the much-argued and protested Equivalencies, was a rank just under Maj. Weiter's; and one over his. Ben drew himself up with a breath, thinking, with part of his brain: Son of a bitch deep-spacer Attitude, and minded for half that breath to make an issue of interservice protocols; but the rest of his brain was still wondering if the Fleet could have any legitimate interest in him and hoping all he had was a pocket full of EIDAT-screwed orders. So he saluted, got a flip of the hand and walked to the inner door, that clicked open on a long bar of a desk and a sober-faced clerk who said (efficiency, at least) "Lt. Pollard?"

"Yes." Manners. Finally. He took the offered escort to a side office. Jackson took the salute, offered him a seat. Young guy. Pleasant, serious face.

Better, he thought.

"Thank you, sir."

Jackson folded his hands on the desk, "Lt. Pollard, —I'm sorry to be the bearer of bad news: a friend of yours has been involved in an accident."

"*Friend* of mine?" That was a complete mental shift. He honestly couldn't think if he had a friend. Not lately. Bird was dead. *Sal?*

"Name of Dekker," Jackson said and Ben all but said, *Shit!* before he remembered he wasn't in the Belt and swallowed it.

"Fatal?"

"Serious. He's asking for you."

"For *me?*" He was vastly relieved it wasn't Sal. Distressed if Dekker'd gotten in trouble. He didn't hate Dekker. Not really. Dekker had enlisted with him, gone off into some secret pilot training program . . . real hot piece of equipment, Dekker had said.

Jackson said, "His doctors feel it might be some help, a familiar face. . . ."

He thought, Oh, God, I don't want to do this. I don't want to see the guy again—I *hate* hospitals . . . I don't *like* blood—

But there it was, the brass had made a humanitarian move, no way to explain all the old business between them—it could drag up too much he didn't want on record; if Dekker had killed himself in some top-secret operation he was sincerely sorry, and if he was all Dekker could dredge up for a request—well, hell, the guy had saved his neck, sort of, back in the Belt—

And cost Bird's life, damn him, however indirectly.

"Sorry to drop this on you," Jackson said.

"Not a problem. Truth is, we weren't friends. —But I guess I owe him to drop over there."

"I've got a travel voucher for you."

"Travel voucher."

"B dock."

"Oh, now, God, wait a minute—" B dock wasn't on Sol One, it was on an auxiliary station three and more days out, on Sol Two. Ben reached for his pocket, right then. "I can't do that. I'm sorry. This is a priority rating. There's an agency officer coming for an interview this week. I can't leave."

Jackson laid an envelope on top of his. "There's a B dock shuttle leaving at 1205. That's your travel voucher and your leave. It's already signed and cleared."

"Sir, —that's six *days* even if I get a same day turnaround." He gingerly eased his letter from underneath and laid it gingerly to the side, in Jackson's view, where the United Defense Command logo showed. "This is from HQ Geneva. It says I'm a military priority."

"This one's from Captain Keu, in this office. On a classified priority. You're going."

"Dekker isn't a friend of mine!"

"He's listed you as next-of-kin."

"We're not related! God, —he's got a mother right here on the station, Astrid, Ingrid, something like that. Talk to her!"

"He's in a classified program. Only certain people are approved for contact in a next-of-kin emergency. You're it. You're not to call anyone. You're not to talk to anyone. Your CO will be advised simply that you're on humanitarian leave—"

"I'm UDC essential personnel!"

"Show me an assignment."

Shit!

"So you're going."

"What about my interview?"

"That's not my information flow. I'll log it as a query."

"Look, this is important. If I miss this slot I could wait six months!"

Jackson shrugged. "We all have our hardships, lieutenant."

"Look, this is a screw-up. It's an absolute screw-up. God, Dekker and I don't even *like* each other."

Cold as a rock. "I don't have that information. Transport will pick up your baggage at your quarters. Just leave it. Report to the shuttleport by 1145."

"It's near 1030 right now. It's twenty minutes to quarters—"

"I'd be on that shuttle, Lt. Pollard. When you get to B dock, report directly to the FleetOps office on the dock, give them this pass and they'll see you get straight to the hospital. Don't mistake that instruction."

"Listen, —sir, you know what happened—Dekker wrote me in as a joke. He never thought they'd be using that information. It's a damn joke!"

"If it is, I'm sure they'll straighten it out at the other end. I'd be moving, lieutenant." Jackson stood up and handed him the two envelopes as he rose. "Good luck."

"Yes sir," Ben said, took his papers and his orders, saluted the son of a bitch and left.

Collected his reader from the front desk, and made a fast, desperate consultation of the trans schedule while he was walking to the doors.

Twenty minutes to his apartment, thirty to the shuttle dock, ten to pack. If he risked a phone call to Weiter to request a rescue, it was a 90% certainty that Weiter couldn't do a damned thing against FSO before 1145 *or* later and he'd be screwed with Weiter for putting *him* in a Position. You didn't crack a security screen. Not if you hoped to keep your clearance in UDC computer tech.

They'd get him back in maybe six days?

Hell. Six days too late if he was on humanitarian leave on B dock when the UDC filled the Stockholm post. He'd get the scraps, the cold left-overs after Meeker got posted; and Hamid; and Pannelli— The next best choice he had was to appeal to Weiter when he got back and hang on as staff til something else came through, oh, six months, even, eight months on, who knew?

Dekker had screwed up, the Fleet was evidently about to lose its investment in him—and, not in his most copacetic state, Dekker had asked for him?

Ben thought, with every thump of the trans on its homebound course: I'll kill him when I get my hands on him, I'll fuckin' kill him.

Ben hated institutions, *hated* hospital smells and institution colors and most of all he didn't look forward to this, in his first hour on B dock. He felt like hell, he'd slept in a damn cubbyhole of a berth hardly larger than a miner-ship spinner, his feet had swelled, he'd had sinus all the way: he'd spent too long in the null-*g* in his life and his body had a spiteful overreaction to the condition. They didn't issue pills and stimsuits for a three-day shuttle trip, no, that prescription's not on your records, lieutenant, sorry . . . If you'd just checked with medical—

It was damned well going to be on the record when he left Sol Two. Talk to the doctors in this hospital, get some damn good out of this end of the trip . . . because he meant to be on that shuttle on its turnaround tonight. Six hours was plenty of time to see Dekker, and get out of here.

—after three days of floating in a three-berth passenger module on a cargo shuttle, ahead of a load of sanitation chemicals and spare parts. He'd had no one to talk to but a couple of machinists who were into some vegetarian religion and hooked on some damn VR game they wanted to explain to him; and he had had ample time to drift weightless in the dark and think—too much time to imagine this meeting, and what kind of damage a pilot could take in an accident. Missing limbs. Blood. He hated blood. He really got sick at his stomach if there was blood . . .

They'd had some sort of missile test that had gone bad out here. Nobody said what. There'd been a lot of long faces in Technical. A lot of emergency meetings last week. Dekker couldn't have been involved in any missile test. A pilot trainee didn't have anything to do with missile tests. Did he?

Jackson had done the talking. But why in hell did a Fleet captain sign the order and bust him out here? What was Dekker that the Fleet cared? The Fleet was fighting for its life in the Appropriations Committee. Dumbass pilot cracked up and UDC Priorities got overridden—for *humanitarian* reasons?

Not in the military he knew. That was the tag end that had disturbed his sleep and his thinking moments all the way out here. Their high-level interest in this affair was what had his stomach upset, as much as the stink of disinfectant and pain and helplessness in this place. He didn't like this. God, he didn't like this, and if Dekker wasn't dead he was going to strangle him bare-handed for writing him into that damned blank.

God, he was.

Reception desk. He presented his orders to the clerk and got a: "Lt. Pollard. Yes, *sir,*" that did nothing for his stomach or his pulse rate. The receptionist got him a nurse, a doctor, and Dekker's attending physician, all in increasingly short succession. "How is he?" Ben asked the last, bypassing long introductions. "What happened to him?" and the doctor said, starting off down the hall:

"No change."

"So when did this happen?"

"That's classified."

More white coats. More people leaning into his face. They wanted him to open his eyes, but Dekker knew the game. They wanted answers to fill the blanks they had on their slates, but they wanted their own answers, the way they wanted the case to be.

Company doctors. He'd been here before. And they wouldn't listen. He asked, "Where's Cory?" because sometimes he couldn't remember what had happened, or he did, but it was all a dizzy blur of black and lights. The ship was spinning. He fought to get to the controls, because he had to stop that spin, with the blood filling his nose and choking his breath, and his hand dragging away with the spin, his grip going—

"Cory? You damned bastard, *stop!*"

But sometimes he came loose from that time and he was in hospital, or he was going to be, soon as Ben and Bird got him there, and they would lie to him and tell him there never had been a 'driver ship and he never had had a partner named Cory.

The Company had lied to him. They said he was hallucinating, but it was all lies. And sometimes he thought the hospital was the hallucination, that it was all something his conscience had conjured to punish him for losing his grip on the counter and for losing the ship.

For losing Cory.

And Bird.

Sometimes he was back in the shower, and sometimes tied to the pipes, because he was crazy, and he couldn't figure out how the ship had come to the hospital.

Thirty days hath September, March eleventh, and November. . . .

There were green coats now. Interns. He hoped for Tommy. But Tommy wasn't with them. "Where's Tommy?" he asked. "Why isn't Tommy on duty? —God, it's afire, isn't it? Meg? Meg, wake up, God, don't die on me—"

"Ens. Dekker, you have a visitor."

"I don't want any fuckin' visitor. Get away from me. Get out of here."

"Ens. Dekker, —"

"Tell him to go to hell! I don't want any damn Company lawyer! —Put Tommy back on duty, hear me? I want Tommy back." They grabbed hold of his arms, they were going to put the restraints on. Tommy wouldn't do that. Tommy would ask, Are you going to be quiet, Mr. Dekker? and he would say, Yes, yes, I'll be quiet, and Tommy wouldn't use them.

Wouldn't. But Tommy wasn't with them. And they did. They told him then if he wasn't quiet they'd have to sedate him. So he said, "I'll be quiet," and shut his eyes.

"Dekker," Ben said. And he opened his eyes. Ben was leaning over his bed. Ben was in uniform. UDC. That was different. But odder things happened in this place. He didn't blink. Things changed if you did. Finally he said, "Ben?"

"Yeah."

There was a ship out there. He remembered that. "Ben, we've got to go back. Please, we've got to go back, Cory's still out there—"

Ben grabbed a fistful of his collar, leaned close and said, in a low voice, "Dekker, shut it down right now or I'm going to kill you. You hear me?"

He said, "That's all right." He *felt* Ben's hand on him. He *saw* Ben's face. He knew where he was then, Bird was asleep and Ben was about to beat hell out of him. But that was all right. He really liked Ben, most of the time. And there hadn't been much to like where he'd been.

What could a guy do? Ben disengaged himself, and Dekker caught his hand. He pulled free and got out of the door to get his breath.

The doctor was out there, several doctors this time. "He knows you," Dekker's surgeon said. Higgins was his name. "You're the first person he *has* recognized."

"Fuckin' hell! Then he's cured. I'm out of here."

"Lt. Pollard," another doctor said, and offered his hand. "Lt. Pollard, I'm Dr. Evans, chief of psychiatry."

"Fine. Good. He needs a psych. That's all that's going to help him!"

"Lt. Pollard, —"

"Look, what do you want from him? The guy's schitz, completely off the scope. He doesn't know where he is, he doesn't know what happened—"

"Lt. Pollard." The psych motioned off down the farther hallway. "There's coffee in the lounge. You've had a long flight."

The psych wanted him to sit down and be reasonable, which he was in no mood to be. But coffee appealed to his upset stomach and his sleep-deprived nerves. And it was not at all a good idea to have a psych telling the local CO you'd been hysterical. You didn't need *that* on a record behind another service's security screen. So he went with the psych, he went through the dance—"White or black, sugar?" "That's enough, thanks,"—until he could get the weight off his feet, sink into a chair and try not to let Evans see his hands shake while he was drinking.

"So what happened to him?" he asked, before Evans could fire off his own questions.

"That's what we want to know."

"So how'd he get like this?"

"That's another question."

Deeper and deeper. Ben stared at the doctor and scowled. "So a door got him. Is that it?"

"A simulator did."

Flight simulator? Dekker? "Hell of a simulation, doctor."

"Didn't lock the belts, strong dose of sedative in his bloodstream."

Shit. Pills again.

Evans said: "We'd like to know how he got there."

Or maybe not. "You mean somebody put him there?"

"It's one possibility."

"Guy has a talent for making friends. Yeah. There's probably a dozen candidates."

"Why do you say that?"

Psych question. He thought, Because he's a fuck-up. Because he has this way of getting himself in trouble and slapping the hand that helps him. But that led to more questions; and screwed Dekker worse than he was with this guy, to whom he owed nothing yet. He said, finally, "Say I didn't really know him that well."

"He listed you as next-of-kin."

"It was a joke. The guy's full of them. Lot of laughs."

"We don't rule out suicide."

Dekker? he thought. Dekker? Suicide? The idea was more than unlikely. It upset him. And he didn't figure that, either why they could think that—if they knew Dekker, which they might not; or how Dekker could come to that—here, in this place that swallowed people down without a word.

"You don't agree?"

He shrugged. "It's not him. It's just not him."

You didn't come from where Dekker came from—didn't survive what he'd survived—and check out like that—in a damn sim. Something wasn't right, not with the questions, not with Dekker lying in there thinking he was back in the Belt, not with this whole max-classified operation that took a will to live like Dekker's and put him in that bed, in that condition.

Dekker had looked at him like he was what he'd been waiting for, and said, to his threat of killing him bare-handed, That's all right . . .

Every time you got near the guy there was a disaster, Dekker attracted disasters, you could feel it, and, God of all the helldeck preachers, he wanted on that shuttle tonight. Do this effin' job, get Dekker to figure out where he was, and when he was, make him talk to the psychs, and get out of here while there was still a chance of making that interview—and getting out of this mess.

"I'll talk to him," he said.

"You're sure you're all right about that?"

Another psych quiz. Correct answer: "A long trip with no information, run in here straight from the mast, I was a little shaken up myself." He tossed off the rest of the coffee, got up and pitched the cup into the bin. "I'm fine to talk to him. What do you want out of him?"

"His health."

"Yeah, well, he'll pull it out. Knock him down and he bounces."

"Don't stress him, lieutenant. I really don't advise another confrontation. He's been concussed. We want to keep that blood pressure under control."

That was about worth a laugh. Dek was already stressed. Dek was in an out-of-control ship in a 'driver zone with his partner lost. He said soberly, "I've no intention of upsetting him."

The doctor opened the door, the doctor walked him back to Dekker's room and signaled an orderly for a word aside in the hallway.

Ben walked on in, pulled a chair over and sat down by Dekker's bed. Dekker's eyes tracked his entry, stayed tracked as he sat down, he wasn't sure how focused. Dekker had been a real pretty-boy, a year ago, fancy dresser, rab hair, shaved up the sides. Still looked to be a rab job, give or take the bandage around the head; but the eyes were shadowed, one was bruised, the chin had a cut, lip was cut—not so long back. The hollow-cheeked, waxen look—did you get that from a bashing-about in a simulator a few days ago?

"You look like hell, Dekker-me-lad."

"Yeah," Dekker said. "You're looking all right."

"So what happened?"

Dekker didn't answer right off. He looked to be thinking about it. Then his chin began to tremble and Ben felt a second's disgusted panic: dammit, he didn't want to deal with a guy on a crying jag—but Dekker said faintly, shakily, "Ben, you'll want to hit me, but I really need to know—I really seriously need to know what time it is."

"What time it is?" God. "So what'll you give me for it?"

"Ben, —"

"No, hell, I want you to give me something for it. I want you to tell me what the hell you're doing in here. I want to know what happened to you."

Dekker gave a shake of his head and looked upset. "Tell me the time."

Ben looked at his watch. "All right, it's 1545, June 19th—"

"What year?"

"2324. That satisfy you?"

Dekker just stared at him, finally blinked once.

"Look, Dekker, nice to see you, but you really screwed everything up. I got orders waiting for me back at the base, I got a transfer that, excuse me, means my whole career, and if you'll just fuckin' cooperate with them I can still catch a shuttle in a few hours and get my transfer back to Sol where I can stay with my program. —Dek, come on, d' you sincerely understand you're screwing up my life? Do me a favor."

"What?"

"Tell the doctors what happened to you. Hear me? I want you to answer their questions and tell them what they want to hear and I don't, dammit, I want to be on that shuttle. You want me to call them in here so they can listen to you explain and I can get out of here?"

Dekker shook his head.

"Dekker, dammit, don't be like that. You're a pain in the ass, you know that? I got to get back!"

"Then go. Go on. It's all right."

"It's not the hell all right. I can't get out of here until you tell them what they want to know! Come on. It's June 19th. 2324. Argentina's won the World Cup. Bird's dead. Cory's dead. We came out here on a friggin' big ship neither of us is supposed to talk about and Gennie Vanderbilt is top of the series. Do you remember what put you here?"

"I can't remember. I don't remember—"

"Because you climbed into a friggin' flight simulator tranked to the eyeballs—does that jar anything loose?"

A blank stare, a shake of the head.

Ben ran a hand over his head. "God."

"It's just gone, Ben. Sometimes I think it's the ship again. Sometimes it's not. You're here. But I thought you were before. What are they saying about the sim?"

"Dekker, —" He gave a glance to the door, but the doctor-types were conferring outside. He said, in a low voice: "You're not hooked on those damn pills again, are you?"

Dekker shook his head. Scared. Lost. Eyes shifted about. Came back to him.

"Ben, —I'm sorry. Please tell me the time again."

He didn't hit Dekker. He leaned forward and took Dekker's hand hard in his despite the restraints and said, very quietly, "It's June 19th. Now you tell me the year, Dek. I want the year. Right now. And you better not be wrong."

Dekker looked seriously worried. A hesitation. A tremor of the lips. "2324."

"Good. You got it memorized. Now there's going to be a test every few minutes, hear me? I want you to remember that number. This is Sol Two. You had a little accident a few days back. The doctors want to know, that's not so hard to hold on to, is it?"

"I can't remember. I can't remember, Ben, it's just gone . . ."

"Shit." He had a headache. He looked at Dekker's pale, bruised, trusting face and wanted ever so much to beat him senseless. Instead he squeezed Dekker's hand. "Dek, boy, listen. I got a serious chance at

Stockholm, you understand me? Nice lab job. I'm going to lose it if you don't come through. I really need you to think about that simulator."

Dekker looked upset. "I'm trying. I'm trying, Ben. I really am—"

Something was beeping. Machine up there on the shelf. Doctors were in the door. Higgins said, "Lt. Pollard. He's getting tired. Better leave it. —Ens. Dekker, I'm Dr. Higgins, do you remember me?"

Dekker looked at *him,* and said faintly, "Ben?"

"You do remember him," Ben said. "Hear me? Or I'll break your neck!"

"Don't go."

"He'll be back tomorrow."

"The hell," Ben said. "Dekker, goodbye. Good luck. I got to catch a shuttle. Stay the hell out of my life."

"Lieutenant." That was Evans. "In the hall."

He went. He got his voice down and his breathing even. "Look, I've done my job. I'm no doctor, you're the psych, what am I supposed to do?"

"You're doing fine. This is the first time he's been that sure where he is."

"Fine. I've got orders waiting for me on Sol One. I haven't got time for this!"

"That's not the way I understand your orders. You have a room assignment—"

"I haven't got any room assignment."

"—in the hospice a level up. It's a small facility. Very comfortable. We'd prefer you be available for him 24 hours. His sleeping's not on any regular pattern."

"No way. I've got a return order in my pocket, my baggage is still right back there in customs. Nobody said anything about this going into another shift. That wasn't the deal."

"Nobody said anything about your leaving. You'd better check those orders with the issuing officer."

"I'll check it at the dock. I'll get this cleared up. Just give him my goodbyes. Tell him good luck, I hope he comes out all right. I won't be here in the morning."

"Hospice desk is on level 2, lieutenant. You'll find the lift right down the corridor."

Ben had been there awhile. Ben had told him—

But he couldn't depend on that. Ben came and Ben went and sometimes Ben talked to him and told him—

Told him about an accident in the sims. But if it was a sim then maybe people he thought were dead, weren't, even if they told him so. The doctors lied to him. They regularly lied, and Tommy didn't come back. They kept changing doctors, changing interns, every time he got close to remembering. . . .

Only Ben. Ben came and he started to hope and he knew that hope was dangerous. You didn't hope. You just lived.

Ben asked him was he on drugs. He had been once. He had been crazy once, now and again, but Ben and Bird had pulled him out. The ship was spinning. Cory was out there alone, and somebody had to pull him out—

Ship was spinning. Pete was yelling. And Cory—

Ben said he would kill him if he was crazy and he hoped Ben would do that, if he truly was, because he didn't want to live like that.

Ben said remember. But he couldn't remember any specific time in the sims. He could remember an examiner giving him his C-3. He could remember the first time he'd seen the boards. Remembered pushing beams at Sol. Supervisor had said all right, he could do that: he was under age, but they needed somebody who wouldn't ram a mass into the station hull. His head was bandaged, his ribs were. His knees ached like hell, he thought because he had hit the counter, trying to hit the button, but he wasn't sure of anything. You blinked and you got green numbers and lines, and if you followed them too far you never came back. Midrange focus. Back it up, all the way inside.

There'd been an accident and the ship had blown up. And his partners were dead. Or maybe never existed. It was a sim. Bright ball of nuclear fire. And he was here and they were in it, and it was all green glowing lines out there, whipping and snaking to infinity.

He remembered faces now. People he thought he liked—Bird. Meg and Sal. Cory, and Graff. Pete and Elly and Falcone. Faces. Voices. Falcone yelling, Hey, Dek, see you tomorrow.

But Falcone wouldn't. Elly wouldn't. They never would.

"You damn bastards!" he yelled. "*Bastards!*"

Interns came running, grabbed hold of him. "No," he said, reminded what happened when he yelled. "No. *Tommy!*"

"Get the hypo," one said, and he got a breath, he got a little sanity, said, "I'm not violent. I don't need it. It's all right. Let go, dammit! Get the doctor!"

They eased up. They stopped bruising his arms and just held him still.

"Just be quiet, sir. Just be quiet."

"No shots. No damn shots."

"Doctor's orders, sir."

"I don't need one. I swear to you, I don't need one."

"Doctor says you're not getting any rest, sir. You better have it. Just to be sure."

He looked the intern in the face. Big guy, red face and freckles, lying across him. Out of breath. So was he. And two other large guys who were leaning on him and holding his legs.

"Sorry," he said, between breaths. "Don't want to give you guys trouble. I really don't want to. I just don't want any shot right now."

"Sorry, too, sir. Doctor left orders. You don't want to be any trouble. Right?"

"No," he said. He shook his head. He made up his mind he had better change tactics. Agreeing with them got him out of this place. It would. It had. He couldn't remember. It was only the drugs he had to worry about.

"Just hold still, sir. All right?"

"Yeah," he said, and the hypo kicked against his arm. Stung like hell. His eyes watered.

He said, "You fuckin' get off me. I can't breathe. Let me up, dammit."

"Soon's you shut your eyes, sir. Just be quiet. You loosened a couple of John's teeth yesterday. You remember?"

He didn't remember. But he said, out of breath, "I'm sorry. Sorry about that. I'm better. A lot better."

"That's good, sir."

"Friend of mine was here," he said. But the drug was gathering thick about his brain. He said it again, afraid he might not remember when he waked. Or that it hadn't happened at all.

He went to sleep when they drugged him and he waked up and he never knew where or when. He was going out now. He felt it happening. And he was scared as hell where he would wake up or what would be true or where the lines would lead him.

"Ben," he cried, "Bird. Ben, come back— Ben, don't go—they killed my partners, Ben, they fuckin' killed us—"

"This isn't validated," the check-in clerk said, and slid the travel voucher across the desk in the .6 *g* of 8-deck. "You need an exit stamp."

Ben took the voucher with a sinking heart. "What exit stamp? Nobody said anything about an exit stamp. There's no exit stamp in the customs information."

"It's administrative, sir. Regulation. I have to have a stamp."

"God. Look, *call* Sol One."

"You do that from BaseCom," the clerk said. And added without expression: "But you need an authorization from your CO to do that, sir."

"And where do I get that?" You didn't yell at clerks. It didn't get you anything to yell at clerks. Ben said quietly, restrainedly: "My CO's on Sol One—I need the UDC officer in charge."

"This is a Fleet transport voucher."

"I know it is," Ben said. "But this uniform is UDC. Is it at all familiar to you? Where's the UDC officer in charge?"

The clerk got a confused look, and focused behind him, where someone had come into the office, to stand in line was Ben's initial reckoning; but whoever it was said, then, "Lt. Pollard?"

Voice he'd heard before. A long time ago. He turned around, a little careful in the .6g, saw a blue uniform and a black pullover, a thin, angular face and nondescript pale hair. Brass on the collar.

The trip out from the Belt. The *Hamilton.* And Jupiter's well.

Graff. Fleet Lt. Jurgen Graff. Carrier pilot, junior grade.

"There's an office free," Graff said, meaning very evidently they should go there. Now. Urgently. A Fleet lieutenant wanted to talk to him, and he was stuck on Fleet orders in something that increasingly felt like a deliberate black hole?

"I've got a flight out of here at 1800. They're talking about an exit stamp. I need some kind of clearance."

"You don't have a flight out of here. Not this one."

He slowed down, so that Graff had to pull a stop and look at him. "Sir, I need this straightened out, with apologies, sir, but I've got a transfer order waiting for me back on Sol One, I was told not to communicate with my CO, I'm *not* Fleet personnel. I understand the interservice agreements, but—"

"Five minutes."

"I'm UDC personnel. I want to see a UDC ranking officer. Sir. Now."

"Five minutes," Graff repeated. "You don't want your friend screwed. Do you?"

"My friend— Sir, I don't *care* what happens to my *friend.* I've got an appointment waiting for me back on Sol One, and if I lose it, *I'm* screwed. I'm just a little uneasy about this whole damn arrangement, —sir. This isn't what I was told."

"There's another shuttle out the 22nd. 2100 hours."

Ben caught a breath. Three days. But Graff's moves meant business and you didn't argue a security matter on the open dock—no. Even if it was blackmail. Extortion. Kidnapping.

Graff waited. He came ahead. He went with Graff into a freight office and Graff waved the lights on.

"Yes, sir?" he said.

"We need him," Graff said. "We need him to remember."

"Sir, I just graduated from TI. If I'm not back there for the interviews they're going away. They're going to assign those slots and I'm stuck teaching j-l programming to a class full of wide-eyed button-pushers, —sir. Excuse me, but I've not been in contact with any officer in my chain of command, I've gone along with this on the FSO's word it had notified my CO. I'm not sure at this point I'm not AWOL."

"You're not. You're cleared."

"I've got your word on that. I haven't seen any order but the one that had me report to the FSO on One. What have you done to me?"

"You have my word. I'll get a message to your CO."

"You mean they haven't?"

"I'll double check. We've played poker, haven't we, Mr. Pollard?"

"Yes, sir." Days of poker. Him. Dekker. Graff. No damn thing else to do on a half-built carrier.

"This is poker," Graff said. "For the major stakes. How *is* he?"

"What does it matter? What's he into?"

"Say I need him sane."

"He's never been sane."

"Don't joke like that. In some quarters they might take you seriously."

"I am serious. The guy's good, but his tether on reality's just a little frayed."

"Maybe that's what it takes to do what he does."

He stood there close to Graff, looking into Graff's sober face in this very unofficial office and suddenly wondering who and what Graff was talking about and what Dekker *did* regularly do that had put him where he was. He said, carefully, "Dekker got lost out in the Belt. Banged around a lot. Real disoriented."

"We know that."

And how much else? Ben wondered. God, how much else? News didn't escape the Belt. Security didn't let anything get out. Even yet. Everything about the mining operation out there was under wrap. You didn't know how much the Fleet might know. Or what tiny, inadvertent slip would let them guess what they'd done back there and what they might have been involved in that might screw his security clearance for good.

"I knew this man a handful of months. I've seen him like this before—when he first got out of hospital on R2. I can't make him make sense til he wants to make sense. I couldn't then. Nobody can."

"You made a good advance on it. Three days, lieutenant. I want him to talk."

Breath came short. "Do I get to beat it out of him?"

"Let's be serious, lieutenant."

"What am I supposed to be asking? Have I got a clearance to hear it? Or what happens when he *does* talk? What am I looking for?"

"As much as you can know—and it's not been released yet—there was an accident. Dekker wasn't in it. Friends of his were. Dekker's crew was lost."

"Oh shit."

"Top command subbed in another pilot with Dekker's crew on a test run. The test didn't go right. Total loss. Dekker was hospitalized, treated for shock. The day he got out—he either climbed into a simulator under the influence of drugs or something else happened. It's a matter of some interest—which."

Ben chewed his lip. Missile test, they'd said on Sol One. Tech committee meetings. Place crawling with brass and VIPs. Hell. "So isn't there an access record?"

"Computers can be wrong. Can't they?"

Ben's heart rate picked up: he hoped to hell there wasn't a monitor hearing it. He tried to think of some scrap to hand Graff, for good will's sake. He finally said, "Yes. They can be."

"I want him functioning," Graff said. "Say you're on interservice loan—at high levels. It could be good. It could be bad. To take maximum advantage of that . . . you need to deliver." Graff pulled a thick envelope from his jacket and held it out to him. "He listed you next-of-kin. So you have a right to see this."

"I'm not his next-of-kin. He's got a mother—"

"She's specifically excluded. Don't worry. There's nothing in this packet outside your security clearance."

He took it. He didn't want to.

"I wouldn't leave that material lying about unattended," Graff said, "all the same. —You've got your quarters in hospital. I can't order you not to use the phone. But if you do, if you contact anyone else, do you understand me, you're not behind our screen any longer. Take my personal advice: get back to the hospital and stay there—and don't use that phone."

He looked at Graff a long, long moment. Lieutenant j-g. Carrier command officer. A tech/1 to a tech/2's rank. But he had the impression

Graff was leaning on some executive and clandestine authority to do what he was doing. It was in Graff's tone, in the clear implication he should avoid his own chain of command.

"Whose office does this originate in, sir? You mind to tell me how official this is? Who's in charge?"

"Ultimately, the captain."

Two and two suddenly made four. Keu. Sol FSO. He looked Graff in the eyes and thought—I don't like this. Damn, I don't. He said,

"Is your captain the only authority that's covering me?"

Graff said, "No."

Conrad Mazian? The EC militia commander who was romancing his way through the UN hearings? "In which service, sir? I want to know. I need to know that. I want orders in writing."

"Ben. Take my word. I'd go back to quarters, immediately, if I were you. I'd stay quiet. I'd do everything I could to finish my job. If I were in your place." Graff opened the door, and shut off the lights. "If you need me, for any reason—tell Dr. Evans."

The keycard worked, at least. The room in the hospice was an institutional cubbyhole with a bunk, a phone, an ordinary flat-vid.

And no baggage.

Delivered, customs had said. Customs had showed him the slip. Delivered at 1500h. God only where.

He set down the soft drink he had carried up from level 1. He looked at his watch. 1845h.

He picked up the phone and went through hospital downside to call customs.

"This is Lt. Benjamin Pollard. I was just there. My baggage isn't here. Is it still being delivered?"

"Who did you talk to?"

He sat down on the bed. He pulled a vending machine sandwich from his pocket, laid it on the table by the soft drink, and pulled out the customs claim ticket. "The claim number is 9798."

A pause. *"It's been delivered, sir."*

"You didn't deliver it to HOS-28."

"That's what's on the ticket, sir."

"That's not what's in HOS-28, soldier. I want to know where my baggage is right now."

"That's all the record I have, sir. You could check with Lost Baggage at 0700."

"This shift doesn't find baggage, is that it? It just loses it?"

A moment of silence. *"I'll make a note of it, sir."*

"Thank you."

He punched out. He did not break the phone. He took a sip of his soft drink and unwrapped the sandwich.

No official assignment, no cafeteria open at this hour, no card with food privileges. He had fifty on him. Period. And Mr. Lieutenant j-g Jurgen Graff and his unnamed captain hadn't seen to that detail.

God, he didn't like the feeling he had. Bet that Graff *had* contacted Maj. Weiter? Hell if. Bet that the UDC knew where he was right now?

He looked at the phone and thought how he could call the UDC CO here. He could do that. He could break this wide open and maybe be a hero to the UDC—or get caught in the middle of something, behind a security screen that didn't have Stockholm anywhere inside it. A screen confined to *this* place. Right now he could plead total ignorance. Right now he had a transfer order signed by Keu and a Security stamp on it and he could plead he had regarded the order exactly the way it said in the Interservice Protocols. And he could do what they wanted and get out of here.

Dammit, he didn't know why Dekker was crazy. Anybody who wanted to fly little ships and get shot at was crazy. If even the simulator could half kill a guy—

He could have said get Dekker off the drugs. He could have said don't sedate him—but Dekker knew too much about him, damn him, Dekker knew enough to babble things that could end up on *his* record, if Dekker got to talking to the psych; and if Dekker had told certain things to Graff, God—Graff could have been sifting everything he had said against information he had no idea Graff had, and weighing it for truth. Graff could have had technical backup doing it, big-time, interactive logic stuff you had no good chance to evade without a clearer head and a calmer pulse rate than he had had in that interview—

God only, what Dekker had involved himself in. Or why someone might have wanted Dekker dead.

Or what might happen if he picked up that phone right now and tried to get through to the UDC office—via hospital communications.

He didn't know enough about how the lines were drawn here. He didn't *want* to know enough. Do what Graff wanted and be on that shuttle on the 22nd, that was all. Any way he could. And if the UDC did land on him—spill everything immediately. Total innocence. No, sir, they showed me orders, they said it was cleared—

Somebody subbed a pilot on a test run? And somebody put Dekker into a simulator drugged out of his mind?

Bloody hell.

He pulled out the envelope, from inside his jacket. Opened it and pulled out cards and pictures, a couple of licenses and old IDs.

Flight certification. Picture of Dekker and three other people. Group shot. All in Fleet uniform. Woman and two guys besides Dekker. All smiling. Arms over each other's shoulders.

Old vid advert for a truly skuz sex item. God. We all have our secrets, Dek-lad, . . .

Picture of Sol Station. Picture of a couple of people outside a trans station. Picture of Mars Base from orbit. If there'd been any of Cory Salazar, Dekker had lost those, a long time ago.

Datacard. The phone had a reader, but he shoved the card into his own. Personal card showed vid rentals. Commissary charges. Postage charges. Bank records. Bits and pieces of Dekker's life since they'd parted company. Lad had 5300.87cc to his account and no debts. Not bad. Not rich either.

The other datacard was old notes and mail. Not much of it. Notes from various people. One letter months ago from Ingrid Dekker. Four, this last year from Meg Kady.

So Meg did write him. He would never have figured Meg for the letter-writing kind.

Would never have figured Meg for a lot else, either.

He keyed up Meg's last letter, scanned at random through what must have cost a Shepherd spacer a mint to send:

. . . *can't complain. Doing fine. I'm working into the crew, got myself onto the pilot list* . . .

Sal and I dropped into The Hole, just on a look-see. Maybe it's what we are now. Maybe it's just the place is duller. It doesn't feel the same—

So what does? he thought, and thought about Sal, and good times in The Hole's back rooms. But Sal Aboujib probably had herself a dozen guys on a string by now, swaggering about in rab cut and Shepherd flash, visiting pricey places like Scorpio's—if Scorpio's still existed. Sal had her a berth, had her a whole new class of guys to pick from. And Ben Pollard never had gotten a letter from Sal Aboujib. A hello from Dekker once, months ago. He'd said hello back. Only communication they'd had. And it was on here. *Hope you're doing all right. Everything fine.* Only long-distance letter he'd ever gotten, tell the truth. And what did you answer, to people you didn't want to be tied to? Good luck, goodbye, Dekker?

Bills. Note from one Falcone—*Dek, we don't like it either. But noth-*

ing we can do right now. They want a show. We'll sure as hell give them one.

He skimmed back to the letter from Ingrid Dekker. A short one. *Don't come here. I don't want to see you. You went out there by your own choice and maybe it wasn't any of it your fault what happened, but things are hard enough, Paul, and I don't need any more trouble. Stop sending me money. I don't want any more ties to you. I don't want any more letters. Leave me alone.*

Shit.

He set the reader on his knee, gave a deep breath, thinking—Shit, Dek —He'd grown up on his parents' insurance himself, both of them having been so careless as to take the deep dive with their whole crew. At first he'd really resented them doing that, thought if they'd given a damn about their kid they wouldn't have been that careless, but he'd stared into Jupiter's well himself once—and he *knew* how subtle and sudden that slope was, in the pit of his stomach he knew it, now, and dreamed about it, on bad nights.

But his mama had never written him a letter like this one, and in that cold little spot marked Who's left to care, he guessed why Dekker might have written him as next-of-kin: Meg with her letters about how she was working into the crew and everything was going fine for her—Dekker wouldn't risk having another woman writing him, saying, Get out of my life, you skuz. Dekker already knew what Ben Pollard thought. And if Dekker was in trouble that needed a next-of-kin—whose life was he going to interrupt, who might remotely even know him?

He cut the reader off. He sat there in a cardboard cubby of a room with no damn baggage and for a moment or two had remorseful thoughts about Paul Dekker. Wished maybe he'd written a line or two more, back then, like—hell, he didn't know. Something polite.

What friggin' time is it?

Two *months* in a miner-ship with Dekker off his head asking him the time every few minutes. So here he was back there again—locked into a hospital with Dekker. One part of him felt sorry for Dekker and the other panicked part of him still wanted to beat hell out of the fool and get out of here. . . .

Dammit, what am I supposed to do with this damn card? Why didn't Graff give this stuff to the psych?

Sub in another pilot, did they? Why, if not Dekker's attitude? And *who* did it, if not the CO who's supposed to want this stuff from Dekker? Real brand-new ship, Dekker said once. That's why the Fleet had wanted him. He'd been real excited about it—wanted it more than anything in his life—

And a crew's dead and Dekker's screwed like that?

He sat there on the side of the bed desperately, urgently, wanting off Sol Two, he didn't at the moment care where. This whole deal had the stink of death about it.

Serious death, Sal would say.

No shit, Sal. What do I do with the guy?

CHAPTER 3

"Mr. Graff, urgent word with you. Down the hall. Sir. Please."

0645 and the breakfast line in the green room was backed up to the door. Hardly time for coffee in the fifteen minutes before he was due in Tanzer's office and Jurgen Albrecht Graff punched white coffee instead of black for his stomach's sake. "Can it wait?" he asked without looking at Mitch, and caught the cup that tilted sideways and straightened it in time. Held it while it filled.

"No, sir. A number of us want to talk, sir. Urgent business."

Spit and polish. From Mitch. There was no one else in the rec nook of the mess hall and no reasonable chance of being overheard in the clatter of trays. "Tanzer wants to talk, too. I have an appointment in fifteen."

"Hell." Mitch was Shepherd, aggressively Shepherd, shaved up the sides, couple of earrings. Bracelet. "I swore you'd be there. Sir."

Graff lifted out the cup, said, "All right, five," and stole a sip as he walked with Mitch out the main door and down the hall to the conference rooms. Door to 6a was open. Mitch's tech crew was there, Pauli and Jacoby, Jamil and his longscanner, Trace. Graff recognized a delegation when he saw it. Tanzer had said, Don't discuss the hearings. Patently that was not the intention here.

Mitch shut the door. "Sir. We're asking you to get one of us in front of the committee."

"Won't happen," Graff said. "No chance. You want to get a haircut, Mitch?"

"Hell if."

"That's an Earth committee. Blue-sky as they come. They won't communicate."

"Yeah," Jacoby said. "Is that why Tanzer killed Pete and Elly? Couldn't let a Belter pull it off?"

"Ease off, Jacoby."

"They won't let us in hospital. You seen Dekker? You *seen* him, lieutenant?"

Pauli muttered: "Wouldn't be surprised if Tanzer ordered him put in that machine. Didn't want him at the hearings."

"Shut that down," Graff said. "Right now."

Mitch folded his arms, set a foot on a chair, and said, "Somebody better hear it. They didn't want any Belter son of a bitch in front of the cameras. Dekker couldn't fly it? Then why didn't they sub the *crew,* ask them that!"

"Mitch, I hope somebody does have the brains to ask it. But there's nothing I can do. They're not going to ask me that."

"Hell if, sir! Tanzer's pets are killing us. You want me to shave up like a—" Mitch looked at him—him and his regulation trim, and shut the epithet off unsaid. "You get me in front of that hearing and I'll look like a UDC accountant."

"Mitch, I'm in a position."

"You're in a position. You're running safe behind shields—sir. We're the ones with our ass on the line."

Pauli said: "And they can't automate these sumbitches any further. Why don't they ask somebody who knows?"

"The designers will. Staatentek's here. They'll ask. That much I'll get a chance to tell them."

"Ask 'em about the sim!"

Female voice: Trace. "They're not interested. This is going to be a whitewash start to finish."

"The designers have to talk to us, Trace. We'll get our word in."

Mitch said: "The *engineers* have to talk to us. The execs and the politicrats won't and they have the say."

"Mitch, I can't listen to this."

"Tanzer is a hidebound blue-skyer son of *a* bitch who thinks because he grew up with a rulebook up his ass is a reason to try to tell any spacer his business or to think that the salute-the-logo dumbasses they've pulled in off the Guard and the system test programs could do the job with these ships—"

"They can fly, Mitch."

"Yeah, they can fly. Like Wilhelmsen."

"Nothing *wrong* with Wilhelmsen. Listen to me— Shut it down, and listen: if we have a technical at work, we want to find it, we don't want to whitewash *that* either. We have something more at issue here than Wilhelmsen."

"Yeah," Pauli muttered. "Tanzer."

Mitch said, "Nothing wrong with that ship. Everything wrong with the pilot. And they aren't going to find the solution to what happened to Wilhelmsen in Tanzer's fuckin' *rulebook*. Sir."

"Let's just find out, shall we?"

"Just make the point with them, lieutenant: Wilhelmsen wasn't set with the crew. Wilhelmsen should have said not ready, *he* was the pilot, he had the final say-so, demo be damned. It was his *responsibility* to do that."

"Yes, it was his responsibility, but it wasn't in his judgment to do it, or he would have done it—the guy's dead. He got it the same as the rest, Mitch. Let's give the experts a chance to figure out what."

"What chance have they got, if they're not getting the information? Their *experts* are blue-sky as Tanzer is!"

Jacoby said: "It's the At-ti-tude in the UDC brass. They murdered Wilhelmsen and Wilhelmsen murdered that crew, that's what they need to hear!"

"All right! All right! But there's nothing I can do to get you in there right now, and if you act the fools and screw this, they'll pull those design changes and you'll be flying targets. Now leave it! Get off my tail! Give me a chance! *That's* the order. I've got a meeting."

There was quiet. It wasn't a happy quiet. Graff handed the coffee to Mitch. "You drink it." He started for the door in a dead silence and looked back. "It's my life too, guys. You shit me, a carrier's gone. *Program's* gone. You understand that?"

They weren't used to hearing Helm Two talk like that. Not at all. There were sober faces.

Mitch said, "No offense, lieutenant."

Graff passed a hand over his close-cropped hair. Said, "Hey, I have to deal with 'em, guys," and ducked out, with an uncomfortable feeling of being square in the middle—merchanter and neither Shepherd nor regular UDC. Not part of the rab the EC had exiled to the Belt, not part of the EC, either, in the sense the rab had resisted it—didn't even understand the politics in the '15, but he was getting to.

Fast.

They'd hauled the Shepherd pilots into the Program for their expertise. They weren't eighteen-year-olds, and they damned sure weren't anybody's boys. You didn't use that word with them. Didn't *lead* them, no way in hell. You fed them the situation and showed them where it was different from what they knew. You showed them the *feel* of it, and let it sink into their bones and they *showed* the interactive systems new ways to conceptualize. They designed a whole new set of controls around the Shepherds, and software to display what they saw in their insystem-trained heads.

Explain that to Col. Glenn Evan Tanzer, of UDC R&D. God, he wished the captain were back here, that *one* of the captains would turn up; Kreshov hadn't shown insystem for weeks; and exactly how it happened that one of the captains wasn't here at B Dock, at the same time a stray investigative subcommittee had outflanked Keu at Sol and gotten here unchecked—he didn't know. He couldn't even swear FleetCom was secure from the UDC code experts. Shepherds thought so, but he wouldn't commit any more to it than he had.

Not now. Not lately, in Sol System, where the enemy was mindsets that wouldn't understand the realities in the Beyond. The Belt was closer to The Beyond than it was to Earth.

And closer to it than Tanzer by a far shot. Always Tanzer—who'd been sitting here in R&D so long they dusted him.

0657. By the clock on the wall. He walked down the corridor, he walked into Tanzer's office, and Tanzer's aide said, "Go right in."

He did that. He saluted, by the book. Tanzer saluted, they stared at each other, and Tanzer said, "Lt. Benjamin J. Pollard. Does that name evoke memory?"

Shot across the bow. Graff kept all expression off his face. "Yes, sir. Friend of Dekker's. Listed next-of-kin on his card."

"Is that your justification for releasing those records to Sol?"

"Captain Keu's orders, sir. He sees all the accident reports."

"Is this your justification for issuing a travel voucher?"

"I didn't issue the travel voucher. Mr. Pollard's presence here isn't at my request."

"Lt. Graff, you're a hair-splitting liar, you're a troublemaker and I resent your attitude."

"On the record, sir, I hardly think I can be held accountable—"

"That's what you think. You're sabotaging us, you're playing politics with my boys' lives, and you have no authorization to bring in any outsider or to be passing unauthorized messages outside this facility to other commands."

"That is my chain of command, sir. Dekker is my personnel, and Keu is my commanding officer. Sir. I notify him on all the casualties. What Captain Keu does is not in my control. And if the question arises, I will testify that in my opinion Dekker was not in that simulator by choice. Sir."

Tanzer's fist came down on the desk. "I'm in command of this facility, *Lt.* Graff. The fact that your commander saw fit to leave a junior lieutenant in command of the rider trainees and the carrier does not give you authority over any aspect of this operation, and it does *not* give you authority to issue passes or to take communications to anyone outside of BaseCom, *do you understand me?*"

"Where it regards your command, yes, colonel. But I'm responsible to Captain Keu for the communications he directly ordered me to make and which I will continue to make, on FleetCom. Lt. Pollard is here on humanitarian leave in connection with Fleet personnel. He's Prioritied elsewhere. He's here temporarily and he has adequate Security clearance to be here."

"He's also UDC personnel."

"He's under interservice assignment. On leave. And not available to R&D."

"A friend of Dekker's. Let me tell you, I've had a bellyful of your recruits, and I'm sick and tired of the miner riffraff and psychological misfits washing up on the shores of this program. Your own captain's interference with design has given this program a piece of junk that can't be flown—"

"Not true."

"—a piece of junk that works in the sims and not in the field, lieutenant, because it doesn't take into account human realities. That firepower can't be turned over to adrenaline-high games-playing freaks, Mr. Graff, and that machine can't rely on the 50%'ers on the sims—how many ships are you going to lose on that 50%? Four billion dollars per ship and the time to train the crew, and you're going to gamble that on 50% of the time the pilot's nerves hold out for the time required? We're pushing human beings over *their* design limits, and they're dying, Mr. Graff, they're ending up in hospital wards."

"Wilhelmsen didn't die of fatigue, colonel, he died of communications failure, he *died* of not working with his own crew. He schitzed—for one nanosecond he schitzed and forgot where in hell he was in his sequence. There's an interdict on that move—it's supposed to be in the pilot's *head,* and it failed, colonel, *he* failed, that's the bottom line. Dekker—"

"Dekker ran that same flight on sim and he's lying delirious in hospital. Don't let me hear you use that word schitz again, lieutenant, except you apply it to *your* boy. There's the problem in that crew. There's the troublemaker that had to prove his point, had to shoot his mouth off—"

"Dekker didn't run that sim. And the word is *concussion,* colonel. From the impact of an unsecured body in that pod. He didn't *forget* to belt in."

"He was suited up."

"The flightsuits keep your *feet* from swelling, colonel: Dekker's been exposed to prolonged zero *g.* The other crews say—"

"He was up there on drugs, lieutenant! Read the medical report! He was high on trank, he was in possession of a tape he had no business with, and he and his attitude got in that pod together, let's admit what happened up there and quit trying to put Dekker's smartass maneuver off on any outside agency. There wasn't one."

"I intent to find out what did happen."

"Do you? Do you? Let me lay this word in your lap: either you come up with proof that'll stand up in court-martial, or this investigation is closed. Dekker climbed into that pod on drugs, because he has an Attitude the same as all the other misfits this facility's been loaded with, he believes he's cornered the market on right, he's a smartass who thinks his reflexes make up for his lack of discipline, and if you drop that chaff in the hearing you won't like the result. If you want this program to fly, and I assume you do, then you'd better reflect very soberly what effect your appearance and your testimony this afternoon is going to have on your captain's credibility—on the credibility of your service and the judgment of its personnel. Don't speculate. Keep to the facts."

"The facts are, Dekker saw what was happening, he called the right moves. It's on the mission control tape. . . ."

"You're so damned cocksure what your boys can do, mister, but it's easy to call the right moves when you're not the one in the pilot's seat. *You* won't sit those controls. *You* won't fly those ships. *Will you?*"

Fair question, except they'd been over that track before. "That's exactly the point. I'm not synched to a rider crew. Cross-training would risk both ships."

"The truth is, lieutenant, your *Fleet* doesn't want its precious essential personnel flying a suicide ship, your Fleet won't let go of its hare-brained concept before it stinks. Your Conrad Mazian isn't a ship designer, he isn't an engineer, he's a merchant captain in a ragtag militia trying to prove it's qualified for strategic decisions. This ship needs interdicts on a pilot that's stressing out."

"That ship needs its combat edge, colonel. If Welhelmsen had had an AI breathing down his neck he'd have had one more thing on his mind: Is the damned thing going to take my advice or not? At what mission-critical split second that I happen to be right is it going to cut me out of the loop? You can't cripple a ship with a damned know-it-all robot snatching control away because the pilot pushed the *g*'s for a reason that, yes, might be knowingly suicidal, for a reason that wasn't in the mission profile. Besides which, longscan's after you, and what are you going to do, give a Union longscanner a hundred percent certainty an AI's going to interdict certain moves? If he knows your cutoffs, he knows your blind spots. If he knows you can't push it and he can, what's he going to do, colonel?"

"When the physiological signs are there, you're going to lose that ship, that's a hundred percent certainty, and nobody else is going to be exceeding that limit."

"Wilhelmsen was leaning hard on the Assists. He could have declined that one target, that's inside the parameters, that's a judgment a rider's going to have to make. But he'd have looked bad for the senators. He wanted that target. That's an Attitude. There's a use for that in combat. Not for a damned exhibition."

"Wilhelmsen was saving the program, lieutenant, saving *your* damned budget appropriation, in equipment that's got six men in the hospital and seventeen dead. You don't push machines or human beings past the destruct limit, and you don't put equipment out there that self-destructs on a muscle-twitch. The pilot was showing symptoms. The AI should have kicked him out of the loop right then, but it can't do that, you say he can't have it breathing down his neck—a four-billion-dollar missile with a deadman's switch, that's what you've got—it needs an integrative AI in there—"

"Watch the pilots cut it off. Which you can't do with that damned tetralogic system you're talking about, it's got to be in the loop talking to the interactives constantly, and no matter the input it got after, its logic systems are exactly the same as the next one's, same as the ships are. The only wildcard you've got is the humans, the *only* thing that keeps the enemy longscanners guessing. The best machine you've got can't outguess the human longscanner—why should you assume they're trying to outperform the pilot?"

"Because the longscanner can't kill the crew."

"The hell he can't!"

"Not in that sense."

"Your tests don't simulate combat. That's what we've been telling you—you keep concentrating on the fire rate, always the damned fire rate and you're not dealing with the reason we recruited these particular crews. Nobody at Lendler Corp has been in combat, none of your pilots have been, the UDC hasn't been, since it was founded—your tests are set up wrong!"

Not saying Tanzer himself hadn't been in combat. Red in the face, Tanzer got a breath. "Let's talk about exceeding human limits, lieutenant: what happened out there was *exactly* why we've got men in hospital over there who can't walk a level floor without staggering, it's why we've had cardiac symptoms in men under thirty, and those *aren't* from four-hour runs." A jab of the finger in his direction. "Let me tell you, lieutenant, I've met the kind of attitude your command is fostering among the trainees. Show-outs and ego-freaks. And I wish them out of my command. You may have toddled down a deck in your diapers, and so may Mazian's ragtag enlistees out of the Belt, but how are you going to teach them anything when they already know it all and you acquired your know-how by superior genes? You can't lose 50% of your ships and crews at every pass. 96% retrievability, wasn't that the original design criterion? Or isn't that retrievability word going to be in the manual when we put this ship on the line?"

"If a Union armscomper gets your numbers you have zero retrievability, colonel, that's my point. You have to exceed your own numbers, you have to surprise your own interfaces in order to surprise that other ship's computers and that means being at the top of the architecture of your Adaptive Assists. The enemy knows your *name* out there. Union says, That's *Victoria,* that's Fitzroy or Graff at Helm, because *Victoria* wouldn't go in with Helm Three. They know you and they know your style, and it's in their double A's, but you innovate and they innovate. One AI sitting on top of the human and his interfaces is like any other damn AI sitting on top of the interfaces—there aren't that many models, the enemy knows them all, and the second its logic signature develops in the enemy's intelligence about you, hell, they'll have a fire-track lying in wait for you."

"Then you'd better damn well improve your security, hadn't you?"

"Colonel, there are four manufacturers in friendly space for this tetralogic equipment and we can't swear there's not an Eye sitting right outside the system right now. Any merchanter who ever came into system could have dropped one, before the embargo, and it's next to impossible to find it. Merchanters are your friends and your enemies: that's the war the Company made, and that's what's going on out there—they don't all declare their loyalties and a lot of them haven't got any, not them and not us. They'll find out the names. They'll find out the manufacturers and the software designers. They'll learn us. That's a top priority—who's at Helm and who's in command, and if it's even one in four brands of tetralogic—"

"All the more reason for interchangeable personnel."

"It doesn't work that way! You don't go into an engagement with anybody who just happens to be on watch. You *try* to get your best online. No question. You don't trade personnel and you don't trade equipment. You haven't time at .5 light coming down off jump to think about what ship you're in or what crew you're with. I'm telling you, colonel, my captain has no wish to raise the substitution as an issue against your decisions, but on his orders, as judiciously as I can, I am going to make the point that it was a critical factor. We can*not* integrate a computerized ship into our operations. In that condition it *is* no better than a missile."

"You haven't the credentials to say what it is and isn't, lieutenant. You're not a psychiatrist and you're not a computer specialist."

"I am a combat pilot. One of two at this base."

A cold, dark silence. "I'll tell you—if you want to raise issues this afternoon, I'm perfectly willing to make clear to the committee that you're a composite, lieutenant, a *shell* steered by noncommand personnel and an absentee captain, and you clearly don't have the administrative experience to handle your own security, much less speak with expert knowledge on systems you've never seen. I've held this office for thirty years, I've seen all sorts of games, and your commanding officers leaving that carrier to subordinates and your own abuse of your commanding officer's communications privileges is an official report in *my* chain of command. This is *not* the frontier, this is *not* a bare-based militia operation, and if your service ever hopes to turn these trainees into competent military personnel you can start by setting a personal example. Clean up your own command and stop fomenting dissension in this facility!"

"I do *not* accept that assessment."

"Then you can leave this office. And if you are called on to testify, you'll be there as one of the pilots personally involved in the accident, not as a systems expert. You'd be very unwise to push past that position—or you'll find questions raised that could be damned embarrassing to your absentee superior and your entire service. I'm talking about adverse publicity, if you give grounds to any of these senators or to the high command. Do you understand that? Because I won't pull any punches. And the one security no one can guarantee is a senator's personal staff."

"Are you attempting to dictate my testimony, colonel? Is that what I'm hearing?"

"In no wise. Give my regards to your captain. Good *day,* lieutenant."

Something had come loose. Banging. The tumble did that. Dekker reached after the cabinet, tried to get to the com.

Hand caught his arm. Something shoved him back and he hit pillows.

Bang from elsewhere.

"Hey, Dek. You want eggs or pancakes?"

He couldn't figure how Ben had gotten onto the ship. Ben had rescued him. But he didn't remember that.

"Eggs or pancakes?"

"Eggs aren't real," he said. "Awful stuff."

"They're real, Dek-boy. Not to my taste, living things, but they're real enough to upset *my* stomach. Eggs, you want? Orange juice?"

He tried to move. Usually he couldn't. But his arms were free. He stuffed pillows under his head and Ben did something that propped the head up. Ben went out in the hall and came back and set a tray down on the table, swung it over him.

"Eat it. That's an order, Dek-boy."

He picked up a fork. It seemed foreign, difficult to balance in .9 *g.* His head kept going around. His arm weighed more than he remembered and it was hard to keep his head up. But he stabbed a bit of scrambled egg and got a bite down. Another. He reached for the orange juice but Ben did it for him, took a sip himself beforehand and said, "We got better at Sol One."

Maybe it was. Maybe he was supposed to know that. Ben held the cup to his lips and he sipped a little of it. It stung cuts in his mouth and it lit his stomach with a sugar impact.

"Keep it up, Dek-boy, and they'll take that tube out."

He didn't know there was a tube. Didn't know how Ben had gotten here. Or where they were now. Didn't look like The Hole at all. Didn't look like R2 hospital. He reached after the fork, took another tentative nibble at the eggs. God, he was weak.

"Where's Bird?" he asked.

"What year is it, Dek-boy? I warned you there'd be a test this morning."

He shut his eyes. Opened them and Ben was still there. In this room. He recalled something like that. Ben was going to beat hell out of him if he missed.

"2324."

"Good boy. Have some more oj."

"Can't." His stomach suddenly felt queasy, when he thought about that number. Number had to be wrong. He waved the cup away and watched Ben drink it.

Ben, in a UDC uniform.

He was going crazy. It was 2324. Ben didn't belong here.

Ben said, "You remember Meg and Sal?"

"Yeah. Sure."

"Meg writes to you, doesn't she?"

"Yeah, sometimes."

"Real love affair."

"We're friends."

"Yeah," Ben said. "You looked it when you said goodbye. Remember saying goodbye?" He took an envelope out of his pocket. Held up a handful of cards and pictures. "Remember these?"

He'd seen them before. They'd lied to him, the doctors had. They made all these things up. They told him they were his, he'd thrown them across the room.

Now Ben had them. Ben held up a picture of him with people he didn't remember and he couldn't look at.

"What are their names?"

He shook his head.

"Woman's Elly?"

The name jolted. Elly was dead. Pete and Falcone.

"Pete?"

Guy on the right. Big grin. Pete smiled like that. Pete had his arm over the shoulder. But he couldn't remember the photo.

"Which one's Pete?"

"I don't know." But it was a lie. Ben just didn't belong with them. Everything was scrambled. Cory and Ben and Bird. He was afraid Meg was going to be in that picture if he went on looking at it.

Blood. Exploding everywhere. Beads floating, fine mist.

He squeezed his eyes shut. The eggs didn't sit well at his stomach. Everyone in that picture was dead. He was in there too.

"Who's the other guy?"

"Falcone."

"Said not to worry about him. Didn't he? Left you a note? You remember?"

He shook his head. He shoved the table away, tried to get up. Ben pushed him back against the pillows and a stabbing pain went through his skull.

He grayed out for a moment. When he came back Ben was quietly finishing his toast. Ben said, "You ready to talk now?"

The cup hit the grid. Sideways. Two out of five. Graff lifted the cover up and righted it before the coffee hit, collected his overdue morning caffeine and turned in the general noise of the end of breakfast, straight into Villy's intercept.

UDC Flight Chief. *Captain* Alexandro Villanueva—senior test pilot for the UDC, who said, all friendly, "Hear you and the old man went one this morning."

Fast. Must have ricocheted off Tanzer's wall, Graff thought, and shrugged in mid-sip while Villanueva stuck his card in the slot and punched up a coffee. He said, "We differed."

Villanueva rescued his cup. "Damn thing."

"Ever since they changed the cups."

Villanueva took the coffee out and let the cover drop, said, quietly, "You know, back when we were doing the A-89, we had one of these runs of trouble. Lost twelve guys in six months. The old man just sat in that office and filled out the reports: you never saw him crack—but it broke him up. Same now. He wants to pull this program out. But we've got to come out of this with an answer. A right answer."

"Redesign isn't it." He got on well enough with Villanueva. Villanueva had started out calling him son—never did think he'd quite gotten the man out of the mindset. Gray hair on Captain Villy, legitimately come by, rumor had it: handful of crack-ups and a few pieces of luck—if dealing with Tanzer daily didn't do it. They kept trying to promote him to a desk, God only wish he'd get Tanzer's post and run the whole program, not just test ops—but Villy kept on making test runs himself, one of the UDC pilots who had real respect among the Shepherds.

"Graff," Villanueva said, "dammit, we're vulnerable on this project, we're real vulnerable. Politicians are gathering like sharks. I know the old man's hard to deal with. But let's not hang the differences out in plain sight today."

He thought about Mitch. About the frustration among the Shepherds, who wanted to fight Tanzer. And that did no good. "They won't likely ask me anything but where I was, where the targets were. That's all in the electronic record. Cut and dried, isn't that the expression for it?"

Villanueva stood there a moment. Just looking at him. He expected Villanueva to say something in answer, but instead Villanueva walked off with his coffee and didn't look back.

Maybe he should have given more back. Used a different expression. Read the signals otherwise. He didn't dislike the man, God knew he didn't dislike him. The man had been trying to say something, but somehow in the inevitable screw-ups between blue-skyer and spacer—he had the feeling the signals had gotten fuzzed.

Villanueva went over to a table with his own men. Sat down. Graff walked over to the other side, where a couple of the Fleet's own gray heads inclined together. Demas and Saito. Nav One and Com One—no credence at all to the Equivalencies that the Fleet had had settled on them. *Commdr.* Demas, as happened. But Nav One meant it was Demas did the major share of the course plots, with the backing of eighteen techs interfacing with scan and longscan at any given instant, which meant that a prototype carrier on a test run knew so precisely where it was and where everything else was that a Lt. j-g at Helm couldn't screw up if he worked at it.

Except with a wrong word to the UDC R&D chief.

"Think I just picked a wrong word with Villy. Does 'cut and dried' describe what they're going to ask at the hearings?"

Com One said, her almond eyes half-lidded, "Probably. 'Rigged' might too. On, is the man?"

Demas said, "A lot On. Deep in. Drink your coffee, Helm. Present for you." Demas laid a bolt on the table. Fat one.

Damn. "What is that?"

"That, J-G, is a bolt. It was lying next the wall in a dark little recess in the carrier's main corridor. Where the construction crew just installed the number eighteen pressure seal."

Thing was good as a bullet lying there. "I want to see the count sheet. I want the last crew that worked in there. Damn those fools!"

"Station labor. Gravitied brains. What do you ask?"

Ben said, "You remember Graff?"

"Yeah," Dekker said.

"What do you remember?"

"The trip out from the Belt. Here."

"Good boy. Where are we?"

"Sol Two," he said. Ben told him so. He had to believe what Ben told him: Ben was the check he had asked for, Ben was what he got and he had to believe everything Ben told him—he told himself that, this morning, Ben showed him pictures and showed him letters in the reader, that he remembered reading. The ones from Meg, the note from Falcone, the morning—

The morning they pulled him off the demo and put somebody else in.

Nothing you can do, Falcone had written. Left the note on the system. Came back like a ghost—after the accident. After—

"You remember where the sims are?"

"Which ones?"

"You tell me."

He felt tired, wrung out. He lay back in the pillows and said, "Couple downside. They're all the procedurals." Tried to think of exact words and remembered Ben was a licensed pilot too. "Ops stuff—stuff you need your reflexes for—it's in the core."

"Null-*g* stuff."

"Null-*g* and high-*g*." His eyes wanted to drift shut. His mind went around that place as if it were a pit. He could see the chamber in the null-*g* core, the sims like so many eggs on mag-lev tracks, blurring in motion. Lot of *g*'s when they were working. . . .

"When's the last time you remember using the sims in the core?"

Difficult question for a moment. Then not so hard. "Watch before the test. Wilhelmsen and I—"

"Wilhelmsen."

"He was my backup."

"Friend of yours?"

Difficult to say. "Chad . . ."

"Wilhelmsen?"

He nodded, eyes shut. "Son of a bitch, but he was all right. Didn't dislike him. We got along."

"So they subbed him in. You watch the test?"

He didn't know. Completely numb now. But the monitor on the shelf was showing higher points to the green line.

"You went into shock. They put you in hospital."

Wasn't the way he remembered. Wasn't sure what he did remember, but not that shock was the reason. No. He hadn't seen it.

"They give you drugs in the hospital?"

He nodded. He was relatively sure of that.

"Give you a prescription when you left?"

"Dunno."

"They say they did."

"Then I guess they did."

"You guess. Were you still high when you left the hospital? Did you have drugs with you?"

"I don't remember."

"What time of day was it?"

"Don't remember, Ben, I don't remember." But something was there, God, a flare on the vid, a light the cameras couldn't handle. Plasma. Bright as the sun. Pete and Elly, and Falcone and the ship.

"You all right?" The monitor was beeping. "—No! Let him alone. It's all right! Leave him the hell alone."

Orderly was trying to intervene. He opened his eyes and looked toward the door, trying to calm his pulse rate, and Ben leaned over and put his hand on his shoulder. Squeezed hard.

"You get in that sim by yourself?"

"I don't know."

"Somebody put you there?"

"I don't know. I honestly don't know, Ben. I just can't remember."

"Come *on,* Dek, *think* about it. You got into that core. You remember that? You had to get that far. What happened then?"

He shook his head. He kept seeing dark. Flashing lights. Green lines and gold. Heard Cory saying, Nothing you can do, Dek, nothing you can do . . .

They were back in The Hole. In his room behind the bar. Had a drawerful of pills. . . .

He put a hand over his eyes, then stared at the ceiling and looked over at Ben again to be sure where he was and when he was. But the black kept trying to come back and the lines twisted and moved.

'Driver ship, a k long. Loads of rock going to the Well at tremendous *v.*

Cory was dead. Dead a long time. So was Bird. He thought that Bird was dead. Fewer and fewer things were coming loose and drifting.

He pressed his hands over his eyes until it made sparks of color in the dark of virtual space. Red. Phosphenes. Was that what they said the lights were?

Spinning, of a sudden. He grabbed the bed.

Ben said, "God, watch it!"

Something was beeping. Ben said, to someone at the door, "He had a dream, that's all."

* * *

"Want you there this afternoon," Graff said to his Nav One; and to Saito. Saito said,

"This won't be like our procedures. An answer-what's-asked. This is Earth. Don't mistake it."

Graff took a sip of cooling coffee. "I couldn't. The old man hasn't sent us a hint, except Pollard, and Pollard doesn't know anything. I don't know if that's a signal to raise that issue or not—but I can't understand the silence. Unless the captain's leaving me to take the grenade. Which I'd do. Little they could do anyway but transfer me back. But he should tell me."

"No grenades," Demas said. "—No chance of Dekker talking?"

"Pollard's honestly trying. All I know."

"You sure he's the captain's? He could be Tanzer's."

Graff remembered something he'd forgotten to say, gave a short laugh. "Pollard's a native Belter."

"You're serious. Tanzer knows it?"

"Knows he's a friend of Dekker's. That has him the devil in Tanzer's book. What's more, this Belter claims he's a Priority 10 tracked for Geneva."

Demas' brows went up.

Graff said, "Bright. Very bright. Computers. Top security computers."

"Tanzer can't snag a Priority like that."

Saito said, "Not without an authorization. I doubt Tanzer can even access that security level to realize what he is."

"The captain set up Pollard with a room in the hospital. I told him to stay to it and Dekker's room and keep his head down. With a security clearance like that, he understands what quiet means, I think. He's got an appointment waiting for him—if he can get out of here before he becomes a priority to Tanzer."

"You signal him?"

"Every word I could prudently use. There were some I didn't. Maybe I should have. But he's UDC. You don't know where it'll go, ultimately."

"No remote chance on Dekker?"

"No chance on this one. Too much to ask. They've requested the log. They're going to ask questions on the carrier—they'll want to ask questions about the trainees. But they won't talk to them. They're not scheduled. Trainees don't talk to the EC. Trainees they're designing those ships around don't talk to the committee because the committee is only interested in finding a way that doesn't admit we're right. Another schitzy AI. Another budget fight."

"The Earth Company makes a lot of money on shipbuilding," Demas said. "Does that thought ever trouble your sleep?"

"It's beginning to."

The captain wanted to bust Demas up to a captaincy. Demas insisted he was staying with Keu. The argument was still going on. The fact was Demas hated administration and claimed he was a tactician, not a strategist, but Demas saw things. Good instincts, the man had.

Saito said, quietly: "Committee will be predominantly male, predominantly over fifty, and they won't understand why the captain didn't leave Fitz in charge and take me and Demas with him. *That's* what you're dealing with."

Fitzroy, Helm One, was answering questions for the committee at Sol One. Graff said, glumly: "Tanzer's threatening to make an issue out of *their* command rules."

Demas shook his head. "Let him make it. That'll get me to the stand surer than the nav stats would. And I don't think he wants that."

One could wish. But one couldn't get technical with the legislative types. With the engineers, yes. "They'd talk to Demas. But the engineers couldn't talk policy to the legislators. Couldn't get through their own management."

"I keep having this feeling they're going to blindside us."

"You'll handle it. No question. Easy done."

Keu's silence was overall the most troublesome thing. Graff finished off his coffee, took the bolt and pocketed it. "Paperweight. Every paperpusher should have one. —Tell the construction boss I want to talk to him, in my office, right now."

"Ought to give him the thing at max *v*," Demas said.

"When we find the foreman who faked the parts count—I'd be willing." Graff headed for the door, tossed his cup in the collection bin.

Ben was back. Ben had been in the hall awhile. Ben sat down with his chair close to the bed, put his hand on his shoulder.

"How're you doing, Dek?"

"All right."

"You were remembering, you know that? Pete and Elly? You remember that?"

Ben scared him. "I was dreaming. Sorry, Ben." If he was dreaming he could be in the Belt. Or the ship. But Ben shook at his shoulder and said,

"Dek, how did you get in the sim? What were you doing in there? I got to get out of here. I got twelve hours, Dek."

Sim chamber. Pods spinning around and around. Racket. Echoes. Everything tried to echo. And Ben said he had twelve hours. He didn't want Ben to leave. Ben came and Ben went, but as long as he knew there was a chance of Ben being there he knew what he was waking up to.

He said, "It's June 20th, isn't it? Isn't it, Ben?"

Ben took a fistful of hospital gown, under his chin, and said, "Dekker, remember what fucking happened. I got to be on that shuttle. It's my *life* at stake, you copy?"

He tried. Ben let him go, smoothed the covers, patted his shoulder. Didn't ask him anything for a moment. Ben was upset and he earnestly tried to pull the sim chamber out of the dark for Ben. But it wasn't there.

Just that fireball. Second sun. They said it wasn't Wilhelmsen's fault. Maybe it wasn't. You died when you overran your limits.

"Target," he said. Ben said, "What?"

He said, "Target. Missed one. . . ."

CHAPTER 4

The hearing was set up in A 109, not the biggest of the classrooms—dressed up with tables and a couple of UDC guards with sidearms—to do what, Graff asked himself bitterly, shoot down anybody who'd tell the truth out of turn?

Limited seating, they called it. No public access. That meant the workmen and the mechanics that worked for the EC, the vendors and the man who sold meat pies on 3-deck were barred, and those of them with security clearances still had to pass metal detectors. It meant that any military personnel showed if the committee knew they existed, and sent them passes: that meant ranking officers and the few like himself whose names were on the duty list the hour of the disaster. But there were passes issued for aides and for official representatives of the several services. And that meant the Fleet had Saito and Demas.

And the Shepherd trainees had Mitch and Jamil. They'd taken off the jewelry, taken off the earrings—couldn't hide Jamil's tattoos, but Jamil's single strip of black hair was braided tight against his scalp, and both of them were as regulation as the Shepherds could manage.

There were the various heads of department, maintenance chiefs, the ones who had security clearances. There was a big carrier schematic on one screen, others showing details of the docking ports. And an undetailed model on the table. Just the flat saucer shape. Manta shape, the blue-skyers called it. He'd seen a picture of the sea-dwelling creature and he saw why. Thin in one aspect to present minimum profile to fire or to high-*v* dust when it needed, broad and flat to accommodate the engines and the crew, and to lie snug against a carrier's frame.

Black painted model. The real thing was grayer, reflective ceramic. But they didn't advertise the coating. Thirty crew aboard when, please God, they got past the initial trials, thirty crew, mostly techs, mostly working for the longscanner. Core crew was four. The essential stations. The command personnel. The ones whose interfaces were with the active ship controls and the ones they had to risk in the tests.

The carrier dropped into a star-system and launched the riders—trusting that realspace ships, launched like missiles, with more firepower than ability to maneuver at *v,* could do their job and make a carrier's presence-pattern a far, far more diffuse element for an enemy's longscan computers.

And trusting the human mind could keep going for four hours on intermittent hyperfocus at that *v* with no shields, only a constantly changing VR HUD display and a firepower adequate to take out what threatened it—if reactions were still hair-triggered after that length of time immersed in virtual space; if human beings still had consistent right reactions to a dopplered infostream of threat and non-threat and every missile launched and potentially launched. A longscan of a fractional *c* firefight looked like a plaid of intersecting probabilities, overlaid cones or tri-dee fans depending on your traveling viewpoint; and you overran conventional radar, even orders from your carrier: all you had was calc, com, and emissions.

Put an Artificial Intelligence above the human in the decision loop? Use a trained pilot for no more than resource to his own Adaptive Assist systems, with no power to override? Like hell. Sir.

He took a seat next to Demas and Saito, he cast a look down the row at Mitch and Jamil, and let the corner of his mouth tighten, surreptitious acknowledgment of their effort at diplomacy.

The committee filed in. Over fifty, Saito had said, and all male. Not quite. But the balance of the genders was certainly tilted. There were a handful of anxious execs from the designers and military contractors, from Bauerkraftwerke, who had designed the rider frame and some of the hardware; Lendler Corp, simulator software; Intellitron, which produced the longscan for both carriers and riders; Terme Aerospatiale, which did the Hellburner engines; and Staatentek, responsible for integrative targeting systems, computers and insystem communications. All of which could be pertinent. Lendler and Intellitron and Terme Aerospatiale were all Earth Company, but God only knew what side they were on. They'd doubtless been talking up the military examiners since last night: there'd been a UDC briefing.

"That's Bonner," Saito whispered, indicating a white-haired shave-headed UDC officer. Gen. Patrick Bonner, Graff understood. Tanzer's direct CO. Ultimate head over R&D, not a friend. And what was he saying to an EC contractor, both of them smiling and laughing like old friends?

People got to their seats. Bonner gave a speech, long and winding, a tactic, Graff thought, designed to stultify the opposition. Or perhaps his own troops. Not here to fix blame, Bonner said. Here to determine what happened and what caused it.

Introductions. Graff found himself focusing on the walls, on the topographic details of Bonner's receding hairline, the repeating pattern in the soundproofing, on the nervous fingers of the rep from Bauerkraftwerke, which tapped out a quiet rhythm on the table.

Statement of positions: Bauerkraftwerke insisted there was no structural flaw, that its engineers had reconstructed the accident and there was nothing to do with failure of the frame or the engines. Terme Aerospatiale agreed. Lendler said its simulation software wasn't at fault. Staatentek, the patent holder of the local AI tetralogic, maintained that the random ordnance software, the communications, the targeting software, had not glitched. Nobody was at fault. Nothing was wrong.

But a redesign in favor of the tetralogic control couldn't be ruled out.

Bangs and thumps again. "Ben?" Dekker called out. Ben had said he would be there. But he waked up in a corridor, on a gurney, with restraints he didn't remember deserving. "Ben!"

A nurse patted his shoulder and said, "It's all right, your friend's just outside."

He hated it when the illusions started agreeing with him. He lay still then, listening to the rattle and clatter. Someone said, from over his head, "We're going to take you in now," and he didn't know where. He yelled, "Ben! Ben!" And somebody said, "Better sedate him."

"No," he yelled. "No." And promised them, "You don't need to."

"Are you going to be all right?" they asked him.

"Yeah," he said, and lay there getting his breath. But there was a whine of hydraulics and a clank, and they shoved him into a tube, telling him: "You have to stay absolutely still . . ."

Like a spinner tube, it was. Like back in the belt, in the ship. He lay still the way they told him, but it got harder and harder to breathe.

Flash of light. Like the sun. He heard a beeping sound that reminded him—that reminded him—

"Elly—Elly, Wilhelmsen, don't reorient, screw it, *screw it,* you're past—"

"He's panicking," someone said.

He screamed, at the top of his lungs, *"Wilhelmsen, you damned fool—"*

Fifteen-minute recess. Break for restrooms and the corridor and the hospitality table.

Mitch moved close enough to say, "They're dithering, sir."

Graff said, "Ease down. Not here."

"They're saying it can't be flown. That's a damn lie."

"Ease down, Mitch. Nothing we can do out here." He had Saito at his elbow. He could see Tanzer down the hall with Bonner, in hot and heavy discussion.

Demas came back from the phone in the office. Said: "A word in private."

Graff said, "Mitch. Be good," and took Saito with him, farther up the hall. "You get him?"

"Couldn't get hold of Pollard. Talked to Higgins. The neurosurgeon wanted to run another brain scan. Higgins and Evans agreed. Dekker went off the edge, he's under sedation. Higgins says he remembers the accident. Nothing further. He may never be able to remember how he got in that pod."

"Damn."

"You've got to tell it plain, Helm."

"Break it wide open? We don't know what the captain wants. We don't know and if it were safe to use FleetCom he would."

Saito said, "It can't be worse. At this point I'd advise going past protocol. Worst we can do is alienate Bonner and a few handpicked legislators who came out here with him. This is a setup. But it has records. The contractors are here defending their systems. And there may be a few line-straddlers in the senatorial party."

That was a point. Bonner was already alienated. This was likely a breakaway group of legislators Bonner favored putting in here to hear what Tanzer put together—but the fact that they let him talk at all was either a try at getting something incriminating out of him; or maybe, maybe there were members of the group that wanted more than one view.

"God only knows what we're dealing with. No Pollard, no Dekker. It's a small hand we're playing. All right. I'll tell Mitch. Wraps are off."

Past lunch and beyond, and Ben paced the waiting room. He'd read all the damned articles available to the reader, he'd become grudgingly informed in the latest in microbiologic engineering, the pros and cons of seasonally adjusted light/dark cycles and temperature in station environments, the ethics of psychological intervention, and the consequences of weather adjustment in the hurricane season to the North American continent, not to mention five posture checks for low-*g* workers. He'd occupied himself making changes in a program he had stored on his personal card, he'd been four times at least to Dekker's room to see if he was out from under sedation—he'd lost count. You could hear the clangor and rattle of lunch trays being collected—they had a damned lot of hurt and sick people in here, people that had let a welder slip or gotten in the way of a robot loader arm, one guy who'd taken a godawful number of volts closing a hydraulic switch—he heard the gossip in the corridors coming and going, he was saturated with hospital gossip on who was missing what and how the guy with peritonitis was doing today and what was the condition of the limb reattachment in 109?

While the orderlies were having lunch.

Another trip out to Dekker's room. Can't wake him, Higgins said. We've gotten the blood pressure down now. But he's tired. He's just tired—

"I've got a shuttle pulling out tonight—tell the lieutenant I've done everything I can do. I want to see him. I've got to get out of here."

Higgins said, "He's involved in a hearing this afternoon. I don't know if I can reach him. I've left two messages with his office."

"The hell! Doctor, my luggage is still lost, I'm out of money for the damn vending machines—I never got a cafeteria authorization and I'm sick of potato chips—I never asked to come here, Dekker and I never were friends, dammit, I don't know why I'm his keeper!"

Higgins lent him five. Which wasn't the answer he wanted, but it was lunch, at least, and he wasn't going to offend Higgins by turning it down. Supper, he wasn't even going to think about.

Tanzer's turn with the mike. Nobody from the Fleet on that panel and no chance, Graff thought, of doing anything about that, except refusing to allow Fleet personnel to testify and trying to make an issue of it—but he was in a Position on that too, being one of the people on the list to testify; and he hoped the sweat didn't show.

Demas' advice, Saito's, Armsmaster Thieu's, for that matter, who might be called, was unanimous, and that it agreed with his only confirmed that if he was wrong and if he screwed this, the Fleet had to push him out the lock as a peace offering. That was one thing. He understood that kind of assignment.

But the thought that he could screw things beyond recall, offend the wrong senator, say something the media could get hold of and kill the riderships or bring the Fleet under UDC control—either of which would kill any hope of preventing the whole Beyond being sucked into Union's widening influence—that was the possibility that had his hands sweating and his mind chasing random imaginations throughout Tanzer's performance: he kept thinking, I've got to counter that; and, I've got to get that across to the committee, and, God, they're not going to ask me the right questions.

No way Bonner's going to let me answer those questions.

The general's no fool. There's something he's got planned, some grenade planted and ticking, only where is it? With Tanzer?

Tanzer was saying: "It's the task of this facility to evaluate prototype systems and to take them to the design limits. The essential step before we risk human life is advanced, exacting interactive assist simulation. The second step is automated performance testing. And again, the simulations are revised and refined, and procedures and checklists developed in hours of Control Integration Trials, a process with which many of our distinguished panel are intimately familiar. They are also aware that in the world of high-velocity craft we are exceeding human capacities to cope with the infostream. We've overrun human reaction time. We've long since overrun conventional radar. Hence the neural net AA, which adapts and shapes itself threefold, for the pilot's past performance, enemy's past, pilot's current behaviors—and the longscan technique that extrapolates and displays an object's probability. We've developed doppleredcommunications and communications techniques to receive information faster than human senses can sort it, computer assemblies to second-guess the pilot on multiple tasks. The faster we go, the more the pilot becomes an integral component of the systems that filter information via his senses and the Adaptive Assists into the ship's controls. Right now the human is the highest vote in the Hellburner's neural network; but we've long been asking the question at what point the sophistication of the computers to provide the information and the speed and power of the ship to react may finally exceed the engineering limits of the creator—that is, at what point of demand on human capacity to react to data, do we conceive a technically perfect and humanly unflyable machine?"

The questioner, Bonner, said, "Have we done that, in your opinion?"

Tanzer said, "Yes. In my opinion, yes."

"Go on."

"The EC militia came here with a design within the capabilities of the shipbuilding industry, and within the skills of its own pilots to operate. And the design for a companion ship they *claimed* could use off-the-shelf hardware and software—"

Damn him, Graff thought.

"—and serve as a high-velocity weapons platform. It was not, of course, operable as designed. The fleet insists that the unpredictability of human decisions without a tetralogic AI dominating the pilot-neural net interlink is essential to high-*v* combat. And we have six men in hospital and seventeen dead in the realworld discovery process."

Hell.

"We're putting crews into a ship that is in effect a high-*v* multilogic missile, with the sole advantage that the equipment is theoretically recoverable."

There had been dead silence in the room. There was a small muttering now. Don't blow, don't blow, Graff wished Mitch and Jamil. We get our turn.

The gavel came down.

Tanzer went on: "A pilot with twenty years' experience and no faults in the sims ran the course successfully for three hours, forty-six minutes and 17.4 seconds. The accident, which you've seen repeatedly, took place within seven tenths of a second. In the 17th second Wilhelmsen missed one random ordnance target on the approach and reoriented to catch it on the retreat, which he did. At this point telemetry leaves us to guess what passed through his mind—perhaps the recollection he was entering the probability fan of a target in his path. Pulse and respiration has increased markedly over the previous ten minutes. The armscomper and the co-pilot simultaneously indicated alarm as the maneuver started. The armscomper fired off-profile as required and missed. In the next .7 of a second the pilot's telemetry recorded three muscle twitches in conflicting directions causing the craft to undergo successive shocks, and one extreme reaction which caused the pilot and the crew to lose consciousness and sent the ship into a tumble.

"Possibly—Dr. Helmond Weiss will provide more specifics in his testimony—but possibly prolonged hyperception to a micro-focused event like the double miss caused a spatial confusion. . . ."

Pens on TranSlates took rapid notes. Graff kept his notes in his head. And said to himself, on the memory of his own system entries: Wilhelmsen panicked.

"Seven tenths of a second," Tanzer said, "from first mistake to the ship entering a fatal motion. 4.8 seconds later it clipped a targeting buoy at .5 light. There is no recoverable wreckage. Our analysis of events rests entirely on telemetry—in which, ironically, the speed makes the microgaps significant data fallouts."

"Meaning the instruments couldn't send fast enough."

"Meaning our data-gathering had two phases: an infosift rapid transmission and a more detailed concurrent total transmission that was running 28 minutes behind the condensed report. Machines can't transmit that fast. More important, human neurons don't fire that fast. We're using human brains to improve a missile's kill rate at a sustained rate of decision that exceeds human limits. Meaning we can't think that fast that long. We've tried an Assisted handoff to a human co-pilot and it's not practical. The psychological stress is actually increased by the trade, and performance is critically reduced. Either we put an unexpected AI override on the observed physical responses that preceded the incident, or we go back to design and put that ship under a tetralogic AI with the pilot at the interface—as the heart, not the head, of the affair; or, unacceptably, we outright admit that we don't give a damn for human life, and we breed human beings to do that job and tape-train the fear and humanity out of them, the way they do in Union space. There are no other choices."

Down the corridor to the vending machines, a cheese sandwich and a soft drink. Cheese was edible. The fish wasn't even to mention. It had something green scattered through it. Ben sat down, unwrapped the sandwich, tore the indestructible packaging on the chips and sipped his drink.

A guy came in, put chits in the machine. God, he didn't want a couple of orderlies discussing kidney function during his sandwich. . . .

But he caught the haircut and the uniform, took a second look, and found the shave-job staring back at him with sudden sharp attention.

"Pollard?"

The face almost rang bells, but he couldn't place it. The haircut, pure rab, didn't agree with the blue fatigues that said military. Civ docker, he thought. Then he thought: Dekker. Shepherd. And had a sudden notion in what packet of memory that face belonged.

"Mason?" he asked.

"Yeah!" the guy said, hands full. "Word is you're here for Dekker, damn! How is he?"

"Like shit." He indicated the place opposite him at the table and Mason brought his sandwich and his drink over and sat down. Ben asked, "What are you in for?"

"Therapy." Mason wiggled the fingers of his right hand. "Gym floor jumped up and got me. —Dekker's still bad, huh? He *say* anything?"

"Thinks he's in the fuckin' Belt most of the time." Ben took a bite of cheese sandwich, thought about that shuttle leaving at mainday end, and how there wasn't another til next week, wondered if there was a shortcut to the memory Graff wanted, and said, "Keeps asking for Bird and Cory Salazar. What in hell happened to him? *Anybody* know?"

Mason pulled a long face. "Just they pulled him out of a sim-pod bloody and beat all to hell. But we'd lay odds—" Mason looked at him about chest-high and stopped talking in midsentence. Mason filled his mouth with sandwich instead.

"—lay odds, what?"

Mason looked at him narrowly while he took time to chew the bite and wash it down with soft drink. "Nothing."

"What, nothing? What's that look mean?"

"You here as a friend of Dekker's? Or officially?"

"Look, I'm a programmer, not a psych. I was minding my own business on Sol One. FSO hauled my ass out here because Dekker named me next-of-kin. Lt. Graff hands me his personals, doesn't tell me shit else, asks me to find out what happened to him, and that's where I am, trying to find out why he's lying there seeing ET's and angels, so I can get back to Sol One before my posting's gone. What's that look mean?"

Mason said slowly, "You're not here on Tanzer's orders."

"I don't know Tanzer. The FSO jerked me over on a hush-up and hurry. *Humanitarian* leave, on account of Dekker wanted me. What's the UDC got to do with it?"

"Uniform you're wearing isn't exactly popular in some quarters."

"So what are we? Union spies? Not that I heard."

"Say Dekker wouldn't be lying in that bed except for the UDC CO here."

Ben took a look at the door. Nobody around. Nobody listening, unless they routinely bugged the vending machines. "Mason. This is Ben Pollard. Ben who was Morrie Bird's partner. Ben whose ass your ship saved once upon a while. You seriously mind to tell me what the hell's going on and why Dekker rates all this shiz?"

Mason swallowed a bit of sandwich and sat there looking at him and thinking about it. "Say it's a real pressured environment."

"Yeah?"

"The UDC doesn't *like* Belters. You must be the exception."

Belters who might be old, exiled rab, Ben thought, Shepherds who looked like Mason—that haircut wouldn't get a security clearance from the UDC, but he didn't say so. He said, carefully, "There's some feeling, yeah, but I never ran into it. Went into TI, computer stuff—in no pain until they snatched me here. What's this about Dekker and the CO?"

"Tanzer's run the R&D for the UDC insystem stuff since Adam was an Earther, he's got his System, and his friends in high places, til the Fleet signed us in to fly for them. The UDC wanted to do the test and documentation through their facility—all right, they had the set-up and the sims and the knowledge of the suppliers and the technical resources; which is how R&D's got their hands on the ships and put their guys in the seats, because the U friggin' DC is *trying* to get the Fleet demoted to a UDC command."

"I've heard that. Mazian's all over the news trying to get funds. The opposition wants it with strings."

"You've seen the big ships. But the secondary stuff the Fleet's building—top secret stuff, fast. UDC's never flown anything this hot. Design screw-ups, spec screw-ups, materials failures. They cut the budget which means they go to the drawing-board again and make changes—no mind it costs another 150 million for a study and an 80 mil legislative session that could've made up the difference—no, that's fine, that's going in the damn senators' pockets and feeding the contractors. We had one glitch-up with a pump that wasn't up to specs, we got another because security's so damn tight the company making a mate-up device can't talk to the company writing the software, you figure that?"

"Must be the programmer that did the EC security system."

"Listen." Mason's finger stabbed the water-ringed tabletop. "Right now they're six months behind schedule and talking about one damn more redesign on the controls. The UDC bitched and bitched about sim time, said Tanzer's 'boys' were the ones to do the test runs because they had the hours and the experience—you want to talk to *me* about hours? Shit, I'm twenty-seven, that's twenty fuckin' years I've lived on the *Hamilton,* and they give me 200 hours at nav? 200 fuckin' hours, you believe that? They won't log anything you ran up before you were *licensable* at your post. I was nav monkey when I was seven, I was running calc when I was ten, I was sitting relief on the edge of the Well when I was twelve, and *then* they say they're counting only a quarter of the time our ships logged us—as a compromise because it was *civilian* hours? Ninety days a run, thirty heavy, and on call 24 fuckin' hours a day in Jupiter's lap for longer than these sim-jockeys would hold up, and they give me 200 hours? I was 2000 plus on my last run out from R2!"

"That's crazy."

"Yeah, but that's UDC rules. You only get hours for the time you're logged on. Who logs on? Who ever logs on? You do your fuckin' job, you're too busy to log on, with a load coming and the watch rousting you out of your bunk at 2100 to check you're where you think you are, because somebody thinks we got a positional problem, shit if I'm going to log on as officer of record and get my fuckin' *hours* for the UDC. Same shit they're pulling on the merchanters. You know why they don't count real hours on us? Because the UDC's got four pilots can claim real hours on a par with us, and last week they had five."

"The guy with Dekker's crew?"

"Wilhelmsen." Mason leaned closer, said, "Listen, —" And stopped as a nurse came in and carded a soft drink. The nurse left. Mason said, "We've got a lot of pressure. You got maybe four, five hours at a run. Virtual space display. Neural net Assist. Real sensory overload. Hyperfocus, non-stop. And you *don't* sub in some stranger in the last twelve hours before a run, you *don't* have bad feeling between the pilot and the techs, you don't plug in a guy with a whole different visualization system. You want to figure how much pressure Wilhelmsen was under to perform? Shit, he missed a target. He could've let it go. But he was too hot for that. He flipped back to get it, schitzed on where he was, and took three good guys with him. You know why Dekker's in here? Dekker—Dekker told Wilhelmsen's crew to their faces that *he* could have done it."

"Shit."

"No kidding. Wilhelmsen's navigator took severe exception, there were words—"

"Before or after they sent Dekker to hospital?"

"Let me tell you about that, too. Yeah, Dekker was in shock. He was watching it in mission control. But he didn't need any hospital. They wanted him quiet. They wanted him not to say a thing in front of the senators and the VIPs they had swarming around the observation area."

"They."

"The UDC. Tanzer. They doped him down and let him out after they got the last of the VIPs on the shuttle out of here. And twelve hours later they haul Dekker out of the sim that's been running for six—"

Evans walked in. Stood there a moment, then said, "Lt. Pollard. Getting the local news?"

Ben remembered to breathe. And shoved back from the table. "We knew each other, back when. Old news. —Nice seeing you, Mason."

"Nice seeing you," Mason muttered, and got up himself, Ben didn't wait to see for what. He chucked his plastics in the bin and walked out, with a touch of the pulse rate and the cold sweats he'd used to feel in the Belt, when the Company cops were breathing damned close to them.

Infighting with the UDC? A major Fleet project going down the chute and the blue-sky UDC fighting to get its boys in the pilot seat and the Earth Company militia under its command?

He wished he were in Stockholm.

"Lt. Graff," Bonner said, and Graff got up from beside Demas, walked quietly to the table and swore to tell the truth.

"State your name, rank, citizenship, service and age," the clerk said.

"Jurgen Albrecht Graff, Fleet Lieutenant, EC Territories, ship merchanter *Polly d'Or,* assigned militia ship *Victoria,* under Captain Keu, currently Helm Two on the ECS8, uncommissioned, age thirty-eight."

Heads perusing documents, drowsing on hands, came up and looked at him with dawning close attention.

Gen. Bonner said, "Will you state your approximate actual age, for the record, lieutenant?"

Son of a bitch, Graff thought. "Actually, sir, I haven't calculated it since I was fifteen. But I was born in 2286, Common Reckoning, and the first EC president in my memory was Padriac Melton."

"Would you agree you're approximately early twenties, lieutenant, in terms of actual years?"

"I've no access to those records, sir. And it's not relevant to my experience."

"What is your logged experience?"

"Since I was posted to Helm—ten years, six hours a shift. . . ."

"Logged hours, lieutenant."

"—conservatively, 1800 hours, since posting. Not counting apprenticeship. Not counting working during dock, which is never logged."

Bonner's face was a study in red. "*Logged* records, lieutenant. Answer the question as asked or be held in contempt."

"As far as I know, there are documents behind those hours, sir. The *Polly d'Or* is likely somewhere between Viking and Pell at the moment, and she maintains meticulous log records. *Victoria*'s whereabouts the Fleet commander could provide, if you'd care to query—"

"I doubt this committee has the patience, lieutenant. And let's state for the committee that your logged hours on Sol Two records are substantially less. Can we at least agree that you're not a senior officer, and you were in physical control of the carrier during the test run?"

"General." Saito's quiet voice from behind him, mild dismay registered on the faces of the panel. "Una Saito, Com One, protocol officer on *Victoria*. —Lieutenant, as a matter of perspective, where were you born?"

Bonner said, "Ms. Saito, whatever your rank may be, you're in contempt of this committee. Be seated before I have you ejected."

Graff said, looking at all those frowning blue-sky faces, "Actually, sir, if it's relevant, I was born on the sublighter *Gloriana*, on its last deep-space run."

There was a murmur and a sudden quiet in the room. Graff sat there with his hands folded, not provoking a thing, no, and Bonner, give him credit, gave not a flicker.

"So you would maintain on that basis your experience is adequate to have managed the carrier on a critical test run."

"I would maintain, sir, that I am qualified to take a starship through jump, an infinitely riskier operation."

"You're qualified. Have you *done* it?"

"Yes, sir. I have. Once on initiation, eighteen times on hand-off on system entry."

"Yourself. Alone."

"Helm on *Victoria* is backed by 49 working stations, counting only those reporting in chain of command to Helm."

"I'll reserve further questions. Senator Eriksson?"

"Thank you." This from the Joint Legislative Committee rep. "Lt. Graff, Eriksson from the JLC technical division. Medical experts maintain that hyperfocus is not sustainable over the required hours of operation."

"It's routine for us. If—"

"Let me finish my statement, please. Medical experts have stated that the ERP Index indicates mental confusion—stress was taking its toll. As a starship pilot you have systems which defend against impacts. You have an AI-assisted system of hand-offs. You have a computer interlock on systems to prevent accidents. Based on those facts, do you not think that similar systems are necessary on these ships?"

"Senator, all of those interlocks you describe do exist on the rider, but let me say first that a starship's autopilot override is at a 2-second pilot crisis query in combat conditions, the rider's was set at 1 for the test, and that while the carrier does have effect shields, the size of the rider makes it possible to pass through fire zones in which the carrier's huge size makes such passage far riskier. The armscomp override isn't necessary, of course, because a rider's available acceleration isn't sufficient to overtake its own ordnance, but it does have a template of prohibited fire to prevent its ordnance hitting the carrier or passing through a habitation zone. The AI-driven autopilot did cut on when it detected a crisis condition in the pilot, which, as I said, was set at 1 second for this test. The AI queried the pilot—that's a painful, attention-getting jolt. It waited a human response—long, in the AI's terms, again, 1 second before it seized control. It was already tracking the situation on all its systems. It knew the moves that had caused the tumble. It knew the existence of the next target. It knew it was off course, but it had lost its navigation lock and was trying to reestablish that. The buoy's existence was masked for the test, but the AI realized it couldn't save the test: it entered another order to penetrate the virtual reality of the test to sample the real environment, accessed information concealed from the pilot and reckoned the position of the target buoy as potentially a concern, and correctly assigned it as a hazard of equal value but secondary imminence to the threat of the ship's high-*v* tumble. It reasoned that elimination of the target required the arms function, while evasion of the target required the engines, and that the motion exceeded critical demands of the targeting system. A subfunction was, from the instant the AI had engaged, already firing engines to reduce the tumble, and tracking other firepaths. It was doing all that, and attempting to locate itself and its own potential ordnance tracks relative to interdicted fire vectors—realspace friendly targets. Fire against the target was not set for its first sufficient window: the condensed telemetry of its calculations is a massive printout. The AI was still waiting for the window when its position and the target's became identical."

Took a moment for the senator to figure what that meant. Then an angry frown. "So you're blaming an AI breakdown?"

"No, sir. Everything from the AI's viewpoint was coming optimal. A human with a clear head couldn't have outraced the AI in targeting calculations or in bringing the ship stable enough to get a window. A human might have skipped the math and discharged the chaff gun and the missiles in hope of destroying the object by sheer blind luck, but the AI had an absolute interdiction against certain vectors. It didn't even consider that it could violate that—that range safety could have taken care of the problem if it arose. Somebody decided that option shouldn't be in its memory, and this being a densely populated system maybe it shouldn't have been. But that ship was effectively lost from the moment the pilot reacted to his crew's apprehension. That communications problem was the direct *cause* of the accident—"

Bonner said, "Excuse me, senator. The lieutenant is speculating, now, far outside his expertise. May I remind him to confine himself to what he was in a position to witness or to obtain from records?"

He didn't look at Bonner. "A communications problem set up by a last-minute substitution of pilots."

The committee hadn't heard that. No. Not all of them had, at least. And from Shepherds he knew were back there in the room, there was not a breath, not an outcry, just a general muttering, and he couldn't turn his head to see expressions.

The senator said: "What substitution, lieutenant?"

"The crew trained as a team. The Fleet pilot was replaced at the last moment by a UDC backup pilot the colonel lifted out of his own crew and subbed in on Fleet personnel. The Fleet captain in command objected in an immediate memo to Col. Tanzer's office—"

Bonner said, "Lieutenant, you're out of line. Confine yourself to factual answers."

"Sir. That is a fact upheld by ECS8 log records."

Somebody yelled from the back, "Do they show the Fleet laid those targets and set that random ordnance interval?" Several voices seconded, and somebody else yelled, "You're full of it, Jennings, you don't break an ops team! You never sub personnel! Tanzer killed those guys sure as a shot to the head!"

The gavel came down.

Somebody shouted, over the banging, "The Fleet set up the course. Check the records! The Fleet had orders to set the targets closer together to screw the test!"

And from nearer the front, as the MP's and Fleet Security moved in, "*Wilhelmsen* screwed the test—those targets were all right! He lost it, that's all!"

Bonner was on his feet shouting, "Clear the room. Clear the room. Sergeant!"

*   *   *

Institution green. Ben had seen green. Had eaten real lettuce, drunk lime (orange juice was better) and had real margaritas the way they could make them on Sol One, but he still wasn't sure why inner system liked that color that mimicked old *Trinidad*'s shower paneling, whether that shade was what Earth really favored. He sincerely hoped not. He honestly hoped not. But if Earth was that color wall to wall he'd take it over B Dock hospital corridors and vending machine suppers.

Dekker was still hyperbolic—swung on an intern, threatened the nurses, called the CO a psychopathic control junkie—

"How many fingers?" the intern had asked, holding up two, and Dekker had held up his own, singular—which was Dekker, all right, but it hadn't won him points. The intern had checked his pulse, said it was elevated—

Damned right it was elevated. "You're being a *fool,*" Ben said, while they were waiting for the orderly with the trank. He grabbed Dekker by the arm and shook him, but Dekker wasn't resisting. "You know that, Dek-boy? Use your head. Shit, get us *out* of this place!"

"Sorry," Dekker said listlessly, "sorry." And stared off into space until Ben shook him again and said, "You want to spend your life in here? You want a permanent home here?"

Dekker looked at him. But the orderly came in and gave him the shot. Dekker didn't fight it. And after the orderly went away Dekker just lay there and stared past him.

"Dek," Ben said, "count their fingers. Walk their damn line. *Remember* how you got in that damn sim. Maybe the lieutenant can get you out of here. Just play their game, that's all."

And Dekker said, while Dekker's eyes were glazing, "What's the use, Ben? What's the use anymore?"

That *wasn't* like Dekker. Wasn't like him at all. But Dekker was out then, or so far under as made no difference. They said people drugged out could hear you, and that under some kinds of trank maybe you didn't have the same resistance to suggestion: Ben squeezed Dekker's arm hard and whispered, right in his ear, "You're going to do what they say and get yourself out of here. Hear it?"

Dekker didn't give any sign he did. So it was out to the hall again, 1805h, and no likelihood Dekker was going to come around again this evening.

He might lie to the doctors, Ben thought, he might *tell* them Dekker had remembered, make something up—prime Dekker with it and hope Dekker had enough of his pieces screwed together to remember it. If he could figure out what they wanted to hear. *Say* it was Wilhelmsen's crew that attacked him, that was the signal he was picking up. That was what the Fleet wanted.

But not what the UDC wanted. And what the Fleet wanted wasn't any ticket to Stockholm, no.

Damn, damn, and damn.

Meanwhile Dekker got crazier, no knowing what drug they were filling him full of or what it was doing, and if he could get hold of Graff he'd tell him check the damn medication for side effects, it wasn't helping, it was making Dekker worse; he'd stopped trusting Higgins, and Evans hadn't been available since yesterday—

He'd seen this before, damn if he hadn't when an organization got ready to throw a man out with the garbage—some skuz in power had taken a position and bet his ass on it, and now the skuz in power had stopped wanting the truth, since it didn't agree with the positions he'd taken—

So you trashed the guy who knew what was going on; you pinned the blame on him as far as you could; you shunted out anybody who might be sympathetic—Evans' departure from the scene—and from where Ben Pollard was standing it didn't look as if Graff or the Fleet had any serious influence left in the hospital—not enough at least for Graff to get his ass in here and ask Dekker himself, which signal he should have picked up from the beginning if he'd had any antennae up.

Not enough to do a thing about the stuff they were shooting into Dekker, who, if the Fleet knew it, wasn't outstandingly sane to start with.

Triple damn.

"Good night," some nurse said to him. "G'night," Ben muttered, half looking around. Good night was what Earthers said to each other. Good night was where this guy had come from. The place of green and snow and rain. Tides and beaches.

He'd seen growing plants. Been into the herbarium on Sol One. Amazing sight. Guided tours, once a week. Keep to the walkway, don't pick the leaves. But the Guides demonstrated how some of them smelled. Flowers would take your head off. Leaves smelled strange. He wasn't sure he liked it. Grease and cold metal smelled one way, and that was home. This hadn't been, hadn't smelled quite edible, not quite offensive, not at all smell like anything he'd known. The ocean was what he wanted, not any damn woods full of stinking plants: snow that was water freezing, not methane, or the scary stuff you got when a seal was chancy.

Snow was the result of weather, which was the result of Coriolis forces, which he understood, and atmospheric rollover, which he theoretically understood—he thought about that, pushing the button for another damned cheese sandwich, he thought about a city that was like helldeck without an overhead, with the tides coming and going against its edges and snow happening—that was what he thought about for company on the walk home.

Didn't think about Dekker lying trank-dead in bed, or Dekker saying, What's the use, Ben? What's the use anymore—

When Dekker had hung on to life harder than any son of a bitch of his acquaintance. And when other sons of bitches were playing games with a defense system they called important—dammit, the services played games, with a war on? And the whole human race could find itself in a war zone if the Fleet *didn't* keep the mess out past the Oort Cloud?

The Earth Company was playing damn games again, that was what, in another of its corporate limbs, the friggin' Company and the UDC and the Fleet, that couldn't find his luggage, was politicking away as usual and throwing out a guy like Dekker who was sincerely crazy enough to want to fly a ship like that into combat.

He'd fought fools in administration before. And they were beatable, except there was such a supply of them.

He'd fought Systems before, and they were beatable, if you knew the numbers, or you could get at them. But damn, he'd tried to stay clean. Even with that EIDAT system, that begged for a finger or two in its works. Use the numbers he had to get to Graff?

Graff couldn't do anything or Graff would have done it. Possible even that Graff had screwed him from the start of this.

Get to Keu's office? Not damned easy. And no guarantee the Fleet even at that level could do anything.

Go to the UDC CO and screw Dekker by blowing his own service's hope of getting him back?

Walking the corridor to his so-called hospice quarters, he thought how if going to Tanzer would get him a pass out of here on the next shuttle, damned if it wasn't starting to look like a good idea. Screw Dekker? Dekker was already screwed. So what was one more, given he couldn't help the guy?

He held sandwich, chips, and drink in one arm, fished his card out of his pocket with his right hand and shoved it into the keyslot.

The message light was blinking on the phone, bright red in the dark. He elbowed the button on the room lights, shut the door the same way, and went to the nightstand to set his supper down—

Found his luggage, maybe. He couldn't think of a call else he had in, unless Dekker'd taken a spell of something.

Couldn't be he'd broken anybody's neck. They had him too far out for that. Please God.

He plugged in his personal reader—never use a TI card in an unsecure device—and keyed up playback.

TECH/2 Benjamin J. Pollard
CTS/SS/UDC 28 BAT 2
CURRENTLOC: UDC SOL2B-HOS28
1719JUN20/24 SN P-235-9876/MLR 1923JUN20/24
TRANSFER TO: ACTIVE DUTY: UDC SYSTEMS TESTING
RANK: TECH2/UDC SOL2B-OPS/SCAN G-5: PILOT RATING C-3 WITH 200 EXPERIENCE HOURS LOGGED.
REPORT TO: 2-DECK 229, BARRACKS C: JUN21/24/0800h: ref/ CLASSIFIED: OUTSIDE COMMUNICATION SPECIFICALLY DENIED.

He sat down. He had that much presence of mind. He punched playback again with his thumb, and the same damned thing rolled past.

Transfer? Systems Testing? Pilot rating?

Shit!

The committee wanted another go. Immediately. The shuttle was two days on its way from Sol One, due in at maindawn, and, informed it wouldn't be held, senatorial demands notwithstanding, the committee decided to keep going through maindark, if that was what it took. You didn't snag a senator for a five-day to Sol Two—no famous restaurants, no cocktail lounges, no "facilities" the way they legendarily existed downworld: the senators had important business to do, the senators wanted out and back to Sol One and down to Earth and their perks and their privileges, and they'd talk with the company reps over gin and tonic the whole way back.

Graff had hoped, for a while, after things went to hell, that some few members of the committee might want to ask *him* questions over gin and tonic, if they had the clout to ask him in for a go-over; or rec-hall coffee, if they had the clout just to get past Bonner. He'd kept his phone free. He'd hoped until he got the notification of the resumption of the sessions—the committee wanted a chance to review testimony and wanted certain individuals to "stand by" a call.

Demas and Saito weren't on the list. Mitch and Jamil certainly weren't. No audience. No guarantee there would be any questions Bonner didn't set up. Graff sat there tapping a stylus on the desk and thinking about a fast call to Sol One via FleetCom; but that was still no use—if the captain hadn't noticed a shuttle-load of senators, contractor executives, and UDC brass headed to Sol Two's B Dock, there was no hope for them; and if the captain hadn't known something about the character and leanings of said senators and contractors and Gen. Patrick Bonner, Fleet Security was off its game. So the lieutenant had to get his butt out there right now and give the senators what they asked as best he could.

So the lieutenant in question put his jacket on, straightened his collar, and opened the door.

"Mr. Graff."

Face to face with Tanzer.

"I'd like a word," Tanzer said as he stepped into the hall.

"About my testimony?" He *didn't* have an Optex, didn't own one and it wasn't legal for a private conversation; but he hoped Tanzer would worry.

Tanzer said, "Just a word of sanity."

A trap? A smear, if Tanzer was carrying a hidden Optex. He could refuse to talk; he could tell Tanzer go to hell; but he had to face Tanzer after the committee was long gone. "Yes, colonel?"

Tanzer said, quietly, "You could screw this whole project. You're a junior, you don't know what you're walking into. And you could lose the war—right here, right in this hearing. I'm advising you to answer the questions without comment—*no,* I'm not supposed to be talking to you, and no, I can't advise you about your testimony. By the book, I can't. But forget that business in the office. We both want that ship. We don't want it canceled. Do we? —Can we have a word inside your office?"

No, was his first thought. There were aides milling about down the hall. There were potential witnesses. But not knowing what Tanzer wanted to tell him could be a mistake too. Bugs, there weren't, inside. Not unless the UDC was technologically one up, and he didn't think so. He opened the door again, let Tanzer in and let the door shut.

Tanzer said, directly, "The companies aren't going to support finding a basic design flaw; that's money out of *their* pockets, do you understand me? That's not what we're going to push for."

Tanzer and a 4-star? Politicking with a Fleet j-g? What in hell was going on at Sol One? "I wasn't under the impression that *was* seriously at issue."

"You don't understand me. Those companies don't want the blame.

They're perfectly willing to put the accident off on the service. To call it mishandling—"

Oh-ho.

"A control redesign, existing technology—that, they'll go for. As long as it's *our* design change, out of our budget. You listen to me. This is critical. We've got some Peace-nows kicking up a fuss—they want to grab that appropriation for their own programs. They're talking negotiation with Union. Partition of the trade zones. They've got some tame social scientists down in Bonn and Moscow talking isolation again."

They'd talked it off and on for two hundred years. But Union was very interested in Earth's biology. *Very* interested.

"They won't get it."

"They can dither this program into another five-year redesign with political deals. The Earth Company can end up deadlocked with the UN. We need the AI on top to let us get some successes with this ship—make it do-able, so we can go public as soon as possible. The thing can have another model, for God's sake, build the old design and lose ships to your heart's content, *after* we've got the first thirty out of the shipyards and trained pilots who know its characteristics. Prove your point and have your funerals, it'll be out of our hands, but let's get this ship online."

"The effect will be training your pilots to pull it short—to worry when they're taking a necessary chance. Combat pilots can't have that mindset; and you *can't train* with that thing breathing down your neck."

"You're not a psychiatrist, lieutenant."

"I'm not an engineer, either, but I know the AI you've got won't accommodate it, you're talking about a very complicated software, a bigger black box, and that panel's already crowding armscomp, besides the psychological factors—"

"Cut one seat. One fewer tech. The tetralogic's worth it."

"That's ten fewer objects longscan can track, and that's one damned more contractor with an unproved software and another unproved interface to train to."

"That's *nothing* getting tracked if the ship doesn't get built, lieutenant, come down to the point. You're not going to get everything you want."

"If you want to cut a deal, you need to talk to the captain, I'm under his orders."

"What are his orders?"

"To keep that ship as is."

"Or lose it? You listen to me. You don't have to agree. Just don't raise objections."

"Talk to my captain. I can't change his orders."

Tanzer was red in the face. Keeping his voice very quiet. "We can't reach your captain."

"Why?"

"We don't know why. We *think* he's in committee meetings."

"Go to Mazian's office, colonel, I can't authorize a thing."

"We've been trying to reach *him,* lieutenant, and we've got your whole damned program about to destruct on us, out there—you'd better believe you're in a hot spot, and I wouldn't take you into confidence, you *or* your recruits, but we can't afford another shouting match for the committee. We're trying to save this program, we're not arguing the value of human hands-on at the controls: you know and I know there's no way Union's tape-trained clones are any match for real human beings—"

"They're not that easy a mark. Azi *still* aren't an AI with an interdict."

"They'll crack. They'll crack the same as anybody else. Their program's going to have the same limitations."

"They won't crack, colonel, they're completely dedicated to what they're doing, that's what they're created for, for God's sake—"

"You listen to me, lieutenant. I was in charge of the program that put your *Victoria* out there and I don't need to be told by any wet-behind-the-ears what a human pilot is worth, but, dammit! you automate when you have to. You don't hold on to an idea til it kills you—which this is going to do if you screw up in there. You can lose the whole damned *war* in that hearing room, does that get through to you?"

"Colonel, in all respect to your experience—"

"You go on listening. Yes, we had to have a show, yes, I subbed at Wilhelmsen. Your boy Dekker's got problems. Serious problems." Tanzer pulled a datacard from his breast pocket.

"What's that?"

"A copy of Dekker's personnel file. It's damned interesting reading."

Damn, he thought. And hoped he kept anxiety off his face. It couldn't be Fleet records—unless there was a two-legged leak in the records system.

"Reckless proceeding and wrongful death." Tanzer pocketed the card again. "You want the reason I subbed him? There's a grieving mother out there that's been trying to get justice out of that boy of yours. Rape and murder—"

"Neither of which is true."

"I had, if you want to know, lieutenant, specific orders to pull Dekker off that demo, because Dekker's legal troubles were going to surface again the minute his name hit the downworld media—and it would have."

"On a classified test. He lost a partner out in the Belt. The incident isn't a secret in the Company. Far from it. Don't tell me you didn't know that, if you've got that record."

"The name was going to surface, take my word for it. He's politically hot, too damned hot to represent this program—*that's* why I pulled him from that demo, lieutenant, and you had to ignore my warning. Stick to issues you're prepared to answer and leave Dekker the hell out of this. Cory Salazar. Does the name mean anything to you?"

"ASTEX politics murdered Salazar."

"Tell that to the mother. Tell that to the mama of the underage kid Dekker seduced out there."

"That wasn't the way it happened, colonel."

"You want to tell Salazar's mother that, —lieutenant? You want to tell that to a woman who's on the MarsCorp board? I couldn't put him in front of the media. I *had* to pull him off that team. You understand me? I'm trusting you right now, lieutenant, with a critical confidence, because, dammit, you've raised the issue in there and you'd better have the good sense to back off that point, waffle your way out of it and come into line if you want to keep your boy inside these walls. If he gets to be a media issue, he's dead. You understand that?"

"I understand Wilhelmsen died, I understand a whole crew *died* for a damned politicking decision—"

"You think I don't care, Lieutenant? Your boy Dekker's got a political problem *and* a mouth. And we've got a ship that kills crews and somebody's *mother* breathing down our necks, wanting your boy's head on a platter. You hear me? I didn't screw Dekker. Your captain put him in that position, I didn't. Damned right I pulled him from what was scheduled to go public, and damned right I shut him up before he got to the VIPs we had onstation."

"By shoving him into a pod unconscious?"

"No, damn you. I didn't."

Not lying, if he could rely on anything Tanzer said. Which he was far from sure of. "You told him *why* you pulled him?"

"Trust that mouth? No. And don't you. Hear me? He got into that pod on his own. Leave it at that. Attempted suicide. Who knows? I won't contest that finding. But you shut it down with that. I know he's popular with your recruits. I know you've got a problem. But let's use our heads on this and you quieten matters down and get *off* that issue."

Damn and damn. Call the captain, was what he needed to do. But they *weren't* sure the UDC wasn't eavesdropping. And if Keu *was* currently caught up in committee at Sol—

Ask Tanzer if FleetCom was secure? Hell if.

"We'd better get in there," Tanzer said and opened the door and walked out.

Son of a bitch, Graff thought, what do I do? Demas is on board, Saito's on her way up there. . . .

He walked out, shut the door. Tanzer was down at the corner of the hall with Bonner, the two of them talking. He looked at his watch. One minute from late, the committee was about to convene. He could no-show, he could send Bonner word he was going to be late.

They could say any damned thing without hindrance then, finish the meeting without him in the time it would take to get FleetCom, let alone confer with the captain.

He'd faced fire with steadier nerves. He'd made jumpspeed decisions easier with a ship at stake. There was no assurance Tanzer had told him the truth, or even half of it. There was no assurance they had ever tried to get Keu, or Mazian, there was no assurance it was anything but a maneuver to silence him and ram something through, and there was not even absolute assurance they'd told the truth about political influence stalking Dekker, but if it was, God, somebody had found a damned sensitive button to push. If the Fleet didn't back Dekker, if the Fleet let Dekker take a grenade—the likes of Mitch and Jamil wouldn't stand still for it, there'd be bloodshed, no exaggeration at all, the Belters would take the UDC facilities apart first and work their way over to Fleet HQ. Betray them—and there was no trusting them, no relying on them, no guarantee the metal and the materials were going to go on arriving out of the Belt, and damned sure no crews to handle the ships.

Now he didn't know what Bonner was going to do in that hearing room. Or Tanzer. And he wasn't in a position to object—he felt he was heading into a trap, going in there at all, but he followed them in and sat down in a decimated gathering.

Not a friendly face in the room. Not a one.

Bonner called the session to order, Bonner talked about high feelings over the tragic accident, Bonner talked about the stress of a job that called on men to risk their lives, talked about God and country.

Blue-sky language. Blue-sky thinking. *Up* to an Earther didn't refer to phase fields, *war* was two districts on a plane surface in a dispute over territory, and the *United Nations* was a faction-ridden single-star-system organization trying to tell merchanter Families what their *borders* were: explain borders to them, first.

You had to see a planet through optics and think flat surface to imagine how *ground* looked. He hadn't laid eyes on a planet til he was half-grown. He never had figured out the emotional context, except to compare it to *ship* or *station,* but there was something about being fixed in place next to permanent neighbors that sounded desperately unnatural. Which he supposed was prejudice on his side. Bonner talked about a righteous war. And *he* thought about ports and ships run by Cyteen's tape-trained humanity, with mindsets more alien than Earth's.

Bonner talked about human stress and interactive systems, while he thought about the Cluster off Cyteen, where startides warped space, and a ghostly malfunction on the boards you hoped to God was an artifact of that space, while a Union spotter was close to picking up your presence.

Bonner got Helmond Weiss on the mike to read the medical report. Telemetry again. More thorough than the post-mortem on the ship. Less printout. Four human beings hadn't output as much in their last minutes as that struggling AI had. Depressing thought.

Then the psych lads took the mike. "Were Wilhelmsen's last decisions rational?" the committee asked point-blank. And the psychs said, hauling up more charts and graphs, "Increasing indecision," and talked about hyped senses, maintained that Wilhelmsen had gone on hyperfocus overload and lost track of actual time-flow—

. . . making decisions at such speed in such duration, it was pure misapprehension of the rate at which things were happening. No, you couldn't characterize it as panic. . . .

". . . evidence of physiological distress, shortness of breath, increase in REM and pulse rate activated a medical crisis warning with the AI—"

"The carrier's AI didn't have time to reach the rider?" a senator asked.

"And get the override query engaged and answered, no, there wasn't time."

Playback of the final moments on the tape. The co-pilot, Pete Fowler, the last words on the tape Fowler's, saying, *"Hold it, hold it—"*

That overlay the whole reorientation and firing incident, at those speeds. The panel had trouble grasping that. They spent five minutes arguing it, and maybe, Graff thought, still didn't realize the sequence of events, or that it was Fowler protesting the original reorientation.

You didn't have time to talk. Couldn't get a word out in some sequences, and not this one. Fowler shouldn't have spoken. Part of it was his fault. Shouldn't have spoken to a strange pilot, who didn't know his contexts, who very well knew they didn't altogether trust him.

The mike went to Tanzer. A few final questions, the committee said. And a senator asked the question:

"What was the name of the original pilot?"

"Dekker. Paul Dekker. Trainee."

"What was the reason for removing him from the mission?"

"Seniority. He was showing a little stress. Wilhelmsen was the more experienced."

Like hell.

"And the crew?"

"Senator, a crew should be capable of working with any officer. It was capable. There were no medical grounds there. The flaw is in the subordination of the neural net interface. It should be constant override with concurrent input from the pilot. The craft's small cross-section, its minimum profile, the enormous power it has to carry in its engines to achieve docking at highest *v*—all add up to sensitive controls and a very powerful response. . . ."

More minutiae. Keep my mouth shut or not? Graff asked himself. *Trust* Tanzer? Or follow orders?

Another senator: "Did the sims run the same duration as the actual mission?"

Not lately, Graff thought darkly, while Tanzer said, blithely, "Yes."

Then a senator said: "May I interject a question to Lt. Graff."

Bonner didn't like that. Bonner frowned, and said, "Lt. Graff, I remind you you're still under oath."

"Yes, sir."

The senator said, "Lt. Graff. You were at the controls of the carrier at the time of the accident. You were getting telemetry from the rider."

"Yes, sir."

"The medical officer on your bridge was recorded as saying Query out."

"That's correct."

"What does that mean?"

"It means she'd just asked the co-pilot to assess the pilot's condition and act. But the accident was already inevitable. Just not enough time."

Blinks from the senator, attempt to think through the math, maybe. "Was the carrier too far back for safety?"

"It was in a correct position for operations. No, sir."

"Was the target interval set too close? Was it an impossible shot?"

"No. It was a judgment shot. The armscomper doesn't physically fire all the ordnance, understand. He sets the priorities at the start of the run and adjusts them as the situation changes. A computer does the firing, with the pilot following the sequence provided by his co-pilot and the longscanner and armscomper. The pilot can violate the armscomper's priorities. He might have to. There are unplotteds out there, rocks, for instance. Or mines."

"Did Wilhelmsen violate the priorities?"

"Technically, yes. But he had that choice."

"Choice. At those speeds."

"Yes, sir. He was in control until that point. He knew it was wrong, he glitched, and he was out. Cold."

"Are you a psychiatrist, lieutenant?"

"No, sir, but I suggest you ask the medical officer. There was no panic until he heard his crew's alarm. That spooked him. Their telemetry reads alarm—first, sir. His move startled them and he dropped out of hype."

"The lieutenant is speculating," Bonner said. "Lt. Graff, kindly keep to observed fact."

"As a pilot, sir, I observed these plain facts in the medical testimony."

"You're out of order, lieutenant."

"One more question," the senator said. "You're saying, lieutenant, that the tetralogic has faults. Would it have made this mistake?"

"No, but it has other flaws."

"Specifically?"

"Even a tetralogic is recognizable, to similar systems. Machine can counter machine. Human beings can make decisions these systems don't expect. Longscan works entirely on that principle."

"Are you a computer tech?"

"I know the systems. I personally would not go into combat with a computer totally in charge."

The senator leaned back, frowning. "Thank you, lieutenant."

"May I make an observation?" Tanzer asked, and got an indulgence and a nod from Bonner.

Tanzer said: "Let me say this is an example of the kind of mystical nonsense I've heard all too much of from this service. Whatever your religious preferences, divine intervention didn't happen here, Wilhelmsen didn't stay conscious long enough to apply the human advantage. Human beings can't defy physics; and the lieutenant sitting behind his carrier's effect shields can maintain that spacers are somehow evolved beyond earthly limitations and make their decisions by mysterious instincts that let them outperform a tetralogic, but in my studied and not unexpert opinion, there's been altogether too much emphasis in recruitment based on entry-level skills and certain kinds of experience—meaning a practical exclusion of anyone but Belters. The lieutenant talks about some mysterious unquantifiable mentality that can work at these velocities. But I'd like to say, and Dr. Weiss will back me on this, that there's more than button-pushing ability and reflexes that make a reliable military. There is, very importantly, attitude. There's been no background check into volunteers on this project . . ."

Dammit, he's going to do it—

". . . in spite of the well-known unrest and the recent violence in the Belt. We have a service completely outside the authority of the UDC trying to exclude the majority of Sol System natives from holding a post on weapons platforms of enormous destructive potential, insisting we take *their word*—" Tanzer's knuckles rapped the table. "—that the policies and decisions of the UN, the world governments, and even Company policy will be respected and observed outside this system. It's imperative that these ships *not* remain under the control of a cadre selected by one man's opinion of their fitness for command, a man not in any way native to Earth or educated to Earth's values. The Fleet is pushing qualifications arbitrarily selected to exclude our own military in command positions, for what motive leaves me entirely uneasy, sirs."

Some things a man couldn't hear and keep his mouth shut. "General," Graff said. "I'd like to make my own statement in answer to that."

"This isn't a court of law, lieutenant. But you'll have your say. In the meantime, the colonel has his. —Go on, colonel."

Graff let go a breath and thought, I could walk out, now. But to what good? To what living good? I'm in it. The Captains can disavow what I say. They can still do that. But Tanzer wanted to cut a deal. Tanzer wanted me to agree on the redesign and what good is my agreement to them, what could it possibly influence if this committee's already in their pocket?

Tanzer said, "There are two reasons why I favor a tetralogic system. This ship is too important and too hazardous to civilian targets to turn over to personnel in whose selection our values have never been a criterion. I've been asked privately the reason for the substitution—"

My God, here it goes.

"In the recess I've also been asked the reason for the morale difficulties in this old and time-tried institution. Gentlemen, it lies in the assumption that these machines are flyable only by super-humans personally selected by Conrad Mazian and his hand-picked officers. Earth is being sold a complete bill of goods. Conrad Mazian wants absolute control of an armada Earth is sacrificing considerably to build. What's the difference—control of the human race by a remote group of dissidents—or by a merchanter cartel with a powerful lobby in the halls of the Earth Company administration? These ships and the carriers should be under UDC command and responsible to the citizens of the governments that fund them, not to a self-appointed committee of merchantmen with their own interests and their own priorities."

Bang went the gavel. The growing murmur from the committee and the aides and witnesses ebbed down, and Tanzer went on:

"You've seen an unfortunate incident in this hearing room, resultant from what the Fleet calls discipline, beginning with the concept of command by committee and ending with the uniform variances that permit Belter enlistees to dress and act like miners on holiday. The carrier that is allegedly on operational alert at this moment for the protection of Earth itself doesn't even have its senior pilot at this facility, while Captain Keu is on an indefinite leave to Sol One. *Junior* lieutenant Graff insists he's qualified in an emergency—but his heads of station outrank him, a prime example of merchanter command order, and if he says decisions have to come at light speed, and he can't have an AI breathing down his neck, what does he say about a committee of senior officers calling the shots for him on the flight deck?"

He stood up. "I *object,* general."

"Sit down, lieutenant." The gavel banged. "Before I find you in contempt of this committee and have you arrested."

He sat. He was no good in the brig. The captain and the Number Ones needed to hear the rest of it. Accurately.

Tanzer said: "We need a disciplined system that can let us substitute a pilot, a tech, a scan operator, *anybody* in any crew, because this isn't the merchant trade we're running, ladies and gentlemen, it's war, in which there are bound to be casualties, and no single man is indispensable. There has to be a chain of command responsible to legitimate policies of the Defense Department, and in which there is absolutely no leeway for personalities too talented and too important to follow orders and do their job."

He couldn't stay quiet. "You mean downgrade the ship until cargo pushers can fly it!"

Bang went the gavel. "Lieutenant!"

* * *

Echoes in the core. High up in the mast sounds came faint as ghosts; not like R2 where half-refined one shot through zero-cold, and thundered and rumbled like doom against the chamber walls. In this vast chamber sims whirled around the chamber on mag-levs and came like tame, dreadful flowers to the platforms, giving up or taking in their human cargoes—

You carded in before you launched. The pod's Adaptive Assists recognized you, input your values, and you input your tape for the sim you were running. You fastened the one belt that locked the others. But something was wrong. The pod started to move and he couldn't remember carding in, couldn't think through the mounting pain in his head and the force pinning him to the seat—

"Cory!" he yelled. Tried to yell. "Cory, hold on!"

But he couldn't reach the Abort. Couldn't see it, couldn't reach it, and the damn sim thought the belts were locked. "Mayday," he called over com, but it didn't answer. Someone had said he'd earned it. Maybe Ben. Ben would have. But he didn't think Ben would have done this to him . . .

"You're a damn screw-up!" someone yelled at him. "You screwed up my whole damn life, you son of a bitch! What'd I ever do to deserve you?"

Sounded like his mother. But his mother never grabbed him by the collar and hit him. That was Ben. Ben was the way out and he tried to listen to Ben, it was the only chart he had that made any sense now . . .

Ben said, "What day is it, damn you?" And he honestly tried to remember. Ben had told him he had to remember.

"I object vehemently," Graff said, calmly as he could, "to the colonel's characterization of myself, my captain, my crew and my service. I challenge the colonel's qualifications to manage this program, when he has had no deepspace experience, no flight time at those speeds, no experience of system transit at those speeds; and neither have any of the medics who've testified. This—" He clicked a datacard onto the table, and remembered with a cold chill the one Tanzer was carrying. "This is *my* personal medical record. I call that in evidence, on reaction times and general qualifications."

The gavel came down. "I'll thank you to reserve the theatrics, lieutenant. This committee is not impressed. You've asked to make a statement. Make it. I remind you you're under oath."

"*Yes,* general. I call the general's attention to the fact that he did not so admonish the colonel. Can we assume it was an oversight?"

He expected the gavel. Instead Bonner leaned forward and said very quietly, "The colonel knows he's under oath. Make your statement."

"It's very brief. The colonel ordered me not to tell the truth to this committee."

There was a moment of silence. Bonner hadn't expected that shot. He should have. Bonner said, then, "Are you through, lieutenant?"

"No, sir." He thought of Dekker. And the bloodied sim-pod. And wondered if he would see another day in this place. "I intend to answer the committee's questions. If it has any."

A long silence, subjective time. Then a senator asked, "You think you could have flown the rider?"

"If I were trained to do that, yes, ma'am."

"You couldn't, say, step from the carrier into the ridership. Given the familiarity with the interfaces."

"I've had years of training for the mass and the characteristics of a large ship. Cross-training could confuse me. Jump makes you quite muzzy. You're riding your gut reactions quite heavily in those first moments of entry. Certainly so in combat."

Another: "You think a training program can produce that kind of skill, here, in a matter of months."

"No, sir. Not without background experience, I don't. That's why the Fleet didn't recruit from the local military. Test pilots like Wilhelmsen—he could have done it. I've no wish to downplay his ability. He was good. We'd have taken him in a moment if the UDC had wanted to release him. Or if he had wanted to go."

"Are you doing the recruiting, now?" Bonner asked. "Or speaking for Captain Mazian?"

"I'm agreeing with the colonel, sir, based on my knowledge of Wilhelmsen's ability. But that ability can't be trained in the time we need; we need prior experience. We particularly need crews that can *feel* insystem space. The Shepherds and the miners and insystem haulers aren't trainees as the term implies; and they're not eighteen-year-old recruits who think a mass proximity situation is an exam problem."

"What *is* a mass proximity situation, lieutenant?"

God.

"A collision alert, sir." It was the least vivid description that leapt to his mind. He had no wish to offend the senator. The senator laughed, like a good politician, and leaned back.

Another asked, "Lieutenant?"

"Yes, sir."

"To *what* government do you hold loyalty?"

A handful of days ago he would have said something about historical ties, a center for the human species. But he didn't want to get into abstracts. Or create any apprehension of an outsider viewpoint. He looked the senator in the eyes and said quietly, "To Earth, sir."

But the answer appeared to take the man aback; and it struck him then for the first time that he was looking at Earth, at this table: a row of incomprehensible special interests. None of them could *see* Earth from the outside—the techs from subsidiaries of the Earth Company; the senators from the Pan-Asian Union and Europe. Bonner, from the Western Hemisphere. (Who first defined east and west? he wondered, hyperfocusing, momentarily as bereft of referents as they were, taking in everything. Politics of dividing oceans? And why not north and south—except the ice?)

The same senator asked, "And these recruits from the Belt? To whom are they loyal?"

Touchy question. A good many Belters were political exiles from Earth. He said, "I'm sure they'd tell you, individually, whatever their concept is. The human race, certainly. The one that nature evolved on this planet, not the one from labs on Cyteen."

"Loyalty to themselves, would you say?"

He quoted Bonner. "Isn't that the issue of the war, senator? Freedom of conscience?"

Silence from Bonner. Deathly silence.

"If this design goes AI," Graff continued quickly, wishing for Saito's eloquence, "so the enemy can predict it; or if some legislative compromise replaces our command with officers who don't know jump-space tactics—we'll die, ship by ship. Then let the UDC hold the line with no carriers, no deepspace crews. Lose us and you won't have the merchanters. You won't have the far space stations. We're the ones that have risked everything carrying out your orders, trying to hold the human race together. What's on Cyteen isn't *like* us."

Bonner said, "Lieutenant, tell me, what do *you* care if Earth ceases to exist?"

He said, halfway into it before he remembered whose quote it was, " 'If Earth didn't exist, we'd have to create one.' "

Emory of Cyteen had said, a now-famous remark: "We all need to be from somewhere. We need a context for the genome. Lose that and we lose all common reference as a species."

But the committee didn't seem to recognize the source. Likely they couldn't recall the name of Cyteen's Councillor of Science—or conceive of the immense arrogance in that statement. Cyteen *was* terraforming, hand over fist. Ripping a world apart. Killing a native ecology, replacing it—and humanity—with its own chosen design. He'd seen the classified reports. And he wasn't sure Bonner had. Mazian was taking those records to the highest levels of the Company and the UN.

A senator said, "We're here to discuss technology. The fitness of a machine."

"The fitness of the men who fly it," Bonner said, "is also at issue."

The pod reoriented. Flesh met plastics. Dekker tried to defend himself, but something grabbed his collar, held him. Someone shook him, and said, "Straighten up, you damned fool, or I'll hit you again."

"Trying to," he told Ben's hazy image, and tasted blood in his mouth.

"Why in hell?" Ben asked him. "Why in hell'd you have to ask for me?"

"Dunno, dunno, Ben." Blood tasted awful. He tried to get his breath and Ben shoved him back against the pillows. Ben looked like hell.

Ben still had his fist wrapped in his collar. Ben gave him another shove. "I can't blame whoever shoved you in that simulator. You're a pain in the ass, you know that? You're a damned recurring pain in the ass!"

"Yeah," he said. He didn't want his lips to tremble, but they did, and tears stung his eyes. A long, long time he'd been alone. There'd been others, but they'd died, and Ben hadn't, Ben wouldn't, Ben was too hard to catch and Ben wouldn't get himself killed for anybody. He trusted Ben that way. Ben was too slippery for the sons of bitches.

Someone shadowed the doorway.

"Need to check his blood pressure, sir."

Somebody had said something about Have a nice trip. Someone who'd told him go to hell. . . .

He caught at the bed. Caught at Ben's arm as Ben started to get up and turn him over to the nurse. "No."

"Your blood pressure's getting up, Mr. Dekker."

"Screw it. —Ben, —"

"Lieutenant."

He swung his legs off the bed, made a try at getting up and the room went upside down. The nurse made a grab after him, he saw the blue uniform, and he elbowed it aside. He caught himself with a grip on the edge of the bed.

But Ben was gone. Ben had left him, and the nurse got a hand on his shoulder and his arm. "Just lie down, Mr. Dekker. Lie down. How'd he get in here, anyway? Visitors aren't supposed to be in here."

He didn't know either. But a lot of things happened here that shouldn't. And he hadn't been dreaming. Ben had been there. He had a cut inside his lip and a coppery taste in his mouth that proved it, no matter what the nurse said about visitors. He lay down and ran his tongue over that sore spot, thinking, through the shot and everything, Ben's here, Ben's here . . . and knowing it was Sol Two where Ben had found him: Ben hated him; but Ben had got here, Ben talked sense to him and didn't confuse him. Even if Ben wanted to beat hell out of him. He *liked* that about Ben—that for all Ben wanted to go on beating hell out of him, Ben hadn't. Ben had held on to him. Ben had shaken him and told him where rightside up was and told him to get there. Only advice he'd trusted in days. Only voice he'd wanted to come back to, since—

—since his crew died. Died in a fireball he wasn't in. Couldn't have been in, since he wasn't vapor.

Somebody'd said, later, Enjoy the ride, Dekker.

He couldn't remember who. Someone he'd known. But the voice had no color in his mind. No sound. And he couldn't recover it.

They said, shadows leaning over him, "Need to keep that blood pressure down, Mr. Dekker," and he said: "Screw all of you, I don't need your help," and kept his eyes shut.

Whine of mag-levs. You got that through the walls. There was light out there, but it didn't diffuse, despite the distances across the huge sim chamber, where a solitary pod was working. There was a safety stand-down in effect. Lendler Corp techs were doing an inspection on this shift, remoting the pod from the number two access. You could see the light on, far across the chamber.

Easy ways to get hurt out there. Pods pulled a lot of *g*'s, positive and negative. Graff touched the cold plastics of the dead panel, drifting in the zero *g*, antagonizing an already upset stomach, and watched the pod, figuring how hard a body could hit, repeatedly, during that gyrating course. Dekker was strong for his slight frame. Only thing that had saved him. God only knew how conscious he'd been, but enough he'd protected his head somehow. And his neck and his back and the rest of his bones. The meds who hadn't seen the inside of the pod had said the belts must have come loose. But the belts had been locked together under Dekker, deliberately to fool the safety interlocks, by somebody who hadn't left prints—unless it was the last man to use the pod, and that was Jamil, who hadn't a motive that he knew. Belts locked underneath Dekker—otherwise the pod wouldn't have moved. The MP's report had said, Suicide is not ruled out.

Suicide, to have a MarsCorp councillor on your case?

Suicide, to call Tanzer a bastard?

Don't let it get to you, Saito had said, when he'd called the carrier to tell them the hearing was over. Midge had hand-carried his report to the ship and a long transmission had gone out to the captain by now. Tanzer was going to rebound off the walls tomorrow.

But the report was at Sol One by now. So far as what he dared send the captain, the most urgent matter was one name, of everything related to the accident: Salazar. The rest was in Dekker's file. Beyond that, Keu needed to know how Bonner and Tanzer had run the hearing; needed to know how his Helm Two had answered the questions, right or wrong.

Helm Two had underestimated Tanzer, that was the fact, Tanzer had thrown him a last-minute set of choices in which his refusal to go against Keu's orders, and a lone lieutenant's blind run through a mine-field, Tanzer had said it, might just have lost the program tonight, lost the war for the whole human race, literally, right in that hearing room this evening—if somebody wiser and better at politics couldn't somehow take the pieces and put them together with more skill than he had mustered in front of that committee.

He was tired, God, he was tired, and he had had no business coming here. He wasn't doing entirely rational things now, he'd sent word with Midge where he was going and put com on alert, but he hadn't come to the Number Ones for aid and comfort and he was refusing to, knowing nothing they could tell him was of any use, since they didn't know any more than he did what was going on. He'd made some critical judgments left and right of the course he'd hoped to hold in the hearing and in his dealings with Tanzer, and he was avoiding their input til he'd mapped out the sequence and sense of those judgment calls, that was what he suddenly realized was pushing his buttons right now—he wanted to know the answers; and if he could shove Bonner and Tanzer into a move of some kind, even an assassination attempt, he'd know, all right; he'd have proof: more than that, the senators might have it, before they left here at maindawn: Explain that one, cover another attempted murder, Bonner, while the committee's still on station . . .

Otherwise, if Tanzer was only tracking him and more innocent than he judged, let Tanzer sweat what he was up to—looking for clues, maybe, trying to find something to prove Dekker's case, something politically explosive. Legal troubles in Dekker's past—it was all backgrounded, solved, just one of the connections Dekker had had and left when he left the Belt. He didn't go off Sol Two, he took no leaves, but there had been no particular reason for Dekker's name to rouse any anxieties in Defense—certainly no reason to fear him getting to the media. Dekker was allergic to cameras and microphones, Dekker certainly didn't want publicity bringing his name up again, any more than Defense did; and evidently there'd been a decision to take Hellburner public if the test succeeded. So someone high in the Defense Department had said pull him.

That being the case—the line certainly led to Salazar; and Salazar lived behind the EC security wall, the same EC that they were fighting for. That was a worry, and a real one, if the woman had penetrated security channels and found out *what* Dekker was working on, and where he was.

There was—top of the list regarding Dekker's injuries—Wilhelmsen's crew. Dekker hadn't been tactful. Dekker was, Pollard had said it, volatile. There was a lot of that in the crews they'd recruited—including the UDC test pilots. You could begin to wonder was it a pathology or a necessary qualification for this ship—or was it the result of ramming crews together in a handful of years, the few with the reflexes, the mental quickness—the top of the above-average in reaction time, who didn't, even on a family ship, necessarily understand slower processors, or understand that such slower minds vastly outnumbered them in the population? He'd told Tanzer, You can't train what we need . . . he hoped he'd gotten that across at least to one of the committee, but there was no knowing—he'd never excelled, himself, at figuring people: he'd certainly failed to realize how very savvy Tanzer could be in an argument.

He had his pocket com. The captain might send him word at any hour, please God, and give him specific instructions, either for a bare-ass spacewalk or a steady-on as he was bearing and he'd rather either right now than chasing might-have-beens in circles. After a jump you got a solid Yes, you'd survived it. But right now he could wonder whether the FSO was still operating on Sol One, or whether something might have gone wrong at levels so high the shockwave had yet to hit Sol Two. For all he knew the committee had *been* the shockwave of a UDC power grab and he'd just self-destructed in it.

Or why else hadn't they heard anything? Or why, according to the news that he had heard before he'd left the office, was Mazian still smiling his way from council to council in the European Union, and making no comment about the accident, except that a "routine missile test" had had a problem.

The pod flashed by, unexpectedly, filling the viewport. His heart jumped. He watched the pod whip across the far side and felt queasy after the visual shock. Dekker's pod had been running on the mission tape. Dekker had seen the accident. They'd treated him for shock, he'd gotten out of hospital and turned up here, at shift-change, in a pod repeating the exact accident set-up. On loop. Was there anything *in* that, but vindictiveness?

Higgins said only that Dekker had lucid moments. No recollection, most times no awareness even where he was. Cory Salazar had died out in the Belt. Dekker was back in that crack-up. Over and over and over.

Check-in records had listed no UDC personnel as in the area. The mission sims tape was checked out to Dekker—as mission commander, he'd had one in his possession. Dekker had been in hospital. One would have expected that that tape had been with his effects. Security should have collected it, with the tapes in all crews' possession, living and dead. But Library hadn't checked Dekker's in: Dekker was alive, and unable to respond to requests for the tape, Security said, they'd decided not to seek an order to get it from his effects—which would have had the Provost Marshal's staff going into Dekker's locker while Dekker was alive, a violation of policy in the absence of charges.

A hatch door crashed and echoed at the distant end of the access tube. The lift had just let someone in. The Lendler Corp techs, maybe, moving up to this bay. But the light was still on over there. And the pod was still running, the mag-levs whiting out anything but the loudest sounds.

Damn, he thought, Tanzer might be a fool after all. He might *have* his answer, all right: and if he and his didn't make the right moves now, he might *become* the answer. He'd gotten colder, standing here, and he had a sudden weak-kneed wish to be wrong about Tanzer—he hadn't thought through what he'd done in the hearing yet, he wasn't ready or willing to make gut-level choices in a physical confrontation. He closed his fist around the bolt in his pocket—he'd collected that from the desk; he drifted free and took out the pocket com he'd collected too. "D-g, this is 7-All, sim bay 2. QE, C-2-6, copy?"

"7-All, this is Snowball, C-2-6, on it, that's 03 to you, dammit, seal that door!"

Saito was on com. Saito must be lurking over Dan Washington's shoulder and the pocket com was wide open now and logging to files on the carrier. Saito wasn't as accepting of hare-brained excursions as

Dan was, Saito must have gotten uneasy, and, onto Helm Two's side excursion, was probably calling Demas in, besides having Security closer than he'd set them. But they would or wouldn't come in, depending on what Saito heard. Meanwhile he watched the hand-line quiver along the side of the lighted tube. Someone was on it, now, below the curve of the tube. Several someones, by the feel as he touched it.

First figure showed in the serpentine of lights, monkeying along the line. Not UDC. Their own. Flash of jewelry, light behind blond hair.

Friendly fire incoming, then. Not UDC: Mitch. He drew a breath, focused down off the adrenaline rush toward a different kind of self-protection, said to the com, "Snowball, easy on," before Security came in hard. More of them behind Mitch: Jamil, Almarshad . . . Pauli. A delegation. The Shepherds didn't have access to query over com. Saito was sure to give him hell; the Shepherds had tracked him, never mind Tanzer's "boys" might have—it wasn't a good time he was having right now; and he hoped it wasn't a breaking problem that had brought them here. He couldn't take another.

He held his position as the Shepherds gathered in front of the open door, drifting hands-off on the short tether of their safety-clips, in the frosty-breathed chill and the low rhythmic hum of the mags. "Hear it was bloody," Mitch said.

"How did you hear? What's security worth in this place?"

Jamil shrugged, tugged at the line to maintain his orientation. "2-level bar. Aerospatiale guys with a few under their belts. Saying Bonner's pissed. Tanzer's pissed. Bonner told some female committee member it wasn't really important she understand the technicals of the accident, or the tetralogic, she should just recommend the system go AI."

"Damn," he said, but Jamil was grinning.

"Happens Bonner mixed up his women *and* his Asians. Turned out *she's* Aerospatiale's number two engineer."

He had to be amused. He grinned. And he knew that via his open com, Bonner's little faux pas was flying through the carrier out there, for all it was worth. So the J-G wasn't the only one who could talk his way into trouble.

But that was one engineer and one company, with no part of its contract at issue: Aerospatiale was the engines, and they weren't in question.

The Belter trash, as they called themselves, wanted to know how it had gone. Correction, they knew how it had gone. He didn't know how they'd found him, didn't know what they expected him to say. He hadn't delivered. Not really. They couldn't think he had.

"What are you guys doing here?"

They didn't know how to answer, evidently: they didn't quite look him in the eye. But maybe he halfway understood what was in their minds—a feeling they'd been collectively screwed, the way the Belters would say. And that together was better than separate right now.

"How did you find me?"

Mitch said, "Phoned Fleet Security. *They* knew."

CHAPTER 5

2-Deck 229 was a tacky little hallway in a tacky little facility that met you with a security-locked, plastic-protected bulletin board that said things like NO ALCOHOL IN QUARTERS and REMEMBER THE 24-HR RESTRICTIONS, along with SIM SCHEDULE and LOST CARD, DESPERATE, BILL H. SMITH.

Humanitarian transfer, hell. You couldn't shoot a Fleet officer. Wasn't legal. Couldn't even kill Dekker, who didn't know what was going on, who just looked at you and said, Yeah, Ben. All right, Ben. Like you could do anything you wanted to him, the worse had already happened.

Bloody *hell.*

He found Barracks C. He walked in, where a handful of guys with a vid-game looked up and got up and stared at him, a solid wall of hostility.

"Lost?" one of them asked.

"I'm fuckin' *assigned* here," he muttered, and got dismay and frowns.

"No such," one said, Belter accent thick and surly. "UDC shave-head? You got the wrong barracks, loo-tenant."

Fine. Great. He said, in deep Belter brogue, "Not my pick, mate, they do the numbers."

Wasn't what they expected out of a UDC mouth. Postures altered, faces did.

"You wouldn't be Pollard, would you?"

He'd hoped to get his assigned bunk, nothing more. But there was no good making enemies here. He said, grudgingly, "Yeah. Benjamin J.," and saw expressions go on changing for the positive. Not the reaction he generally got from people.

"Pollard." The head troublemaker came over. "Almarshad." A gesture to left and right, behind him. "Franklin and Pauli. What's the word on Dekker?"

Dekker didn't attract friends either, not among people who really knew him; and when a guy introduced himself the way Almarshad did you should worry about bombs. He shook Almarshad's offered hand, said, conservatively, "Not the best I've ever seen him," and watched reactions. *Looked* like they were friends of Dekker's. And it was true Dekker was a Cause in the Belt. A Name—among people who *didn't* know him. Not with Shepherds, much as he knew, and that was what this set looked to be—but it could be Dekker had found a niche in this classified hell.

Franklin asked,

"He say who hit him?"

Or these guys *could* be the committee that put Dekker in hospital, for all he knew.

He said, again carefully, "Bounced on his head too often. I don't know. *He* doesn't. —Friends of his, are you?"

Almarshad seemed to comprehend his reserve, then, frowned and said, "He's got no enemies in this barracks. You keeping that uniform?"

He hadn't many allegiances in his life. But, hell, the UDC fed you, gave you everything you could dream of, held out the promise of paradise, until Dekker helpfully dropped your name in the wrong classified ears—which landed you up to your ears in an interservice feud; and now some Shepherd-turned-bluecoat wanted to make an issue of your uniform? Hell, yes, you could take offense at being pushed. "Yeah, I'm keeping it. Far as I know."

"Shit," Pauli said with a roll of his eyes, and turned half away and back again with an outheld hand. "Tanzer give you your orders?"

"I don't know who gave me my orders. Captain over FSO *Keu* got me out here. The *Fleet* got me out here. Humanitarian leave. Now it's a fuckin' humanitarian *transfer,* I can't find my fuckin' baggage, I can't find my fuckin' bunk, I got no damn choice, here, mister! I'm supposed to be in Stockholm! I'd rather be in Stockholm, which I won't now! —I'm a security Priority *10,* and they got me in here for reasons I don't know, with a damn classified order I'm probably securitied high enough to read. But you don't question orders here, I'm certainly finding that out!"

A hand landed on his shoulder. Almarshad. "Easy. Easy. Pauli means to say welcome in. Tanzer's a problem, we know who you are, we know damn well you're not his boy."

"I don't fuckin' *know* Tanzer!"

"Better off," Franklin said under his breath. "Where've they got you? What room?"

"We got rooms." Thank God. "Said just—here."

"You're Dekker's, then. A-10. Demi-suites. If you count four bunks and a washroom."

Personally he didn't. But he'd been prepared for worse in the short term. He said, "Thanks," and took the pointed finger for his guide.

Hell if, he kept saying to himself. Hell if I'm going to stay here. Hell if this is going to be the rest of my life, —Mr. Graff, sir.

He'd flunked his Aptitudes for anything remotely approaching combat, deliberately and repeatedly: he couldn't pass basic without a waiver for unarmed combat on account of a way-high score in technical; he'd worked hard to clean the Belter accent out of his speech and to fit in with blue-skyers and here he was resurrecting it to deal with some sumbitch Shepherd who'd have walked over him without noticing, back in R2. Get into technical, get his security clearance—get connections and numbers, the same as he'd had in R2, that was his priority. His CO back in TI, Weiter—Weiter had connections, Weiter had to let him make his rating in very fast order, and George Weiter had had the discriminating good sense to screw the regs, bust him past the basics and into levels where he could learn from where he was and get at those essential, top-level access numbers.

No guns, damned sure, nothing to do with guns. He'd made sure of that.

And here he was busted to a pilot trainee rating? It was crazed. It was absolutely insane. It was *going* to get fixed. Get to Weiter—somehow. Get to somebody up in HQ. In Stockholm. Fast.

He located A-10, at the corner of the hall, opened the door—

And found his lost luggage in the middle of the darkened room.

"Shit! Shit, shit, *shit!*"

The shuttle was in Servicing, the politicians, the engineers, the corporate execs and the general were tanking up in Departures, and now reality came due. Now it was back to dealing with Tanzer on a daily, post-hearing basis, and the Fleet's independence notwithstanding, when the UDC CO sent a See Me at 0800h, the Fleet Acting Commander had to show up.

"He's expecting you," the aide said. Graff said a terse Thank you, opened the door and walked into the fire zone.

"Lt. Graff," Tanzer said.

"Colonel," Graff said and stood there neither at ease nor at attention while Tanzer stared at him.

Tanzer rocked his chair back abruptly and said, "I expect cooperation."

"Yes, colonel."

"'Yes, colonel,' what?"

"Whatever's good for the program, colonel."

"And what do you think that is, now, would you say?"

"Colonel, you know my opinion."

The chair banged level. "Damn your opinion! What are you trying to do to this program?"

"Trying not to lose a carrier, when its riders fail. I'll be in it. You won't, colonel."

"I won't, will I? I'm on the line here, you sonuvabitch."

"Not for the same stakes, colonel, forgive me."

"You son of *a* bitch."

After a sleep-short night that opening was extremely welcome. Tanzer was angry. Tanzer wasn't satisfied with what had gone down. That could be good news—if it wasn't the demise of the program Tanzer was foreseeing.

Tanzer said, with a curl of his lip, "Two more of your recruits are in from the Belt, I'm *sure* you'll be delighted with that. And Lendler Corp is recommending the Fleet change its security regulations with the sim tapes. And who in hell transferred Pollard into your command?"

"*My* command?"

"Your command, your captain's command, your navigator's command for all I know, who knows who's in charge in your office? You have a UDC trainee in your program, Mr. Graff, do you want to tell me just how that happened?"

He wasn't sure whether Tanzer was in his right mind. Or what in hell was going on. He said, "I don't know. I'll look into it."

"I'm already looking into it, I'm looking into it all the way to TI and Geneva. What do you say to *that,* Mr. Graff?"

"I don't know either, colonel. I'll find out."

Tanzer gave him a cold, silent stare. Then: "You find out and you come tell me. It's one of those things I like to keep up with, who's where on this station. Just a habit of mine. I think you can understand that. Hearing's over. I'd like to clear the record, just get everything back in appropriate boxes. I think you can understand that too, can't you, lieutenant?"

The passenger shuttle was going out, that was the maddening thing. But there was absolutely no question of Ben Pollard getting to it: it was ferrying the brass out from the hearing, the hearing was evidently over, Dekker hadn't remembered a thing he could take to Graff and get out of here, so evidently *that* wasn't his ticket out—and, dammit! he wanted to talk to Graff, wanted to ask Graff to his face what kind of a double-cross had caught him in this damned illicit transfer. But Graff had been "unavailable" during the hearing. Graff's aides had only cared to ask if he had any report yet. Of course he'd had to say no; so Lt. Graff hadn't seen fit to return his calls yesterday; Lt. Graff wasn't in his office this morning—

While the transfer orders he'd gotten said, Outside contact specifically denied.

So what was Outside? Sol One FSO? Sol One UDC? —Graff's office?

In a moment of wild fantasy he thought of risking his clearance, his career and a term in the brig, getting to the Departure lounge by hook or by crook, snagging some UDC officer bound out of this station and protesting he'd been kidnapped: contact Weiter on Sol One.

But there were serious problems with that scenario. Abundant problems. Chief among which was not knowing what he was dealing with, or what Dekker was involved in, or how much of that hearing had involved Dekker specifically and how much had involved a program in trouble.

He didn't unpack. He'd just looked for a change of clothes—he'd been washing clothes in hospice laundry every day, wrapped in a hospice towel while they dried, thank God he'd had his shaving kit and two changes of shirts and underwear in his carry, but, God, he was glad to get his light station boots and his pullover, and find the textcards he'd packed—

And his personal computer, which thank God hadn't been damaged. They'd searched his luggage. They'd probably searched his computer files. Probably had to call in the station techs to read his to-do list, which now wasn't going to get done, if he couldn't get out of this. He entertained dark thoughts of finding a phone and using a handful of codes, but he didn't want the output directed to any terminal he owned. Or to his barracks. He figured all he'd better do with the phone was find out what was in his file right now, which would happen the minute he used his card.

All right. But we're *not* putting our only copy in, are we?

You couldn't copy a personal datacard. Copying was supposed to screw it. EIDAT said. Writing outside your personal memo area was supposed to screw it.

But EIDAT said a lot of things about security to its customers that didn't apply to its programmers: a few alterations to the 00 and the card would copy—if you had the Programming OS on the card, which wasn't supposed to fit in the MEM area. But if you got creative with the allocations it would. *Not* that he didn't trust the integrity of the UDC command here, *not* as if they just might have a watch on a Priority 10 right now that might notice him going out to the Exchange and buying a card with his remaining vending chits. But he could certainly sacrifice the chess gamecard—even in the paperless and police-controlled Belt, Customs had never quite apprehended gamecards and vidcards as write-capable media.

Yeah.

Quick sand-down of the gamecard edge on the nailfile he carried, a little application of clear nailpolish, available locally, at certain contact points—and you could write to it quite nicely. The cheerful, bright commercial label said it was a patented gamecard, a lot of worn-at-the-edges cards were out there that did show the critical contacts. EIDAT certainly didn't want to advertise the procedure even to the police, because people with access to EIDAT systems code didn't ever pirate gamecards. No. Of course not.

He stuck the datacard in the second drive and had his datacard copy in a nice secure place in quarters before he went out to the wall phone in the barracks main hall. He stuck his datacard into the slot. The write-function clicked. The new readout said CAF, MKT and MS-FUNC. PRIORITY MS was blinking.

He keyed MS and the hash mark. It said, ***Report to Lt. Graff's office, 0900h.***

And funny to say, when he tried to call over to Graff's office on a level 10, his level 10 authorization wouldn't work. Son of a bitch, he thought, smug, amused, *and* furious. He had to do it on a lowly level 3. They *had* fried his accesses. And he was illegal as hell now, with that other card as a holdout. Question was—*which* service had pulled his security clearance.

So Graff wanted to talk to him. And it was 0848 right now. He had about time to get his ass over to Graff's office, and find out such facts as Graff was willing to tell him about his transfer—

Which he was about to do when he caught sight of the two females lugging duffles into the barracks main hall—one dark-skinned, one light, one with a headful of metal-capped braids and one with a shave-strip of bright red curls.

My *God* . . .

He hung up. He had the presence of mind to take his card out of the slot. He stood there while two of the most unlikely recruits in the solar system came down the center aisle to the catcalls of the bystanders, saw them look right past him as if he was part of the landscape.

"Sal!" he called out. "Meg!" and saw two pairs of eyes fix on him, do a re-take of him and the uniform. Baggage hit the floor. The two best-looking women he'd ever slept with ran up, grabbed him, both, and kissed him breathless, one and the other.

Couldn't hurt a man's reputation. Whistles and howls from the gallery. He caught his breath, besieged with questions like what was he doing here, what was this about Dek, and how was he?

Questions without an easy answer. "What are *you* two doing here?" he asked, and got a stereo account: they'd gotten the word Dekker was in some kind of accident, they'd gotten word they were shipping a carrier out—

"God, that thing *moves*—" Sal said.

"So we rode it in and transferred over on the shuttle," Meg said. "And these damn MPs have got to stall us up with questions, shit! officers and VIP's all over the place. —How's Dek, for God's sake, he got all his pieces?"

"Everything you'd be interested in. —You enlisted?" *That* didn't fit his expectations, didn't fit what he'd been reading in Dekker's letter file.

"They hail us down," Sal said, "in Jupiter's own lap, a carrier pulls up and says, Have you got Kady? And wants to talk to us. Wants to talk to Meg. And Meg talks to the Man, and we get this news Dek's in hospital—some kind of crack-up, they're saying, and they'd kindly give us a ride insystem—"

Shepherds began to ooze over. One said, "Well, well, look what pulled in. Hiya."

Meg looked. Sal did. Ben didn't know the face, but Sal struck an attitude and said, "Well, well, *look* at familiar faces—they let you in, Fly-by?"

Laughter from all about. Not a nickname. Fly-by seemed to favor. "God, how'd *you* get past?" Belter accent, Shepherd flash. "I thought they had criteria."

"You skuz," Sal said, but it didn't have the edge of trouble. Sal put a hand on the skuz's shoulder, gave his arm a squeeze. "Jamil's a sumbitch, but he's an all right sumbitch. This is Ben Pollard."

"Got the whole team, but Morrie," another said. "Damn on!"

"Ben, where d' we sleep?" Meg asked. There were immediately other offers. "Take you up later," Meg said. "I got a date at the hospital, if I can get the pass they said I had—"

"Get you to the room," Ben said, and, catching two elbows, hauled them along to 10-A. Good-natured protest followed from the rear, but it died, and a couple of guys, Jamil included, overtook them at the door, set down the baggage and made themselves absent. "Thanks," he said; discretion was not dead here. "Thanks," Meg called back, while he was opening the door. He put a hand on Sal's back, got Meg's arm and got them inside, into privacy.

"What've we got?" Sal said. "Is my radar working, or what?"

"It's working," he said. "We got a sumbitch in charge, same damn sumbitch switched Dekker out and some guy in on a test run and cracked up Dekker's crew, *Dek-baby* thinks he's in the fuckin' Belt looking for Cory, and *I* got a meeting with Fleet Lieutenant J. Graff right on the hour." He had a sudden idea, fished his temp hospital card out of his uniform pocket, and held it up in front of Meg. "This is a pass. You're me, just put it in the slot at the main desk, won't trigger an alarm and in the remote chance they should ask, tell 'em Graff sent you. Dekker's in room 114. They pulled him out of a simulator beat to hell and concussed and there's some chance he didn't climb in there on his own, by what I can guess. Tell him straighten up. Tell him where he is, tell him I said so, tell him I'm going to break his neck next time I see him—*I've* got five minutes to make the lieutenant's office. . . ."

"Somebody did it to him?" Meg asked.

"Hey. You know Dek. There's got to be a waiting list." He recalled the atmosphere outside, and said, "We got to talk. Fast. Sit. The lieutenant can wait five."

The sounds came and went. 2324. 2324. Dekker tried to remember. He said it to himself to remember. And maybe he was losing track of time, but it seemed to him breakfast had come and gone and Ben hadn't come this morning. That upset him. Ben kept saying he couldn't stay, and maybe he'd just gone wherever Ben had to go to. He didn't even want to know where that was. He just wanted to go back into the dark if they'd let him alone, if there wasn't anybody going to come but doctors with tests and interns and if there was nothing to do but lie here and listen to the halls outside.

"Dek?" Female voice. "Dek?"

Voice he knew. Voice that shouldn't be here. So he was losing it. But if he was starting to hallucinate again maybe Ben wasn't gone. He came up out of the dark to see.

She was scarily real, Meg was, leaning over him. "How you doing?" she asked, and he said, "Dunno," because he didn't. She smelled real, she looked real, she sounded real. She asked him, "Anything wrong with the jaw?"

"No," he said, wondering why she asked, and Meg leaned down and kissed him the way she'd kissed him goodbye once, which caught him short of breath and half-smothered and no little dizzy as it went on, but if this was going to turn into one of those dreams, he didn't mind, he'd go out cold this way.

He got a breath, finally, he had Meg up close to his face, running a finger down his cheek, saying, "You been through some severely bad business, Dek. But it won't happen again. I'm here. Sal's here. Ben's here. We won't let the bastards get to you."

Good news. He really wanted to believe it. But he didn't let himself sink into the fantasy all the way. He only flirted with the idea, asking warily, "How'd you get here?"

She settled her hand on his, gave his fingers a squeeze. "They sent to me in the Belt, said, You got a friend in trouble, you want to come, and I said, Sure. Why not? I could do with a change."

So she wasn't leveling with him. That could only mean his subconscious couldn't think of an answer. Second question: "What about Sal?"

"Sal said she couldn't trust me on my own, said she'd keep me honest."

Her fingers on his felt warm and solid. She was in Shepherd civvies, she had this fondness for big earrings and he didn't remember the ones she was wearing. He wasn't artistic, he couldn't make up ones he didn't know, spiral and gold with some kind of anodized bar down the middle. He couldn't make up the blue eyeshadow and the pink. He wouldn't put those colors together with red hair. But it looked good. She did. And her really, truly being here was crazier than his thinking she was.

Third question. "Where's Ben this morning?"

"Ben's in the lieutenant's office. Ben's real pissed. Something about his security clearance and him supposed to be in Stockholm—didn't altogether make sense, but he was going to go complain. —What's this about you arguing with a simulator?"

Panic hit him. But he didn't know why he should be afraid of Meg. Or Ben. Or why there was a gap around his recollection of the sim room. Sounds. Mag hum and sudden motion. Ominous. Something had happened under that sound.

"There's been a hearing," Meg said, "senators all over the place. They're leaving. Ben asks if you'd like to tell them anything. Says if you could tell them how you got banged up it might be a good idea."

Senators. Mission control. Rows of instruments. Instruments on the sim panel, just the same.

"Shit," he breathed, feeling a cold sweat come on him. But it was all right, the memory was gone again. He willed his heart to slow down, stop fluttering like that: they filled him full of drugs if they caught his pulse up, and if they caught Meg here, Meg could be in trouble —Meg might not come back. People went out the door and you didn't know if—

—the Company'd let them back.

No. Not the Company. Tanzer. The UDC, that ran this place. . . . "Ben explained a skosh," Meg said, rab-speak, long time back, it seemed now. The Inner System had changed so, even in the few years he'd been to the Belt and back. "You don't got seriously to say: I know about the accident. But you got to get out of here, Dek, you got to get yourself straight. Ben said I should ask you the date."

"2324," he said, and found it suddenly worth a laugh, with what breath he could find. "2324." Meg didn't know why that message from Ben should be funny, and he couldn't explain, he hadn't the coherency to explain, he kept seeing the readouts in the spex in front of him, green and red and gold, and, *dammit,* he could make it, he could've made it, but when he tried to imagine past that point the controls wouldn't work, weren't going to work again until he could get his hands on them and change those numbers. . . .

Meg shook his shoulder. "Heads up, Dek. First thing you got to do, you got to get straight. Ben said you didn't get into that pod on your own. That you should remember for him. He really needs that, Dek."

Sim room. Noise. And the memory just stopped. Got his pulse rate up again. "Can't. Can't get hold of it, Meg. Meg, —"

She leaned close and whispered in his ear, "You want to go back to barracks and you and me do a little rec-time? Mmmn?"

Offer like that—from Meg—could raise a corpse. Meg's touch on his cheek could. He thought about the barracks, had a sudden cold jolt, thinking of Meg there, and Ben and Sal; and not the faces he remembered. A whole puzzle-piece of his life just lifted out, gone, and another one clicked in, not the same shape, there were still dark spots—there'd been another puzzle-piece before that; but it was close, it was damned close. Pete and Elly and Falcone, they wouldn't have understood Meg. Wouldn't have gotten on with her, not easy. Might not get on with Sal or Ben. Cory either. He looked Meg in the eyes and remembered his blood pressure, realized he wasn't wearing the sensor.

Several things clicked into place. Where he was. How he hadn't gotten his shot this morning, either. How he was clearer-headed now than he'd been since—

More panels. Instruments red-lighting. Alarms screaming. Inner ear going crazy.

"You all right, Dek?" Finger along his cheek. "You're white. You want me to call a doctor? Dek?"

He shook his head, suddenly sure of that. He sucked in a breath and got an elbow up under him, to see if his head was going to spin. Weak, God. Meg was trying to help him, saying he should lie down. But he didn't think so, he had a bad feeling about lying down and letting Meg call a doctor, they'd give him shots again and he'd go to sleep and go on sleeping—

He shoved up onto his hands, swung his feet over the edge. The room was tilting, felt like the pod, but he kept his eyes on the line where the wall met the floor. He sat there getting his breath and making the room stay steady.

"You sure you better not get back in that bed?"

He moved his arm. That shoulder had hurt. Didn't now, as much. He kept his eyes on that line and said, "Want to get up, Meg. Just give me a hand."

She did that. He didn't need it to lean on. He just needed it steady. Second reference point. He made it to his feet, risked a blink, then shut his eyes and stood there a moment. He opened them and took a step, with Meg's help. "Shot to hell," he muttered. "Too much zero g."

"Does that to you," Meg agreed. "Going back to it?"

"Inner ear's playing me tricks." Another step. A third. He took a breath, let go her hand and took a fourth.

"They ought to have had you walking. Especially a spacer. Especially you. What're the doctors worth in this place?"

A moment of vertigo. He got it back again. "Meg, how in hell'd you get here?" Months to get in from the Belt. They'd told her he was in trouble? Time threatened to unravel again. Except—

"Just caught a passing carrier. You got people real worried about you, Dek. Important people."

Carrier could make that passage in a handful of days. Better than that, the rumor was. And a carrier pulled Meg out of the Belt? Out of a berth she'd risked her neck to get? "Meg, make 'em send you back, don't get mixed up in this, I don't want you, I don't want you here—"

"Hell if, boy-doll. Anyway, I signed the papers. Going to make me an officer—"

"Oh, shit. Shit, Meg!" The room went spinning. He just stared at Meg's face for a reference point and kept his feet and knees from moving. "You were where you wanted."

"Yeah, well. It's not all al-tru-istic. —You want to sit down, Dek?"

"No." A shake of his head that risked his balance. "No. I'm all right. I need to stand up. They won't let me stand up. Have I got any clothes in that locker?"

Meg looked. He didn't dare track on her. She said, "No."

"Meg, I want you to go to the lieutenant. . . ."

"Graff?"

"Graff. I want you to go to him—" The place could be bugged. But there was nothing else to do. "I want you to tell him I need help. I don't trust what they're giving me. I want out of here."

"This then or now, Dek? Who's doing this?"

He tried a step and another one. His heart was pounding. Sounds came distant and strange. He walked as far as the door, opened it, and gambled his stability on a look at Meg. "You remember your way out of here?"

"Yeah."

"I'll walk you to the door. Five on ten I don't get that far. But you'll know, then, won't you?"

"Shit, Dek."

"Yeah." He took her arm. She grabbed his hand. "Let's walk, huh?"

"Aboujib," Graff said, and put out his hand for a non-reg handshake. Dark-skinned, exotic as they came to Inner System eyes, and by Ben Pollard's recommendation and the enlistment records, a Company-educated disciplinary washout who'd gotten another kind of rep among the Shepherds. Jamil had been by to give him a quick word. Pollard had shown up for his appointment with Aboujib in tow—one Meg Kady was "visiting Dekker" on Pollard's pass. ("It'll work in the lock," Pollard had said, with airy disregard of UDC security, but Pollard was *not* unconcerned, Pollard had just smiled, put a thoroughly stripped personal card on his desk and said, "I'm screwed, sir. Do you think you could just possibly get somebody to do something about this? *They* just put me in your command, sir, I'm UDC, and I'm mortally worried the colonel's going to want to talk to me.")

Hell in a handbasket. As the Earthers said. And here was the *rest* of Dekker's former crew, in on the Sol One shuttle without a word of explanation, warning, or advice what to do with them?

He wasn't highly pleased with the captain right now. Not pleased with Tanzer, not pleased with the situation, and not pleased to know one of the pair was loose in hospital on somebody else's Fleet pass.

But Jamil had been damned cheerful, saying, "We got us a couple of recruits, lieutenant. —Mitch is going to die."

It could give a man the feeling something was passing by him. And that things were careening out of control. "Welcome in, Aboujib. Scan-tech, is it?"

"Yessir." Aboujib had a solid grip, a steady eye, a distractingly quirky dimple beside a pretty mouth—and she was outside his crew and off limits, endit, right there. Not many women among the Shepherds and a consequent shortage of women in the program; and one of Dekker's former partners?

The captain had put Dekker's unit together again. That was what was happening. Keu wasn't saying a thing—so FleetCom wasn't secure: the captain was just doing it, case by case: somebody had moved a *carrier* in from the Belt, for God's sake, or *Victoria* was back in-system: no other way to ferry Aboujib and Kady here since the accident.

Which could mean the captain hadn't been on Sol One for the last week; could mean Mazian had interrupted his diplomatic receptions to take a hand; or it might mean Keu had help: cooperative command in action—Col. Tanzer, *sir.*

He said, "Very glad to have you aboard, Aboujib. . . ." and the phone beeped. His calls were routing through the carrier's board and that wasn't to be ignored. He picked up the receiver, said, "Graff here," and heard:

"Lieutenant?" Thin voice. Strained. *"Dekker. Need some help, sir."*

"Shove it!" he heard in the background. Female voice. And something happened.

A hand came under Dekker's arm. Pulled. The nurse took hold of Meg's arm and lost that grip. Fast.

"You want those fingers, mister, you keep 'em the fuck *off my arm.*"

The nurse had hit an alarm, or something: a light was flashing. But Dekker knew where he was, he knew who was keeping his balance for him and he'd trust Meg in the black deep of space. He said, "Door, Meg. Now."

"He's not released," the nurse said. Other meds showed up. *Higgins* arrived at the desk, looked at Meg and said, "Who are *you?*"

"Ben Pollard right now," Meg said. "Ben's getting my pass straightened out."

"Get security," Higgins said to someone in the hall. "Lt. Dekker, they'll take you to your room."

"No such." He held his feet. "I'm going." Head was killing him. But standing was easier. "Where's my uniform?"

Security showed up, MPs, UDC. An MP grabbed for Meg, and next thing he knew he'd grabbed the MP—the guy looked at him, he looked at the guy with his fist doubled, but the MP with a fistful of his pajamas wasn't about to hit a hospital case. So he kept his hold on the MP, the MP kept his hold on him, and they stared at each other while the interns tried to drag him away. "You tell Tanzer fuck himself. Hear? —Meg? Get. Get out of here."

They told her, "You're under arrest. You're not going anywhere," and Meg said,

"Hell if. Spiel on, chelovek, a judge is going to hear every word of this. You seriously better not bruise him."

"Now wait a minute." Higgins pulled the MP off—tried to: he wasn't about to let go his only anchor, and Higgins was upset. "All right, all right, calm down. Everybody calm down. Lt. Dekker, let go of him."

Things were graying out. But he got a breath and held on, said, rationally, he hoped, "I'm walking out of here and I'm going back to my barracks."

Meg said, "Dek, calm down."

Her, he listened to. Kept his grip the way the MP held on to him and listened to Meg say, "He had a seriously bad time with Company doctors. Fed him full of prescription drugs, while he was spaced. You let him go. He'll be all right."

"I'm not a damn mental case, Meg."

Higgins said, smooth as silk, "We're not maintaining that. He's had concussion and broken bones. If you're a friend of his, persuade him back to bed."

"I've been in bed too damned long. Won't let me up, won't let me walk—"

"You've been to therapy, lieutenant. Don't you remember?"

Scared him. He *wasn't* sure. He didn't argue with what they might be able to prove. Or fake records for. He was afraid he was going to pass out, and end the argument that way. "I want my release. Now."

Higgins frowned, bit his lip. Finally, "I'll release you to your CO. Personally. If he wants you. Ms. —?"

"Kady. Margritte Kady. Meg, to whoever." She stuck out her hand. Higgins looked confused and angry. "Higgins, is it?"

He ignored the hand. "Do you mind explaining who the hell you are and where you came from?"

"Manners," Dekker said. Still with his grip on the MP, he looked the man close in the eyes and said, "You want to let go? I want to let go."

Man wasn't amused. Man said, "Doctor?"

"Let him go."

Took a bit just to get his hand unclenched. The MP's uniform had a circle of sweaty wrinkles. The MP refused to straighten it. Man was cold and thin-lipped, and mad as hell. UDC was full of those types. He reached for Meg's hand and said, "Let's go."

"There are forms to fill out," Higgins said. "And a physical."

"Had one," he said, walking—he hoped Meg knew where the door was: he didn't. He halfway expected the MP was going to have his way after all. He remembered he was in pajamas when he saw the door. He didn't know any way back to the barracks but the Trans. Didn't know how he was going to stay conscious through that ride. Little bit of *g* it pulled would wipe him out.

But Meg steered him for a bench by the door and set him down. "You just stay there a minute. I'm going to go back there and call your CO. Isn't anybody coming near you. —Is your CO going to pull you out?"

"Yeah, yeah, I think he's already got somebody coming."

"Then I'll stand here and wait. If you're sure. —You going to be all right?"

"Yeah," he said. His teeth had started to chatter. He was barefoot. The pajamas weren't worth much. Meg took off her coat, put it around his shoulders, and made him hold on to it. She left him a moment and came back with a blanket, God knew how.

She said, "Higgins is severely pissed. He's on the phone. But the nurse is all right. Nurse asked if you wanted a chair."

Nurse was the one he'd hit. More than once. He shook his head, with some remorse for that—and regret for missing his chance at Higgins. Meg tucked the blanket around him, and under his bare feet, and sat down and offered him a warmer place to lean. They'd never been to bed together, had just been letter writers, at 830 million k remote from each other. They'd discovered they were attracted to each other too late to do anything about it, except that goodbye kiss. And now a hello one, a hug and a place to lean on, when he'd gotten to the absolute bottom of his strength. Meg never found him but what he was a mess. And here she was, he'd no idea how. She hadn't come straight with him. And maybe sitting here with her like this was all another hallucination. If he was hallucinating this time he didn't want to come back again, didn't want to fight them, didn't want to get even, didn't want to prove anything to anybody. Just sit, long as he could, long as he could hold himself awake.

Meg said, "Well, well, *blue* uniforms, this time. That us?"

He focused stupidly on figures the other side of the glass. On one young, fair-haired . . . Graff, for God's sake. With Fleet Security.

He bit his lip til it hurt enough. He said, "Don't let me fall, Meg," and stood up, letting go the blanket, as Graff came through the Perspex doors. "Lt. Graff, sir."

Graff looked at him, up and down, Graff frowned—you could never tell what Graff was thinking. Could have been of skinning him alive, for all he could read.

Meg said, "They've been drugging him to the gills, sir. He never did do well with that."

Graff said to the MPs. "Take him to the ship."

"Barracks," Dekker said, then was sorry he'd objected. He'd take anywhere but here. But he didn't know the ship. He wanted somewhere he knew. He wanted people he knew, namely Meg, and Sal, and Ben.

"Just long enough for a check-up," Graff said. "I want you on record, Dekker. From the outside in. You behave yourself, hear? No nonsense."

"Yessir," he said. He let Security take hold of him, he sat down and they said they were going to borrow a chair; he heard Graff tell Meg Welcome in; and: "Hereafter, don't start a war. Wait for the UN to declare it."

"Yessir," Meg said. Which wasn't a word he ever recalled from Meg Kady. But Meg had enlisted. The fool. The absolute fool, if that was the price of Meg's ticket here. He felt tears in his eyes, thinking about that.

But damned if he could figure out how she'd managed it, all in all.

Time had gotten away from him again. It kept doing that. So maybe he was, the way Ben said, crazy.

CHAPTER 6

Welcome back," they said, "welcome back, Dek." Jamil and Trace, Pauli and Almarshad and Hap Vasquez—they intercepted him at the door when he was only calculating how much strength he had to get to his own quarters and fall into bed. Jamil warned the rest about grabbing hold of him, thank God, most of all thank God for Ben and Meg and Sal Aboujib showing up out of the depth of the room to rescue him from too much input too fast . . . he was tracking on too much: he knew and didn't know in any detail what he'd said to the guys or what they'd said to him, and for one dislocated moment he really thought Pete or Elly or Falcone was going to turn up in the barracks; they always had . . .

But they weren't going to do that ever again, dammit, end report, o-mega; he was here on this wave of time, and by a break of bad luck they weren't, and he was going to fall on his face if the guys didn't let him get to his quarters. He'd spent hours out in a null *g* sickbay, been prodded and probed and sampled and vid-taped from angles and in a condition he didn't want on the evening news, and his imagination until now had only extended to lying down in quiet, not running an emotional gauntlet of friends of dead friends—who could see how absolutely he'd been screwed over, dammit, when he should at least have gotten some of theirs back. He didn't know what had happened to him in hospital, not all of it; he didn't know what he'd admitted to, most of all he couldn't remember what had put him there, and by that, he'd evidently let the lieutenant down, too, in some major way . . .

"Come on," Meg said, and he walked across a tilting, unstable floor, around a corner, down a short hall to a familiar door and a room that had been—images kept flashing on him out of a situation he didn't remember—cold and empty the last time he'd left it, clothes in the lockers nobody was going to use anymore. . . .

Now it was alive with voices and faces out of a period of his life that never should have recrossed his track, except it was like a gravity well, things didn't fly straight, they kept coming around at you again and he didn't even know the center of mass. That should be a calculable thing. He should be able to solve that problem, with the data he had. . . .

"Get him in bed," Meg was saying, "he's severely spaced," and Ben said, "Damned fool had to walk it, where's his head anyway?"

Ben never minced words. He could cope with Ben far better than he could Sal Aboujib, who, after Ben had got him onto his bunk, pinned him with hands on either side of him, looked him in the face so close he was cross-eyed and said, "Oh, he's still pretty. Dek, sincerely *good* to see you. So good you're in one piece—"

"*Let* him alone. God!" Meg shoved Sal aside. "Man's severely had enough for a while. Go get his supper. Do you mind?"

Numb at this point. Completely numb. You hyped, and if things wouldn't calculate, what could you do but handle the things you could? He said, "Not reg."

Sal said, "Nyet. Lieutenant cleared it. Sandwich all right, Dek? Chips?"

"Yeah, I guess." Sandwich meant fish of some kind and that nauseated him. Then he thought of what he did want. What he'd wanted in his lucid moments in the hospital. "Hamburger and fries. —" And simultaneously remembered what happened to Belters who ventured the quick food in the cafeteria. "You watch the hamburgers, Sal. It's real stuff—"

"Dead animals," Ben said, and shuddered.

"Fish are animals," Meg declared.

"No, they're not."

The argument went completely surreal. The noise did. He was lying here and people promising to get him a hamburger were arguing Belter sensibilities, enzymes and whether fish were intelligent. "Milkshake," he said. But he was tired and he wanted to get under the sheets he was lying on, which took far too much effort. He just shut his eyes a moment and something warm settled over him. Blanket. And a weight pressed the mattress beside him and an arm arched over him.

He focused blearily on Meg. "Why in hell did you come here? You got no business here—"

"We'll talk about it later."

"We'll talk about it while there's still a chance, before you get into the security stuff—" The meds would say his blood pressure was getting up again. His eyes were blurry. He made the effort to lean on one arm, the one that hadn't been recently broken, and gathered all the detail of a face he'd never thought he'd see again. He'd wanted her once. He didn't know if he still did—didn't want to want her. Didn't know if he could take another dead friend. "Damn thing's a meatgrinder, Meg, the colonel's an ass—"

"Yeah, so Ben said. —Are you getting out? Seems to me you got a serious excuse here. Thinking about a Medical?"

His mind went blank on that. He couldn't see himself doing anything else. He couldn't see himself shoving freight around, going back to pusher work. But the future he'd had before the accident was black and void in front of him, just—not do-able now. For the last year he'd chased after being the first pilot to run that course. Making it. He'd believed that, even through the funerals of those who hadn't. And that wouldn't happen, couldn't happen, now, everybody was dead but him—

"You *want* to get out of the service?" Meg asked him.

He kept trying to look at that dark ahead. And finally he shook his head. No, he didn't want out. He didn't know what he was going to do, but he didn't want out of the Fleet—didn't know who might go with him next run, didn't know what they could pull together into a crew that wouldn't take another one apart—didn't want that. Maybe that was why he couldn't see where he was going. Crew was gone, they might well drop him back in training, let him shape up with Meg and Ben and Sal from the beginning up—granted Tanzer didn't kill the program.

Meanwhile some other crew would make that first run; and the second; and the third—he'd take the controls after someone else had flown the ship and it was documented and tame enough for the second line to try.

And maybe that was sanity. Forget his notions: maybe it wasn't what he'd trained for, wasn't what he'd wanted, but it was a way back into the cockpit, forget the naive confidence he'd had in his invincibility. He wasn't a kid anymore. God hope he wasn't a fool anymore, who had to have that number one status or kill himself and everyone with him.

He gave up the prop of his arm, fell back again and gathered the bedspread and pillow under his head. He looked in Meg's eyes and didn't see a woman who was young and mind-fried with love—just a friend, a sane, brave friend, who was older than he was, and whose reasons he didn't honestly know.

"Meg, I'm serious, don't want to offend you. Good to see you. Good you came. But if you've got any loophole out of enlisting, any way in hell back to the berth you had, you should go back. . . ."

"Five hundred-odd million k, I come for this man. What about those letters you wrote? 'Getting along fine, a real chance at something, the first thing in my life I know I want to do—' "

"That was bullshit. It's like anywhere else. We got a fool in charge."

"Yeah, well, we dealt with fools before. Got no shortage of 'em in the Belt. Some have even got seniority."

"They got plenty of it here. —Too damn many funerals, Meg. I'm sick to death of funerals—"

"Death is, jeune rab. Better to burn than rot."

Plasma spreading against the dark. Whiteout on the cameras. He said, urgently, "Meg, go back where you've got a life, for God's sake. You've got a berth—"

"—without shit-worth of seniority."

"Well, you won't get any here. They won't count your hours, just give you a flat 200. Spend your whole life out in the Belt and that's all it's worth. They'll screw you any way they can."

"Mmmnn. Yeah. Sal's seriously pissed about that—but she's computers anyway. Straight quantifiable skills stuff. *I* was an EC shuttle pilot, remember? Earth to orbit. LEO to Sol One. You name it, I ran it, four years riding the gravity slopes. And it's all in the EC's own infallible records. Here, I *got* seniority."

"Shit," he said, cold inside, he didn't know why, except Meg was hell to stop when she had an idea, and Tanzer was a damned fool. It'd be like the UDC, to look at just that record of Meg's hours and do something seriously stupid. Like put a shuttle jock on the combat line. "Meg, you don't know. We got innate stupidity here, serious innate stupidity. The equipment's a real stress generator, you understand me? They made the sims realtime to start, but the UDC guys won't spend four, five hours in the sims, hell, no, we're too short on sim-time for that, and we got guys too *experienced* to need that, so what do we do? We pitch the sims down to be do-able. *Comfortable.* Spread the time around. You read that?" His head ached. His voice was going. The capacity to care was. "They're killing us. Take guys with reflexes to do the job, and then they fuck with the sims till you got no confidence in them. That's a killer, Meg, that's a damn killer, ship's so sensitive you can screw the thing if you twitch—"

"You fly it?"

A memory chased through his nerves, oxygen high and an adrenaline rush, hyperfocused—

"Yeah," he said, voice gone shaky with memory. "Yeah. Mostly the sims. But twice in the ship." And he knew why he wasn't going to take a Medical. Better to burn, Meg had said. And he did that. He did burn.

Door opened. "Mustard or ketchup?" Sal's voice. "Got one each way. . . ."

"Mustard," he said, grasping after mundane sanity. The smell ought to make him sicker than hell, the hospital food hadn't smelled of grease and he'd all but heaved eating it. But maybe it was the company: maybe it was the smell that conjured the cafeteria and the sounds and shoptalk over coffee: he suddenly wanted the burger. He took a real chance with his stomach and his head and hitched his shoulders around against the wall so he could sit up to eat, and handle the milkshake. A sugar hit, carbohydrates and salt, a guaranteed messhall greaseburger with dill pickles, chili sauce, tomatoes and mustard—

"How can you *eat* that?" Ben asked. "God!"

Meg said, "Shut up, Ben," and took the ketchup burger herself.

Earth system, Meg had to be, then. Rab, rad, and, Meg had said it once, falling behind the wave of change on Earth: go out into the Belt and you stepped back a century at least—old equipment, a hodgepodge of antique fads and fashion—rab-rad gone to Shepherd flash and miner Attitude. But Meg was old genuine rab, he believed it, the rab they'd gunned down at the Company doors when he was a kid. So Meg had come home to hamburgers and ideas she was so far out of the current of, he hurt for her. And he was scared for her.

Damn right she was a pilot. The Fleet was raking up all the recruits they could beg or bribe away from the Shepherds, and they'd evidently made her an offer, given her her hours—a fool friend, an almost-lover near young enough to be her son, cracked up in hospital, needn't have been any part of it. Couldn't go by what Meg said. Couldn't. She had a lot of virtues, but strict accounts wasn't one of them. It was enough she'd come to the hospital to get him. It was enough she'd stand there and risk arrest and losing everything to get him out. Meg was like that. Might go, might stay. But if she stayed—

—if she stayed—

He got most of the hamburger down. He got down half the shake and half the fries. He sat there in a room with Ben and Sal talking about computers and the UDC, and Meg wolfing down the first hamburger she must have had in years, and looking not a bit changed—a few more lines around the eyes, maybe. And when he had to put the rest of his shake aside, he shut his eyes for just a moment and sat there, and thought about Cory. He thought about Bird, and the Belt. He thought he was there for the moment, but it wasn't a serious drift, just remembering. Safe.

Want to break his damn neck, Ben thought. Skuz ate the mess and went out cold, no wonder. Poor dead cow. Fish *weren't* intelligent. Thank you.

Sal leaned on his arm and whispered a thoroughly indecent proposal, which reminded him what he hadn't gotten in the last year, what with the course work and the computer time and all—a proposal that didn't make a man think all that clearly about the value of his life and the necessity of getting out of this hellhole . . .

"Yeah," he said thickly, directing thoughts to getting his ass out of here *and* snagging Sal into the TI—and down to Stockholm. Sal was damned good. In several senses. "Yeah. —Meg, *hate* to leave you with the skuz there, —d' you mind sitting on him?"

"Any way he can make it," Meg said smugly. "Us freefallers are adaptable—how's yourself, Ben?"

He *was* out of practice. Polite society did that. He actually felt his face warm. "Hell, ask Sal in a while."

Sal hooked her arm in his and said, "Details later. Serious interpersonal relations. —You got a notion where, mate?"

"Whole damn room to ourselves," he said. And elbowed the door open.

Dek said, "You want to dispose that?" and handed Meg the remnant of the milkshake. She went to the bath to dump it and came back to find Dek on his feet rummaging a locker—his, she figured, and hoped he wasn't thinking of getting dressed. Her own back ached with the *g*-shift off the shuttle—she'd gotten soft, living on the *Hamilton*'s c-force decks. It was the little muscles that hurt, the ones you used pulling your body around in freefall, a lot of them in unusual places, and she seriously didn't want to face the guys outside. . . .

"You're not going to walk," she said; he ignored the question, lifted a stack of folders in the top of the locker and said, sounding upset, "The tape's gone."

"What tape?"

"Sim tape. I guess they took it back to library. Damn sure they've been through here."

"They?"

"MPs. Crash investigators. Whatever."

"They already had the hearing, Dek. VIPs left this morning."

He was looking white. He leaned one-handed against the locker frame and looked at nowhere. "I'm tracking, Meg."

Meaning quit treating him like a spacecase. Joli jeune rab, face like a painted angel and a body language that said Screw *you*—in any sense you wanted to take it.

A lot like herself, truth was. But there had to come a moment in a lifetime when a person looked in the mirror and knew age had happened; and Dek was her mirror—that body and that face that carried all its worry-lines in muscle, not engraved permanently beside the mouth or around the eyes. Age had sneaked up on her; and Dek's mama wasn't older, she'd bet on it. So might be he didn't want any forty-year-old woman putting the push on him. With his looks he'd have his pick of anybody out there, and probably had had, all his life—probably had damned well enough of everybody who saw him wanting him, and no few laying uninvited hands on him—pretty guy had that problem no less than anybody else; maybe more, because *he* was supposed to like it.

So back off the kid, Magritte Kady, and shut the hell up—he's tired, he's probably sick to death of being hit on, probably thinking hard how to finesse a middle-aged woman out of his bed tonight; and not doing real well with the words, is he?

Dek didn't say anything. He wandered into the bath, ran water, came out again with his face and the front of his hair wet, and looked at her with eyes like a lost, battered kid's.

She said, "Nothing comes with the package. I came here to haul your ass out. Not laying claim to it by any right. Isn't as if I didn't get something—I got back to inner system, didn't I? So no debts. I owed you."

Disturbed him, that. She saw the frown. He said, "How's the arm?"

Half-thinking, she rotated the hand, lifted the arm. "Works."

"Reflexes?"

She shrugged, moved the thumb that was a little stiff. "Age is, jeune rab. It does hit us all."

"*You* aren't old, Meg."

Gallant jeune fils, too. She didn't let the face react. Just the gut felt pain. She told it shut up and laid out the truth. "Still not saying I should have been at the controls, on my best day. You pulled our asses out of a bad one, Dek, you got what I never had: if you want me on your team, all right, I'll back you; or if you want me or Sal off it, you say that too, right now, plain as plain, because I owe it to Sal. I'm forty and counting, arm isn't what it used to be and it won't be again. Sal's young but she's got experience to collect. That's what you get. Can't lie to you. No good doing that. . . ."

He came closer. Looking into his face was a send-off; looking into his eyes was the deep dive, gravity well, painful as slow compression. His face went out of focus as he leaned and kissed her on the cheek—deeper hurt, that. But the jeune fils didn't, couldn't know. . . .

"Call it even," he said, then, "Paid is paid," —but his hands traveled down and behind her. Came a light kiss on the mouth that shook a forty-year-old's good sense. Another one that—

God.

"Don't *do* that," she said shakily, when she had a breath, and meant to crack some half-witted joke about their relative ages, but he said, "Bed, Meg," and pulled her down on the bunk with him.

Not real copacetic, no, the jeune fils had far more ideas than substance left, but clothes and covers went one way and the other, boots thumped out from under the sheets, and a bunk that wasn't designed for two meant real caution about putting an elbow into his sore spots. She did. But he said never mind, hell with the ribs, he didn't care, if he was hallucinating he didn't want to wake up, she could fly him to hell and gone, he'd take the trip—

Didn't care. That was the operative word, that was the danger word she was hearing from him—but she didn't know what to say on the instant but to punch him on the leg and say, "I'm damn well here, jeune rab. Shut up."

Struck him funny, somehow. Didn't recall as she'd ever seen him laugh like that, and there wasn't much healthy about it; but he sort of snuggled down then, hugging her close, said, "Anything you want, Meg, whatever you like," and started drifting out, little at a time.

Murmured, finally, "Cory, —" But she didn't take offense. Man'd busted his ass trying to save Cory Salazar, done everything for his partner a man could do and then some, and what would you want in a man—that he'd forget, now, and switch Cory off like a light?

Not any partner she'd ever give a damn for.

So she ruffled his hair, said, "Hush, it's Meg," and he said, with his eyes shut, "Meg, for God's sake get out, go back, don't get mixed up in this, dammit, you had a berth—"

"Yeah. They were going to make me senior captain. You got my knee pinned, you want to move over, Dek?"

Bed with Aboujib was a long, long experience. You didn't get away easy—tech-nique, Sal called it; and he didn't know—he was here, where the competition back at TI couldn't eavesdrop; and Sal wasn't a critic, Sal just took what was—Sal was all over you and kink as hell, maybe. You couldn't be ice with Sal, maybe that was why he was thinking suddenly, amid his attentions to Sal, that he *truly* didn't want Stockholm to see this side of Ben Pollard—that wasn't real sincerely in his right mind, feeling as he did for the moment that he'd actually missed R2's sleaze and neon, that he'd *missed* Mike Arezzo's synth-egg breakfasts and the noise of helldeck—

Stockholm was a VR image. Stockholm was special effects, there wasn't an Earth and you couldn't get to it, the Company only made it up to explain the universe—got its Earth-luxuries out of fancy tanks, it was all synth for all he knew, what the hell difference whether it was a cow or a tank culture, he wasn't going to eat what had blood running through it—hell, Earth was full of eetees no less than Pell, and what was Ben Pollard doing trying to fit in with people who ate hamburgers and ran a department that bought a damned EIDAT?

Ben Pollard was trying to stay alive and stay out of the war, that was what he'd been doing. Ben Pollard was back on helldeck, the bubble had burst, and what turned up but Sal Aboujib, the Fleet's own damnable *doing,* screw the bastard who was responsible for this—

Hell, when it came down to it, Dekker was *responsible* for it, it didn't matter the UDC and the Fleet had gotten their shot in, Dekker could reach out from the hereafter and screw his life up with one little touch, the way he'd screwed Cory Salazar's—way he'd screwed the program up—

Off chance that part wasn't his fault, but you didn't protect yourself by figuring a mess of this magnitude that Dekker just happened to be in the middle of—didn't have Dekker's fingerprints all over it. Wasn't that the guy necessarily did anything, he didn't have to do it, he just *was.* Like gravity and infall, things went wrong in his vicinity. . . .

Sal cut off his air, and lights went off awhile. When he came down he was halfway tranquil, catching his breath, and said—it still bothered him: "You know, you could've written once."

Sal didn't answer that one right off. She came over on top of him and made a cage out of her elbows beside his head. Her braids hit him in the face. Her lips brushed his nose.

"That's no answer."

"Didn't figure you wanted one," Sal said.

Fair answer, one he hadn't thought of. Fact was, when he was trying to settle in with inner-system pets and sorting the threats from the bottom-enders he hadn't had but a few twinges of regret for helldeck—tried to clean the Belt out of his language, tried not to dream about it, just wanted to see those clean green numbers in his head, different life, Aboujib. Different aims. . . .

So he didn't answer that. He just said, "Here's seriously screwed. Dekker's involved. Thought you had better sense. Thought Meg had. I can understand her, maybe, got to be hell getting seniority out there, but *you're* Shepherd, you got the connections, you didn't have to dump and come—"

Sal slid down, slid over, rolled onto one elbow, all shadow, braid-clips a-wink in the dim light. Eyes eclipsed and looked at him again.

"Weren't treating her right, Ben. She took it. But, tell the truth, she wasn't seriously happy on the *Hamilton.*"

"Personalities?"

Sal traced something with a long fingernail on the sheet between them. Second eclipse. And glance up. "Could say. Guys put the push on her. Guys said—" Shift of the eyes toward the door and a lowered voice. "Said it was damned good she'd got shot, it put Dek at the controls. . . ."

"Shit."

Sal shrugged. "Probably true. She says it is. But that's the Attitude, you understand? She took the jokers. She took the shit. But they said she'd got an affinity for gravity wells, didn't want her flying in Jupiter's pull—big joke, right?"

Severely big joke. The idea of infalling a gravity well made him nervous as hell. Going down to Stockholm, if he got there, as happened, he intended to drink a lot of cocktails before the dive—because *he* was Shepherd—a Shepherd orphan, as happened, thank God he'd been on R2 when the ship went. But sometimes, on his worst nights, he dreamed of metal groaning, bolts fracturing, the sounds a ship would make when compression began—pop, and *bang* and metal shrieking—

Yeah, Shepherds made jokes. Shepherds defended the perks and prerogatives they got from the Company for flying where others couldn't. And Meg was insystemer, *inner* systemer, even blue-sky; and there on Sal's ticket. . . .

So Dekker got the credit with the Shepherds, for one hell of a flight; and Meg, who'd nearly got her arm blown off for the cause—got the shit: *Dekker* hadn't asked for a post with the Shepherds, that was the Attitudinal difference. . . .

"She wanted to come," Sal said. And gave a long breath. "Couldn't let her go alone."

"To find Dekker? She didn't effin' *know* him. She didn't—"

Pi-lut, he thought then. Meg was a pilot same as Dekker, didn't care about anything but to fly. And the Shepherds didn't want her at controls?

Double shit. But things the other side of the wall still didn't make sense in that light.

"So she's in *bed* with the guy?"

A movement of sheet, shrug of Sal's shoulders. Silence a moment. Then: "Hormones."

"What kind? That's the question."

"Like he's the best, you know what I mean? Beating him'd—I dunno, it'd prove a lot of things."

"God." He fell onto his back to think about that a tick.

"I mean," Sal said, "if even the Fleet had offered her back then what they'd offered Dekker—if they'd just *offered,* she'd have been gone. But she was lying in pieces and patches, as was—couldn't blame them, really, but it severely did hurt. . . ."

Up on his elbow again. He was hearing craziness he might have to fly with. "She's not any damn twenty-year-old, Sal, if you want to talk hormones, here, you got to have a whole different wiring. Reactions aren't there. They're not going to *be* there for any sane human, Sal, the guy's flat crazy, it seems to be a pre-rec on this ship—"

Silence a moment. Sal was all shadow and maybe anger, you couldn't know when you were talking to a cutout in the dark. Finally Sal said, with a definite edge to her voice, "She's not any twenty-year-old, but she was *damned good,* Ben, you weren't out there with us, you didn't see how she'd finesse a rock—and we got shit, Ben, the Company gave us *shit* assignments, because we were worse than freerunners, we were freerunner *lease* crew, and they were trying to run us broke, to crack the ship-owners, that was what they were up to. We never got one good draw from that 'random assignment procedure'—Meg had a record on Sol, Meg was on the Company's hit list because Meg was rab, Meg didn't dress by the codes, Meg didn't think by the codes, Meg wouldn't kiss ass and they screwed her, Ben, same as B.M. screwed her, same as the *Hamilton* screwed her— So here the damn Fleet comes in and says,

By the way, will you come in and haul Dek out of his mess? —Didn't even say, You want to fly for us? Said, You want to come haul this chelovek out of his funk and we'll cover your record? That's all, that's all they promised, Ben. And she got this look—shit, what was I going to do? She'd stuck by me. Maybe it's time somebody went with her."

He'd never heard Sal talk that way—Sal with an attack of Obligations. But, shit-all, —

That thought led down a track he didn't want to take, something about old times, about what they'd had on helldeck, confidence that came of knowing the guy you were sharing a ship with wasn't out to screw you—whole damn universe might be out to do that, but your partner wouldn't, your partner had to have the same interests you did, and you just didn't cheat on him.

You just didn't cheat on him. . . .

He rolled out of bed, buck naked and cold in the draft from the vents, he walked over to the other bunk and leaned his arm against it, because if he stayed in that bed he was going to start thinking about Morrie, and he didn't like to do that, not in the middle of the dark.

So Sal was being a fool. So Meg thought she could get the years she'd lost back again and the system wouldn't screw them all.

Rustle from behind him. Movement. Arms came around him, and the chill myriad clips of Sal's braids rattled against his back.

"Cold out here, Ben."

"I want out of here, dammit, I'm not aptituded for combat. I got a place in Stockholm . . ."

Sal said, holding him tight, "What's Stockholm?"

CHAPTER 7

Maindawn and in the office early, trying, before the mainday rush hit, to make sense of the reports from the designers and the sims check. Graff took a slow sip of vending machine coffee, keyed the next page on the desktop reader. The report writer liked passives: "will be effectuated," "will be seen to have incremented," and especially convolutions: "may have been cost-effective in the interim while result-negative in the long-range forecast—"

Graff keyed the dictionary for "forecast." It said something about 1) terrestrial weather patterns and, 2) prediction. The latter, he decided, but keyed it up; and found something, as he'd suspected, different than his own definition of "prediction." These were the people who designed the computers and the software that ran the sims, for God's sake, and they were giving him messages about Old Earth weather patterns and fortune-telling?

He tried to read these reports out of Tanzer's staff. He felt responsible in the captain's absence. He worried about missing something. He worried about not understanding Tanzer face to face, and these were the only lessons in blue-sky usage on his regular reading list.

"Effectuated," he could guess from particles. And he didn't have that small a vocabulary. He *didn't* use that many semicolons in his reports; he wondered was his style out of fashion; and he wished not for the first time that he'd had at least one of the seminal languages—given the proliferation of derived meanings, that was what Saito called the problem words, cognates; and metaphor. All of which meant a connection between "forecast," planetary weather, and the Lendler Corp techs who, between working on the sims and writing reports, danced a careful and convolute set of protocols between his office and Tanzer's—"effectuate," hell. "Obfuscate" and "delegate" and "reiterate," but nothing *effectual* was going to happen with that investigation except Lendler Corp gathering evidence to protect itself against lawsuits from the next of kin.

Save them the trouble. Stick to Belters. Belters didn't sue Corporations, Belters didn't have the money or the connections to sue Corporations.

But come into *their* territory—

Lendler didn't want to do that. Didn't want to interview the Belters. Even when he had it set up.

The phone beeped. He hoped it was Saito coming on-line: he could use a linguist about now—and he could wish Legal Affairs hadn't left their office to a junior: the Fleet needed to enlist a motherworld lawyer, was what they needed, maybe two and three of them, since they never seemed unanimous—he'd had the UDC counsel on the line last night, talking about culpabilities and wanting releases from the next-ofs—

"Lt. Graff?" Young male voice. Familiar male voice. *"Col. Tanzer on the line."*

He'd never been in the habit of swearing. But association with the Belters did suggest words. He kept it to: "Put him on, Trev."

Pop. *"Lt. Graff?"*

"Colonel?"

"I'm looking at the file on Paul Dekker. Just wondered if you had any last-minute additions, before we write our finish on this accident business."

"I'd appreciate that, colonel, as soon as we finish our own investigation."

"Dekker's been released from hospital, I understand, on your orders."

Possibility of recorders. Distinct possibility. "Released to Fleet medical care. His blood showed high levels of tranquilizer and pain medication. My medical staff says it was excessive. Far excessive. The word malpractice figured in the report."

A moment of silence. *"Blood samples taken after he was in your doctors' care, lieutenant. I'll inquire, but you'll excuse me if I choose to believe our own personnel. File a separate report if you like. Call the Surgeon General. It's completely of a pattern with the rest of your actions. But you may find some of those chickens coming home to roost very shortly."*

Another one for Saito. But the gist of it got through, quite clearly.

Tanzer said: *"The phone isn't the place for this discussion. I'll see you in my office in ten minutes. Or I'll file this report as is, without your inspection, and add your objection in my own words."*

Moment of silence from his side. A moment of temptation to damn Tanzer for a bastard, hang up, and call the captain on uncoded com. He might be a fool not to have done that: Tanzer made little moves, niggling away at issue after issue, day after day; *damn* the man, he could be recording the conversation right now. But caution won. Follow the forms. "I'm on my way," he said.

The sojers had this perverse habit called reveille, which meant after the com scared hell out of you and you hauled yourself bleary-eyed awake, you ran for the breakfast line before the eggs disappeared—Meg had gotten into that routine on the ship coming here, got a few days spoiled on the shuttle, and here she and Sal were again—standing in line, the only females in sight, with two guys who drew their own kind of attention.

Orientation, the lieutenant had told her, outside hospital. Keep him busy. Push him, but not too hard. Don't let him off by himself.

Which meant they were a kind of bodyguard, she supposed. Against what, she wasn't sure—against Dek's own state of mind, high on the list: too much death, Sal put it, for anybody to tolerate. Everybody he'd gotten really close to, except Ben and her, had died; he'd watched it happen every damned time; and last night he was telling her to try to de-enlist, get out of his life?

Only convinced her how seriously she meant to follow the lieutenant's orders and keep a tag on him.

So Dek was supposed to show them around, get them acquainted with the classrooms and the VR labs and the library, get their own cards picked up. *Lab* schedule, soon as they could get settled, hell and away different than *she'd* learned flying, but that was the way they did it in the Fleet: Dek said you took a pill and they hooked you up to a tape and they fed the basics of the boards into you by VR display like programming some damned machine—

"Confuses you at first," Dekker was telling them, in the breakfast line, the other side of Ben. "Reactions cross what you know, you face it the next day and you don't remember learning something new—your hands know. They use it just to teach you the boards. The brain takes a while to get used to it—a while to know it knows. Handful of people can't take the pills. But it's rare."

She listened. She tried to imagine it.

"They're experimenting with that stuff over at TI," Ben said. "Hell if they're going to mess with *my* head. I'm a Priority 10. Programmer. Security clearance. Damn chaff, that's what's going on, it's that screwed-up EIDAT they're using—drop me in here and *my* level isn't in the B Dock system, oh, no, all it knows is pi-luts and dock monkeys, so I got to be one or the other, right? Right." Dollop of synth eggs onto Ben's plate. "So it lets some damn keypusher screw with my assignment. Does somebody over at Sol wonder where I am? Not yet. Personnel isn't supposed to think, oh, no, *they* trust the EIDAT. I got a post waiting for me, God hope it's still waiting. —What the hell *is* that stuff?"

"Grits," Dek said.

"Was it alive?"

"It wasn't alive." Dek slid his tray to the end of the line and drew his coffee.

"You want me to carry that?" Meg asked.

"I'm *fine,*" Dek said, and stuck his card in the slot. "That's present and accounted for. Laser scans the bottom of the containers, figures your calories and your allotments—dietician's worse than—hell." Reader's read-line was blinking.

"You have a message," the checkout robot said, as if Dek couldn't read.

" 'Scuse." Dek carried his tray over to a corner table, quiet spot, Meg was glad to note, following him, while Ben waited for Sal to check through—a skosh too many Shepherd eyes in this place for her personal comfort, all picking up every move they made. Hi, Dek, they'd say soberly, sounding friendly enough. Giving her and Sal the eye, that was a natural—women being severely scarce here; and sort of glossing Ben.

But the UDC boys looked at Ben and looked at them and heads sort of leaned together at tables, she could see it going on all over that other corner of the hall, thick with UDC uniforms.

Dek set his tray down. "I'll check that message blinker. Probably your stuff. Hope it's your stuff."

As Sal and Ben showed up with their trays and set them down.

"What's he doing?" Ben asked with a glance over his shoulder. "You don't ask what a message is before breakfast, you never ask what a message is before breakfast—"

"Thinks it could be our accesses." Meg set her tray down and cast a glance at Dek over by the phone, a skosh anxious, she couldn't even tell why, except Dek had had this edge in his voice: he was On about something, she read it in his stance and his moves, and she hadn't been able to read all the codes that had popped up. She said, still on her feet, "Ben? You capish the code on that blinker?"

"Accesses stuff," Ben said, sitting down.

"Uh-oh," Sal said.

Understatement. Serious understatement. Dek hit the phone with his open hand. "Scuze," Meg said, and went that direction.

Dek snatched out his card, and ricocheted into her path. "What is?" she asked, catching at his arm. "Dek?"

"They clipped me, Tanzer's fuckin' *clipped* me, the son of a bitch." Dek shoved her and she didn't know whether to hang on or not—her hand stung as he blazed past her. But that didn't matter. Dek going for the door like a crazy man—that seriously mattered. Dek knocking into guys inbound—

Mitch, for God's sake—

Dek got past. Hot on his track she hit the same obstacle, who didn't give way a second time. Neither did the other guys. "Kady," Mitch said, not friendly. "I heard they'd gotten desperate."

"I got a seriously upset partner—out of my *way,* dammit!"

"So what's with Dekker?"

"Something about getting clipped."

"Shit!" Mitch said, and: "Pauli," to the big guy behind him, Shepherd from the hall yesterday. She remembered. "Haul his ass back here. Fast."

"What's going on?" Sal asked as she and Ben showed up with a handful of other curious.

"Dekker's been clipped," Mitch said. "Just calm down, we're going to see what the lieutenant says about this."

Hell if she understood "clipped," she didn't know Pauli from trouble, she knew Mitch too damn well, but Mitch's outrage at least sounded to be on Dek's side and stopping Dek seemed to be a priority on their side too. Pauli-whoever took out in the direction Dek had gone, and she went with, at a fast walk.

First corner showed an empty hall; but Pauli broke into a jog for a side corridor as if he knew where he was going, she caught up, and spotted Dek, all right, traveling at a fair clip himself.

"Dek!" she called out; and he stopped, took a damn-you stance and stared at them cold as cold.

All right. *That* was the surly young sumbitch she knew. She panted, "You got friends, chelovek, capish? Slow down. Deal with people."

Dek looked half poised to walk off. Pauli said, "Is it true? They pulled you?"

"Yeah." Dek's mouth didn't look to be working real well, he clearly didn't want to talk; but about that time Ben and Sal showed up with some of the other Shepherds from the messhall, Ben with:

"What's going on? —Dekker, are you being a spook?"

"Ben," Meg exclaimed. Sal said the same. But Dek made a disgusted wave of his hand and managed to unlock his jaw.

"Nothing's wrong, nothing's the hell wrong. Sorry I got you here. Sorry I got you into this."

A sane woman had to get things off personals. Fast. "Ben, Sal, this is Pauli, friend of Mitch's; Pauli: Ben Pollard, Sal Aboujib. Say how-do, and somebody answer a straight question, f' God's sake. What's going on here?"

"The damn UDC," Dek said, "that's what's going on. Tanzer's just tossed me out of the program."

"He can't do that," Pauli said. "Screw him. He can't do that."

Somebody else said, "No way, Dek." And another one: "Mitch is on his way to talk to the lieutenant right now. No way that's going to stick."

Dek wasn't highly verbal. He was white, and sweating. Sal said, quietly, with her arm in Dek's: "You want to go back to the room, Dek?"

Ben said: "Screw it, he's got a breakfast sitting back there, we all got breakfast back there, if nobody's grabbed it."

Leave it to Ben. Sal had a crazy man halfway turned around and stopped from strangling the colonel and Ben wanted his effin' breakfast. Dek was looking at Ben like he was some eetee dropped by for directions.

"You mind?" Ben asked him impatiently.

"Yeah. All right," Dek muttered. And went with him.

God, both of them were spooks.

"I'm looking at Dekker's record," Tanzer said, tapping a card on his desk, "right here: the medical report and his disciplinary record—including his violent behavior here in hospital, his defiance of regulations in the sims—"

"His behavior, colonel, was thoroughly reasonable, considering the level of drugs in his system. Drugs with possible negative psychological impact considering his history—which is in that file. That from *my* medical experts. He has grounds for malpractice."

"This is the accident report." Tanzer shoved a paper form across the desk at him. "Sign it or don't, as you please. I'll spare you the detail. I'm *not* calling the hospital records into question, I'm *not* charging him with flagrant violations of security with that type, I'm *not* charging him for disregard of safety regulations. I *am* concluding there was no other person involved in the sims accident but Ens. Dekker."

He kept every vestige of emotion from his face. "How are you proposing he got into that pod?"

"I'm supposing he got in there the ordinary way, lieutenant, the same as any fool can climb in there. He just happened to be on trank. These are the records of his admission—he was flying before he got in there."

"Was put in there."

"He was in illegal possession of a tape that should have been back in library—"

"He had license to possess that tape, colonel. He'd been in hospital, he'd just been released, in condition *your* medics knew when they let him out with a prescription drug in his system—"

"Whatever drugs were in his system, he put there, before he decided to go on a sim ride."

"Pardon me if I don't rely on those doctors' word, colonel, or their records."

"Rely on whatever you like. I'll tell you one thing: Dekker's barred from the sims."

"He's going in there on my orders, colonel."

"Check your rules, lieutenant. The sim facility and its accesses are under UDC direction."

"You restrict one of my people from the sims, colonel, and the case is going clear to the Defense Department."

"Then you better start the papers moving, lieutenant, because he's barred. And if you give a *damn* for your program you won't file—that's my unsolicited advice, because you don't want him in public. Take my word for it you don't want him in public. But until I get cooperation out of your office, you don't get cooperation out of mine."

"Do I understand this as blackmail? Is that what you want? My signature, and Dekker's back in?"

"I wouldn't put it that way. But let's say it might signal a salutary change of attitude."

"No deal. *No* deal, colonel. And you can stand by for FleetCom to be in use in fifteen minutes."

"Good. About time you woke up your upper echelons. Tell them they've got a problem with Dekker. A serious problem."

Trays were still sitting. They came into the messhall and guys stopped and stared in that distant way people had when they were trying to spy on somebody else's trouble. Talk stopped, mostly, and started again, and Dek didn't look at anybody, didn't talk to anybody, just sat down at his place at table and put the straw in his orange juice.

Ben gave her a tight-jawed look. Table was still all theirs. Pauli and the guys had gone off toward the breakfast line, but they hadn't made it: they'd gotten snagged, talking to guys over by the wall, all Shepherd. There were UDC guys on the fringes—tables were either UDC or they were Shepherd, Meg marked that suddenly: there wasn't another mixed table in the whole damned hall.

She didn't like the quiet. Didn't like the feeling around them. Dek was having his eggs. Ben was having toast. Sal gave her a look that said she was right, everybody else was crazy but them.

Young woman, blond hair in a shave-strip, came up, set her tray down, said, "You mind, Dek?"

Dek shrugged. That one sat down. "Trace," the interloper said, looking her way, and offered her hand across the tray as a dark-skinned Shepherd kid took the seat next to Sal: "Almarshad. Friends of friends."

Pauli sat down, him with no tray, and said, "It's us Tanzer's after. —Pollard, you mind to answer whose side you're on?"

Hell of a question, Meg thought. She watched Ben frown and think, then say, with a cold sweet smile on his face: "Hell, I'm not in Tanzer's command. I'm Security-cleared. I'm Computer Technical, out of TI. I'm due somewhere else, and if I get there, frying Tanzer's ass'd be ever so little effort. So why doesn't somebody get me out of here?"

"Hear you were a good numbers man," Pauli said.

The frown came back. "Damned good," Ben said. Ben wasn't lying. "But I'm not flying with him. I'm not flying with you guys. I'm not friggin' going *near* combat . . ."

"Small chance you'll have in my company," Dek said under his breath. "If they get this mess cleared, it'll just be one more thing they find. Dammit, Pete and Elly—what in *hell* is it with me that—"

Pauli's hand came down on Dek's wrist and shut him up. Thank God, Meg thought. She didn't know the danger spots here, but her personal radar was getting back severe oncomings.

Hadn't even gotten back to the office before he had a hail from behind and a "Lieutenant, we've got to talk to you—"

No doubt what it was before Mitch and Benavides overtook him. Graff said, "Dekker's banned from the sims, is that what this is about?"

"Tanzer's doing?" Mitch asked—and didn't ask was it his.

"*Col.* Tanzer," he reminded them. "In the office, Mitch. Let's keep it out of the corridors—"

"It's in the corridors, sir, it's all over the messhall. The UdamnDC doesn't care where it drops its—"

"Mitch. In the office."

"Yessir," Mitch said meekly; and the delegation trailed him down the corridor and around the corner to his own door. He could hear the phone beeping before he even got the door open. He got to his desk, picked up the handset.

"Graff here."

Saito's voice, *"J-G, we have a problem. Paul Dekker's been restricted."*

"I'm aware, I assure you. Word to the captain. FleetCom. Stat. Code but don't scramble. Tell the captain we'd urgently like to hear from him."

"Aye."

He hung up. He looked at Mitch. "Where is Dekker right now?"

"Messhall," Mitch said. "Granted Pauli and Kady could catch him."

"Catch him."

"He wasn't damned happy, and he was headed spinward."

"You catch him. You sit on him if you've got any concern about this program."

Quiet from the other side. Then: "We enlisted. We signed your contract. We've got plenty of concern about this program, lieutenant, we're damned worried about this program, —we're damned worried about a lot of things."

"First time I've asked this, Mitchell. Follow orders. Blind. Just do it."

Mitch looked at him a long time. So did the others. Finally Mitch said,

"We'll follow orders. —But what the hell are they *doing,* lieutenant? D' you hear from the captain? Do we know anything? What's happening at Sol?"

"You want it flat on the table—I don't know what the situation is, I don't know whether the captain's tied up in the hearings or what. I'm asking you, I *need* you to go back to your labs, follow your orders, show up for sims—get everybody back on routine. Like nothing's going on. Like nothing's ever gone on."

Long silence then. Long silence. And finally Mitch broke contact.

"Yeah," Mitch said. "You got it. You got it. But Dek's damned upset."

"Tell Dekker my door's open, I know what happened and I'm on it. May take a bit. But he's going back in there."

Opened his mouth on that one. If you made a promise like that to these men, you'd better plan to keep it.

Like dropping into system, he thought; sometimes you had to call one fast. He thought it over two and three times, the way you didn't have time to reflect on a high-*v* decision—but the fallout from this one was scattered all through the future, and he didn't know whether he was right to promise a showdown—for one man.

Damned if not, he decided. You could count casualties by the shipload—in an engagement. But if it was your own service taking aim—damned right one man mattered.

Whole roomful of tranked-out fools sitting at consoles, making unison reaches after switches, unison keystrokes, as far as Ben could tell. "Damn *spacecases,*" he said, with a severe case of the willies. Deeptech, they called it, VR with drugs and specific behaviors involved; and hearing about it wasn't seeing thirty, forty people all sitting there with patches on their arms and faces and elsewhere and in private places, for all he knew: forty grown people making identical rapid moves like the parts of some factory machine. "Talk about Unionside clones. . . ."

"Just basic stuff," Dekker said. They were in the observation room, looking out through Spex that reflected their disturbed faces—disturbed, in his case, and Meg's and Sal's. Dekker, professional space-out, tried to tell them it was just norm.

"Spooky," was Sal's word too. "Seriously spooky."

Ben asked uneasily, "They do computer work that way?"

"Basic functions," Dekker said. "Basic stuff. For all I know, they do: armscomp, longscan—'motor skills,' they call it. They teach the boards that way. Some of the sims are like that, when there's one right answer to a problem. Anything you can set up like that—they can cut a tape. It's real while you're seeing it. Damned real. But you move right. You do it over and over till you always jump right."

Wasn't the answer he wanted to hear. He said, "*I'm* not taking any damn pill. I'm already right. Righter than any guy this halfass staff has got, I'll tell you. You let them muck with your head?"

"Just for the boards," Dekker said, and cut the lights as they left. "Just to set the reactions. 'Direct Neural Input,' they call it. You do the polish in sims, and you do that awake—at least you're supposed to . . ."

Two years he'd known the guy and he realized he'd never actually heard Dekker's sense of humor. He decided that was a joke. A damned bad one.

Meg asked, "So what if it sets a bias that's not *right,* once upon some time?"

"You aren't the only one to worry about that. Yeah. It's a question."

"So what are they doing? Set us up to jump on the average we're right?"

"That's part of what they call 'documentation'—meaning there's nobody who's flown the ship."

"Nobody?" Sal asked; and Ben nearly managed unison.

"Docking trials, yeah. They got that part. Straight runs. Milk and cookies. Rotate and reorient. Do it in your sleep. But *not* with armscomp working. You got enough problem with system junk."

"Like a damn beam-push through the Belt."

"You got it. At that *v* it's a lot like that. Only where we're going—there *aren't* any two-hundred-year-old system charts. You get stuff off the system buoy when you drop into a known system, where there's regular traffic, but out at the jump points, there's chaff you just don't know's there. And maybe stuff somebody meant to dump—ship-killers, scan-invisible stuff, you don't know."

"Shit." Cold chill went down Ben's back. "These guys ever *made* a run with Mama shoving you?"

"A lot of these guys have done it—if you mean the combat jocks. Yeah. That's what it's like. And we just run ahead and blow the sumbitches they dump out of the carrier's path."

"You're kidding."

"That's what she does."

"That's the damn stupidest thing I ever heard!"

"That's why they like us Belter types. Shipkillers and rocks—no difference. Same gut feeling for how rocks move—same thing that makes a good numbers man or keeps a Shepherd out of the Well, that's what they want."

"Hell if, Dekker, hell *if*! Not *this* Belt miner!"

"You a good miner?" Dekker had the nerve to ask.

"A live one! On account of I never *let* MamBitch boost us like a missile—except once. In which you figured, you son of a —"

Meg said, "Hell, Ben, they *give* you guns. . . ."

"Yeah, and it won't work—that's what they're doing in there, they're brainwashing those poor sods, they brainwashed *him,* for God's sake, blow rocks out of the way, hell! They got *that* on those tapes?"

"Not yet," Dekker said, just as quiet and sober as if he was sane. "But they'd like to. Get the reactions right on *one run,* so they can bottle it and feed it into the techs—word is, that's what they want to do, ultimately. Get one crew that can do it. And they'll teach the others. Hundreds of others."

"God," Sal said, and hooked a thumb back at the human factory. "Like *that*?"

Dekker shrugged. "That's what they think."

"That's what they think," Ben muttered. The human race was shooting at each other. Dekker said Union was building riderships, too—

"I thought the other *side* was where they wired you to a machine and taught you to like getting blown to hell. Not here. Not on *this* side, no *way,* Dek-boy. What the hell are we fighting for? That's Union stuff in there!"

"They developed it, what I hear."

"God."

" 'Not yet,' " Meg quipped.

"Damn funny, Meg."

Ben looked at Dekker, looked at Meg and at Sal, with this sudden sinking feeling—this moment of dislocation, that said he was surrounded by crazies, including the woman he went to bed with; including every hotshot Shepherd tight-ass in this whole establishment, *and* the CO, *and* the lieutenant.

"What's it do to your reflexes?" Meg said.

Dekker said, "Screws 'em to hell. Scares shit out of you. Like I said at breakfast. Hands move, you don't know why, you threw a switch, you don't know why. Moves are right. But you got to convince yourself they are. You can't doubt."

"Any chance it came around on this Wilhelmsen?"

Dekker didn't answer that for a second or so. Ben wasn't sure about keeping his breakfast. "Yeah," Dekker said. "But that's the one thing you never better think. You *never* think about it. Not in the sims. Especially in the real thing—"

Dekker's voice wandered off. He stood there with his hand on a door switch and looked off somewhere, just stood there a breath or two—then drew a larger breath and said,

"Worst enemy you've got—asking whether your moves are right. You just can't doubt—"

"Yeah," Ben said, with the sudden intense feeling they had to get him out of this hallway before a guard saw him or something. "Yeah, right. Why don't we go tour somewhere else? Like what there is to *do* on this station?"

Dekker looked at him like he'd never thought of such a thing. "Don't know that there is. This isn't One."

"What I've seen, it isn't even R2. What do you do for *life* in this can? Play the vending machines?"

"Not much time for social life," Dekker said faintly. Which reminded him there hadn't been outstanding much in TI, either. Even attached to Sol One, where there was plenty.

"Not much where we've been," Meg said. "Either."

They walked down the hall in this place full of labs where human beings learned to twitch like rats, to guide ships that moved too fast to think about, and you couldn't help thinking that helldeck on R2, for all R2's faults, had been the good old days. . . .

"So what *do* you want to do, Dek-boy? I mean, granted we all get our wants, —what's yours?"

Scariest question he'd ever asked Dekker. And Dekker took a while thinking about it, he guessed, Meg sort of leaning up against Dekker, one visible hand on his arm—where the other one was might have something to do with his concentration. . . .

But Dekker said, real quiet, "I want to be the one cuts that tape. I want to be the one that does it, Ben."

He wished he hadn't asked. Sincerely wished he hadn't asked. Sincerely wished Meg would put her hand somewhere to disrupt the boy's concentration and shake him out of his spook notions.

"There a chance?" Meg asked, quiet too; and he thought, God, it's in the water, they got to put it in the water—

Dekker didn't answer that one right off. "If they let me back in the sims, there is . . ." And a few beats later. "But I'm not doing it with you, Meg. I can't do it with you."

Silence from Meg. Then: "Yeah."

"I don't mean that." Dekker stopped cold, took Meg by the shoulders and made her look at him. "I mean I don't want to. I can't work with you. . . ."

Meg didn't look real happy. Meg was about as white and as tight-lipped as he'd ever seen her. Meg shoved his hands off. "You got a problem, mister? You got a *problem* with me not being good enough, that's one thing, you got a *problem* about setting me on any damn shelf to look at—that's another. You say I'm shit at the boards, that's all right, that's your damned opinion, let's see how the Aptitudes come out. I'll find a team and I'll fly with somebody, we'll sleep together sometimes, *fine.* Or I'll wash out of here. But you don't set me on any damn shelf!"

After which Meg walked off alone down the hall, sound of boots on the decking, head down. Not happy. Hell, Ben thought, with a view of Dekker's back, Dekker just standing there. Sal was with him—he wondered that Sal didn't go with Meg; he was still wondering when Dekker lit out after Meg, walking fast and wobbling a little.

"You make sense out of either one of 'em?" he asked Sal.

"Yeah," Sal said. "Both."

Surprised him. Most things came down to Belter and Innersystemer. So maybe this was something he just wasn't tracking. He asked, for his own self-preservation: "Yeah? I know why *he's* following. I don't know why she's pissed."

Sal said, "Told you last night."

"He didn't say she couldn't fly. He said—"

"He said not with him. Not on his ship. She'll beat his ass. That's what he's asking for."

Talking was going on down the hall, near the exit. Looked hot and heavy.

Sal said, "She'll pass those Aptitudes. You never seen Meg mad."

He thought he had. Maybe not, on the other hand. Meg was still lighting into Dekker—boy was a day out of hospital, shaky on his feet, and he didn't look as if he was holding his own down there.

Then Dekker must've said something, because Meg eased off a little.

Probably it was Yes. Probably. Meg was still standing there. Meg and Dekker walked off together toward the security door, so he figured they'd better catch up.

The other side of the door, Meg said, "We got it worked out."

Ben said, "Not fair, man's not up to this." Dekker looked as if he wanted holding on his feet, as was. But Dekker said,

"Going to try for that tape, Ben. You want to test in?"

He threw a shocked look back at the doors, where roomfuls of walking dead were flying nonexistent ships. "To *that?* No way in hell. Non-com-ba-*tant,* do you read? No *way* the UDC is risking my talent in a damn missile. I'll test for data entry before I do that—"

"What's Stockholm got?" Sal asked. "They say *Pell's* got a helldeck puts Sol to shame. Got eetees and everything."

"Yeah?" He was unmoved. "I've seen pictures. Can't be that good in bed."

"Got real biostuffs, just like Earth. There's Pell, there's Mariner Station—"

"Yeah, there's Cyteen going to blow us to hell or turn us into robots. Don't need to go to Cyteen—our own service is trying to do it to us . . ."

Seriously gave him the willies, that did. Get into his mind and teach him which keys to push, would it?

A programmer didn't need any damned help like that.

No answer, no answer, and no answer. Graff was beyond worrying. He was getting damned mad. And there was no place to trust but the carrier's bridge, *with* the security systems engaged—but workmen had been everywhere, the UDC had very adept personnel as capable of screwing up a system as their own techs were of unscrewing it—and it was always a question, even here, who was one up on whom. "I *know* the captain knows about Dekker," he said to Saito and Demas and Thieu—age-marked faces all; and the only reassurance he had. "Pollard, Aboujib, Kady all shipped in here—you'd think if he *is* moving them, they'd be couriering something, a message, two words from the captain—"

"Possibly," Saito said, over the rim of her coffee cup, "he feared some shift of loyalty. Dekker is the keypoint. None of them have met in over a year. Friends and lovers fall out. And Pollard is UDC."

"They came. Dekker's leavetaking with Kady was—passionate to say the least. Pollard joined him here. Protocol says none of this is significant?"

"They're not merchanter. That's not what's forming here."

Puzzles, at the depth of things. Silence from the captain, when a word would have come profoundly welcome. He looked at Demas, he looked at Armsmaster Thieu, he looked at Saito. Com One. If *Victoria* spoke officially, it was Saito's voice. If the Fleet spoke to Union or to blue-skyers, it was Saito, who made a study of words, and customs, and foreign exactitudes—and psychologies and expectations.

"What *is* forming?"

Saito shrugged. "That's the question, isn't it? I only point out—you can't take our social structure as the end point of their evolution. Blue-skyers and Belters alike—their loyalties are immensely complex. Ship and Family don't occur here. Only the basis for them. Difficult to say what they'd become."

"Prehistory," Demas murmured.

"Prejudice?" Saito asked softly.

"Not prejudice: just there's no bridge between the cultures. The change was total. Their institutions are seminal to ours. But they don't *need* kinships, they don't *need* to function in that context. Their ancestors did. We've pulled our resource out of the cultural matrix—"

"Matrices. Wallingsfordian matrices."

God, they were off on one of their arguments, splitting theoretical hairs. Demas was a hobbyist, and the carrier's bulletin board had a growing collection of Demas' and Saito's observations on insystem cultures. He hadn't come shipside for Wallingsfordians versus Kilmer or Emory.

"Saito. *Is* the captain setting up something you know about?"

A very opaque stare. "I'd tell you."

"Unless you had other orders. *Has* the captain been in contact with you? Am I being set up?"

A moment more that Saito looked at him and never a flinch. "Of course not."

Hard day?" Villanueva asked, at the dessert bar.

"Could say." The one claim you could make for Earth's vicinity was more varieties of sweet and spice than a man could run through in a year. And Graff personally intended to try during his tenure here—a tenure in which combat was beginning to look preferable. "What's this one?" he asked of the line worker, but Villy said, "Raisin cake. All-spice, cinnamon, sugar, nutmeg—"

"You have it down." Graff was fencing. He was sure Villy wasn't here entirely for the dessert. He didn't want the lecture. He didn't want the inquiry. He was, however, amazed at Villy's culinary expertise.

Villy shrugged. "You guys always ask. —How's Dekker doing?"

"All right till the colonel clipped him." He weighed asking. He couldn't stand the suspense. "Did he send you?"

Hesitation. "Could say that."

"What's he after?"

"He's saying put the boy back into lower levels. Use Mitchell's crew, use me and mine. He says he takes your point, no command substitutions, no crew subs until we get this thing operating."

"Why doesn't he make his own offers?"

"Seems us pi-luts talk better to each other, at least where it concerns capabilities. You want the truth—I suggested he lay off the substitutions."

"Wish you could have done that earlier."

Villanueva gave him a look back. "Truth is, I did."

Graff picked up his tray and tracked Villy to the tables in the officers' mess, said, "Do you mind?" and sat down opposite him before he had an answer.

"Be my guest," Villy said.

There had to be looks from other tables, assessing their expressions, the length of their converse. Graff said, urgently, "It's no deal, Villy. I can't. Your colonel's got *no* right to pull him—"

Do him credit, Villy didn't even try to defend the technicality. "Mitchell's crew and mine. No subs. When Dekker passes the medicals and the reaction tests—ask the colonel then. He'll put him back on. Just wait till the boy quiets. For his own sake. For the program's."

"Whose medicals? Yours or ours?"

Villy evidently hadn't considered that point. "I'll talk to the colonel. Maybe we can arrange something. We *can't* afford another set-back. You know it and I know it. We've got to pull this thing together before we lose it."

"I'm willing. But I want the heat *off* Dekker's tail. The kid's had enough."

"No argument here."

A bite of cake. Time to reflect. "Captain Villy, —do you personally *know* what happened in the pod access?"

Villy didn't answer that one straightaway either. "If I knew it was us I wouldn't say. If I didn't know anything, I wouldn't have an answer. What does that tell you?"

"You dance well."

Villy laughed, not with much humor. Tapped the table with his finger. "We got the senatorials and the techs out of here. We've got the program back in our hands. We're *not* going to get another design. That's the word."

First *he'd* heard. Had they won one? "No redesign?"

"That's the whisper going down the line. Heard it from the Old Man. We don't get the AI. Rumor is, we're going for another run in the sims, try to build a stricter no-do into the pilot, not the machine."

Graff leaned back, heart thumping. Took a breath. He couldn't tell whether Villanueva was happy with that situation or not. "So what's your opinion?"

"Go with it. That's what I'm saying. Your best. And ours. We try to set the tape, best we can. Then we fly with it. —You won it, J-G. Enjoy it."

The nickname was traveling. And he wasn't sure he'd won anything: he'd gotten extremely wary of concessions from Tanzer's office. But Villy said:

"We're not happy with the situation—I don't trust your tape-teaching, and that's evidently what they're leaning on, heavier and heavier. I don't *like* the damn system, I still don't think drugging down and walking through any situation is any cure for some kid hitting his personal wall—we can't guarantee your reflexes, or mine, are going to be in every guy that's ever going to run through this program."

Old argument. Graff said softly, delicately, "That's why we're getting them where we're getting them." But he didn't say, And we'll fill out the primary pilot list outside Sol System. You didn't say that. On the captain's orders you didn't. Earth didn't want to know that.

No.

"Listen," Villy said, "you know and I know we're reaching the bottom of the barrel. People don't go out to be miners and Shepherds because they're upstanding citizens. They're ex-rab, they're asocials . . . These two girls you got in—both of them have records . . ."

The rab was some kind of Emigration movement. Pro-space. Anti-Company. It had turned violent, ten years ago, big blow-up, company police had panicked, opened fire on a crowd . . .

"Dekker has a record," he reminded Villy. "He's also popular in the Belt. The Company system out there was crooked. He beat it. You know what the UDC's setting up, making his life difficult? It's certainly not the best PR move the UDC could make. And Kady and Aboujib were part of Dekker's crew out there, such as survived—another pilot and a numbers man, as the Belters call it: good ones, for what the record shows."

Villy made a wry expression, took a sip of coffee. "May be. We'll see—once the boy's back in the sims. Personally, I hope he makes it. He's a son of a bitch, but Chad didn't dislike him."

"Wasn't any animosity on either side, that I know. Dekker got along with Wilhelmsen."

A pause. "J-G, off the record—between you and me: do you really buy it that Chad's crew dumped him in that pod?"

"I don't buy it that Dekker went crazy when he saw the ship blow. Not till the MPs tried to make him leave mission control, get him away from the senators and the VIPs. After that, no, he wasn't highly reasonable. Would you be? So he said something that wasn't politic—people *do* that. Other people don't necessarily try to kill them in cold blood. *No,* I'm not accusing the crew. I find it almost as unlikely as Dekker doing it to himself. You've got to understand, Villy: this kid spent a couple of months in the dark, in a tumble, in the Belt—*bad* accident. He couldn't get the ship back under control. This isn't a guy who's going to suicide *that* way, of all the ways he could pick. And no Belter's going to do that to him. Not the way they did it. So you tell me what happened."

Villy thought about that one, thought about it very seriously, by all he could tell. Then: "Let me tell you about Chad's crew. They're professionals, Rob's got a father he's supporting, guy got caught in a tractor accident, insurance won't pay anything but basics; Kesslan and Deke are real close with Rob—they're not going to risk it, for one thing, even if they were that mad, which I don't think they were. I think they understood Dekker's outburst. Might not have liked it, but understood it. Murder just doesn't add."

Made some sense—granted the father had no means of support; which he personally didn't know—nor understand, inside Earth's maze of cultures and governments, any more than he understood the motives and the angers that bred in the motherwell.

"Won't say," Villy added, "that there aren't some others Dekker could've touched off. But *don't* try to tell me it was Chad's crew."

"I respect your judgment." Mostly, that was the truth. "But what do we do? Dekker doesn't deserve what's happened. His crew didn't deserve what happened. Wilhelmsen—didn't deserve what happened. Let me tell you, in that hearing, I never tried to suggest that Wilhelmsen was primarily at fault, because I never believed it. He was good. It was *exactly* what I said: that substitution killed him and it killed the rest of them."

Villy was listening, at least. Maybe it was something in the coffee. Reason seemed possible of a sudden and he hammered it home. "It's not possible, it's not the way things *work* at light speed, Villy, it can't be, you can't treat people like that. An ops team is a living organism. You don't split it and expect it to perform with anything like efficiency."

Long silence. A sip of coffee. "We've changed the damn specs so often it's a wonder anything mates with anything. The mechanics are overworked, they can't *do* the maintenance in the manufacturers' specs, on the schedule they're being handed, with the staff they've got. That's the *next* disaster waiting to happen and nobody wants to listen to them. We've got a program in trouble."

"We've got a human race in trouble, Villy. I've *been* there, I've *seen* what we're fighting—I don't want that future for the species, I don't happen to think that social designers can remake the model we've got—"

But when you thought about it, just trying to talk to Villy—you began asking yourself—*Haven't we, haven't we, already? Hasn't distance, and hasn't time?*

Like to take you outside the well, like to open your eyes, Captain Villy, and let you feel it when you drop out and in. They'd never get you back here again. . . .

Because the part of Villanueva there was to like, came alive when he was talking about his job. You saw that sometimes in his face.

"You have no attachment," Villanueva said, "no feeling for being *from* this planet."

"I've met what isn't," Graff said.

Interest from Villy. Quirk of a brow. "What are they like?"

"They're them. We're us. Sociable fellows. They don't fight wars."

"So why are you in this one?" Villanueva asked. "Earth didn't ask for this—not our business, a plane clear to hell and gone away from us. Earth Company brought us this thing. The old bottom line. They rooked us into it. Rooked you in too? Or what made you enlist?"

Good question. Complicated question. "Our ship's routes. The ship I was born to. *Polly d'Or.* Didn't ask for trouble, but they tried to cut us out, wanted to regulate where we came and went—retaliation for the Earth Company's visas. Economics on one scale. Our ship on the other."

Villy still looked confused, still didn't get it.

"We'd lose everything. The Fleet's what keeps those routes open. Only thing that does. They can't enforce their embargo."

"Hell and away from us."

"Now. Not forever. Lucky you have us. It'll come here—eventually it'll come here."

"Not everybody believes that."

"Nobody outside this system doubts it. You'll deal with Cyteen—on your terms. Or on theirs. Their technology. You want your personality type changed? They can do it. You want your planet re-engineered? They can do that. They *are* doing it—but we can't get close enough to find out what. We don't get into that system anymore."

"We."

"The merchanters they don't own."

"You ever been down to a planet?"

He shook his head.

"Ever thought about it?"

"No."

"What are you afraid of?"

The question bothered him. He was in a mood right now. Maybe it was Tanzer. Maybe it was because he'd never really thought about it.

"Maybe all those people. Maybe being at the bottom of the well, knowing I can't get myself out of it."

Villanueva frowned, said, finally, "I grew up under blue sky. But if they get me down there I can't get out either. Trying to retire me to the damn HQ. I want this ship to fly. It'll be the last one I work on. I want this one to fly. That's my reason."

"We got a few slots, Captain Villy."

A glance, a laugh. "Old guy like me?"

"Time's slower out there. Remember I'm in my forties."

Villanueva pushed back from the table, leaned back in the chair. "Damn you, you're trying to seduce me."

He felt a tight smile stretch his mouth. "We're the only game there is. You don't want to die in the well. Take you out, Captain Villy. Don't let them send you down. . . ."

"Damn you."

"Think on it."

Villy set his elbows on the table. "About the Dekker business—"

He *was* merchanter—before he was militia, before he was Fleet. And you did try to get it screwed down tight, whenever you talked deal.

"Dekker's back in the program."

"Marginally back in the program. Contingent on the medicals."

"Our medicals."

"Coffee could use a warm-up. Yours?"

Rec hall, the term was, but it was the same messhall, they just pulled the wall back and opened up the game nook next door: dinner started at 1800h, canteen and a bar opened at 2000h if you could keep your eyes open that late, which Dekker didn't think he could, even if it was one of the rare shifts his duty card wouldn't show a No Alcohol Allowed. He was walked out, talked out—"Get the man a sandwich and shove him in bed," was Meg's advice; and he was in no mind to argue with it.

There were a few empty tables left in the middle. They drew their drinks. "Stake out a table," Dekker advised them. "Nobody'll take it if your drinks are sitting."

Ben was in the lead; Ben stopped and hesitated over the choice of seats in front of them. "They got a rule where you sit or what?" Ben asked, with a motion of his cup forward. Dekker looked, numbly twigged to what was so ordinary a sight it didn't even register: all UDC at the one end of the hall, from the serving line; all Fleet at the other.

"This end," he said.

"There some rule?" Ben repeated.

"They just do." Sounded stupid, once you tried to justify it. "Not much in common." But you didn't sit at the other end. Just didn't.

"Plus ça change, rab." Sal gave a shake of her metal-capped braids, set down her drink and pulled back a chair. "You sit, Dek. We'll do. What shall we get? Cheese san? Goulash? Veg-stew?" Fast line or the slow one, was what it amounted to.

"Dunno." He hadn't known how sore he was till he felt a chair under him, and now suddenly everything ached. The walking tour of the facility was a long walk, and bones ached, shoulders ached, head ached—he said, "Chips and a chicken salad—automat, if you don't mind." Do them credit, the cooks kept the stuff as fresh as you could get on the line; or the rapid turnaround did. Something light sounded good, and come to think of it, sleep began to. He wasn't up for a long evening. In any sense. He hoped Meg wouldn't take offense.

They'd done all the check-ins, gotten Meg and Sal scheduled for Aptitudes tomorrow—Ben had outright refused to sign up, declaring they could damned well get his Aptitudes from the UDC, or court-martial him for failure to show for tests: not an outright show of temper with the examiners, no, just a perfectly level insistence they look up his Security clearance, Ben said; turn up his assignment to Stockholm . . . Benjamin Pollard wasn't taking any Fleet Aptitudes until they showed him his old ones or put him in court.

Damned mess, he reflected, sorry for Ben, truly sorry for what had seemed to a pain-hazed mind his only rescue. Ben's talk about court-martial upset him. Ben's situation did. And all the lieutenant would say, when he had in fact gotten a phone call through to him, was: We'll work with that. Let me talk to the examiners, all right?

He ground at his eyes with the heels of his hands, listened to the dull buzz of conversation and rattling plates over the monotone of the vid, and wondered if there was anything unthought of he could do, any pull he personally had left to use, to get Ben back where he belonged—as much as that, if there was anything he could do to send Meg and Sal back home—no matter that Meg really *wanted* her chance at the program. He'd been on an emotional rollercoaster since this morning, he'd been ready to go back to routine and they'd stopped him; they'd told him the lieutenant was fighting that, and he'd been ready to come from the bottom again—til, God, Meg hit him with the business about flying either with him or against him.

He didn't want her killed, he didn't want to lose anybody else—he didn't want to be responsible for any life he cared about. He kept seeing that fireball when he shut his eyes; in the crowd-noise, he kept hearing the static on Cory's channel, in the tumbling and the dark—because Meg's threat had made it imminent, and real.

The hall seemed cold this evening. Somebody had been messing with the temperature controls, or the memories brought back the constant chill of the Belt. He sat there rebreathing his own breath behind his hands, knowing (Ben had a blunt, right way of putting it) knowing he was being a spook, knowing he hadn't any right to shove Meg around, or tell her anything—no more than he'd had any right to take Ben's name in vain or ask for Meg and Sal to come here—he supposed he *must* have asked for Meg, too, since they were here, even if he couldn't figure why the Fleet had gone to that kind of trouble—

Except the captain had wanted him to testify in that hearing Ben had told him about, the one it was too late to testify in, even if he could remember—which he couldn't.

So he'd let the captain down, he'd let the lieutenant down—in what cause he didn't know; he only knew he'd disrupted three lives.

So Meg *hadn't* been happy where she'd been, so the *Hamilton* wouldn't let her right to the top of the pilot's list: you didn't get into that chair just walking aboard, Meg had to have known that, Meg must have known what to expect, coming in on a working crew with its own seniorities and its own way of doing things . . .

So you took a little hell. So you stuck it out. Everybody took hell. He hadn't been all that good at keeping his head down and taking it, but, God, he'd started a police record when he was thirteen: he'd been a stupid kid—and Meg had done a stupid thing or two, run contraband, something like that, that had busted her from the Earth shuttle to the Belt; but he and Meg were both older, now, Meg ought to know better and do better—he'd made it in the Belt; so had Meg—so she had to have damn-all better sense than she was using—

"You all right?" Meg asked. They were back with the sandwiches. He took a drink of the cola, wished he hadn't gotten an iced drink.

"Yeah," he said, chilled. He took his sandwich and unwrapped it while they sat down with their trays. Something on the vid about the hearings. "Missile test," they called it. That was Hellburner's cover story. They talked about hearings adjourning on Sol One. . . . He wished they'd change the channel. Watch the stupid rerun movies. Had to be better. The message net had to be better.

"What else do we need?" Meg was asking. "What about these tests tomorrow? Is there anything we can do to prep ourselves?"

"Nothing but a lot of sleep. Relax. They put you through anything on the carrier? They did, me."

"Didn't see a damned soul on the carrier, except at mealtimes. We played gin most of the way."

"Nice guys," Sal sighed, "and the reg-u-lations said we couldn't touch 'em."

That got a frown out of Ben. And Sal's elbow in Ben's ribs.

Meg said, "So what *do* we do? What's it like?"

"They hook you up to a machine, like medical tests, eye tests, response tests, hand-eye, that sort of thing."

"Hurt?" Sal asked.

"Yeah, some."

"You going to study up?" Sal asked Ben.

"I'm telling you, I'm not taking them. I'm not showing. *Let* them court-martial me, it's exactly what I want."

"Ben, —"

Guys stopped by the table. C-Barracks. Techs. Mason, among them, nudged his shoulder with his tray. "Dek," Mason said. "How you doing?"

"All right," he said, "pretty tired."

"Good to see you. Real good to see you. . . ."

"Pop-u-lar," Ben said when Mason and his guys had moved on. "Just can't figure how. All these people get to know you and they haven't broken your neck."

"Ben," Sal said, defending him. But it didn't sting, couldn't even say why, just—it didn't. Ben didn't ask for help, Ben didn't ask for anything—Cory had been a lot like that. Ben was going to fight his way out of this mess on his own, and that was at least one piece of karma he wouldn't have to worry about.

"Best—" he started to say. And caught a name on the vid, sounded like Dekker. He picked up *Sol Station,* and . . . *lodging a complaint—*

"Ms. Dekker, what specifically are you alleging?"

God. It *was.* She looked—

"Dek?" Meg asked, and turned around to look where he was looking, at the vid, at a woman in a crowd of reporters. Blond hair was faded. Face was lined. She didn't look good, she didn't look at all good . . .

Something about MarsCorp, something about threats, an investigation into phone calls . . . Some organization backing a suit—

Sal said: "What's going on?" and Meg: "Shhh."

He couldn't track on it. Didn't make sense. Something about losing her job, some civil rights organization launching a lawsuit in her name—

"It's his mother," Ben said; he said, "Shut up, dammit, I can't hear—" But he could see the background, see the MarsCorp logo, he knew *that* one—MarsCorp offices on Sol Station, police, reporters, some guy who said he was a lawyer—something about her son—

Picture jumped, tore up. The local station cut in with the channel 2 program information crawl—but he wasn't finished yet, wasn't damned finished yet . . .

"They cut it off!" He shoved the chair around to get up, get to a phone, saw the shadow of the tray and the sense of balance wasn't there. He staggered, hit it, food went everywhere, cup bounced—"Shit!" He was flat off his balance, elbowed the guy trying to hold his feet, guy grabbed at him and he didn't want a fight, he just wanted the phone. "Get out of my way!"

"You son of a bitch!" The guy had his arm. Ben and Meg and Sal grabbed for him, Ben saying something about Let him go, the man's upset; but the guy wasn't letting him go, the guy swung him and he grabbed for a handhold on the UDC uniform, about the time there were a whole lot of other chairs clearing, and Fleet was all around them. A high voice yelled, "You damn fools, stop it—"

Wasn't any stopping it. The UDC guy hit him, and he hit the guy with everything he had, figuring it was the only blow he was going to get in—couldn't hear anything, with guys coming over the tables, guys pushing and shoving and punches flying past his head—he didn't want to be here, he *wanted* the damned phone, *wanted* the truth out of the station, that was all—

Lights were flashing on and off, shouting filled his ears, fist rattled his skull and gray and red shot across his vision as arms came around him and hauled him out of it.

He wasn't breathing real well, couldn't half see: he yelled after Meg and Sal in the melee, couldn't tell who he was hitting when he tried to break free—

"Dekker!" That was the lieutenant. So he was in deeper shit; but more imminently of a sudden, he had his wind cut off as they bent him over a table. Something cold clicked shut around his wrists. That scared him: he'd felt *that* before . . . and it got through to his brain that the guys holding him were the cops, and Graff's voice made him understand that help was here, the fight was over, and the lieutenant wanted him to stand still. He tried to; which meant they got the other wrist, locked the cuff on, and at least pulled him back off the table so he could get a breath . . .

"The guy shoved him." Meg's voice rang out loud and clear. "Wasn't Dek's fault, he was just trying to get up—it was an *emergency,* f' God's sake. This ass wanted to argue right of way!"

Guys started shouting all around, one side calling the other the liars.

"Clear back!" Voice he knew but couldn't place. His nose was running and he sniffed. Couldn't say anything, just tried to breathe past the stuffy nose and the clog in his throat.

"What happened here?" the Voice asked—he blinked the haze mostly clear and saw a lot of MPs, a lot of angry guys standing along the wall with more MPs and soldiers. What Happened Here? drew shouting from all around, Meg and Sal profane and high-pitched in the middle of it, how the guy'd bumped him, how his *mother* was in some kind of trouble on the news . . .

Had to talk about his *mother,* God, he didn't want an audience, didn't want to talk about his mother in front of everybody. He tried to look elsewhere, and meanwhile the lieutenant was saying they'd better move this out of here, *he'd* take him in custody—

Please God. Anywhere, fast.

The other voice said: "I think we'd both better get this moved out of here," and he made out the blurry face now for Captain Villy, with a knot of UDC MPs and a whole lot of trouble. They were holding Meg, and Sal, and Ben, among a dozen mixed others. "Move 'em," Villy said, and there were Fleet Security uniforms among the lot. He started to argue for Meg and Sal and Ben; but: "Dekker," Graff said sharply, and said, "Do it."

He did it. He kept his head down and walked where they wanted him to, he heard Graff at the top of his lungs chewing out the rest of the guys in the messhall and Villanueva doing the same, telling them they were all damned fools, telling them how they were on the same team—

Yeah, he thought. Yeah. Tell 'em that, lieutenant.

Himself, he didn't want to think what was going on back at Sol Station, didn't want to think what he'd just done back there in the messhall; he kept his mouth shut all the way to the MP post, and inside; him, and Ben and a whole crowd of their guys and the UDC arrestees; but when they tried to take Meg and Sal into the back rooms:

"I want *Fleet* Security—laissez, laissez, you sumbitch—ow!"

And Sal screamed how she was going to file complaints for rape and brutality. . . .

The MPs got real anxious then. "Where's Cathy?" one asked, and a guy got on the phone and started trying to scare up a female officer, while Meg argued with them about holding on to him, "Dammit, let him go, he's just out of hospital, for God's sake—man got up and bumped a tray, his mother was on the news—"

God. "Meg, shut *up.* It doesn't matter!"

"That sumbitch shoved you!"

At which the sumbitch with the custard all over him started yelling at Meg, somebody shoved, Sal started yelling, and he couldn't do anything, he was cuffed, same as Ben was, same as the UDC guy was, except they'd made the mistake of not doing that with Meg and Sal.

"Meg," he yelled. *"Meg!"*

They got rough with Meg, they got rough with Sal, he kicked a guy where he saw a prime exposed target and they shoved him up against the wall, grabbed him by the hair and by the collar and shoved him into a chair.

"She didn't *do* anything," he said, but nobody was listening to him. He said, "None of them *did* anything. . . ."

They got Meg and Sal out of the room. Ben and the other guy, too, and left one guy to stand and watch him. He was dizzy, the adrenaline still had his head going around, and his nose dripped a widening circle on his shirt. He tried to sniff it back, breathing alternate with that disgusting sensation; and in his head kept replaying as much as he'd heard on the vid about what was going on with his mother. . . .

A lawsuit, for God's sake—but she wasn't anybody to show up on vid, with lawyers from—what the hell organization was it?

The Civil Liberty Association? He didn't know who they were, but she'd looked like hell, hair stringing around her ears, makeup a mess. He kept seeing her blinking at the strong lights and looking lost and angry. He *knew* that look. She'd worn it the last time she'd bailed him out of juvenile court.

. . . *I don't need any more trouble,* she'd written him. *Stop sending me money. I don't want any more ties to you. I don't want any more letters. . . .*

He had never taken leave back to Sol One: there was a serious question, Legal Affairs had warned him from the beginning of his enlistment, whether once he came onto Sol Station where lawyers could get to him with papers, he could escape a civil process being served . . . or whether the Fleet could prevent him being arrested. The Fleet had put him behind a security wall only because having him on trial wouldn't *sit* well with the Belt, where they mined the steel; and the EC cooperated because letting Cory Salazar's case get to the media would raise questions about a whole long laundry list of things about ASTEX and MarsCorp the Earth Company itself didn't want washed in public. Anything to keep him out of court—

Because damned right there was a connection between his mother and MarsCorp, it was *him,* it was Cory Salazar's *mother,* who'd wanted to have a daughter, had one solo and tried to run that daughter's life and now her afterlife as a personal vendetta against the pusher-jock who'd romanced her collegiate offspring out of her hands.

Hell if that was the way it had been. Cory had dreamed of starships, Cory'd hated her mother's laid-out course—college to a MarsCorp guaranteed success track—so much that Cory couldn't run fast enough or far enough to escape it. Maybe starships had only been a kid's romantic answer—but Cory had come to the Belt because she'd thought she could double and triple her money freerunning—she'd lured *him* along for a pilot, and they'd nearly done it, until Cory ran head-on into the corrupt System her mama had wanted her to sit at the top of—and it killed her.

That was the bloody truth. *That* was the thing Alyce Salazar wouldn't see. He'd wanted to tell her so: he'd imagined how he'd say it if he got the chance, maybe talk to her sanely, maybe just grab her and shake some sense into mama, so she'd do something about the system that had killed Cory.

But Legal Affairs had nixed any such move, said plainly, Don't communicate with her. Don't attempt to communicate with her. And made it an order.

So now Alyce Salazar had communicated with his mother: he knew that was the case, because his mother wasn't dedicated to finding trouble, his mother was the absolute champion of Never get involved . . .

The side door opened. A team of medics came in, with: "Let's have a look at you," so he sat where they wanted and let them look at his eyes with lights, and into his ears, and his mouth. They got the nosebleed stopped, at least, then said they'd better have him down in the clinic for a thorough go-over.

"No," he objected, suddenly panicked. "There's nothing wrong with me."

But they took him anyway.

Aboujib, assault with a weapon, incitement
Basrami, assault

Bissell, assault
Blumgarten, assault, assault on an officer
Brown, assault with a weapon
Cannon, assault, incitement
Dekker, instigation of riot, assault
Franklin, assault with a weapon
Hardesty, assault
Hasseini, assault, verbal abuse of an officer
Jacoby, assault with a weapon
Kady, assault, assault on an officer
Keever, assault, destruction of government property
Mason, assault
Mitchell, assault, assault on an officer
Pauli, assault, incitement
Pollard, assault with a weapon
Rasmussen, verbal abuse; (hospital)
Schwartz, assault
Simmons, assault
Vasquez, assault; (hospital)
Zeeman, aggravated assault

Graff read the list, handed it to Petrie, the junior out of Legal Affairs. "I want interviews, any way you can get them. Record everything. I want them now, I want any releases you can get, I want them an hour ago. And I want condition, instigator and perpetrator on our hospital cases."

"Yessir." Petrie put the list in his case. The temper must be showing. Petrie didn't stop for questions of his own. The door shut.

Demas, resting against the counter, said, "Doesn't seem there was anything premeditated: the channel 3 news boss recognized a correspondence of names on the Sol One news feed, suddenly realized it was sensitive, and jerked the report off the air—*bad* decision. Dekker happened to be in the messhall, the vid happened to be channel 3. Charlie Tyson happened to be behind him with a tray; Dekker jumped up—bang into the tray. Tyson blew up, Dekker blew, the whole messhall blew."

"I want a tape of that news broadcast, I want to know what's going on with Dekker's mother, I want to know what she's involved in."

"You want it in capsule now?" Demas asked. "I've got the essentials."

"Go."

"Dekker's mother got fired two days ago. She was a maintenance worker—electrician—for SolCorp. The maintenance office claimed incompetence—the record is apparently inaccessible—she claimed she was a victim of MarsCorp pressure inside the EC, claimed Salazar's agents had been harassing her on the phone. She showed up in front of the MarsCorp office with lawyers and reporters, MarsCorp called Security, and a MarsCorp spokesman went on camera to charge Ms. Dekker with sabotage and threatening phone calls—apparently Ms. Dekker had been doing some work inside the MarsCorp sector and got some phone numbers, by what Ms. Salazar charges. Ms. Dekker claims they've been harassing her—calls on her off watch, that kind of thing. Ms. Dekker's got some civil rights organization on her side, they're charging Ms. Salazar used pressure to get Ms. Dekker's job on personal grounds. End report."

"Harassing phone calls. Is Ms. Salazar *on* One?"

"She was eight days ago, at the time Ms. Dekker claims she got two of the calls. She's in London at the moment, Ms. Dekker claims she asked for a trace on the calls. The station office claims there was no such request and says their records *show* no calls to Ms. Dekker's residence." Demas folded his arms. "Ask how sophisticated Ms. Salazar's employees might be."

"I take it there are ways to evade those records."

"Abundant methods—limited only by the sophistication of the operator and the equipment. This is a woman who maintains apartments in *two* space stations and a couple of world capitals, on two separate planets. I would not match a station electrician against her technical resources."

"We've been sleeping through this one. I need a structural chart of MarsCorp and the EC. With names and kinships." Damn, the Security chief was—where else?—with the captain. "Can we get that through our own channels?"

"We can try. It's going to be a maze. Kinships, I'm not sure are going to be systematized anywhere. They're illegal, remember—where it regards government contracts. Personal friendships are illegal."

"Are anomosities?"

A humorless laugh. "Unfortunately there's no such rule. Among those cards on your desk is the Alyce Salazar file such as we have it—with Saito's compliments. Some of the information may be in there. It's going to take Legal Affairs to—"

"—unravel the MarsCorp connections?"

Demas nodded. "If they can."

"Meanwhile there's the next shuttle to One. I want somebody on it. I want somebody to go personally to the captain's office—if there still is an office—and *get* a report to him we're sure isn't intercepted. And I want some message back here that isn't wearing a UDC uniform or Belter chain and claiming they don't know a thing. I should have done it when Pollard came in here."

Demas looked thoughtful. "I'll look up the schedule."

"Due in at 0900h on the 27th, out at 2030h the 29th, we've got a service hold for scheduled maintenance. They're claiming it's booked full outbound. There's always some contractor holding seats. If we've got any pull—get one."

He'd gotten used to being handled like a piece of meat. He'd gotten used to cameras and doctors and cops. They made a vid record of the new skin on his shoulder and the finger-marks on his arm. They asked him who'd hit him, he just shook his head, didn't even have to come out of his haze to talk to them. They took samples of his hair, his skin, his blood, and whatever fluid they could wring out of his body; "Pulse rate just won't go down," one of them said. "That's on his hospital records."

"What do you *expect*?" he asked, only time he'd opened his mouth except for a tongue depressor, and one of them said he should calm down.

"Yeah," he said. His stomach was upset from the poking around they were doing. He tried to go on timing out, just go away and blind himself with the lights and not to let his heart flutter, the way it felt it was doing. Couldn't think about anything if you wanted to fake out the meds. Think of—

—Sol One. His mother's apartment. But that was no good. His mother was in trouble, thanks to him . . .

—*Way Out.* But that ship was dead. Like Cory.

Think of stupid stuff. Name the moons of Saturn. Jupiter had used to work, but he'd learned that real estate too intimately.

Docking fire sequence for a miner ship. Range and rate of closing.

Finally one said, "Name's Parton. Fleet Medical. How are you doing, Lt. Dekker?"

Fleet. He said, "The lieutenant agree with this?"

"The lieutenant doesn't agree with fighting."

So he was in trouble. With everybody. He slid a glance over to the wall, where he didn't have to look at Parton or get in an argument, and wondered distractedly if he could get a word out of the news channel if he could just get permission to make a phone call. . . .

But the medic, Parton, was talking with the other medics—said, of the blood pressure, "Yeah, he does that. Doesn't like hospitals. Doesn't like UDC medics, if you want the plain truth. . . ."

Not real fond of any meds right now, —sir. Can I get up?

But he didn't ask that, he didn't think it was smart to ask, at this point. He got an elbow under him—they had him lying on a table freezing his ass off, and he only wanted to relieve the ache in his back. But a hand landed on his shoulder: it had a UDC uniform cuff. MP. He lay back and stared at the lights and froze in silence until the Fleet medic came back and stood over him.

"Lieutenant's orders: you go where you're told to go, you don't argue, you don't say anything about the incident to anybody but our legal staff, you understand?"

He said, burning with embarrassment, "Something about my mother on the news, can anybody for God's sake find out what happened to my mother?"

"Lieutenant's aware of that. He's making inquiries."

"What about the other guys? Pollard and Kady and Aboujib—"

"They're fine."

"They arrest them too?"

"Riot and assault." Parton looked across him, over his head. "Lieutenant wants him *with* his unit. The three he named."

"Kady and Aboujib are women."

"They're his unit, sergeant."

Long silence. Then: "I'll have to ask the major."

Age-old answer. Dekker shut his eyes. Figured they'd be a while asking and getting no. "It's protecting me from Kady you better worry about," he told them. Bad joke. Nobody was laughing. He wasn't amused either. Meg had a record of some kind. Meg had just gotten it cleared, got a chance to fly again. Ben had his assignment in Stockholm. . . .

His mother used to say, *You damned kid, everything you touch you break—*

You messed up my whole life, you self-centered little brat—why can't you do right, why can't you once in your life do something right, *you damned screw-up?*

Long time he lay there freezing, with a knot in his gut, replaying that newscast for the information he could get out of it, telling himself they couldn't prove anything on his mother, she'd at least got some kind of lawyer, so she wasn't without help—

He'd got a little money ahead, he'd saved it out of his pay, he wasn't spending anything. He'd tried to give it to her before, for what he'd cost her, but she hadn't wanted it. Maybe he could get Ben to send it to her. Maybe she'd take it from Ben—she was going to need funds fast, if she wasn't drawing pay, she never got that far ahead of the bills, and even if she had free legal help, it wouldn't pay for food . . .

"Word is, he can't go in a cell with the women," the MP said. "Regulations. We can put him with Pollard. . . ."

He didn't argue. Parton only said he'd report that refusal to the lieutenant.

Parton left. The UDC medics got him up. The MPs locked a bracelet on his wrist that they said he wasn't to mess with, and took him out and down the hall to the cells.

Guys from his barracks yelled out, along the way, "Hey, Dek!" and he looked numbly to the side. Mason and Chiv were there. Pauli. Hardesty. And across the aisle—a guy he didn't know, familiar face, who looked murder at him. So he didn't look. He walked where they wanted him, they took the cuffs off when he'd gotten to Ben's cell and they opened the door and put him in.

Ben gave him a sullen look. He didn't figure Ben wanted to start a fight in front of the MPs. So he got over in the corner, there being just a double bunk and a toilet, and Ben sitting on the bunk: he sank down on the floor with his back to the corner, feeling the bruises and feeling the silence from the bunk.

MPs stood there a moment more looking at him. He had the fanciful notion that after they left Ben was going to get up and come over and kill him. But he didn't truly think so. Hit him—yeah. He expected that. He even wanted it. Anything to stop him thinking about the mess he'd made.

The MPs went away.

Ben said, "The place is probably bugged."

Which meant Ben wouldn't kill him—not in front of any cameras. He sat there with his knees drawn up to his chest so tight he couldn't move and felt numb.

"You going to sit there?"

He didn't know what else to do. Didn't care about climbing up to the top bunk. He was comfortable enough where he was—comfortable as he was going to get.

"You sure got a way of finding it, you know that?"

"Yeah," he said. It cost to say, "Sorry, Ben," but he did it, past the knot in his throat. He hadn't said it often enough, maybe, over the years, and a lot of the people he should have said it to—it was too late to tell.

Ben didn't say anything for a while. Finally: "You break anything?"

"No." He wasn't sure about the ribs, and the lately-broken arm and the shoulder ached like hell, but the meds hadn't taped anything, or sent him back to hospital, so probably not. He just generally hurt.

"Son of a bitch," Ben muttered. Ben might hit him after all. Ben's chances of getting out of here and back to his security clearance had sunk, maybe, as low as they could go. Ben had nothing to lose.

Ben muttered, "Get out of the damn corner. You look like hell."

He made a tentative move of his legs. But he was wedged in. Couldn't do it without more effort than he wanted to spend. So he shook his head, just wanted to be left in peace awhile. Didn't want an argument . . . or he just wanted this one to play itself out and come to some distracting conclusion.

"Damn." Ben got up, came over and grabbed him up by one wrist and the other, turned him back to the bunk and shoved him onto it.

Bang went his head against the wall. He just rested where he'd hit and stared at Ben, Ben with this thoughtful expression he couldn't figure out. Mad, he expected. But he didn't want to deal with complexities or have Ben trying to con him. And Ben's frown didn't look as angry as Ben should. "You sick? You want the meds?"

"I've had 'em." He curled into the corner where the bunk met the wall, tucked up and tried to project a thorough Leave me alone.

Ben sat down, put a hand on his ankle and shook him. "You all right?"

"Yeah." He jerked his leg, Ben moved his hand, and he sat there with his arms across his gut, because he felt the pieces coming apart, the one reliable guy he knew was after him in a way that didn't mean Ben had just gone friendly—oh, no, Ben had just changed the rules; Ben was after something, maybe his neck, maybe just after using him to get what he wanted: Belters were like that, that were born there. You could partner with them. You could deal with them. But you didn't ever take for granted they thought the way you did.

"Your mama's in some kind of trouble, is she?"

"Her trouble."

Ben said, "Sounds to me like Salazar."

They'd gotten altogether too friendly one watch, on the ship, on the trip out from the Belt. Their lives had been changing. Late one night he'd told Ben a lot of things he wished now he hadn't. Early as the next wakeup, he'd known it was a mistake. "Leave it the hell alone, Ben. It's not your business."

"Not my business. You *are* a son of a bitch, you know that, Dekker?"

"Yeah," he said. "I've been told."

"Listen, Dekker, —"

"I said let it ride!"

"What *else* does your mama have to do with MarsCorp?"

"She fixes the damn circuits, all over Sol One. She's an electrician—they don't ask her politics or her religion before they send her into an office—maybe she screwed up a job—"

"MarsCorp? Come *on,* Dekker."

"MarsCorp, the Vatican for all I know, I don't know what she's into, I don't know what's going on, they cut the damn news off, weren't you listening?"

"Dekker, —I want you to say nice things to the cops, I want you to use your head, I want you to say I'm sorry to the nice UDC guys and yessir to the colonel and don't the hell get us in any more heat, you understand me?"

"Yeah," he said. Simple demands, he could cope with. He got his back into the corner and his knees tucked up out of Ben's convenient reach. Didn't like guys touching him. He was sure Ben didn't mean it any way but Pay Attention, but he didn't like it. "It's my fault. The whole damn thing's my fault, I got that loud and clear, all right? I'm sorry you got involved."

Ben hit his foot. Another Pay Attention. "Dek-boy, you are in deep shit here, have you noticed that? Stop thinking about your mama, *you* have got enough shit to occupy your time. I do not want you to screw up in front of the lieutenant, I do not want you to mouth off to the MPs, I do not want you to get us in deeper than we are. You copy that? Now, for all those watching, we are going to agree there is involved in this a Name that they won't want in court, no more than they did when they the hell raked you into the Service and gave *me* my slot at TI. That Name is, let us agree, Salazar. So we are not going to court-martial, we are not going to see any outside lawyers, we are behind the thickest fuckin' security wall in the inner system, and I think it would be a most severely good idea not to antagonize the Fleet at this point, since the UDC is for some whimsical reason not all that happy with you. Do you follow?"

Jaw wasn't working all that well. He nodded. He couldn't stop thinking about his mother. He couldn't help thinking how a lot of people would be alive if he'd never existed and how people connected to him might have better lives now if he was dead and Salazar didn't have anybody to go after.

Ben said it right—Salazar couldn't get a message to him through ordinary channels, so she sent one on the news. I'm here. I'm still waiting. I'll get what you care about until I can get you. . . .

He didn't track on everything Ben said—but that, *that,* he understood. He wanted to get to a phone. He *wanted* permission from someone to get a call out.

Which was exactly what Salazar wanted. So he couldn't do that. *Couldn't,* dammit. Not without thinking more clearly than he was right now. . . .

Let her have him, maybe, do something so the Fleet would throw him out and all the Belter and Shepherd types who'd protected him wouldn't want to, wouldn't give a damn if he went to trial. . . .

Then, if they ever let him testify, he could tell mama Salazar to her face she'd killed her own kid. Only revenge Cory would ever have—unless you counted a few execs out of jobs. But they'd find others. The Company always found a place for the fools. Ben said so. And he believed it. They just promoted them sideways, somewhere they hadn't a rep—yet. The Company took care of its own.

"Severe mess," Sal said with a shake of her braids. Meg concurred with that.

"Sloppy place," she said, looking around at a scarred, dirty cell. "The tank over at One is ever so nicer." She felt a draft from a torn coat sleeve, and leaned her back against the wall, one leg tucked. They weren't in prison coveralls. The Es-tab-lish-ment was still trying to figure what to do with them, she supposed, on grounds of her previous experience with such places. "D' you s'pose the lieutenant has got a plan, or what-all?"

"I sincerely do hope," Sal said. Sal had an eye trying to swell shut. A cut lip. Sal did not look happy with her situation. Sal looked, in fact, intensely scared, now the adrenaline rush was gone and they were sitting in a cell with a riot charge over their heads.

"It was a set-up," Meg said. "Don't you smell set-up? I never saw a room blow so fast. Just a skosh peculiar, they let Dek out and they run him back in, and *us* so seriously important and all? *We're* the ones they shagged a carrier to get here. Are they going to forget us? Nyet. Non."

Sal was still frowning. "Amnesia's been known. Strikes people in office, most often. I hear they got no vaccine."

"Faith, Aboujib. *Believe* in justice."

Sal snorted. Almost laughed.

"I believe, Kady, I *believe* we are in un beau de fuck-up here. . . ."

Truth was, she was scared too. But scared didn't profit you anything when it came to judges and courts, and she'd said it to Sal—the Fleet hadn't gone to all this trouble to invite them to a messhall brawl.

"I believe in they hauled our asses a long, long way to haul Dek in out of the dark. *That* is a truly remarkable al-truism, Aboujib."

"Des bugs."

"Bien certain they would. Bien certain someone's playing games. Dekker's mama lost her job. Does this rate news? Does this rate the peace movement lawyers giving interviews in front of the MarsCorp logo? Nyet. But there it was."

"You think somebody made it up? Faked it?"

"Nyet. *Peace* movement, Aboujib. *Peace* movement is involved. Does not the antenna go up? Does not an old rab ask herself why and what if?"

There was a spark of interest in Sal's dark eye. The one that showed. Sal didn't say a thing, but: "Rab is. The Corp is. Amen."

"That chelovek in the suit, that lawyer? That's a plastic. You mark."

"Why's he with Dekker's mama?"

Scary to think on. Truly scary. Sal looked at her, Sal as Belter as they came, and Shepherd; and how did you say the motherwell's mind in Sal's terms?

"Think of helldeck. Think of all those preachers, them that want to save your soul. And they each got a different way."

Another snort. "Crazies."

"On Earth they got their right. That's why they got it still on helldeck. On Earth you got a right to say and do. So they say and do. On Earth you can say a straight-line rock won't hit you. And maybe it won't. It might be too heavy. Might fall. You understand?"

A straight-line rock was one thing to a Belter. Fall was a contradiction in terms. You didn't have rocks on station, where things *fell.* And *fall* didn't go straight-line. Thoughts and puzzlement chased through Sal's expression, and rated a frown.

"What I said. Crazy."

"A rock might fall on its own before it hit you. You got to know its size to know."

"Why'd it move?"

"Because some crazy threw it at you. Bare-handed. But it might fall first."

"So. On station, natürlich."

"In the motherwell, *everything*'s like that. Gravity and friction are always in the numbers. Not a lot of blue-skyers can figure those numbers. Things just happen because they happen and sometimes they don't happen and you don't know why, so you were lucky or you weren't. You don't know. Very few can comp it. Ask a peacer what the answer is. He'll tell you it's not war. Ask him how you'll get no war. He'll say don't make one. Half the time it works. You got, however, to convert the other side to this idea. Ask a peacer how to make peace. He'll say, Don't fight. Half the time that works too."

"Guy was going to beat hell out of Dek."

"Yeah, well, this rab did have such a thought. And I sincerely wasn't going to sit and watch it."

"So why're the peacers paying for a lawyer for Dekker's mama?"

"Peace on Earth's like that rock. You got to calc things you don't, in space. You got to ask, primarily, *whose* peace, whose way, how long? But Earthers don't, generally. Blue-sky's used to not calcing all the factors."

"Trez sloppy," Sal said.

"The Corps don't *like* you to calc all the numbers. Neither do the helldeck preachers. Listen all you like, you sojer-boys with the bugs. You sleep down with the Corp, you get up with fleas. How good's *your* addition?"

"There is no excuse," Tanzer said, "there is *no* mitigating circumstance except your personal decision to release Dekker from hospital without psychiatric evaluation, without appropriate procedures. The man's a fuse, lieutenant. *You* knew that. Or don't you read your personnel reports?"

Graff didn't ask how Tanzer had. He said, patiently, standing in front of Tanzer's desk: "Dekker didn't do anything. He got up in a hurry and bumped a man he didn't even know. . . ."

"This is a finger you want on the trigger of the most sophisticated weapons system ever devised? Can't navigate from a chair in the messhall? Is that his problem?"

"Your news service released a story without a next-of notice. Was that deliberate?"

"Is it a death situation? I think not. Your boy can't tolerate a little stress? What in *hell* is he doing in this program? He blows and your whole side of the messhall comes out of the seats—"

"Your man did the grabbing and the shoving. Don't try that one. It was simultaneous. There are too many witnesses."

"Your *witnesses* were all in the middle of it. Your latest recruits were instigators. Is that what you call leadership? Is that what you call a co-operative relationship? Damned right, I don't put all the blame on Dekker, *I* don't blame the boy you dragged out of hospital and put into a high voltage situation, *I* blame the officer who made that boy a cause, which is damned well what you've done with your attitude and, for all I know, your direct statements to your command. You piled the pressure on that boy, you put those women in the middle of it, you set him up to draw fire—he was guaranteed to blow the first time he got *any* load more than he had. So his *mama* lost her job, damned right his mama lost her job—she was calling MarsCorp board members at two in the morning, *threatening* phone calls, you read me? She's a space-case—like mother, like son, if you want my opinion. It's congenital!"

"You have no basis for any such conclusion."

"Haven't I? I'm telling you right now, right here, he's never getting back in a cockpit and you aren't giving any more orders in a UDC premise, not in the messhall, not the offices, not the classrooms, not the corridors or the hospital. Try *that* one, lieutenant. Take *that* one to your captain and see what he has to say."

He had *no* instructions how to play that one. He wasn't a lawyer. He didn't know whether Tanzer could legally do that. He wasn't in charge of policy. He didn't know whether he should use Fleet Security to guarantee access. It was down to that. The phone rang—thank God for two extra seconds to think while Tanzer jabbed a button and growled an irritable, "I'm not to be disturbed."

"Sir," the secretary said, on intercom, *"your line."*

Unusual. Tanzer picked up the phone to listen in private and his expression smoothed out and went completely grim.

"When?" Tanzer asked; and: "Any other information?" And, "Find out, dammit, however you have to."

After which Tanzer hung up, glowered at him and said, "Get yourself and your crew up onto the carrier. Right now."

"Incoming?" A strike at Sol? Union missiles?

Tanzer's fist slammed the desk. "Get your ass out of this office, lieutenant, and get it the hell up to the carrier where you're *supposed* to be competent!"

Incoming was no time to stand arguing, and arguing with Tanzer was no way to get information through the carrier's systems; but if it was Union action there was no way he was going to make the carrier's deck before criticality. "Phone," he said, and reached for the one on the desk. The colonel made to stop him, and he held on to it with: "Dammit, they need a go-order. —Carrier-com," he told Tanzer's secretary. "Fast," —after which the secretary muttered something and he heard the lighter, fainter sound of Fleet relays. "This is Graff," he said the instant he had a click-in. "Status."

"J-G," Saito's voice came back faintly. *"You're on a UDC line."*

"Yes." Short and fast. "Colonel's office." It *wasn't* an incoming—he knew that in the first heartbeat of Saito's remark about his whereabouts and he knew in that same second that UDC was a codeword on its own. Saito said, calmly: *"Stand by,"* and the phone popped and went to com-noise.

"This is FleetCom Command. ECS4 ETA at Sol Two 2 hours 3 minutes. Command of Sol Two facilities has passed to Fleet Command. UDC personnel are being—"

The message went offline. Went on again. *Somebody* in the outer office had a nervous finger.

"—with Fleet personnel. This message will repeat on demand. Key FleetCom 48. Endit."

He looked at Tanzer, who *didn't* know. Who was worried, clearly. And mad. Tanzer's secretary said, in his ear: *"Lt. Graff, this is Lt. Andrews. The colonel has an urgent message. Would you turn over the phone?"*

"For you," he said, and passed the handset to Tanzer. Stood there watching Tanzer's face go from red to white.

Number *4* carrier was incoming from Sol One, *not* at cap, but as much as they meant anyone's optics to see at this stage. The captain?

"Get a confirm on that," Tanzer said to whoever was on the line.

Tanzer wasn't looking at him. He could ease things or complicate matters—here in this office. He could end up with what had happened in the messhall played out on dockside—at gunpoint, if he and Tanzer both wanted to be fools. He put on his blankest, most proper expression—was very quiet when Tanzer finally hung up and looked at him.

"I trust our messages were similar," he said, with—he hoped—not a flicker of offense. "May I suggest, sir, we present this to personnel in a quiet, positive manner. I'd suggest a joint communiqué."

Tanzer didn't say anything for a moment. Then, with a palpable effort: "I'd suggest we keep this quiet until we can sort it out."

"Colonel, I appreciate the difficulties involved. FleetCom is handling approach and docking. In the meanwhile my command has its own set of procedures, primarily involving dock access at this point. I'd suggest we move your security into a secondary position and move ours into supervision of debarcation facilities."

"I've no authorization to do that. You'll *wait,* you'll bloody wait!"

"I'll wait," he said, trying to add up in his head what all the Alpha and Beta Points on this station were, and what he could do to secure records without creating an incident he was virtually certain Fleet Command didn't want. "On the other hand, that carrier will dock in a little less than two hours, by which time I have to have a secure perimeter, colonel, that's mandatory under our procedures."

They'd done it at Mariner, they'd done it at Pell, and he had no doubt, now, that it was his mandate to secure that area here, as quietly and peacefully as possible. It was only now sinking in that a transfer of command *had* happened, but how it had happened, he had no idea. The thought even occurred to him that it might be a lie—a final, extravagant lie—that maybe things had gone critical—on Earth or at the front, and they were pulling what they had, while they had it. That was what the whisper had been, always, that there might not *be* the time they needed to build the riderships or the full number of carriers; and then they could take their choice—let the Fleet die, let Earth fall, and lose themselves in space or in the motherwell, anonymous and helpless; or run with what they had, and gather the marines and the trainees they knew would be targets . . .

And run and spend their lives running—

Danger-sense had cut in, for whatever reason: his brain was suddenly doing what it did when hyperfocus was coming up, no reason, except Saito's evasion yesterday, and the colonel's being caught completely by surprise. If negotiations had been underway—it was a shock to Tanzer, or Tanzer acted in a way that didn't make sense.

So he took a quiet leave, out through the anxious secretary's office—he stopped to say, "Andrews, for your own sake, *don't* spread anything you may have heard,"—and saw nervousness pass to estimation and fear.

Into the corridors, then—feeling the air currents, sampling the ambient. No panic in the clericals, nothing evident. The carrier had left Sol, presumably with notice to insystem defenses—then word had flashed via FleetCom, and presumably a UDC message from some quarter had chased that transmission to the colonel. Maybe Saito and Demas hadn't known what was about to happen.

Or maybe they had. Maybe they always had.

He walked quietly to his office, he checked in on FleetCom and asked Saito again: "Snowball, this is 7-All, status."

"7-All, that's LongJohn, we've got a Code Six."

Stand down but stand by. And LongJohn wasn't any of their crew.

LongJohn was Jean-Baptiste Baudree, *Carina.* Mazian's Com Two. "That's a copy," he said; thinking: *Damn.* What's *he* doing here? It's not the captain, then. What aren't they saying? "Status," he insisted; and got the information he next most wanted:

"7-All, that's Jack."

Edmund Porey?

Lieutenant Edmund Porey?

He hung up and, with a pang of real regret, stopped trusting Saito and Demas.

CHAPTER 9

Lt. J-G Jurgen Albrecht Graff
SB/Admin
2152h JUN24/23; FGO-5-9
Command of Sol B has been transferred to FleetOps. You are hereby ordered to render all appropriate assistance, including securing of files and records, under direction of Comdr. Edmund Parey. . . .

Commander. The hell!

And Jean-Baptiste? *Mazian's* second-senior?

Thoughts ran down very scattered tracks since that message. Thoughts needed to, on an operational level: Tanzer was only marginally cooperative, communicating through his secretary, BaseCom was a steady stream of query and scant reply from the UDC at Sol One—one assumed: a great deal of it was going in code one assumed FleetCom couldn't breach.

Tanzer had been blindsided, that seemed evident. And maybe FleetOps had had to keep the junior officer in the far dark to carry it off, but it was evident, at least as best he could put matters together, that the business with the committee and the general had been a flanking action—try to stir up some chaff, maybe throw a rock into the Sol One hearings. Who knew?

Certainly not the junior lieutenant. Possibly the Number Ones had. Certainly the captain had—and kept silent in spite of his repeated queries, which Saito of *course* had sent, the way he'd ordered Saito to do . . .

Damn and damn.

The deception shook him. You relied on a crew, you dumped all your personal chaff and trusted, that was what it came down to. You assumed, in throwing open everything you had, that you had some kind of reciprocity. Never mind the gray hair he didn't have. The *Fleet* could decide he was expendable. The *Fleet* could use him any way it had to. But they put you in charge, you made what you thought were rational decisions and if the people who were supposed to be carrying out your orders weren't doing that, you trusted they'd at least trust you enough to tell you—before you assumed you had a power you didn't, and put yourself and them into a no-win.

You did the best you could in a touchy situation and they promoted *Edmund Porey* two ranks in the last year?

God, what did the man do? The Captains had to know Porey. *Had* to. Were they blind?

But Nav Two on *Carina* had a good head for Strategic Operations—Porey was back and forth to the Belt, Porey was ferry-captain on the carriers as they moved in for finish, which made him currently one of the most experienced with the ships, and Porey was probably working tight-in with Outsystem and Insystem Surveillance: that had to be where he got the merits. Clever man. *Clever* man, Edmund Porey was, and, clearly now, command-track, which he himself would never be: hyperfocus and macrofocus weren't the same thing—not by a system diameter they weren't.

So Porey had the stuff. Clear now how desperately they needed a mind of Porey's essential qualities.

Clear now whose command he just might end up serving Helm for. The captain hadn't trusted him. So they brought Porey in over his head?

He didn't want to think about that. Instead, he arranged his priorities and issued his orders, *trusting* they were getting through. It gave him the same surreal feeling he'd had writing his will, for the handful of personal possessions he did own—that past the time those instructions were carried out, his personal existence was going to be very much different.

He had ordered the records secured. That first. There were a lot of extremely upset UDC security personnel on the loose. There had very nearly been an armed stand-off. The UDC ordered erasure on certain files, he was quite certain. He was equally certain he had been too late to prevent that, during the time of the stand-off and queries flying back and forth between his office and Tanzer's—he was sure UDC security had done exactly what they should have done, and that he had not been able to prevent it (although outside of going hand to hand with UDC personnel and cutting through a lock he didn't know what he could have done) would be written down for a failure on his part.

He had not let them throw the database into confusion. That was a plus. He had not lost the library tapes. That also.

He had ordered personnel in detention transferred; he had taken hospital and testing records under Fleet protection. He might order the release of detainees, but the disposition of those cases as a policy issue was not within his administrative discretion. He did not *like* the new commander. He, however, did not personally approve of creating administrative messes, which, counting his administrative style and Porey's, might be the worse for the difference. He advised the UDC officers that all facilities *were* passing under Fleet administrative command, and personally phoned the UDC provost marshal and UDC Legal Affairs to be certain that all legal proceedings were frozen exactly where they were: no sense letting anything pass into record that need not.

Demas called, to say that the carrier was braking, directly after ceasing acceleration. Demas said that there was a contingent of marines aboard needing gravitied accommodations.

"I copy that. What's the head count?"

"Two thousand."

That was a carrier's full troop complement. They wanted miracles. He called Tanzer, he listened to the shouting, he calmly requested invention, and ordered an emergency galley set up in an idle SolCorp module, ordered its power-up, ordered an Intellitron communications center linked in as FleetCom relay for the marine officers, ordered the Fleet gym given over to troop exercise, the Fleet exercise schedule combined with the UDC, on alternate days; located every class-4 storage can in Sol-2, shifted all class-4 storage to low-g and ordered station ops to consolidate the remainder and clear section D-2 for set-up as habitation. Sol-2 civil Ops bitched and moaned about access-critical supplies.

"I assure you," he said coldly and courteously, "I appreciate the difficulty. But human beings have priority over galley supplies . . . That is a problem. I suggest than you move your dispenser equipment to 3-deck to handle it. There *are* bottles and carts available . . . —Then get them from maintenance, or we'll order them. I'm sure you can solve that. . . ."

Meanwhile, the thin nervous voice of approach control tracked the carrier's braking, in a tone that said approach control wasn't used to these velocities. Inner system wasn't a place merchanters ever moved at anything like that *v.* Merchanters drifted into the mothersystem at a sedate, mind-numbing leisure, sir, while bored techs and mechanics did whatever repair they'd had on backlist—days and days of it, because the mothersystem with all its traffic had regulations, and a starship, which necessarily violated standard lanes, made mothersystem lawyers very anxious. The mothersystem was a dirty system. The mothersystem had a lot of critical real estate, the mothersystem had never accurately figured the astronomical chances of collision, and the Earth Company had made astronomically irritating regulations. Which they now saw Exceptioned. That was the word for it. Exceptioned, for military ships under courier or combat conditions.

The ECS4 wasn't even at hard stretch. But station was anxious. If braking utterly failed (astronomically unlikely) that carrier would pass, probably, fifty meters in the clear. But tell them that in the corridors, where the rumor was, Security informed him, that the carrier was aimed straight at them.

Porey, the bastard, might shave that to 25 meters, only because he hated Earth system. But Porey never said that in outside hearing.

Porey had other traits. But leave those aside. Porey was a strategist and a good one, and that, apparently, was the priority here. Not whether Edmund Porey gave a *damn* about the command he'd been given. Not whether he had any business commanding here, over these particular mindsets.

The Shepherds were *his* crews, dammit, down to the last two women the captain or someone had finagled in here.

Fingers hesitated over a keypad.

The captain. Or someone. *Anyone* in Sol system must have known more than he had. What in *hell* was going on?

He had a call from Mitch Mitchell on the wait list. He returned it only to ask, "Where are you?"

"Sir?" Mitch asked. *"What's going on? What's—"*

He said, "Where are you?"

Mitch said, *"Your office in two minutes."*

"You don't read, Mitch. Where?"

"Coffee machine in one."

Not that long to work a carrier into dock, not the way they'd learned it in the Beyond, especially when it was a tube link and a straight grapple to a mast. The carrier used its own docking crew—marines, who simply moved the regular staff aside. More and more of them. A familiar face or two: Graff recognized them, if he couldn't place them. *Carina* dockers. Mazian's own crew. A lot of these must be.

Lynch, the sergeant-major identified himself, close-clipped, gray-haired, with no ship patch on his khaki and gray uniform, but Graff recalled the face. He returned the salute, took the report and signed it for transmission of station Secure condition.

More of them were coming off the lift. "Sgt.-major," he said, with a misgiving nod in that direction. "We've had a delicate situation. Kindly don't antagonize the UDC personnel. We've got a cooperation going that should make your job easier."

"The commander said take the posts. We take 'em, sir."

He frowned at the sergeant-major. Darkly. Kept his hands locked behind him, so the white knuckles didn't show. "You also have to live here, Sgt.-major. Possibly for a long while. *Kindly* don't disturb the transition we have in progress. That also is an order."

A colder face. A moment of silence. Estimation, maybe. "Yes, sir," Lynch said. *Carina* man for certain. Dangerous man. Close to Mazian. Lynch moved off, shouted orders to a corporal.

Steps rang in unison. Breath steamed in the air in front of the lift. Marines were headed for the communications offices, the administrative offices, the lifesupport facilities, simultaneously.

The lift let out again. Armored Security and a scowling close-clipped black man in a blue dress jacket.

Graff stood his ground and made his own bet whether Porey would salute or put out a hand.

It was the hand. Graff took it and said, "Commander."

"Lieutenant. Good to see you." He might have been remarking on the ambient temperature. "I take it the report is in our banks."

"It should be. I take it you heard about the interservice incident. We have personnel in the brig . . ."

"The colonel's office," Porey said, shortly, and motioned him curtly to come along.

Quiet in the cell block, deathly quiet for a while. Then someone yelled: "Hey, Pauli."

"Yeah?"

"You know that five you owe me?"

"Yeah?"

"Cancel it. You got that sumbitch."

"That sumbitch is in here!" another voice yelled. "That sumbitch is going to whip you good, Basrami!"

"Yeah, you got a big chance of doing that, Charlie-boy. How was dessert?"

"Your guy can't navigate an aisle! What's he good for, him and his fe-male pi-luts? Couple of Belter whores, what I hear—"

Dekker stood at the bars, white-knuckled, Ben could see it from where he sat. From down the aisle Meg's high, clear voice. "You a pi-lut, cher, or a mouth?"

"You come in here to save Dekker's ass? Bed's what you're for, honey. It's where you better stay."

Ben winced. Meg's voice:

"Fuck yourself, Charlie-boy, but don't fuck with me. What are you, a tech or a pilot?"

"Pilot, baby, and you better stay to rock-picking. You're out of your league."

Chorus of derision from one side of the cell-block. Shouts from the other. Dekker hit the cross-bar with his fist, muscle standing hard in his jaw, and from down the row, Meg shouted:

"You got a bet, Charlie-boy."

Wasn't any way she wouldn't take a challenge like that. Her and Sal. Ben felt his gut in a knot, saw Dekker lean his head against the bars, not saying anything, that was the danger signal in Dekker. And somebody down the row yelled.

"Hey, Dekker! You hearing this?"

Shouting over the top of it. Dekker had to answer, *had* to, way the rules worked, and Ben held his breath and crawled off the bunk, not sure what he was going to do if Dekker blew.

"Dekker? You hear?"

Man couldn't talk. Ben added those numbers fast, yelled out: "He's ignoring you, mouth! You're boring."

"Funny he had a lot to say when Chad bought it! That right, Dekker? That right?"

Ben shoved his arm, not hard. Dekker was frozen. Hard as ice. Staring into nothing. Other guys were yelling. Something hit the middle of the aisle and rattled to a stop. And Dekker looked like a guy hit in the gut, wasn't saying anything, wasn't defending himself, was letting others do it. Another shove wasn't going to push him into thinking. God only knew what it might do. He had the look of a man on the edge of cracking and Ben didn't know what to do with him, he didn't know how to answer the catcalls and the shouting that was going on, he hoped to hell for the MPs to come in and break it up. Wasn't any more from Meg. He could hear Sal's voice in the middle of it, but he had a desperate feeling he was in a cell with half a problem and Sal had the other half . . .

"Hey, Custard Charlie," somebody yelled. "You want to run the sims full hours? Take you on."

That was a hit. Belters tagged you and you stayed tagged until you burned it off—and then it could come back years later.

"Take you on, take Dekker and his women on, any day, any day—what about it, Dekker? You got a voice, pretty-boy? Where's your ladies?"

"Ladies" included one UDC shave-head in the mix, Ben figured, but he wasn't going to get into it, wasn't his business, wasn't going to win a thing.

But Dekker came alive then, shouting, "We got enough of that Attitude, mister, we got too damn many *dead* with that Attitude. I *liked* Chad, you hear me, you son of a bitch? I liked him all right, it was your own CO set him up." Dekker's voice cracked. He wasn't doing highly well right now, but at least the jaw had come unwired. He hit his fist on the bars, turned around and said to the ceiling or the walls, Ben didn't think it was to him, "God, they're making me crazy—they're trying to make me crazy."

Wouldn't touch that line, Ben told himself, and held his breath, just stood out of the way while Dekker walked the length of the cell and back.

"Hey, Dekker," another voice yelled. "You son of a bitch, was that your mama on the news?"

Shit. Dekker was at the bars and that knot was back in his jaw. "You want to discuss it? Is that Sook?"

"No way," another voice yelled out. "Sook's not guilty. That was J. Bob."

Catcalls went one way and the other. Shouting racketed up and down the hall, until starting with the far end, it got suddenly quiet. Quiet traveled. Ben leaned against the bars and tried to see what was going on, and all he could make out was UDC uniforms and MPs.

"That's better," someone said. "*Keep* it quiet. Fleet personnel are being released—"

A cheer went up.

"—to Fleet Security, for your own officers to sort out. You'll file outside, you'll give the officers your full name, your serial number, your rank, in that order. You'll be checked out and checked off . . ."

"Where do *I* go?" Ben muttered, suddenly with the notion he didn't necessarily want to go into a pool of UDC detainees with a grudge. "Shit, where do *I* go?"

"You go with me," Dekker said. "You're in our barracks, you go with me."

Doors had started opening. You could hear the clicks and the guys moving out.

Their door clicked. Dekker shoved it and they both walked out. Walked down the hall toward the MPs and it was only UDC guys left in the cells on the right, staring at them. They're not going to let me out, Ben kept thinking, they're not going to let me out of here . . .

"Wrong flock, aren't you?" an MP asked him; but the other said, "That's all right, that's Pollard."

It wasn't highly all right. Hell if it was. He was all but shaking when they got through the doors and out of the cell block, into the outer hall where sure enough, a couple of Fleet Security officers were waiting with a checklist. "Dekker," Dekker muttered, "Paul F. . . ." and didn't get further than that before the senior officer said,

"Dekker, go with the man. —You Pollard?"

Ben nodded. Saw one of the Security officers motion Dekker toward another set of doors, saw Dekker look at him and had this panicked sudden notion that if he let Dekker off alone *something* stupid was bound to happen—Keu and the lieutenant had tagged him with Dekker, and the only way to ensure Dekker didn't drag him into worse trouble was to stay with him. "Excuse me," he said, "but I have orders to keep an eye on him—*lieutenant*'s orders . . ." Highest card he knew.

But the guy said, "You have the *commander*'s orders to go to your barracks and stay put until further notice. The lieutenant's not in command now. Comdr. Porey is."

He must have done a take. He felt his heart stop and start. "*Commander* Porey?"

"Follow orders, mister. This whole station's under the commander's orders. The UDC's command's been set aside."

He wasn't the only one in the area now. Mason and Pauli had shown up under escort. "Hot damn," Mason said.

But Ben thought, with a sinking feeling, Oh, my God. . . .

Graff was extremely glad he didn't have to hear what happened inside what had, until an hour ago, been his office. Occasional words came through the closed door, while he stood outside in the hall with Tanzer's aide Andrews, neither of them looking at each other, with MPs and Fleet Security at their respective ends of the corridor.

It was not a happy situation. He didn't like Tanzer. But he felt only discomfort in seeing the man finally walk out of the office white-lipped and red-faced. Tanzer swept up Andrews and walked back the way he had come, with, as Graff understood Porey's intentions, *no* transfer out of here, no resignation accepted, and a hardcopy of an order from Geneva that in effect put Edmund Porey in charge of Tanzer's office and Tanzer's program.

He still didn't know how it had happened, or what might have shifted in the halls of power, as the captain would put it. He hadn't talked to Demas or Saito in any informality, hadn't exchanged internal security with the marine details and Porey's own Fleet Security force.

And not a word even yet from the captain. Which might be because he didn't rate one in their list of priorities. But which left him wondering again—what wasn't perhaps wise to wonder.

Since Porey had issued no request for him, since Andrews and Tanzer were gone, he walked down to the intersection of corridors and to the messhall, only observing the temper of things. There were very few out and about, but Security, and aides.

Tone down the dress, he'd advised Mitch. Between you and me; but pass it on—things are going to shift. Minimum flash. Minimum noise for the next few days. Observe this man before you make *any* push at him. Do you read me? I'm not supposed to be telling you this. If it gets out that I did, it will be to my damage. Do you understand me?

Longest solemn silence he'd ever gotten out of Mitch. Then Mitch had tried to ask him specifics—who is this guy? What in hell—excuse me, lieutenant, —but what in hell's going on with the program?

Apparently, he'd thought to himself, politics of a very disturbing bent. But he'd said to Mitch, I don't know yet. It's a wait-see. For all of us.

He went to the messhall, as the most likely place to find anyone out of pocket, anyone who had missed the barracks order, or thought he was the universal exception—an attitude more likely with Belters than with UDC or merchanters, and he was resolved none of his trainees was going to get swept up by Security—

None of his had *met* Porey's idea of Security. None of his own Security people got nervous at a joke. Ease off, they'd say. That's enough. They'd call the Belter in question by name or nickname, like as not, and get a generally good-natured compliance—

Not now. Not with these men, not with Lynch. He didn't know where they'd pulled this particular batch of marines in from, but they didn't have the look of basic training—Fleet Command had pulled something in from the initial set-up squads, he'd bet on it, though he'd have to get into Fleet Records to find out, but these weren't eighteen-year-olds, they weren't green and they sized up an officer they didn't know before they even thought about following his orders. . . .

Merchanters, maybe. But serving as line troops—when the Fleet needed every skilled spacer they could recruit? His stomach was upset. He carded a soft drink out of the machine and spotted a pair of marines at the administrative entrance, the galley office. What did they think, the cooks were going to take the cutlery to the corridors?

Exactly why those guards were standing there. Damned right. Tell it to Porey that the guys weren't going to go for the knives. Tell it to Lynch. A sight too much real combat readiness and overreaction in the ambient, thank you. A sight too much readiness in these troopers for any feeling that things were safe or under control.

"J-G."

Demas. Behind him. He took a breath and a drink, and disconnected expression from his face before he turned around. "We're on standby," he said, disapproving Demas' leaving the ship unofficered, before he so much as realized they weren't the primary ship at station any longer; Demas said, "LongJohn's on. We've got a while."

He nodded, tried to think of somewhere pressing to go, or something he had else to do, rather than discuss the situation with Nav One.

"You all right, Helm?"

As if he were a child. Or a friend.

"I'm tired," he said, which might cover his mood; but it sounded too much like a whimper. He didn't like that. He didn't like Demas conning him. He said, point-blank: "How much of this did you know?"

Demas' face went very sober, very quickly. It took a moment before he said, "Not who."

He hadn't expected honesty. He hadn't expected *that* answer. So Demas wasn't happy with the new CO either. And Demas was indisputably the captain's man. That came clear of a sudden.

He asked, under the noise of the heat pumps, "When did this get arranged?" and watched Demas avoid his eyes. Or look anxiously toward the marines—who might have Security audio, he realized that of a sudden. Damn, he wasn't *thinking* in terms of hostile action, it was their own damned *side,* for God's sake. But Demas was clearly thinking about it.

And Demas was the captain's man.

Demas said, in a low, low voice, "The Company pulled every string it had, in every congress on the planet. You want to go out to the ship, J-G?"

Of a sudden he had a totally paranoid notion, that Demas and Saito might be reeling him in for good, getting him where he couldn't get into trouble—where he couldn't *cause* trouble. Arrest? he asked himself. —Have I done that badly—or been that completely a fool?

"Hear this," the com said suddenly. *"This station and all station facilities, civilian and military, have passed under Fleet Tactical Operations, by action of the Joint Legislative Committee. Military command has been transferred as of 1400h this date to the ranking Fleet Officer.*

"Let me introduce myself. I am Comdr. Edmund Porey. I am not pursuing the interservice incident that marred the station's record this afternoon. I am releasing all personnel from detention with a reprimand for conduct unbecoming . . ."

The glove first.

". . . but let me serve notice that that is the only amnesty I will ever issue in this command. There are no excuses for failure and there is no award for half-right. If you want to kill yourselves, use a gun, not a multibillion-dollar machine. If you want to fight hand to hand, we can ship you where you can do that. And if you want to meet hell, gentlemen, break one of my rules and you will find it in my office.

"Senior officers of both services meet at 2100 hours in Briefing Room A. This facility is back on full schedules as of 0100 hours in the upcoming watch. Your officers will brief you *at that time. Expect to do catch-up. If there are problems with this, report them through chain of command. This concludes the announcement."*

He looked at Demas, saw misgiving. Saw worry.

He thought about that request to go up to the ship, and said, "Nav, I *understand* these people. I've worked with them. You understand? I don't want any mistake here."

Demas looked at him a long moment—frowned, maybe reading him, maybe thinking over his options, under whatever orders he had, from the captain, from—God only knew.

"J-G, —" Demas started to say. But there were the guards, who might well be miked. Demas put a hand on his arm, urged him toward the door, toward the corridor, and there wasn't an office to go back to, unless he could get one through Porey's staff. Demas' hand stayed on his arm. He had a half-drunk cup in his other hand. He finished it, shoved it in the nearest receptacle as they passed.

Demas said, in a low voice, "Helm, be careful." Squeezed his arm til fingers bit to the bone. "Too much to lose here."

"The Shepherds'll blow. One of them's going to end up his example. If you want to lose the program, Nav—"

"Too much to lose," Demas repeated; and a man would be a fool to ignore that cryptic a warning. He let go a breath, walked with less resistance, but no more cheerfully; and after a moment Demas dropped his hand and trusted his arrestee to walk beside him.

"Ens. Dekker," the man said, letting him into Graff's office. But it wasn't Graff at the desk. It was Porey, for God's sake—with a commander's insignia. Didn't know how Porey was here, didn't know why it wasn't Graff standing there, but it was Fleet, it was brass and he saluted it, lacking other cues. He'd dealt with Porey before, had had a two-minute interview with the man on the carrier coming out from the Belt and he didn't forget the feeling Porey had given him then; didn't find it different now. Like he was somehow interesting to a man whose attention you just didn't want.

"Ens. Dekker," Porey said, with his flat, dark stare. "How are you?"

"Fine, sir."

"That's good." Somehow nothing could register *good* in that deep, bone-reaching voice. "Hear you had a run-in with the sims."

"Yes, sir."

Long silence then, while Porey looked him up and down, with a skin-crawling slowness a man couldn't be comfortable with. Then: "Bother you?"

"I'm not anybody's target, sir."

"And you lost your crew."

"Yes, sir."

"Hear they were good. Hear Wilhelmsen was."

"Yes, sir."

"So what are you?"

Nerves recently shaken, shook. He didn't know what the answer was, now. He said, "I want to fly. Sir."

"What are you, Dekker?"

"Good. Sir."

"You're going back in that chair. Hear me? You're going to go back in and you're going to forget what happened here. You want to fly?"

"Yes, sir."

"Then you do that. You take that crew we've put together for you and you get back in that sim and you *do* it, do you hear me?"

He wasn't thinking clearly. Nobody he'd ever been in a room with gave him the claustrophobic feeling Porey did. He wanted this interview over. He wanted out of this office . . . he wasn't up to this.

"Do you hear me, Dekker?"

"Yes, sir," he said.

"Then you go do that. I want results. You say you're the best. Then *do* it. Do you hear me?"

"Yes, sir," he said.

"You're dismissed."

"Yes, sir," he said again, and then remembered Meg; and Ben; and Sal. "But with another *crew,* sir, than the one I've been given . . ."

"The Fleet's assembled the crew you have at cost and expense, Ens. Dekker. We're told they're good. We'll see it proved or we'll see it disproved—in the field."

"They're not ready, sir." He shoved himself forward, leaned on the desk and stared Porey in the face. "They haven't had the year I've had, they're not up to this, they haven't flown in a year at least. . . ."

Porey said, "That's what the sims are for."

"What are you after, a body count?"

People didn't talk to Porey that way. He saw the slight surprise in Porey's eyes, and something else, something that chilled him before Porey said,

"I'm after whatever you've got. As much as you've got. Or you die. And your crew dies. That's understood, isn't it? We're Test Systems here. And you test the systems. Do you want them to live? Then you don't question me, you *do* it, mister. Do you have that?"

"It's not reasonable!"

"I'm not a reasonable man." Porey's eyes kept their hold. "I never have been. I never take second best. Have you got it, Ens. Dekker? Or are you talk, and no show?"

He trembled. No human being had ever made him do that, but he shook and he knew Porey could tell it.

"We give you everything you ask for, Dekker. Now you *do* what you say you can do, you pull the Hellburner out. You *do* it. Don't give me excuses. I don't hear them. Am I ever going to hear your excuses?"

"No, sir."

"You're meat, til you prove otherwise. Prove it. Or die. I don't personally care, Dekker."

He couldn't get his breath. He couldn't think, he wanted to strangle Porey so bad. He choked on it. Finally: "Yes, sir. I copy that clear. Am I dismissed, —sir? Because you fucking *need* me, don't you, *sir*?"

Porey kept staring at him. Looked him up and down. Said, "Aren't you the *bitch,* Dekker?" and finally made a backhanded move that meant Get out. Dismissed.

He took it, saluted, turned and walked out, oxygen-short, still on an adrenaline burn, and shaking, while he was still remembering Porey from the ship, remembering that Graff had said even then: Don't get close to him.

Then he hadn't been able to figure whether Graff had meant that literally or figuratively, but he had a sinking feeling he'd just made a move that amused Porey—in the sense of defying Porey's expectations. That was an intelligent man—maybe the most intelligent man he'd ever met; maybe too intelligent to mind who lived and who died. He believed what Porey had said—he believed lives didn't matter in there, lives didn't matter in this station at the moment, law didn't matter . . .

Guards fell in with him, the same that had brought him there. He hadn't even any notion where they were taking him, but they escorted him to the main corridor and told him go to barracks, everybody was confined to barracks.

Deserted corridor. Deserted conference rooms. Guards posted line of sight along the curvature. The vacancy of the corridors was surreal. The echoes of his own steps racketed crazily in his ears. The downside of the adrenaline surge left him dizzy and chilled.

Another several turns, more empty corridors. Guards at the barracks section door asked for his ID. "Dekker," he said, and pulled his card from his pocket, turned it over numbly, all the rush chilled out of him. "Off duty. Just out of detention."

The soldier guards said go through. He went, through the corridor into a barracks main-room crowded with people he knew, people he liked, guys who grabbed his arm and wished him well. He thought,

If you only knew what I've done to you . . . . . .

And almost lost everything when Meg got through the crowd and flung her arms around him. Cheers and catcalls from the company, egging her on for a kiss he didn't shy away from, but all at once he was leaning on Meg, not certain which way was up. Dark was around him, that hazed back to light and the faces—

You all right? someone asked him, and he tried to say he was. Guy belongs in bed, somebody else said, but he said no, and they shoved him at a chair and told him the galley was sending food to barracks and in the meanwhile things had to be better, they were under *Fleet* control, they were trying to straighten out the duty roster and figure who was on what tomorrow . . .

Meg hauled a chair up facing his, grabbed his hands and made him look at her.

"Dek. You tracking, cher?"

"Yeah," he said. He wanted a phone, he wanted—he didn't know now whether he could cope with the news station or his mother. He kept hearing echoes, like the sim room. Someone saying, *Enjoy the ride, Dekker.* But the voice never had any tone. It drowned in the echoes.

He kept seeing the accident sequence on the tape. Not threatening, just a problem. He kept thinking about his mother, the apartment, the dock at R2. He kept seeing mission control, and a silent fireball. And the dizzy prospect down the core, all lines gone to a vanishing point. Fire pattern in the sims. Intersecting colors. Green lines. Track, and firepoints. He shook his head and took account of the room again, guys he ought to love, if he had it left. But maybe he was like Porey. Maybe he didn't have it, or never had had. More comfortable not to have it. More comfortable to love the patterns more than people. Patterns didn't die. They just evaporated. People went with so much more violence . . .

"God, he's spaced. Get him on his feet."

"We're going to *fly* with this moonbeam?" Arm came around him, hauled him for his feet, and he didn't resist it. "I tell you, I should've been in Stockholm, should've got my transfer—I *hate* this shit." Friends here. People he trusted. People he'd betrayed in there with Porey, because he'd been a damned fool.

"Man's got to eat."

"Somebody ought to call the meds."

"*No* meds." He'd had enough. He walked. He got to his room. He hit the bed.

"Didn't search the room," he thought he heard Meg say. "Didn't mess up the drawers, I mean, these MPs are politer than Company cops."

"Peut-et' they're just neater," Sal said; and Ben:

"There wasn't a search."

"How do you?" Sal started to ask. And said: "Silly question. Trez dim of me."

Electronics and flash-scan assured privacy, even against fiber and remotes. Security swore so. Graff could feel secure in this cubbyhole next the carrier's bridge, if he could trust present company.

Ask Demas and Saito who they belonged to? They'd say—Captain Keu. Of course. Saito would say it without a flicker. One preferred to hope and reason that was the case, rather than ask a pointless question.

"Tanzer's actually dispatched a resignation," Saito said, apropos of the situation within the station, "but it came back negative out of Geneva. That means the UDC wants him where he is. Which could be show of opposition: they could replace him three days from now. Or they want him where he is because he knows where the records are and what's in them, which could be useful to them here. They lost a big one. Forces inside the JLC lost a big one."

"We *didn't* know," Demas put in, doubtless reading minds, "when it would shift. That it might—one hoped."

He considered a question, shot a sidelong glance at Demas and asked pointblank: "And Porey? Where does he fit?"

Demas broke eye contact, just momentarily. Saito's face was absolutely informationless.

Saito said, then, "Porey is highly successful."

"At *what*?" Anger betrayed him into that bluntness, anger and the memory of dealing with them differently. "At covering his trail, evidently." If they were Porey's or about to be, he was laying a firetrack in his own path, he knew he was, but he had his personal limit of tolerance. And he disturbed them. Even Saito flinched, looked down, saying:

"Some things are excused, as long as the results are evident. Some patterns of behavior simply do not come through in social context. . . ."

"Other things," Demas said with unexpected harshness, "are blindly ignored. The captain is head of Strategic Operations. The captain is *too valuable* to assign back to Hellburner, so says the EC. Porey is available. He could be promoted into qualification. *That* is what happened, J-G, plain and simple."

He looked at Demas, saw fire-flags left and right of this conversation and knew he could self-destruct here. He took a chance on them—a last chance. "Who wanted him? Who?"

"—promoted him? Who *does* promote by executive order these days?"

Mazian. Who *wasn't* the best of the militia captains: Keu was; or Kreshov, maybe. But Mazian was the promoter, Mazian was the one who could smile his way through corporate and legislative doorways, Mazian could say things the way they needed to be said . . .

"The Earth Company," Saito said, "has SolCorp, LunaCorp, ASTEX, all space-based entities. But it also has its hands deep into the whole EuroTrust industrial complex—Bauerkraftwerke, Staatentek . . . the list is extensive—that have very good reasons to want extension of their facilities outside the reach of pressure groups and watch committees—meaning, into space. Those Earth-based companies give the EC an enormous influence inside the Joint Legislative Committee. The citizen pressure groups are enormously naive, usually single-issue. They think they move events. But in general the JLC is riddled with influence-trading, purchase decisions made on relationships, not quality. . . ."

"Ancient terrestrial lifeform," Demas said. "Dinosaur. Vast body. Little brain. It flourished on an age of abundant food supply."

"I've heard the word," Graff said.

"Not to overwhelm you with local history," Saito said, "but the UDC is a composite creature that never did function well. The Earth Company created us to oppose Cyteen's secession; but it never imagined a splinter colony could raise a population base of Union's size and it never imagined the light barrier would fall so quickly."

"More," Demas said, "it didn't understand the ship-building capacity of an enemy with no social debt. Ships cost Union nothing but sunlight, ultimately. Do you want more facilities? Create more workers."

"But now the EC understands," Saito said, "at least enough to frighten them. The special interests understand enough to see their interests are threatened. Now everybody wants to manage the crisis. Everybody wants to safeguard their power base. Everybody believes there's fault, but it's most certainly someone else's. The free-traders are making headway."

"Union-run merchanters," Graff muttered. "Long *we'd* last. And they'd be nothing to Union but a supply source. Cyteen manage Earth? There'd be short patience."

"Possibly they'd founder of bewilderment. —But that *is* the truth, J-G: the Company brought us here because Earth doesn't *believe* in star-travelers unless it sees us: and its own problems absorb its attention. The EC needed the demonstrable presence, the face and the voice to make the outside real to these people. And whether they've believed their own myth, or simply view Mazian as manageable—he's gotten far more important than we planned."

He was listening to sedition. To conspiracy. The captains had sent Mazian downworld, they'd chosen their spokesman—who excelled mostly at salving over wounded egos, at getting the captains to make unified decisions. It was merchanter command structure: Mazian was only the Fleet's Com One. . . .

"They're putting him in single command," Demas said.

"God." He didn't believe it. He couldn't believe it. But Demas went on:

"The EC stamps his personnel choices as a matter of course. Yes, he does the things that have to be done. But he's not following the rules we laid down."

"Hellburner has all but foundered," Saito said, "on citizen groups that *fear* the EC, who've insisted the UDC do what it doesn't have the personnel to do—"

"They've run us out of time," Demas said. "So now, *now* the EC steps in and gets us the power to do something—but it's Mazian they give it to. The captain's still sitting at Sol One with a mess on his hands, the whole UDC administrative system suddenly shoved inside our operations, but—"

"We begged him," Saito said, "to break with Mazian, to repudiate his personnel assignments, catch the commercial back here and take command of the carrier, the *hell* with Mazian's reputation with the EC."

His heart was beating faster and faster. He was sure what he was hearing, and surmised what must have been passing, God, on Fleet-Com—

"But the captain won't do it," Demas said, "won't expose dissent among the captains. Not now, he says: with Earth, appearances and public belief are everything. If we don't get the riders and the rest of the carriers funded in this legislative session, we're back to the spooks and the rimrunners."

He was still reeling from the first shock. Nerves wanted to hype and he tried to hold it. "What in *hell* did the captain want me to do here? Was I supposed to foul it up so badly he'd have to take it over? —Or is Porey what I won us?"

"That rump session of the committee wasn't supposed to come here," Saito said. "You handled it as well as it could have been handled. You were sincere. You were indignant. You were the epitome of the Fleet's integrity and professionalism. You didn't know anything to the contrary."

"So now we've got Mazian's hand-picked command here? Mazian's put *Edmund Porey* over a program that's already self-destructing? Have you worked with this man? I *have.* I was in the Belt with him."

"We're extremely concerned," Demas said. "We're concerned about those carriers out in the Belt, and at Mars, that have yet to have officers assigned. Yes, they'll bring in our people. But fifteen of the captains will be UDC. That was the deal that was cut."

His stomach turned over. A second time. "You're serious."

"That is the deal. Fifteen of the carriers—with Earth-born command."

"Who do they have?"

Saito made a ripple of her fingers. "They'll have a selection process. Earth believes in processes."

"That's fifteen dead ships—first *time* they take them past Viking."

"J-G, this is the crash course on truth in this venue. Mazian projects well. As a strategist he's even competent. But thank God for the Keus and the Kreshovs. They'll keep us alive. They may even keep Mazian alive."

"I've got a—" —kid on the verge of insanity, he was about to protest, when he recalled he didn't *have* anything, he didn't *have* a command, so far as he knew. "Dekker's not going to work well with Porey. Dekker's the best we've got. *Mitch* is not going to work well with Porey. He's the next. We're going to lose this program."

"No, we're not," Demas said. "Porey's in command of the program. Porey's put *you* in charge of personnel."

"*Me?* Where did you hear this?"

"Say it went through channels."

"Did he do the picking? Or was my selection—"

"Compromise. Though in Mazian's view I think you're to keep us in line," Saito said. "Technically, we equal his rank. But we're not command personnel. We're not designated as such, by the captain. Consequently the captain can recall us at will and Porey can't take us under his command—or get us assigned to that carrier. I'm afraid that isn't *your* case."

"We're concerned for that," Saito said. "But there's nothing we can do, but advise, where our perspective is of use."

He was glad he'd not had time for supper. He thought he might lose it, if that were the case.

"All personnel?"

"All flight and technical associated with the program. Tanzer's still there, of course, but he's promoted sideways, still in charge of R&D, but Hellburner's being lifted out of R&D—"

"Into *what*?"

"Fleet Ops. The parts manufacturers and the yards are being given a go-ahead, on a promise of funds tied to test success. They're pushing this ship for production, we're funded for one carrier's full complement, but no further; and the plain fact is, we're out of time. Latest projection is—we're going to see the first carrier-rider system in the field in six, seven months. Theirs or ours. Naturally we have our preference."

"What in hell are they asking me to do with these people?"

"Mazian sets the priorities. Porey carries them out. You keep the crews sane."

"You mean I promise them *anything.* Have I got a shred of authority to carry it out?"

For the second time, Demas evaded eye contact. "I'd say it's more than we can do. But, no, in effect, you don't."

"Is he asleep?" Ben asked quietly—made a trip to the bathroom while Sal was drowsing and stopped for a look-see. Dekker looked skuzzed, thoroughly, face down in the pillows. Meg was using his reader, scanning through Dekker's manuals—there was a lot of study going on in the barracks, over cold dead hamburgers and breaded fish. The smell out there could gag you. And the atmosphere was crazed. Guys *glad* they were going to fly this thing—the pilots and the lunatic lead techs who made up the core crew.

He should have counted, he told himself. He'd been a numbers man. He should have added it—and panicked when the number of him and Dekker and Meg and Sal tallied four, same as the other core crew units out there.

"He's out," Meg said. "Cold. Thank God. Man's seriously needing his sleep."

He came and sank down on the edge of the other bunk, said, ever so quietly, "You like this guy?"

Meg shrugged. You never got unequivocal out of her or Sal. But she was here. She'd risked her neck and her license for him. Partner, yeah. But Meg didn't do things for one reason, or even two. A solid part of it was in that datacard, was in the way Meg looked right now, sharp and serious and On as he'd ever seen her.

He didn't say what he'd sat down to say: Flunk that damn test. He slid a glance at Dekker and back and said, "You know, you better carry a pocket wrench."

Any Belter knew what a wrench was for, on helldeck. Meg's mouth quirked.

"The CO's crazy," he said very quietly. "I flew out here with that guy."

"So did we."

"*That* where they got him? Belt garrison?"

She shook her head. Whispered, "That carrier came in from deep. We dunno where. All the time we were on there, we saw crew, never but once saw him."

"What'd you think?"

Meg frowned. "Didn't like the signals."

He said, under his breath, "We got a serious warning. Don't know what that guy's problem is, but it is. We saw him far more than once. Just watching us. The body language. He wants his space, he wants yours. Smiles and laughs but he doesn't smile, you know what I mean? He watched Dek real close. Dek didn't like him."

"Grounds?"

"Just that." He didn't think the place was bugged. Events hadn't proven it and it was too egocentric to think Porey's security had made a straight line to their quarters. But he got uneasy with the topic. He said, "Helldeck radar, maybe. Guys you'd insist do the EVA, if it was the two of you in a miner can, you know what I mean?"

Meg got real dead grim. "Ask Sal about that kind." And then bit her lip like she'd said too much of Sal's business. "Yeah. Same signals. You ever ship with Sammy Wynn?"

Awful thought. Guy with some serious personality faults, that wouldn't get better on a long, lonely haul. "I wouldn't share a bar table with Sammy Wynn. Whatever happened to him?"

"Spaced by now, I hope." She stopped and looked aside as Dekker turned over and buried his head in a pillow. Time to go, Ben decided, before they woke Ens. Moonbeam. He stood up, stood still til he knew Dekker wasn't going to wake up.

"You going to take the Aptitudes?" Meg asked him.

Sore spot, that. "Yeah," he admitted. And went back into the room with Sal. He had signed the assignment roster out there. He hadn't intended to tell them. But what had happened here, with the UDC CO busted out of command, himself being caught behind a Fleet Security wall . . . he didn't give a real thought to a transfer right now. He could test into something administrative. Damned sure the Fleet wouldn't want him going back under the UDC curtain with what he'd witnessed here, if by any means they could finagle hanging on to him—and it certainly looked as if they had the clout. He *didn't* have the instincts or the nerves for combat, he'd proved that before, and that was bound to show. Drugged you down, they did, even for the basic test. Hooked you up to a machine and read your responses and your answers. You couldn't fake this one. They said.

He passed the door back into his room, sat down on the bed carefully, so as not to wake Sal. Low light, scatter of braids on the pillows, innocent-as-a-babe profile with parted lips, slight snub nose—dammit, the conniving kid was his partner, he *liked* being with her, he'd found a piece of himself clicked back into place when she'd come walking into the barracks—and being without her again was a dreary thought. He earnestly, honestly liked Sal; *and* Meg; which he'd never said about anybody but Morrie Bird; and God help him, he could even get acclimated to Dekker, or just plain nerve-dead.

Fact was, skuz as this whole place was, somehow the echo and the racket and the coming and going in the barracks fit him like an old sock—fact was, he *liked* the racket and the activity and the accent he'd grown up with echoing off the bulkheads. Pressure here was from fools higher-up, different than TI's carpeted, high-voltage corridors, where competition was cutthroat and constant.

But this wasn't any damn mining run this group was prepping for. At TI your highest chance of fatal injury was sticking your finger in a power socket or ODing on caffeine. Here—

God, they weren't even sure the damn ship would *work.* Rumor out in the hall was that they were going max *v* with the program and they still hadn't proved any crew could run it once—let alone fly it in combat.

That was crazy. And he wasn't—even if insanity got the rest of them.

Sal—go out there and turn herself into a missile? Sal and Meg end up in a fireball? Hell if, if he could stop it. But he didn't know how to; couldn't stop Meg, damn the woman, if Dekker couldn't. And if Meg went, Sal went, and if Sal went—

Oh, hell, he was *not* a fool. There were women in Stockholm. There'd be a way to get down there, even through Fleet Command—if he just got Aptituded into strategic technical.

Stockholm women wouldn't ask stupid questions like What's the Belt? They'd have university degrees and stand and watch the tide come in and the snow fall and . . . think it was all damned ordinary.

Hell. Bloody *hell* with women. *Dekker* was saner. At least Dekker knew what he wanted.

CHAPTER 10

Insert card please," the neutral voice said. The phone clicked. Dekker held the receiver and waited. And waited. Meg and Ben and Sal were in Testing. His day didn't start until 1015, when he had an appointment with Evaluations. Which meant he could go to the gym to try to settle his breakfast and his nerves; or try a phone call, see if he could get a personal call through to Sol One, on FleetCom, in spite of the security crackdown.

"Ens. Dekker." Human voice this time. *"Is this an official call?"*

"I'm trying to call my mother." He *hated* to sound like a strayed six-year-old. *Mother* always felt strange to him. Mama he'd long outgrown, though it came naturally to Belter ears. "It's a next-of. There was something on the news. —Look, can you put me through to Lt. Graff? He knows the situation."

"—I'm not being obstructionist, Ens. Dekker. I'm aware of your situation, but I am required to get an authorization for personal calls."

God. Everyone in the solar system knew his business. "Yeah, well, can you *do* anything, FleetCom? The lieutenant's not outstanding easy to find this morning."

"I'll page him."

"Everybody's paged him," Dekker muttered. "I'll card in every little bit, I'm going down to gym 3A."

"I'm sorry. The gym is now off limits to Fleet personnel. Use the one on 3-deck, section 2."

"How do I get my clothes out of the locker in 1A?"

"Check with the office on 3-deck."

Everything was on its ear. "Thanks," he said, glumly, and went four sections and took a lift in—it was about as much exercise as he wanted, just walking it. But one thing he'd learned in his tour in the Belt, if you could crawl to the gym, you crawled there and worked out; and if you got the spooks or the nerves—you went there and burned the chill off, you didn't let your mind go in loops—never let that start, not when you worked in cold, dark places, with things that went bang all too commonly.

The office there had his gym clothes, everything in sacks with old locker numbers. They had his name on the gym records. They had lockers already assigned to him and his crew. . . .

He hadn't had a run of things that worked in weeks. It gave him a moment of ridiculous cheerfulness. He had the whole gym to himself for the hour, everybody else being in sims or in special briefings—he wasn't fondly looking forward to his own session with the meds upcoming. Warm up the sore spots and go in there with the adrenaline burned out of him, was the plan—lunch on carbohydrates and go into Evaluation at 1300 warmed-up and hyped, and blow hell out of their damn tests . . . he could do it. The doctors had kept him flat on his back too long, he'd dropped five kilos on the hospital food, and Custard Charlie Tyson had gotten a couple of good hits in, but he could do it if he could get the chill out of his bones.

Light workout with the hand weights raised a sweat. Coordination was shot. That *wasn't* good. He leaned on his knees a moment, trying to get his wind back and the rubbery feeling out of his arms, getting madder and madder at the meds, at the UDC, at the Fleet that had busted Graff over to a desk job and put in a bastard with an Attitude—

Temper wasn't helpful. Demas would say that. Calm down, Dekker. Use your head. Adrenaline's for speed, not stomach acid.

Yeah. But it didn't help when the knees wanted to cave in, when you had serious worries about three fools who'd gotten themselves into a Situation for his sake, and had a CO who'd flat *warned* him he didn't give a damn for their survival—

Stomach acid, hell, he wanted to beat the shit out of Porey, that was why he was shivering. And if he did that, with all the esoteric consequences of people he knew and didn't know, it wouldn't stop bastards from being bastards, and wouldn't get Porey out of here, he'd only make it worse.

He didn't want to be in this situation. He didn't want to be anybody anyone else relied on for anything: he was schitz as hell. He was crazy. Ben knew it. He didn't see why Fleet Command couldn't see it. He didn't know why he'd ever been made an issue, or put where they'd put him, except the Shepherds had needed somebody crazier than they were to press their differences with the insystemers—and people who wouldn't have given a damn about him back in the Belt, found a use for him here. He wasn't Paul Dekker to them: he was this to one group and that to another and nobody really knew shit about him. . . .

Hi, Dek, good to see you, Dek, how you doing? He couldn't stand it any more—because Ben was right, they didn't know him, didn't know he was a screw-up, a damn dumb pusher-jock who didn't think before he opened his mouth. Only value he had to anyone, the fact that his nerves jumped faster than average. Only thing he was good at, that ship—*that* was all that had mattered to him; Pete and Elly and Falcone had had themselves, and they'd gone together—the Fleet had thrown them together, they'd tested high, that was all. And they were good and they'd worked together, but he was burned out this morning, he didn't even know whether he'd ever felt anything with them but comfort, and that was cheap—

He didn't know why Ben had decided to take the damn test this morning. Ben had skuzzed out on him. If Ben had held out, Ben might have persuaded Sal and Sal *might* have reasoned with Meg—

Like hell. *He* hadn't seduced Meg out here. At least Meg and Sal weren't his fault. The ship had done that. Some lying bastard in the Fleet had done that, who'd told Meg they'd give her a choice—

Yeah. A chance. Thanks.

Drug made you seriously spaced. You had sensor spots patched all over you, in places that made a body most emphatically wonder if it was procedure or the femme tech having a few loose circuits of her own—

"Do it where?" she remembered asking. But the examiner, that was a guy, nice-looking grayheaded man, asked her to match up all these shapes and holes—God, she hadn't done this one in years. "I'm not good at this," she said. "I don't *fly* little cubes."

Neither did he, he said. At least he had a sense of humor. So she ran the test and she tracked on discrimination stuff that flashed on screens, they moved her to another station and belted her in and the computer spun her around and around—easy piece, nothing hard at all. Til the floor dropped out from under her and *then* the thing went through its paces.

Wanted you to draw a straight line? Right.

Wanted you to get up and walk one?

Yeah. Maybe.

Sit in the spin chair again. Wait for the light and press the button while the chair spins?

Siren blast. Right before the light flash.

Dirty trick, sumbitch. Dirty trick. Flash again. Flash, flash. Pause. Flash.

Hold the yoke and the toggles, make the VR lines meet? This was a good one. Hadn't done this one before. . . .

Weight escaped his balance and bounced. Dekker ended up on one knee, caught a breath and waited for the room to stop spinning before he went to pick it up and rack it and lock it in. Good show he was going to make for the meds in an hour. He drew long breaths, sat down and felt after the towel to mop his face.

Stars came out of a vast dark. Lights on the panel glowed with information. . . .

It was in his head, the same as, in the Belt, you got to seeing rocks in your sleep, not rocks as they existed in the deep dark, but the way they were in the charts, the courses they ran, falling sunward, faster and faster, and then more and more slowly outward—

He wiped the sweat that stung his eyes. He heard somebody come in, challenged at the office for numbers and names. "Yeah," he heard someone say, far away and a door shut . . .

Echo. Door opening and closing. He'd seen a shape. He'd talked to someone. But he couldn't remember to whom. He chased the memory. But the voice that came back lacked all tone:

Just checking. Do what you were doing. . . .

Who in *hell* would he take that answer from?

Piece of nonsense. He *could* screw this test. They wanted him to discriminate a damn lot of advancing lines and dots? Easier if the sensors didn't itch.

He muttered, "Quick way to solve this. Who programmed this?"

Examiner said, "Don't talk."

"This is a piece of *shit,* major. Begging pardon." Zap. "Damn arcade game."

"Watch that one."

"This is fuckin' *armscomp!* I'm not testing for this—"

Zap.

"You're not damn bad, lieutenant . . . But you're not real modest, either."

"I'm damned *good.* But I'm not killing things."

"You have a moral objection?"

He put hands and eyes on autopilot and left them to search for screen-generated threats. At definable intervals. Random number generator in the virtuals, for God's sake. "I got a moral objection. I got a moral objection to getting shot at."

"Exactly what we're looking for."

He thought about that reasoning. He thought about screwing the test, while he was zapping stupid dots. Faster now. "Screw it, you severely got a pattern in here."

"I've been telling them that."

"Tell you something." Zap. "I'm supposed to be in Stockholm. Somebody skuzzed my records." Zap. "Matched me up with the lunatic." Zap. Zap-zap-zap. "Oh, hell."

"See? Not all a pattern. You missed that one. Getting cocky, were you?"

Faster now. "Son of a bitch," he said.

"You have two hands, two keysets. Brain can do both operations. Hands can. How good are you?"

"Damned moonbeam partner of mine," he muttered. "You give me programming. I'm telling you—anywhere else is a waste—" Zap. "I don't want combat. —I *know* what this mother's doing—"

Zap/zap/zap—

Hand on the other pad. Interrupt to Command level and invoke the chaos o/i off the internal generators. Obsolete as a security device, but certainly an improvement on *this* antique.

Resume. Let them figure that one. Let their *techs* come in and patch it if they didn't like it.

"Where did you get that code?"

"Telepathy," he said. "Sir. I told you. I *belong* in Stockholm."

Watch the lights, track the dot, do you have any blurring of vision, Mr. Dekker?

Have you had any headaches?

Stand here, stand there, look at the light, bend over, Mr. Dekker . . .

He escaped with a grudging Release on his card and an admonition to take his mineral supplements, got to a phone outside the med station and put the card in to check the readout for messages. Lunch, he thought, might bring people to check their messages. Might get a phone call, however muzzy, from Meg, telling him how she was doing.

None from Graff; none from Meg or Ben or Sal. No authorizations. Just a reminder of his appointment in Evaluations.

And a note from the gym that he hadn't carded in his preferred time slot and was he interested in team volleyball?

Hell.

Marine guards at every intersection. Corridors everywhere had a decided chill. God, there were even guards in the messhall. . . .

He started in, saw Mitch and Pauli and the guys at the tables and they saw him.

Upset him. He couldn't say why. He walked by for politeness' sake—"Sit down," they said, offering him a chair. But he couldn't face lunch of a sudden, in this place—too many faces in the room, too many people trying to be friendly who didn't know all that was going on with him, and the guards and the UDC watching him from the other end of the room. He muttered, "No, I'm on medicals right now, just time for a soft drink, thanks."

"Got anything back on the tests?"

Wasn't a thing stirred in C-barracks but what everybody was in it. "No. Not yet." He patted the back of Mitch's chair and made his escape to the rec-area foyer, where he could card a soft drink and a granola bar that tasted like cardboard and hit his stomach like lead.

They probably were talking about him back there. And he couldn't talk to them, couldn't deal with them until he knew what he was, whether he was going to clear the tests himself, whether his partners were passing theirs—he wasn't anyone, until he knew who he was working with, what he was, where he'd be, what they'd assign him to—

Fly again, yeah. Porey would see to that. Front of the line-up. Or the bottom—at Porey's discretion. He'd opened his damned mouth, he'd forgotten for a critical second he had partners who could be in danger from what he did or promised—

Couple of UDC guys came over and carded a candy bar. Names were Price and McCain. Techs. They hardly even looked at him, but he was sweating. He kept thinking, If I'd kept my mouth shut, if I'd done what the colonel wanted, if I'd only once ducked my head and played the game—

Tray banged somewhere. The room felt cold. His mother had said,

Paul, what is it with you? Why do you always end up in the middle of it?

He wished to God he knew that. He wished to God he could go over there with the other guys and sit down and be what they wanted him to be, but he couldn't even tell them what he'd done or what he was waiting to find out—

Please God, they'd Aptitude somewhere down the list, somewhere out of immediate usefulness, and he could go maybe to Chad's crew, patch things up with them, he couldn't think of a match-up else he could make that might have a chance. He should have offered *that* to Porey, Porey wasn't crazy—he didn't want to lose another ship, for God's sake: Porey probably would have called it a good idea—good for morale, pull the program together. UDC *and* Fleet.

He should still propose that to Porey—talk to Chad's guys himself in advance, if he could get them to talk to him . . .

God, why couldn't he think about people? He was all right with machines, all right with anything that reacted in just one way when you touched it—he could understand that. He just—

—couldn't figure how to stop himself before he said things. When he opened his mouth it was wrong, when he didn't say anything it was wrong, he never got it figured out, some people just understood him and most didn't, and the ones that did were always in trouble because of the ones that didn't. Sum of his life, that. Evaluations said he was smart. So why couldn't he get that right? Like go in there and apologize to Porey and take what he had coming?

Because when he walked up against a guy like that something went snap inside, he went hyper and he *couldn't* think, that was the whole damn problem—

So calm down, don't do that?

It was why the Fleet had recruited him, it was what they trained him to do, split-second, hyped and half crazy, and they wouldn't understand he didn't come with an off switch . . .

Except maybe Graff understood. But Graff wasn't answering pages today . . .

Damn him.

A little hyped. They said, You can relax now. But there wasn't any sleep. Just the boards, alive with lights. Hands knew where to go and went there. Hell of a way to teach. But they said, "This is a sim tape. Familiarization. It won't prioritize for you. Just give you the handedness of the boards. . . ."

"Got it, yeah. No trouble."

"Don't fight the sims, Kady. You want to bring that pulse down."

"Yeah. I'm not fighting it." Happy as hell. God. I *want* this thing, don't want to screw it up—God, I don't want to screw it—

"Calm."

"Yeah, yeah." So *don't* get excited, Kady, don't go after it, ride with it, just float and enjoy it—

"Lot better, lot better, Kady. How're you doing?"

She laughed. Laughed like an idiot.

"You all right there? You know what you're doing?"

Her hands were reaching. She wasn't doing it. But she didn't object. The sequence made complete sense. "Jawohl, mate, piece of easy, there."

Clumsy direction, then. Her hand shook. "Shit!"

Boards went dark. Direction stopped. She grabbed for the B-panel and the fuse conditions, and the examiner said, "Abort, abort, it's all right."

"What did I do?" Her heart was going half light. The drug made her light-headed and she hated the sensation.

"Tape error. Not yours. Relax."

Made her mad. They had no right to screw up. But you didn't get mad while you were at the boards, you paid attention. All attention. Save mad for later.

"Ms. Kady." New voice. "That was a system abort. Don't worry about it. You can stand down."

"Thank you." Cold and calm. Same as you did when something went seriously wrong. She flipped the board-standby switch. Habit. Fool, she thought. It was a toy-board anyway.

"Thank you." Another delay. "You can get up. Go to the room with the red light showing. You are in .9 gravity."

"I think I can remember that," she muttered.

"Some don't."

"Thanks." Anger was the immediate reaction. She was embarrassed to beg; but, putting her foot off the platform: "Do I get another try on that abort?"

A hesitation. Somebody had blanked a mike. Then: "How are you feeling?"

"Good enough for another try." Self-disgust. "If I can get one."

"Get back in the chair, then."

Thank God. She was all but shaking. And damped that down. Fast.

"Pulse is up, Ms. Kady."

"Yeah. Re-start."

"Hyped as hell," came a mutter from the earplug. Faint. Then at normal volume: "The yoke is an automated assist. It *is* changing its responses. Do you perceive that?"

"Yeah." Absolute relief. They hadn't told her the sim could do that. "But I got my own numbers. Let's shorten this. What are you, IMAT?"

"IMAT or CSET. A or B, select your format, input your actual license level."

"No problem." She took B, ran her numbers in, hoping she remembered them, hoping she was still that sharp, and watched the readout for response profiles. "Shit! Excuse." 12.489 sudden *g*'s on a tenth of the yoke range. She cut it back, re-calced in her head, thinking she could have a seriously pissed examiner if she dithered too long, but dammit, she needed the fine control on that hairline correction in the sims and you had to have it wide enough if they threw you an emergency. *Hell* of a thrust this sim was set for—different than shuttle controls by a long way . . .

Forgot to ask if time counted. Too late to spare a neuron. You did it right, that was all, you did it real, hell with them . . . set the controls to your own touch and take the time it took, they should have effin' *said* if there were criticalities not on the instruments—it was a new kind of adaptive assist, *piece* of nice, this was. . . . All kinds of interlocks and analyses it could give you. Mining in the Belt, you adapted your jerry-built and most egregiously not AI ship by whittling a new part out of plastic, and what you saw on your boards was a whole lot of hard-to-read instruments, not an integrated 360° V-HUD with the course plot and attitudes marked in glowing lines. *This* thing was trying to find out your preferences, arguing with you when its preconceptions thought it knew you. But it would listen. —Damn it, machine, soyez douce, don't get cheek with me . . . used one of these things ten plus years ago, she had, but, God, that had been an antique, against this piece . . .

"All right." She calmed her breathing rate. Panel lights lit. Scopes lit. "Go!"

Numbers hemorrhaged.

"God!"

"Nothing yet?" Dekker asked the desk on his mid-test break; and the secretary in Testing said, "No, sir. No result yet."

"Are they out yet? Have they left?"

"I don't think so, sir."

He tried FleetCom. He had a new comtech and had to explain everything again. "I just want to know if the lieutenant's ever checked in."

"He's in a meeting," FleetCom said.

"Has he gotten his messages?"

"I think he has. Excuse me. . . ."

On hold again, when all he wanted to do was hang up; and he didn't want to offend FleetCom by doing that before the tech got back to him. He wished he hadn't called. Five-minute break from his own Evaluations, it was 1456 by the clock, the granola bar and soft drink were wearing extremely thin, and he was regretting it. *If* he could get off the phone, he could get down the hall to the vending machines.

No word on his partners. Aptitudes was a four-hour session. You could take a little longer coming out from under the trank if you reacted. . . .

God, he didn't know what to—

"Ens. Dekker? Sorry to keep you waiting. I did get hold of the lieutenant. He says see him in his office at 1400. That's 21a, Admin."

"I'm in Evaluations til 1700. I'm in the middle of tests—"

"Excuse me. . . ."

Hell!

He put a hand over his eyes, he leaned against the counter and waited. Looked pleadingly at the secretary across the desk, then: "Do they *ever* take this long on Aptitudes?"

"I don't know, sir. I've only worked here for four . . ."

"Ens. Dekker? I'm *sorry . . . the lieutenant says he can't talk at 1700, he's got another meeting."*

"Will he clear a phone call for me to One? That's all I want."

"I think he wants to talk to you about that."

Shit. "Look—" He shut out the light and the secretary's presence with the palm of his hand. Tried to think. But he kept seeing fireballs. Hearing that door clank. "Is that all he wants? The phone call? Or does he want—look, can *I* talk to him online? Two minutes."

"He's in a meeting, sir. Just a moment."

He was late by now, by two minutes. You weren't late in Evaluations. You didn't antagonize the examiners. Who were UDC to begin with.

"The lieutenant says he needs to talk to you. He says at 2200."

"2200." Graff didn't plan to sleep, maybe. "Right. Thanks. Yeah. I'll be there."

"My partners aren't out of Test *yet,*" Dekker said. "They went in at 0600. It's 2202 and Testing doesn't answer questions. . . ."

"They're all right," Graff said, quietly, from the other side of the desk. "I can tell you that much."

"So *what* do you know?"

"That they're being very thorough."

"They're not reacting to the drug or anything—"

"No. They're all right. I did check."

It wasn't regulation. He wasn't convinced. He wasn't at all convinced.

Graff said: "On the other matter—"

"I just want to call my mother. Make sure she's all right." He kept his frustration to himself. He didn't want to push Graff. He was running short of friendlies in Admin.

Graff said, "I got your message. I understand. There's a good possibility her phone calls are being monitored by the police. Possibly by someone less official."

"Who?"

"All we know," Graff said, "is the same thing you saw in the news. We're investigating. I could wish this lawyer weren't involved—personally. Is your mother a member, a contributor—of that organization?"

"I don't know. I don't think so. —Are you asking me her politics?"

"You don't have to answer that."

"She hasn't got any politics that I know of. She didn't when I lived there. I don't think she would change."

"She was never politically active. Never expressed any opinions, for or against the government, or the Earth Company?"

Bit by bit the line of questioning made him uneasy. It wasn't like Graff—at least as he knew Graff—to probe after private information. He didn't think it was necessarily Graff's idea—and that meant whoever was investigating. So he offered a bit of his own reasons: "I was rab when I was a kid, the clothes, the haircut—Kady says I was a stupid plastic, and I guess I was; but I thought I was real. I used the words. My mother—got hot about it, said politics was all the same, didn't matter what party, all crooked, she didn't want any part of it—told me I was a fool for getting involved. They'd shot these people down on Earth. I think—"

—Meg was there, he almost said. But that was more than Graff needed to hear—if a deep spacer cared about the Company, the Earthers trying to emigrate . . .

"Think what?" Graff asked.

He couldn't remember his thread for a moment. He shrugged. "Doesn't matter. She's just not the kind. Works a full shift, mostly over, if you want extras you have to do that—and that was all she wanted.

A nice place. Maybe a station share. Security. That kind of thing. You wouldn't get her involved in anything."

"You know the Civil Liberty Association?"

"No, sir. I never heard of them."

"They're the ones funding your mother's lawyer. They're headquartered in Munich. They support lawsuits in certain causes, that's mostly what they do. Their board of advisers has some of the same associations as the Sun Party, the Peace Front, the Karl Leiden Foundation—the Party of Man—"

He shook his head. "I don't know anything about them. I doubt she does."

"They're Earth-based Internationals: of several related groups, only the Civil Liberty Association and the Human Research Foundation maintain offices off Earth. They apparently do each other's business. So I understand. I'm no expert in terrestrial affairs. But I thought you should know, this organization does have political overtones that aren't friendly to the program or to the Fleet."

"What do you want me to do?"

"I only thought you should be aware of the situation."

Deeper and deeper. He thought of saying, I'm in no position to restrain her from anything. I can't do your politics for you. But it was all on their side and nothing on hers. And probably the lieutenant didn't want a blunt question, but it wouldn't be his first offense this week. "So hasn't the Fleet got strings it might pull?"

"Possibly."

"So what do you want me to say to her?"

"Nothing. Nothing on that score. I just want you to be aware of these things."

Why? In case of what, for God's sake?

"Do you still want to call her?" Graff shifted a glance toward the phone on his desk.

He had never believed of himself that he was smart, no matter what Evaluations told him—if he was smart, he wouldn't be here now, put on the spot to make an excruciatingly personal phone call in front of a man he'd thought he trusted, whose motives he didn't now entirely understand.

And, God, he didn't want to talk to her . . . he was fast losing his nerve.

"Do you want to do that?"

"Yes, sir," he said, before all of it evaporated. "If you can get me through."

Graff took up the handset and punched in. "FleetCom. Route this through our system, FSO, Sol One. —Number there?"

"97 . . . 2849. Dekker, Ingrid. Routing can find her." 2210 mainday and she ought to be home. She didn't have a nightlife—at least she hadn't had, when he'd been living at home.

"Takes a bit," Graff said, and gave him the handset. "It's going through, now."

He held it to his ear. Listened to the clicks and the tones. His heart was beating fast. What in hell was he going to say? Hello, mother?

Click. Click-click. Beep.

"There's a noise on the line."

"A beep?"

He nodded.

"Somebody's got it monitored. FleetCom's picking that up."

Hell. It was going through. He listened for the pick-up. But the answering service came on instead. *Ms. Dekker is out at the moment. Kindly leave your name and number. . . .*

You'd know. "Mother. Mother, this is Paul. I'm sorry to hear about the trouble you're having. . . ." It was hard to talk coherently to a machine, hard to think with that steady beep that meant the police or somebody else was listening. "I don't know if I can help, but if you just want to talk, I'm here. I'd like to talk to you. I'd like to help—" He wondered if he should mention money. But while he was thinking, it clicked off and connections broke, all the way back along the route, leaving him the sound of static.

"She wasn't home," he said, and gave the handset back. "I left a message on the machine."

"Anything that comes through—you *will* get. I promise you."

"Thank you." They'd taught him to say thank you. Please. Yes, sir. No, sir. Stand straight. Answer what you're asked. They'd told him he wouldn't fly if he didn't. His mother hadn't had that advantage in dealing with him. He didn't remember he'd ever said Yes, ma'am or Please or whatever boys were supposed to answer to their mothers. Fuck you, he'd said once, in a fit of temper, the week she'd bailed him out of juvenile court, and she'd slapped his face.

He'd not hit her. Thank God, he'd held it back, he hadn't hit her. Only respect he'd ever shown her, that last year . . . and if they shipped him out from here—the only respect he might ever have a chance to show, except that phone call.

"Forgive me," the lieutenant said. "I have to ask this—in your judgment, is it possible—is it remotely possible she did make threats against MarsCorp?"

Ingrid Dekker wasn't a walkover. She wasn't going to stand and take it—not without handing it back. "If they threatened her. But she wouldn't—wouldn't just take it into her head to do that, no, I don't believe that." I have to ask this . . .

At whose orders . . . sir. . . .

"Are you close to your mother—still?"

God. He didn't want to discuss it. But the lieutenant had been on his side, Graff if anybody was still his lifeline. He didn't want to put his mother in a bad light. She was the one in trouble and she needed all the credit she could get. He said, looking at a spot on the front of Graff's desk: "I was a pain in the ass, sir. She said if I went to the Belt I didn't need to come back. I—was sincerely a pain in the ass, sir. I was eighteen. I was in with a rough crowd. —I was stupid."

Graff didn't say anything to that, except: "Have you corresponded with her?"

"No, sir." He stared fixedly at that spot on the desk, wondering if they might search his room and bleed his datacard for it, next use he made. Maybe they already had. "Not recently. —I've got about four, five k I'd like to send over to her account. If I could do that. She's not working, she's going to need the money."

"I'll talk to Legal. See what the procedures are. —As I said, we're going to be looking into the case. If there are strings to be pulled, maybe we can pull them."

"I appreciate that, sir."

"Are you ready to get back to work?"

"Yes, sir."

Graff keyed something on the deskcomp. Glanced at it. "I don't know if they can get your friends back to quarters this watch. But you're their unit commander, you have access there on any shift, if you want to check up on them."

Not back to quarters? Not in this watch? His heart did a tic and a speed-up. He looked at Graff, met a level, I can't-tell-you kind of stare.

"What are they *doing*?" he asked Graff. "They're in there for Aptitudes—it's a four-hour test, for God's sake . . ."

"You have access there."

"I've *been* over there. They wouldn't tell me a damn thing!"

Graff had never been one to hold back information, not under Keu, and not under his own administration. Now . . .

"I suggest you go over there," Graff said. "That's all I can say."

* * *

Didn't *like* the damned drugs. Didn't effin' *like* the floating feeling. Told you stuff you didn't want to hear. Told you you'd effin *die* if you screwed it . . . and Ben didn't want to die, he sincerely didn't want to die . . .

"Fire!"

His heart took a jump, he felt neg *g*, he went spinning away—you should feel blood pooling in your head and your feet and he didn't, didn't feel anything right except cold breeze on his face and his lungs getting air again—

He could see light. Felt somebody holding his sleeve. He was flat on his back in *g* and *Dekker* was holding on to him, saying, "It's all right, it's all right, Ben—"

Wasn't who he wanted to wake up in the arms of. He stared at Dekker, with his heartbeat still thumping away like explosions, and recalled they were surrounded by dots all but six of which were trying to kill him—

—except he was in bed and Dekker wasn't flying the ship.

He took slow assessment of this fact. He took a look around the ceiling of a disgustingly barren room, recalled signing his name, and them telling him Sal was in, and him talking to the tech and screwing with the sim, because he'd been mad as hell and wanting to get court-martialed and wanting to go to bed with Sal Aboujib if he had to get shot at to do it—only viewed backwards, as he had to see it now, that sequence didn't highly make sense.

Neither did Dekker sitting on his bedside. He'd come here to sit with Dekker. He wasn't in the hospital. He was in the sims lab and Dekker, with this scared look on his face, was holding him by the wrist.

"Ben."

"Yeah?" He began to think he'd better wake up.

"Ben. You all right?"

Dekker asking really worried him.

"Don't agitate him," somebody else said. "You know the rules."

"Trying to give him a heart attack, what's the damn hurry?"

There wasn't any answer. Dekker took hold of his hand. Said, "Shit . . ."

Dekker holding his hand? He'd really rather not. Unless he was dying. He didn't feel like he was dying. He stared at Dekker, made his fingers bend and his hand drew back and decided in this moment of clarity that he wanted his foot on the floor.

"Ben. Ben, —don't do that."

Froze right there. Face down in the bend of Dekker's arm. And couldn't think how to get out of that situation.

"Skuzzed," Dekker said. Light came back. Dekker swore at nothing in particular. That was all right. Saved him the bother.

"Aboujib did pass," he wanted to know.

"Yeah."

"Meg?"

"Yeah. I got three of you. Same condition." With which Dekker got up and stalked out.

That was Dekker, all right. Boy had a lousy temper.

"Shit!" he heard from the hall.

CHAPTER 11

2345h and all Dekker wanted was his own bed, didn't want to talk to anybody, just skuzzed through the door into a darkened barracks, went straight to his quarters around the corner and down the corridor, and got undressed on autopilot—wasn't even thinking clearly when he heard the stir outside. A knock came at his door and he stared at it and blinked.

Second knock. He thought, What in hell? and opened it, on Mitch and Pauli and Trace and God-only who else the shadows behind them were.

"Want to talk to you," Mitch said, and Dekker leaned his forearm on the doorframe and reasoned that even if he could talk them into leaving him alone now, it was too late, the adrenaline he thought he'd run out of was up again, sleep was gone, leaving just caffeine-ragged nerves and a body shaking with chill and exhaustion. Didn't have a shred of embarrassment left, Trace there and all—he just said hoarsely, "What?"

"The rest of your guys didn't come in?"

"No."

"Dek. What's going on?"

"I don't know what's going on, I don't know any more than the rest of you guys." Struck him then, though, that a lot of the aforesaid guys had risen to his defense in the messhall, a couple of them had gone to hospital and a lot of them had suffered serious inconvenience on his account—so they had some right to knock on his door in the middle of his sleep and want a piece of his hide.

Mitch asked: "Is it true they're going to bust your guys right into active? They're going to put Pollard and Kady and Aboujib straight in?"

Wasn't hiding any damn thing around here. He'd been trying to get the same admission out of Testing and he couldn't do it, *or* find out who the order came from that had shoved his crew straight out of Aptitudes into the board-sims—he stared at Mitch a beat or two, muttered, "Something like."

" 'Something like.' They're going to take Kady's hours for legit?"

"Mitch, I don't know what they're taking for anything, nobody's told *me* a damn thing, I don't know what your source is, but it's more than I know . . ."

"So where are they right now?"

"In the labs sleeping it off. They started in at 0600 and they got through somewhere around 2200, that's all I know, except they're Aptituded in, that's the only official word I have on anything." He got short. His temper was on the edge. But he hadn't reassured anybody. And maybe they'd heard something: he hadn't been in the rumor mill all day, he'd been chasing around in places rumors didn't get to—back and forth between offices and Evaluations. And rumor was evidently saying for fact what he suspected and couldn't get the labs or the techs to admit to. . . .

Shove them up into Mission Ready, with him?

God, Porey wouldn't do that. Porey'd said himself that he wouldn't lose another ship: the Fleet couldn't afford it. They weren't going to do that. . . . They *couldn't* do that. . . .

"Rumor is," Jamil said, "the Fleet thinks your guys have the stuff, so they're just going to go with them, put them right in on the pods—"

"They can't do that," Dekker said. It came out a thin, helpless kind of voice. "No way. They haven't got ships to throw away on a notion like that—"

"Rumor is," Mitch said, "they were running some kind of new tape off Pete and the guys during the mission, rumor is the Fleet thinks they can take that tape and sub it for the whole damn training sequence—"

Legs nearly went out from under him.

"Seems," Jamil said, "they wanted crew that hadn't been *biased* by all this prior training—"

"Shit, no. . . ." He couldn't feel anything below the gut. He got a couple of breaths and managed to stay on his feet. "This is shit, guys, I don't know where you got this, but this is shit. No way are they going to do that . . ."

Trace said, "First we got Tanzer, now we got a guy thinks he can program us like computers?"

"*Where'd* you hear this stuff?"

"In the slightly off chance," Mitch said, "that we're dealing with bugs, we decline to answer that in specific. But we thought you'd like to know."

"Shit—" He wasn't doing too well with words. His teeth started chattering. "I got to talk to the lieutenant. . . ."

"It's Porey we have to make a dent in."

"Good luck with that," Trace said.

"We can not show up tomorrow. The whole lot of us."

Dekker shook his head, made a wave of his hand, suddenly struggling to get control of his jaw. "N-no. This is a m-man m-makes ex-examples. Trust me that I kn-know."

"God, the man's freezing," Trace said. "Get him a sheet or something."

"I kn-know what I'm *t-talking* about. You don't pull a st-strike—he'll p-pick one of you—" Pauli got past him into his room. But he kept looking at Mitch. "Guy's a control freak. I m-met him. F-flew out here with him . . ." A blanket settled around him. He made a stiff, half-successful grab after it. But it did nothing for his chill. He let Pauli pull him back toward the bunk, while Mitch said, "You guys go on. Let's get his door shut. . . ."

Mitch stayed, and Pauli did, and Jamil and Trace. Dekker sat down on the bed, tucked the blanket around him. Mitch said: "The man's making an example, all right—he's going to kill you, you understand that? High team gets the next run. That's us or that's you, Dek. You can kill yourself in sims, if one of those girls screws up."

"They aren't damn b-bad . . ."

"Listen, *Pollard* may know what he's doing, Pollard had a background, but they hauled these girls in here for no other reason than they were with you in the action out there and they're somewhat famous in the Belt. They've got *no* place in the program. Fleet's listening to helldeck gossip, *no* solid background in hours—"

"They survived."

"Yeah, they survived whoring their way around helldeck. That's what they did for a living, Dekker, I don't know if you heard, but that's the plain truth."

He didn't believe he'd heard that. That was how it got as far as it did. "Screw *you,* Mitch, you keep your opinions to yourself."

"All right, all right, they're friends of yours, I'm sorry. But you came in there new. You ask Pollard where these girls got their credit. With him, with Morrie, with any ship they ever handled . . . no bad karma for it, but they didn't make their keep with the runs they made—"

"You stow it, Mitch. I *worked* with them."

"You never flew with them. Never knew shit what they could do, and now because they were with you, they got a rep the Fleet takes for granted—"

"They *passed* the Aptitudes, Mitch, the examiners shoved them right into the board sims, you're telling me any of *us* sailed through into the sims?"

"Hey. Maybe their brain-tape works. Maybe you *can* program human beings to act just like a robot—just like the damn AI they tried to hang over our heads. They don't build one, they make *us* one. But what happens under fire, Dek? What happens when the answer isn't in any damn *tape,* and those girls don't know it? That's when it's going to make a difference. . . ."

"Meg's the coolest head under fire I ever saw. Meg saved our *asses* on R2, and *you* weren't there, Mitch, *you* couldn't get to us, if you want me to bring that up—"

"Well, you can thank God she caught a bullet, because if Meg Kady had been flying, she might have taken out the *Hamilton.* Don't blind yourself, Dek. She was a second-rate miner jock who got caught running contraband—she's got a helldeck rep and now they're going to hype her and Aboujib and Pollard on some tekkie tape and put you head to head with us. I don't want to see you crack up. I don't want to see those girls hurt. I don't have a personal grudge against them, I just have a real gut reaction when I see somebody running totally on rep and getting somebody else fuckin' *killed,* Dek, and sending this program down the out-chute."

"Maybe we'll see," he said, set his jaw and looked elsewhere, because he didn't have anything left to say on the subject and he was too tired and too shaken to punch Mitch out. There were things he could say, like firstly, Where were you, Mitch, when we were depending on you? But he didn't honestly know that answer, he'd been too charitable to ask; and he didn't want a war with Mitch.

Mitch is a mouth, he told himself, Mitch was born with an Attitude—he wouldn't deal with *me,* except I'm the competition, and he has to take me seriously. It's Shepherd, that's all it is—Meg's insystemer and she's flash and they don't like her style, that's the problem—

Jamil said, "Dek, you have to protect yourself. I don't personally know whether Kady and Aboujib have got it, I think Pollard probably does, but not the way they need to have it now. The examiners didn't bust them through into the sims because they're good, they busted them through because they were *told* to, that's the truth, Dek, and we're worried, we're worried for you, we're worried for your crew, we're worried for the reason that we signed up for this program in the first place, because we're in the center of some serious games, here—we got congresses playing games with a ship we could fly if they'd get the hell off our backs and quit screwing with the way we work—"

"We don't want to see you killed," Mitch said. "We don't want to see anybody else killed. You better find out what's going on. You better find out what your crew's capable of—before you put your lives on the line out there, that's what I'm saying. The lieutenant hasn't got any power to do anything about anything right now. But he might tell you the truth and he might listen. And he might pass what he knows to the captain—who is the *only* authority we can think of who might pull the plug on this damned tape—"

"It's what they use Unionside," Trace said. "That's where they got the tech. They don't even know what they're doing with it, that's my guess, they just got it, they can't come up with a fix on the program, and now they're going to try this, they're going to make *you* the guinea pigs. You've got to lay back, Dek. Lay back and lay out and don't *try* to take those guys realtime . . ."

Mitch took Jamil's arm, hauled him to the door. Trace lingered, just stood there, the only female in the group, with, he suddenly uncharitably surmised, other intentions than argument.

"Go on," he said, "out."

"Dek, I know they're friends of yours, that's what—"

"Trace. Get the hell out. Now. And turn out the lights."

She turned out the lights. She left. He fell back on the wreckage of the bedclothes and felt the cold hit his chest and stomach—thought about getting up and putting the bed back in order, but he didn't, right now, have the fortitude. He just rolled over in the blanket and tried to fall unconscious, if sleep was out of reach; but images rolled over and over like riot behind his eyes, the argument with Meg about her flying, Graff sitting there and telling him Get over to Testing, Porey saying, You're meat, until you prove otherwise. . . . But the sequencing of events didn't make sense. They'd *brought* Meg and Sal here to wake him up, they'd had to start from the Belt directly after the accident, directly after he ended up in hospital—they'd brought Ben from closer in and Ben had gotten here faster, that was all, but they must have started at the same time.

They'd had the hearing, Graff had said, and they'd wanted him to testify. But he hadn't. And still Porey had come in to take the program over. And they had tapes. Tapes they'd made off Pete and Elly and Falcone on the mission, leading up to the wreck—

Union tech, then, the same deep-drug tech that they'd sworn once they could beat—but the ship wasn't up to specs and the program was screwed and they had to keep their funding going, *had* to keep getting the ships built—

So the Fleet had seized control and they had to have another pony show? They swore to somebody they'd get the program turned around and to do that they had to hold out some brand new tekkie trick that was going to win the war so they could get the money?

They wanted to try out the tech on *unbiased* crew—and for that, they hauled in Meg and Sal clear from the Belt, pulled in Edmund Porey *and* a carrier, blasted away from Sol Station like a bat out of hell an hour after the riot in the messhall landed him and half the program in the brig?

Then Porey had wanted to talk to *him,* personally, when he hadn't, that he knew, talked to Mitch, or any of the other recruits in any private interview?

Porey knew him—personally, at least insofar as they'd met during his trip out from the Belt in the first place; Porey had ferried him out from the Belt—it wasn't impossible that Porey had had his hand on his career long before this . . . maybe even suggested him for the program when they enlisted him: he had no idea, but Porey had been in a position to have done that. Maybe *that* was why the interview in the office, that had gone so badly; maybe Porey was justifiably angry that he'd been in the center of controversy, when Porey had brought him here specifically to keep him out of media attention, because of the Salazar mess—

Then his mother, devoutly noninvolved, got fired—and went after MarsCorp; and peacer groups showed up with lawyers to back her suit?

He lay shivering in his bed, thinking, Why? on the frenetic edge of exhausted sleep. Everything looped back, as if he was the gravity well nothing could escape. . . .

There were so many things that didn't make sense. There were so many pieces of his life being gathered up and shaken—everything that went wrong from here to Pell seemed to have his name on it, in bright bold caps. Paul F. Dekker.

A guy couldn't have that kind of luck, no way in *hell* one stupid miner-jock could just chance to be where carriers moved and officers intervened—

And Graff just happened to care so much he went to all the trouble to collect his friends to rescue him?

Like hell. Like hell, lieutenant, sir.

"What was I going to say to him?" Graff asked. "Ask these people and they might give you what you want, but dammit, you don't deal with them like that."

Demas said, in his null-*g* unmonitored sanctuary in the heart of the carrier, "Nothing you can do, J-G. No way to stop it even if you'd known in advance. This was decided at much higher levels."

"Did you know? *What* do you know?"

Demas shook his head. "I don't and I didn't. I would guess there was consultation. I would hope there was consultation of more than Porey with his own captain, but knowing what Mazian decides these days, I have some trepidation on that account. But who knows? Tapetech works for Union."

"Not at the *cost,*" Graff said, and looked left at a sound that in no wise belonged in this place. "Saito, —"

"Medicinal," Saito said. The bottle Saito had just uncapped broke five regulations Graff could think of immediately: it was glass, it was private property in an ops area storage, it was liquid, it was alcoholic and it probably hadn't passed local customs.

It was, however, null-stopped, and Saito sailed it his direction. "You're not on call. Jean-Baptiste is on the line, we're still on stand-down. You need your sleep and your morality won't let you. So join the rest of us and turn it in."

"So where do you do that? Fleet HQ? There must be a waiting line. It seems a damned busy traffic this year."

"There's nothing we can do. No help to the boy, ruining yourself. If we were attacked this instant you're worthless. Best you know it beyond a doubt."

He took a sip and made a face at the sting; and in the midst of his indignation, realized flavors still evolving on his tongue, an unfolding sensory sequence, the way Earthly flavors tended to do—nothing simple. Nothing exactly quantifiable. From instant to instant he liked and loathed the taste. He found it significant that the sensory overload could reach even through his present mood to say it was rich, it was expensive, it was—if you could synthesize it—only one of endless variations on which a whole trade flourished—from a gravity well in which Conrad Mazian had been sunk for weeks.

"This place *corrupts,*" he murmured. "It's the motherwell of corruption. When did we forget what we came here to prevent?"

"Take another, J-G. Edmund Porey is in charge of the people in charge of the tape. He brought the tape, he brought the applications techs. They're officially *Carina* crew."

"What are we fighting to keep away from? What in *hell* are we fighting to keep out of Sol System?"

Demas caught the bottle that drifted from his hands, took a sip and sent it on to Saito, third leg of their drift-skewed triangle. Demas said, "I earnestly recommend sleep, J-G. Perhaps a night of thorough debauch—we might manage that. There's absolutely nothing else we can do."

"We can help the boy. We can at least do something about his next-of's situation."

"Technically Ingrid Dekker is not, you know, next-of. Pollard is. Dekker explicitly took her out of that status . . ."

"For her safety. *He* knows the situation. That's why he didn't call on her."

Saito frowned, cradled the bottle in her arms. "I've been over and over the Dekker file. There is a remote possibility someone at Sol One leaked the story about Dekker's accident. The information was at Sol One via FleetCom and one can never assume there was no leak. One hopes not. But it's remotely possible she might have found out, and she may have learned about Salazar's proceedings against her son. She might have taken action of her own—but there is that last, troubling letter from the mother to Dekker—in his file. . . ."

"In which she tells him not to communicate? But he disregarded it."

"He doesn't know we monitor these things."

"He should suspect. —You think she may have attacked MarsCorp, in revenge for her son?"

"Difficult. Difficult case. Neither Cory Salazar nor Dekker had a father of record—not an uncommon situation for Mars, much less so for Sol One. Sol's still very tied to the motherwell. In all senses. Ingrid Dekker had a son. Had she named a father, tests would have established paternity. That man would have had financial and legal liability—under local law."

"Possibility she didn't know?"

"Possibility she didn't know or didn't want to say. It would extend legal rights to the child. She took full financial responsibility. She had the child—again, her choice."

Graff frowned, revising attitudes. He had no idea who his own father was, but his mother had had a cheerful account of possibilities, all from one ship—who had not the least liability in the matter: not for him and not for his cousins of the same stopover. Who might even be half-sibs, but who cared?

Earth certainly did.

"Mother," said Saito, "has nothing to do with ship-loyalty. Not in the least. Unitary family. He grew up in a two- or three-room apartment alone with one woman. No sibs, no cousins, no other kin—not an abnormal situation. Not the local ideal either."

Claustrophobic, what he could feel about it. He watched Saito take a drink and sail the bottle back to him.

"Dekker did not get on well in school," Saito said. "Fell in with a group of young anti-socials—read, quasi-rab—and got caught vandalizing station lifesupport—a series of smokebomb incidents, as happened. One might assume it was their idea of political statement."

"A very stupid one." He had read the file, though not with Saito's interpretation. Sabotaging one's own lifesupport hardly qualified as intelligence—and Dekker was far brighter than that. Or should have been.

"He got very little education. It's all classroom theory, there. Very little hands-on. Dekker doesn't learn by lecture. His episode with the court nearly had his mother fired and deported, for a minor out of control—"

On a merchanter ship, it would have had the youngster scheduled for a station-drop and a go-over by psychs. Possibly with mother or cousin in tow, but not absolutely. There was no use for such a case aboard—

But Dekker was not insane. Quite remarkably sane, considering his upbringing. Graff took a sip and frowned, passing it on to Demas.

"She spent her personal bank account on lawyers and bond for the boy's behavior," Saito said. "She enrolled him in vocational training. Electronics, her own profession. He ducked out of that and got a position pushing freight. Lied about his age. Made very little money, but he was out of trouble. He went back to school—probably found out he needed the math for a license—and apparently became an upstanding citizen, though by this time he was in remedial in all his subjects. . . ."

"One brush with the rab. And no other troubles," he said, "until the Belt."

"Until he absconded with Alyce Salazar's daughter—with whom he'd been a correspondent since his return to school."

"Mmmn," said Demas, "the miraculous reform."

"And no record there," Saito said, "until Cory's death. A model citizen. Solvent—"

"On Ms. Salazar's money."

"But solvent. A hard worker. He had been on Sol before he left. Had, one suspects, a habit of pushing himself beyond the legal limits on his license. . . ."

"Certainly a talent," Graff murmured, thinking . . . "Why did no one at Sol ever Aptitude him?"

"With that score in social responsibility, I don't think anyone ever thought of tracking him for ops."

"A mortal waste."

"Earth has a million more who want the slot. They can afford human waste."

"Dekker's a statistical anomaly."

"Especially in that population. But they didn't recognize the profile. Sports or trouble, that was their analysis. And he was off the team very quickly. He wasn't physically adept, of course. And temper didn't serve him well. You do not frustrate that lad. But you know that."

Morbidly interesting, Graff thought, to know what a profile like his own might have meant—in the motherwell. "Pressure on the genome."

Demas muttered: "Emory? Or Wallingsford?"

And Saito: "Don't we fight this war for that distinction?"

"Who knows why we fight? Because we stayed by the Company? But what's the Company? Not wise, nor representative of the motherwell. Nothing I've met tells me that answer." Demas passed the bottle again, to Saito.

Graff asked, "Can we help his mother? We've civilians working in FSO. Maybe she could be employed there."

"There's that peacer contact. She certainly won't pass our security clearance with that attachment."

The bottle came back to him.

"Because she's naive and desperate, she's a security risk? She wouldn't have access to the FSO lunch schedule."

Saito said: "Being Dekker's kin and outside our wall is a security risk. And there's the vid. The Dekker affair may have died out of the media—but watch them remember it now. Command will be extremely reluctant to solidify that association. The peacer connection—"

"Our employing her could be an interesting embarrassment to their side."

"And there's the claim of harassing Salazar."

A most uncomfortable thought occurred to him. "You don't think Salazar could have hired Ms. Dekker's lawyer, to control *both* sides of the lawsuit?"

"Not legal, of course—to pay both sides' legal help. That much is true even in Sol System."

"Possible, though. Isn't it? Their system of exchange makes a private transaction hard to trace."

"Oh, it's even possible the peacer groups see Salazar as a way to their objectives; possible that the money is flowing to this conflict from the peace and the defense committees. Mars is relatively leftist, relatively isolationist. They see their interests remote from the EC as a whole. Pursue some of these groups deeply enough and you come out the door of their opposition."

"Moebius finance," Demas said. "These groups survive on fund-raising. Particularly their executives and staff. How could these people survive without each other?"

Completely paranoid.

"The enemy of my enemy," Demas said, and took the bottle up, "threatens both our livelihoods. And of course the Fleet is innocent in this game. Earth's parliaments and congresses understand Mazian. Mazian gains command of R&D. Of Sol Two. God, one wonders what traded hands."

Graff thought privately, and dared not say, even to them: Our integrity. Our command. Mazian was going to fill the captaincies with his choices—

Porey among the first.

Fingers felt all right. Wasn't sure about the ownership of the hand, though. Schitzy experience, that was. Meg held her eye from blinking with one set of fingers and tried to apply the pencil without blinding herself—Dek had been kind enough to make a supplies run from the quarters to the lab-dorm, only thing she'd asked of him last night: Get our makeup, God, we got to look like hell—

"Dek was a skosh bizzed last night," she said to Sal, who was putting earrings in, stealing a bit of mirror past her shoulder. "Don't you think?"

"Man's doing all right."

"You?"

You had to catch Sal like that, blindside. Sal met her eyes in the mirror, wide-open.

"So, Aboujib?"

Sal said, scowling, "Scared as I hoped to be, give me a damn field of Where-is-its? and a: Some of these things are rocks, Aboujib, and some of these things are missiles? I never memmed a field faster in my damned life—"

"Pass?"

"Hey. I didn't have a heart attack. —Kady, I got seriously to talk to you about your sojer lessons. They're severely *real,* these sumbitches."

She would have turned around. But mirrors was the best place to catch Sal. "Truth, Aboujib. You want to go back to the *Hamilton*?"

She saw the hesitation. The little nip of a lower lip. "Without?"

And had this moment with her heart up in her throat. She'd passed, dammit, they'd told her. Finally got a chance at a ship and a guy she got on with, and, dammitall, here was Sal pulling in the other direction, she saw it plain.

And it was a lot of hours with Sal, a lot of bad times and a lot of good, but on the other hand there was Dek—there was Dek, who—God. . . .

Sal's frown had gone. The lower lip rolled out in a rueful sulk. "I dunno, Kady, I dunno how you talk me into these things."

"Aboujib, come serious. You want to be back there."

"I tell you what. I want, I seriously want, a little damn couple fitnesses on that simulation. They got no mem-check, there's not a damn interset macro in there—maybe they been getting this thing from *Shepherd* types. Ought to ask a freerunner about rocks, Kady, ought to ask us how not to go boom in a fire-track—"

"I'm not asking that."

"Well, I'm not the hell going back to the *Hamilton.* Leave you here with the guys?" Frivolous. Deliberate. The mask was back and Aboujib's long eyes were half-lidded. "*I* lay you bets, Kady." Flick of a nail against a large earring. "Ben didn't flunk that mama. Not our Ben. Scare hell out of him the way they did me—and they get a class A per-for-mance. So with this child. Miner nerves, here. Don't tell *me* fire-track. They're saying I got to set up the positionals? Somebody else is going to have his finger on the fire-button? Shit-all. I want the *guns,* Kady."

"Effin' right I passed, Dek-boy. No question I'd pass if I wanted to. Ap-ti-tuded, hell, they put me in *armscomp,* are you satisfied?"

Dekker wasn't. He sincerely didn't want that. He watched Ben shaving in this dormitory the labs afforded their test subjects and kept his chilled hands in his pockets.

"Sorry doesn't cover it. I know. But—"

Ben looked around at him. "You worried, Dek-boy. Tell me why you're worried."

He wasn't sure he ought to say that either—since Ben didn't know; since self-doubt was the deadliest creature you could take into the program. The program was full of egos. Ben's was fairly healthy.

"So what's the matter?" Ben prodded him.

He had to say something—because somebody would, back in barracks. "Say the Fleet has that new program—say they came up with this tape stuff . . ."

"You mean what they gave us wasn't reg?"

He was supposed to be a fast thinker. He wasn't doing well this morning. Mute as a rock, he was.

"Look, Moonbeam, what in hell are they up to? Gives a guy a real uneasy feeling, that look of yours, and you're the lousiest liar I know of."

"It's supposed to work, that's all I know."

Ben gave him a long, suspicious stare.

"All I know," Dekker said; and Ben said,

"Hell if. What's going on?"

"Nothing," he said. "Nothing but they want results. Fast. And the heat's on my tail. But it doesn't get to you guys. It doesn't."

"Yeah? They put you in command, did they, of the whole friggin' Fleet?"

"No. Porey said it. They don't want to lose another ship. And I swear to you, —I won't lose another crew."

CHAPTER 12

Glowing lines converged. Dekker blinked sweat and the simulator manufactured an uncharted rock on split second Imminent for the carrier.

Missed the bastard and redirect to take it out on the fly—

Got it, got the beta target before the bloodflow caught up with his knees.

Targets coming.

Carrier showed up on the scope. That was the priority—your carrier showed and you got the come-home, and you were done, far as you could clear it a path, granted you could get through the effect shield without glitching.

Soft and smooth—you got the slight buffet as you came through the shield, momentary LOS of everything on the boards and you had to know its *v*, the extent of those shields, how close you were going to be when you came through the envelope—damned close, *damned* close.

Touch. Slight mismatch. Within tolerance. Probe caught.

Mate.

Power down.

Good run, solid run. Not flashy, except that UO and making that shot. He could cut the sim, meltdown and unbelt, he'd earned it *and* a hot shower. Fine control when you'd been hyped was hell, and switch-off was the co-pilot's job, if there'd been a co-pilot this sim—he wouldn't lose points on that. But he was a fussy sumbitch. He set his switches. He set every effin' one.

Damn, it felt good. Felt solid.

Home again.

He shifted his legs as the pod opened and he could unbelt and drift out. Breath frosted, while sweat still ran under the flightsuit.

Take *that* in your stats, Tanzer.

Card game went on, Ben and Sal running up favor points on Almarshad's and Mitch's guys, and the spectators drifted down there. "Hey, Dek," came back, but Dekker tried to ignore it and concentrate on his math and his set-targets for tomorrow's run.

Conversation floating back from the table said, "It's one thing in sims. Live fire's going to be something else."

"You just hit 'em," Ben said, and took a card. "Dots is dots."

"No way," Wilson said. "Ask Wilhelmsen."

"They don't have to," Mitch said, and a chill ran through Dekker's bones. He was thinking what to say to shut that up when Meg said, acidly, "Dunno a thing about Pete Fowler, mister. Nice guy, I s'pose, and I highly 'preciate his help, but he's not the one does the thinking."

"Still not live fire, Kady."

"Ease off," Dekker said, and shoved his chair back.

"Hey," Mitch said. "No offense."

"Doesn't bother me," Meg said, and dealt out cards. "Testosterone's not the only asset going. Shepherds seriously got to rethink that."

"Meg," Sal said.

"Hey. I'm easy."

"You been easy, Kady."

Meg pursed her lips. "You a virgin, Mitch? I swear I don't know."

"Hold it, hold it," Ben said.

"The program's making a serious mistake," Mitch said, "putting you girls in here. Tape can't give you the wiring, Kady, there's a *reason* they never pulled women in on this program—"

"Yeah," Meg said acidly. "Look at the scores, Mitch."

"Meg," Dekker said.

"Tape off a real *pi-lut,* Kady."

That tore it. "Mitch," Dekker said.

"No, no," Meg said coolly, "not a problem, Dek. Man's just upset."

"Bitch."

"Yo," Sal said. "You want to match score and score, Mitchell?"

"Just hold it," Dekker said into the rising mutter from Mitch's crew and Almarshad's. "We don't need this."

"We don't need any damn *tape,*" Mitch said, "and we *damn* sure don't need any tape off any women. *Reactions* aren't there. You're never going to see a female pilot on this ship, Kady, you don't see 'em in the carriers, you don't see 'em in the riders, and you're never going to. You'll crack under fire, you're going to screw this whole damned program, on a rep you didn't earn."

Meg said, with a riffle of cards, "Cher, you got a truly basic misconception, there. Ship's aren't shes, they're hes—you got to make love to them the right way, got to keep 'em collected so you *both* get there . . ."

Laugh from some of the guys, thank God. Wasn't funny at the table. Mitch was pissed. Mitch was being a son of a bloody bitch, was what he was being, hurt feelings, and a mouth that made you want to knock him sideways.

But Mitch gathered up the cards Meg dealt. "You're in over your head, Kady."

"Cher, I had a shuttle go dead once, lost a motor on lift, landed in the Seychelles, and *that* was a bitch. I haven't sweated since."

"Bullshit."

"Yeah. Tell me yours."

Mitch glowered a moment, then laid down a card and said, "Well-divers are fools."

"You got that," Meg said. "I resigned it."

"Didn't resign it," Sal said. "They threw you out."

"Huh. I was getting tired of it. Too much same stuff. You seen Luna once, you've seen it. Big damn rock."

"Smug bitch," Mitch said, in better humor. Dekker eased back and found himself shaking, he was so wound up. But Meg wasn't. Cold as ice, or she hadn't any nerves between her hands and her head. Couldn't tell she might want to knife Mitch Mitchell—

But he'd lay odds Mitch knew.

"Damn, damn. You got a rhythm in this thing."

See those programs, see how that infodump selected for the human operator, and how it prioritied—*that,* that was a serious question. They'd had a problem like that in TI, putting a human into the supercomputer neural-net, without letting it take over infoselection. This one sampled the human needs as well as the environment and it wasn't doing all it could. The data behind it was flatline. He pushed it, and it gave him the same input.

"You're not supposed to critique it, Pollard. Just stick to the manuals."

"Screw the—begging your pardon. But I *worked* on something like this. Staatentek program or independent?"

"Classified."

He bit his lip. Didn't raise the question of his clearance.

"Just a minute, Pollard."

Just a minute was all right. He sat and stared at the screen that offered such interesting prospects: infodrop for the human decision and infocompression for the computer. Reality sampling against a chaos screen in a system Morrie Bird's prize numbers man found achingly familiar, after a stint in TI's securitied halls. . . .

Screw supply systems modeling, this thing talked to him with a familiar voice.

This isn't sim software, he thought. Main program's elegant. *This* is real, isn't it? Ignore the cheesy recorded randoms, son of a bitch—the system under this is a piece of work—

He said, to the air, "Staatentek didn't do this, did they?"

No answer for a minute. Then a different voice: "Pollard. Leave the programs alone."

"You can *feel* the randoms. I didn't have to look for them."

A pause. "That's very good, Pollard. What would you suggest we do about it?"

Obvious answer. To the obvious question. The Belt. The numbers. The charts. The *feeling* you got for the system—the way the rocks moved. Real rocks, with the Well perturbing what the Sun ruled. . . .

. . . Shakespeare; and Bird . . .

Ben, leave the damn charts—

"Pollard? What would you do?"

"I'm sure you have," he said. "Use Sol."

"Or Pell. Or Viking. You haven't met Tripoint, Pollard. Would you like to see Tripoint? That one's an excellent example. . . ."

Balls hit and rebounded on the table. Ben walked around the other end, considering his next shot, gave a twitch of his shoulders, estimated an angle, and took careful aim with the cue.

"Mmmn," Sal said. Ben was sure it was Sal's voice behind him. Muscles were absolutely limp this evening. He was a little off his game—give or take a year's hiatus. Dekker, the skuz, had had practice. Keep the run going. He didn't want the cue in Dekker's hands, not from what he'd seen.

Two in succession. It was rec hall, bar in the middle—a lot of UDC guys on Permission down there, drowning their sorrows. Fleet at this end, some of them too. And a scatter of marine guards—more khaki around the corridors than Ben personally found comfortable, thank you.

Real wringer of a sim this afternoon, he'd earned a beer, dammit, but they had him up again tomorrow, same with all of them.

Opened his big mouth and they'd reset the sim, all right.

Dots and more dots, in a space where the effin' familiar *sun* didn't exist . . .

Spooky situation. Wanted to feel it out and you were busy tracking damn dots.

Gentle shots. Balls rebounded. "Come on, come on—"

"Ouch," Sal said.

Shit.

Dekker drew a breath. Armscomper *wasn't* the opponent you'd choose in this game. Pilot versus armscomper got bets down, never mind he'd had practice Ben swore you didn't have time to take at TI.

Hell if. Ben had learned it somewhere, helldeck, maybe. And a Belter didn't show you any mercy. You damn sure didn't want to let him get the cue back.

He saw his shot. Lined it up. Bets were down. Favor points. Military didn't let you play with money. And nobody had any.

Click and drop. Sighs from half the spectators. Muted cheers from the rest.

Second shot. Ball dropped, balls rearranged the pattern. He was sore when he bent to survey the situation, but it was a good kind of soreness, kind you got from a hard run. Never had realized there was good pain and bad. He'd felt the other kind. Too damn much.

Click.

"Right on, Dek!"

Meg and Sal had bets on opposite sides.

He grinned, took aim.

Click. Perfect bank.

Sudden disturbance, then, in the ambient. Dekker felt it, looked up as everybody else was looking, at a handful of UDC guys who'd showed up at the table. Marines were in motion, starting to move between.

Rob Childers. Kesslan and Deke. Chad's crew. A marine said, "Let's not have any trouble. Get on back there."

Rob said, "Dek."

He felt a sudden queasiness in the approach. A sense of confrontation. The marines weren't pushing. They weren't letting the UDC crew closer, either, and there was starting to be noise, other UDC guys moving in.

"Wait a minute," Almarshad protested, thank God somebody on their side had the sense to say something, offer a hand to object to force; and he had to move, himself, had to do something in the split second.

He dropped the cue to his left hand, took a nonbelligerent stance.

"Dek," Rob said and held out his hand.

Put him entirely on the spot. Marines didn't move, didn't know who was who or what was happening here, he scoped that—scoped the moment and the move and the necessity to do something before they all ended up in the brig.

"Rob," he said, and went quietly past a confused marine and took the offered hand, looked Rob in the face and wondered if Rob *was* the one who'd tried to kill him, or if Rob knew who had. He took Kesslan's hand, and Deke's. The music system was grinding out a muted, bass-heavy beat, that had the silence all to itself.

"Too much gone on," Rob said. "Both sides."

He had to say something. He took that inspiration, said, "Yeah. Has," and couldn't find anything else to say.

"Let you get back to your game," Rob said.

"Yeah. All right." He stood there while the room sorted itself out again, Rob and the rest of them going back to their side. He never managed to say the right thing. He didn't know what he could have said. He felt a hand on his arm—Meg, pulling him back to the table, while Franklin muttered, "Shit all."

"They do it?" Mason asked him under his breath.

He gave it a desperate thought, trying to believe they were innocent. But he remembered getting hit, remembered the pod access, and couldn't be analytical about the dark, and the pain of broken bones, and the toneless voice that said, in the back of his memory. Enjoy the ride, Dekker.

Tape going into the slot. The voice said, Let me—

Let me, what?

Wasn't anybody but the pilot handled the mission tape.

Didn't make sense.

He didn't answer Mason. He got down and lined up his shot again, determined. Made it. There was a sign of relief. He was relieved too. Was all he asked, for his pride's sake. Didn't want to show how rattled he was. He focused down and made a run of three, before a ball trembled on the verge of a drop. And didn't.

"All *right,*" Ben said, out of a sigh and a stillness. Ben sounded less than satisfied. Everything seemed paler, colder, he didn't know why. He stood by Meg and Sal, arms folded, and watched Ben make a straight run.

UDC MPs looked in on the situation. You could hear the music over the voices. When things were normal, you couldn't.

He wanted a drink, but regs didn't let him have one. He thought of desperate means to get one, but if they caught you at it, you were screwed. He didn't want a session with Porey. Didn't.

Bets got finalized. He'd bet himself, as happened, so had Ben; and Sal could collect. But something passed between Meg and Sal, and Meg took his arm and said Sal was taking a wait-ticket—

"You better get to bed," Meg said, and he'd have paid off, he wouldn't have minded, he was halfway numb at the moment—her change in arrangements made him think maybe he was better with Sal, who wouldn't pry—Sal and he never had gotten into each other's reasons for anything.

But Meg had set up what she evidently thought was a rescue, and he gave himself up and went off with her.

She was upbeat, cheerful, talking about the game, not a single question who that had been or why—must have gotten her information on her own, because Meg didn't favor ignorance, depend on it: she got him to bed, was willing to go slow if he'd had the inclination: he didn't; and wrapped herself around him after and snuggled down to keep him warm, about the time Ben and Sal came trooping through.

"Shhh," Meg hissed, and they were immediately quiet, quiet coming and going to the bathroom—the front room had its drawbacks; but he was on the edge of falling asleep, suddenly exhausted.

Glad he'd made some sort of peace, he decided. Even if their move had put him on the spot and forced what he wasn't ready for.

Likely they weren't the ones who'd ambushed him. He hadn't been sure of that when he'd taken Rob's hand; and even if he was somewhat sure now, he couldn't come to peace with it, couldn't forgive them, could he, if there was nothing to forgive in the first place, if they were innocent and it was somebody else he saw every day in the corridors, ate with in the mess hall. Maybe whoever had put him in hospital had been in the crowd getting a further kick out of his confusion.

He'd lost an argument or two when he was a kid—he'd lived through the chaff he had to take, he'd faced the guys again—they'd been two years older: he'd lived in fear and gotten hell beaten out of him a couple of times by the same guys before he'd made them believe they were going to take so much damage doing it they didn't want to keep on his case—not the ideal outcome he'd have wanted, but at least he could believe he'd settled it, at least he'd made a point on them and at least they didn't give him any more trouble.

But out there in front of everybody, they'd put him directly on the spot, damn them—yeah, he could have acted the touchy son of a bitch Ben said he was, told them go to hell and had the program in a mess and the lieutenant ready to kill him. He'd had an attack of responsibility, he decided finally. Mature judgment or something. His mother had sworn he'd never live that long.

But it didn't solve his own problem. Just theirs. He was still walking around not knowing, still a target for another try, God only when, or on what provocation. In the meanwhile he knew those he'd trust with his life, and those he just didn't know. In the meantime somebody was off scot free and probably laughing about it.

"You all right, cher?" Meg stirred beside him, massaged a shoulder. He realized the tension he had, then, probably as comfortable as a rock to be next to.

"Yeah." He tried to relax. "Cold."

Meg put a warm arm over his back. "Roll over, jeune fils. No questions. Do. We got sims in the morning. Big day. Relax."

Couldn't understand why she put up with him. Couldn't understand why Ben did, except Sal was with Meg. He wished he could do better than he did, wished he could say they weren't in a mess of his making. But it was. And they were. And Meg somehow didn't care he was a fool.

The rec hall was quiet. It was a Question whether to acknowledge what had happened or ignore it; but the former, Graff decided—word having drifted his way via Fleet Security via Sgt.-major Lynch. Probably word had drifted to Porey too and no orders had come. But it was Personnel's business to take a tour, while the alterday galley staff was cleaning up. Music was still going. Most of the participants were back in barracks, hopefully.

"Quiet here?" he asked a marine on watch.

"Quiet, sir."

"Any feeling of trouble?"

"No, sir. Not lately. Real quiet, sir."

He made no approach toward the last few celebrants—a few UDC, a few Fleet personnel, a little the worse for drink, at opposite ends of the hall. He wasn't there on a disciplinary. But he meant to be seen. His being there said command levels had heard, command levels were aware.

Dekker hadn't blown it, by all he'd heard. He didn't know where the idea had started. He didn't know that it had done any good, but at least it had done no demonstrable harm.

Someone walked in at his back, walked up beside him.

"Tables still standing," Villy said.

"Noted that."

"Hope it lasts," Villy said. "Difficult time."

Villy had never said anything about the change in command. Like having your ship taken out of your hands, Graff thought, like watching it happen on, Villy had said, the last big project he'd ever work on.

What did you say? What, in the gulf between his reality and Villy's, did one find to say?

"Good they did that," he said. "I hope it takes."

CHAPTER 13

Big empty section of the mast—you'd know where you were blindfolded, null-g with the crashes of locks and loaders and the hum of the core machinery, noises that made the blood rush with memories of flights past and anticipation of another, no helping it. Meg took a breath of cold, oil-touched air, a breath that had the flightsuit pressing close, snug as a hardened skin, and hauled with one hand to get a rightside up view of what Dek had to show them, screen with a live camera image from, she guessed, optics far out along the mast.

Big, shadow-shape of the carrier—wouldn't all fit in the picture—with spots on its hull picked it out in patchwork detail, all gray, and huge—

And on the hull near the bow, a flat, sleek shape clung, shining in the floods.

"That's it?" Ben asked.

"That's it," Dek said. "Her. Whatever you want to call it. They built three prototypes. That's the third. That's the one that's make or break for us. Crew of thirty, when we prove it out. Four can manage her—in a clean course, with set targets. Most of her mass is ordnance, ablation edge, and engine load. You've had the briefings."

Meg stood by Sal's side and got a shiver down the back that had nothing to do with the cold here. Beautiful machine, she was thinking; Sal said, Brut job, and meant the same thing, in a moment, it sounded as-if, of pure gut-deep lust. Wasn't any miner-can, that wicked, shimmery shape.

And most imminently, in the sim chamber behind the clear observation port, the pods, one in operation, a mag-lev rush around the chamber walls, deafening as the wall beside them carried the vibration.

"Damn," she breathed. But you wouldn't hear it.

"The pods you see moving," Dek said, over the fading thunder, "that's the tame part. That rush is the dock and undock. They can take those pods more positive or neg *g*'s than your gut's going to like. But that's not the dangerous part. That pod, there, the still one—" He pointed at one floating motionless, away from the walls. "That's the real hellride. Could be at ¾ light, what you know from inside. That's the one they mop the seats on. That's the one can put you in hospital—unstable as hell in that mode—screw it and you'll pull a real sudden change."

"Thanks," Ben said. "I like to hear that, damn, I like to hear that."

Meg said, "Going to be all right. No problems. Hear?"

But Dek looked up at that pod in a way she kept seeing after he'd turned away and told them it was up the lines to the pod access—like an addict looking at his addiction, and a guy scared as hell.

"Take you on the ride of your life," was the way he put it.

"Now wait a minute," Ben said. But Dek took out on the handlines and Sal snagged Ben's arm with: "Now, cher, if we don't keep with Dek and Meg here, they'll assign us some sheer fool pi-lut we don't know the hell who . . . Do you want to go boom on a rock? No. Not. So soyez gentle and don't distract the jeune fils."

"No," Graff said, "no, colonel, I *don't* know—I've got a meeting with him . . ."

"He's got no right," was the burden of Tanzer's phone call. Which didn't over all help Graff's headache. Neither did the prospect of dealing with *Comdr.* Porey face to face.

"I'll pose him the question," he told Tanzer. Couldn't honestly blame the colonel this morning—discovering that his carefully constructed sims schedule was in revision, that Villanueva's team had been opted straight off test systems into the priority sims schedule and three others of the test systems crews had been bumped off the sims schedule entirely, in favor of Dekker and three raw recruits, who'd been given access-on-demand, on any shift.

The officer in charge of Personnel ought to know what was happening. One would logically think so.

The officer in charge of Personnel hung up the receiver, put on his coat and took his hangover headache down the corridor to the CO's office.

Marine guards let him in. Porey was all smiling, smooth congeniality.

"Jurgen," it was. And an offered hand as Porey got up from his desk. One had to take it or declare war. "I've been going through the reports. Excellent job you've done, getting us settled into station. I don't find a thing I'd change. Sit down, sit down . . ."

"Thank you," Graff said, and sat, wondering whose name those actions had gone out under in the report to FleetCommand—wonder, hell, he *knew* what games Porey was playing, with the reports, with his smiling good grace: Porey's aides never knew what they'd meet when they walked into his office, the smiling bastard or the shouting, desk-pounding sumbitch, but either one would knife you. It was, knowing your career could hinge on Porey's approval, damned easy for a staffer to start twitching to Porey's cues. He could see it working in *Carina* junior crew out there, in the marine guard—he could see it going on all around him, suggesting that it might be wise for him to play Porey's game too; suggesting that this man, clearly on his way to a captaincy, and certainly in Mazian's good graces, could be a valuable contact . . .

Except that he'd seen this game going on since they were both junior lieutenants, and he felt the urge to puke.

He said, with a fixed smile, "Edmund, do you think your staff could possibly give Personnel any sims schedule changes a day in advance? Tanzer is *not* happy. I could have minimized the disturbance."

"Didn't that come to you?" Porey was all amazement.

"No, it didn't come to me. I had to hear it from Tanzer. I *don't* like dealing with the UDC when I don't know what's going on. It makes me feel like a fool. And I don't *like* that, Edmund, I truly don't."

Satire on Porey's own style wasn't what Porey was used to meeting. Porey had a thinking frown as he sat down, guarded amusement at the edges of his mouth: everything for effect, most especially the expressions on his face. Peel Porey layer by layer and you never got to center.

"Matters of policy," Porey said, rotating a paperweight in his fingers, "are handled in this office. Tanzer has no power that you don't give him. If you choose to coddle him, that's your decision. Not mine." The paperweight stopped moving. "The assignment of personnel and priorities, however, is mine. Relations with the UDC—use your talents at diplomacy. I'm sure you're up to it."

Distraction and a shot across the bow. "By the Procedures, Personnel involves health and welfare, neither of which works when my office has no say in reassignments or systems changes." Attack on his own. "In consideration of which, I want a briefing on the tape-learning procedures from the techs that came in with you. I don't have time to read science reports."

"Jurgen, my staff hasn't time to handle delicate egos, Tanzer's or yours."

"Or three hundred fifty-six Shepherds who've been rooked out of their seniority, lied to by the UDC, shafted by the legislature and killed out there on the course because nobody's ever damn listened to them. Edmund, we have tempers at critical overload here, and a blow-up isn't going to look any better on your record than it looks on Tanzer's. If you want a riot, these are the ones that will do it. They're not kids, they've had too many fools in command over them here and in the Belt to trust anybody now on credit. They don't reject authority: they're looking for it, they *want* it—but don't expect them to follow orders til they know the ultimate source is sane."

Porey didn't say anything for a moment. He wasn't stupid and he cared about his own survival. That was one thing you could believe in.

Porey said softly, "You're an honest man, Jurgen. How do you plan to get out of Earth system alive?"

"By keeping my CO from making mistakes."

Long, cold stare. A slow smile. "You don't have any resentment, do you, for my being installed here?"

"I'm not command track. I never pretended to be."

Still the stare. "You think I'm pretending?"

"I don't think you're pretending anything. I *know* you."

Feed the fantasy—and the anxiety. Porey didn't like to be known, but he liked to be respected. The man did have an ego. A parsec wide. Porey smiled slowly, in a way that almost touched the eyes. "Good. A vote of confidence from you, I appreciate, Jurgen. I truly do."

Odd chill of unease as the pod cruised up to the access. Thump of the pressure seals. Hydraulics as it opened and offered its dark, screen-lit interior. Ordinary sounds. Shadows moved on the white plastic of the control console as Dekker put the tape in and he felt an irrational urge to look behind him, as if his crew wouldn't be there.

No damned reason to get nerves. But it had been Pete on the line beside him, all the times before. It wasn't now. It wasn't Elly, it wasn't Falcone. It was Meg, on Pete's tape, and Ben and Sal—they belonged here. He made himself believe that, stop remembering what had been . . .

For no reason, a piece of the puzzle snapped in, unbidden. Null-g. Shadows on the console. He felt the blow at the base of his skull. He knew where he had been—at the entry. Knew where they'd been. Shadows. Two of them . . .

Dammit. Not the time to be woolgathering. He looked back at Ben—Ben looked scared, but Ben looked On, tracking wide and fast on the pod, taking in everything, the same as Meg and Sal. All business—the way they were when the jokes stopped and they were thinking and absorbing. He gave them the lecture tour, the buttons on the console, the read-out window, the authorizations procedure—"Card and tape in the slot for a check-out. It reads your ID, takes your personal numbers and sets, and double-checks the tape for authorizations. Ready?"

"Are you serious?" Ben said. Then: "Yeah. Yeah. Go."

He caught the handholds on either side of the entry, angled his feet for inside and eeled into his station. "Sal," he called back, over the hum of a passing pod, caught her by the arm as she sailed into the dark, shadow against the lights, a glitter of braids tied into a cluster, for safety's sake. He aimed her for the far side of the four-wide cockpit. "Ben." Same as Ben came feet-first through the hatch, for the seat between him and Sal. Meg came last, for the seat between him and the hatch, settled in. Green-lit gold on plain stud earrings. Green dyed her side-shaved profile, green turned her red curls black. Ringed fingers found the belts and buckled in, eyes glowed wide and busy in the light of the screens, assessing the instruments.

He drew his own belt over—he waked reaching for them at night, with a recurring nightmare of drifting free. Suit braces powered up as he plugged in, and the helmet cut off side vision. It was deep-field V-HUD now. Switches on, power up. "Comfortable?"

"Yeah," from Meg. "As possible," from Ben.

Belts were tight. Second tug, to be sure. Orientation run. Starting over, primer stuff—only he wasn't the neo this run. There was something surreal in the moment, in the familiar lights, in the ordinary sounds of the pod, the dark masquerading as routine. They were On. Anxious. Wanting to be right. But he kept expecting other voices.

"This thing got any differences?" Meg asked, last-minute.

He shoved the tape into the console, pushed LOAD. "One. See that yellow ABORT, upper left? Doesn't exist on the real boards. It'll stop the pod—if you don't get a response from me, or if you detect anyone in trouble, you hit that. Takes you right back to the bay."

"Cher," came Meg's low voice, "you just do. I got confidence in us."

"More 'n I got," Ben muttered. "Hold it, hold it. I'm not set yet."

"Response check, thing doesn't glitch, but be sure. Boards are all in test mode."

Passengers was all they were required to be; but that wasn't Meg's style, wasn't Ben's or Sal's either. He tried his own boards, set his arms in the supports, heard Meg's voice saying, "I got it, right on." Ben muttering, "Don't screw it, Dek-boy. Yeah, I'm on, on, go."

Sal's, saying, "Hit it, Dek."

Dark, flash of lights—

He kicked the thumb switch on his keys. Readout glowed green against the dark. Finger moves on opposite hands, the undock sequence switch.

Bang! of grapples. Mag-levs and human voices mixed—a 6 *g* shove butt-first for ten eternal seconds to a sustained straight-at-the-spine shove at +9 *g*.

Green lines wove fast and faster . . . the pod was alive and the tons of thrust were mag-lev sim, but it was all in his hands, responsive to a breath, a stray thought, a moment's doubt—where he was, when he was, who he was with—

He didn't want to do this.

Serious panic, a flash on instruments in chaos—

Then. Not now. Now was now. Not a time to lose track, God, no—

Focus down. Focus wide. Attention to the moving lines, that's all—

"Politics," Porey said, "pure politics. Let me explain it to you. Fifteen of the fifty carriers have to be UDC—that's the deal we cut, and that's what we have to do. The accident *gave* us Hellburner, and that tape's going to *give* us the program. The parliaments on Earth want *responsible* individuals in policy positions—read: no captains will violate policy laid down by the JLC. And this won't change in the field."

Graff stared at Porey. He thought he'd heard the depth of foolishness out of Earth.

Porey made a small, sarcastic shrug. "They have our assurances. And if the news services should call your office, Jurgen, and since you're over Personnel, they might, the answer you give is: No, of *course* these ships are launched at carrier command discretion, with specific targets. No, they will never be deep-launched, with less specific orders. That tactic won't work."

"You mean I lie."

"I mean the Joint Legislative Committee's expert analysts say not. The changing situation over time—read: the commanders of individual ships making decisions without communicating with each other—would make chaos of strategic operations. So it can't be done. End report. The JLC analysts say it's not appropriate use of the riders. The legislators don't *like* what these ships can do, combined with the—irregular character—of the crews we've picked to handle them. These crews are, historically, trouble Earth got rid of. Earth's strategic planners are obsessed by the difficulty they've discovered of conveying their orders to ships in the Beyond—they've apparently just realized the time lag. They can't phone Pell from here and order policy about—"

"They've always known that."

"The ordinary citizen hasn't. The average businessman *can* get a voice link to Mars now. Or the Belt—if he wants one."

Lag-com was a skill, a schitzy kind of proceeding, talking to a voice that went on down its own train of logic with no regard to your event-lagged self. That was one of the reasons senior Com and psych were virtually synonymous. And Earth hadn't realized until now you couldn't talk to a launched rider—or a star carrier? He refused to believe it.

"Lag-com has finally penetrated the civil user market," Porey said, "since *we* increased the pace of insystem traffic. Earthers are used to being told the antenna's gone LOS, used to being told Marslink is out of reach for the next few months, used to shipments enroute for years and months—supply the market counts but can't touch. Their shipborne infowave was so slow as to be paralytic, before we started military operations insystem. The last two years have upset that notion—this, from the captain. So if anyone asks you—of *course* we're going to have a strong mother-system component in FleetCommand. Of course riderships will never make command decisions. We're going to loop couriers back to Earth constantly."

"Mazian's *promised* this?"

"The same as they promised us. —Jurgen, you have far too literal a mind. This is a game. They play it with their constituents. The legislature's technical advisers are under influences—corporate, economic, political . . . but you've met that. They certainly won't deviate from party line. Where does the funding for their studies come from, anyway?"

Lights flared, green numbers bled past in the dark. Do the run in his sleep, Dekker kept telling himself, piece of easy. But it didn't stop the heart from pounding, didn't stop hands and body from reacting to the situation on-screen—you didn't brake the reactions, you didn't ever, just presented the targets to your inert armscomp, accepted Ben was going to miss most of the time and tried not to let that expectation ever click into the relays in your brain.

"Screw that," he heard Ben mutter, and all of a sudden got input on his aux screens, targets lit, armscomp prioritizing.

Chaff, he determined. Then targets flashed and started disappearing. Longscan was coming from a living hand, not the robot inputs. He heard "Shit!" from Ben and saw the scan image shift, tracking fire. Meg's gold data-sift to his highside HUD was making sudden marginal sense. Not like Pete. . . . Not the same. . . . "Doing all right, doing all right," he muttered, "just—" Heart jumped. Hands reacted. Sim did—

He stopped the bobble before his vision cleared. Guys weren't talking, someone had yelped, short and sharp, but the dots that meant conscious were still lit, data was still coming up on the screens, fire was still happening, longscan shaping up. Had three scared guys in the seats. Next four shots were misses. His fault. He'd pulled a panic, lost it—had no time now to be thinking about it—targets—*dammittohell!*—

"The UDC," Porey said, rocking back his chair, "believes in a good many myths. We don't disabuse them. And, yes, this room is secure."

"What else haven't we said? What *else* hasn't filtered out here? Or is this a longstanding piece of information?"

"The ECS4," Porey said, "is fully outfitted. *Fully* outfitted. We're operational, and we have a com system they can't penetrate. To our knowledge—they haven't even detected its operation. Installation on the ECS8—is waiting a shipment. Communications between you and FSO have been, I understand, infrequent. That situation is going to improve."

"When?"

"Estimate—two months, three."

"Until then? Edmund, —I want to know. Who pulled Kady and Aboujib out of the Belt? Who opted Pollard in? Where did this damned new system come in?"

"Exact origin of those orders?" Porey asked with a shrug. "I'm sure at some high level." Meaning Keu or Mazian, which said no more than he knew. "But the reason for pulling them in—plainly, they were Dekker's crew, we know things now about Hellburner we didn't know. We've adjusted the training tape to reflect that, we've chosen a crew with a top pilot to start with a—tragically—clean slate. It's the best combination we can come up with."

"Not to rush into schedule. Dekker's just out of hospital. Look at his psychological record, for God's sake. You're putting an outrageous load on this crew."

"I leave that to the medics. They cleared him. He's in."

"Cleared him with how much pressure from command?"

"What are you suggesting?"

"That there's too damned much rush on this. That Dekker's not ready to go into schedule."

Porey leaned back in the chair, frowning. "You expressed a curiosity about the tape system. Have you ever *had* deep-tape, Jurgen?"

"No." Emphatically. It occurred to him at the moment that Porey could order that even in his case. And he didn't like the thought.

"Ordinary DNI tape isn't so different from deepteach. Less detailed, in general. But the real difference is the class of drugs. Deepteach trank suppresses certain types of brain activity. Eliminates the tendency to cross-reference with past experience. General knowledge is still an asset. Specific training isn't. Hostility to the process certainly isn't. The other trainees have both handicaps. They've been trained otherwise and they won't trust a tape telling them differently. But this crew knows nothing else. They have general knowledge. They're not afraid of it. So their judgment can override the tape."

"Theoretically."

Another shrug. "So the technicians assure us: that with no trained response to overcome—they can do it and not panic. We cut a new tape from what succeeds—and bootstrap the others."

"You bring this *tape* business in," Graff said, "you slip it on a novice crew without an explanation—then you want to shove off Belt miner reactions on Shepherd crews that've risked their necks for a year training for these boards? What do I say to these people? What's the official word? Because the rumor's out, Edmund, they didn't take that long to put two and two together."

Porey looked at him long and coldly from the other side of what had been his desk. "Tanzer's complaining. You're complaining. Everybody's bitching. Nobody in this facility wants to take this program to implementation. I have other orders, Jurgen. If crews die—they'll die in the sims. We do not lose another ship on display. We haven't, as happens, another ship we can lose."

"We haven't another core crew we can lose, either. Where are you going to get recruits if you kill our best with this damned tape? Draft them out of Earth's pool? Persuade the Luna-Sol cargo runners to try what killed the Shepherds?"

"Maybe you don't have enough confidence in your recruits."

"I have every confidence in them. I also know they've never been cut free to do what they know—not once. They're a separate culture from Earth, separate from Mars, separate even from the Belt. The UDC regulated them and played power games with their assignments and their schedules. The JLC changed the specs and cut back the design. These crews *thought* when the Fleet came in here that somebody was finally on their side. So what do I tell them when they ask about this tape? That we took it off the last spectacular fatalities? That's going to give them a hell of a lot of confidence."

"Dekker should trust it. The tape did come from his crew. And he certainly knows the crew we've given him."

"The crew we've given him never worked ops together. They were *financial* partners. Everyone seems to have forgotten that!"

"Dekker's confident."

"Confident, hell! Dekker's numb. He's taken the chaff that's come down from the UDC, his crew's dead, somebody tried to kill him, he's got a personal problem with a MarsCorp board member, which is why the UDC pulled him from that demo in the first place, on somebody's orders I still haven't heard accounted for. You put him into the next mission and what guarantees you won't get the same communiqué Tanzer got: Pull Dekker, keep him out of the media, take him out of the crew that's trained for that run—and then what will you do? Fold like Tanzer did? Or tell the EC to go to hell?"

Cold stare. Finally Porey said, "I'm aware of Dekker's problem."

"Is that all? You're *aware?*—Do you realize his mother and the peace party lawyers are all over the news right now? The case is active again. Do you think that's coincidence? Salazar doesn't care what she brings down."

"I'm aware of Alyce Salazar."

"So are you going to pull Dekker? Or are you using him as test fodder? Doesn't matter if he cracks up in the sims, it solves a problem—is *that* it?"

"You have a personal attachment to this boy—is that your problem?"

No re-position. Straight through. Straight through. He got a breath and tried to tell himself it was all right, it was only a sim. A last target.

Miss. Sal said, "Damn," and: "Sorry, Ben."

"Yeah, yeah," Ben said.

"Dekker." Sim chief's voice. You didn't hear them break in like that,

they didn't remind you they existed unless you were totally, utterly screwed. *"Dekker. What's the trouble?"*

Pod was in neutral now. They wouldn't abort you cold—a shift like that messed with your head. But nothing further was going to happen in the sim. Virtual space was running, green lines floating in front of his eyes, but without threat. His heart was going like a hammer. Breaths came in gasps.

"Muscle spasm."

He lied to the sim chief. Chief was going to order them in, no question. New crew—he could well glitch *their* reactions—He'd never, never gotten called down over com. Never gotten a stand-down like this.

"Going to order a return. Your crew all right?"

"Crew's fine." He didn't get any contradiction over com.

"You want to push the button?"

Abort was quicker. Abort would auto them to dock. His nerves wanted that.

"I'll go manual. No abort." Hell if he was going to come in like a panicked neo. He got his breathing calmed. He lined them up, minute by excruciating minute. He brought it as far as basics. "Meg," he said then, "take it in. Dock it, straight push now. Can you do that?"

"Got it," Meg said. "Take a breath, Dek."

Three more minutes in. Dock was basic—now. Lesson one. Punch the button. Mind the closing *v.* They'd killed one man and a prototype module getting that to work realtime, before Staatentek admitted they had a problem.

Whole damned program was built on funerals . . .

"Doing all right, Meg."

He unclenched stiff fingers. Watched the numbers run, steady, easy decline in distance: lock talked to lock and the pod did its own adjustments.

Bang into the grapples. System rest.

A damned pod, not the ship, but he was having trouble breathing as the hatch opened, to Meg's shutdown—

"Shit!"

His heart jumped. "Easy, easy," he told her, as she made a frantic reach at the board. "Lock's autoed, not your fault, not your fault, it's automatic on this level."

"Not used to these damn luxuries." Breath hissed between her teeth. "Got it, thanks."

No word out of Ben. Ben wasn't happy. Sal wasn't. He could feel it out of that corner. He thought about saying Don't mind it, but that wasn't the case, you damned well had to mind a screw-up like this, and they did. He thought about telling them some of those were his fault, but that wasn't what they needed to set into their reactions either. He just kept his mouth shut, got the tape, grabbed the handholds and followed Meg out the hatch.

Caught Meg's attention, quick concerned look. He shied away from it, hooked onto the handline and heard Ben and Sal exit behind him. He logged the tape out on the console, teeth clenched against the bitter cold.

"Cher," Meg said, gently, hovering at his shoulder, trying for a look at him or from him, he wasn't sure and he wasn't coping with that right now.

"We'll get it," Sal said. "Sorry, Dek."

They were trying to apologize to *him*. Hell.

He started to shiver. Maybe they could see it. Maybe they were realizing how incredibly badly he'd screwed that move—or would figure it once their nerves settled. He didn't know how much to tell them, didn't want to act like an ass, but he couldn't put his thoughts together—he just grabbed on to the handline and headed off down the tube, not fast, but first, so he didn't have to see their faces.

He heard Ben say, "Damn temper of his. Break his neck, I'd like to."

"Hey," Meg said, then, "we screwed up, all right? We screwed it, we screwed him up, he's got a right."

He wanted to tell Meg no; and he wanted to believe that was the answer; but he couldn't. He handed off at the lift, waited for them.

Sal said, "Dek, we'll get it. Trez bitch, that machine. But we'll get it, no problem."

"Yeah." First word he'd been able to get out. He punched the lift for exit level, snatched back a shaking hand toward his pocket.

Meg was looking at him, they all were, and he didn't want to meet their eyes. He stared at the lift controls instead, watched the buttons light, listened to the quiet around him, just the lift thumping on the pressure seals.

"So?" Tanzer asked, on the phone; *"Does this mean a run-around or does it mean you've found an answer to my question?"*

"There is an answer, colonel. Negative. The orders come from outside this base. We can*not* change policy."

"Policy, is it? Policy? Is that what we call it now, when nobody at

this base can answer questions? What do *you know, lieutenant?* Anything?"

Graff censored what he knew, and what he thought, and said quietly, "I repeat, I've relayed your objections. They've been rejected. That's the answer I have to convey, colonel, I'm sorry."

"Damn you," Tanzer said, and hung up.

He hung up. He sat for a long few moments with his hands folded in front of his lips and tried to think reasonably. No, he could not call the captain. FleetCom went through Porey now. No, he would not go running to his crew—and maybe that was pride and maybe it was distrust of his own reasoning at the moment. He was *not* command track. He was *not* in charge of policy. He was *not* in authority over this base, *not* in authority over strategy, and *not* in the decision loop that included the captain, who somehow, in some degree, had to know what was going on here—at least so far as Demas and Saito had said: they'd warned Keu, they'd pleaded with him, and Keu—had refused to rein Mazian back, had *let* Mazian make his promises and his assignments.

So what was there to say? The captain had refused to disapprove Porey's command. The captain had refused Demas, refused Saito . . . who was he, to move Keu to do anything? Perhaps the captain was more farsighted, or more objective, or better informed.

Or more indifferent.

Porey was aware of Dekker's problem? And Porey shoved Dekker and a novice crew toward mission prep?

Bloody damned *hell*!

"You blew it," Porey said.

"Yessir," Dekker said on a breath. "No excuses."

" 'No excuses.' I told you I wouldn't hear excuses, and I wouldn't hear 'sorry.' You're the pilot, you had the say, if you weren't ready you had no mortal *business* taking them in there."

"Yessir."

Porey's hand came down on the desk. He jumped.

"Nerves, Mr. Dekker. What are you going to do about it?"

"Get my head straight, sir."

Second blow of Porey's hand. *"You're a damned expensive failure, you know that?"*

You didn't argue with Porey. The lieutenant had warned him. But too damned many people had told him that.

"I'm not a failure, sir."

"Was that a success? Was taking trainees into that sim and screwing them up a *success*?"

"No, sir."

"Nothing's the matter with you physically. The meds found nothing wrong with you. It's in your *head,* Dekker. What did you claim after Wilhelmsen cracked up? That you *knew* better? Do you still know better?"

"Yessir."

"Can you do the run he did?"

"Yessir."

"You're no use to me screwed up, you are no damned use, mister. I've got other crews. I've got other pilots. And let me tell you, if you don't straighten yourself out damned fast, we've got one more way to salvage you. We've got one more tape we can use, *which* I haven't, because you said *you* were better, because the techs said untrained personnel were better on tape, but if you're no other good to anyone, Dekker, then we might just as well put you right down in that lab and input what *might* improve your performance. You know what I'm talking about?"

He guessed. He managed to say, "Yessir."

"I'll make a promise to you, Dekker. You've got one week. I'm not restricting you, you can do any damned thing you want, I don't give a damn for the regulations, for the schedule, for whatever you want to do. You've got carte blanche for one week. But if you don't pull those sim scores right back where you were before your 'accident,' then we put you into lab, input *Wilhelmsen's* tape into your head, and see if it improves your performance. You understand that?"

"Yessir."

"Are you clear on that?"

"Yessir."

"Then get the hell out of here and *do it,* Dekker, while the labs try to straighten out the damage you've done to your crew. I don't want to see your face right now. I don't know if I want to see it again."

CHAPTER 14

SEQ. 285t-III. Dekker, Paul F. Authorized.

He waited, clinging to the line, felt like a fool inputting the card and checking the tape serial number on the display for the second time, but the cold feeling in the pit of his stomach refused to go away, and nothing seemed right, or sure enough.

Couldn't *remember* if he'd done it. Things he'd done weren't registering. He was thinking on things other than here and now and the number didn't damn matter. There wasn't a training tape he couldn't handle.

Come apart on an orientation run, for God's sake? Their input couldn't have overridden his displays if he hadn't let it, and they were apologizing to him for screwing up? If he was glitching on their input, he could have spared a hand to shut them out. He could have let go the damned yoke and recovered it at leisure. The number one sim was a walk down the dock if you didn't seize up like a fool—

Muscle spasm. Point zero five second bobble—not wide enough to invoke the braces or trigger an abort on a sleeper run like that; and he'd spaced on it—in that five-hundredth second, he'd been in the Belt, he'd been back at Sol, he'd been with Pete and the guys and lost with Cory—God only where his head had been but he hadn't known his next move. He'd blanked on it, without reason, without warning.

Pod drifted up, opened for him. He grasped the handholds and slid into the dark inside—respiration rate coming up. Sweat starting. He could feel it on his face, feel it crawling under the flightsuit as he prepped the boards. Belts, confirm. Power up, confirm. Single occupant, tape 23b, Dekker, P, all confirm.

He adjusted the helmet. The dark and the glowing lights held a surreal familiarity. It was no time. It was every time.

Some drugs came back on you, wasn't that the case?

But the guys weren't with him now. If he screwed it he screwed it by himself. Wasn't going to let them do to him what they'd done to Meg and Ben and Sal, wasn't going to take that damned tape—

No.

"Dekker."

Sim chief again.

"Dekker, you want to stand down for an hour?"

Didn't like their telemetry. Picking up his heartbeat.

"No. I'm all right."

"Dekker."

Series of breaths. "Porey's orders. Free ticket. I'm all right, let it go."

Seemed like forever that light stayed red.

They had guys over in hospital that couldn't walk straight, that never would fly again . . .

Had guys in the mental ward . . .

Sim chief was probably checking with Porey's office.

Calm the breathing down.

Light went from red to green.

Punch it in.

GO!

"Dek," it was, "how'd the run go?" and "Dek, you all right?"

He winced, shrugged, said, Fine, working on it.

And stopped the lift on three-deck, made it as far as the nearest restroom and threw up non-stop.

From Meg, back in barracks, a shake at his shoulder: "Dek, cher. Wake up. Mess call. You coming? You'd better come."

He hauled himself out of half-sleep and off the bunk, wobbled into the bathroom to pop an antacid—the meds didn't restrict those, thank God—and to scrub normal color into his face. He walked out again to go with Meg, navigated ordinary space, trying not to see the glowing lines and dark, not to hear the mags or feel the destabilizing jolts of thrust.

Familiar walls, posters, game tables, drift of guys out to the hall. Ben and Sal gave them a: Come on, you're late, and he wondered suddenly where this hall was, or why he should stay in it, when there were so many other like places he could be—spaced, he told himself, sane people didn't ask themselves questions like that, sane people didn't see the dark in the light . . .

"Hey, Dek, you all right?"

Mason. "Yeah. Thanks."

Hand on his shoulder. Guys passed them in the hall.

"He all right?" Sal asked.

"Yeah," he said. Somehow he kept walking as far as the messhall, couldn't face the line. "I'm just after coffee, all right? I'm not hungry."

They objected, Meg said she was getting him a hamburger and fries, and the sumbitch meds and dieticians would log it to her, the way they did every sneeze in this place, maybe screw up her medical records. He waved the offer off, went over to the coffee machine and carded in.

Nothing made sense to him. Everything was fractured. He was making mistakes. He'd glitched the target calls right and left this morning.

It *had* been this morning. It had to have been this morning . . . but he'd run it so many times . . .

He walked back toward the tables, stood out of the traffic and muttered answers to people who talked to him, not registering it, not caring. People came and went. He remembered the coffee in his hand and drank it. Eventually Meg and Sal came out of the line, so did Ben, and gathered him up.

Meg had the extra hamburger. "You're eating," she said. "You want the meds coming after you?"

He didn't. He took it, unwrapped it, and Ben hit him in the ribs. "Pay attention, Dek-boy."

"Huh?"

"Huh," Ben echoed. "Salt. Pass the salt. God. You are a case today."

"Thinking," he said.

Ben gave him a look, a shrug in his direction. "He's thinking. I don't think I've ever seen that before."

"Ben," Meg said.

"Dekker. Pass the damn salt."

"Shit!" *Wasn't* approved com, the sojer-lads got upset, but *she* was upset, so what?

"It's all right, it's all right," the examiner said. "You're doing fine, Kady."

"Tell me fine, I screwed my dock . . ."

You couldn't flap the voice. "It gets harder, Kady. That's the object. Let's not get overconfident, shall we?"

"Overconfident, my—" She was shaking like a leaf.

Different voice. Deep as bone. "You shoved a screen in over your pilot's priority. Did your pilot authorize that?"

Hell, she wasn't in a mood for games. She thought she *knew* that voice. It *wasn't* the examiner.

"Kady?"

"Had to know," she muttered. Hell, she was right, she'd done the right thing.

"Not regulation, Kady."

Screw the regs, she'd say. But she did know the voice. There weren't two like it.

"Yessir," she said meekly, to no-face and no-voice. Dark, that was all. Just the few yellow lights on the V-HUD and the boards, system stand-down.

"You think you can make a call like that, Kady?"

Shit. "Yessir."

Silence then. A long silence. She waited to be told she was an ass and an incompetent. She flexed her hands, expecting God only—they sometimes started sim on you without warning.

Then the examiner's quiet voice said—she wasn't even sure now it was alive—

"Let's go on that again, Kady."

She couldn't stand it. "Was I right?"

"Your judgment was correct, Kady."

"Ms. Dekker, do you have proof of your allegations?"

"Talk to my lawyer."

"Is it true your son is in a top secret Fleet project?"

"I don't know where he is. He doesn't write and I don't give a damn."

"How do you feel about Ms. Salazar's allegations—"

More and more of it. A Paris news service ran a clip on Paul Dekker that went back into juvenile court records and the other services pounced on it with enigmatic references to "an outstanding warrant for his arrest" and his "work inside a top secret Fleet installation."

Graff punched the button to stop the tape, stared at the blank screen while Demas hovered. FSO had sent their answer: Regarding your 198-

92, Negative. Meaning they'd turned up nothing they cared to say on the case—at least nothing they trusted to FleetCom—or him.

"Influence-trading," Demas said. "Scandals of the rich. Young lovers. Salazar and her money against the peacers. The public's fascinated."

The Fleet didn't need this. He didn't. Dekker certainly didn't. A bomb threat involving Salazar's plane, the peacers denying responsibility, the European Police Agency finding a confidential report in the hands of the news services. Rode the news reports outside Sol Two almost as hot and heavy as the Amsterdam Tunnel collapse.

While Demas and Saito only said, Hold on, Helm. Hold on. *Don't* make a problem, the captain doesn't need a problem.

"I honestly," Demas said, "don't think Dekker needs to see this particular broadcast, regardless of any promises."

"She's never called him. Never returned the call."

"Lawyers may have advised against. I'd advise against. Personally, J-G."

"I knew you would."

"So you didn't ask."

"I don't know Earth. Now I wonder if I even know Dekker. He's never asked me, either—whether there was word."

Light and dark. The AI substituted its interlink for crew, he was *fine* till the randoms popped up, till he saw the wicket he had to make and the pod reacted—bobble and reposition, reposition, reposition—

Fuckin' *hell*!

Screwed it, screwed it—screwed that one—redlight—

You're hit. Keep going. Don't think about it.

Chest hurt, knees hurt, right arm was numb. Damn hour and five sim and he was falling apart—

Made five. Lost one.

Randoms again. Five minutes down. God, a chaff round. . . .

Blinked sweat. Tasted it. *Hate* the damn randoms, hate the bastards, hate the Company, dammit—

Overcorrection. Muscles were tired, starting to spasm, God, where was the end of this run?

Couldn't hold it. HUD was out, the place was black and blacker—

"Dek, Dek, wake up," from the other side of the door and Ben, with the territory behind his eyes all full of red and gold and green lines and red and yellow dots, hoped Meg would just put a pillow over the sumbitch's face. Beside him, Sal moved faintly.

"Dek!"

"Shit," Sal moaned, and elbowed him in a muzzy catch after balance.

"Dek? Come out of it."

"Son of a bitch," Ben muttered, felt a knee drop into the cold air outside the covers and set a foot on the floor, hauled himself to his feet and banged into the chair by the bed.

"Ben?" Sal murmured, but the blow to the hip did it. He shoved the door open into the dark next door and snarled, "Dekker!"

Dekker made a sound. Meg gave a sharp grunt above a crack of flesh and bone meeting. The son of a bitch had got her.

"Dekker!" He shoved past a smooth female body to get a shove of his own in, got a grip and held it. "Dekker, dammit, you want to take a cold walk?"

Same as he'd yelled at Dekker on the ship, when Dekker got crazy. He had one hand planted against a heaving, sweating chest, right about the throat, and Meg had cleared back, gotten to the light switch. He couldn't see anything but a blur, and he didn't let up the pressure—if Dekker moved to hit him Dekker was going to be counting stars, he had his mind made up to that. Dekker was gasping for breath—eyes open now.

"Spooks again," Meg panted.

"I'll say it's spooks, this is the damn spook! I dunno why you sleep with him."

The inside door opened and Sal came in at the periphery of his vision. He heard Meg saying, "It's all right, it's just surface," and kept his own hold on the lunatic, who still looked spaced and shocky. Dekker's heart was going hard, felt like detonations under his hand. Dekker's eyes had lost their glaze, started tracking around him.

Drifted back again, looked halfway cognizant.

"Let up," Dekker said.

He thought about that. He thought about Meg saying for the last damn week Dekker was just confused, and Sal saying back off and give him some space. While Dekker kept a sim schedule the other crews were talking about. He gave Dekker a shove in the chest. Hard.

"Let up, hell. I'll solve your problem, I'll break your neck for you. You hit Meg, you skuz, you know that?" Dekker didn't say anything, so he asked, for Dekker's benefit, "You all right, Meg?"

"Yeah."

"Hell of a bruise coming," Sal muttered.

Dekker set his jaw again, didn't exactly say go to hell, but that was the look he gave, along with the impression he might not be in control of his voice right now. When Dekker shut up, you either kept a grip on him or you got out of his way. So he kept his hand where it was, asked, civilly, "You still talking to him, Meg?"

"Wasn't his fault, Ben." Mistake. Meg sounded shaky herself, Meg had evidently gotten clipped worse than he thought, and that wobbly tone upset Dekker, he saw that. Dekker quit looking like a fight, just stared at the ceiling, gone moist-eyed and lock-jawed.

Great.

He gave Dekker another shove, risking explosion. "You want to, maybe, get a grip on it, Dek-boy? Or you want to schitz some more?"

Dekker made a move for his wrist, not fast, just brushing him off. He let Dekker have his way, stood back and let Dekker sit up with his head down against his knees a moment, to wipe the embarrassment off his face.

"You know," he said, pressing his advantage, "you do got a serious problem, Dek. You busted Meg who's trying to help you, the meds are bitching you're pushing it too damned hard— you seriously got to get your head working, Dek-boy, and we got to have a talk. Meg, Sal, you want to leave him with me a minute?"

Dekker looked away, at the wall. Sal shoved Meg out of the room and Dekker didn't look happy with the arrangement, didn't look at him when the door shut, just sat in bed and stared elsewhere.

Towel on a chair. Ben got it and wrapped it around himself—wasn't freezing his ass off, wasn't matching physique with pretty-boy, either—wouldn't effin' be here arguing with him, except he was supposed to go back into pod-sims with a guy who couldn't figure out what time it was.

"Just drop it," Dekker said.

"Drop it, huh? Drop it? Wake me up in the Middle Of, and I should drop it? We're getting back in that pod at 0900, I'm not seriously inclined to drop it!"

Dekker leapt up off the bed and shoved him. "Just fuck off! Fuck off, Ben, all right? —I'm resigning."

Took a second for that to make sense. Didn't look as if Dekker was going to shove him twice, didn't look as if Dekker was anything but serious. Resign from the Fleet? You couldn't. From the program? Moonbeam had cold feet of a sudden?

Serious problem here, damned serious problem, from a guy who had dragged him into this so deep he couldn't see out, whose neck he had every moral right to break already; Dekker was piling the reasons higher, except Dekker wasn't exactly copacetic enough for a fight at the moment, and there were two women in the other room, primarily Meg, but Sal, too, who would take severe exception to his murdering the skuz.

"Resigning," he echoed Dekker.

Dekker leaned an elbow against the wall, wiped his shave-job mop out of his eyes and muttered, "Before the sim. First thing I can get anybody on mainday."

"When did this notion take you?"

Dekker's jaw locked again, visibly. Knot of muscle. Nowhere stare. But you waited and it would unlock, sometimes in ways you didn't want, but he waited. Dekker took a second swipe at his hair, and stood with his hand on the back of his neck.

"I haven't got it, Ben, that's all. I'm schitzing out."

"Yeah?" He wasn't eager to climb into that pod with a lunatic, he didn't know why in hell he had this urge to pull Dekker out of his funk and assure he was going to have to do that—it was instinct kept him here, to hold the seams of the partnership together, maybe, what they had right now being better than the hellish situation they *could* have. "Schitz I'm used to. You want to explain this new idea?"

"Doesn't need explaining. I can't cut it anymore. Can't do it."

"Nice of you."

"Yeah."

"Dekker, you are the absolute *nicest* son of a bitch I ever met, God, what do we do to deserve how nice you are? We are stuck in this fool's outfit, they're feeding us this damn experimental tape on account of they got it off your crew and *you* skuz out on us. Do you think they're going to give up on the investment they got in us? —No, they're going to put us out on the line with some only skosh saner fool and take stats on how long we take to make a fireball! Thanks, thanks ever-so for the big favor, Dek, and mercy for the vote of confidence, but you got to excuse us if we don't all break into party, here."

"I'm sorry." Dekker turned his back on him, leaned a second against the bathroom door, then went in and shut the door.

"Dekker, —"

Didn't like that sudden cut-off. Didn't like that, I'm sorry, out of the son of a bitch. There weren't locks on the doors. Not in this place. So he hauled the door open.

Dekker was bent over the sink. Mirror-Dekker looked up, white as death, with a haggard expression that scared hell out of him.

"You contemplating anything stupid, Moonbeam?"

"What time is it, Ben? You know what time it is?"

"You know what the hell time it is."

"Not all the time, Ben, not all the fuckin' time I don't know what time it is, all right? I'm losing it!"

"You never knew where it was in the first place."

"It's not funny, Ben. It's not damn funny. Let me the hell alone, all right?"

Hell if. He grabbed Dekker by the elbow and steered him out of the closet of a bathroom, Dekker balked in the doorway and Ben slammed him hard against the doorframe. "Listen, Moonbeam, you don't need to know where the hell you are, that's Meg's department. You don't need to wonder what's coming, that's Sal's. You don't need to know a damn thing but where the targets are and get *me* a window, you hear me? Time doesn't mean shit to you, it doesn't ever have to mean shit, you just fuckin' do your job and leave ours to us, you hear me?"

Door opened. It was the marines or it was Meg to Dekker's rescue. But Dekker wasn't fighting the hold he had, Dekker was backed against the bathroom doorframe with a kind of consternation on his face, as if he'd just heard something sane for once.

"Ben, back off him."

"Yeah, yeah, he's all yours, I got no designs on him." He let Dekker go and Dekker just stood there, while Sal grabbed his arm and said, "Benjie, cher, venez, venez douce."

Hell of a mouse Meg had on her cheek. Meg was wearing a towel around the waist and not a stitch else when she put her arms around Dekker's neck and said something in his ear, Come to bed, probably—but he wasn't sure that was what Dekker needed right now, Dekker needed somebody to bounce his head off the wall a couple more times, if it wouldn't wake the neighbors.

"Cher. Come on."

Sal tugged at him. He went back to their room, Sal trying to finesse him into bed. Ordinarily nothing could have distracted him from that offer. But he was thinking in too tight a loop, about Dekker, the sim upcoming, and the chance of a screw-up. He sat down on the edge of the bed. Sal massaged his back, then put her arms around his neck, rested against his shoulders.

"Meg'll handle him," Sal said.

"Meg should take a good look at him. Sal, we got a problem. Major. He says he's quitting."

"Quitting!"

"You want to lay bets they'll let him? No. Nyet. No way in hell. We got ourselves one schitz pilot. I got nightmares. He's got 'em. He's been pushing himself like a crazy man—"

"Put Meg in?"

"I think we better consider it. I think Meg better consider it—at least on the one tomorrow. I don't know if they'll stand for it. But that's our best current idea, if we're going to get in there with him."

Sal gave an unaccustomed shiver. "They give us that damned tape. Hell, I'm used to thinking, Ben. I'm used to making up my own damn mind. I can't. I don't know that I am. It's a screw-up, soldiers no different than the corp-rats, you get the feeling on a screw-up."

"You're doing all right."

"The scores are all right. But I still never know, Ben, I don't get anything solid about what I'm doing, I don't ever get that feeling."

He didn't either. He hauled Sal around in front of him, held on to her, Sal being warm and the room not.

Sal held on to him. He buried his face in Sal's braids and tangled his fingers in the metal clips. "Dunno, Sal, I dunno. I've done everything I know. Meg should screw him silly, if he wasn't so skuzzed."

"Won't cure everything, cher."

"Makes a start, doesn't it?"

"He's a partner," Sal said.

"Yeah. Moonbeam that he is."

"Soldier-boys aren't going to listen to him or us."

"Dek-boy's on total overload. I've seen this guy not at his best and this is it. He's not stupid. Lot of tracks in that brain—that's his problem. All he has to do is follow one and he's in deep space so far you need a line to bring him back. But none of them pay off. His crew's dead, he's still hurting, not a damn word out of his mama, Porey's on his back, we're in deep shit, and he's not thinking, he's just pushing at the only track he's got. The only one that'll move. Don't give this boy *time* as a dimension. He's just fine—as long as it's *now.*"

"Yeah. Yeah. I copy that. What do they say, hyperfocus and macrofocus?"

"And dammit, you don't let this boy make executive decisions. Paper rank's got nothing to do with this. It's who *can.* Effin' same as the merchanters."

"Meg?"

He hesitated over that. Didn't have to think, though. "Meg's Meg. Meg's the ops macrofocus. The Aptitudes pegged her exactly right. Meg always knows where she is. Knows two jumps ahead. Dek's the here and now, not sure what's coming. No. I'm the exec."

Silence a moment. Maybe he'd made Sal mad. But it was the truth.

"So how do we tell *them*?" Sal asked.

"Sal, —you want to switch seats tomorrow morning?"

She sat back and looked him in the face, shocked. "God, you're serious. They'd throw us in the brig."

"Is that new? No, listen, we can do it: same boards, different buttons. You got eight different pieces of ordnance, that's the biggest piece of information to track on. I can diagram it for you. Inputs, you got two, one from Meg if you got time to sight-see, one from longscan, which you know what that looks like . . ."

"Ben. What *are* you up to?"

"Surviving this damn thing." A long, shaky breath. Going against military regs wasn't at all like scamming the Company. But it did start coming together, now that he was thinking about the pieces. "Because I want the damn comp. Because, screw 'em, it's what I *do.* Because I think that ET sumbitch in there effin' knows we're in the wrong spots and it doesn't feel right to him and it's killing him. I don't know this crew that died, but I can bet you, one of them was the number one in this unit, no matter who they had listed. That guy died and they bring us in and put Dekker in charge? No way."

"What's that make me, mister know-all? Why in *hell* did they Aptitude me longscan and you the guns?"

He'd spent a lot of time thinking on that. He reached up and laced his fingers with Sal's. "Because you want 'em too much, because you *enjoy* blowing things up. —Because that's *not* what the tests want on that board."

She let go. "Where'd you get that shit?"

"Hey. Helldeck psych. Cred a kilo. And I know what the profiles are. I'm from TI. TI *writes* these tests. They got this Command Profiles manual, lays out exactly what qualifications they want in fire-positions and everything else. Enjoying it'd scare them shitless. We're *not* inner system. You got to *lie* to the tests, Sal, you got to psych what they want us to be and you got to be that on those tests—*only* way you get along."

"Meg—Meg is doing all right with this stuff. Tape doesn't bother her."

"Meg's an inner systemer, isn't she? She knows how to tell them exactly what they want to hear. Meg's doing what she wants. We're *not.*"

"So what do we do? Is Aptitudes going to listen, when they *made* the rules?"

"Lieutenant might." If Graff could do anything. If it wasn't too late. He was scared even thinking about what occurred to him. But running into a rock was scarier than that. And that was likely. A lot of scary things were likely. Like a crack-up tomorrow morning. Stiff neck for a week after Dekker's twitch at the controls.

"Should we go talk to him?"

"No. Not direct." He eased Sal off his lap, went and got a bent wire out of a crack in the desk drawer.

"What—?" Sal started to ask, and shut up fast. She watched in silence as he bent down and fished his spare card out of a joint in the paneling.

He put it in the reader, typed an access, typed a message, and said, "'Scuse, Sal. Taking a walk."

Sal didn't say a thing. He opened the door, went out through Dekker's and Meg's blanketed, dark privacy—towel and all.

"Ben?" Dekker asked.

"'S all right," he said, "forgot something."

He slipped out to the corridor, around to the main room of the barracks, and around to the phones.

Linked in. Accessed the station's EIDAT on system level. With a card with a very illegal bit of nailpolish on its edge.

"What in hell?" Dekker asked when he came through again.

"Hey," Meg said. "Easy."

He got through the door and Sal didn't ask a single question, not while he folded up, not while he put the card away in its hiding spot behind the panel joint. You grew up in ASTEX territory, you learned about bugs and you developed a fairly sure sense when you might be a target for special monitoring. He didn't honestly think so. But he took precautions and hoped to hell the bugs, if they existed, weren't optics.

Most of all he hoped the lieutenant was one of the good guys, because the lieutenant was no fool: the lieutenant knew enough to figure who around here could get into the system and drop an unsigned message in his file. They didn't *have* TI techs above a 7A in this place. He'd checked that, already.

CHAPTER 15

Shouting in Porey's office again. Dekker sat on the bench outside, between a couple of marine guards, and stared at the opposite wall, acutely aware of the traffic in the main corridor, people stealing glances in this direction—you got a feeling for notoriety, and disaster, and you knew when you'd achieved it. Wake up to a stand-down and a see-me from Graff, who had nothing to tell him, except that somehow the Aptitudes in his unit were skewed, that they wanted to see Ben and Sal back in Testing, and Graff was due in a meeting with Porey, immediately. Which left him here, in the hall, listening to war going on in the office, and he hoped it didn't aim at Graff. Mutiny in the Shepherd ranks, if that was the case—Graff was the *only* point of reason in their lives since the disaster of the last test; and personally, he wanted to kill Porey. They told him he was supposed to go fight rebels from a planet clear to hell and gone away from Earth and right now the targets he most wanted were Comdr. Edmund Porey and whoever had screwed up Ben and Sal, if that was what had happened.

Something crashed, inside the office. He tried not to twitch, found his hands locked, white-knuckled. The guards exchanged looks, dead expressionless.

Marines weren't anxious to go in there either.

* * *

Weights rang back down into the pod, and Meg collapsed on her back on the bench, nerve-dead. Patterns still danced behind her eyelids, but the adrenaline was gone, it was only phosphenes.

Message came from the lieutenant, and Dek had been outright shaking when he'd read it. *Bad* shakes. Thank *God* Ben had done—whatever Ben had done. Sal was close-mouthed on it—but she had the idea it involved last night, phones, and messages Dek would have highly disapproved.

Weights banged, close to her head. Her eyelids flew open. *Mitch* was standing over her. Hell of a start, even if he was decorative: the son of a bitch. *She* had as little to do with Mitch as possible. Ben and Sal had gotten called in to Testing. Dek . . .

"What's this about Dekker getting scrubbed?"

Mitch wasn't alone. The other traffic in the gym wasn't casual. A delegation gathered around—Pauli, Franklin, Wilson, Basrami, Shepherds, all of them on her case; Shit, she thought, and sat up, looking for a way to shut this action down. "Maybe you better ask the lieutenant. I dunno."

"Word is there was a fight last night."

Double shit. Damned thin walls. "Wasn't any fight. A discussion. That's our business."

Pauli said, "Discussion that scrubs a crew?"

Basrami said, "Word is, the lieutenant gave him a mandatory stand-down. The lieutenant's been climbing all over Testing. Saito's still there, with Porey's com chief. Now the lieutenant's talking with Porey and Dek's hanging outside with the guards. Doesn't look arrested, but he doesn't look happy."

More information than she'd had. The grapevine in this place was efficient except in her vicinity.

Mitch asked, "So what's going on, Kady?"

"All I know," she said, "we got the stand-down before we got to breakfast. They wanted Ben, they wanted Sal in Testing, they wanted Dekker in Porey's office. They didn't want me, so I came here to blow it off."

"Come off it, Kady."

"It's the truth! I don't know a damned thing except Dek's been severely pushing it. Could be a medical stand-down—I hope to hell it's a medical. Porey's been on his back. He hasn't said, but *we* screwed a sim, he talked to Porey, and he's run hard since. You want to tell *me*?"

Silence from the guys. Then Mitch said, "They giving any of this special tape to him?"

Nasty question. "Not that I hear. I don't think so. —No. There's been no time like that in his schedule."

"Are they going to?"

Scary question. "Him, they don't need to, do they? He knows what he's doing."

"Just asking," Mitch said.

"Yeah," she said. "Well, whose would they give to him? Tell me that." Five on ten they made the same and only guess she could, and the idea scared hell out of her. "They took my mates into Testing. They told Dek report in. They didn't tell me an effin' thing. I'm either the only one right in the universe or I must be one of the problems." Which shaded closer to her private anxiety than she wanted. She got up, picked up her towel, for the showers. "So if you got any news, you owe me."

"Nothing," Pauli said. "Except a serious concern for the program. And Dekker."

Belters rarely said "friend." You didn't say, I care, I love, I give a damn. They wouldn't do that. But they came asking. Even that skuz Mitch. Made her think halfway better of Mitch, and that gave her another cause to worry.

"Yeah," she said. "Thanks. If I hear anything, either."

The door opened. Graff said, stone-faced, "The commander wants to see you."

"Yessir," Dekker said.

No questions. Graff was negotiating with an unreasoning, unreasonable son of a bitch and didn't need trouble from another source. He got up and walked in, saluted, and Porey said, all too quietly, "You may have had a problem, mister. This whole damn program may *have* a problem. So I want an answer, I want a single, completely straight answer: If you were second-guessing the Aptitudes, where would *you* have expected Pollard and Aboujib to fit in the crew profile?"

"Ens. Pollard's a computer tech, theory stuff." He had one sudden chance, maybe, to do something for Ben, which would drop the lot of them down the list, break Meg's heart and save all their skins. He debated a split second, then: "UDC Technical Institute. I'd have thought he'd be handling the computers. —To be honest, sir, I'd have thought he'd go somewhere up in Fleet Ops—they were going to send him to Stockholm. He's got—"

Porey snarled, "We've got *enough* UDC hands in this operation right now. What about Aboujib? Co-pilot?"

He didn't know what all this was about. Not enough to maneuver with. "Ben taught her numbers. I'd expect she's good. Longscan or arms-comp. She's—" He flashed on Sal's frustration with the scan assignment. "I don't know—don't know. What she wants—is the fire button." His mind was on what Porey had said about Ben. He thought he might have done Ben harm, bringing in the Stockholm business. He made a desperate, uninvited counter. "Sir, I haven't got any doubts about Ben Pollard. He went UDC because they had his program, but he's Belter. He wouldn't do anything but a hundred percent for his partners."

Porey left a cold, cold silence. He didn't know what he was arguing for or against, or who was on trial. Porey just stared. "If," Porey began, and the phone beeped. Porey grabbed up the handset, snarled, "This is a conference, damn you—" and the face went expressionless while Dekker had time to think, Something's happened . . .

Graff was paying the same kind of attention. Porey said, "Procedures. Stat. —Estimate," and looked grim as he hung up and stood up. "Pod's hung."

"God." Dekker thought Porey wanted the door—grabbed for the switch.

"Dekker!"

"I can help, sir, . . ."

"No!" Porey said. And there was no argument.

Meg hauled clothes on, still wet—damn sweater hung on an earring. She finessed it loose the painful way and got her head through—

Mitch, the skuz, was standing in the locker room door.

She jerked the sweater down. "Getting your thrills, Mitch?"

"Serious talk, Kady. Question. Couple of touchy questions."

Private, the man wanted. Hell of a way to get it; and time was, Mitch didn't get two seconds, but Mitch didn't look like trouble, Mitch looked like business, and curiosity was killing her. "So? Give."

"What is their damn *hurry* with Dek, do you get any feel?"

She bit her lip. Shook her head. "Neg. No. What are you asking?"

"Is Ben on our side?"

"Absolute. *No* question, and Sal and I fly with him."

Mitch ducked his head, looked up with the straightest eye contact she'd ever had out of him. "Ben made a phone call last night. Dek got pulled this morning. You know about that?"

"Yeah. Ben could have slipped it to the lieutenant—about two jumps ahead of me, you want the truth."

"That schedule of his. Did he set it? Is it his choice? Or is Porey doing it?"

"Much as I know it's his schedule." It was sensitive territory. She wasn't sure she wanted to discuss any crew business with Mitch, who was Dek's competition in this place. But Dek had her scared to hell, that was what she had said to Sal and that was what made her confess now. "I can believe Ben might have stopped him. I just hope it didn't land either of them in trouble."

"Second touchy question. You apparently aren't too damn bad. How much of it do you think is tape?"

"I was *good* before I came here, mister."

Mitch held up a hand. "No offense. Straight q & a—they're talking about shoving it on the rest of us, I want to know from the ones that know—does that damn thing really work?"

Sounded like an honest question. "Different way to learn, same way you guys learn, what I hear, this Neural Input stuff. I don't know what's the difference, except we trank deeper—by what I hear. How could I tell? I don't get the other kind."

"Rumor is they're running you guys up to mission level sims. They're saying they're using you guys for guinea pigs because you came in cold, as far as these boards. That if it works with you—we're next and we got no choice. Now they're hauling Pollard and Aboujib back into Testing? Makes the rest of us damn nervous, Kady."

Made her nervous when he put it that way.

"You *know* anything about Pete Fowler, you ever have any—weird feelings off that stuff?"

"I'm not *being* him, Mitch, I'm not any damn dead guy. That's not what's going on. . . ."

"He was twenty-nine, he was a good, fast thinker, he was regular for Elly Sanders—she was the longscanner. You want any more? Pete's faults? His virtues? I can tell you. He was a nit-picking sumbitch about the checklist. . . ."

"I'm telling you I don't know anything about Pete Fowler. I damn sure haven't got a fix on Sal and I always was a stickler for doing—"

"Mitch!" somebody yelled, out in the sims. "They got a pod hung!"

"Oh, *shit,*" Mitch said, and he was running—*she* started running after him, scared as hell, no idea what they could do, why they were going—but it was somebody she knew in that damned thing, and she moved.

"What's the status?" Porey asked, leaning over a tech—Security ops had eight monitors and four of them were black, except for green letters showing CORE-21, that was the sims area, anybody who worked up there knew that section, and Dekker knew it, made a guess what those black monitors showed before Porey got his answer.

"They cut the power, sir," the ops tech said, "Chief Jackson got the spin shut down. Cameras are working, they're on another generator, but all the pods are full crewed and frozen out there til they get power back on."

The core was totally dark, even the access areas—requests for personnel movement going out over com, the same sequence that must have attended his own accident, Dekker thought glumly—like standing off and watching it happen to him.

"Do we have a recovery team out there?" Porey asked, and the tech answered that they were still trying to organize that—only way they had to haul you back if a pod had to totally crash was suit up and go out there; the construction workers that formed the rescue squad were coming in from their off hours and from work around the carrier—

"Too damned long," he said, he didn't care if he was out of turn: "I know the systems, sir, I'm used to a suit—"

"You're *not* going out there," Porey said, and adjusted the com in his ear, scowling, eyes showing the least anxiety while he listened to something elsewhere. "—You have one?" he asked someone invisible. "Suiting now?"

They'd found somebody closer. Dekker drew a controlled breath, then, still wanting to *do* something; but rescue was evidently getting into motion. Black monitors. No emergency lights—the fool engineers had put the viewport shutters on the main power. Power was cut, completely, complete black in the chamber, no ventilation in the pod, no heat, no filtration for anybody out there. God hope the mags weren't all crashed.

"Patch through the suitcom," Porey said. Graff said to the tech at the boards in simulation Control, "Give us audio, here. Are we getting anything out of the pod?"

"We don't get anything. Whole core section's on that generator."

"What the hell kind of engineering is that, dammit to bloody *hell,* what kind of operation do we have here?"

"An old one," Graff said. "Lot of patch-jobs."

"Piece of junk," Porey muttered. "Nothing moves, does it?"

"Not the shutters, not the internal lights—there's a requisition to get them on another circuit, but the engineers have found a problem doing that."

"Can they power up with the rest of those pods sitting out there?"

"Should be able to," Graff said, while Dekker kept his mouth shut.

Should be able to, once they got the one pod clear. If it didn't, if they were all crashed, everybody was in trouble. Imminent trouble.

"One man's not enough out there," he said tautly. "They've got no locators, those are all killed with the power. . . . Sir, in all respect, I know what I'm doing. . . ."

"Shut *down,* Dekker, you're not going up there."

A dim seam of light showed at the edge of one monitor—lock door, he figured, on a leech and hand-battery. Audio cut in, unmistakably a suit com, heavy breathing, little else, and a white star appeared in both monitors: suit-spot shining in all that black.

Sim chief's voice, then: *"You're going across the chamber, zenith climb about ninety meters . . . sensor range within . . ."*

"Copy that." Female voice, unexpectedly. Familiar voice that sent a sinking feeling to the pit of his stomach as the star shot off at a fair speed. Scary speed.

"Don't hurry it, don't hurry it . . ." from the chief. *"Dammit, slow down."*

Meg didn't. Meg was hotdogging it, scaring hell out of him and the sim chief—miner showout, but habitual: a miner knew his distance without his eyes, by reckonings they didn't teach in construction, and she wouldn't miss: blind in the dark, she wouldn't miss: that was the push she was used to—and she was counting and calcing.

"Shouldn't argue with her," Dekker muttered, sweating it. "She knows her rate, she's feeling it . . . tell the chief that."

"Is that Kady?" Graff asked. "Dekker, is that Kady out there?"

"Yessir."

"Get her the hell out of there!" Porey said into the mike. "This is Comdr. Porey. Get her out of there. *Now*!"

Took a little relaying of instructions. Meg developed a problem with her mike. Didn't fool Porey, didn't fool anybody, but there wasn't a thing Porey could do from here. Meg was closing into sensor range, you could hear the pings on audio and see the rate drop.

Then number two monitor showed a faint haze of detail. Chamber wall and a pod directly in Meg's suit spot, he'd bet his life on it.

"She's all right," he said, feeling the shakes himself. "Sir, she knows her business."

Porey wasn't saying a thing about the transmission difficulties, wasn't giving any orders now, he just muttered, "Kady's on notice with me, you make that clear, Mr. Graff."

"Yes, sir," Graff said.

Word came from another channel that the Pod Rescue Unit was

being deployed. At least some of the rescue squad had gotten there, and was launching the track-guided equipment that could tow the pod.

Meanwhile an engineer was giving instructions and Meg started identifying and freeing up the bolts that released it from its track.

"Shit . . ." came over the com; and froze his heart.

"What's the matter?" the chief asked; but he could see it for himself, the pod's number decal—number three. The pod they'd been scheduled for.

"That's Jamil," he said, to whoever cared, and looked for a chair free. But there wasn't one. "Jamil and his guys took our slot—said they could use the time . . ."

Didn't take much calc to find a lighted, open hatch, and Meg beelined for it, braked and took a shaky bent-kneed impact, another showout miner-trick, with a hand-up catch at the rim of the lock to stop the rebound. She cycled the lock on battery power, breath hissing with shivers—it wasn't cold coming through the suit, not this fast, it was shock starting to work, in the loneliness of the airlock. Let the rescue crew do the maneuvering with the PRU, the chief had said, they wanted her out of there and that lock shut before they powered up the mags and she agreed, she didn't know shit about the tow system: it was on now, it was moving, bound for a pod access lock where meds were waiting, and they weren't going to need her unless the mags were definitively crashed.

Moment of intense claustrophobia then, just the ghostly emergency light, then a door opened into a brightly lit ready-room full of guys willing to help with the suit.

She got the helmet off, drew a breath of icy clean air and got a first welcome bit of news—power-up was proceeding, pods were answering; they for sure weren't going to need her again out there, and she could unsuit and take the lift out to gravitied levels and the lockers. Good job, they told her, good job, but they were busy and she got herself out of the way, let them tend the suit, unaccustomed luxury for a miner-jock, and boarded the lift out of there.

Slow, slow business in the recovery of the pod, and they could only watch, in 1-deck Security ops. Dekker hung at Graff's back and Porey's, listened to the output from the rescue team on the open speaker.

They were working into dock now, at access 3. *"That's copy,"* he heard a voice say, and flashed on cold, on dark, on inertia gone wild—

Enjoy the ride, Dekker. . . .

"That's him," he said of a sudden—had everyone's attention, and he looked at Graff, who understood what he meant, Graff surely understood.

"ID that man," Graff snapped, "isolate that voice. —Mr. Dekker—" as he headed for the door. "Hold it."

"Dekker!" Porey said atop Graff's order, but he'd already stopped and faced them.

"I want you to listen," Graff said. "I want you to pick out that voice, all the voices that might be involved."

"Is he meaning the attack on him?" Porey wanted to know, and Graff nodded, leaning over the master com in ops. "Yes, sir, that's exactly what he means. —Play it back, ensign."

"That's copy," the recording said, among others, and Dekker said with absolute conviction, "Yes. That one."

"Who's carded to that area right now?" Porey asked. "Nobody's leaving that area without carding out, hear me?"

"Yes, sir," the com tech said; and relayed to Fleet Security.

"Not everybody's carded in," Graff said. "They probably let medics and techs in wholesale—anybody with a security badge . . ."

"Sir," the tech said, "I think I've got it pinned. That output's on e-com, I've got the serial number on the unit."

"Track it."

Time to indulge the shakes and the unsteady breathing, alone in the lift. *"They're getting telemetry,"* Meg heard, on the com track that was probably going out to every speaker in the mast. *"Four heartbeats."* Best news yet. Thank God, she thought, queasy in the steady increase of *g* against the deep fast dive the car was taking. She clenched her teeth and collected herself, watched the level indicator light plummet until the car came to rest and the door opened on warm air and bright light.

She expected Mitch and a handful of guys; but the room was packed, everybody who could cram themselves in, all wanting news. "Four heartbeats," she told them, which they might have heard, she couldn't tell if the com was feeding through, there was so much racket. She wasn't prepared to be laid hold of, wasn't expecting Mitch of all guys to pat her heavily on the shoulder and say how miner-jocks had their use—other guys did the same, and all she could get out was a breathless, desperate: "Jamil. Jamil took our sim slot . . . anybody seen Dek?"

Nobody had. She was shaking, embarrassing herself with that fact, but she couldn't stop the chill now. A big guy whose name she didn't even know threw his arm around her shoulders, hugged her against his side, and yelled out to get a blanket, she was soaked with sweat.

I'm all right, she tried to say, but her teeth kept chattering. Seeing that number out there had put a shock reaction into her—she wasn't used to shaking; wasn't used to *time* to think when she was scared, or, worst, to knowing there wasn't a damned thing she could do personally to help those guys or Dek. . . .

The blanket came around her. "Tried to kill us," she said between shivers. "Wasn't any fucking accident, Dek was supposed to be in that pod . . . That was *our slot* Jamil took . . ."

"Sims tech Eldon A. Kent," Graff said, reading the monitor, "out of Munich, trained in Bonn . . ."

"I want a piece of him," Dekker said. God, he wanted it, wanted to pound the son of a bitch so fine the law wouldn't have pieces left to work with. "Just let me find him."

"Certainly answers the questions about access," Graff murmured, reading over the data on the monitor. "Free access to the pods, a lot of the techs let each other through, never mind the rules. He's Lendler Corp, he comes and goes—what were you *doing* up there suited, Dekker? What were you doing with the mission tape?"

Piece suddenly clicked into place. Bad memory. Whole chunk of memory. "Wanted to look at the tape, just wanted to look at it—" The disaster sequence. The maneuver Wilhelmsen had failed to make. "Damned set piece. They wanted it to work, they kept training us for specifics. I told them that, I . . ."

"They."

"The UDC. Villy."

"So you went to the ready room, or up to the access?"

"The ready room. To run it on the machine there. They wouldn't let me in the labs, I was off-duty. I just wanted to *look* at the sequence—"

"Where did this Kent come in?" Porey asked.

"While I was running the tape."

"Alone?"

He shook his head. "Guy was with him. I know the face, I can't remember the name—"

"And they came in while you were reading the tape. What did they say?"

"They said they were checking out the pods, they were looking for some possible problem in the sims. They wanted me to go up to the chamber and answer some questions . . ."

Graff asked: "Did you suit to fly? Was that your intention?"

"I—I hadn't—no. I just had the coveralls. I hadn't brought a coat."

"You suited because of the cold, you mean."

"Yes, sir."

"You went up there," Porey said. "What happened?"

"They said put the tape in, I did that, they hit me from the back. Said—said—'Enjoy the ride.' Sir, I *want* these guys . . ."

"Absolutely not," Porey said. "You don't go after them. That's an order, mister."

"Commander, they're up there right now with Jamil and his guys, they've got their asses to cover—"

"Mr. Dekker."

"They're with Jamil!"

"Mr. Dekker, shut *up* and believe there are reasons more important than your personal opinion. We have a program with problems, a ship with problems, and what happened to you and what happened up there isn't the only thing at issue. They're Lendler Corp technicians; and they didn't take a spontaneous dislike to you, do you read that, Mr. Dekker? Lendler Corp has a multitude of Fleet contracts, which has UDC contracts, which leaves us with serious questions, Mr. Dekker, does it penetrate your consciousness that there may be issues that have a much wider scope than your need for vengeance or my personal preferences? If things were otherwise, I'd turn you loose. As is, you keep your mouth shut, you keep it *shut* on this and let Security handle it. We'll get them. It may take time, but we'll get them. We want to know whether there's a network, we want to know if there's any damage we don't know about, we want to know if there *is* a connection to you personally or if you just have incredible luck, do you understand that, Mr. Dekker?"

"Yessir," he said, past a choking anger. "Yessir, I understand that."

"Then you see you keep your mouth totally shut about what you know. You don't even tell your crew; and believe me I mean that. —Mr. Graff?"

"Sir."

"Escort Mr. Dekker to my office. I'm not through with him."

"Walk slowly," Graff said, on the way out of ops. Porey was back there on com calling in senior Security, he was well sure: Fleet Police already had the pod 3 access as secured as it could be with medics at work; they had the answer they'd been looking for and the mess only got wider, with tentacles into God knew what, Lendler, any *other* corporation. You didn't take a highly educated technical worker and suddenly turn him into a saboteur and hand-to-hand murderer, not overnight, you didn't; which meant Kent was other than a peaceful citizen, Kent was skilled and malicious, and *somebody* in Lendler Corp had gotten him credentials and arranged for him either to get here or to stay here, at the time a lot of Lendler Corp had transferred out—Porey was right on this one. They had, as Villy was fond of saying, pulled a string and got a snake. Potential faults in the equipment, faults in the programming, faults in the assignments, and Porey still hadn't closed on the monumental coincidence of his pulling Dekker from the test today in the first place, *why* he'd had sudden misgivings on this day of all days . . .

The message that had turned up in his personal file, with no identifying header *or* record, damned sure hadn't been a spontaneous generation of the EIDAT system, and his stomach was increasingly upset, with guilt over the concealment of that security breach, and the conviction exactly who had inserted that message—along with a cluster of Testing Labs files nobody outside highest security clearances should have been able to access at all.

Bias in the tests, Earth-cultural bias in the Aptitudes, consequently in the choices and reactions trained into the UDC *and* the Shepherd enlistees—a bias that didn't want aggression on the fire-button or command decisions out of the pilots: he'd only to run an eye down the questions being asked and the weight given certain answers to see what was happening; and before the accident phone calls had already been flying back and forth between Sol One and B Dock: Porey had already invoked military emergency on Intellitron in as fine a shade of a contract clause as a merchanter could manage—demanding access to programs Intellitron had held secret thus far: Pending mission. Medical question. Emergency. Credit Edmund for the nerve of a dockside lawyer . . . and meanwhile, aside from the possibility of active sabotage, they had to wonder how many *other* examples of misassigned crews they were going to find, they had a clear notion *why* the UDC crews had had problems, and knew, thanks to Pollard, why the whole program might have a serious problem—which he couldn't, for Pollard's sake, confess.

Friendliest Edmund Porey had ever been to him, after he'd broken the news and Porey had absorbed it. And, dammit, he didn't want Porey's kind of friendship—he didn't want Porey deciding he could help Porey look good, and putting in a request for him on staff, God help him, even if it meant a promotion. Not at that price. And it looked that way now, it looked increasingly that way, with no word from his own captain, no evidence Keu was still in charge over at FSO.

Be careful, Demas had told him last night. Don't succeed too conspicuously.

"Mr. Dekker."

A breath. "Yessir."

"Coincidence in this instance is remotely possible."

"Yes, sir."

"You don't believe it."

"No, sir. I absolutely don't."

"You're probably asking yourself why you were so lucky—why I pulled you from tests."

Another breath. Maybe Dekker hadn't gotten that far. Maybe Dekker was still tracking on the past, pulling up damaged memory—maybe Dekker was thinking of revenge, or Porey, or the multitudinous accesses corporate connivance could infiltrate that a Fleet pilot wasn't educated to suspect . . .

"The reason I did pull you—we found a bias in the Aptitudes. I'm telling you something that's classified to the *hilt,* understand. If it gets to the barracks the wrong way, with no fix, it could affect performance. Fatally. You understand me? We're on a knife's edge here, right now. We don't need loose talk. On any topic."

A worried glance. "Yessir."

"I'm telling you this because I suspect one of your crew made the discovery and communicated it to me, secretly, which is *also* not for general consumption, and when the commander briefs you, don't let him know you know either—*how* I heard could bring one of your crew before a court-martial, do I make myself absolutely clear on that?"

"Yessir." Dekker's voice was all but inaudible.

"The public story has to be that, having experience with this ship, we're going to be re-evaluating certain crews for reassignment—"

"Break crews? Is *that* what we're talking about?"

Damnable question. Touchy question, considering the Wilhelmsen disaster. He paused in the corridor short of the marine guards outside Porey's office, outside their audio pick-up, he hoped, or their orders to eavesdrop on an officer. "Not by fiat. I'm asking for any crews who might want assignments reevaluated—in the light of new data. No break-up of existing crews unless there's a request from inside the crew. We recognize, believe me, we recognize the psychological investments you have."

"Why in hell—" Dekker caught a breath, asked, in bewildered, betrayed tones: "Why didn't you catch it before this?"

"Mr. Dekker, when we began this program, in an earlier, naive assumption of welcome here, we *trusted* the UDC to know Sol mindsets better than we did. We were absolutely wrong. We didn't understand the prejudice involved, against the people we most needed. And your crew is the most foreign to their criteria. More so than Shepherds. Maybe that explains how it turned up with your group. But what I've told you can't go any further. Hear me?"

Dekker drew a shaky breath. "Yessir."

"I have to take your word, Mr. Dekker. Or, understand me—court-martial Ben Pollard."

"I'm giving you a two-day stand-down, Mr. Dekker," Porey said, the friendliest Dekker had ever seen the man, the quietest he'd ever imagined him. It still didn't include warmth. "I don't want you *near* the labs for forty-eight hours."

Graff said, from the side of the room, "I'd recommend longer."

Frown from Porey, who rocked back in the desk chair. "We haven't got longer. You have a mother a great deal in the news . . . which you know. You may *not* know there's a special bill proceeding through a JLC committee, that requires the military to surrender personnel indicted for major crimes, are you aware of that, Mr. Dekker? —Does that concern you?"

A complete shift of attack. Another assault on memory. Sometimes he thought he lost things. "My mother, sir, . . ."

"He's not gotten the headlines," Graff said. "His schedule's been non-stop for days . . ."

"Your *mother,* Mr. Dekker, has a battery of very expensive peacer lawyers, your mother is a cause that's burned a police station in Denmark and gotten a MarsCorp chartered jet grounded in Dallas on a bomb threat—do you know that?"

No, he didn't. He shook his head and Porey went on.

"The whole damned planet's on its ear, there's a lot of pressure on the legislative committee, and you're essential personnel, mister. Your crew is an essential, high-tech experiment that through no particular fault of yours, has taken a direct hit from a damnably persistent woman and a nest of lying political *fools* in the UDC, who are in bed and fornicating with the politicians who appointed them to their posts, the same politicians who are fornicating with the shadow parliament and the peacers in Geneva. That bill is a piece of currency in this game. We have to avoid you becoming another piece of currency in this affair, a damned media circus if they extradite you, and that means getting anything done with this project has assumed a sudden certain *urgency,* do you follow me?"

He saw the lieutenant out of the tail of his eye. Graff wasn't looking at him. Hadn't told him . . . God, *how* much else had Graff kept from him?

Porey said: "We're talking about a fault in the Aptitudes, and I want your well-considered opinion here, Mr. Dekker, whether you want a go-with as-is, or whether you personally want to make a personnel switch. *Both* your crew members are demonstrably capable in the seats they've trained for—but 'capable' is a fragile substance in a Hellburner crew, you understand me?"

"Yes, sir," he managed to say. "Extremely well. Pollard and Aboujib?"

"Exactly."

"Can I talk to them?"

THUMP of Porey's hand on the desk. "You're the pilot! Gut decision! Which?"

An answer fell out. "I'd ask them, sir."

"Correct answer," Graff muttered, looking at the floor.

Hard to argue with Porey. Hard to think in Porey's vicinity. But there was Graff. Graff agreed with him . . . Graff handed him secrets that could mean Graff's own career; and Graff had failed his promise to tell him if there was news from Sol One . . .

Porey said, "Then we'll put the decision up to them, since that's where you want it. No preferences. You've lost one crew. Let's see if this one's worth the investment. Meanwhile, Mr. Dekker, do some thinking about your own responsibilities—like executive decisions. Do you make executive decisions, Mr. Dekker?"

"Yessir."

"Do you remember your instructions, regarding what you've seen and heard?"

"Yes, sir."

"What are they?"

"Silence. Sir."

A hesitation. A cold, cold glance, as if he were a morsel on Porey's plate. Then a casual wave of the hand. "Dismissed. Two day stand-down."

"Yessir." Anger choked him of a sudden, out of what reserve of feeling he wasn't sure. But it wasn't at Graff. He refused at gut level to believe Graff had deliberately lied to him. The service had. The out-of-reach authorities had, and not for the first time in his life. He saluted, turned and reached for the door.

"Mr. Dekker," Graff said, from the side of the room. "Excuse me, sir. —Mr. Dekker, outside, a moment."

"Yessir." He wasn't enthusiastic. He didn't want to talk. But Graff followed him outside, between the guards.

"Mr. Dekker, I failed a promise. —Do you want the information, on your mother's whereabouts?"

He nodded. Couldn't talk. He was acutely conscious of the guards on either hand; and Graff steered him well down the corridor, toward the corner, before he stopped. "Your mother is on Earth at the moment—everything funded by the Civil Liberty Association, as far as we can tell."

"Why?"

"The peace movement finds the case useful—the Federation of Man, for starters—as I warned you might happen; there is a financial connection between certain of these organizations, the CRA, the Greens and a number of other organizations—"

"It doesn't make sense! She's not political!"

"I'm afraid it's rather well left the original issue. It's the power of the EC that's in question. There've been demonstrations at the Company offices in Bonn, in Orlando, Tokyo, Paris—"

More and more surreal. "I don't believe this. . . ."

"There's a great deal of pent-up resentment against the Company, economic resentments, social resentments—so Saito tells me: mass population effect: the case came along, it embodied a concept of Company wealth and power against a helpless worker. The Company is understandably anxious to defuse the situation; they've offered a settlement, but concession seems to have encouraged the opposition. Salazar's plane was forced to land in Dallas because of a bomb threat, that's what the commander was talking about: whether that was a peace group or a random lunatic no one knows. I can't overstate the seriousness of what's happening downworld."

"She's never been on Earth. She can't have any idea what's going on . . ."

"We certainly wish she had decided against going down."

"Did she ever call back?"

"No: my word on that, Mr. Dekker, I swear to you. Most probably her lawyers advised her against it. Most probably—considering who funds them."

"I've got to call her! I've got to talk to her—"

"Reaching her, now, through the battery of bodyguards and security around her, on Earth—I earnestly advise against it. I don't think you can get through that screen. If you do it's almost certainly going to be monitored, very likely to be placed back on the news, by one side or the other in this affair."

"God. Where is she—right now, where is she?"

"Bonn, as of this morning. Mazian is in the same city. There are peacer riots and demonstrations. The news services are crawling all over the city. If you want to communicate with her, you just about have to do it through news releases, and it's not the moment for it. We're imminently concerned about this extradition bill getting through. We don't want the maneuvering going public, and it could if you make a move. One believes the legislators aren't stupid. No one is spelling out to the media what effect the bill will have, no one is saying outright that it's aimed at you in specific, incredibly the news services haven't put it together yet or don't even know about it. It's all proceeding in committee, so far; Salazar publicly making speeches on the fear of some 'criminal element' with a finger on the fire button. Earth is extremely worried about that point."

"Do they know what we are? Do they understand this ship?"

"The general public knows now it's no missile project: no one believed we could maintain cover after the hearings, yes, it's leaked, what it is—senatorial aides, company representatives, nobody's sure exactly what; but we're completely public; and the program, with what we've found out in the last three hours, is in such disarray we can't *take* another round of hearings. The coalition that put command of this facility in our hands is extremely shaky—as I understand it. If political reputations are threatened by the wrong kind of publicity, certain key votes could shift—and we could be massacred in the legislative committee. That, aside from your personal welfare, is why the Company and Fleet Command are extremely anxious to stop that bill; certain citizen lobbies are very fearful of wildcat attacks from the Fleet provoking a military strike at Earth; and even *knowing* it's a certain faction in MarsCorp pushing that bill, certain key senators desperately need a success in this program to play against it or they can't—politically—stand the heat of standing against the bill."

"What do they want from us? I'm not a criminal! Jamil and his crew aren't criminals! I want to know who's trying to kill me that doesn't fucking *care* if they get my crew along with me! Nobody's going to do a damned thing about those guys that did this, are they—are they, sir?"

"Keep your voice down. The guards have audio. We don't even know at this point that it wasn't a simple mechanical. Those systems have been under heavy use. But I'll grant you we don't think that's the case. That's one problem. And I'll tell you between us and no further. I had a real moment of doubt at the outset whether to make an issue of the Aptitudes with your crew or let it ride the way it was. The temptation to let it stand and save this program one more major setback was almost overwhelming—but I know, and I think you know, this system is operationally too sensitive and strategically too critical to accept half right. I hate what happened to Jamil. I wish I'd ordered a general stand-down—but hindsight's cheap. As it is, the pod sims are in stand-down, we've got a question of other sabotage possible—what you've given us is very valuable; but we're running short of time to develop a case, and we're going to have to find answers for a pack of legislators, it's dead certain. Right now I don't want you to think about any of this. I want you to take the stand-down, get a night's sleep, and remember what you know is dangerously sensitive. You understand me on that point?"

"Yessir."

"I have confidence in you," Graff said, turned and walked him back to the marine guards. "Corporal. One of you take Mr. Dekker where he wants to go. Get him what he needs. —I suggest it's a beer, Mr. Dekker. I strongly suggest it's a beer. Tell galley I said so. Check with me if they quibble."

"Yes, *sir,*" the marine said. "This way, sir."

"Beer, sir," the guard said, had even gotten it for him and brought it to him at a table back in the galley, quiet refuge in a flurry of cooks and a clatter of pans around them—and in consideration of the Rules around this place, and politeness, and the damned regulations—Dekker shoved the kid's hand back across the table, with: "Sip, at least. Where I come from—fair's fair."

"Nossir," the corporal said, and shoved the beer into his hand. "We can, any evening, and you guys can't, and, damn, you guys earn it."

Misted him up, he'd had no expectation of that, and he hid it in a sip of beer. Guy he didn't know. Young kid who was going to ride that carrier out there with two thousand other guys and get blown to hell if he made a mistake.

Guy's name was Bloomfield, T.

And if Graff could have done anything personal for him—he was grateful to the lieutenant for Cpl. Bloomfield, who didn't know him, had no personal questions, didn't chatter at him, just let him sip his beer. He felt the alcohol go straight for his bloodstream and his head:

after months of abstinence he was going to be a serious soft hit. He thought about going back to barracks and catching some sleep, he thought about his crew and Jamil and the guys he knew; and he wanted quiet around him, just quiet, no one to deal with, and when they got to the changes they were going to make in assignments—that wasn't going to happen.

He wondered where Meg was, most of all, finally said to Bloomfield, "You have a com with you. You think you guys could locate a female about my height, red hair, shave job. Fleet uniform . . . ?"

"*That* one," Bloomfield said reverently. And kept any remark he might have to himself. "Yessir." And got on the com and said, "This is Bloomfield. Anybody on the com know where the redhead is?"

Remarks came back, evidently. Bloomfield listened to something on the earplug, struggled for a sober face, and asked, looking at him: "You want her here, sir?"

He managed a laugh. "Tell her it's Paul Dekker asking. Cuts down on casualties."

CHAPTER 16

You knew it was bad, Mitch put it, and trez correctly so, Meg thought—when they gave the whole barracks a beer pass, and brought cans and chips into the sacred barracks to boot. Pod sims were severely crashed, mags could be down a week, if sabotage *wasn't* the cause, as was the running speculation in the barracks: in which case, plan on longer.

Beer helped the mood, though: the ping-pong game got highly rowdy, a couple of armscompers not quite in their best form, but at least everybody was laughing. Word from hospital was guardedly optimistic—the meds weren't talking about life and death with Jamil and the guys now, but how long they'd be in hospital, about the percentage they could expect to come back and how soon. Jamil was conscious, Trace was. In the ruckus around the table, nobody questioned Ben and Sal slipping late into barracks. Ben just settled down soberly on Dek's other side with: "Heard the news. Bad stuff," while Sal went for beers.

"Meg pulled them out," Dek said. "Got to them fast as anybody alive could. And the sim chief was on fuckin' duty this time, didn't have to *stop* to get fuckin' Tanzer's fuckin' authorization, he just braked the other mags and cut the power, was all. The worst part's the stop, I can tell you that. —They go on and switch you guys, or is somebody going to tell me what they did, or what?"

Dek had had considerably more than one beer, not a happy drunk, but direct.

"Yeah, they switched us. Damned right they did."

At which Dek looked at Ben and Meg recognized it was a good thing Sal came back with the beers.

Dek asked: "Why in *hell* didn't you tell me?"

Ben took his beer and Meg held her breath. Ben said: "Because they could've said no deal. And you already knew."

"I didn't know."

"Yes, you did. Give me armscomp, hell, I don't want the guns . . . why'd they give me the guns? I'm a numbers man. So Sal said, 'Want to trade?' and I said, 'You friggin' got it, give me the comp and I'll get you the fire-tracks . . .' "

"Bull*shit,* Ben." Dek's voice wobbled of a sudden. "What are they going to do about it, then?"

Like he *didn't* know. Like he hadn't told her, in a couple of minutes during which Cpl. Bloomfield had been calling the hospital, checking on Jamil.

"Come on, cher." Sal squatted down with her beer and patted Dek on the knee. "Screw the regs. Ben's the numbers, Ben's always been the numbers—"

Ben said, "Armscomp and longscan's integrated boards, what's the difference, who's punching up, who's punching in? They ran us switched, as a pair, didn't have an iota of trouble with the sim—Sal's got to get the feel for the ordnance, but she's on it . . ."

"It's not a free lunch, Ben."

"Close as. I got my hands on that *system,* Dek-boy, I got a system runs like it's friggin' elegant—"

Ben was in serious lust. Dek looked at him. Dek was going to hit him, Meg thought, poised to grab. But Dek didn't.

Sudden *quiet* from the ping-pong match. Rapid fall-off of noise from the door inward, and she looked, where, God, it was *UDC* uniforms incoming, senior guys; and the lieutenant was with them. Guys were coming to their feet. They did.

"Villanueva . . ." Dek murmured. The redoubted Captain Villy, then.

"At your ease," Graff said—official voice, that. *Something* sure as hell was up. Nobody moved. "Personal message first," Graff said, "Jamil says he's coming back. Says he and Dekker are in a race."

Fly-by was a show-out, but, God, that was good news: he was no cheap write-off and neither was his crew. Cheers at that. A faint laugh out of Dek.

"As you know," Graff continued, "the mag interfaces took damage in shut-down, repair crews can handle that . . . but the larger question is what caused the pod to hang, and we are not putting crews back into the moving sims until we can pinpoint a cause and ensure operational safety. This does not, however, mean the program is at stand-down."

Whole room must be breathing in unison, Meg thought. Good on everything they'd heard so far. But there were the UDC uniforms.

—Just hope to God they aren't putting us back under Tanzer.

"—Lab-sims will continue as scheduled. We have also made selection of Fleet crews for a carrier operations exercise—"

"Test run," Dekker muttered, at her side. Translation from a lot of sources, to the same effect.

"—starting within the hour." Quiet settled. Quickly. "In the meanwhile we are taking steps to integrate Fleet and UDC instructional *and* operational personnel. You will see UDC personnel in Fleet areas, eventually in barracks: on which matter I want to say something specific—"

Rising murmur of dismay. The lieutenant waited, frowning.

"There was an incident reported to me, out of rec-hall, an attempt from a UDC crew to meet this company halfway, which was reciprocated with good grace. As a pilot myself, I appreciate the criticality of operational confidence in fellow personnel—let's be blunt: confidence of that kind was a casualty of the Wilhelmsen run.

"But what went wrong with this program does not serve this program; and when you're heads-up and hands-on, what doesn't serve this program doesn't serve *you* or the carrier you're defending. I don't have to spell out to you the reality for the future: that you will be working with UDC crews, whose lives will be equally at risk, including the lives of personnel aboard your carrier. Competition is well and good where it brings out extreme effort. But the relationship between the four core crew members of this ship will be extended eventually to the complete thirty-member support team aboard, who will rely on core crew: in the same way, a carrier's four Hellburner crews will have to rely on each other, and on that carrier and its internal support crew, for survival. There is no more serious business. Those of us from merchanter background have never quarreled with your style or your customs—and we refuse to quarrel with the personal customs of our sister service out of the inner system. *Whatever makes a crew work,* is that unit's business and only their business: that's the position we've always taken. That's the position we expect you to take now, because when you're out there in the wide dark, friends, your personal *style,* and whether you're from Sol's inner or outer system, doesn't make a damn bit of difference. The reliance you have on the crews making up your defensive envelope—that's all you've got. Those are your brothers and your sisters. And the uniform will not matter."

Murmur from the barracks, worried murmur.

Graff cut it off with: "The *names* of the pilots . . ." and got instant quiet. ". . . of the three crews selected, given alphabetically: Almarshad, . . . Dekker, . . . Mitchell. Those crews: pack immediately and board ECS4 within the hour; your quarters in this barracks will remain in your name, sacrosanct. You have no mass limit for this particular run: the carrier's engines will not notice your handweights or your case of soft drinks, for that matter; but remember that all electronics aboard must be listed with the duty officer, and alcohol and medications of any sort must be dispensed by carrier staff only.

"Other crews will keep listed schedules. That's all, guys, have a good evening. We'll have a further briefing after breakfast call."

"Lieutenant!" Mitch called out. "Is that as in—*test flight?*"

"It's as in keeping this program going, Mr. Mitchell. You'll get more specific briefings after you're aboard. That's all I can tell you. I won't be making this trip. You'll be under the orders of Comdr. Edmund Porey, specifically. Goodbye, good luck, good outcome."

"Porey!" Sal breathed.

"What in hell are they doing?" Ben muttered, which was what *she* was thinking. "They're crazed," Dek said, and called out, "Lieutenant!" started across the room.

And stopped, still, arms at his sides, just stopped, for no reason she could see. The lieutenant was still standing there, looking straight at him with a worried expression, but Dek didn't ask his question and the lieutenant didn't give his answer.

"Shit!" Sal said, and went for Dek before she had the brains to, as Graff walked out with Villanueva, and guys were coming up and accosting her and Sal and Ben with congratulations—noisy and excited gatherings around Almarshad and Mitch and their guys, speculation flying . . . upbeat: the whole program had crashed on them, and now everything was moving faster than anyone thought.

"Dek." She got his attention and he looked sane—sane and a little shaken. Ben overtook and asked: "What are we *doing* in this sort-out?"

"We have to pack," Dek said for an answer, which meant, to an old Company hand, We can't discuss it here.

* * *

Another time-glitch, the station's smooth pale surfaces to the carrier's spartan corridors, foam steel and color codes, lights that worked only when there was presence, hand-lines rigged every which way, and déjà vu on every surface. The rigging crew had been kind enough to supply a hand-line with a color cue and Dekker followed it, herding the duffle along, the head of his little column, Mitchell's group and Almarshad's. Long, long way from the entry to the rider loft: the lifts wouldn't take them where they wanted to go so long as the carrier core was crashed, and the rules wouldn't let you do miner-tricks, not on Porey's ship, he had that by experience. You slogged it the hard way, and expected sore arms.

Ship's officer was ahead, check-in point. "Welcome aboard," they got; and a copy apiece of the ship's internal regs; and the standard information on alcohol, volatiles, explosives, electronics, and live animals or plants.

"Inner perimeter take-hold for power up . . ." rang out on the speakers—inner perimeter didn't mean them; and the petty officer said, "Core's going to engage for you. You can take the lift, captain's compliments."

Captain's compliments. He took a breath, exchanged glances with his crew, thinking, Bloody hell . . . because extravagant gestures from Porey were highly suspect. The man *liked* causing pain: he'd met what he'd taken for examples of the type, but cheap talent, compared with Porey's position and intelligence and potential. He didn't want to be on this ship, he didn't want to be under Porey's command, even feeling as he did now that Porey was a competent commander—he knew in his mind that they were aboard for security reasons, not because of the test; and they weren't mission candidates, he'd said as much to his crew in the privacy of their quarters, but the way this was starting out, this move on Porey's part—was Porey in games mode. You bet your life in your nerves and your skill, and they had Porey jinking like this to start with, yanking them out, putting UDC into the barracks when he damned well *knew* they were worried about UDC security? A dozen guys with combat nerves, trained to deal with this kind of thing, and what in hell was Porey up to, making maneuvers on the ones trying to make his program work?

Snake, he thought as he punched the lift call. It's politics, it's damned, stinking politics, that's what it smells like—he's afraid I'll talk, he wants me where he can control com, where I can have another accident if it comes to that—man'll do anything, nothing in him you can get hold of, nothing gets to his eyes except when people squirm—he enjoyed it this morning, when he knew he'd got a hit in, and I hadn't done anything, he's *that* kind . . .

The siren blasted the thirty-second warning. Surreal sound, one he'd heard a handful of times in his life, when he'd ridden out from the Belt.

"Helluva surprise," Almarshad muttered. "Nobody sets foot on this carrier but the commander's own staff, what any of us have heard, not even the lieutenant. Don't they trust each other or what?"

Almarshad wasn't thinking about surveillance. Wilson wasn't, either, who said, "Wish the lieutenant was going," as if Porey wouldn't eavesdrop. Dekker felt a cold fear, of a sudden, that not all of them might come back down this particular lift again. Mitch's crew and Almarshad's: the mission team and the backup, that was the order of things he could see, and he had a sudden claustrophobic sense he couldn't go through with this, couldn't watch this, couldn't stand another watch in mission control while something went wrong . . .

The deck vibrated with the engagement of the core. The lift door opened to let them in.

Motion instead of thinking—a moment of dumping thoughts and negotiating the door, null-*g*. He got himself and his crew and their baggage in with two other teams, grabbed the take-hold in the corner next to the lift controls and stared at the panel, read the instruction and warning stickers on monofocus and didn't blink, because he could lose himself right now, lose where he was, and when this was, and what he had to do . . .

G increasing. "Hold on," he said, as the indicator approached the loft exit. The car hit the interface, jolted into lock with the personnel cylinder. The door opened . . .

Wood and sleek plastic. Carpeted burn-deck . . .

Looked like the Shepherd club on R2. Like exec offices.

"My Gawd," Meg breathed at his back. "Is this us or Porey's cabin?"

"It's us," he said in shock, "it's evidently us."

Wasn't real wood, it was synth, but it was good synth. There was a tended bar, an orderly with trays of food and null-capped liquor—there were more orderlies to take their duffles and carry them away . . .

"Shee-it," came from Sal. And Ben:

"Class *stuff*, here."

Reality was completely slipping on him. He gave up his baggage to the orderly who caught a look at his nametag and took the duffle away—no wide spaces, the whole huge loft was diced up into safer, smaller spaces, by what he could see from his vantage; it hadn't been like this the last time he'd been aboard. Bare girders on the ECS5—no paneling, no carpet, no interior walls and no orderly with cheese and crackers and margaritas and martinis. The Shepherds were right in their element: Mitch said, "All *right,*" and moved right in on the bar; and Ben didn't blink, Ben had been living the soft life on Sol One; Meg and Sal had been with the Shepherds—

But he hadn't. This wasn't real. Not for him. It wasn't ever supposed to be for him . . . there were people who had luxuries and people who didn't have, by some rule of the universe, and he couldn't see himself in a place like this . . .

"As you were." Porey's voice, deep and live. He looked around at the outer-corridor entry, as the commander walked in. Porey strolled past Mitch to the bar and picked up a cheese and cracker, popped it in his mouth. Nobody moved. Nobody thought to salute. It was too bizarre, watching Porey walk a tour of the very quiet area.

"We had a problem. We still have a *problem,* gentlemen. —Ladies. —We have sims down—again. We have one of our best teams down—again. This wasn't your fault. Fixing it, unfortunately, is your responsibility. Seeing you have time and opportunity to focus on the job at hand—is mine. I've pulled you out here, and I am pulling this carrier out of station. Our final Hellburner prototype is mated to the frame, we're proceeding with deliberate speed, we've advised the necessary powers that there will be a test, and we are, frankly, using the time to make our final selection. Three units will be using traditional lab sims, which we can manage aboard this ship, and using sims *in* the actual prototype, daily, shift after shift. Mr. Dekker's unit will be using something different in addition, which we are watching and evaluating. Selection will be solely on the basis of scores and medical evaluations.

"Alcohol is not a prohibition during this watch. It will be available from time to time as schedules permit; but I suggest you not have a hangover in the morning: schedule will start with orientation to the library, the loft, the prototype—

"About which, remember you people are the best of the best—a carrier's survival and the accomplishment of its objectives is in large part your mission. You will live very well here, as you can see: core crews and technicians will occupy these quarters, with adequate staff to assure your undivided attention to your duty, which is solely the operation of your craft, the protection of your carrier and the achieving of strategic and tactical objectives. Additionally, privilege is extended in special facilities to your maintenance personnel, your library research technicians, and your communications and analysis personnel—you will sit at the top of a pyramid of some seven hundred staff and crew, with information gathering and processing facilities interfaced and cross-checked with the nerve center of the carrier itself. Everything you need. Anything you reasonably request. And, yes, *tactical* and targeting decisions will be part of your responsibility, in consultation with the captain of this ship. You will learn to make those decisions in close cooperation with carrier staff, decisions which were not, until now, your responsibility. Command believes your expertise in gravity-bound interactions and object location is an invaluable resource; and you will no longer receive cut-and-dried mission profiles. You will construct them yourselves. This is a policy change reflecting a change in the source of policy: how long we can maintain that control of policy rests directly on your successful completion of this mission.

"In the meanwhile, enjoy yourselves, ask the staff for anything within reason, and consult your individual datacards for further briefings." The second half of the cracker and cheese. Porey walked slowly toward the exit. And stopped. "Enjoy yourselves, gentlemen. Ladies."

Scared hell out of a guy—Porey, as Meg would put it, doing courtesy.

"Shit," Ben said, closing ranks with him and Meg; and Sal said, close after, "So that's Porey up close."

"That's Porey," Dekker said.

"Po-lite chelovek," Meg said. "Nice place, and all. . . . You wouldn't ever think it, would you? Son of a bitch."

A massacre, a slaughter of the innocent. Graff braced his finger against his lips, watched the vid in dismay, the crowd, the peacers shouting, the blond woman with the stringing hair looking distractedly left and right over the crowd like something trapped. Reporters asked, "Is your son the model they're basing this tape on? Are you in communication with him?" Ingrid Dekker shook her head in bewilderment, saying, "I don't know. I don't have anything to do with him, nothing he did has anything to do with me . . . it's never had anything to do with me . . ."

God.

He sat there, watching the alien scene, steps of some ornate building, a cathedral, they said, in London, the placards and banners, the sheer mass of human beings . . .

À bas la Compagnie, they were yelling. Down with the EC.

And elsewhere on Earth's life-rich surface, a UDC spokesman was claiming that the attitudes of the rab movement were infiltrating the Fleet, that the real aim was to disarm Earth's local forces, that the Earth

Company was attempting to use the Fleet and the whole construction push in the Belt to take political control of the UDC and establish a world dictatorship . . .

Disaster. Utter political disaster.

"The tape is the damning thing. Someone's given out details. Someone in a position to know what we're doing—"

Saito said, "Don't discount Tanzer. The UDC has those records at their disposal, a lot of damaging data. We had to accept the UDC structure in place, and after the takeover, we knew it was a bomb waiting to go off."

"What side are they on, Com, for God's sake? Do they think it's a bloody game we're playing?"

"Their power is in question. Their sight has unquestionably shortened. The question whether or not they're in control of the EC or whether the EC is in control of Earth's policy—it's a very large, a very sensitive, issue in this system. The EC has enormous power, a constituency spread over the stations and the refineries and worlds outside this system. And we outsiders only know the EC. But there are governments, many governments on Earth, that consider the situation out there solely the EC's war."

"But it *is* the EC's war. Do any of us doubt it's the EC's war? The EC's cursed emigration restrictions created the mess, *they* motivated the dissidents to move out, *they* insisted on micromanaging at lights distance. Every stupid decision they ever compromised their way into creating this war, but the fact is something very foreign is coming *here,* that's the point. They're worried about tape-training off a rab model because the *rab* movement is foreign? The rab isn't azi. The rab isn't designed personalities. The rab isn't an expansion into space so remote we don't know what may come out of it or what in hell they're going to provoke . . . *Belters* are foreign? They should worry about me, Com. *I'm* foreign. *I'm* more alien than anything they've ever met!"

"Maybe they do worry. Maybe that's what that mob in Geneva is really saying. Give us back our control over things. Make it stop. Make it the way we always thought it was."

"It never was. Not for one moment was the universe the way they imagined."

"Of course it wasn't. But they thought they knew. They thought they controlled it all. Now they know they don't. And that poor woman—is the symbol of their outrage."

"Alyce Salazar has to be the EC's greatest internal liability. Why in *hell* do they go on letting her take the offensive?"

"Principally because Mars wants its independence. Because Mars has gotten quite different, quite alien from Earth. That's what I've turned up on the Salazars."

"Cyteenization?"

"Something like. Something like the Belt—with nostalgic conservatism as the engine, instead of the radical reform that drove the rab to the Belt. They cling to an Earth that never existed. They're the pure article, more Earther than Earth is—maintaining the true opinion, the true Earthly tradition. Never mind the outbackers are eccentric as they come. The corporate management runs the government, quite conservative, quite protective of their personal interests and their family influence."

"I thought that was illegal."

"It is. But it's the driving force in Martian society—who's in whose camp. Understanding what the daughter's desertion meant to Alyce Salazar—simplistically, face-saving has to be a large part of her motive, by what we've turned up. The girl escaped her mother's authority by literally slipping through customs and eluding her mother's personal security: that was one blow to the Salazar corporate image; more extravagantly, she embarrassed her mother by dying, quite publicly, quite firmly associated with Belter rab in a fullscale Company disaster. The daughter was clearly a dynastic hope on her part—a bid to extend Salazar's influence into another generation. A lot of Salazar alliances were built on that assumption."

"Which had to be revised at the daughter's death."

"Which to a Martian corporate, was a major disaster. A threat to her immediate control. It's radicalized the Salazar influence: she's—certain people think, calculatedly—offended certain elements that oppose the Company. The consensus I'm getting from intelligence is she's not mad, she calculatedly created a cause and an opposition to force the EC itself down her path in a move to come out of this more powerful than she was. That's what we're dealing with. She's maneuvering for power equal to the EC president—and the EC so far is paralyzed, because of who's backing her. They can't betray the conservatives in Bonn, or it erodes a structure they've built up over decades. The conservatives there are in fear for their lives over the radical resurgence. And *that* promotes Company hardliners, like Bertrand Muller. Muller is for the war, incidentally. He wants us to 'recover Cyteen.' "

"My God."

"He calls it a colony. What do you want? He's ninety years old, he formed his current opinion on his fortieth birthday, and he says the Company police who fired on the rab were defending civilized values."

"We're in the hands of lunatics."

"Of financiers. Far worse."

CHAPTER 17

Hit it, hit it, hit it—"

Breathless dive down the handlines for the seats, one, two, three, four . . . in place, switches up . . .

Launch. Surreal burst of static while the screens and the V-HUD spieled numbers and lines . . .

"Shit!" from Ben. You couldn't cure him—or Sal; and there wasn't a miracle, they'd screwed the first run, the second and the third, but damn, Meg thought with half a neuron to spare, it felt better of a sudden . . . wasn't garbage she was screening, it was starting to shape itself—

Objective wasn't *there,* God, intelligence gaffe—

Time to sweat. Ben was on it, logicking his way for the current location. Dek said, "What the hell?" and Ben confirmed a fire-zone. Virtual ordnance blasted out into virtual reality and she figured—yes!

"Got it, got it, got it—"

"Watch that mother!"

Fan of junk in the carrier path. Dek repositioned and gave Sal the window on a roll to the main objective, and Meg input him the latest calc in long vision, new definition to the hostile fire-paths he was ready to see, more precise positions she was inputting to Sal and to him.

Feeling too good, too damn good, you didn't cut a rip like that, couldn't sustain it . . .

Couldn't get overconfident, the damn sim kept throwing them targets and you couldn't *believe* you were getting them, effin' sim had to be playing with them . . .

Couldn't go on this way—she was the only one in the crew who had time to worry, worry was the job description, taking the long view, mission objective, degree of criticality, sight and target, sight and target, priority was seen to, ride home couldn't be this—

"Shit!"

Whole list of hits. It had felt too good all the way through, and Dekker shook his head, looking at the outcome, all of them gathered around the table, getting the same news. Objective achieved, path cleared, flock of surprises locked and taken out . . .

"Too soft," Ben muttered. "Too soft, this thing. I don't like it. It's not supposed to fall down like this . . ."

Dekker rocked his chair on its hinge, propped a knee against the table and surveyed his crew, the chart-table with its windowed displays—not the stuff they'd worked with in the station, not the hard plastic chairs and the scrub-boards and the antique display system: anything they wanted, Porey said, and for himself he still had crises of disbelief.

And moments of slipping reality—like this one, that showed him faces he knew with reactions that just weren't wrong . . . Pete and Elly and Falcone riding in the cockpit with them an hour ago, if he wanted to be spooked about it; but that *wasn't* really what had happened: the carrier had that tape lab down the corridor, the way the carrier had a lot else it hadn't let out, and his crew spent hours there, but they didn't drug deep anymore, they didn't need to, that was the story from the tape-techs. Done was done and their sessions were simply reaffirming the synched reactions, making sure—Meg said—they didn't pick up any bad habits in live practice. . . .

Live practice. Hell of a way to word it, considering.

They ran the sims in the prototype itself up to four hours a day, its V-HUD and instruments linked realtime to the carrier boards and the sims library, thanks to what Ben called the effin' difference between the UDC's EIDAT and the Fleet Staatentek. Ben seemed personally vindicated in that—what it all meant, he wasn't sure, but it ran.

And they did, not the first time, damned sure, the screw-up had been what Meg called egregious and Sal called words he'd never heard. Until, this sim-run . . .

This run, he looked at the result and the fact Ben had psyched that relocated target right and laid the probability fan right *over* the son of a bitch, dead center—that was a fluke, but Ben swore he'd had a good hunch—which was what Elly had used to say. Same words. That was a spook-out, too; but it was another fluke. The cockpit wasn't haunted and his crew didn't see spooks in the mirror. He slept with Meg with no illusions it was Pete Fowler, hell if, Meg would say. You didn't confuse one with the other . . .

And that still wasn't what worried him. It was what Ben said, it wasn't supposed to fall down this easy. They were out here on no other reason than keeping *him* away from the media, he told himself that once a day and he managed to relax and worry about Mitch and Almarshad, who were the ones in jeopardy—*still* catching glitches; and the crew who was dogging it and trying to come up from scratch and a couple of total disasters pulled a hundred percenter?

He'd thought he knew the answers, he'd eased off, kicked back, taken it for granted he was just going to steer while everything was going to go to hell and they started handing him stuff that fit together.

Adrenaline had come up, hold-it-steady had become tracking-on, this last run; he was still hyped and on his edge and he hadn't been this alive down to the nerve-ends since—

Since he'd screwed the sim. You knew all along something was wrong with our set-up, Ben kept insisting. And by comparison, now it wasn't wrong, and he couldn't sit still and couldn't help remembering how it felt to be a hundred percent On, and right . . .

With a crew he *cared* about, dammit, more than he'd ever cared about human beings in his life, and too damn many deaths and too many lost partners, with a chance to make runs *they'd* plotted, the way the UDC hadn't let them do it, and that perfect run lying on the table saying . . . Can't do it twice. Complete fluke. Can't pull it off again . . . System can't be that perfect. Something's wrong.

His gut was in knots and his suspicion began to be, in two blinks of an eye and the work of an overhyped brain, that it could be working because his team had come in with miner-experience, something the lofty Shepherd types with their fancy tech hadn't had, or—

Or the tape off his dead partners worked, and Porey *hadn't* given up when they'd had to downgrade the crew to basics—it wasn't basics anymore. They'd either pushed the sim to the limit—or it had lied to them. And he didn't put that past Porey, he didn't put anything political past Porey, if he wanted to prove something to some committee in charge of finance . . .

They were on the damned *list,* that was what, they always had been, that son of a bitch had jerked him sideways and just kept going with his crew. What was it, a confidence-building exercise? Another damned psych-out for more damn political reasons? He felt sick at his stomach.

"You all right, Dek?"

He looked at Meg, realized everybody was looking at him.

"Dek," Ben said, "you aren't spooking on us, are you?"

He shook his head solemnly. "It's August eighth, Ben."

"Huh?" Sal said. Meg frowned. But Ben said,

"It better be, Moonbeam. It had effin' better be."

"Yes, sir," Graff said at the table, hands folded, looking straight at two very anxious senators and a busy background of senatorial aides. There was a committee, inevitably if there was a glitch, there was a committee, thank God currently meeting at Sol One, in the comfort of class 1 accommodations: it wanted answers and this was the forerunner, the shockwave.

"*Why* is a junior lieutenant left in command of this base? What in *hell* does your base commander think he's doing taking that carrier out? We give you the authority you ask for, and immediately the program goes to hell in a handbasket, while the officer in charge removes a carrier and declares he's going to test, without notifying the UDC or the Joint Committee, *with* a highly controversial figure aboard, conveniently unavailable to an ongoing investigation, while a distorted version of the whole damned training program leaks to the media? What kind of circus are you running here?"

His stomach was in knots. He missed certain of the references. Demas and Saito had advised him certain things to say, certain points to make, the direction he should go with these men. But Demas and Saito didn't know one truth he knew. Neither did Porey and neither did the captain.

"Sir," he began on that track, "with all respect, I deny that the breach was in our Security."

"Are you suggesting the UDC leaked it? What about Dekker's phone call to Sol One? What about other phone calls from other Fleet personnel?"

He hoped to hell there wasn't a recorder going. "Let me explain, sir. Fleet personnel are contained in a security cocoon within the former administrative apparatus. Our personnel are issued cards which do not work with civilian accesses, which can't access BaseCom or the internal phone system without going through FleetCom, which is physically aboard the carriers, if there were anyone outside this facility for them to call, nearer the Belt. The one exception was Dekker, who—"

They began to interrupt and he kept going. "—who made his only call to his mother in my office, on my authorization, and I recorded the call in its entirety in case any question arose about that contact. The UDC system is run through BaseCom, which is linked by other means to station central. Those are the principal routes information can take. There is the shuttle, and there is contact between human beings who can walk from one place to another. If information flowed from this faculty, it took one of those routes."

On which they had evidence, except a member of a Fleet unit also had accesses he wasn't supposed to have . . . that Fleet Command didn't know about . . . which, if he confessed it now, was damning to him, to the Fleet, to Dekker's crew at minimum, to the Fleet's credibility and their support from the legislative committee, at worst.

While at least at some level the UDC and potentially the legislature knew about Pollard's security clearance—and might possibly know he'd somehow retained system access—if Pollard himself weren't under higher orders.

God, he should never have held his information source secret from Porey. Never.

"I suggest you use the channels you have to find *out* what's going on, lieutenant. *Somebody* in your command with real authority had better get his ass into this station, find out where the leak is and get this program off the evening news. You're public as *hell,* reporters are demanding to come over here in herds, we've got a very fragile coalition that worked hard to give you what you asked for, and let me tell you very bluntly, lieutenant, if anything goes wrong with this rumored upcoming *test* you've lost the farm. You cannot disavow another failure, your captains can't pass the buck to junior officers. Do you understand that? Am I talking to anyone who remotely understands the political realities of this situation?"

"*Yes,* sir, I do understand." No temper. "I am thirty-eight unapparent years of age, sir, and older than that as you count time. I was in command of this base during the last hearings, I was lately the director of personnel in this program, I *am* currently in charge of this facility and the testing program, and of the investigation, and we do have an answer, at least to what happened to Jamil Hasseini and his crew." He reached in his pocket and held up a yellow plastic washer. "This caused the so-called accident."

He had their attention. At least.

"How?"

"Operations records showed a hang-up in an attitude control. This plastic washer turned up to block the free operation of the yoke. In a null-*g* facility, you may know, maintenance has to be extremely careful to log and list and check every part, down to the smallest screws and washers, that they take into the facility. These are experienced null-*g* workers. We don't know by those records how long this little part has been there—whether it was there from the time the pod was assembled and it by total accident floated over a course of years undetected into the absolutely most critical position it could take in the control system—or whether it was placed there recently."

"Sabotage, in other words."

"We view it as more than suspicious. Paul Dekker was assigned to that pod."

"So we've heard."

"How much have you heard?"

"Maybe you'd damn well better tell us what there is to hear. We hear Dekker was assigned there and pulled at the last minute. Again. Why? How?"

"By my order, as chief of personnel. I made a routine final check on the crew stats: they were coming out of a period of orientation and lab sims. I felt we might be rushing it, in terms of fatigue levels. A stand-down under those circumstances is routine. Routine—except that this was the time his replacement crew was going into sims with him. Except that the same individuals we suspect of sabotage had access to that area. Civilian employees: Dekker's given a positive ID on one of them as guilty of assault in the last so-called accident. We're talking about deliberate sabotage and premeditated murder committed on Dekker—"

"With what motive?"

"I doubt it was personal. We've two employees of Lendler Corp under surveillance. We don't know all their contacts, yet. But they had access on both occasions."

Frowns. "Can you prove anything?"

"We're developing a case. But you see the problem we've been working against."

"Your security is supposed to be on top of things. People come and go where they like here, is that the way it works?"

"People with security clearances, yes, sir—in this case clearances granted by the UDC, interviewing people on Earth, where we have no screening apparatus. We're reviewing the systems, and the clearances, but there are 11338 civilians on B Dock, hired by the UDC and overseen by various offices. We're naturally giving Lendler Corp a higher priority in our review, but that doesn't mean information can't go out of here through another route."

"Meanwhile Dekker is unavailable."

"He is unavailable."

"And you have no proof of this sabotage."

"Their access. Dekker's testimony. The washer. Circumstantial evidence placing them in the area."

"You know what that's worth."

"A good reason not to let out what we know or make charges we can't substantiate. We're gathering evidence."

"Meanwhile these purported saboteurs are at work on this station."

"Yes, sir. Of necessity, they are."

"And Paul Dekker's out there on that carrier. —Is he in any way involved in the upcoming test?"

"Certainly he'll be in observation and advisement. All crews have that assignment during a run. Whether he'll be assigned the run or not—that's dependent on evaluations."

"He *can't* be the one to take the controls. That name can't be prominent in this program. —Have you *no* comprehension?"

"Senator, political decisions in crew choice caused the last disaster to this program. And I can't believe I'm hearing this all over again."

"I can't believe what I'm hearing from the junior command officer on this base. I can't believe your persistence in putting this man into the glare of publicity. Let me make it clear to you, lieutenant, careers are going down in flames if there's a second disaster. We've backed you, we've delivered votes in the JLC, we've patched together the coalition that gives you what you asked for and damn you, you serve us up Dekker for a witness to sabotage and Dekker for the representative of your program, and leak to the press, while you're 'developing a case' you daren't bring to court. Are you aware what's happening on Earth? Are you *aware* of the fire-bombing at the EC heaquarters? Are you aware of the bill pending in committee?"

"The extradition bill? Yes, I'm aware of it. And both acts of sabotage were aimed at him—by people who didn't even know him. This is no personal grudge on the part of the saboteurs, senator, it's politically motivated murder, the same as the substitution that killed his crew was politically motivated, by people who may not have known where their orders came from. Now we have another coalition, as I understand it, part of which is working for this bill, but somebody else clearly doesn't want him in court—somebody in a position to obtain security clearances wants him dead, and if we break the Lendler case into the open right now, it's going to be a string that reels more and more information into the spotlight—it's as explosive as the Dekker case and for identical reasons. *That's* why we haven't expelled these individuals. We know where they are. We suspect who they work for."

Temper. Saito had warned him. He got it under control. He faced the senators and the busily note-taking aides with a cold stare, and saw anger and consternation on both senatorial faces.

"I also want to know," he said, "how this exact information about Dekker's being pulled from the sim got to the Joint Committee. Was it out of Stockholm?"

Silence for a moment. The other senator said, harshly, "Through the media, lieutenant. Not the way we prefer our briefings."

"Haven't you the power to find out those sources?"

"No. We haven't. There are *laws.*"

"To cover illegal activity? I find that incredible."

"We want to know who made this decision to test. *Is* there a test? Or is this whole maneuver a cover for this Dekker person?"

"There assuredly will be a test."

"With Dekker's crew?"

"Possibly."

"Let me tell you what this looks like to us. It looks like a do or die proposition, a harebrained go-for-broke damned stupid risk, on your senior captain's perception that the Fleet's losing prestige in Europe and your facility here is shut down! We can't *get* you another ship to wreck, lieutenant, we can't continue our support in the face of this stupid risk of lives and equipment!"

Senior captain? Mazian? "The program is *not* shut down, sir. If you perceive that, you've been misled."

"The simulators are wrecked, you're vulnerable to sabotage, you're sending out crews who aren't ready—"

"No, sir. I'm delighted to report that all necessary equipment is functioning. There's been no hiatus in the program. All our crews are at work, including the UDC teams, integrated with ours."

A silence. Doubt, curiosity, and deep offense. He had his own doubts, of these men Saito called essential and friendly and to be trusted with the truth, these fools who wouldn't so much as talk to Saito, because *Saito* wasn't a command officer and *Saito* wasn't in charge.

"This doesn't agree with our information."

"I hope I have better news, then, sir. Our crews are keeping schedules, we are bringing our other senior crews, including UDC personnel, up to mission-ready; and when they're ready they will go. Officially, I know nothing about the upcoming test. I won't know the time until I'm told. But assuredly it will go. And any media attention to this facility will find everything in operation."

A modicum of respect, perhaps. A reassessment, a reevaluation what situation they were dealing with, certainly.

"Maybe you'd better explain yourself, lieutenant. With what equipment? With this *tape* you've come up with? Are we brainwashing our crews?"

"Crews at mission ready have to practice daily to maintain those skills. With the damage to the sims, Fleet Command opted to use the Hellburner prototype, patched to the shipboard simulators."

"When was that authorized?"

"The patch?"

"The shipboard facility. The chamber."

"Not chambers, sir, nothing like. I'm not privy to the details, but this is equipment we brought with us into the system, that we regularly use. Combat crews on stand-by also have to practice, virtually daily, to keep their edge. We certainly can't stop a carrier's operations or use its physical self for exercises. Naturally we have the equipment."

"Then why in *hell* haven't we been using it all along? Why spring it now? Why this whole damned, accident-riddled program?"

"Politics, sir." He hoped he kept all satisfaction off his face. "As the situation was told to me, we were ordered at the outset, over our captains' explicit protests, to submit our trainees to the UDC Systems Test protocols, to their aptitude criteria, their rules and their existing equipment during testing of the prototypes. As I believe, there was a major policy battle over that point in the JLC, and we lost."

Total quiet in the room. The clicking of the aides' keys had stopped.

"You never said explicitly," the other senator put in, "that you *had* the equipment."

"There was some fear," Graff said, "that the UDC might use its position to demand control of that equipment. In a situation in which we are not to this hour solely in control of communications system accesses, in which we've had sabotage, attempted murder of our personnel, assignment of flight personnel on criteria purely ideological in nature—plus the security breach—we are trusting your discretion on this point and we trust there will not be another leak. What we train on is a very dearly held piece of information. If our enemy knows what equipment we have—we are, in the vernacular, screwed. We protested, through every channel we trusted, that the station facilities here are a hundred fifty years old, with maintenance problems that eat up funds for improvements we asked for. The decision to put the rider training into the hands of the UDC, to use Lendler's data conversion system for the pods in the first place—was as I understand, a purely political decision. We asked to review the software. We were not trusted to make that input. *We . . . were . . . not . . . trusted."*

Another silence. An angry silence on both sides. But it wasn't productive anger. Graff shifted back in his chair. "I'm not a diplomat. My captain left other officers here who are. But they aren't command track by UDC rules. So I pass their word on to you. As for the operational crews of all the ships—you gave us a requirement to have carriers on standby to defend this system—and I can tell you with absolute certainty I would be grossly irresponsible to take that carrier's controls after months of total stand-down. We're in constant training, all ops crews and staffs are in training during any stand-down; and the UDC has never provided carrier control sims. It's certainly no secret."

"Where did you obtain this other equipment?" Anger. Still, a genuine offense, and he answered with careful exactness:

"I haven't been on that carrier and I honestly don't know the source."

"Where would you expect that carrier to obtain it?"

"The black market."

"Whose black market?"

The question seemed naive. "The one out *there,* sir. Outside this solar system. There's very good equipment available."

"I find this outrageous. *Union* equipment? Is that story true?"

"We have manufacturers. We're not primitives looking for Earth's expertise, my God, senator. We *provided* the designs that are making your corporations money."

"Are you using Union equipment?"

"Senator, we don't look for the label. If it works, if it's better, we use it. If we can get our hands on Unionside equipment, we're delighted, and they'd be extremely upset, if they knew it. They don't want us using their programs."

"Are you creating tape?"

"Of course. They're creating tape over in the UDC. In TI. They're creating tape in Houston, for physical rehab patients—"

"You *know* what we're asking. These people with their fingers on the fire button—are you saying, lieutenant, that the tape training your crews are being given is being adjusted to the personality of some single individual, and among those individuals may be Paul Dekker?"

"Physical reaction tape doesn't affect personality. That's a complete misapprehension."

"It's a public perception. Truth doesn't matter. Public perception does! You're going to use a rab agitator, a man linked to riots in Bonn and Geneva—"

He held his voice steady and his hands from clenching. "A young man who knows nothing about riots in Bonn, who was qualified for a pilot's license before his enlistment, which one would hope the ECSAA doesn't do for criminals—"

"Oh, come on, lieutenant! The ECSAA licensed every miner in the Belt!"

"Dekker was a pusher pilot at Sol One, in your own space, by your certifications. He's an outstanding young officer who's distinguished himself by his work and his dedication to this program. And if he meets mission criteria, he will be a source for training material. Skill—"

"He's too politically sensitive. It's already too public. God! Why do you people persist in shoving this man in our faces? Are you actively *challenging* the legislature?"

He shook his head. "Your creativity, sir, with all respect. Any choice made on political and not operational grounds reduces this ship's chances of survival. If this test fails, the EC has no alternative and no further resources to offer us. I'm authorized to tell you we will have no choice at that point but to pull out entirely and abandon our defense of the motherworld. That's precisely where it stands."

"Dammit!"

"Yes, sir. I agree with you. But no one but our predecessors had a choice."

Things kept on surreal, so far as Dekker was concerned, time-trip to a place he'd never been, and the little things got to you: the moment in the shower you couldn't remember where you were: the split-second during mission prep the whole scene seemed part of the station, not the carrier. Nothing felt safe, or sure. You ran the prep, you ran the sims, you scribbled away on your plans, you ran the sims, and every once in a while they gave everybody a day down and you could put your feet up, play cards and enjoy a light beer, because the carrier pilots were using the equipment, but the whole thing cycled endlessly.

You could believe at times you were in the war, the other side of the Hinder Stars. Or in Sol Station's carpeted corporate heart, where orderlies served you food you didn't even recognize, arranged in pretty patterns on the plates. Your bed turned up made, your clothes turned up clean and the bar when it was open served free drinks. Wasn't so bad a life, you could get to thinking. But debt for this had to come due, either to Porey or to God, or to somebody.

Hit two hundred-percenters, back to back, and he started thinking, the sims are lying to us. They're jerking us around, trying to give us confidence—

They want their damn theory to work, they're targeting the tape they're giving us at the exercises, that's why we're getting scores like that, that's why it's not happening to the other teams—

Some damned fool in an office somewhere could believe a lie and put us out there, when it's all lab stuff that looks good . . .

"Dek, what are you guys having for breakfast?" Call from the end of the narrow room, down by the display.

Damn, they'd posted the scores.

Lot of guys went and had a look. "Hell," he groaned, but it wasn't ragging this time, it was a rueful shake of heads and a:

"Dek, looks like you got the run."

"Not yet," he said to Almarshad.

"No, I mean you got the run. You're posted. Mitch is back-up one, we're two, half a point between us."

Blood went to his feet. He sat there, with his crew, who weren't celebrating, who just looked at him; and got up as Mitch and Almarshad came over and congratulated him, not looking happy, not taking it badly either. It was too serious for that, too damned uncertain for that.

"Not a thorough surprise," Mitch said. "Sounds like we're headed for girl-tape for sure." Ragging it a little close to the edge, that. But he took Mitch's offered hand, and Meg let him lay a congratulatory hand on her shoulder after. "Kady. Class job, you guys. Sincerely."

Meg looked as if she'd swallowed something strange. Sal just looked smugly satisfied, and gave Mitch a kiss on the cheek.

Ben said, "I can't believe this. I can't believe this. What am I doing here?"

CHAPTER 18

His mother had said often enough, You don't care, Paul, you just don't care about people, there's got to be something basic missing in you—

Maybe there was. Maybe he didn't feel things other people did. Maybe machines were all he came equipped to understand, all that was ever going to make sense to him, because he couldn't stay away from them . . . he honestly couldn't live without doing this . . .

He couldn't turn it loose. When he was away from the ship, he could think reasonably about it, and know that it was a cold way to be, and that if he could be something different and he could be back in the Belt with people he cared about, doing nothing but mining, he could be happy—he'd *been* happy there; he could have been again, in the right company . . .

But when he got up here in null-g, in the rider loft, with the four Hellburner locks staring him in the face, and the ship out there, behind number 1, then everything was different, every value and priority was revised. The ship was a presence here. Was waiting to be alive; and he was, in a way he wasn't in the whole rest of his life. He was scared down in the gravitied quarters, scared out of his reason, and he realized he'd gotten everyone who cared about him in one hell of a mess; but up here—

Up here he knew at least *why* he'd made the choices he had, right or wrong, he knew why he'd kept going, and why the pods made him afraid—just that nowhere else was this. Nowhere else had the feel this did. It didn't altogether cure being scared, but it put the fear behind him.

This was where he would have been on that day, dammit, except for Tanzer, except for Wilhelmsen being put in the wrong place, at the wrong time . . . it felt as if his whole life had gone off-line since then, and he was just now picking up again where it should have been, with the people he should have had: time that had frozen on him, was running again, the mission was in his pocket, and right now the only thing he was honestly afraid of up here was being pulled from the mission again—

But nobody in command would mess with him—not now. It wasn't Tanzer in command. He was too vulnerable. He was somebody, finally, that people couldn't shove aside, when all through his life people had been trying, and they couldn't do that again. If he did this—if he lived through it—

If he made good on everything he'd promised.

"Dekker."

Porey's voice, echoing over the speaker, making his heart jump.

"Sir?"

"Mission dump has gone to your files. We have incoming."

Cold hit his gut, raw panic negated every reasoning. It couldn't happen. It wouldn't happen, it wasn't true . . .

"I said incoming, Dekker. Get your ass into library! Fast!"

He grabbed a new grip on the zipline for the lift and hit the inner lift wall, *damn* the drilled reaction, he didn't believe it, damn, he didn't believe it. *"We're not betraying position,"* the voice from the speakers said. *"We're allowing forty minutes, that's all we can allow, for library access, plot, and confirm. Get with it."*

"You're lying! Sir! This is a test run, this is a damn *test,* you don't have to pull this on us!"

Silence from the lift speaker. Lift crashed into the frame, jolted him and the whole compartment around to plus 1 *g,* and he caught a grip on the rail.

"Damn you!" he yelled at the incommunicative com. "Damn you to hell, commander, *—sir!* Where's this incoming?"

But nothing answered him.

"I swear to you it wasn't our guys," Villy said on the way to the officers' conference room, to a meeting Graff would as soon have skipped.

"That's official from the colonel. He didn't leak it, nobody on staff did that he can trace. That's what he wants me to say."

"What do *you* say?" Graff asked.

"He's not lying." Villy didn't sound offended by the question. Villy's eyes, crinkled around the edges with a lot of realtime years, were honest and clear as they always had been. You wanted to believe in Alexandro Villanueva the way you wanted to believe in sanity and reason in the universe. But Villy quoted Tanzer at him and it was suddenly Villanueva's own self Graff began to worry about, now, about the man who, over recent weeks, he'd worked with as closely and as cooperatively as he worked with his own staff—sorting out the tempers, the egos, the simple differences in protocols: they'd mixed the staff and crews in briefings and in analysis sessions, they'd given alcohol permissions in rec on one occasion, holding the marine guards in reserve—and nobody'd been shot, nobody'd been taken to the brig, and no chairs had left the floor. More than that, they had a remarkable sight ahead of them in the hall, that was Rios and Wojcak in UDC fatigues and Pauli in Fleet casuals and station-boots, engaged in conversation that involved a clipboard waved violently about.

No combat. Sanity. Cooperation, if a thin one. There was a secret, highly illegal betting pool going among the crews, odds on *which* crew was going to draw the test run, and a sizable pot, from what Fleet Police said, the UDC crews leaning heavily toward solid, by-the-book Almarshad and the Fleet tending to split between Mitchell and Almarshad and no few still betting on Dekker as the long shot. He hadn't taken the action on that pool that regulations demanded; Villy hadn't; more remarkable, *Tanzer* hadn't, if Tanzer knew, which he personally doubted—Tanzer didn't know everything that was going on these days, Villy directly admitted there were topics he didn't bring up with Tanzer, and it was too much to hope that Tanzer had learned anything about dealing with the Shepherds or changed his style of command. It was Villy's discretion he leaned to—had been leaning to it maybe more than he should have. Maybe he'd only been naive, looking too much for what he hoped and too little for the long years Tanzer had built up a network in this place.

Fact was, same as he'd told the committee, there were too many chances for leaks, too many contractors, too many technicians, too many station maintenance personnel with relatives in Sol One or, God knew, in Buenos Aires or Paris. It was worth their jobs to talk, the workers knew that, they'd signed the employment agreements, but they were human beings and they had personal opinions, not always discreetly.

Shuttle was coming in—approaching dock. They might be rid of the senators, but they had reporters incoming. FleetCom had broken the news of the impending test. The senators had no wish to get caught here, they were packing to leave, had their last interviews with the Lendler personnel today (God hope they didn't give anything away) and the shuttle would be at least six hours in maintenance and loading, latest report.

None too soon to be rid of the lot, in his book.

"We have any new data on the hearings at One?" Villanueva asked him. "Anything from the JLC or the technical wing?"

"Nothing. Not a thing yet."

Steps behind them in the hall, rapid, as they reached the briefing room. Late arrival, Graff intercepted it, turned to glance and met an out-of-breath Trev, out of FleetCom. Evans handed him a printed note.

It said: Reporters are on the shuttle. All outbound system traffic on hold. Test is imminent.

Hell, he thought. And: Why didn't the captain warn us? FSO has to have known, FSO has to have signed the press passes . . .

"Reply, sir?"

"None I want in writing. Tell Com One I said so and what in hell. Those words. Stat."

"Yessir," Trev said, and cleared the area at max speed.

Which left Villy's frown and lifted eyebrow.

"Reporters, on the inbound shuttle," he told Villy. "The test's been announced, I don't know by whom . . . System traffic is stopped. We're stuck with the shuttle, the senators, and the reporters."

Villy's look couldn't be a lie. "They've been inbound for three damned *days!* This isn't a leak, this is a damned publicity set-up! What kind of game are you guys running over at FSO?"

"That's what I'm asking FleetCom. Bloody *hell,* what are they doing to us?"

"Damn mess," Meg muttered, in the ready room, looking at the lighted plot-screen—Dek was a bundle of nerves, holding to the handgrip beside her and memorizing that chart with the only drug-training he'd ever had, the bit that helped you focus down and retain like crazy. Ben was swearing because he hadn't got his specific numbers out of carrier Nav yet, Sal was talking to the ordnance clerk; and Meg muttered her own numbers to voice-comp, while suit-up techs tugged and pulled at her in intimate places. You didn't even do that basic thing for yourself, you just memmed charts fast as you could and talked to the systems chiefs and techs who you hoped to God had done their job.

The helmet came down over her head, and other hands twisted the seal. 360° real-HUD came active, voice-link did. She evoked her entry macro, that prepped her boards long-distance, dumped her touch, her patterns, her mem-marks on the plot-screen fire-path to the Hellburner systems.

Mitch's crew and Almarshad's were in flight control, two beats of argument between them whether it could possibly be real, whether they might actually have a realspace system entry launched at high *v* from far out; or whether intelligence reports foretold something about the drop in—the consensus was test, set-up, but *they* couldn't take it as a test run, didn't dare believe the ordnance that would come at them was anything but real. The sketchy fire-track was running right past Earth's moon, not the kind of thing Sol System traffic control was going to like, and that meant a wide-open track with a shot at Earth that if they didn't get a fast intercept on that incoming ship—the doomsday scenario: they could lose the whole motherwell in less than ten minutes, that was what shaped up on their data. Billions of people. All life on earth. The enemy wouldn't *do* that. They were human beings . . .

But life in the Belt and the gossip from Fleet instructors argued there were minds out there more different than you ever wanted to meet. And you could never, ever bet on them doing the logical—

Siren went off, the board and take-hold, "Hell!" Ben cried, because they were going, there was no more time, the carrier was going to hit the mains and the next input they got was going to be off carrier ops, the carrier's longscan/com team that was their data-supply and their situation monitor, them and the back-up teams doing *her* job for the sixty-minus seconds it was going to take them to board and belt.

She grabbed the dismount line behind Dek, in crew-entry order, hindmost, and hung on as the door slammed wide and the line meshed with the gears, hell of a jerk on the arm. You held on, was all, as the singing line aimed you for the mounting bars at the hatch, one, two, three, four, tech lines ringing empty, the Hellburner's tech hatch open, but receiving no one. Carrier technical crew shouted good wishes at them as they shot past and one after the other hit the stop, pile-up of hand-grips—inertia carried them in—she hit the cushions last, heard the hatches shut when she slipped the toggle, both ports, confirm on the seal by on-panel telltales as she was snapping the only manual belt; second toggle and they went ops-com, linked with the carrier, sending and receiving a blitz of electronic information. "We're go," Dek said, and instantaneously the carrier mains cut in with a solidity that shoved them harder than the pods ever had, 10+ in a brutal, backs-downward acceleration.

Carrier was outputting now, making EM noise in a wavefront an enemy would eventually intercept in increasing Doppler effect, and to confuse their longscan they were going to pull a pulse, half-up to FTL and abort the bubble, on a heading for the intercept zone—that was the scary part. That was the time, all sims aside, that the theoretical high *v* became real, .332 light, true hellride, with herself for the com-node that integrated the whole picture.

They tranked you down for jump. They didn't for this move. They told you what it was going to be, they pulled disorientations and sensory assaults, and learned the mem-techniques from the starship crew, and hoped you could get the threads back when you came out—but meanwhile you just kept talking to the computer and the carrier and moving your markers with the joystick, laying the strike and the strategy as if you were seeing it tamely on the light-table instead of on monitors, with numbers and grids floating in glowing colors. Reality became hyper-extended vision, into mathematical futures, chaos of nature, two intersecting presence-cones of human action that had to narrow at a proximity to Luna that was truly harrowing.

Hard to breathe. The flight-suit squeezed the ribs in efficient pulses, oxygen flowed—damned sure not the pod this time. This was real—this was—

Moment that the brain skipped . . . moment that they weren't—anywhere, and all the data left the brain void. A voice said, like God, *Stand by sep, Hellburner;* she recalled that procedure, scanned her crew's LS, TAC and STAT data glowing gold at the upper periphery of her midrange vision and said, mechanically as any machine, "Sep go, that's go, go . . ."

Bang!

"We have absolutely identical interests," Villy said to the gathered reporters, while Graff folded his arms and leaned against the wall by the door. Captain Villy rested elbows against the podium and said in that voice that had to be believed: "Let me explain where the UDC stands. Yes, there've been problems in the past. As a test crew, in this facility, we've seen ideas that worked and we've seen ideas that didn't—we've worked with a lot of bright-eyed young pilots and techs that came in here all impatient to be trained in equipment we ran when it didn't have all the buttons they put on it—who never gave a damn about what we knew so long as the buttons worked. That's the truth. And I'll tell you, having the future operational crews shoved in here to be part of the testing procedures—that's been a hell of an adjustment for us—but the Fleet did call this one right. The physiological demands of this equipment are hell; and the crews that can fly this baby are going to be so scarce in the general population they're probably going to give some of us a chance to be honest working crew."

Tidbits of real News. Graff pricked up his ears, saw Optex record lights like so many blinking eyes among the reporters.

"They say the other guys have to grow 'em in vats, and eighteen years from now we're going to see their hand-raised clone pilots in the cockpit. That eighteen years is the lead we have, because they tell us the merchanters that won't take our side, won't take the Union side either. Union doesn't have the insystem crews we do—they're a lot more mechanized, their mining equipment's state of the art, a lot of robots. Their miners sit on big ore-collectors, they don't have our antique equipment and consequently they never developed the pool of experienced insystem crews like we drew in from our asteroid belt—"

"What about this tape?" a reporter asked, out of turn. "What about this Union mind-tape?"

"It's not Union," Graff said from near the door, and drew an immediate concentration of steady red lights. "It's ours, and it works only on the reflexes, a glance left or right at the panels, mathematical formulae and routines, nothing as organized thought or attitudes . . . It covers the same kind of memorizations you do in school—" He trusted they did such things in schools. These reporters were Earth's equivalent of com and he doubted they had any experience in common. He wanted Saito down here, but Saito was on the carrier, where FleetCom with a test proceeding mandated she be; Demas was God knew where—Demas had taken refuge in Ops, he was willing to lay bets . . .

Com said in his ear: *"Mission is go-for with Dekker. Rider is sepped. We're coming up in station systems."*

"I copy," he told the bone-mike. "I'm on my way to mission control."

Reporters were still looking at him. Optex lenses were all turned his way, and Villy was watching him from the podium.

"Mission's away," he said, removed the uncomfortable security com from his ear, and added, with a certain suicidal satisfaction, "Team leader *is* Dekker," and watched all chaos erupt.

* * *

"All *right!*" Ben sounded finally satisfied with the numbers and Dekker gave a little breath of relief—a relief that Ben probably wouldn't understand. Smug, that was Ben when he relaxed; but Ben wasn't smug now, he was On and anxious, all the way.

"We just keep running quiet awhile, Dek-boy. A real hold-steady here, minimum profile, just keep us out of their acquisition long as we can—carrier's gone up ahead, going to fire a decoy and brake hard."

The carrier's vane-config showed clear, that was the immediate worry on this maneuver—the carrier was going to pull an axis roll: a thing the size of some space stations was going to do a total reverse, pass them again at close range, rotate a second time and tail them at a distance . . .

"This is a set-up," Meg complained, "we got too many numbers on this, Ben. It's got to be a set-up . . ."

"Dekker a murderer?" Graff said, tracking past the spex windows of mission control to the profile screens and the working teams and his own trainees at the boards. They'd established the reporters in the viewing area, gotten the senators a secure spot in a VIP observation point, and on the displays in mission control a situation was unfolding neither party yet comprehended. "No. He happens to be the survivor of three documented attempts on his life, two of which put him in hospital, one of which killed Cory Salazar."

Not the loudest voice, but the one he chose to hear: "That contradicts what Councillor Salazar charges—"

Probability fans were changing color on the screens, rapidly narrowing. "It is, nevertheless, the truth. The evidence against Paul Dekker was fabricated by the identical agencies responsible for covering up a strike-breaking police action that took seventeen other lives documented in 2304 sworn affidavits and complaints."

"From Belters?" Bias dripped from the question, and sharpened focus and temper for a split-second.

"From civilian and military eyewitnesses and victims living and dead in Earth Company records. There are *no* grounds for the charges against Paul Dekker—they're old history, investigated and officially dismissed when the agencies that made the charges were dissolved by legal action for corruption, wrongful death, and labor abuses. As for the culpable parties, they were relieved of command and stripped of their licenses, but unfortunately that was the *only* action taken. I suggest you ask Ms. Salazar why she's never named them in her pending suit."

"Why didn't she?"

"I couldn't speculate on her motives."

Ten and twenty questions at once. Riot, as reporters a moment ago drifting along the spex wall suddenly elbowed each other to get Optex pickups to the fore. *Let* the Company raise hell, let the Fleet ship him to the battle zone—please God, ship him to the zone, away from reporters, cameras, Edmund Porey, and self-serving senators demanding dinner in the VIP observation area.

Then someone shouted from the hall, "They're releasing the separation footage!" and bedlam surged in the other direction, reporters trying to get into mission control, jamming in the doorway. Two stayed to ask:

"Who authorized this test, lieutenant?"

"Not in my need-to-know, I'm afraid. Insystem traffic near Luna shows lift delayed for thirty minutes on the monitor up there. That has to come from very high levels."

"Who can authorize it?"

"Sol One Stationmaster, for the lowest level."

"If—"

The barrage of questions and dicing of information kept up. He stood there with his gut in knots. It was go now, no likely recall of the rider. Mission parameters were showing on the screens, dopplered transmission from the carrier, and from the rider, via the carrier. Course was laid for intercept from the ecliptic, of a zenith system entry shielded from the carrier by Earth's own security zone . . .

Worst-case scenario in system defense—an attack coming into Earth's vicinity, and not a damned thing on the transmissions to say the case wasn't real . . . worse, there was an incoming showing on the one screen his eye knew for real-case. Something *was* inbound or they'd gotten insystem traffic management to lie, and it didn't. Ever.

Ship felt good, felt *good* all the way, zero no-calls and zero glitches on the boards. Clean, wide sep from the carrier and for a while they would keep the carrier's rate inside its shields, pretending to the enemy that separation was still to come. Attitude assemblies were all answering test-calls. Dekker lost himself in the internal config-confirms, in the numbers that were the immediate future—Meg was there to tell him where he was, Ben was shaping further future, and Sal was working up the fire-path, armaments taking program, talking to Meg's boards which would talk to his V-HUD when the time came. Right now body-sense was expanded into the ship, time was cut loose and independent of circumstance—the track and the fire-points were shaping up further and further into the diagrams spread in his far vision—but he was only generally aware of that: he was seeing that interval as leisurely information-building minutes diving toward a split-second hype-point, where he had to be ready to execute a sequence of immaculately timed moves to confuse the enemy, position the fire platform, and get their asses safely past a line of answering fire scarily close to Luna, with a *v* that overrode both Luna's pull—and the available energy of their own missiles.

Which was all Sal's problem.

They aren't *doing* anything, the reporters objected with increasing frustration, even anger, and Graff said, finally, with a heart going faster and faster, eyes fixed on the monitors beyond the spex panes: "Oh, yes, they are. They're maintaining output silence. The carrier's doing all the transmission, noisy as it wants to be. They launched something on either side before they braked, one's a decoy, one's the rider, and the rider doesn't want to be seen yet, that's the name of the game—even we don't know which it is, because they haven't told us and motion hasn't started."

Questions broke out, a shouted confusion.

"Yes, we have no doubt they're still conscious. See the four dots on the screen, all doing fine . . ." Trajectories were widening their perspective on the screens and one reporter noticed the obvious. "That's going straight through Luna space—is that Luna space?"

"All system traffic's suspended. The firepaths will have been cleared and safed."

"What if—"

Chatter kept up. Media seemed to abhor a thinking silence.

He watched the situation on the screens, thinking, Damn, who's feeding them their orders? But he heard no calculations emanating from FleetCom. He suspected the carrier armscomper had primed them for this—set up the incoming *and* the response: he personally suspected that anything and everything Porey did was with mirrors; but he kept his mouth shut and hoped to God no reporter got onto that question.

And the firepaths *were* damned close to Luna . . . the reporter was right, they were terrifyingly close, from the viewpoint of civilians not used to starships at entry and exit *v*—close, and with a maneuver that, if they did it—damn, it was Russell's Star, replayed—

Long, long time on a hold-steady. Easy to become hypnotized, if not for the nuisance chatter on internal com. Dekker did the small breathing exercises that kept him aware of time—nothing but freefall at fractional light, minimal signature, nothing noisy, no output at all, no input but the passive recept of the carrier and its boards that advised them things they couldn't output to see.

Couldn't prove it wasn't real, what they were receiving. You couldn't assume it, daren't assume it.

"What we're going to do imminently, Dek-boy, we're about to do a little round the corner shot at this sumbitch. Luna's shadow's your boost point, God, I hope you get it right . . ."

"Copy that," he muttered. "Do your own job, Ben."

"Ordnance up," Sal said. "Meg. Dek, that's your plot-points, you copy?"

Dots and lines were multiplying in his midvision now, floating in space, designating essential fire-points, orientation, mass decrease. Considerable decrease: Hellburner was 90% fuel, engines, ablation surface, and ordnance.

"He's got it," Meg said. "Here we go, guys. —Initiate."

Pulse of the main engines. Missiles launched with a shock through the frame, one and two away . . . straight toward the moon. Adrenaline stretched time and distances.

"T-1," Ben was saying, calling out the major coordination points.

Second pulse, high-*g* RO, intermittent accel and launches directly down their backpath toward their carrier, staccato hammer of missiles away, Hellburner's mass diminishing fast.

Second RO, braces engaged. Had to hold the track with immaculate numbers—crossing the carrier firepath now, edge on, minimum profile.

"Son of a *bitch,*" Ben yelled, as the emissions recept picked up launch, but their four missiles had kicked off the frame on the mark and Dekker swung into his scheduled Profile RePosition with an instant eighth less mass and a violence that blurred vision. "Track!" Ben yelled at Sal. "Track!"

"Got it, got it, got it," Sal cried, onto a steady stream of profanity, as their chaff gun opened up down the hostile firetrack straight for the incoming. "Burn it!" Ben yelled, and Dekker shoved it to +10.5 instant *g*s ahead, on the instant, rotated sideways as they were.

Countered. Graff watched the fire bursts, listened to the dispassionate voice of FleetCom confirm the intercept.

It looked so slow on this scale—so incredibly slow. But his heart knew the speed at which things were moving, his gut was in knots, he wanted his own hands on controls, he wanted that with every breath he took—

They were on. God, God, they were making it. So had Wilhelmsen—this early on. Another ReOrient and they were still throwing fire . . .

But, damn! the lines intersected, and of a sudden—missiles near Luna were off the scope of a sudden—

Range safety? or hostile action?

"Test stop," came over the speakers. *"The test has been terminated . . . this is FleetCom mission control . . ."*

Disaster? Graff felt cold all over. Couldn't have. The plot was still tracking.

"The incoming is confirmed as EC militia merchanter Eagle, *proceeding at* V *to maintain effect shields against inert chaff which will not, repeat not, intersect civilian traffic. Luna-vectored ordnance was destroyed by the range safety officer. At no time was this ordnance capable of reaching the lunar surface: technical explanation will follow. The remaining ordnance is being cleared from the area by destruct commands issued by range safety. Rider ordnance trajectories have been computed as intersecting* Eagle *presence and moment with three major strikes, sufficient to have eliminated the incoming threat. This concludes a successful test of the Hellburner prototype. In-progress System traffic will resume ordinary operations in fifteen minutes . . ."*

Impossible to hear in the spectator gallery, after that. Crews and techs inside mission control were out of their seats, pounding each other on the backs with complete disregard of uniform or gender. "Damn *on!*" Villy roared from the other side of the spectators, Optexes were going, reporters were shouting questions—a few of them loudly incensed about the apparent proximity to the moon.

God, he just let it go. Gave fragments of answers, how he felt—damned happy; had he been nervous—wanted to be *out* there, he said, all the while tracking on the screens, the celebrations, the communications from FleetCom telling Hellburner 1 there was no need to brake, the carrier was on direct intercept, and from UDC System Defense saying that lift traffic would resume in areas declared cleared, starting with alpha zone, near Earth's atmosphere.

Was it an unwarrantable risk to Luna? a reporter wanted to know. He said, tracking on the politics as well as the damned brilliant straight-line shot, "In the first place, it was never going to hit the moon. It was moving past the moon faster than it was moving toward it. By the laws of physics it absolutely couldn't hit the surface."

"If something had gone wrong with the missiles—"

"They didn't have enough fuel to reach the moon soon enough to hit it. It's absolutely impossible."

"But they could reach the carrier."

"The carrier could run into them. The range officer got it well within the safe zone. If it had failed to detonate, there were two back-up systems; and, I reemphasize, the ordnance was not infalling Luna, no more than the ship itself was. The armscomper knew exactly what she was doing."

"She," a reporter pounced on the question, but another shouted:

"Was it a successful test, when the duration was half an hour *less* than the Wilhelmsen run, at a slower speed?"

"The rider *eliminated* the threat. It had nothing left to shoot at. There's no point in continuing beyond mission accomplished."

"But could they have kept going?"

"No doubt whatsoever. And let me point out, they were slower, but their target was moving at system entry speeds. Wilhelmsen's targets were only randoms, from known fire points, nothing this realtime. But he gave us data that helped us. It wasn't a pointless sacrifice—never a pointless sacrifice." Tanzer had just shown up in mission control, Tanzer accepting handshakes of his staff, beyond the sound-damping spex, and the whole press corps was suddenly trying to figure out how to get where they weren't going to be admitted. Villy clapped him on the shoulder in passing and escaped the intercepts, while another Optex pickup arrived in his face with,

"Ms. Salazar has denounced the choice of Paul Dekker as the source of tape for the program and called for the disfranchisement of the Fleet. How do you feel about that?"

"My answer? If that incoming had been Union, that ship and that young pilot and crew would have prevented global catastrophe. A single barrage of inert matter falling on Earth at half light would create ecological disaster." Stock answer, stock material, the science people had calc'ed it years ago: he knew not a damned thing about climates, truth be told.

A reporter followed up: "Earth was not in actual danger."

"Earth was in deadly danger if that had been a Union ship. But Hellburner demonstrated its ability to deflect any such attack. Their course was right on intercept with that incoming militia ship, you can see it on the display up there. This was a live ordnance test, but nothing at any time was aimed at Earth or Luna."

"What if it went off-track?"

"That's why there are range safety officers." He didn't want to say what he suspected, that if the destruct sequences for the rider's missiles hadn't been dumped to *Eagle*'s computers by the Sol system buoy on entry, the range safety officer on the ECS4 had to have had a few extremely anxious moments once the shots went around the limb of the moon. That volley had come very close to sending the missiles out of communication with the carrier. But the crew hadn't pulled any punches. No crew could afford to think in those terms. Ever.

"Lieutenant, lieutenant, do you think—"

"Excuse me. . . ." He was getting a burst of new information off FleetCom on the screens and over the PA, and another line of comflow in his ear from Saito, saying . . .

Panic over much of Europe, assumption the test was real, public reactions yet uncertain . . . But Mazian was in front of the cameras in Bonn, with pronouncements of what a Union strike would have meant for Earth, . . . calling Paul Dekker and his crew phenomenally skilled, heroes of Earth's own defense forces, a combined Fleet-and-*UDC* crew . . .

"Good run. Still room for improvement."

Porey's voice; and Dekker wanted to tell him go to hell for the trick they'd pulled. Destruct the ordnance, damned right they'd had to, he'd been scared as hell they might hit a friendly ship; but a Belter didn't *have* ordinary nerves, and he'd not been a hundred percent convinced until they'd gotten the congratulatory communication from FleetCom that it had been the scheduled test.

Didn't know what to do with the nerves now, things were still dragging along, interminable time stretch: not so hard a job, this run, but that was the problem, wasn't it? You didn't *get* the hellish repositions and redirects when you were working with Ben and Sal, when your copilot was thinking ahead of the pilot's problems so he didn't get called on for those moves—only *one* of those shifts he'd had to rip, they'd hyped the *v* sideways hard after Sal's best shot and Ben was still muttering about realspace feeling real, and soreness setting in.

Meg said, "We're in the pocket, right in the pocket, now, Dek, you don't have to do a thing til the bow-shock. —Incidentally, compliments from Capt. Kreshov, on *Eagle,* he says it was a damn pretty job, his words. —Thank you, sir. The team appreciates the compliment. —We got a drink offer from his armscomper . . ."

"Sounds good," Ben said. "Yeah!" from Sal.

Himself, he wasn't highly verbal, just tracking on the approaching carrier—Ben decided it was a frigging party, all of a sudden, Sal and Meg evidently had; and he could strangle Ben. They weren't through until they'd been through the realtime shields, nothing virtual about it this time: carrier coming up like a bat behind them, Baudree's showing out, no different than the rider jocks, except Baudree was carrying multiples of their mass, and when he contemplated dock after what he'd been through he felt sweat running on his forehead and a tension cramp knotting his leg.

Meg switched him out of the Fleet Com loop to carrier-com, then, the range blip and the docking schematic a total preoccupation in his 360° V-HUD compression, carrier Helm talking to him now, wanting his attention, while he left Meg and Ben to watch elsewhere.

"Just hold steady and we've got you."

Moment of panic. Hard to shift time-perception. It wasn't going fast now. Everything took forever and a tiny bobble was disaster. You didn't screw it at this stage. Didn't, please God, didn't.

"Bow shock in 43 seconds."

"Copy that. Go." He couldn't afford to think they'd done it . . .

Not yet.

"That's capture and dock," FleetCom's dispassionate voice said. *"Thank you, Mr. Dekker. Excellent job."*

Graff found himself breathing again.

"We're going into our checklist." Dekker's voice. The reporters had gotten to recognize it. Had picked up on the tension in mission control and Villy had finally gotten it through, the shift the pilot had to make between nanosecond events and docking at relatively slow docking approach. "We had two funerals getting this down pat," Villy muttered. "It's no piece of easy the kid's working—hell of a buffet when you cross the shields."

Another flurry of technical questions. Graff looked for an escape, saw the door to the VIP area open and the two senators walk out—instant recognition from the press, instant convergence in that direction. Shouts and questions.

"We were invited to observe this test." The senior senator, Caldwell. "To see how the taxpayers' appropriations have been spent. I must say we've had a compelling demonstration of the effectiveness of the technology, outstanding performance . . ."

"J-G," Demas said, in his ear. *"Bonn. Our suspect did work for MarsCorp."*

He ducked for the corridor, deserted Villy and the senators for a small nook near a couple of marine security guards. "Say," he asked the security unit. "Have we got a case?"

"I don't know if we have a case, but he has former close associates in the Federation of Man, and the UDC background check didn't

go that deep, he was passed in under Lendler security, and hear this, J-G, the UDC 'took Lendler's word for it,' unquote. 'All their personnel have to have a clearance.' Unquote. Marscorp is 45% of Lendler's business: the atmospherics softwares, for a start."

Bloody hell, he thought. The information had hit his brain. The implications were still finding sensitive spots in his nervous system. "Took Lendler's word for it." "All their personnel have to have a clearance." Political implications, far beyond the Dekker affair.

"You're serious."

"Mars is threaded all through this. But so is the Federation of Man. Eldon Kent has two cousins in that association. Lendler's records on him are so-named classified—which we can't penetrate without filing charges."

"Not yet. Not yet. God."

Saito cut in on the channel. *"J-G. The carrier is returning to dock."*

"We're deep in reporters. Tell the commander that."

"I'm sure he knows," Saito said.

Damn! he thought, but he kept it off his face, he hoped, at least. He stood very still for a moment, heard Caldwell saying, inside, ". . . a tribute to the skill and dedication of Earth's industry and innovation—"

CHAPTER 19

Mains cut in, hard, and Dekker gave himself up to the force, just breathed the way one had to and trusted, figuring at this point if the carrier hit a rock or took them to hell, he wasn't afraid anymore, he just stared at the blank, black VR in front of him, sensory deprivation . . . they were planning to fix that, arguing about what a crew wanted, coming off hype, whether they wanted anything at all but a VR off the carrier's boards, but Dekker personally voted just for the vid of the carrier surface, that was the only thing he wanted to see, he was convinced of it now, only thing a rider crew was going to want was constant reassurance that they were snugged up against the frame and locked, and that the clanks that rang through the hull were the autoservice connections and the ordnance servos, ready to shove ordnance up into the racks if there were a need to launch the prototype a second time immediately, which, thank God, there wasn't, and the servos didn't.

Tired, now, just tired. The carrier pulsed down to system speeds, and announced a reposition on a new vector. Slow as humans lived, now, Dekker supposed, but things were moving faster than he could track or understand—

Which was the universe at ordinary, Meg would say, if Meg was talking, but none of them seemed to have the energy to talk right now, just trying to ride through the braking and not think, he supposed, all of them coming down off hype, and exhausted.

Second accel. He made the deep sustained breaths and shut his eyes. Black around them and black inside: reality had caught up to him, and Cory was dead. Long time back. Another life. Pace the breaths and count, the way you had to with a shove like that, to keep conscious. Hotdogging from Baudree, far as anybody could do that with a mass like this—

"What in hell's he doing?" Ben asked plaintively. "Where are we going?"

"Going back to base," Meg said.

"You got read-out?"

"Nyet. But you *feel* the direction, rab."

"Come off the mystic stuff. Nobody 'feels' the direction."

"Hey. There's ways and ways to feel it, cher, we did it. Where else they got to take us? —And there's those of us that feel the sun. Those that lived close to her—"

"Hell if, Kady."

"Nothing mystic. We got magnetics. Science boys say so."

"That's shit."

"Dunno. But the sun's starboard by 15 and high by 5."

"Trez garbage, Kady."

"Hey. Trez mystique, Pollard."

"Could get us a comlink," Sal grumbled. "Bloody damn hurry, they could let us come aboard. I got a serious bet on with Mitch's guys. And we're alive to collect . . ."

"*What'd* you bet?" —Ben, alarmed.

Familiar voices in the dark. He was safe here. Porey was outside, Porey who wanted him to make decisions, when Ben and Meg were the ones who decided—exactly the way Graff said about merchanter crews, and he couldn't understand why Porey expected him to follow UDC rules; he didn't *want* the say, just fly the ship, that was all, and he'd done that, hadn't he? He'd done the part he wanted, and for his part, he didn't care where they went from here, whether Meg was right or whether they were going to turn up somewhere out in real combat, he wanted to talk to Mitch and the guys, just a real quiet chance at the crews they'd worked with, chance to store it down, debrief—forget the things he'd been through.

But that wasn't the way it worked. God, that was still to go through, the meds were going to haul them in and go over them with a microscope. And he'd gotten spoiled, he wanted the massage, the stand-down and the beer and somebody else to make up his bunk, the kind of treatment you got on the carrier, that was what, he'd gotten spoiled . . .

But the barracks was where he lived. He looked forward to messhall automat cheese sandwiches . . . french fries and a hamburger and a shake, one thing Porey's fancy cooks couldn't come up with, not with the right degree of grease. You had to have things like that or you didn't know you were alive, and not in some passing dream . . .

Eyes were watering, tear tracks running down his face. He didn't know why. He just listened to carrier ops, com chatter between base ops and here, and traffic control; and Meg was right, they were routed in.

Did it, he kept telling himself, the dark was proof of that, the feel of the ship was proof of that. He'd done what he wanted to do, the most outrageous thing he'd ever planned to do, and he didn't know what was left but to be free to do it.

Didn't even have to teach how. Tape would do that. He just had to get it together for the next time they let him fly. . . .

"We find—" Graff said, to the gathering of Optexes, "when we bring in an integrated crew—the sum of the one is reliably the sum of the rest. People in this profession, given the chance to pick their own partners, sort themselves, I don't know how otherwise to express it. You don't work with anybody under your ability, where you know your life is on the line. Yes, they're all four that good . . ."

"This *crew* is tape-taught," a reporter said. "What does that say about human skill?"

"Let me explain for any of you who're thinking of tape in the classic sense, the *tape* we're referring to is really the neural net record: you go in with what you did before, matched to a performance you want; and the neural assist system shapes itself around you—that's why we work with just four people at this stage. They're physically programming the systems."

"By their feedback."

"Exactly. The tetralogics won't do what these people do. They brought instincts and experience no tape can teach. The experts and the computers all have to ask *them* what the right reaction is—*that's* what the tape is, that's all it's doing, recording and learning from the humans in control . . . storing all the responses as a norm some other human being just may exceed. . . ."

The reporters liked that idea. You could see it in the mass mark-that orders to the Optex loops, the shouted questions, the sudden comprehension on their faces. They wanted a confirmation of themselves, *that* was what they wanted for their viewers, another human yearning, a sense of synch with the chaos systems around them. "You're saying there's something unquantifiable, something about the human factor . . ."

"The human component governs the computers, that's the way it is in the starships, that's the only way this ship is going to do what it was created to do. That's what the whole design fight has been about and that's what this crew's just proved."

A vid byte they could use. The carrier was in dock. Presumably the rider crew and the backups were on their way down and the reporters were ready; he was theoretically the sacrifice, stalling and pacifying the reporters with running commentary, but, damn! he'd scored a point.

On the viewscreens and the monitors, images of Bonn and Paris and London, demonstrations by the Federation of Man and the leading peace groups, claiming Earth itself had been at risk, never mind high-*v* ordnance was aimed the other way: that same fear of near-*c* in system that discouraged the trade they might have had—people were frightened, stunned by the rapid approach, reporters already asking (personal applications always chased a new idea) why they languished three days on a shuttle ride that the carrier could cover in thirty minutes . . .

They had more questions. He saw the lift indicator showing operation, and nodded in that direction. "They're coming onto station."

Attention deserted him for the lift area: marines and Fleet Security had an unbreachable line of athletic bodies setting up a clear area, through which Villy, on similar advisement, showed up with Tanzer and the senators in tow, trailed by a still ecstatic crowd of Fleet and UDC crews from mission control—a complete media show-out, Graff thought with an uneasy stomach; and damned Porey to bloody hell for the decision to come straight in—but what else was it all for, after all? Risk Dekker, risk the prototype, risk *Eagle* with its thousand-member crew, for that matter, not to mention oversetting local regulations and stirring up the peacers with what they thought was a burning issue—

"Lieutenant." Tanzer arrived on his left hand.

"Colonel. We seem to have done it."

Tanzer shot him a look as if he were weighing the courtesy "we" that he hadn't even considered in saying. The senators were in earshot. He'd delivered Tanzer an unintended, face-saving favor and Tanzer looked as if he were trying to figure what he wanted in exchange.

"We *have* done it," Tanzer said, as the lift doors opened.

Dekker and his crew walked out still in their flight gear, all pale and tired-looking, but cheerful till they confronted the shockwave of reporters, questions, and Optexes—nobody, dammit, had even warned them what was waiting: Porey had let them walk into it. Graff dived forward; and the other core crews surged through and grabbed them, slapping backs and creating a small island of riot inside the cordon of security. He hung back a little, let the crews have their moment—saw Dekker both dazed and in good hands, the reporters not getting past the guards, just jostling silently for position with the Optexes as he finally took his turn with the crew, shook hands and congratulated them. There was glaze in their eyes. The four of them were still hyped and lost and not coping with the timeflow—he knew the look, he felt it, he ached to insulate them from this, get them quiet and stability. . . .

"Good job," he said. "Good job, all of you."

"Thank you, sir," Dekker breathed, and looked past him where—he turned his head—the vids showed riot in Bonn and Paris, just wide-tracking, lost.

"Ens. Dekker," the reporters shouted, "Ens. Dekker, how do you feel right now?"

Dekker turned his head to look at the reporter, honestly trying and failing, Graff read it, to accept one more slow-moving attention track. "I—" he began.

A reporter said, "Ens. Dekker. Ens. Dekker. There's a news crew standing by with a link to Bonn. Your mother's with the crew. Are you willing to speak to her, tell her how you feel at this moment?"

Damn! Graff thought, and shot another glance at the vids, where placards and banners called for peace, where a blond woman with a look as lost as Dekker's gazed into the lenses and then to the side, probably toward a monitor.

"Talk to her," the reporter said, "you can talk, she'll hear you—do you hear us, Ms. Dekker?"

"Yes," Ingrid Dekker said. *"Yes, I hear you. . . ."*

"I hear you," Dekker said faintly, and the whole area shushed each other to quiet.

"Paul? Paul? Is that you?"

"Yes." God, he was going to fracture—Graff saw the tears well up, saw the tremor. "Are you all right, mother? Are they treating you all right?"

Ingrid Dekker bit back tears. *"I wanted to return your call."*

"I wanted to call again. They said the lawyers wouldn't—"

Somebody shoved between Ingrid Dekker and the interviewer, said, *"That's enough."*

"Let her alone!" Dekker cried. "Damn you, take your hands off her—"

The picture jolted, the broad shadow of peacer security for a moment, Ingrid Dekker's voice crying, *"Paul, —Paul, I want to go home!"*

Kady got hold of Dekker. Aboujib did; and Pollard said, on Optex, "Those sons of bitches."

"We'll see if we can get Ms. Dekker back on," the interviewer was saying; and addressed his counterpart in Bonn. "Can you get to Ms. Dekker to ask—?"

Dekker was in shock, reporters shoving Optex pickups toward him, marines under strict orders not to shove back. That face was magnified on monitors all around the area, pale and lost, then Senator Caldwell's face was on the screens, reporters asking him his reaction.

Caldwell said, gravely: *"It's clear Ms. Dekker had something more to say, and the Federation leadership didn't want her to say it. I see enough to raise serious questions about how free Ms. Dekker is, at the moment . . ."*

Serious questions, Graff thought, choking on his own outrage. Serious questions whether Porey's timing for noon in Bonn, when Mazian was there, with the peace demonstrators, was anything like coincidence.

—God, run the test right past Luna in a move the peacers were bound to protest, have the reporters set up, the questions primed—

Then send Dekker and a crowd of excited crews head-on into the media for a reaction, when Porey damned well *knew* he was spaced?

He couldn't pull Dekker out directly, couldn't order Security to oust the reporters, daren't look like censorship on *this* side of the issue. He went in, took Dekker's arm with Optexes on high gain all around him. "Someone will do something." Which rang in his own ears as one more damned promise he didn't know how he was going to keep.

Dekker gave him a bleak, blank stare. "I don't want to leave, sir. If they can get her back I want to talk to her."

The mikes got that, too. Kady said, out of turn, "They don't want her loose. That's clear."

But all that showed on the Bonn monitors was a shut wooden door, and a reporter outside it, with no sound going out, talking, while demonstrators elbowed and shoved.

And all that showed on theirs was Dekker's stricken face, Dekker saying, dazedly, "They lied to her. They lied to her all the way . . ."

* * *

"It's playing," Demas said, leaning against the counter, "it's playing over and over again, around the planet, as the world wakes up. Dekker's a handsome kid, doesn't at all hurt his case. Or ours."

Graff wanted to break something—Demas' and Saito's necks, if he didn't recognize in Demas' glum expression an equal disgust. He looked at the vid, seeing Ingrid Dekker's bewildered distress, her son's—"Let her alone!" Over and over again.

As a weapon, Ingrid Dekker had turned in the hands of her wielders, and bit to the bone. Dekker was no longer the faceless Belter exile, he was the pilot who'd pulled a spectacular success with the Hellburner, he was a kid with a human grievance and a mother held prisoner by causes and politicians, and the demonstration organizer who had shoved Ingrid Dekker away from the reporters was under heavy condemnation and refusing questions.

Demas was right: it didn't hurt that Dekker had the face of a vid star and sincerity that came through the body language. The crew hadn't played badly either: the rumored split in the UDC/Fleet ranks, Ben Pollard with his UDC insignia on his flight-suit, Kady and Aboujib in flash and high tech, all of them profoundly concerned and angry at a human issue. . . .

While on the evening and morning news around the world, Alyce Salazar was doing damage control, covering her partisans, claiming that the Fleet had manipulated the media (truth) and that, quote, the important issues were being ignored in a rush to sympathy for a lying scoundrel who'd conned her daughter . . .

Dekker might be seeing it—he'd ordered open media access for appearances' sake while reporters were here, if no other reason; and had no argument from Porey. The vid was going out over all the station, their local authority doing no screening whatsoever.

"J-G," Demas said, "honestly, *I* didn't know until they ordered me to take charge of Security, right when the test started. They did query Saito, early on, for an assessment of Dekker's personnel record, his cultural makeup—"

"They. Did the captain know?"

"I don't know what there is to know. My guess is, Mazian sent Porey in here to figure the odds. If it was good enough, go, shove the best team in the ship and make the run; and if it turned out to be Dekker, meet the political chaff head-on, no hiding it, aim him straight for the cameras and damn all Salazar could do."

"Pardon me, Nav, but the *hell* the timing was random! High noon in Europe, in Bonn? Mazian's there. He knows the schedule. He *knew* it would draw instant fire!"

"I don't think he planned the scene with Dekker's mother."

"I don't put it past him."

"I think you give him too much credit. Some things just drop into your lap. But Mazian did want the protests—according to Saito. He wanted to solidify the issue, Saito says, so that it has substance, and then shoot that substance to hell. Make the peacers take a specific position and prove them wrong."

"Dekker's mother."

"Dekker's mother is a side issue. An opportunity I'm sure they'll take advantage of. Not mentioning Salazar. The EC wants Salazar stopped, in such a way it *won't* break Mars out of the union . . . and we have the Kent business with MarsCorp's fingerprints all over it."

"And daren't use it, dammit, we daren't even arrest Kent and Booten, we don't know—"

A stray thought crossed his mind.

"What?" Demas asked in his silence. "Don't know what?"

He leaned back in his chair and looked at the vid, where another instant opinion poll was playing. A radical shift in the numbers in the last 5 hours, plus or minus 3 points of accuracy. People believed the things they'd seen. 45% believed Paul Dekker was innocent and 46% now believed there was a significant threat of the war reaching Earth.

He said to Demas, apropos of nothing previous, "I want a statement prepared, a public relations version of Dekker's file. In case. I don't like unanticipateds, Nav."

"You've got it. But the Company will black-hole it. Salazar is too sensitive an issue. And far too powerful. She's using the issues, she's *not* the grieving mother, she's a politician. Kent . . . has got to be a professional. And if we've got him, there'll be others—inside the Earth Company offices, for all we know."

"All the same," he said.

He offered Demas a thin smile, and Demas took himself and his securitied briefcase back to the carrier, to Saito, to whatever lines of communication they were using to reach the captain with or without Mazian's knowledge.

They knew now what had killed Wilhelmsen: Ben Pollard had put them onto it and Porey's question to Dekker had shown it plain as plain. Wilhelmsen had been UDC command track. Pete Fowler had been the shadow behind Dekker's status, the real decision-maker—and the UDC had put them into the same cockpit. But they couldn't put that story in the release to the media—they dared not confuse the issue. Dekker was the point man, the—what had Saito said—the face the public knew? Dekker was the command officer of record in both crews; and that was the way the story was going to Earth.

Himself, he put on his jacket and went to evening rec, where there was a general liberty in force, with most of the reporters packed in with the senators on the shuttle, about six hours distant from the crews, thank God.

Thanks to some other agency, he was trapped with eight of them on station for at least a week. And damned if he was going to deal with them blind.

Beer and vodka were permissible; and Mitch and the UDC's Deke Chapman were doing a *v*-vid arcade game, noisy and rude, with bets down and the marine guards in on it, when a command officer walked in on it unannounced . . .

"Graff," Meg said, the whole room drew a breath, seemed to decide it was a friendly tour, and went back to an abated roar; Vasquez offered the lieutenant a beer.

"Sip," Graff said, in the way of a Shepherd who was on duty; so Graff got his sip to a cheer from all about, then said, quietly, "Pollard. Word with you. Outside."

Quick frown from Sal.

"No trouble," Graff said. "Just an operational. As you were, everybody."

Jokes on that score, no disrespect at all, just guys on an R&R from death and destruction. Meg slid into her chair again, caught Dek's hand, because he was looking spaced again—

Let down, she understood that. Only thoroughly happy moment he'd had in his life, by all she knew; and they'd hit him head-on with that business with his mother and the peacers. He looked her in the eyes now as if she had the answers—as if, as the rab would say, she was the word and the know-how.

And maybe she had been that, once, for a lot of people—maybe she'd been more, once, than she ever let on to those who checked on such things—but the generations changed, the whole human race spun and raced toward tomorrow after tomorrow, and if you were twenty-five now you didn't know the rab that had been the young and the foolish and the seekers after personal truth. The rab is, they'd used to say—after the Company man had said, No dealing with rabble. The rab is, and the rab will be, and screw the corp—

Was it lover or her personal tomorrow—looking into her eyes and hanging on the words?

"She'll get out," she told him, because she knew it was his mama he was brooding about; and maybe Cory. He didn't have many tracks left when he got this far down. She hit his arm, and said, "Rab is and rab does, jeune fils. And they shot us down. Don't forget that. Shot you down. I got nothing to teach you about being screwed."

"She never *cared* about politics, Meg!"

"We got to do, got to do, jeune fils. Life is, death is, and that's all; but we're here and they got to deal with that. They got to deal with us."

Dek had been a kid when the rab had lost its innocence, and the blood had run on the Company steps. Severely young, Dek still was, in some ways. She couldn't be, again; and she told it cold and plain as she'd learned it herself: "There's no *luck,* jeune rab, things don't brut *happen* for no damn reason, and you aren't it, forgive, cher. But nobody at this table, not me and not you and not Sal, is that important, that God is going to screw up somebody else's life to get you. I dunno who, I dunno why, but we've eliminated God as a suspect. . . ."

Dek managed a laugh, a grin, and picked up his beer with his hand shaking. He drank a sip without spilling it. At least.

"Hey," Sal said, "They got the whole UN Human Rights Commission asking to talk to your mama. . . ."

"But if they get her out she's not safe, Salazar's people tried twice to kill me and got Jamil—"

"Cher rab, are they going to risk stirring things up now? They got their ass on the line. They want quiet, soon as they can hush this up. When the corp-rats get caught, they always want a real quick silence."

He let go a sigh, shook his head.

Sal elbowed him. "Take you on, cher. Billiards or poker?"

Poker, it was. Ben pulled a chair back, set his beer down, said, cheerfully, "Deal me in," and collected looks from his crewmates. He kept the smugness off his face—the reason was for Sal's ears, for Dekker and Meg once the stuff went public—as would happen, he was sure, when Security found out what to do with the file that had landed in their laps.

Dekker asked, "What did they want?"

"Oh, nothing."

"Come on," Sal said.

"Oh," Ben said, picking up cards, "just a little tekkie stuff." *Good* hand, it was. There were nights a guy was On, and this was it.

Damn, there was stuff going to hit the news tomorrow.

"Tekkie stuff, hell," Sal said. "What was it?"

"Just a little advice." And access numbers and a nailpolish-sealed card. He laid down chips.

Didn't have to go to Stockholm to prove the Staatentek over the damned EIDAT, damn no. *Elegant* equipment, they had on that carrier.

"What advice?"

He smiled, thinking about the morning news, and MarsCorp, and Salazar's personal memo file, and the wonderful, damning things it held.

"Don't buy stock in EIDAT, Lendlor or MarsCorp. Even at discount."

"What have you got?" Dekker asked sharply.

Wider smile. "A winning hand, Dek-boy, odds are—a winning hand."